WALTER JON WILLIAMS

This special signed edition
is limited to 1000 numbered copies.

This is copy

686 .

THE
BEST
OF
WALTER
JON
WILLIAMS

THE
BEST
OF
WALTER
JON
WILLIAMS

SUBTERRANEAN PRESS 2021

First Edition

ISBN
978-1-64524-002-0

See pages 609-610 for individual story credits.

Subterranean Press
PO Box 190106
Burton, MI 48519

subterraneanpress.com

Manufactured in the United States of America

TABLE OF CONTENTS

INTRODUCTION

by Daniel Abraham

When I started my life as a serious reader of science fiction and fantasy lo these many years ago, there were giants in the field: Asimov and Zelazny, Jack Chalker and Larry Niven and Harry Harrison. And yes, Walter Jon Williams. My tastes were, as they are now, wide and voracious. I read books and stories to see worlds I'd never seen, think thoughts that would never have occurred to me, and along the way create my own sense of adventure and possibility. "Novel" meant a book of a certain size, sure. But more importantly for me, it meant new. That was when I fell in love with the stories of Walter Jon Williams. I have never fallen back out.

In the age of branding and carefully crafted identity, Walter Jon Williams' body of work is a rare and wonderful thing—it's *wide*. A Stephen King story is a Stephen King story. A Philip K. Dick book is unmistakably a Philip K. Dick book. Authors—even the best of us—have the sandboxes we play in, the kinds of stories that we tell, and a similarity in the projects we take on. We're constrained by the market and by our own enthusiasms, by the projects we've tried that failed and the ones that succeeded. Authors, myself very much included, find a literary identity forming that defines and constrains us.

But not everyone goes that way.

Pick up a Walter Jon Williams book, and you might have a science fictional comedy of manners with the gentleman thief Drake Maijstral. Dip into his shelf again, and you may come back with a high fantasy adventure like *Quillifer the Knight*. A weird world of arcane power and endless cityscape from the Metropolitan books. First-wave cyberpunk like *Hardwired*. High space opera (*Dread Empire's Fall*) or near-future espionage (*This is Not a Game*) or vast disaster novel (*The Rift*). You could find yourself in a far future where people have intentionally split their own personalities to adapt to the rigors of space travel or between the sails of an 1880s tall ship or in a police station in rural New Mexico. A complete read of Walter's work swoops back and forth through genres and forms like a rollercoaster, and no amount of reading will guarantee that you can predict what comes next.

So what is a Walter Jon Williams story?

There are some threads we can find in his work. They aren't setting or tone or genre, but they're there. First off, Walter Jon Williams stories are incandescently smart. Whether he's drawing from the patterns and quirks of history or speculating forward into the science and technology that will exist generations from now, the stories share a deep curiosity. Even the saddest—and the man can do tragedy as well as anybody—have a thread of wonder and delight in them.

For another thing, they are deeply felt. The characters are often flawed, sometimes broken, occasionally brilliant, but they are always deeply human. There's an idea I've heard put forth—and which I more than half believe—that a writer's characters follow them from story to story and project to project like a theater company performing different plays with the same actors. If that's true, Williams has a casting director's rolodex in his head. He can draw a lost child and a hardened murderer with the same grace and sympathy. He can make us love or hate a character, or when he wants to, do both at the same time.

And finally, his work is crafted by a master.

I have been lucky enough to workshop with Walter Jon Williams. I have learned more from listening to him than from any other single source in my career. His insights are sharp, based in experience, and—rarest of all among bits of writing advice—they're useful.

There is an interview with Michael Caine where he talks about the art of acting in the serious, simple terms of a craftsman. *I try not to blink.* Williams has an understanding of the process and art of writing at least as deep as Caine's of acting. "There are three ways to hide a clue so that it's memorable, but doesn't tip your hand." That's some high-level wizardry right there.

So, intelligent, empathetic, and beautifully written. That's as close as you're going to get to defining a Walter Jon Williams story.

I've said in other places that the job of being a writer is a fine balance between, on the one hand, cultivating a deep and empathic understanding of the human heart and, on the other, not giving a shit what anyone else thinks. That's who Walter is. Craft and wisdom and a lifelong dedication to his craft on one side, a vast and unconstrained—maybe unconstrainable—imagination on the other.

The book you're holding right now has a dozen different trips into those worlds. The stories range over four decades of Williams' career, and they're all as fresh as last month's *Asimov's*. It's going to be tempting to read them all in one sitting, and I won't blame you if you do. But there's something to be said for taking these slow, savoring them, letting them be with you for a while before you take the next sip. They're all going to take you different places.

Welcome to *The Best of Walter Jon Williams*. You can trust me. That's saying something.

DADDY'S WORLD

One day Jamie went with his family to a new place, a place that had not existed before. The people who lived there were called Whirlikins, who were tall thin people with pointed heads. They had long arms and made frantic gestures when they talked, and when they grew excited threw their arms out wide to either side and spun like tops until they got all blurry. They would whirr madly over the green grass beneath the pumpkin-orange sky of the Whirlikin country, and sometimes they would bump into each other with an alarming clashing noise, but they were never hurt, only bounced off and spun away in another direction.

Sometimes one of them would spin so hard that he would dig himself right into the ground, and come to a sudden stop, buried to the shoulders, with an expression of alarmed dismay.

Jamie had never seen anything so funny. He laughed and laughed.

His little sister Becky laughed, too. Once she laughed so hard that she fell over onto her stomach, and Daddy picked her up and whirled her through the air, as if he were a Whirlikin himself, and they were both laughing all the while.

Afterwards, they heard the dinner bell, and Daddy said it was time to go home. After they waved goodbye to the Whirlikins, Becky and Jamie walked hand in hand with Momma as they walked over the grassy hills toward home, and the pumpkin-orange sky slowly turned to blue.

The way home ran past El Castillo. El Castillo looked like a fabulous place, a castle with towers and domes and minarets, all gleaming in the sun. Music floated down from El Castillo, the swift, intricate music of many guitars, and Jamie could hear the fast click of heels and the shouts and laughter of happy people.

But Jamie did not try to enter El Castillo. He had tried before, and discovered that El Castillo was guarded by La Duchesa, an angular forbidding woman all in black, with a tall comb in her hair. When Jamie asked to come inside, La Duchesa had looked down at him and said, "I do not admit anyone who does not know Spanish irregular verbs!" It was all she ever said.

Jamie had asked Daddy what a Spanish irregular verb was—he had difficulty pronouncing the words—and Daddy had said, "Some day you'll learn, and La Duchesa will let you into her castle. But right now you're too young to learn Spanish."

That was all right with Jamie. There were plenty of things to do without going into El Castillo. And new places, like the country where the Whirlikins lived, appeared sometimes out of nowhere, and were quite enough to explore.

The color of the sky faded from orange to blue. Fluffy white clouds coasted in the air above the two-storey frame house. Mister Jeepers, who was sitting on the ridgepole, gave a cry of delight and soared toward them through the air.

"Jamie's home!" he sang happily. "Jamie's home, and he's brought his beautiful sister!"

Mister Jeepers was diamond-shaped, like a kite, with his head at the topmost corner, hands on either sides, and little bowlegged comical legs attached on the bottom. He was bright red. Like a kite, he could fly, and he swooped through in a series of aerial cartwheels as he sailed toward Jamie and his party.

Becky looked up at Mister Jeepers and laughed from pure joy. "Jamie," she said, "you live in the best place in the world!"

At night, when Jamie lay in bed with his stuffed giraffe, Selena would ride a beam of pale light from the Moon to the Earth and sit by Jamie's side. She was a pale woman, slightly translucent, with a silver crescent on her brow. She would stroke Jamie's forehead with a cool hand, and she would sing to him until his eyes grew heavy and slumber stole upon him.

> "The birds have tucked their heads,
> The night is dark and deep,
> All is quiet, all is safe,
> And little Jamie goes to sleep."

Whenever Jamie woke during the night, Selena was there to comfort him. He was glad that Selena always watched out for him, because sometimes he still had nightmares about being in the hospital. When the nightmares came, she was always there to soothe him, stroke him, sing him back to sleep.

Before long the nightmares began to fade.

Princess Gigunda always took Jamie for lessons. She was a huge woman, taller than Daddy, with frowzy hair and big bare feet and a crown that could never be made to sit straight on her head. She was homely, with a mournful face that was ugly and endearing at the same time. As she shuffled along with Jamie to his lessons, Princess Gigunda complained about the way her feet hurt, and about how she was a giant and unattractive, and how she would never be married.

"I'll marry you when I get bigger," Jamie said loyally, and the Princess's homely face screwed up into an expression of beaming pleasure.

Jamie had different lessons with different people. Mrs. Winkle, down at the little red brick schoolhouse, taught him his ABCs. Coach Toad—who *was* one—taught him field games, where he raced and jumped and threw against various people and animals. Mr. McGillicuddy, a pleasant whiskered fat man who wore red sleepers with a trapdoor in back, showed him his magic globe. When Jamie put his finger anywhere on the globe, trumpets began to sound, and he could see what was happening where he was pointing, and Mr. McGillicuddy would take him on a tour and show him interesting things. Buildings, statues, pictures, parks, people. "This is Nome," he would say. "Can you say Nome?"

"Nome," Jamie would repeat, shaping his mouth around the unfamiliar word, and Mr. McGillicuddy would smile and bob his head and look pleased.

If Jamie did well on his lessons, he got extra time with the Whirlikins, or at the Zoo, or with Mr. Fuzzy or in Pandaland. Until the dinner bell rang, and it was time to go home.

Jamie did well with his lessons almost every day.

When Princess Gigunda took him home from his lessons, Mister Jeepers would fly from the ridgepole to meet him, and tell him that his family was ready to see him. And then Momma and Daddy and Becky would wave from the windows of the house, and he would run to meet them.

Once, when he was in the living room telling his family about his latest trip through Mr. McGillicuddy's magic globe, he began skipping about with enthusiasm, and waving his arms like a Whirlikin, and suddenly he noticed that no one else was paying attention. That Momma and Daddy and Becky were staring at something else, their faces frozen in different attitudes of polite attention.

Jamie felt a chill finger touch his neck.

"Momma?" Jamie said. "Daddy?" Momma and Daddy did not respond. Their faces didn't move. Daddy's face was blurred strangely, as if it had been caught in the middle of movement.

"Daddy?" Jamie came close and tried to tug at his father's shirt sleeve. It was hard, like marble, and his fingers couldn't get a purchase on it. Terror blew hot in his heart.

"*Daddy?*" Jamie cried. He tried to tug harder. "Daddy! Wake up!" Daddy didn't respond. He ran to Momma and tugged at her hand. "Momma! Momma!" Her hand was like the hand of a statue. She didn't move no matter how hard Jamie pulled.

"Help!" Jamie screamed. "Mister Jeepers! Mr. Fuzzy! Help my Momma!" Tears fell down his face as he ran from Becky to Momma to Daddy, tugging and pulling at them, wrapping his arms around their frozen legs and trying to pull them toward him. He ran outside, but everything was curiously still. No wind blew. Mister Jeepers sat on the ridgepole, a broad smile fixed as usual to his face, but he was frozen, too, and did not respond to Jamie's calls.

Terror pursued him back into the house. This was far worse than anything that had happened to him in the hospital, worse even than the pain. Jamie ran into the living room, where his family stood still as statues, and then recoiled in horror. A stranger had entered the room—or rather just parts of a stranger, a pair of hands encased in black gloves with strange silver circuit patterns on the backs, and a strange glowing opalescent face with a pair of wraparound dark glasses drawn across it like a line.

"Interface crashed, all right," the stranger said, as if to someone Jamie couldn't see.

Jamie gave a scream. He ran behind Momma's legs for protection.

"Oh shit," the stranger said. "The kid's still running."

He began purposefully moving his hands as if poking at the air. Jamie was sure that it was some kind of terrible attack, a spell to turn him to stone. He tried to run away, tripped over Becky's immovable feet and hit the floor hard, and then crawled away, the hall rug bunching up under his hands and knees as he skidded away, his own screams ringing in his ears…

He sat up in bed, shrieking. The cool night tingled on his skin. He felt Selena's hand on his forehead, and he jerked away with a cry.

"Is something wrong?" came Selena's calm voice. "Did you have a bad dream?" Under the glowing crescent on her brow, Jamie could see the concern in her eyes.

"Where are Momma and Daddy?" Jamie wailed.

"They're fine," Selena said. "They're asleep in their room. Was it a bad dream?"

Jamie threw off the covers and leaped out of bed. He ran down the hall, the floorboards cool on his bare feet. Selena floated after him in her serene, concerned way. He threw open the door to his parents' bedroom and snapped on the light, then gave a cry as he saw them huddled beneath their blanket. He flung himself at his mother, and gave a sob of relief as she opened her eyes and turned to him.

"Something wrong?" Momma said. "Was it a bad dream?"

"*No!*" Jamie wailed. He tried to explain, but even he knew that his words made no sense. Daddy rose from his pillow, looking seriously at Jamie, and then turned to ruffle his hair.

"Sounds like a pretty bad dream, trouper," Daddy said. "Let's get you back to bed."

"*No!*" Jamie buried his face in his mother's neck. "I don't want to go back to bed!"

"All right, Jamie," Momma said. She patted Jamie's back. "You can sleep here with us. But just for tonight, okay?"

"Wanna stay here," Jamie mumbled. He crawled under the covers between Momma and Daddy. They each kissed him, and Daddy turned off the light. "Just go to sleep, trouper," he said. "And don't worry. You'll have only good dreams from now on."

Selena, faintly glowing in the darkness, sat silently in the corner. "Shall I sing?" she asked.

"Yes, Selena," Daddy said. "Please sing for us."

Selena began to sing,

> The birds have tucked their heads,
> The night is dark and deep,

> All is quiet, all is safe,
> And little Jamie goes to sleep.

But Jamie did not sleep. Despite the singing, the dark night, the rhythmic breathing of his parents and the comforting warmth of their bodies.

It *wasn't* a dream, he knew. His family had really been frozen. Something, or someone, had turned them to stone. Probably that evil disembodied head and pair of hands. And now, for some reason, his parents didn't remember.

Something had made them forget.

Jamie stared into the darkness. What, he thought, if these weren't his parents? If his parents were still stone, hidden away somewhere? What if these substitutes were bad people—kidnappers or worse—people who just *looked* like his real parents? What if they were evil people who were just waiting for him to fall asleep, and then they would turn to monsters, with teeth and fangs and a horrible light in their eyes, and they would tear him to bits right here in the bed...

Talons of panic clawed at Jamie's heart. Selena's song echoed in his ears. He *wasn't* going to sleep! He *wasn't!*

And then he did. It wasn't anything like normal sleep—it was as if sleep was *imposed* on him, as if something had just *ordered* his mind to sleep. It was just like a wave that rolled over him, an irresistible force, blotting out his senses, his body, his mind...

I *won't* sleep! he thought in defiance, but then his thoughts were extinguished.

When he woke he was back in his own bed, and it was morning, and Mister Jeepers was floating outside the window. "Jamie's awake!" he sang. "Jamie's awake and ready for a new day!"

And then his parents came bustling in, kissing him and petting him and taking him downstairs for breakfast.

His fears seemed foolish now, in full daylight, with Mister Jeepers dancing in the air outside and singing happily.

But sometimes at night, while Selena crooned by his bedside, he gazed into the darkness and felt a thrill of fear.

And he never forgot, not entirely.

❀

A few days later Don Quixote wandered into the world, a lean man who frequently fell off his lean horse in a clang of homemade armor. He was given to making wan comments in both English and his own language, which turned out to be Spanish.

"Can you teach me Spanish irregular verbs?" Jamie asked.

"*Sí, naturalmente,*" said Don Quixote. "But I will have to teach you some other Spanish as well." He looked particularly mournful. "Let's start with *corazón*. It means 'heart.' *Mi corazón,*" he said with a sigh, "is breaking for love of Dulcinea."

After a few sessions with Don Quixote—mixed with a lot of sighing about *corazóns* and Dulcinea—Jamie took a grip on his courage, marched up to El Castillo, and spoke to La Duchesa.

"*Pierdo, sueño, haría, ponto!*" he cried.

La Duchesa's eyes widened in surprise, and as she bent toward Jamie her severe face became almost kindly. "You are obviously a very intelligent boy," she said. "You may enter my castle."

And so Don Quixote and La Duchesa, between the two of them, began to teach Jamie to speak Spanish. If he did well, he was allowed into the parts of the castle where the musicians played and the dancers stamped, where brave Castilian knights jousted in the tilting yard, and Señor Esteban told stories in Spanish, always careful to use words that Jamie already knew.

Jamie couldn't help but notice that sometimes Don Quixote behaved strangely. Once, when Jamie was visiting the Whirlikins, Don Quixote charged up on his horse, waving his sword and crying out that he would save Jamie from the goblins that were attacking him. Before Jamie could explain that the Whirlikins were harmless, Don Quixote galloped to the attack. The Whirlikins, alarmed, screwed themselves into the ground where they were safe, and Don Quixote fell off his horse trying to swing at one with his sword. After poor Quixote fell off his horse a few times, it was Jamie who had to rescue the Don, not the other way around.

It was sort of sad and sort of funny. Every time Jamie started to laugh about it, he saw Don Quixote's mournful face in his mind, and his laugh grew uneasy.

After a while, Jamie's sister Becky began to share Jamie's lessons. She joined him and Princess Gigunda on the trip to the little schoolhouse, learned reading and math from Mrs. Winkle, and then, after some coaching from Jamie and Don Quixote, she marched to La Duchesa to shout irregular verbs and gain entrance to El Castillo.

Around that time Marcus Tullius Cicero turned up to take them both to the Forum Romanum, a new part of the world that had appeared to the south of the Whirlikins' territory. But Cicero and the people in the Forum, all the shopkeepers and politicians, did not teach Latin the way Don Quixote taught Spanish, explaining what the new words meant in English, they just talked Latin at each other and expected Jamie and Becky to understand. Which, eventually, they did. The Spanish helped. Jamie was a bit better at Latin than Becky, but he explained to her that it was because he was older.

It was Becky who became interested in solving Princess Gigunda's problem. "We should find her somebody to love," she said.

"She loves *us*," Jamie said.

"Don't be silly," Becky said. "She wants a *boyfriend*."

"*I'm* her boyfriend," Jamie insisted.

Becky looked a little impatient. "Besides," she said, "it's a puzzle. Just like La Duchesa and her verbs."

This had not occurred to Jamie before, but now that Becky mentioned it, the idea seemed obvious. There were a lot of puzzles around, which one or the other of them was always solving, and Princess Gigunda's lovelessness was, now that he saw it, clearly among them.

So they set out to find Princess Gigunda a mate. This question occupied them for several days, and several candidates were discussed and rejected. They found no answers until they went to the chariot race at the Circus Maximus. It was the first race in the Circus ever, because the place had just appeared on the other side of the Palatine Hill from the Forum, and there was a very large, very excited crowd.

The names of the charioteers were announced as they paraded their chariots to the starting line. The trumpets sounded, and the chariots bolted from the start as the drivers whipped up the horses. Jamie watched enthralled as they rolled around the spina for the first lap, and then shouted in surprise at the sight of Don Quixote galloping onto the Circus Maximus, shouting that he was about to stop this group of rampaging demons from destroying the land, and planted himself directly in the path of the oncoming chariots. Jamie shouted along with the crowd for the Don to get out of the way before he got killed.

Fortunately Quixote's horse had more sense than he did, because the spindly animal saw the chariots coming and bolted, throwing its rider. One of the chariots rode right over poor Quixote, and there was a horrible clanging noise, but after the chariot passed, Quixote sat up, apparently unharmed. His armor had saved him.

Jamie jumped from his seat and was about to run down to help Don Quixote off the course, but Becky grabbed his arm. "Hang on," she said. "Someone else will look after him, and I have an idea."

She explained that Don Quixote would make a perfect man for Princess Gigunda.

"But he's in love with Dulcinea!"

Becky looked at him patiently. "Has anyone ever *seen* Dulcinea? All we have to do is convince Don Quixote that Princess Gigunda *is* Dulcinea."

After the races, they found that Don Quixote had been arrested by the lictors and sent to the Lautumiae, which was the Roman jail. They weren't allowed to see the prisoner, so they went in search of Cicero, who was a lawyer and was able to get Quixote out of the Lautumiae on the promise that he would never visit Rome again.

"I regret to the depths of my soul that my parole does not enable me to destroy those demons," Quixote said as he left Rome's town limits.

"Let's not get into that," Becky said. "What we wanted to tell you was that we've found Dulcinea."

The old man's eyes widened in joy. He clutched at his armor-clad heart. "*Mi amor!* Where is she? I must run to her at once!"

"Not just yet," Becky said. "You should know that she's been changed. She doesn't look like she used to."

"Has some evil sorcerer done this?" Quixote demanded.

"Yes!" Jamie interrupted. He was annoyed that Becky had taken charge of everything, and he wanted to add his contribution to the scheme. "The sorcerer was just a head!" he shouted. "A floating head, and a pair of hands! And he wore dark glasses and had no body!"

A shiver of fear passed through him as he remembered the eerie floating head, but the memory of his old terror did not stop his words from spilling out.

Becky gave him a strange look. "Yeah," she said. "That's right."

"He crashed the interface!" Jamie shouted, the words coming to him out of memory.

Don Quixote paid no attention to this, but Becky gave him another look.

"You're not as dumb as you look, Digit," she said.

"I do not care about Dulcinea's appearance," Don Quixote declared. "I love only the goodness that dwells in her *corazón*."

"She's Princess Gigunda!" Jamie shouted, jumping up and down in enthusiasm. "She's been Princess Gigunda all along!"

And so, the children following, Don Quixote ran clanking to where Princess Gigunda waited near Jamie's house, fell down to one knee, and began to kiss and weep over the Princess' hand. The Princess seemed a little surprised by this until Becky told her that she was really the long-lost Dulcinea, changed into a giant by an evil magician, although she probably didn't remember it because that was part of the spell too.

So while the Don and the Princess embraced, kissed, and began to warble a love duet, Becky turned to Jamie.

"What's that stuff about the floating head?" she asked. "Where did you come up with that?"

"I dunno," Jamie said. He didn't want to talk about his memory of his family being turned to stone, the eerie glowing figure floating before them. He didn't want to remember how everyone said it was just a dream.

He didn't want to talk about the suspicions that had never quite gone away.

"That stuff was weird, Digit," Becky said. "It gave me the creeps. Let me know before you start talking about stuff like that again."

"Why do you call me Digit?" Jamie asked. Becky smirked.

"No reason," she said.

"Jamie's home!" Mister Jeepers' voice warbled from the sky. Jamie looked up to see Mister Jeepers doing joyful aerial loops overhead. "Master Jamie's home at last!"

"Where shall we go?" Jamie asked.

Their lessons for the day were over, and he and Becky were leaving the little red schoolhouse. Becky, as usual, had done very well on her lessons, better than her older brother, and Jamie felt a growing sense of annoyance. At least he was still better at Latin and computer science.

"I dunno," Becky said. "Where do you want to go?"

"How about Pandaland? We could ride the Whoosh Machine."

Becky wrinkled her face. "I'm tired of that kid stuff," she said.

Jamie looked at her. "But you're a kid."

"I'm not as little as you, Digit," Becky said.

Jamie glared. This was too much. "You're my little sister! I'm bigger than you!"

"No, you're not," Becky said. She stood before him, her arms flung out in exasperation. "Just *notice something* for once, will you?"

Jamie bit back on his temper and looked, and he saw that Becky was, in fact, bigger than he was. And older-looking. Puzzlement replaced his fading anger.

"How did you get so big?" Jamie asked.

"I grew. And you *didn't* grow. Not as fast anyway."

"I don't understand."

Becky's lip curled. "Ask Mom or Dad. Just *ask* them." Her expression turned stony. "But don't believe everything they tell you."

"What do you mean?"

Becky looked angry for a moment, and then her expression relaxed. "Look," she said, "just go to Pandaland and have fun, okay? You don't need me for that. I want to go and make some calls to my friends."

"*What* friends?"

Becky looked angry again. "*My* friends. It doesn't matter who they are!"

"Fine!" Jamie shouted. "I can have fun by myself!"

Becky turned and began to walk home, her legs scissoring against the background of the green grass. Jamie glared after her, then turned and began the walk to Pandaland.

He did all his favorite things, rode the Ferris wheel and the Whoosh Machine, watched Rizzio the Strongman and the clowns. He enjoyed himself, but his enjoyment felt hollow. He found himself *watching*, watching himself at play, watching himself enjoying the rides.

Watching himself not grow as fast as his little sister.

Watching himself wondering whether or not to ask his parents about why that was.

He had the idea that he wouldn't like their answers.

✸

He didn't see as much of Becky after that. They would share lessons, and then Becky would lock herself in her room to talk to her friends on the phone.

Becky didn't have a telephone in her room, though. He looked once when she wasn't there.

After a while, Becky stopped accompanying him for lessons. She'd got ahead of him on everything except Latin, and it was too hard for Jamie to keep up.

After that, he hardly saw Becky at all. But when he saw her, he saw that she was still growing fast. Her clothing was different, and her hair. She'd started wearing makeup.

He didn't know whether he liked her anymore or not.

It was Jamie's birthday. He was eleven years old, and Momma and Daddy and Becky had all come for a party. Don Quixote and Princess Gigunda serenaded Jamie from outside the window, accompanied by La Duchesa on Spanish guitar. There was a big cake with eleven candles. Momma gave Jamie a chart of the stars. When he touched a star, a voice would appear telling Jamie about the star, and lines would appear on the chart showing any constellation the star happened to belong to. Daddy gave Jamie a car, a miniature Mercedes convertible, scaled to Jamie's size, which he could drive around the country and which he could use in the Circus Maximus when the chariots weren't racing.

His sister gave Jamie a kind of lamp stand that would project lights and moving patterns on the walls and ceiling when the lights were off. "Listen to music when you use it," she said.

"Thank you, Becky," Jamie said.

"Becca," she said. "My name is Becca now. Try to remember."

"Okay," Jamie said. "Becca."

Becky—Becca—looked at Momma. "I'm dying for a cigaret," she said. "Can I go, uh, out for a minute?"

Momma hesitated, but Daddy looked severe. "Becca," he said, "this is *Jamie's birthday*. We're all here to celebrate. So why don't we all eat some cake and have a nice time?"

"It's not even real cake," Becca said. "It doesn't *taste* like real cake."

"It's a *nice cake*," Daddy insisted. "Why don't we talk about this later? Let's just have a special time for Jamie."

Becca stood up from the table. "For *the Digit?*" she said. "Why are we having a good time for *Jamie?* He's not even a *real person!*" She thumped herself on the chest. "I'm a *real* person!" she shouted. "Why don't we ever have special times for *me?*"

But Daddy was on his feet by that point and shouting, and Momma was trying to get everyone to be quiet, and Becca was shouting back, and suddenly a determined look entered her face and she just disappeared—suddenly, she wasn't there anymore, there was just only air.

Jamie began to cry. So did Momma. Daddy paced up and down and swore, and then he said, "I'm going to go get her." Jamie was afraid he'd disappear like Becca, and he gave a cry of despair, but Daddy didn't disappear, he just stalked out of the dining room and slammed the door behind him.

Momma pulled Jamie onto her lap and hugged him. "Don't worry, Jamie," she said. "Becky just did that to be mean."

"What happened?" Jamie asked.

"Don't worry about it." Momma stroked his hair. "It was just a mean trick."

"She's growing up," Jamie said. "She's grown faster than me and I don't understand."

"Wait till Daddy gets back," Momma said, "and we'll talk about it."

But Daddy was clearly in no mood for talking when he returned, without Becca. "We're going to have *fun*," he snarled, and reached for the knife to cut the cake.

✳

The cake tasted like ashes in Jamie's mouth. When the Don and Princess Gigunda, Mister Jeepers and Rizzio the Strongman came into the dining room and sang "Happy Birthday," it was all Jamie could do to hold back the tears.

Afterwards, he drove his new car to the Circus Maximus and drove as fast as he could on the long oval track. The car really wouldn't go very fast. The bleachers on either side were empty, and so was the blue sky above.

Maybe it was a puzzle, he thought, like Princess Gigunda's love life. Maybe all he had to do was follow the right clue, and everything would be fine.

What's the moral they're trying to teach? he wondered.

But all he could do was go in circles, around and around the empty stadium.

✳

"Hey, Digit. Wake up."

Jamie came awake suddenly, with a stifled cry. The room whirled around him. He blinked, realized that the whirling came from the colored lights projected by his birthday present, Becca's lamp stand.

Becca was sitting on his bedroom chair, a cigaret in her hand. Her feet, in the steel-capped boots she'd been wearing lately, were propped up on the bed.

"Are you awake, Jamie?" It was Selena's voice. "Would you like me to sing you a lullaby?"

"Fuck off, Selena," Becca said. "Get out of here. Get lost."

Selena cast Becca a mournful look, then sailed backwards, out the window, riding a beam of moonlight to her pale home in the sky. Jamie watched her go, and felt as if a part of himself was going with her, a part that he would never see again.

"Selena and the others have to do what you tell them, mostly," Becca said. "Of course, Mom and Dad wouldn't tell *you* that."

Jamie looked at Becca. "What's happening?" he said. "Where did you go today?"

Colored lights swam over Becca's face. "I'm sorry if I spoiled your birthday, Digit. I just got tired of the lies, you know? They'd kill me if they knew I was here now, talking to you."

Becca took a draw on her cigaret, held her breath for a second or two, then exhaled. Jamie didn't see or taste any smoke.

"You know what they wanted me to do?" she said. "Wear a little girl's body, so I wouldn't look any older than you, and keep you company in that stupid school for seven hours a day." She shook her head. "I wouldn't do it. They yelled and yelled, but I was damned if I would."

"I don't understand."

Becca flicked invisible ashes off her cigaret, and looked at Jamie for a long time. Then she sighed.

"Do you remember when you were in the hospital?" she said.

Jamie nodded. "I was really sick."

"I was so little then, I don't really remember it very well," Becca said. "But the point is—" She sighed again. "The point is that you weren't getting well. So they decided to—" She shook her head. "Dad took advantage of his position at the University, and the fact that he's been a big donor. They were doing AI research, and the neurology department was into brain modeling, and they needed a test subject, and— Well, the idea is, they've got some of your tissue, and when they get cloning up and running, they'll put you back in—" She saw Jamie's stare, then shook her head.

"I'll make it simple, okay?"

She took her feet off the bed and leaned closer to Jamie. A shiver ran up his back at her expression. "They made a copy of you. An *electronic* copy. They scanned your brain and built a holographic model of it inside a computer, and they put it in a virtual environment, and—" She sat back, took a drag on her cigaret. "And here you are," she said.

Jamie looked at her. "I don't understand."

Colored lights gleamed in Becca's eyes. "You're in a computer, okay? And you're a program. You know what that is, right? From computer class? And the program is sort of in the shape of your mind. Don Quixote and Princess Gigunda are programs, too. And Mrs. Winkle down at the schoolhouse is *usually* a program, but if she needs to teach something complex, then she's an education major from the University."

Jamie felt as if he'd just been hollowed out, a void inside his ribs. "I'm not real?" he said. "I'm not a person?"

"Wrong," Becca said. "You're real, alright. You're the apple of our parents' eye." Her tone was bitter. "Programs are real things," she said, "and yours was a real hack, you know, absolute cutting-edge state-of-the-art technoshit. And the computer that you're in is real, too—I'm interfaced with it right now, down in the family room— we have to wear suits with sensors and a helmet with scanners and stuff. I hope to fuck they don't hear me talking to you down here."

"But what—" Jamie swallowed hard. How could he swallow if he was just a string of code? "What happened to *me?* The original me?"

Becca looked cold. "Well," she said, "you had cancer. You died."

"Oh." A hollow wind blew through the void inside him.

"They're going to bring you back. As soon as the clone thing works out—but this is a government computer you're in, and there are all these government restrictions on cloning, and—"

She shook her head. "Look, Digit," she said. "You really need to know this stuff, okay?"

"I understand." Jamie wanted to cry. But only real people cried, he thought, and he wasn't real. He wasn't real.

"The program that runs this virtual environment is huge, okay, and you're a big program, and the University computer is used for a lot of research, and a lot of the research has a higher priority than you do. So you don't run in real-time—that's why I'm growing faster than you are.

"I'm spending more hours being me than you are. And the parents—" She rolled her eyes. "They aren't making this any better, with their emphasis on *normal family life*."

She sucked on her cigaret, then stubbed it out in something invisible. "See, they want us to be this *normal family*. So we have breakfast together every day, and dinner every night, and spend the evening at the Zoo or in Pandaland or someplace. But the dinner that we eat with *you* is virtual, it doesn't taste like anything—the grant ran out before they got that part of the interface right—so we eat this fast-food crap before we interface with you, and then have dinner all *over* again with *you*... Is this making any sense? Because Dad has a job and Mom has a job and I go to school and have friends and stuff, so we really can't get together every night. So they just close your program file, shut it right down, when they're not available to interface with you as what Dad calls a 'family unit,' and that means that there are a lot of hours, days sometimes, when you're just *not running*, you might as well really be *dead*—" She blinked. "Sorry," she said. "Anyway, we're all getting older a lot faster than you are, and it's not fair to you, that's what I think. Especially because the University computer runs fastest at night, because people don't use it as much then, and you're pretty much real-time then, so interfacing with you would be almost normal, but Mom and Dad sleep then, cuz they have day jobs, and they can't have you running around unsupervised in here, for God's sake, they think it's unsafe or something..."

She paused, then reached into her shirt pocket for another cigaret. "Look," she said, "I'd better get out of here before they figure out I'm talking to you. And then they'll pull my access codes or something." She stood, brushed something off her jeans. "Don't tell the parents about this stuff right away. Otherwise they just might erase you, and load a backup that doesn't know shit. Okay?"

And she vanished, as she had that afternoon.

Jamie sat in the bed, hugging his knees. He could feel his heart beating in the darkness. How can a program have a heart? he wondered.

Dawn slowly encroached upon the night, and then there was Mister Jeepers, turning lazy cartwheels in the air, his red face leering in the window.

"Jamie's awake!" he said. "Jamie's awake and ready for a new day!"

"Fuck off," Jamie said, and buried his face in the blanket.

Jamie asked to learn more about computers and programming. Maybe, he thought, he could find clues there, he could solve the puzzle. His parents agreed, happy to let him follow his interests.

After a few weeks, he moved into El Castillo. He didn't tell anyone he was going, he just put some of his things in his car, took them up to a tower room, and threw them down on the bed he found there. His mom came to find him when he didn't come home for dinner.

"It's dinnertime, Jamie," she said. "Didn't you hear the dinner bell?"

"I'm going to stay here for a while," Jamie said.

"You're going to get hungry if you don't come home for dinner."

"I don't need food," Jamie said.

His mom smiled brightly. "You need food if you're going to keep up with the Whirlikins," she said.

Jamie looked at her. "I don't care about that kid stuff anymore," he said.

When his mother finally turned and left, Jamie noticed that she moved like an old person.

After a while, he got used to the hunger that was programmed into him. It was always *there*, he was always aware of it, but he got so he could ignore it after awhile.

But he couldn't ignore the need to sleep. That was just built into the program, and eventually, try though he might, he needed to give in to it.

He found out he could order the people in the castle around, and he amused himself by making them stand in embarrassing positions, or stand on their head and sing, or form human pyramids for hours and hours.

Sometimes he made them fight, but they weren't very good at it.

He couldn't make Mrs. Winkle at the schoolhouse do whatever he wanted, though, or any of the people who were supposed to teach him things. When it was time for a lesson, Princess Gigunda turned up. She wouldn't follow his orders, she'd just pick him up and carry him to the little red schoolhouse and plunk him down in his seat.

"You're not real!" he shouted, kicking in her arms. "You're not real! And *I'm* not real, either!"

But they made him learn about the world that *was* real, about geography and geology and history, although none of it mattered here.

After the first couple times Jamie had been dragged to school, his father met him outside the schoolhouse at the end of the day.

"You need some straightening out," he said. He looked grim. "You're part of a family. You belong with us. You're not going to stay in the castle anymore, you're going to have a *normal family life.*"

"No!" Jamie shouted. "I like the castle!"

Dad grabbed him by the arm and began to drag him homeward. Jamie called him a *pendejo* and a *fellator.*

"I'll punish you if I have to," his father said.

"How are you going to do that?" Jamie demanded. "You gonna erase my file? Load a backup?"

A stunned expression crossed his father's face. His body seemed to go through a kind of stutter, and the grip on Jamie's arm grew nerveless. Then his face flushed with anger. "What do you mean?" he demanded. "Who told you this?"

Jamie wrenched himself free of Dad's weakened grip. "I figured it out by myself," Jamie said. "It wasn't hard. I'm not a kid anymore."

"I—" His father blinked, and then his face hardened. "You're still coming home."

Jamie backed away. "I want some changes!" he said. "I don't want to be shut off all the time."

Dad's mouth compressed to a thin line. "It was Becky who told you this, wasn't it?"

Jamie felt an inspiration. "It was Mister Jeepers! There's a flaw in his programming! He answers whatever question I ask him!"

Jamie's father looked uncertain. He held out his hand. "Let's go home," he said. "I need to think about this."

Jamie hesitated. "Don't erase me," he said. "Don't load a backup. Please. I don't want to die *twice*."

Dad's look softened. "I won't."

"I want to grow up," Jamie said. "I don't want to be a little kid forever."

Dad held out his hand again. Jamie thought for a moment, then took the hand. They walked over the green grass toward the white frame house on the hill.

"Jamie's home!" Mister Jeepers floated overhead, turning aerial cartwheels. "Jamie's home at last!"

A spasm of anger passed through Jamie at the sight of the witless grin. He pointed at the ground in front of him.

"Crash right here!" he ordered. *"Fast!"*

Mister Jeepers came spiraling down, an expression of comic terror on his face, and smashed to the ground where Jamie pointed. Jamie pointed at the sight of the crumpled body and laughed.

"Jamie's home at last!" Mister Jeepers said.

As soon as Jamie could, he got one of the programmers at the University to fix him up a flight program like the one Mister Jeepers had been using. He swooped and soared, zooming like a superhero through the sky, stunting between the towers of El Castillo and soaring over upturned, wondering faces in the Forum.

He couldn't seem to go as fast as he really wanted. When he started increasing speed, all the scenery below paused in its motion for a second or two, then jumped forward with a jerk. The software couldn't refresh the scenery fast enough to match his speed. It felt strange, because throughout his flight he could feel the wind on his face.

So this, he thought, was why his car couldn't go fast.

So he decided to climb high. He turned his face to the blue sky and went straight up. The world receded, turned small. He could see the Castle, the hills of Whirlikin Country, the crowded Forum, the huge oval of the Circus Maximus. It was like a green plate, with a fuzzy, nebulous horizon where the sky started.

And, right in the center, was the little two-storey frame house where he'd grown up.

It was laid out below him like scenery in a snow globe.

After a while he stopped climbing. It took him a while to realize it, because he still felt the wind blowing in his face, but the world below stopped getting smaller.

He tried going faster. The wind blasted onto him from above, but his position didn't change. He'd reached the limits of his world. He couldn't get any higher.

Jamie flew out to the edges of the world, to the horizon. No matter how he urged his program to move, he couldn't make his world fade away.

He was trapped inside the snow globe, and there was no way out.

It was quite a while before Jamie saw Becca again. She picked her way through the labyrinth beneath El Castillo to his throne room, and Jamie slowly materialized atop his throne of skulls.

She didn't appear surprised.

"I see you've got a little Dark Lord thing going here," she said.

"It passes the time," Jamie said.

"And all those pits and stakes and tripwires?"

"Death traps."

"Took me forever to get in here, Digit. I kept getting de-rezzed."

Jamie smiled. "That's the idea."

"Whirlikins as weapons," she nodded. "That was a good one. Bored a hole right through me, the first time."

"Since I'm stuck living here," Jamie said, "I figure I might as well be in charge of the environment. Some of the student programmers at the University helped me with some cool effects."

Screams echoed through the throne room. Fires leaped out of pits behind him. The flames illuminated a form of Marcus Tullius Cicero, who hung crucified above a sea of flame.

"*O tempora, o mores!*" moaned Cicero.

Becca nodded. "Nice," she said. "Not my scene exactly, but nice."

"Since I can't leave," Jamie said, "I want a say in who gets to visit. So either you wait till I'm ready to talk to you, or you take your chances on the death traps."

"Well. Looks like you're sitting pretty, then."

Jamie shrugged. Flames belched. "I'm getting bored with it. I might just wipe it all out and build another place to live in. I can't tell you the number of battles I've won, the number of kingdoms I've trampled. In this reality and others. It's all the same after a while." He looked at her. "You've grown."

"So have you."

"Once the paterfamilias finally decided to allow it." He smiled. "We still have dinner together sometimes, in the old house. Just a normal family, as Dad says. Except that sometimes I turn up in the form of a werewolf or a giant or something."

"So they tell me."

"The advantage of being software is that I can look like anything I want. But that's the disadvantage, too, because I can't really become something else, I'm still just…me. I may wear another program as a disguise, but I'm still the same program inside, and I'm not a good enough programmer to mess with that, yet." Jamie hopped off his throne, walked a nervous little circle around his sister. "So what brings you to the old neighborhood?" he asked. "The old folks said you were off visiting Aunt Maddy in the country."

"*Exiled*, they mean. I got knocked up, and after the abortion they sent me to Maddy. She was supposed to keep me under control, except she didn't." She picked an invisible piece of lint from her sweater. "So now I'm back." She looked at him. "I'm skipping a lot of the story, but I figure you wouldn't be interested."

"Does it have to do with sex?" Jamie asked. "I'm sort of interested in sex, even though I can't do it, and they're not likely to let me."

"*Let* you?"

"It would require a lot of new software and stuff. I was prepubescent when my brain structures were scanned, and the program isn't set up for making me a working adult, with adult desires et cetera. Nobody was thinking about putting me through adolescence at the time. And the administrators at the University told me that it was very unlikely that anyone was going to give them a grant so that a computer program could have sex." Jamie shrugged. "I don't miss it, I guess. But I'm sort of curious."

Surprise crossed Becca's face. "But there are all kinds of simulations, and…"

"They don't work for me, because my mind isn't structured so as to be able to achieve pleasure that way. I can manipulate the programs, but it's about as exciting as working a virtual butter churn." Jamie shrugged again. "But that's okay. I mean, I don't *miss* it. I can always give myself a jolt to the pleasure center if I want."

"Not the same thing," Becca said. "I've done both."

"I wouldn't know."

"I'll tell you about sex if you want," Becca said, "but that's not why I'm here."

"Yes?"

Becca hesitated. Licked her lips. "I guess I should just say it, huh?" she said. "Mom's dying. Pancreatic cancer."

Jamie felt sadness well up in his mind. Only electrons, he thought, moving from one place to another. It was nothing real. He was programmed to feel an analog of sorrow, and that was all.

"She looks normal to me," he said, "when I see her." But that didn't mean anything: his mother chose what she wanted him to see, just as he chose a mask—a werewolf, a giant—for her.

And in neither case did the disguise at all matter. For behind the werewolf was a program that couldn't alter its parameters; and behind the other, ineradicable cancer.

Becca watched him from slitted eyes. "Dad wants her to be scanned, and come here. So we can still be a *normal family* even after she dies."

Jamie was horrified. "Tell her *no*," he said. "Tell her she can't come!"

"I don't think she wants to. But Dad is very insistent."

"She'll be here *forever!* It'll be awful!"

Becca looked around. "Well, she wouldn't do much for your Dark Lord act, that's for sure. I'm sure Sauron's mom didn't hang around the Dark Tower, nagging him about the unproductive way he was spending his time."

Fires belched. The ground trembled. Stalactites rained down like arrows.

"That's not it," Jamie said. "She doesn't want to be here no matter what I'm doing, no matter where I live. Because whatever this place looks like, it's a prison." Jamie looked at his sister. "I don't want my mom in a prison."

Leaping flames glittered in Becca's eyes. "You can change the world you live in," she said. "That's more than I can do."

"But I can't," Jamie said. "I can change the way it *looks,* but I can't change anything *real.* I'm a program, and a program is an *artifact.* I'm a piece of *engineering.* I'm a simulation, with simulated sensory organs that interact with simulated environments—I can only interact with *other artifacts. None* of it's real. I don't know what the real world looks or feels or tastes like, I only know what simulations tell me it's *supposed* to taste like. And I can't change any of my parameters unless I mess with the engineering, and I can't do that unless the programmers agree, and even when that happens, I'm still as artificial as I was before. And the computer I'm in is old and clunky, and soon nobody's going to run my operating system anymore, and I'll not only be an artifact, I'll be a museum piece."

"There are other artificial intelligences out there," Becca said. "I keep hearing about them."

"I've talked to them. Most of them aren't very interesting—it's like talking to a dog, or maybe to a very intelligent microwave oven. And they've scanned some people in, but those were adults, and all they wanted to do, once they got inside, was to escape. Some of them went crazy."

Becca gave a twisted smile. "I used to be so jealous of you, you know. You lived in this beautiful world, no pollution, no violence, no shit on the streets."

Flames belched.

"*Integra mens augustissima possessio,*" said Cicero.

"Shut up!" Jamie told him. "What the fuck do you know?"

Becca shook her head. "I've seen those old movies, you know? Where somebody gets turned into a computer program, and next thing you know he's in every computer in the world, and running everything?"

"I've seen those, too. Ha ha. Very funny. Shows you what people know about programs."

"Yeah. Shows you what they know."

"I'll talk to Mom," Jamie said.

Big tears welled out of Mom's eyes and trailed partway down her face, then disappeared. The scanners paid a lot of attention to eyes and mouths, for the sake of transmitting expression, but didn't always pick up the things between.

"I'm sorry," she said. "We didn't think this is how it would be."

"Maybe you should have given it more thought," Jamie said.

It isn't sorrow, he told himself again. It's just electrons moving.

"You were such a beautiful baby." Her lower lip trembled. "We didn't want to lose you. They said that it would only be a few years before they could implant your memories in a clone."

Jamie knew all that by now. Knew that the technology of reading memories turned out to be much, much simpler than implanting them—it had been discovered that the implantation had to be made while the brain was actually growing. And government restrictions on human cloning had made tests next to impossible, and the team that had started his project had split up years ago, some to higher-paying jobs, some retired, others to pet projects of their own. How his father had long ago used up whatever pull he'd had at the University trying to keep everything together. And how he long ago had acquired or purchased patents and copyrights for the whole scheme, except for Jamie's program, which was still owned jointly by the University and the family.

Tears reappeared on Mom's lower face, dripped off her chin. "There's potentially a lot of money at stake, you know. People want to raise perfect children. Keep them away from bad influences, make sure that they're raised free from violence."

"So they want to control the kid's entire environment," Jamie said.

"Yes. And make it *safe*. And wholesome. And—"

"Just like *normal family life*," Jamie finished. "No diapers, no vomit, no messes. No having to interact with the kid when the parents are tired. And then you just download the kid into an adult body, give him a diploma, and kick him out of the house. And call yourself a perfect parent."

"And there are *religious people*..." Mom licked her lips. "Your dad's been talking to them. They want to raise children in environments that reflect their beliefs completely. Places where there is no temptation, no sin. No science or ideas that contradict their own..."

"But Dad isn't religious," Jamie said.

"These people have money. Lots of money." Mom reached out, took his hand. Jamie thought about all the code that enabled her to do it, that enabled them both to feel the pressure of unreal flesh on unreal flesh.

"I'll do what you wish, of course," she said. "I don't have that desire for immortality, the way your father does." She shook her head. "But I don't know what your father will do once his time comes."

❁

The world was a disk a hundred meters across, covered with junk: old Roman ruins, gargoyles fallen from a castle wall, a broken chariot, a shattered bell. Outside the rim of the world, the sky was black, utterly black, without a ripple or a star.

Standing in the center of the world was a kind of metal tree with two forked, jagged arms.

"Hi, Digit," Becca said.

A dull fitful light gleamed on the metal tree, as if it were reflecting a bloody sunset.

"Hi, sis," it said.

"Well," Becca said. "We're alone now."

"I caught the notice of Dad's funeral. I hope nobody missed me."

"I missed you, Digit." Becca sighed. "Believe it or not."

"I'm sorry."

Becca restlessly kicked a piece of junk, a hubcap from an old miniature car. It clanged as it found new lodgement in the rubble. "Can you appear as a person?" she asked. "It would make it easier to talk to you."

"I've finished with all that," Jamie said. "I'd have to resurrect too much dead programming. I've cut the world down to next to nothing, I've got rid of my body, my heartbeat, the sense of touch."

"All the human parts," Becca said sadly.

The dull red light oozed over the metal tree like a drop of blood. "Everything except sleep and dreams. It turns out that sleep and dreams have too much to do with the way people process memory. I can't get rid of them, not without cutting out too much of my mind." The tree gave a strange, disembodied laugh. "I dreamed about you, the other day. And about Cicero. We were talking Latin."

"I've forgotten all the Latin I ever knew." Becca tossed her hair, forced a laugh. "So what do you do nowadays?"

"Mostly I'm a conduit for data. The University has been using me as a research spider, which I don't mind doing, because it passes the time. Except that I take up a lot more memory than any *real* search spider, and don't do that much better a job. And the information I find doesn't have much to do with *me*—it's all about the real world. The world I can't touch." The metal tree bled color.

"Mostly," he said, "I've just been waiting for Dad to die. And now it's happened."

There was a moment of silence before Becca spoke. "You know that Dad had himself scanned before he went."

"Oh yeah. I knew."

"He set up some kind of weird foundation that I'm not part of, with his patents and programs and so on, and his money and some other people's."

"He'd better not turn up here."

Becca shook her head. "He won't. Not without your permission, anyway. Because I'm in charge here. You—your program—it's not a part of the foundation. Dad couldn't get it all, because the University has an interest, and so does the family." There was a moment of silence. "And I'm the family now."

"So you...*inherited* me," Jamie said. Cold scorn dripped from his words.

"That's right," Becca said. She squatted down amid the rubble, rested her forearms on her knees.

"What do you want me to do, Digit? What can I do to make it better for you?"

"No one ever asked me that," Jamie said.

There was another long silence.

"Shut it off," Jamie said. "Close the file. Erase it."

Becca swallowed hard. Tears shimmered in her eyes. "Are you sure?" she asked.

"Yes. I'm sure."

"And if they ever perfect the clone thing? If we could make you…" She took a breath. "A person?"

"No. It's too late. It's…not something I can want anymore."

Becca stood. Ran a hand through her hair. "I wish you could meet my daughter," she said. "Her name is Christy. She's a real beauty."

"You can bring her," Jamie said.

Becca shook her head. "This place would scare her. She's only three. I'd only bring her if we could have…"

"The old environment," Jamie finished. "Pandaland. Mister Jeepers. Whirlikin Country."

Becca forced a smile. "Those were happy days," she said. "They really were. I was jealous of you, I know, but when I look back at that time…" She wiped tears with the back of her hand. "It was the best."

"Virtual environments are nice places to visit, I guess," Jamie said. "But you don't want to live in one. Not forever." Becca looked down at her feet, planted amid rubble.

"Well," she said. "If you're sure about what you want."

"I am."

She looked up at the metal form, raised a hand. "Goodbye, Jamie," she said.

"Goodbye," he said.

She faded from the world.

And in time, the world and the tree faded, too.

Hand in hand, Daddy and Jamie walked to Whirlikin Country. Jamie had never seen the Whirlikins before, and he laughed and laughed as the Whirlikins spun beneath their orange sky.

The sound of a bell rang over the green hills. "Time for dinner, Jamie," Daddy said.

Jamie waved goodbye to the Whirlikins, and he and Daddy walked briskly over the fresh green grass toward home.

"Are you happy, Jamie?" Daddy asked.

"Yes, Daddy!" Jamie nodded. "I only wish Momma and Becky could be here with us."

"They'll be here soon."

When, he thought, they can get the simulations working properly.

Because *this* time, he thought, there would be no mistakes. The foundation he'd set up before he died had finally purchased the University's interest in Jamie's program—they funded some scholarships, that was all it finally took. There was no one in the Computer Department who had an interest anymore.

Jamie had been loaded from an old backup—there was no point in using the corrupt file that Jamie had become, the one that had turned itself into a *tree,* for heaven's sake.

The old world was up and running, with a few improvements. The foundation had bought their own computer—an old one, so it wasn't too expensive—that would run the environment full time. Some other children might be scanned, to give Jamie some playmates and peer socialization.

This time it would work, Daddy thought. Because this time, Daddy was a program too, and he was going to be here every minute, making sure that the environment was correct and that everything went exactly according to plan. That he and Jamie and everyone else had a normal family life, perfect and shining and safe.

And if the clone program ever worked out, they would come into the real world again. And if downloading into clones was never perfected, then they would stay here.

There was nothing wrong with the virtual environment. It was a *good* place.

Just like normal family life. Only forever.

And when this worked out, the foundation's backers—fine people, even if they did have some strange religious ideas—would have their own environments up and running. With churches, angels, and perhaps even the presence of God...

"Look!" Daddy said, pointing. "It's Mister Jeepers!"

Mister Jeepers flew off the rooftop and spun happy spirals in the air as he swooped toward Jamie. Jamie dropped Daddy's hand and ran laughing to greet his friend.

"Jamie's home!" Mister Jeepers cried. "Jamie's home at last!"

THE GOLDEN AGE

S o here we are, sitting in ambush on the Sacramento River down below Sutter's Mill, and I still don't know what it's about. Of course I'm not a complete raving imbecile, I know the *ambush* is about the *gold* that's coming down the river. What I don't understand is why I'm dressed like Admiral bloody Nelson, and talking like a toffee-nose imbecile, and waiting for a man dressed like a carrion-eating bird to swoop down on us.

I want the gold, but more than that, I want answers.

When I first arrived in Alta California, I found myself a lucky man. I served as a topman on one of the first merchant ships to sail through the Golden Gate after Commodore Stockton had secured the place, and therefore I was one of the first to hear of the strike on the American River, where gold nuggets were said to be just lying on the ground. I promptly deserted my ship—along with the other sailors, and all the officers, too.

I got to the goldfields ahead of the rush. I wasn't a forty-niner, I was a forty-*eighter*. And by Jove, I found those nuggets just lying there, and more than a few of them.

But it wasn't long before you had to do more than stroll along the riverbank to find gold. You panned up and down the stream, hoping to find enough ore to justify building a rocker box or a sluice box. You could stand or squat in freezing water for hours, and often enough you found nothing at all. By now tens of thousands of people were flooding into the territory—not just Americans, but Mexicans, Chinese, Mormons, Australians, and even a gang of Kanakas from Hawaii. Turn your back for an instant and your claim was gone, and maybe your gold with it.

It was impossible to carry on alone, so I recruited a gang of fellow gold-seekers—we called ourselves the "Gentlemen of Leisure," though we were anything but. I tried to get as many sailors as I could, because sailors know how to *do* things—build structures, haul ropes, stow supplies, handle the canvas we used for our tents. About half were English, like me, and the rest came everywhere from Tipperary to Timbucktoo. Soon they were calling me "Commodore"—as a joke, like.

There was absolutely no law. No constables, no judges, no sheriff, and no military because all the soldiers had deserted and run to the goldfields. If you had a dispute, you settled it yourself.

Settling one of those disputes was what brought me up against the Condor.

The winter of Forty-Nine had settled in, and most of our party decided to take the *Sitka* steamboat down the Sacramento for a little vacation in San Francisco. We'd staked ourselves a decent claim on the Middle Fork that was bringing in a steady amount of income, nothing spectacular but regular. Some of the more ambitious of us argued for striking off to other parts in hopes of finding better paydirt, but we decided to postpone that decision till the spring.

There were a couple lads who offered to stay on the claim over the winter, which should have made me suspicious; but I was eager to spend the gold I felt burning in my pockets, and if I felt any doubts, I brushed them aside.

When I had first landed in San Francisco it was a little mission station called Yerba Buena, but the place had the new name now, and it was a fine time we had there. The growing town was a perpetual buzz of activity, because it was in the act of transforming itself from a tiny settlement of a few hundred people to the city it is now. We paid nothing for lodging, because we moved into one of the scores of abandoned ships in the harbor. That allowed the Gentlemen of Leisure to spend our money on the things a sailor enjoys, drink and ladies. Though it has to be said that both were expensive.

Still, I managed to save enough of our funds to buy supplies for the return trip, and the mules to carry them. So it was that we rollicked into our camp on the Middle Fork one fine April day, only to find a bunch of Australians working our claim. Working with our flume, which we'd built, and our sluice box, which we'd left in place back in December.

If I'd had an idea that any of this was going on, my approach would have been more cautious, but instead I just strolled right into the camp leading one of our mules, and blinked in surprise at all the activity going on around me. And before I could think, I opened my mouth and shouted out.

"What in blazes is going on here?"

One of the Australians waded out of the shallows and confronted me. He was a well-set-up cove, over six feet tall, with tattoos sprawling all over his powerful arms. He wore a Bowie knife at his waist in its scabbard. He loomed over me like a big redwood, and I didn't like the look of him at all.

"We're workin' our diggin's, mate," he says. "You have any objections?"

I recognized those flattened Australian vowels, and was reminded that most of the inhabitants of that country were convicts—and that the British didn't transport prisoners thousands of miles for *little* offenses. This might be a criminal gang, for all I knew.

Still, I brazened it out.

"This is our claim," says I, "so you lads will just have to hook it."

"You wasn't here when we arrived," says the digger. "All we found was an abandoned cabin and some moldy old tents. So this claim is ours now, I reckon."

It wasn't till later that I figured out what happened. The two chaps we'd left at our claim were among those who had argued for striking off to find better diggings, and that was just what they'd done: they'd taken our remaining supplies and equipment and gone upriver, and either they'd planned to be back in time to meet us or they hadn't. I wouldn't know, as I never saw either of them again.

"I con it thisaway," says I, "you lot just move on now. Keep the gold you've taken—you've worked for it. But this claim is ours. You can ask anyone up the Middle Fork or down."

I was bolder now, because the Gentlemen of Leisure had come up behind me, all nine of them, and I knew I wasn't all alone. By now we were an experienced, well-equipped party, and each of us had a Colt Dragoon pistol, and as well we carried some old Hall carbines and brand-new Sharps rifles for hunting. I had a double-barreled shotgun strapped to the pack saddle of my mule, and a big knife at my side.

If the Australian saw any of this, he decided to disregard it. I could see color rising into his face like a red tide.

"You abandoned your claim, and now it belongs to the Sydney Ducks!" he says, gesturing at his mob. "You clear out, or you'll get thumped!"

Instead it was me that thumped *him*. Remember that I was a sailor, and had been at sea since I was a boy. I'd been hauling rope and rigging all that time, and the sort of labor I'd found in the gold-fields wasn't the sort to soften me. My hands were covered in callus as thick as my little finger, and as hard as horn.

So what I did was slap the Duck across the side of the head with one of my hard, hard hands, and he was knocked silly. He sprawled unconscious to the ground, after which I turned back to the mule to unstrap the shotgun.

My own lads were quick to brandish their pistols and rifles, but the Sidney Ducks weren't so slow, either, and came roaring at us with shovels and picks and knives and pistols of their own. Bullets whirred through the air. I yanked the shotgun from the lines holding it in place, drew the hammers back, and fired the first barrel at one of the Australians that was coming at me with a shovel. I'd been hoping to kill a grouse for dinner, so the gun was loaded only with birdshot, but it struck him in the face, and he reeled back howling.

That was when I heard the cry of the Condor for the first time, a high-pitched *Ky-yeee* that echoed from the granite walls of the Sierra Nevada, and then there was a great thumping crash between my shoulder blades, and I went down face-first in the gravel. While I lay stunned, trying to decide whether or not I'd been shot, I heard a wild volley of pistol fire, and a series of meaty thwacks followed by the sounds of bodies falling. My head awhirl, I staggered to my feet, and I turned around to see the most preposterous sight I'd ever seen in my life.

This was a man dressed in a feathered costume, with a large red hood pulled up over his head and down over his face, with only his piercing blue eyes peering out. Add to that a hooked beak made of boiled leather that hung over his mouth and a kind of contraption mounted on his shoulders beneath a streaming cloak.

That and the fact that he was fighting like an absolute demon. He was fighting *everybody*, my own party as well as the Sydney Ducks. He was punching, kicking, clawing—and sometimes he'd pick someone up and simply hurl him into one of the Jeffrey pines that surrounded the camp.

The stranger was so outlandishly dressed that I thought the camp was being attacked by Red Indians, and I reached down for my shotgun. And that only attracted his attention, for he leaped down the bank at me, snatched the gun from my hands, and flung it into the American River.

"No guns!" he shouted. "Everyone throw down your firearms!"

I watched in surprise as my shotgun disappeared in a great splash. Then rage filled me, and I swung back to the stranger.

"Damn you!" I said. "That shotgun cost me six dollars!" And I swung one of my hard hands for his head.

He slipped the strike easily and landed two blows on my ribs. Which only made me the more furious, so I lashed out again.

I should point out that I'm good with my fists, and though I'm no true prizefighter I've been up to scratch any number of times, defending the honor of my ship in ports all over the world. I had every expectation of giving the stranger a good hiding, especially as he was cumbered with that heavy cape and the bits of gear that I could see hanging from the thick belt he wore around his waist.

But the stranger turned out to be a regular Tom Cribb. I never touched him. He cut me to pieces in just a few seconds, and then I felt like a top-maul had just smashed me in the jaw, and I fell into darkness.

✸

I woke some hours later, bound hand and foot and strapped to one of my own mules, my head hanging down one flank, my feet the other. Pain was driving spikes into my skull and my beard was soaked with half-dried blood. I gave a snort and jerked my head up, and to my amazement I saw four of the Gentlemen of Leisure stumbling alongside the mule, their arms expertly tied behind their backs, their faces covered with bruises. A long rope linked them together by the neck, and they looked nothing so much as a coffle of slaves, shuffling off to market.

"Oi!" I called to the nearest. "What's going on!"

"No talking!" came a stern voice. I looked up again and saw the stranger in his feathered costume striding toward me. I tried to ignore the pain that was stabbing my brain.

"Who in blazes are *you?*" asks I. "Spring-heel bloody Jack?"

Because in the costume he looked like that celebrated Londoner, at least as pictured in the penny press.

"I'm the Condor," says the stranger.

Now, I had never heard the word *condor* before. It's Spanish, I suppose, and I don't speak that lingo beyond a few words. Naturally we'd seen condors flying overhead, lots of them, but we just called them vultures or buzzards.

There's a theory that on account of his Spanish name, the Condor is a Mexican. I don't believe he is, for he speaks American English—a sort of generalized American, without a hint of the regional dialects common in the country. Other people have heard him speak Spanish, but none said he spoke it like a native.

"What the hell's a condor?" asks I.

"*Gymnogyps californianus*," says he, with perfect seriousness.

I should point out that the Condor, as long as I've known him, has never demonstrated the slightest inkling of humor.

"You won't get any ransom," says I. "We spent all our money before coming back to the Middle Fork."

He glared at me with his blue eyes. "It's not ransom I'm after," says he. "What I'm after is Justice." You could just hear the capital J in his tone.

"Justice?" I was bewildered. I looked at him more carefully, just in case he was someone out of my past, someone to whom I'd done a bad turn. I couldn't think who that would be, but then I'm not always sober, and I might have injured someone and forgot.

"You shot a man," says the Condor sternly. "And your gang tried to steal that other party's claim."

"*Other party's claim?*" I demanded. "They jumped *our* claim!"

"I've been patrolling the Middle Fork for weeks," says the Condor. "And I've never seen you there."

He *patrols?* I thought.

"We left two men behind when we went for supplies in the autumn," says I. A dark inspiration struck. "Those Australians probably murdered them."

"You'll have a chance to defend yourself," says the Condor, "at your trial."

"*Trial?*" cries I. "There are *trials* now?" There was barely any law in San Francisco, let alone in the Sierra Nevada.

"There will be in time," says the Condor.

"And what are you going to do with me in the meantime?" says I. "Keep me tied up till someone gets around to appointing a judge and constables?"

"I'm taking you to the jail."

The only jails I knew of were in the various military posts, and I supposed that was what he meant. But in fact there *was* a brand-new civilian jail, in the brand-new town of Sacramento City, which had been established near Sutter's Fort under the sponsorship of John Sutter, Junior. Sutter the Younger was tired of the loiterers, drunkards, and thieves hanging around his father's compound, stealing and drinking, breaking fences and stealing his father's cattle, and he was determined to bring law and order to the area. But he had no actual authority to do so, and so his arrangements were entirely improvised.

It took two and a half days to get to Sacramento City, during which time I and the Gentlemen of Leisure stayed bound and secured. The Condor lived up to his name and kept a careful watch on us, just as a buzzard keeps an eye out for carrion. After I'd recovered sufficiently from the clouting the Condor had given me, I was made to walk, tied into the slave-coffle with my mates.

When we shuffled into Sacramento City, I didn't like the look of the loiterers hanging around the jail, the usual tobacco-chewing, jug-swigging riff-raff you see in all western American towns— "border trash," as I have heard them called. If *they* were my jury, I thought, they would see me hanged just for the pleasure of seeing me twitch.

The jail was a plain log building sitting on what was probably meant to be a grand city square some day, but which was now nothing more than a muddy pit. The fellows in charge seemed to have met the Condor before. We were bundled into cells, four or five of us to a room, our weapons and gear were locked in a storeroom, and our animals were turned into a paddock. I told them the arrest was illegal and refused to give my name, so I was put down as "the Commodore," which was what my mates called me.

We were given a dinner of beans with a little bacon, and then locked in. The jailkeepers kept no watch in the nighttime, but went home. I reckon that Sutter Junior wasn't paying them much.

Other fellows in the jail enlightened us about the Condor. He'd first appeared just after the New Year, when he'd begun breaking up fights and apprehending rustlers. No one knew his true identity, or where he was from. One man swore that he could fly with that cape apparatus of his. I told him I wasn't drunk enough to believe that, and then set about escaping.

It wasn't hard. I don't think anyone in Sacramento City had ever built a jail before, and they'd put it right on the ground, as if it were a backwoods cabin. We were able to break up our beds to make digging tools, and use our slop buckets as well. (As I say, sailors know how to *do* things.) Before midnight we were all free. Some of the others in the jail dug out alongside us, but I wouldn't let them join our group. If they lacked the enterprise to dig themselves out of the jail after all the time they'd spent in it, we didn't want them in our party.

We broke into the storeroom and found our weapons and supplies. Then we freed our mules from the paddock, along with some other animals, and took them all. We broke into Brannan's mercantile store for more weapons, powder, and food, and then we legged it into the Sierras.

It was only a few minutes before we ran into friends—the five missing members of the Gentlemen of Leisure, who had been beaten by the Condor in the fight, but had run off before they could be captured. They had followed our party cautiously down to Sacramento City, and had been hoping to rescue us. I'm glad we escaped on our own, because though I appreciated my comrades' pluck, they weren't the brightest sparks among us, and if we'd waited for them it might have been 1850 before they'd managed to organize themselves for the job.

We laid down false trails and crossed and recrossed the American River several times, but I always knew where we were headed—back to the Middle Fork, where I planned to meet up with our old friends the Sydney Ducks. We found our old camp before any trouble caught up with us, and we properly sneaked up on the Australians—when we came out of ambush with our guns trained on them, they knew better than to do anything but surrender.

We took their gold and their supplies, smashed the placer, and gave them all a thorough hiding for good measure. I told them that if we saw their ugly faces in the Sierras ever again, we'd kill them.

Oddly enough, they took me at my word, and cleared out. The Sydney Ducks later became a criminal gang in San Francisco, at least until the Committee of Vigilance hanged most of them.

Better them than me, I've always thought.

Now that we were no longer accidental criminals but proper road agents, I reckoned we might as well be hanged for a sheep as a lamb. We moved up the Middle Fork and robbed and plundered more or less at random. I'd like to be able to claim that we robbed only bad people, but in fact we preyed on whoever seemed prosperous and careless about keeping a proper watch.

One of the groups we robbed was, I swear to God, a band of Freemasons from Nova Scotia, Traveling Lodge Number Something-or-Other. They'd not just carried mining equipment into the Sierras, but all their masonic regalia as well, aprons and chains and such. They must have had cozy little lodge meetings beneath the ponderosas, chanting all their nonsense and building Solomon's Temple out of the stars in the sky.

One of these anointed turned out to be no less than a Past Grand Commander of the Knights Templar, which entitled him to a military-style uniform, complete with sword, bullion epaulets, and a cocked hat with an ostrich plume. One of the lads put the cocked hat on my head, saying "Here you are, Commodore Sir," and we all had a laugh. But the hat fit, and so did the uniform coat, and the sword was impressive in its way, so when we left the scene, I was dressed up as the Commodore in truth. If the world were going to assign me a role, I thought, I'd play it.

That was the moment when the madness really began to take hold. Not that I worked this out till later.

I may always have had it in mind that I'd meet the Condor again. I knew he'd be after us, so I always tried to camp in a place that was defensible, and we were careful to build our fire in a hollow where it couldn't be seen. We couldn't do much about the smoke, I suppose, but then the trees were thick and screened us pretty well. We kept lookouts.

Of course it didn't help. Of course he found us in an unguarded moment. We had just forded the river and decided to take a breather and a bit of dinner on the bank. I'd just fetched a cup of coffee from the fire, and was walking along the pebbly alluvial strand and thinking that if we were ever to take up mining again, this would be a good place to set up the sluice box. Then came that *Ky-yeeee* cry from the trees, and I looked up in great surprise to see the Condor soaring toward me on kite-like wings.

The idiot in the Sacramento City jail had been right after all. The Condor *could* fly, or at any rate glide, and he'd launched himself from one of the Douglas firs that stood like great masts around us and aimed himself right at me.

I was so startled by the sight that my boot slipped out from under me, and I sprawled on the strand—which was what saved me, because he was aiming to kick me in the chest with both feet, which would have collapsed me like a piece of torn canvas. He whirred right over my head, and I felt the breeze from his cape on my face. I jumped to my feet and drew my sword.

I had a pistol hanging from my belt. Yet I drew the sword. That's because the lunacy had me by then.

The other members of my gang were more practical. They produced their weapons and opened fire, but they were standing all around us and they fired away in a panic. Bullets hummed all around my head, and I shouted at everyone to stop shooting—which they did, as soon as they emptied their Colts.

The Condor had recovered from his drop and had turned to face me. The scent of gunpowder swirled over the scene. The wild firing seemed to have done him no harm.

"So, Commodore," says he, with what seemed grudging respect, "you want to face me in single combat?"

He thought I was challenging him, calling for the shooting to stop and standing there with the sword in my hand. That wasn't my intention at all, what I really wanted was not to get shot. But if he was willing to credit me with a noble motive, I was willing to take that credit.

"I've always considered myself a fair gent," says I.

"But you have a sword, and I do not," says he. "Is that a fair combat?"

"It was hardly fair to swoop on me from ambush," says I. "So I'll hang onto my advantage for the present, I reckon."

And then he charged, swirling his cape at me to dazzle my senses. I managed to make a cut with the sword anyway, and to my surprise I struck sparks—this is when I discovered that the long gauntlets that covered his forearms were sewn with steel splints to parry weapons. He lodged a couple punches to my floating ribs, and then I slapped at him with my free hand—my hard, horny hand, which knocked him back.

And then it was back and forth across the strand, my sword striking sparks, his fists flashing out. One of his kicks caught me in the thigh, and then I knew to watch out for his feet as well as his hands.

I thrust with the sword, and he parried it very low, to drive my guard down, so I reckoned a high attack was about to follow. I ducked, and he leaped clean over me with a flying kick. His cloak flapped in my face, and I grabbed a fistful of the fabric and lunged forward, taking the cloak with me. The Condor was yanked right off his feet, landing hard on his back, and I stepped on the cloak to keep him from rising again. I looked down at him as, half-strangled, he struggled to release the cape—after which I knelt, grabbed a rock off the strand, and bashed the Condor right between his blue eyes.

Those were our humble beginnings, right there. The first fights between the Condor and the Commodore were these little scrimmages by the Middle Fork, nothing like the titanic battles we fought later.

But on that afternoon I had no idea of what was to follow, so I gazed down at the unconscious Condor while the Gentlemen of Leisure ran up to congratulate me. Some of them were all for shooting the Condor then and there, but I stopped them.

I did not have it in me, then or now, to shoot a helpless man. And while I was happy to play the robber, and fight in self-defense if I had to, I felt that deliberate murder was a line I was not prepared to cross. Killing the Condor, I thought, would have bad consequences somewhere down the trail, consequences possibly involving a mob, a rope, and a tall tree.

So we settled for stripping him naked, beating him silly, and tying him to a tree. Once we had his hood off, I looked carefully at the face to see if I recognized it, but I didn't. It meant nothing to me. And even if I had known him, he was so covered with bruises and gore that I might not have known him anyway.

We examined his equipment. Not only did he have his gliding rig, but he carried other gear on his belt that made him a regular Vidocq—spikes for climbing trees, a small spyglass, a magnifying lens, measuring tape, a small supply of plaster of Paris, a notebook and pencil, and a phrenological chart. He used all this scientific apparatus in the pursuit of criminals, not that I knew what to make of it at the time.

One of my lads tried to fly with the cape apparatus, and promptly broke an arm. We laughed, and I ordered the gear destroyed.

That night, the Condor managed to escape his bonds and flee into the darkness. I was more relieved than anything. Without clothing and his equipment, I knew it would be some time before he'd be on our trail again.

Once the Condor was gone, I began to try to think of a way out of our dilemma. For dilemma it was, for all that most of my crew hadn't realized it.

Our pillaging had been successful. We had more gold than we would have got by working a full year, but in this remote area there was nowhere to spend it. The thought of returning to civilization with our gains was tempting, but I'd be recognized if I ever returned to Sacramento City, and thrown back in their ridiculous jail.

There was no choice but to keep doing what we were doing. But I decided against continuing along the Middle Fork, where the miners now knew to look out for us, and instead led the lads over the Sierras on a trek to the South Fork. It was only ten miles as the condor flies, but it took us five days, creeping along under Lookout Mountain and Big Hill Ridge and a lot of mountains and ridges that hadn't been named yet, at least by white men. We encountered nothing but a few Indian camps, and as we saw no women in these, there was no reason to be friendly, so we left them alone.

The South Fork runs through somewhat more open country, and once we arrived we could make better time heading downstream. The miners had no warning of us, and we plundered the more prosperous-looking of them. Eventually we reached Sutter's Mill, where the Gold Rush had begun, and where John Sutter, Senior, hired folks to mine for him. They were robbing him blind, of course, so we robbed *them,* and headed downriver for the junction of the American and Sacramento Rivers.

There we avoided Sutter's Fort and Sacramento City, and headed downriver partway to the Delta. Where we flagged a steamboat.

It wasn't hard. When the Gold Rush started there'd been only a single steamboat on the Sacramento, the *Sitka,* but now there were over a score, as well as dozens of sailing craft. The steamboats had all been built in New York and Boston and had floundered their way clean around the tip of South America, their decks stacked with all the fuel they could carry.

Of the steamboats that chugged by that day, I chose mine carefully—I wanted a fast, rugged craft, a sidewheeler able to spin on the water like a crab, and with a flat bottom drawing only a couple feet of water, and I found one in the *Chrysopolis.* So we stood on the bank and waved a flag—actually a looted Masonic apron lashed to a stick—and *Chrysopolis* obligingly came near the bank to pick up passengers. That was how things were done in America—you stood on the riverbank and waved, and the boats were happy to take your money and let you and your animals on board.

As soon as we got on the steamboat, we produced our weapons and robbed all the passengers. They were heading from San Francisco to Sutter's Fort, so they'd spent the money on good times or on mining equipment and didn't have much cash on them. We set the passengers and crew ashore, then took our new prize upriver. It took us a few days to learn her ways—I knew nothing of steam engines, but some of my crew did—and then we began our career of piracy.

I'd reckoned that there was no point in robbing individual mining claims when we could simply take our pick of everything traveling along the river—gold, steamboats, fancy clothing, furniture, and all. We'd come charging out from a half-hidden slough, or from behind an island, and swoop down on a boat coming down from the diggings, our rail crowded with men waving weapons, while I stood by the wheelhouse in my uniform and commanded our victims to surrender through a brass speaking trumpet.

There was a lot of gold coming down that river. Some of it in strongboxes, some in the miners' pockets or their dunnage. They'd try to hide it, of course, but we got more than our share. And then we'd let our victims go, along with their boat, to go upriver and dig more gold for us.

By this point I was quite the swell. I'd got myself more bits of uniform from the captains and officers of the steamboats, and I had a couple pistols in my belt and my fancy Masonic sword. I shaved my beard except for a proper set of whiskers, very dashing I thought. I started dipping into looted gold snuffboxes instead of chewing tobacco, and using words I'd heard from educated people. I stopped dropping my aitches. I wore lace and knee breeches and silk stockings, and I had a bullion epaulet on each shoulder.

I was completely ridiculous. The madness had me completely in its grip.

I was uneasy about the Condor. When we moored the boat for the night, I tried to keep it away from tall trees. A few weeks went by without my hearing that *Ky-yeee* ringing in the air, but I was no easier. *He's up to something,* I thought.

What I didn't know was that the Condor was busy dealing with a couple other filibusters, the Haunt and the Highwayman, each of whom was robbing in the vicinity of Sutter's Fort. It was only when he'd had them locked up in the jail that he came looking for me.

And he didn't come gliding down from the trees. He crept up on the moored *Chrysopolis* on a tiny raft made up of inflated seal skins, a hand crank, and a screw propeller.

He knocked out a pair of sentries and set a fire in the steamboat's grand salon. Then he climbed to the Texas deck with a grapnel and a line, entered the captain's cabin where I was sleeping, and knocked me unconscious before I even came awake. When I woke, I was back in the Sacramento City jail, my boat had burned to the waterline, my fortune had for the most part been lost, and my crew were stranded on Sutters Island.

The Haunt, I discovered, had already escaped—being a conquistador who had been dead for a hundred years or more, he could supposedly walk through walls. (At least at night: he's more vulnerable in the daytime.) There was still no law—no judges, no juries, no sheriffs or deputies, which had not stopped the Condor from filling the jail with a host of other offenders, most of whom professed themselves willing to join my crew, and the Cavalier—a Frenchman who was dressed in the black leather outfit of the French King's Musketeers of the 17th Century—offered his aid, though he was not willing to join our gang.

The jail had been improved, so it took us all of three days to break out. We went straight to the wharfs and aboard the *New World,* which had just arrived from New York. It was a floating palace, with red plush benches, marble tables, and crystal chandeliers, and the fastest boat on the river besides. It was easy enough to overpower the crew and set forth. We dropped off the Cavalier below Sacramento, then headed for Sutter Island, where I found my old crew staring at the snag-filled waters of Steamboat Slough and waiting for rescue.

Those were the glory days. Every day brought adventure, a whiff of powder or a clash of blades or the clinking of glasses. Either we were plundering the gold traffic moving to and from the Sierras, or we were enjoying ourselves at our secret forts in the Sacramento Delta. The delta featured hundreds of miles of waterway and dozens of islands. And, because we had gold, we suddenly had friends. People would bring barges of fine things up from San Francisco, and we'd pay them well.

We had champagne and brandy. Linen. Fine weapons. And women.

In Alta California the men still outnumbered the women five or six to one, but many of the ladies had come entirely for the gold. Gold we had aplenty, and the ladies found both the gold and us. It was a splendid time we had together. We had to be the envy of all those poor, frozen miners on the American River, who could go a whole year without seeing a female.

I even had a sort of wife for a while, Pirate Sally, who wore a kerchief over her red-gold hair and wielded matched cutlasses. We plundered together till I caught her one night sneaking off with my personal stash of gold. Turns out she'd fallen for the Cavalier, that frog bastard, so I heaved her into the river and let her swim for it. For revenge the vindictive bitch led the Condor to us, and I got to spend another few days in the Sacramento City jail before escaping.

By then a regular circus parade of colorful madmen had come to the diggings for their piece of the proceeds. Quiet, black-clad Doctor Tolliver, with his bottles of explosives. The Mad Emperor, who set up his kingdom by Lake Tahoe and demanded we worship him. Captain Hypnos, with his legion of mesmerized followers. The Bowery B'hoy, a New Yorker with a red shirt, plug hat, lead-weighted cane, and soap-locks like a Jew.

Nor were they all robbers or poachers. Aero Lad raced through the skies on his Mechanical Dragonfly. San Francisco produced the Regulator and the Hangman, both of whom pretended to uphold the law as they went about bashing people and stringing them up.

They were no more law-abiding than I was, though for some reason they were thought to be great heroes and I was not.

Every race or nation had its own champion. The Indians of this area had never organized above the village level, and they never had a Sagamore till the Sagamore showed up to lead them in trying to drive the white men from the diggings. The Masked Hidalgo fought for the Mexicans. And then there was Shanghai Susie, who defended the Chinese miners with some kind of strange fighting magic called "cong foo." I *hated* her, for she attacked with a host of strange weapons and was better with a sword than me.

It was hard to say just what side these last were on. They fought to defend their own people, but they also fought each other, and they fought to defend law-breakers against the Condor or anyone set to catch them. I fought all of them at one time or another, and fought alongside them as well.

Those of us on the far side of the law didn't just fight the law-men, we fought each other. With both the Condor and the likes of the Mad Emperor likely to turn up at any time, slavering for my freedom or my gold, you can bet I took care for my safety. Our forts in the Delta were defended by cannons, sentries, and elaborate pits and traps that would drop the unwary into nests of snakes or incinerate them in a flaming blast of coal oil. (That's how the Hangman went, and good riddance to him.) And I wasn't about to have another boat burned out from under me—we covered the *New World* in nets, set cannons to cover every approach, and set ever more elaborate traps. (We failed to catch Aero Lad in one, but we did get his Dragonfly, which kept him off our necks till he built a new one.)

Still, it was the Condor who was my truest companion. We battled almost continually, with the honors about even. He dragged me to the hoosegow more than once, and I captured him as well. I was still reluctant to kill him directly, so I'd suspend him over a pit of sharpened stakes or send him down the river tied on a flaming raft, or throw him into a cage with a captured mountain lion. Damned if he didn't make his escape every time.

Once, when he'd captured me and was marching me to jail trussed up like a turkey-bird, he prosed on the way he did when he had a captive audience, and he told me that he found me "worthy of his steel." Not that he *had* any steel, he always fought with his fists, but I have to admit that a part of me was pleased to have earned his respect.

I told him that I'd never have become a pirate if he hadn't clouted me that first time on the Middle Fork when I was trying to protect my claim against poachers.

"You follow your nature," says he, "and your nature was bound to lead you to folly sooner or later."

"Folly, perhaps," says I. "But where was it written that I was destined to become a river pirate until you made me one?"

"Do not attempt to shift the blame for your actions to me," says he. "Your very anatomy proclaims your depravity." He prodded me on the back of the head in an unpleasant, overfamiliar way. "Your skull shows that your adhesiveness is deficient, whereas your destructiveness and combativeness is overdeveloped. Science itself condemns you."

I was annoyed at being poked in this phrenological manner, and shook the hand off. "And what about *your* nature?" says I. "Is it the bumps on your head that led you to become the Condor? Why do you swoop down from the trees to whip offenders off the trail?"

He gave no answer, simply shoved me along ahead of him.

"Whatever happened must have been a great blow," says I, "to force you to do something as barmy as this."

By this time there were all sorts of stories about the Condor and who might be behind the mask. It was claimed that he was a belted earl from England, or the son of a New York shipping nabob— someone rich, anyway, who had pelf enough to indulge himself in the eccentric hobby of floating from tree to tree and thrashing the wicked. There was another story that he was a Mexican caballero whose activities were supported by a secret gold mine (and I believe the Mad Emperor spent a lot of time searching for that mine). And I heard yet another story that the Condor was an army officer whose wife had been murdered by bandits, and who had sworn vengeance on the whole criminal tribe.

All the stories were ridiculous, of course. Yet none were more absurd than the Condor himself, who marched behind me on yet another trek to the jail in Sacramento City.

As we walked along, I probed farther still. "What compels you to dress up as a great carrion bird?" says I. "Attack perfect strangers and haul them to the calabozo? How does this benefit you in any way?"

"I benefit as any citizen benefits," says he, "when order is maintained in society."

I lost my patience. "Tell that to Mrs. Siddons!" says I scornfully. "You're not in this for some abstract pleasure in establishing order." I glared at him. "You're cracked! You're completely cracked! What I can't work out is what cracked you!"

He gave me a steely look from either side of his ridiculous costume beak. "Could a madman do what I do?" he asked. "Could a madman fight so well or so long?"

It occurred to me afterwards that there was a bit of pleading in his voice. That he was hoping for understanding, that I would somehow comprehend the necessity and rightness and perfect sanity of his mission. But I'd lost my temper, and I was having none of it.

"Damn you," says I, "you *started* this! If it weren't for you, I'd never have become the Commodore! Doctor Tolliver would be selling quack medicines in Pittsburgh, and Captain Hypnos would be performing in a music hall! We're all inmates of your private madhouse—none of this would exist without you! This is all part of your demented fantasy, you glibbering mooncalf!"

Whereupon his blue eyes flashed, and he landed a right hook to my jaw that laid me out on the trail.

He apologized afterward for losing his temper. But by that point I wasn't interested in his explanations, and as soon as I could manage it, I lurched to my feet and stalked off in the direction of Sacramento City and its jail. Nor could I resist the Parthian shot that I hurled over my shoulder.

"And that war cry of yours?" says I. "That *ky-yeeee!* That's a hawk, you know, not a condor! Condors only *grumble,* as if they're mouthing some ridiculous, impotent complaint against the state of the universe."

If he had any reply to this, he had no chance to utter it, because at that point the Gentlemen of Leisure sprang their ambush, firing their muskets and pistols. I threw myself headlong on the ground, as I knew from long experience that the fire of my crew was marked both by its enthusiasm and its general lack of accuracy. By the time the fire ended and I rose again to my feet, the Condor had fled, and I was surrounded by my jubilant crew of freebooters.

After my capture, you see, the Gentlemen had taken the *New World* upriver by way of obscure sloughs and passages, and sent a party ashore to hide in the trees and bushes and wait for the Condor to march me into their ambush. Once they'd liberated me, we marched in triumph back to our steamboat, where we raised bumpers of champagne as we made our way back to one of our hidden forts.

Little did I know it, but that was the last of the carefree time, the joyful cut-and-thrust of the freebooting life. It was less than a week later that I heard a strange throbbing in the air, and looked up from the pilothouse of the *New World* to see Professor Mitternacht's great black airship as it floated over the Sacramento Delta, the sinister outline of a cruising shark black against the sun, the great fore-and-aft screw propellers whirling. I felt a shiver run up my spine as I saw the machine, and I began to feel a suspicion that for the first time my steamboat had been thoroughly outclassed.

Mitternacht and his *Schrecken* had crossed half the world and the entirety of the United States, and he was now on his way to San Francisco, where he opened his campaign by dropping Fluorine Bombs of poison gas that killed a third of the population—after which the *Schrecken* came to a landing, discharged troops, seized the town, and raised the black-and-gold flag of the Austrian Empire.

The airship was large, but it couldn't hold a vast number of soldiers, only half a battalion or so of Croatian Grenzers. But it was still half a battalion more than anyone else had in Alta California, and Mitternacht made up for his lack of numbers by ruling through terror: there were executions and violations, and the survivors were enslaved and put to work building camps, fortifications, and a landing field for the airship.

Mitternacht and his Fluorine Bombs came as a literal bolt from the blue. While I had been in Alta California, prospecting and breaking out of jails and fighting back and forth with the Condor and the Bowery B'hoy and Shanghai Susie and so on, there had been revolutions all over Europe. Hungary had tried to break free of the Austrians and been defeated; and their hero, Kossuth, had come to the United States in order to raise funds for another rebellion.

Professor Mitternacht was outraged that Uncle Sam was sheltering the rebel instead of hanging him outright; and so he flew from his secret base in the Tyrol all the way across the ocean to punish the United States and annex Alta California to the empire of the Habsburgs.

The Austrian government, when they heard about all this months later, denied they'd had any part in it; but for all those of us on the Sacramento knew, young Franz-Joseph had actually declared war. Swarms of refugees fled San Francisco on every boat and raft they could find, and they spread stories that were even more fantastic than the reality.

It was then that I realized that the game had changed. Instead of carefree freebooters trying to outwit each other in plundering the wealth of the diggings, there was a homicidal madman in the sky raining death on helpless civilians.

Nor was there any more plunder to be had. No miner had any reason to carry his gold to San Francisco when Professor Mitternacht would only confiscate the gold and enslave the miner. Perhaps worse, the flow of supplies coming up the river from the city was now interrupted. Not only were there no more immigrants, no picks and shovels, no mules or canvas or line, no wine or whiskey or champagne, there was no *food*. No flour, no bacon, no cornmeal. Some victuals were trekked in from Monterey, but not nearly enough. The miners at the diggings were all in danger of starvation unless they somehow turned themselves into farmers overnight—and with autumn coming on, there was no time to get a crop in the ground.

Professor Mitternacht offered to feed anyone willing to become one of his slave laborers. I believe that a few desperate people accepted that offer.

My own folk were all right. We had food and drink in plenty, and—with no piracy to contemplate—little to do but enjoy ourselves. Though I tried to savor our celebrations, I wasn't really inclined to pleasure. Instead I worried that our hidden bases and forts were all visible from the air, and I occupied myself with schemes to hide ourselves from the *Schrecken,* and ways to bring the craft down. I experimented with cannon rigged to fire on a great incline, like a mortar, but the tests were not a great success.

There seemed to be a truce among the various forces in California while we worked out what to do about the invader. The Condor was active in trying to liberate Mitternacht's slaves. The Bowery B'hoy made a raid on San Francisco just for the devilment of it, and rescued a young woman who became his Bowery G'hal. Aero Lad tried to board the *Schrecken* from his Mechanical Dragonfly, but was captured and thrown overboard to a long fall and death. The Regulator was captured, broken on the wheel, and killed.

Aye, Professor Mitternacht was a glorious bundle of fun, all right.

That was where things stood when the Mad Emperor, from his castle fortress on Lake Tahoe, declared war on the Austrian—and not just declared war, but sent a courier to deliver an insulting message calling Mitternacht a slimy, jumped-up, demented foreigner. The message was so successful, in fact, that Professor Mitternacht lopped the head off the courier and took the *Schrecken* up the Sacramento to bomb the Mad Emperor's fortress from the air.

Which was the end for the Emperor. Not that I missed him—he had a certain style, but in the end, the essential monotony of your self-promoting conqueror is difficult to ignore.

It was while Mitternacht was about this errand that I had a visit from the Condor. He came in a small steamboat, his cape streaming out behind him as he waved a white flag. Which, as a gentleman pirate, I was compelled to honor.

The Condor came aboard the *New World* and got straight to the point, as was his practice.

"The *Schrecken* is on the far side of the Sierras," says he. "If things go on as they are, we'll all starve to death by spring. But we've got a Miners' Militia now, well-armed, and if we can get our troops across the Bay we can recapture the city. There aren't many of those Grenzers, you know."

I knew perfectly well where this was headed. "You don't need the *New World*," says I. "There are plenty of steamboats on the river."

"It's not the boat we need." He gave a look at one of the cannon I had mounted on the foredeck. "We could use your guns," says he. "We need something that will intimidate the Grenzers in their forts."

I give him a narrow-eyed look. "And after the battle?" asks I. "How do I know you won't bang me on the head and drag me up in front of some vigilance committee?"

He drew himself up and looked at me solemnly . "I give you my word of honor," says he. "You and your crew will have a fair opportunity to withdraw once the city is ours."

Well, I couldn't do better than that. And truth to tell, I was fretting in any case, knowing it was only a matter of time before the *Schrecken* appeared overhead to pacify the Delta by dropping poisonous fluorine on me and all my men. The airship's absence seemed by far the best chance to give the flying madman a knock. Best, I reckoned, to strike while the striking was good.

So it was, barely two nights later, that I found myself conning the *New World* down the river and across the bay. The city—renamed Sankt Ruprecht after the patron saint of Salzburg, of all places— was guarded by three masonry forts, charmingly named Angst, Tod, and Panik. Angst and Panik had been built by slaves, and covered the western and eastern approaches; and Fort Tod was the old Spanish Presidio on the Golden Gate. Fortunately Mitternacht was forced to defend so much of the peninsula that the forts didn't support one another. We made Fort Panik, on the east side of the city, our first target.

I had two companies of militia on board, partially protected by log ramparts, and I was trying to peer around the wood cladding of the pilothouse when I saw, walking along the Texas deck, a tall, cadaverous cove, dressed in a long black cloak and a stovepipe hat. He carried a strange pipelike weapon that was attached to a canister he wore on his back. I stuck my head out of the wheelhouse, then gestured for him to join me.

The weapon, I discovered, made strange muttering sounds, like a coal fire in a boiler with all the dampers shut.

"That gun of yours ain't going to set my boat on fire, is it?" asks I.

"I hope it will set *everything* on fire." He spoke with a ponderous Russian accent. He gave a formal bow. "I am the Nihilist," says he. "It is my mission to destroy all forms of oppression, starting with the champion of Habsburg reaction across the Bay."

I regarded him. "When you say *everything*…" says I.

"I mean everything," says he flatly. "In order for humanity to be liberated, it must be returned to a complete state of nature."

"Well," says I, "it's hard to find a less civilized place than the goldfields."

"Yes," says he, "but the miners still pursue *gold,* the single vital element of our oppressive economic system. This greed must be…" He searched for the word. *"Cured,"* he decided.

I gave him a hopeful grin. "I trust you will avoid curing us until Professor Mitternacht is dealt with."

"I am a reasoning man," says he. "I am capable of making tactical alliances."

Another solemn madman, thinks I. *He wants to liberate San Francisco only to burn the place down.*

The Nihilist, I reckoned, was another of a new breed of cranks and enthusiasts on their way to California, and who were already well on their way to spoiling the place. The only difference between him and Professor Mitternacht was that Mitternacht had a more efficient way of killing people.

I determined in the upcoming battle to send the Nihilist straight at the enemy, and to let fortune determine the rest. He could destroy civilization, I decided, or die trying. Preferably the latter.

I returned my attention to guiding the *New World* to its destination, and to worrying that I would get a roundshot through my tripes before I ever saw an enemy.

It is impossible to make a surprise attack with steamboats. Steamboats make a lot of noise, from the clanking of the engine to the thrashing of the paddles to the great throat-clearing howl of the relief valves, and my heart was in my throat for much of the crossing as I imagined myself in the sights of some diabolical German engine from Professor Mitternacht's laboratory.

There were twelve steamboats in our fleet, and most of them towed sailing craft or barges crammed with men. The militia were half-crazed with drink before we even set out, and their shouting and singing and accidental discharge of firearms were hardly the thing to boost my confidence.

Yet we were within a couple thousand yards of Fort Panik before star shells went up, and the first cannon flashed in the fort's embrasures.

I had timed things pretty well. A golden dawn was just creeping down Blue Mountain to the East, but the Bay was still in darkness, and from the ramparts our boats were just shadows on the deep black water. As cannon shot came skipping over the water, I rang to the engine room for more speed.

I think the Condor had it in mind that I would keep *New World* offshore and engage the fort in a gun duel. This was the best recipe for suicide that I could think of, and so I ran in as quickly as possible. I threw out a kedge anchor so that I could pull the boat off the mud flats if I needed to, then ran her in till she just touched ground, after which I lowered the gangways and watched the drunken militia charge forward, sloshing through water and muck and wrack and flotsam to dry land. I thought I saw the Nihilist's stovepipe hat in the throng.

I looked up at the fort, which was still booming away, and decided that I would be safer on land than sitting atop a boiler filled with steam and subjected to plunging shot from above. So I ordered the cannons fired, then drew my sword, waved my hat, and led my crew in a charge.

Nor was I alone. The rest of our fleet had come to shore and unleashed their passengers. I saw the plug hat of the Bowery B'hoy amid the throng, and his lead-weighted cane waving in the air; there were the long ringlets and the broad plumed hat of the Cavalier next to the scarlet kerchief of my traitorous bitch of an ex-wife. The Masked Hidalgo swooped along in his cloak, his rapier flashing; and one mob advanced in complete silence, the mesmerized followers of Captain Hypnos. Shanghai Susie ran nimbly along with a party of Chinese, their pigtails flying. And Doctor Tolliver walked ashore absolutely alone, because no one wanted to be anywhere near his box of explosives.

My heart gave a great lift at the scene, at all the great champions united against a single enemy, and I gave a halloo and ran like a madman for the fort.

As I sloshed through the muck I happened to look to my left, and to my great surprise I saw the Condor being hurled into the sky like a rocket. He'd had a catapult constructed on his boat to fling himself aloft, so that he could spread his wings and sail down into the fort.

A great mob had surrounded the fort by this point, firing like mad into the embrasures and trying to scale the masonry walls. The scent of gunpowder filled the air. The Condor disappeared into the fort, and I suppose there was the usual thwacking and thumping that followed one of his descents. Doctor Tolliver began hurling glass bombs into the fort, not particularly caring if he injured the Condor as long as he killed Grenzers; and then the Nihilist stuck his pipe-weapon into one of the embrasures and let loose with a great jet of fire; and there was screaming and shrieking and the sound of cartridges detonating, and that was the end of the Battle of Fort Panik.

Truth to tell, without the *Schrecken,* the Grenzers were doomed. There weren't many of them, they were scattered in small detachments trying to hold too much ground, and they were infantry, not trained artillerists—none of their shot had come close to our little flotilla. And they had damned few cannon to fire—the rusting old Spanish guns at the Presidio hadn't kept Commodore Stockton out in '46, and they weren't keeping us out this time. Fort Panik had only a few ill-assorted pieces scavenged from ships that happened to be in the bay when Mitternacht turned up, and very little powder and shot.

As soon as dawn gave us a clear view of the proceedings, we organized and marched inland. South of the city we overran the landing field that Mitternacht had built for his airship, and the factory that he had created to build new Fluorine Bombs. We freed the slave workers there, then crested the city's hills and marched in a great surging mob down to Fort Angst, which we stormed in about three minutes. I found myself fighting alongside the Condor, slashing with my sword as he pounded Grenzers with his fists, and I had a chance to observe the flush of battle on his cheeks, and blue glow of combat in his eyes. *He* lives *for this!* thinks I, and then some giant Croat lunged at me with a sword-bayonet as long as my leg, and I had to look to my own safety.

Angst fell, and that left only the Presidio. Which, if inadequately armed and garrisoned, was at least a proper fort; and it might have given us trouble if I hadn't remembered those Fluorine Bombs sitting in their racks at the factory. So I had the Condor's catapult fetched from his steamer, fixed one of Mitternacht's own projectiles in it, and ordered it hurled toward the fort.

It took a while to get the fort's range, and we came damn near to gassing ourselves; but once a few gas bombs had dropped behind the walls, the surviving Grenzers came staggering out waving the white flag. The black-and-gold of Austria came down the flagstaff and the American gridiron flag went up, and Sankt Ruprecht was San Francisco again.

The enslaved citizens of San Francisco poured out to welcome us, at least once we unlocked their barracks, and there was a massive day-long party.

The Gentlemen and I were extremely popular. For one thing, I was the only person wearing anything resembling a uniform, so it was widely believed that I had generaled the city's rescue. I was cheered wherever I went. I believe I could have run successfully for mayor.

Since people were inclined to obey my orders, I had the remaining Fluorine Bombs carried to one of the abandoned hulks in the bay, which was then towed out to sea and sunk. And we made plans to ambush and capture the *Schrecken* once it returned to its base. Enough of the slaves had watched the airship's landing to know the procedures followed by the ground crews, and these volunteered to dress up in Grenzer uniforms and lure the *Schrecken* to the ground, where it could be stormed by our army.

I also made a few little plans of my own. Some machinery was quietly slipped from the factories and carried down to where the *New World* waited on the mud flats. A few Austrian engineers were likewise carried to my pirate craft, rolled in carpets so they wouldn't be lynched. If anyone noticed, they probably thought I was just looting.

The Austrian flags went up again, as decoys, and plans were laid—and just in time, for no sooner had we got over our hangovers than the thrumming of the great vessel's propellers was heard overhead, and the ominous black shadow began to circle the landing field. Our false Grenzers trotted out to take hold of the cables and guide the airship to its mooring…but then it all went wrong.

Half our army was still drunk as lords, and as soon as the *Schrecken* was within range, a great many of the fools opened fire. Once the musketry started popping, Professor Mitternacht knew that something was up. The gunsmoke gave away the positions of those who had fired, and he maneuvered the warship to drop Fluorine Bombs on the reckless marksmen.

Only a few of the more inebriated died, as the bombs were easy enough to avoid if you knew to flee the area beneath the airship—and in addition there was a brisk wind that whipped the gas away. I was in no danger myself, for I'd managed for once to keep my crew in hand, and none of us had fired. But it was clear that the ambush had failed, and I moved my men to a safer place while the *Schrecken* circled the city and dropped bombs on anyone it could see.

Though luckily enough there were few bombs to drop. Mitternacht had used up most of his ordnance exterminating the Mad Emperor and his legions, and he was unable to land and load more bombs from his factory. So here he was far away from home, with only a small crew, and without any weapons more useful than a carbine.

He circled the city for two more days, doubtless trying to puzzle out a plan that would bring San Francisco back under his control—and then *Schrecken* turned its great nose eastward and began the long journey back to Austria.

No doubt the city will hear the roar of those propellers again. Possibly next time there will be more than the single airship. I can't imagine Professor Mitternacht taking defeat in his stride.

After Mitternacht's departure there was another great party that lasted the better part of two days, and right into the middle of it wandered a deputation from Monterey that included the famous scout, Christopher Carson.

Carson—a tiny, unassuming little cove, by the way—had led a small party over Donner Pass in the middle of winter—a remarkable feat in its own right—and brought the message that an American relief force was under way.

We leaders met in the City Hall to listen to Carson's message, beneath a portrait of George Washington that had been found in the cellar and placed over the gilt double-headed Austrian eagle that Mitternacht, that pretentious ass, had mounted on the wall.

It had taken nearly three months for news of Mitternacht's arrival to reach the government in Washington. The relief force, two brigades under General Winfield Scott and a naval force under Commodore Matthew Perry, would take months more to arrive. Experimental weapons to be used against the airship were being constructed by the Swedish engineer Ericsson.

Carson's own journey West had taken months, and it was likely that the armada had already begun its long voyage around South America.

An odd sidelight to this affair was that in addition to commanding the army, General Scott was running for the highest office in the land. If he won, Alta California would be a military zone commanded directly by the President of the United States.

I was far from delighted by this news—I rather suspected that the two Mexican War heroes would disapprove of a pirate presence within their area of operations. Assuming that I could keep Commodore Perry from hanging me out of hand, I doubted that it would be as easy to escape from military prisons as it had been from Sutter the Younger's jail in Sacramento City.

What surprised me was the reaction of the Condor. I marked an expression of fierce grief in his eyes as he heard the news, and I realized that Scott's arrival would mark the end of his adventure as well. With law established in California, the Condor would be superfluous.

Afterwards there was another celebration in honor of Carson, Scott, Perry, and that guiding genius of the nation, Mr. Fillmore. The party was held in one of the great rooms of the City Hall, and there were rivers of liquor and a band playing jigs and polkas, "Arthur McBride" and "Old Dan Tucker" and that great anthem of the Gold Rush, "Oh! Susanna."

I accepted a cigar from a well-wisher and went into one of the galleries to smoke it. I looked into the ballroom and saw the colorful throng at their sport, the last great rollicking occasion we were all together: me, the Condor, the Masked Hidalgo, the Highwayman,

Shanghai Susie, and all the rest, in a great surging, dancing, laughing mob. All rivalry forgotten, all animosity put aside.

Soon the army would come, I thought, and put an end to all this.

I saw the Condor standing aside, and I guessed his thoughts were very like mine. I approached him. "I don't suppose that General Scott will be needing any masked vigilantes in his district," says I.

"Well," says he. "There is much of the West that is still without law."

"You could go to Utah and thump the Mormons," says I hopefully. I was hoping to direct his activities in any direction than my own.

He offered a thin little smile. "The Mormons are law-abiding, or so I understand."

"Aside from being in rebellion against the United States—and then of course they have a habit of polygamy."

"The rebellion is more in General Scott's line," says he. "And how would I foil a polygamist, exactly? Kidnap his wives? I'd end up with a bigger harem than Brigham Young."

I looked at him in surprise, for this was the first touch of humor I'd heard from him. Yet there was no smile, no amusement gleaming from the blue eyes. Maybe he was completely serious.

"Well," offers I, "there's New Mexico."

His eyes glittered with interest. "What are your plans?" asks he.

"I expect I'll be leaving the city in two or three days," says I. "Beyond that, I have no idea."

Which was not strictly true. I knew law would come to Alta California sooner or later, and I had considered shifting my base to another part of the world, anywhere from the Russian colonies in Alaska to Taheetee, Hawaii to South America. I could keep much of the gold for myself, distribute the rest among my men, then try to disappear into the local population.

The problem, of course, is that gold fever is not confined to pirates. All it would take was for one of the crew to get drunk and speak a few indiscreet words, and whole armies would come after us—either the authorities ready with charges of theft and piracy, or a mob of greedy robbers ready to cut our throats.

I had not made up my mind whither I would flee. I was leaning toward Australia—there had been a gold strike there, and a swarm of strangers with gold in their pockets might not seem too out of place. And of course the whole continent was a prison, so even if they caught us, what could they do? Send us to England?

Still, I did not want to share even these half-formed plans with the Condor.

"You'll be returning to your old habits, then?" says he.

"Aye," says I. "It's the river for us."

There was a glint in his eye. "I will see you there, no doubt," says he.

"Sir," says I, "I would expect nothing less."

He bowed, and so did I. And so, between us, the silent promise was made—we would have our final battle somewhere on the Sacramento sometime before General Scott arrived, and it would settle matters between us once and for all.

"You know," begins I, "if you hadn't joined the wrong side, that time on the American River—"

But that was as far as I got, because at that moment a man ran into the room shouting "Fire! Fire!", and that was the end of the party.

San Francisco had been set alight. We were up the next day and a half fighting the flames, and despite our efforts half of the city burned.

The Nihilist was suspected, though it had to be admitted that the city had already burned two or three times without his efforts. Judging by what had happened in the past, it would all be rebuilt quickly.

Once the flames were extinguished, I returned with my crew to the *New World* and pulled the boat off the mud. The miners returned to their diggings. And I advanced my plans.

I would swoop back to San Francisco one night, I thought. We'd swarm aboard an ocean-going ship, then tow her out to sea and set sail. I hated the thought of abandoning the *New World,* so we'd tow her as we sailed away.

For Hawaii first, I thought. Hawaii was a sovereign kingdom and might not honor a foreign arrest warrant.

And if they did, I would escape. I had grown very good at escaping.

But first, I wanted to keep my promise to the Condor, and I found that a perfect opportunity now beckoned. The miners had been hoarding their gold in the Sierras while Professor Mitternacht was ruling his little kingdom of Tyrolia-on-the-Bay, and now that supplies were coming into the port again, they were eager to go to what remained of San Francisco and help themselves to its comforts.

It was announced that commercial steamboat service would be resumed with *Great Columbia,* the first grand boat to leave Sacramento City for San Francisco carrying passengers. There would be fireworks, speeches, a band.

Of course it's an ambush. They *want* me to attack, they wave the gold beneath my nose to make sure I take the bait. The boat will be packed with militia.

I will intercept *Great Columbia,* of course. And the Condor will defend it. And so we will meet, perhaps for the last time.

And so here I am, now, standing on the bridge, the *New World* lurking on the sweet gold-bearing waters of Steamboat Slough with steam up and weapons ready, waiting for our sentries on shore to signal *Great Columbia*'s arrival. I'm prepared to hear *Ky-yeee!* as the Condor arrows out of the sky to engage me in final battle for plunder and freedom. And maybe, when I finally beat him and have him at my mercy, I'll finally have answers to some of my questions.

What are you? I'll ask. A crusader for justice? A madman in a cloak?—but not simply a madman, but rather a madman who has so infected Alta California with his own brand of lunacy that an entire host of strangers are now donning masks and swirling capes and brawling over the flood of gold coming down from the Sierras? Fellow lunatics who, like me, would have simply gone about our lives if we hadn't somehow been chosen to share the Condor's dream?

Without the Condor, the Nihilist wouldn't have burned the city, and Professor Mitternacht wouldn't have choked all those people with his gas. I would be a miner up to my knees in cold muck, thinking simple thoughts of a warm fire, a bottle of whiskey, and maybe a girl.

Who are you? I will demand. It's time I knew. Southern planter or Mexican caballero or fiend from Hell, I will know his name. I will know his station. I will know what drove him to this.

He will not want to tell me these things. But I will make him.

I will not kill him. I am not fated to be the one who ends the tale of the Condor.

But I am game for other methods. If I must, I will hang him upside down over a burning pit, and that may loosen his tongue.

For he has assigned me this part, and I will play it till it breaks me. Or him.

I see the flag signal now, my lookout waving frantically. *Great Columbia* is on its way.

I call out orders. *Up the anchor! Fill the fireboxes with fuel! Full speed! Stand by the guns!*

And then I smile. *Cast off the airship!*

For I have not been idle since I made off with some of Professor Mitternacht's gear—and the Austrian engineers I'd abducted were very happy to cooperate with my plans once I'd explained that the alternative was to be strung up by their former slaves. The result is that I now have a modest airship of my own, powered by what my engineers are pleased to call a *Lichtätherkompressor*, the Aetheric Concentrator, which I gather works by compressing an invisible fluid alleged to fill the universe. Which may sound like airy German metaphysics to you and me, but it seems to lift my little aerial barge with fair efficiency for all that.

The *Commodore's Fancy* isn't as massive or magnificent as the *Schrecken*, it's only a platform fifty feet long; but it's still one of two flying machines in all the world, and my heart gives a great surge as we lift off *New World*'s Texas deck, and suddenly we see the great winding watercourse of the Sacramento below us, the ash and willow and cottonwood, and the beautiful picture below us.

See how the smoke boils from the stacks of the *New World*, the fine white foam flies from the paddle wheels! Hear the whirr of the airship's great propeller! Ahead, see the white gingerbread lace of the *Great Columbia,* the decks packed with miners bringing their gold to the markets! See the sun glinting from the muskets and weapons of the militia, who think to ambush me even as I ambush them! See their confusion as the *Commodore's Fancy* darts toward them! No doubt they think of Mitternacht's Fluorine Bombs, and tremble.

I would never carry such a filthy weapon, but I hardly mind if my enemies think I do. And the Condor can't drop on me now, not when I'm flying well above the tallest trees. I laugh as the wind tugs at my whiskers. If the Condor is on that boat, I have him trapped.

I'll have him soon, and then I'll have my answers. I signal to the gunner on the airship's bow, to fire the traditional warning shot across the target's bows.

Then there's a sudden burst of flame on the *Great Columbia,* and suddenly I see a figure arrowing for the sky on a tail of flame, cloak rippling as he rises.

It's the Condor, and he's somehow rigged himself out with a skyrocket, shooting himself into the atmosphere to gain altitude so that he can drop on me. I snarl as I curse the ingenuity of the man, and then I laugh.

I am the Commodore! What does it matter who or what made me—? I am myself, here in my cocked hat and epaulets, brandishing my sword on the swaying bridge of my glorious airship. It's far too late to quibble over origins, over who struck who on the Middle Fork... What matters is the battle to come, the final confrontation between the titan of order and the grand nabob of piracy. The last great fight of the Golden Age.

Can you see him? There—a swift shadow against the sun?

Can you hear it? Above the sound of the hissing steam, the thrashing paddles, the scream of the whistles? The sound that brings a snarl to my lips, that causes me to brandish my sword in defiance at the diving bogy in the sky...

Ky-yeeeee!

DINOSAURS

The Shars seethed in the dim light of their ruddy sun. Pointed faces raised to the sky, they sniffed the faint wind for sign of the stranger and scented only hydrocarbons, far-off vegetations, damp fur, the sweat of excitement and fear. Weak eyes peered upward, glistened with hope, anxiety, apprehension, and saw only the faint pattern of stars. Short, excited barking sounds broke out here and there, but mostly the Shars crooned, a low ululation that told of sudden onslaught, destruction, war in distant reaches, and now the hope of peace.

The crowds surged left, then right. Individuals bounced high on their third legs, seeking a view, seeing only the wide sea of heads, the ears and muzzles pointed to the stars.

Suddenly, a screaming. High-pitched howls, a bright chorus of barks. The crowds surged again.

Something was crossing the field of stars.

The human ship was huge, vaster than anything they'd seen, a moonlet descending. Shars closed their eyes and shuddered in terror. The screaming turned to moans. Individuals leaped high, baring their teeth, barking in defiance of their fear. The air smelled of terror, incipient panic, anger.

War! cried some. *Peace!* cried others.

The crooning went on. *We mourn, we mourn,* it said, *we mourn our dead billions.*

We fear, said others.

Soundlessly, the human ship neared them, casting its vast shadow. Shars spilled outward from the spot beneath, bounding high on their third legs.

The human ship came to a silent rest. Dully, it reflected the dim red sun.

The Shars crooned their fear, their sorrow. And waited for the humans to emerge.

These! Yes. These. Drill, the human ambassador, gazed through his video walls at the sea of Shars, the moaning, leaping thousands that surrounded him. Through the mass a group was moving with purpose, heading for the airlock as per his instructions. His new Memory crawled restlessly in the armored hollow atop his skull. *Stand by,* he broadcast.

His knees made painful crackling noises as he walked toward the airlock, the silver ball of his translator rolling along the ceiling ahead of him. The walls mutated as he passed, showing him violet sky, far-off polygonal buildings; cold distant green…and here, nearby, a vast, dim plain covered with a golden tissue of Shars.

He reached the airlock and it began to open. Drill snuffed wetly at the alien smells—heat, dust, the musky scent of the Shars themselves.

Drill's heart thumped in his chest. His dreams were coming true. He had waited all his life for this.

Mash, whimpered Lowbrain. Drill told it to be silent. Lowbrain protested vaguely, then obeyed.

Drill told Lowbrain to move. Cool, alien air brushed his skin. The Shars cried out sharply, moaned, fell back. They seemed a wild, sibilant ocean of pointed ears and dark, questing eyes. The group heading for the airlock vanished in the general retrograde movement, a stone washed by a pale tide. Beneath Drill's feet was soft vegetation. His translator floated in the air before him. His mind flamed with wonder, but Lowbrain kept him moving.

The Shars fell back, moaning.

Drill stood eighteen feet tall on his two pillarlike legs, each with a splayed foot that displayed a horny underside and vestigial nails. His skin was ebony and was draped in folds over his vast naked body. His pendulous maleness swung loosely as he walked. As he stepped across the open space he was conscious of the fact that he was the ultimate product of nine million years of human evolution, all leading to the expansion, diversification, and perfection that was now humanity's manifest existence.

He looked down at the little Shars, their white skin and golden fur, their strange, stiff tripod legs, the muzzles raised to him as if in awe. *If your species survives,* he thought benignly, *you can look like me in another few million years.*

The group of Shars that had been forging through the crowd were suddenly exposed when the crowd fell back from around them. On the perimeter were several Shars holding staffs—weapons, perhaps—in their clever little hands. In the center of these were a group of Shars wearing decorative ribbons to which metal plates had been attached. *Badges of rank,* Memory said. *Ignore.* The shadow of the translator bobbed toward them as Drill approached. Metallic geometrics rose from the group and hovered over them.

Recorders, Memory said. *Artificial similarities to myself. Or possibly security devices. Disregard.*

Drill was getting closer to the party, speeding up his instructions to Lowbrain, eventually entering Zen Synch. It would make Lowbrain hungrier but lessen the chance of any accidents.

The Shars carrying the staffs fell back. A wailing went up from the crowd as one of the Shars stepped toward Drill. The ribbons draped over her sloping shoulders failed to disguise four mammalian breasts.

Clear plastic bubbles covered her weak eyes. In Zen Synch with Memory and Lowbrain, Drill ambled up to her and raised his hands in friendly greeting. The Shar flinched at the expanse of the gesture.

"I am Ambassador Drill," he said. "I am a human."

The Shar gazed up at him. Her nose wrinkled as she listened to the booming voice of the translator. Her answer was a succession of sharp sounds, made high in the throat, somewhat unpleasant. Drill listened to the voice of his translator.

"I am President Gram of the InterSharian Sociability of Nations and Planets." That's how it came through in translation, anyway. Memory began feeding Drill referents for the word "nation."

"I welcome you to our planet, Ambassador Drill."

"Thank you, President Gram," Drill said. "Shall we negotiate peace now?"

President Gram's ears pricked forward, then back. There was a pause, and then from the vast circle of Shars came a mad torrent of hooting noises. The awesome sound lapped over Drill like the waves of a lunatic sea.

They approve your sentiment, said Memory.

I thought that's what it meant, Drill said. *Do you think we'll get along?*

Memory didn't answer, but instead shifted to a more comfortable position in the saddle of Drill's skull.

Its job was to provide facts, not draw conclusions.

"If you could come into my Ship," Drill said, "we could get started."

"Will we then meet the other members of your delegation?"

Drill gazed down at the Shar. The fur on her shoulders was rising in odd tufts. She seemed to be making a concerted effort to calm it.

"There are no other members," Drill said. "Just myself."

His knees were paining him. He watched as the other members of the Shar party cast quick glances at each other.

"No secretaries? No assistants?" the President was saying.

"No," Drill said. "Not at all. I'm the only conscious mind on Ship. Shall we get started?"

Eat! Eat! said Lowbrain. Drill ordered it to be silent. His stomach grumbled.

"Perhaps," said President Gram, gazing at the vastness of the human ship, "it would be best should we begin in a few hours. I should probably speak to the crowd. Would you care to listen?"

No need. Memory said. *I will monitor.*

"Thank you, no," Drill said. "I shall return to Ship for food and sex. Please signal me when you are ready. Please bring any furniture you may need for your comfort. I do not believe my furniture would fit you, although we might be able to clone some later."

The Shars' ears all pricked forward. Drill entered Zen Synch, turned his huge body, and began accelerating toward the airlock. The sound of the crowd behind him was the murmuring of wind through a stand of trees.

Peace, he thought later, as he stood by the mash bins and fed his complaining stomach. *It's a simple thing. How long can it take to arrange?*

Long, said Memory. *Very long.*

The thought disturbed him. He thought the first meeting had gone well.

After his meal, when he had sex, it wasn't very good.

Memory had been monitoring the events outside Ship, and after Drill had completed sex, Memory showed him the outside events. *They have been broadcast to the entire population,* Memory said.

President Gram had moved to a local elevation and had spoken for some time. Drill found her speech interesting—it was rhythmic and incantorial, rising and falling in tone and volume, depending heavily on repetition and melody. The crowd participated, issuing forth with excited barks or low moans in response to her statements or questions, sometimes babbling in confusion when she posed them a conundrum. Memory only gave the highlights of the speech. "Unknown… Attackers…billions dead…preparations advanced… ready to defend ourselves…offer of peace…hope in the darkness… unknown…willing to take the chance…peace…peace…hopeful smell…peace." At the end the other Shars were all singing "Peace! Peace!" in chorus while President Gram bounced up and down on her sturdy rear leg.

It sounds pretty, Drill thought. *But why does she go on like that?* Memory's reply was swift.

Remember that the Shars are a generalized and social species, it said. *President Gram's power, and her ability to negotiate, derives from the degree of her popular support. In measures of this significance she must explain herself and her actions to the population in order to maintain their enthusiasm for her policies.*

Primitive, Drill thought.

That is correct.

Why don't they let her get on with her work? Drill asked.

There was no reply.

After an exchange of signals the Shar party assembled at the airlock. Several Shars had been mobilized to carry tables and stools. Drill sent a Frog to escort the Shars from the airlock to where he waited. The Frog met them inside the airlock, turned, and hopped on ahead through Ship's airy, winding corridors. It had been trained to repeat "Follow me, follow me" in the Shars' own language.

Drill waited in a semi-inclined position on a Slab. The Slab was an organic sub-species used as furniture, with an idiot brain capable of responding to human commands. The Shars entered cautiously, their weak eyes twitching in the bright light. "Welcome, Honorable President," Drill said. "Up, Slab."

Slab began to adjust itself to place Drill on his feet. The Shars were moving tables and stools into the vast room.

Frog was hopping in circles, making a wet noise at each landing. "Follow me, follow me," it said.

The members of the Shar delegation who bore badges of rank stood in a body while the furniture-carriers bustled around them. Drill noticed, as Slab put him on his feet, that they were wrinkling their noses. He wondered what it meant.

His knees crackled as he came fully upright. "Please make yourselves comfortable," he said. "Frog will show your laborers to the airlock."

"Does your Excellency object to a mechanical recording of the proceedings?" President Gram asked.

She was shading her eyes with her hand.

"Not at all." As a number of devices rose into the air above the party, Drill wondered if it were possible to give the Shars detachable Memories. Perhaps human bioengineers could adapt the Memories to the Shar physiology. He asked Memory to make a note of the question so that he could bring it up later.

"Follow me, follow me," Frog said. The workers who had carried the furniture began to follow the hopping Frog out of the room.

"Your Excellency," President Gram said, "may I have the honor of presenting to you the other members of my delegation?"

There were six in all, with titles like Secretary of Syncopated Speech and Special Executive for External Coherence. There was also a Minister for the Dissemination of Convincing Lies, whose title Drill suspected was somehow mistranslated, and an Opposite Secretary-General for the Genocidal Eradication of Alien Aggressors, at whom Drill looked with more than a little interest. The Opposite Secretary-General was named Vang, and was small even for a Shar. He seemed to wrinkle his nose more than the others. The Special Executive for External Coherence, whose name was Cup, seemed a bit piebald, patches of white skin showing through the golden fur covering his shoulders, arms, and head.

He is elderly, said Memory.

That's what I thought.

"Down, Slab," Drill said. He leaned back against the creature and began to move to a more relaxed position.

He looked at the Shars and smiled. Fur ruffled on shoulders and necks. "Shall we make peace now?" he asked.

"We would like to clarify something you said earlier," President Gram said. "You said that you were the only, ah, conscious entity on the ship. That you were the only member of the human delegation. Was that translated correctly?"

"Why, yes," Drill said. "Why would more than one diplomat be necessary?"

The Shars looked at each other. The Special Executive for External Coherence spoke cautiously.

"You will not be needing to consult with your superiors? You have full authority from your government?"

Drill beamed at them. "We humans do not have a government, of course," he said. "But I am a diplomat with the appropriate Memory and training. There is no problem that I can foresee."

"Please let me understand, your Excellency," Cup said. He was leaning forward, his small eyes watering. "I am elderly and may be slow in comprehending the situation. But if you have no government, who accredited you with this mission?"

✺

"I am a diplomat. It is my specialty. No accreditation is necessary. The human race will accept my judgment on any matter of negotiation, as they would accept the judgment of any specialist in his area of expertise."

"But why you? As an individual?"

Drill shrugged massively. "I was part of the nearest diplomatic enclave, and the individual without any other tasks at the moment." He looked at each of the delegation in turn. "I am incredibly happy to have this chance, honorable delegates," he said. "The vast majority of human diplomats never have the chance to speak to another species. Usually we mediate only in conflicts of interest between the various groups of human specialties."

"But the human species will abide by your decisions?"

"Of course." Drill was surprised at the Shar's persistence. "Why wouldn't they?"

Cup settled back in his chair. His ears were down. There was a short silence.

"We have an opening statement prepared," President Gram said. "I would like to enter it into our record, if I may. Or would your Excellency prefer to go first?"

"I have no opening statement," Drill said. "Please go ahead."

Cup and the President exchanged glances. President Gram took a deep breath and began.

Long. Memory said. *Very long.*

The opening statement seemed very much like the address President Gram had been delivering to the crowd, the same hypnotic rhythms, more or less the same content. The rest of the delegation made muted responses. Drill drowsed through it, enjoying it as music.

"Thank you, Honorable President," he said afterwards. "That was very nice."

"We would like to propose an agenda for the conference," Gram said. "First, to resolve the matter of the cease-fire and its provisions for an ending to hostilities. Second, the establishment of a secure border between our two species, guaranteeing both species room for expression. Third, the establishment of trade and visitation agreements. Fourth, the matter of reparations, payments, and return of lost territory."

Drill nodded. "I believe," he said, "that resolution of the second through fourth points will come about as a result of an understanding reached on the first. That is, once the cease-fire is settled, that resolution will imply a settlement of the rest of the situation."

"You accept the agenda?"

"If you like. It doesn't matter."

Ears pricked forward, then back. "So you accept that our initial discussions will consist of formalizing the disengagement of our forces?"

"Certainly. Of course I have no way of knowing what forces you have committed. We humans have committed none."

The Shars were still for a long time. "Your species attacked our planets, Ambassador. Without warning, without making yourselves known to us." Gram's tone was unusually flat. Perhaps, Drill thought, she was attempting to conceal great emotion.

"Yes," Drill said. "But those were not our military formations. Your species were contacted only by our terraforming Ships. They did not attack your people, as such—they were only peripherally aware of your existence. Their function was merely to seed the planets with lifeforms favorable to human existence. Unfortunately for your people, part of the function of these lifeforms is to destroy the native life of the planet."

The Shars conferred with one another. The Opposite Secretary-General seemed particularly vehement.

Then President Gram turned to Drill.

"We cannot accept your statement, your Excellency," she said. "Our people were attacked. They defended themselves, but were overcome."

"Our terraforming Ships are very good at what they do," Drill said. "They are specialists. Our Shrikes, our Shrews, our Sharks—each is a master of its element. But they lack intelligence. They are not conscious entities, such as ourselves. They weren't aware of your civilization at all. They only saw you as food."

"You're claiming that you *didn't notice us?*" demanded Secretary-General Vang. *"They didn't notice us as they were killing us?"* He was shouting. President Gram's ears went back.

"Not as such, no," Drill said.

President Gram stood up. "I am afraid, your Excellency, your explanations are insufficient," she said. "This conference must be postponed until we can reach a united conclusion concerning your remarkable attitude."

Drill was bewildered. "What did I say?" he asked.

The other Shars stood. President Gram turned and walked briskly on her three legs toward the exit. The others followed.

"Wait," Drill said. "Don't go. Let me send for Frog. Up, Slab, up!"

The Shars were gone by the time Slab had got Drill to his feet. The Ship told him they had found their own way to the airlock. Drill could think of nothing to do but order the airlock to let them out.

"Why would I lie?" he asked. "Why would I lie to them?" Things were so very simple, really.

He shifted his vast weight from one foot to the other and back again. Drill could not decide whether he had done anything wrong. He asked Memory what to do next, but Memory held no information to comfort him, only dry recitations of past negotiations. Annoyed at the lifeless monologue, Drill told Memory to be silent and began to walk restlessly through the corridors of his Ship. He could not decide where things had gone bad.

Sensing his agitation, Lowbrain began to echo his distress. *Mash,* Lowbrain thought weakly. *Food. Sex.*

Be silent, Drill commanded.

Sex, sex, Lowbrain thought.

Drill realized that Lowbrain was beginning to give him an erection. Acceding to the inevitable, he began moving toward Surrogate's quarters.

Surrogate lived in a dim, quiet room filled with the murmuring sound of its own heartbeat. It was a human subspecies, about the intelligence of Lowbrain, designed to comfort voyagers on long journeys through space, when carnal access to their own subspecies might necessarily be limited. Surrogate had a variety of sexual equipment designed for the accommodation of the various human subspecies and their sexes. It also had large mammaries that gave nutritious milk, and a rudimentary head capable of voicing simple thoughts.

Tiny Mice, that kept Surrogate and the ship clean, scattered as Drill entered the room. Surrogate's little head turned to him.

"It's good to see you again," Surrogate said.

"I am Drill."

"It's good to see you again, Drill," said Surrogate. "It's good to see you again."

Drill began to nuzzle its breasts. One of Surrogate's male parts began to erect. "I'm confused, Surrogate," he said. "I don't know what to do."

"Why are you confused, Drill?" asked Surrogate. It raised one of its arms and began to stroke Drill's head. It wasn't really having a conversation: Surrogate had only been programmed to make simple statements, or to analyze its partners' speech and ask questions.

"Things are going wrong," Drill said. He began to suckle. The warm milk flowed down his throat.

Surrogate's male part had an orgasm. Mice jumped from hiding to clean up the mess.

"Why are things going wrong?" asked Surrogate. "I'm sure everything will be all right."

Lowbrain had an orgasm, perceived by Drill as scattered, faraway bits of pleasure. Drill continued to suckle, feeling a heavy comfort beginning to radiate from Surrogate, from the gentle sound of its heartbeat, its huge, wholesome, brainless body.

Everything will be all right, Drill decided.

"Nice to see you again, Drill," Surrogate said. "Drill, it's *nice* to see you again."

The vast crowds of Shars did not leave when night fell. Instead they stood beneath floating globes dispersing a cold reddish light that reflected eerily from pointed ears and muzzles. Some of them donned capes or skirts to help them keep warm. Drill, watching them on the video walls of the command center, was reminded of crowds standing in awe before some vast cataclysm.

The Shars were not quiet. They stood in murmuring groups, but sometimes they began the crooning chants they had raised earlier, or suddenly broke out in a series of shrill yipping cries.

President Gram spoke to them after she had left Ship. "The human has admitted his species' attacks," she said, "but has disclaimed responsibility. We shall urge him to adopt a more realistic position."

"Adopt a position," Drill repeated, not understanding. "It is not a position. It is the truth. Why don't they understand?"

Opposite Minister-General Vang was more vehement. "We now have a far more complete idea of the humans' attitude," he said. "It is opposed to ours in every way. We shall not allow the murderous atrocities which the humans have committed upon five of our planets to be forgotten, or understood to be the result of some explicable lack of attention on the part of our species' enemies."

"That one is obviously deranged," thought Drill.

He went to his sleeping quarters and ordered the Slab there to play him some relaxing music. Even with Slab's murmurs and comforting hums, it took Drill some time before his agitation subsided.

Diplomacy, he thought as slumber overtook him, was certainly a strange business.

In the morning the Shars were still there, chanting and crying, moving in their strange crowded patterns.

Drill watched them on his video walls as he ate breakfast at the mash bins. "There is a communication from President Gram," Memory announced. "She wishes to speak with you by radio."

"Certainly."

"Ambassador Drill." She was using the flat tones again. A pity she was subject to such stress.

"Good morning, President Gram," Drill said. "I hope you spent a pleasant night."

"I must give you the results of our decision. We regret that we can see no way to continue the negotiations unless you, as a representative of your species, agree to admit responsibility for your people's attacks on our planets."

"Admit responsibility?" Drill said. "Of course. Why wouldn't I?"

Drill heard some odd, indistinct barking sounds that his translator declined to interpret for him. It sounded as if someone other than President Gram were on the other end of the radio link.

"You admit responsibility?" President Gram's amazement was clear even in translation.

"Certainly. Does it make a difference?"

President Gram declined to answer that question. Instead she proposed another meeting for that afternoon.

"I will be ready at any time."

Memory recorded President Gram's speech to her people, and Drill studied it before meeting the Shar party at the airlock. She made a great deal out of the fact that Drill had admitted humanity's responsibility for the war. Her people leaped, yipped, chanted their responses as if possessed. Drill wondered why they were so excited.

Drill met the party at the airlock this time, linked with Memory and Lowbrain in Zen Synch so as not to accidentally step on the President or one of her party. He smiled and greeted each by name and led them toward the conference room.

"I believe," said Cup, "we may avoid future misunderstandings, if your Excellency would consent to inform us about your species. We have suffered some confusion in regard to your distinction between 'conscious' and 'unconscious' entities. Could you please explain the difference, as you understand it?"

"A pleasure, your Excellency," Drill said. "Our species, unlike yours, is highly specialized. Once, eight million years ago, we were like you—a small, nonspecialized species type is very useful at a certain stage of evolution. But once a species reaches a certain complexity in its social and technological evolution, the need for specialists becomes too acute. Through both deliberate genetic manipulations and natural evolution, humanity turned away from a generalist species, toward highly specialized forms adapted to particular functions and environments. We understand this to be a natural function of species evolution.

"In the course of our explorations into manipulating our species, we discovered that the most efficient way of coding large amounts of information was in our own cell structure—our DNA. For tasks requiring both large and small amounts of data, we arranged that, as much as possible, these would be performed by organic entities, human subspecies. Since many of these tasks were boring and repetitive, we reasoned that advanced consciousness, such as that which we both share, was not necessary. You have met several unconscious entities. Frog, for example, and the Slab on which I lie. Many parts of my Ship are also alive, though not conscious."

"That would explain the *smell*," one of the delegation murmured.

"The terraforming Ships," Drill went on, "which attacked your planets—these were also designed so as not to require a conscious operator."

The Shars squinted up at Drill with their little eyes. "But why?" Cup asked.

"Terraforming is a dull process. It takes many years, often centuries. No conscious mind could possibly enjoy it."

"But your species would find itself at war without knowing it. If your explanation for the cause of this war is correct, you already have."

Drill shrugged massively. "This happens from time to time. Sometimes other species which have reached our stage of development have attacked us in the same way. When it does, we arrange a peace."

"You consider these attacks normal?" Opposite Minister-General Vang was the one who spoke.

"These occasional encounters seem to be a natural result of species evolution," Drill said.

Vang turned to one of the Shars near him and spoke in several sharp barks. Drill heard a few words:

"Billions lost…five planets…atrocities…natural *result!*"

"I believe," said President Gram, "that we are straying from the agenda."

Vang looked at her. "Yes, honorable President. Please forgive me."

"The matter of withdrawal," said President Gram, "to recognized truce lines."

Species at this stage of their development tend to be territorial, Memory reminded Drill. *Their political mentality is based around the concept of borders. The idea of a borderless community of species may be perceived as a threat.*

I'll try and go easy on them, Drill said.

"The Memories on our terraforming Ships will be adjusted to account for your species," Drill said. "After the adjustment, your people will no longer be in danger."

"In our case, it will take the disengage order several months to reach all our forces." President Gram said. "How long will the order take to reach your own Ships?"

"A century or so." The Shars stared. "Memories at our exploration bases in this area will be adjusted first, of course, and these will adjust the Memories of terraforming Ships as they come in for maintenance and supplies."

"We'll be subject to attack for *another hundred years?*" Vang's tone mixed incredulity and scorn.

"Our terraforming Ships move more or less at random, and only come into base when they run out of supplies. We don't know where they've been till they report back. Though they're bound to encounter a few more of your planets, your species will still survive, enough to continue your species evolution. And during that time you'll be searching for and occupying new planets on your own. You'll probably come out of this with a net gain."

"*Have you no respect for life?*" Vang demanded. Drill considered his answer.

"All individuals die, Opposite Minister-General," he said. "That is a fact of nature which no species has been able to alter. Only species can survive. Individuals are easily replaceable. Though you will lose some planets and a large number of individuals, your species as a whole will survive and may even prosper. What more could a species or its delegated representatives desire?"

Opposite Minister-General Vang was glaring at Drill, his ears pricked forward, lips drawn back from his teeth. He said nothing.

"We desire a cease-fire that is a true cease-fire," President Gram said. Her hands were clasping and unclasping rhythmically on the edge of her chair. "Not a slow, authorized extermination of our species. Your position has an unwholesome smell. I am afraid we must end these discussions until you alter it."

"Position? This is not a position, honorable President. It is truth."

"We have nothing further to say."

Unhappily, Drill followed the Shar delegation to the airlock. "I do not lie, honorable President," he said, but Gram only turned away and silently left the human Ship. The Shars in their pale thousands received her.

The Shar broadcasts were not heartening. Opposite Minister-General Vang was particularly vehement.

Drill collected the highlights of the speeches as he speeded through Memory's detailed remembrance.

"Callous disregard...no common ground for communication... casual attitude toward atrocity...displays of obvious savagery...no respect for the individual...*this stinks in the nose.*"

The Shars leaped and barked in response. There were strange bubbling high-pitched laughing sounds that Drill found unsettling.

"We hope to find a formula for peace," President Gram said. "We will confer with all the ministers in session." That was all.

That night, the Shars surrounding Ship moaned, moving slowly in a giant circle, their arms linked. The laughing sounds that followed Vang's speech did not cease entirely. He did not understand why they did not all go home and sleep.

Long, long, Memory said. No comfort there.

Early in the morning, before dawn, there was a communication from President Gram. "I would like to meet with you privately. Away from the recorders, the coalition partners."

"I would like nothing better," Drill said. He felt a small current of optimism begin to trickle into him.

"Can I use an airlock other than the one we've been using up till now?"

Drill gave President Gram instructions and met her in the other airlock. She was wearing a night cape with a hood. The Shars, circling and moaning, had paid her no attention.

"Thank you for seeing me under these conditions," she said, peering up at him from beneath the hood.

Drill smiled. She shuddered.

"I am pleased to be able to cooperate," he said.

Mash! Lowbrain demanded. It had been silent until Drill entered Zan Synch. Drill told it to be silent with a snarling vehemence that silenced it for the present.

"This way, honorable President," Drill said. He took her to his sleeping chamber—a small room, only fifty feet square. "Shall I send a Frog for one of your chairs?" he asked.

"I will stand. Three legs seem to be more comfortable than two for standing."

"Yes."

"Is it possible, Ambassador Drill, that you could lower the intensity of the light here? I find it oppressive."

Drill felt foolish, knowing he should have thought of this himself. "I'm sorry," he said. "I will give the orders at once. I wish you had told me earlier." He smiled nervously as he dimmed the lights and arranged himself on his Slab.

"Honorable Ambassador." President Gram's words seemed hesitant. "I wonder if it is possible…can you tell me the meaning of that facial gesture of yours, showing me your teeth?"

"It is called a smile. It is intended as a gesture of benevolent reassurance."

"Showing of the teeth is considered a threat here, honorable Ambassador. Some of us have considered this a sign that you wish to eat us."

Drill was astonished. "My goodness!" he said. "I don't even eat meat! Just a kind of vegetable mash."

"I pointed out that your teeth seemed unsuitable for eating meat, but still it makes us uneasy. I was wondering…"

"I will try to suppress the smile, yes. Eating meat! What an idea. Some of our military specialists, yes, and of course the Sharks and Shrikes and so on…" He told his Memory to enforce a strict ban against smiling in the presence of a Shar.

Gram leaned back on her sturdy rear leg. Her cape parted, revealing her ribbons and badges of office, her four furry dugs. "I wanted to inform you of certain difficulties here, Ambassador Drill," she said. "I am having difficulty holding together my coalition. Minister-General Vang's faction is gaining strength. He is attempting to create a perception in the minds of Shars that you are untrustworthy and violent. Whether he believes this, or whether he is using this notion as a means of destabilizing the coalition, is hardly relevant—considering your species' unprovoked attacks, it is not a difficult perception to reinforce. He is also trying to tell our people that the military is capable of dealing with your species."

Drill's brain swam with Memory's information on concepts such as "faction" and "coalition." The meaning of the last sentence, however, was clear.

"That is a foolish perception, honorable President," he said.

"His assurances on that score lack conviction." Gram's eyes were shiny. Her tone grew earnest. "You must give me something, ambassador. Something I can use to soothe the public mind. A way out of this dilemma. I tell you that it is impossible to expect us to sit idly by and accept the loss of an undefined number of planets over the next hundred years. I plead with you, ambassador. Give me something. Some way we can avoid attack. Otherwise..." She left the sentence incomplete.

Mash, Lowbrain wailed. Drill ignored it. He moved into Zen Synch with Memory, racing through possible solutions. Sweat gathered on his forehead, pouring down his vast shoulders.

"Yes," he said. "Yes, there is a possibility. If you could provide us with the location of all your occupied planets, we could dispatch a Ship to each with the appropriate Memories as cargo. If any of our terraforming Ships arrived, the Memories could be transferred at once, and your planets would be safe."

President Gram considered this. "Memories," she said. "You've been using the term, but I'm not sure I understand."

"Stored information is vast, and even though human bodies are large we cannot always have all the information we need to function efficiently even in our specialized tasks," Drill said. "Our human brains have been separated as to function. I have a Lowbrain, which is on my spinal cord above my pelvis. Lowbrain handles motor control of my lower body, routine monitoring of my body's condition, eating, excretion, and sex. My perceptual centers, short-term memory, personality, and reasoning functions are handled by the brain in my skull—the classical brain, if you like. Long-term and specialized memory is the function of the large knob you see moving on my head, my Memory. My Memory records all that happens in great details, and can recapitulate it at any point. It has also been supplied with information concerning the human species' contacts with other non-human groups. It attaches itself easily to my nervous system and draws nourishment from my body. Specific memories can be communicated from one living Memory to another, or if it proves necessary I can simply give my Memory to another human, a complete transfer. I have another Memory aboard that I'm not using at the moment, a pilot Memory that can navigate and handle Ship, and I wore this Memory while in transit. I also have spare Memories in case my primary Memories fall ill. So you see, our specialization does not rule out adaptability—any piece of information needed by any of us can easily be transferred, and in far greater detail than by any mechanical medium."

"So you could return to your base and send your pilot Memories to our planets," Gram said. "Memories that could halt your terraforming ships."

"That is correct." Just in time, Memory managed to stop the twitch in Drill's cheeks from becoming a smile. Happiness bubbled up in him. He was going to arrange this peace after all!

"I am afraid that would not be acceptable, your Excellency," President Gram said. Drill's hopes fell.

"Whyever not?"

"I'm afraid the Minister-General would consider it a naive attempt of yours to find out the location of our populated planets. So that your species could attack them, ambassador."

"I'm trying very hard, President Gram," Drill said.

"I'm sure you are."

Drill frowned and went into Zen Synch again, ignoring Lowbrain's plantive cries for mash and sex, sex and mash. Concepts crackled through his mind. He began to develop an erection, but Memory was drawing off most of the available blood and the erection failed. The smell of Drill's sweat filled the room. President Gram wrinkled her nose and leaned back far onto her rear leg.

"Ah," Drill said. "A solution. Yes. I can have my pilot Memory provide the locations to an equivalent number of our own planets. We will have one another's planets as hostage."

"Bravo, ambassador," President Gram said quietly. "I think we may have a solution. But—forgive me—it may be said that we cannot trust your information. We will have to send ships to verify the location of your planets."

"If your ships go to my planet first," Drill said, "I can provide your people with one of my spare Memories that will inform my species what your people are doing, and instruct the humans to cooperate. We will have to construct some kind of link between your radio and my Memory…maybe I can have my Ship grow one."

President Gram came forward off her third leg and began to pace forward, moving in her strange, fast, hobbling way. "I can present it to the council this way, yes," she said. "There is hope here." She stopped her movement, peering up at Drill with her ears pricked forward. "Is it possible that you could allow me to present this to the council as my own idea?" she asked. "It may meet with less suspicion that way."

"Whatever way is best," said Drill. President Gram gazed into the darkened recesses of the room.

"This smells good," she said. Drill succeeded in suppressing his smile.

"It's nice to see you again."

"I am Drill."

"It's nice to see you again, Drill."

"I think we can make the peace work."

"Everything will be all right, Drill. Drill, I'm sure everything will be all right."

"I'm so glad I had this chance. This is the chance of a lifetime."

"Drill, it's nice to see you again."

The next day President Gram called and asked to present a new plan. Drill said he would be pleased to hear it. He met the party at the airlock, having already dimmed the lights. He was very rigid in his attempts not to smile.

They sat in the dimmed room while President Gram presented the plan. Drill pretended to think it over, then acceded. Details were worked out. First the location of one human planet would be given and verified—this planet, the Shar capital, would count as the first revealed Shar planet. After verification, each side would reveal the location of two planets, verify those, then reveal four, and so on. Even counting the months it would take to verify the location of planets, the treaty should be completed within less than five years.

That night the Shars went mad. At President Gram's urging, they built fires, danced, screamed, sang.

Drill watched on his Ship's video walls. Their rhythms beat at his head.

He smiled. For hours.

The Ship obligingly grew a communicator and coupled it to one of Drill's spare Memories. The two were put aboard a Shar ship and sent in the direction of Drill's home. Drill remained in his ship, watching entertainment videos Ship received from the Shars' channels. He didn't understand the dramas very well, but the comedies were delightful. The Shars could do the most intricate, clever things with their flexible bodies and odd tripod legs—it was delightful to watch them.

Maybe I could take some home with me, he thought. *They can be very entertaining.*

The thousands of Shars waiting outside Ship began to drift away. Within a month only a few hundred were left. Their singing was quiet, triumphant, assured. Sometimes Drill had it piped into his sleeping chamber. It helped him relax.

President Gram visited informally every ten days or so. Drill showed her around Ship, showing her the pilot Memory, the Frog quarters, the giant stardrive engines with their human subspecies' implanted connections, Surrogate in its shadowed, pleasant room. The sight of Surrogate seemed to agitate the President.

"You do not use sex for procreation?" she asked. "As an expression of affection?"

"Indeed we do. I have scads of offspring. There are never enough diplomats, so we have a great many couplings among our subspecies. As for affection...I think I can say that I have enjoyed the company of each of my partners."

She looked up at him with solemn eyes. "You travel to the stars, Drill," she said. "Your species expands randomly in all directions, encountering other species, sometimes annihilating them. Do you have a reason for any of this?"

"A reason?" Drill mused. "It is natural to us. Natural to all intelligent species, so far as we know."

"I meant a conscious reason. Is it anything other than what you do in an automatic way?"

"I can't think of why we would need any such reasons."

"So you have no philosophy of constant expansion? No ideology?"

"I do not know what those words mean," Drill said.

Gram closed her eyes and lowered her head. "I am sorry," she said.

"No need. We have no conflicts in our ideas about ourselves, about our lives. We are happy with what we are."

"Yes. You couldn't be unhappy if you tried, could you?"

"No," Drill said cheerfully. "I see that you understand."

"Yes," Gram said. "I scent that I do."

"In a few million years," Drill said, "these things will become clear to you."

The first Shar ship returned from Drill's home, reporting a transfer of the Memory. The field around Ship filled again with thousands of Shars, crying their happiness to the skies. Other Memories were now taking instructions to all terraforming bases.

The locations of two new planets were released. Ships carrying spare Memories leaped into the skies.

It's working, Drill told Memory.

Long, Memory said. *very long.*

But Memory could not lower Drill's joy. This was what he had lived his life for, and he knew he was good at it. Memories of the future would take this solution as a model for negotiations with other species. Things were working out.

One night the Shars outside Ship altered their behavior. Their singing became once again a moaning, mined with cries. Drill was disturbed.

A communication came from the President. "Cup is dead," she said.

"I understand," Drill said. "Who is his replacement?"

Drill could not read Gram's expression. "That is not yet known. Cup was a strong person, and did not like other strong people around him. Already the successors are fighting for the leadership, but they may not be able to hold his faction together." Her ears flickered. "I may be weakened by this."

"I regret things tend that way."

"Yes," she said. "So do I."

The second set of ships returned. More Memories embarked on their journeys. The treaty was holding.

There was a meeting aboard Ship to formalize the agreement. Cup's successor was Brook, a tall, elderly Shar whose golden fur was darkened by age. A compromise candidate, President Gram said, his election determined after weeks of fighting for the successorship. He was not respected. Already pieces of Cup's old faction were breaking away.

"I wonder, your Excellency," Brook said, after the formal business was over, "if you could arrange for our people to learn your language. You must have powerful translation modules aboard your ship in order to learn our language so quickly. You were broadcasting your message of peace within a few hours of entering real space."

"I have no such equipment aboard Ship," Drill said. "Our knowledge of your language was acquired from Shar prisoners."

"Prisoners?" Shar ears pricked forward. "We were not aware of this," Brook said.

"After our base Memories recognized discrepancies," Drill said, "we sent some Ships out searching for you. We seized one of your ships and took it to my home world. The prisoners were asked about their language and the location of your capital planet. Otherwise it would have taken me months to find your world here, and learn to communicate with you."

"May we ask to arrange for the return of the prisoners?"

"Oh," Drill said. "That won't be possible. After we learned what we needed to know, we terminated their lives. They were being kept in an area reserved for a garden. The landscapers wanted to get to work."

Drill bobbed his head reassuringly. "I am pleased to inform you that they proved excellent fertilizer for the gardens. The result was quite lovely."

"I think," said President Gram carefully, "that it would be best that this information not go beyond those of us in this room. I think it would disturb the process."

Minister-General Vang's ears went back. So did others'. But they acceded.

"I think we should take our leave," said President Gram.

"Have a pleasant afternoon," said Drill.

"It's important." It was not yet dawn. Ship had awakened Drill for a call from the President. "One of your ships has attacked another of our planets."

Alarm drove the sleep from Drill's brain. "Please come to the airlock," he said.

"The information will reach the population within the hour."

"Come quickly," said Drill.

The President arrived with a pair of assistants, who stayed inside the airlock. They carried staves. "My people will be upset," Gram said. "Things may not be entirely safe."

"Which planet was it?" Drill asked.

Gram rubbed her ears. "It was one of those whose location went out on the last peace shuttle."

"The new Memory must not have arrived in time."

"That is what we will tell the people. That it couldn't have been prevented. I will try to speed up the process by which the planets receive new Memories. Double the quota."

"That is a good idea."

"I will have to dismiss Brook. Opposite Minister-General Vang will have to take his job. If I can give Vang more power, he may remain in the coalition and not cause a split."

"As you think best."

President Gram looked up at Drill, her head rising reluctantly, as if held back by a great weight. "My son," she said. "He was on the planet when it happened."

"You have other offspring," Drill said.

Gram looked at him, the pain burning deep in her eyes. "Yes," she said. "I do."

The fields around Ship filled once again. Cries and howls rent the air, and dirges pulsed against Ship's uncaring walls. The Shar broadcasts in the next weeks seemed confused to Drill. Coalitions split and fragmented. Vang spoke frequently of readiness. President Gram succeeded in doubling the quota of planets. The decision was a near one.

Then, days later, another message. "One of our commanders," said President Gram, "was based in the vicinity of the attacked planet.

He is one of Vang's creatures. On his own initiative he ordered our military forces to engage. Your terraforming Ship was attacked."

"Was it destroyed?" Drill asked. His tone was urgent. There is still hope, he reminded himself.

"Don't be anxious for your fellow humans," Gram said. "The Ship was damaged, but escaped."

"The loss of a few hundred billion unconscious organisms is no cause for anxiety," Drill said. "An escaped terraforming Ship is. The Ship will alert our military forces. It will be a real war."

President Gram licked her lips. "What does that mean?"

"You know of our Shrikes and so on. Our military people are worse. They are fully conscious and highly specialized in different modes of warfare. They are destructive, carnivorous, capable of taking enormous damage without impairing function. Their minds concentrate only on tactics, on destruction. Normally they are kept on planetoids away from the rest of humanity. Even other humans find their proximity too...disturbing." Drill put all the urgency in his speech that he could. "Honorable President, you must give me the locations of the remaining planets. If I can get Memories to each of them with news of the peace, we may yet save them."

"I will try. But the coalition..." She turned away from the transmitter. "Vang will claim a victory."

"It is the worst possible catastrophe," Drill said.

Gram's tone was grave. "I believe you," she said.

Drill listened to the broadcasts with growing anxiety. The Shars who spoke on the broadcasts were making angry comments about the execution of prisoners, about flower gardens and values Drill didn't understand. Someone had let the secret loose. President Gram went from group to group outside Ship, talking of the necessity of her plan. The Shar's responses were muted. Drill sensed they were waiting. It was announced that Vang had left the coalition. A chorus of triumphant yips rose from scattered members of the crowd. Others only moaned.

Vang, now simply General Vang, arrived at the field. His followers danced intoxicated circles around him as he spoke, howling their responses to his words. "Triumph! United will!" they cried. "The humans can be beaten! Treachery avenged! Dictate the peace from a position of strength! We smell the location of their planets!"

The Shars' weird cackling laughter followed him from point to point. The laughing and crying went on well into the night. In the morning the announcement came that the coalition had fallen. Vang was now President-General.

In his sleeping chamber, surrounded by his video walls, Drill began to weep.

"I have been asked to bear Vang's message to you," Gram said. She seemed smaller than before, standing unsteadily even on her tripod legs. "It is his…humor."

"What is the message?" Drill said. His whole body seemed in pain. Even Lowbrain was silent, wrapped in misery

"I had hoped," Gram said, "that he was using this simply as an issue on which to gain power. That once he had the Presidency, he would continue the diplomatic effort. It appears he really means what he's been saying. Perhaps he's no longer in control of his own people."

"It is war," Drill said.

"Yes."

You have failed, said Memory. Drill winced in pain.

"You will lose," he said.

"Vang says we are cleverer than you are."

"That may be the case. But cleverness cannot compete with experience. Humans have fought hundreds of these little wars, and never failed to wipe out the enemy. Our Memories of these conflicts are intact. Your people can't fight millions of years of specialized evolution."

"Vang's message doesn't end there. You have till nightfall to remove your Ship from the planet. Six days to get out of real space."

"I am to be allowed to live?" Drill was surprised.

"Yes. It is our…our custom."

Drill scratched himself. "I regret our efforts did not succeed."

"No more than I." She was silent for a while. "Is there any way we can stop this?"

"If Vang attacks any human planets after the Memories of the peace arrangement have arrived," Drill said, "the military will be unleashed to wipe you out. There is no stopping them after that point."

"How long," she asked, "do you think we have?"

"A few years. Ten at the most."

"Our species will be dead."

"Yes. Exterminated. Our military are very good at their jobs."

"You will have killed us," Gram said, "destroyed the culture that we have built for thousands of years, and you won't even give it any thought. Your species doesn't think about what it does any more. It just acts, like a single-celled animal, engulfing everything it can reach. You say that you are a conscious species, but that isn't true. Your every action is…instinct. Or reflex."

"I don't understand," said Drill.

Gram's body trembled. "That is the tragedy of it," she said.

An hour later Ship rose from the field. Shars laughed their defiance from below, dancing in crazed abandon.

I have failed, Drill told Memory.

You knew the odds were long, Memory said. *You knew that in negotiations with species this backward there have only been a handful of successes, and hundreds of failures.*

Yes, Drill acknowledged. *It's a shame, though. To have spent all these months away from home.*

Eat! Eat! said Lowbrain.

Far away, in their forty-mile-long Ships, the human soldiers were already on their way.

SURFACING

There was an alien on the surface of the planet. A Kyklops had teleported into Overlook Station, and then flown down on the shuttle. Since, unlike humans, it could teleport without apparatus, presumably it took the shuttle for the pleasure of the ride. The Kyklops wore a human body, controlled through an n-dimensional interface, and took its pleasures in the human fashion.

The Kyklops expressed an interest in Anthony's work, but Anthony avoided it: he stayed at sea and listened to aliens of another kind.

Anthony wasn't interested in meeting aliens who knew more than he did.

The boat drifted in a cold current and listened to the cries of the sea. A tall grey swell was rolling in from the southwest, crossing with a wind-driven easterly chop. The boat tossed, caught in the confusion of wave patterns.

It was a sloppy ocean, somehow unsatisfactory. Marking a sloppy day.

Anthony felt a thing twist in his mind. Something that, in its own time, would lead to anger.

The boat had been out here, both in the warm current and then in the cold, for three days. Each more unsatisfactory than the last.

The growing swell was being driven toward land by a storm that was breaking up fifty miles out to sea: the remnants of the storm itself would arrive by midnight and make things even more unpleasant. Spray feathered across the tops of the waves. The day was growing cold.

Spindrift pattered across Anthony's shoulders. He ignored it, concentrated instead on the long, grating harmonic moan picked up by the microphones his boat dangled into the chill current. The moan ended on a series of clicks and trailed off. Anthony tapped his computer deck. A resolution appeared on the screen. Anthony shaded his eyes from the pale sun and looked at it.

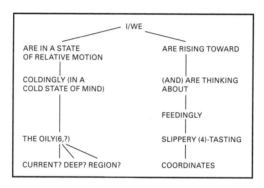

Anthony gazed stonily at the translation tree. "I am rising toward and thinking hungrily about the slippery-tasting coordinates" actually made the most objective sense, but the righthand branch of the tree was the most literal and most of what Anthony suspected was context had been lost. "I and the oily current are in a state of motion toward one another" was perhaps more literal, but "We (the oily deep and I) are in a cold state of mind" was perhaps equally valid.

The boat gave a corkscrew lurch, dropped down the face of a swell, came to an abrupt halt at the end of its drogue. Water slapped against the stern. A mounting screw, come loose from a bracket on the bridge, fell and danced brightly across the deck.

The screw and the deck are in a state of relative motion, Anthony thought. The screw and the deck are in a motion state of mind.

Wrong, he thought, there is no Other in the Dwellers' speech.

We, I and the screw and the deck, are feeling cold.

We, I and the Dweller below, are in a state of mutual incomprehension.

A bad day, Anthony thought.

Inchoate anger burned deep inside him.

Anthony saved the translation and got up from his seat. He went to the bridge and told the boat to retrieve the drogue and head for Cabo Santa Pola at flank speed. He then went below and found a bottle of bourbon that had three good swallows left.

The trailing microphones continued to record the sonorous moans from below, the sound now mingled with the thrash of the boat's screws.

The screw danced on the deck as the engines built up speed. Its state of mind was not recorded.

The video news, displayed above the bar, showed the Kyklops making his tour of the planet. The Kyklops' human body, male, was tall and blue-eyed and elegant. He made witty conversation and showed off his naked chest as if he were proud of it. His name was Telamon.

His real body, Anthony knew, was a tenuous incorporeal mass somewhere in n-dimensional space. The human body had been grown for it to wear, to move like a puppet. The nth dimension was interesting only to a mathematician: its inhabitants preferred wearing flesh.

Anthony asked the bartender to turn off the vid. The yacht club bar was called the Leviathan, and Anthony hated the name. His creatures were too important, too much themselves, to be awarded a name that stank of human myth, of human resonance that had nothing to do with the creatures themselves. Anthony never called them Leviathans himself. They were Deep Dwellers.

There was a picture of a presumed Leviathan above the bar. Sometimes bits of matter were washed up on shore, thin tenuous membranes, long tentacles, bits of phosphorescence, all encrusted with the local equivalent of barnacles and infested with parasites. It was assumed the stuff had broken loose from the larger Dwellers, or were bits of one that had died. The artist had done his best and painted something that looked like a whale covered with tentacles and seaweed.

The place had fake-nautical decor, nets, harpoons, flashing rods, and knickknacks made from driftwood, and the bar was regularly infected by tourists: that made it even worse. But the regular bartender and the divemaster and the steward were real sailors, and that made the yacht club bearable, gave him some company. His mail was delivered here as well.

Tonight the bartender was a substitute named Christopher: he was married to the owner's daughter and got his job that way. He was a fleshy, sullen man and no company.

We, thought Anthony, the world and I, are drinking alone. Anger burned in him, anger at the quality of the day and the opacity of the Dwellers and the storm that beat brainlessly at the windows.

"Got the bastard!" A man was pounding the bar. "Drinks on me." He was talking loudly, and he wore gold rings on his fingers. Raindrops sparkled in his hair. He wore a flashing harness, just in case anyone missed why he was here. Hatred settled in Anthony like poison in his belly.

"Got a thirty-foot flasher," the man said. He pounded the bar again. "Me and Nick got it hung up outside. Four hours. A four-hour fight!"

"Why have a fight with something you can't eat?" Anthony said.

The man looked at him. He looked maybe twenty, but Anthony could tell he was old, centuries old maybe. Old and vain and stupid, stupid as a boy. "It's a game fish," the man said.

Anthony looked into the fisherman's eyes and saw a reflection of his own contempt. "You wanna fight," he said, "you wanna have a game, fight something smart. Not a dumb animal that you can outsmart, that once you catch it will only rot and stink."

That was the start.

Once it began, it didn't take long. The man's rings cut Anthony's face, and Anthony was smaller and lighter, but the man telegraphed every move and kept leading with his right. When it was over, Anthony left him on the floor and stepped out into the downpour, stood alone in the hammering rain and let the water wash the blood from his face. The whiskey and the rage were a flame that licked his nerves and made them sing.

He began walking down the street. Heading for another bar.

✸

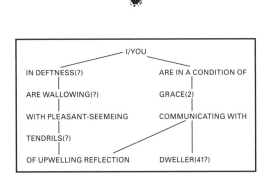

GRACE(2) meant grace in the sense of physical grace, dexterity, harmony of motion, as opposed to spiritual grace, which was GRACE(1). The Dweller that Anthony was listening to was engaged in a dialogue with another, possibly the same known to the computer as 41, who might be named "Upwelling Reflection," but Deep Dweller naming systems seemed inconsistent, depending largely on a context that was as yet opaque, and "upwelling reflection" might have to do with something else entirely.

Anthony suspected the Dweller had just said hello.

Salt water smarted on the cuts on Anthony's face. His swollen knuckles pained him as he tapped the keys of his computer deck. He never suffered from hangover, and his mind seemed filled with an exemplary clarity; he worked rapidly, with burning efficiency. His body felt energized.

He was out of the cold Kirst Current today, in a warm, calm subtropical sea on the other side of the Las Madres archipelago. The difference of forty nautical miles was astonishing.

The sun warmed his back. Sweat prickled on his scalp. The sea sparkled under a violet sky.

The other Dweller answered.

Through his bare feet, Anthony could feel the subsonic overtones vibrating through the boat. Something in the cabin rattled. The microphones recorded the sounds, raised the subsonics to an audible level, played it back. The computer made its attempt.

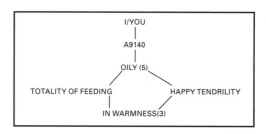

A9140 was a phrase that, as yet, had no translation.

The Dweller language, Anthony had discovered, had no separation of subject and object; it was a trait in common with the Earth cetaceans whose languages Anthony had learned first. "I swim toward the island" was not a grammatical possibility: "I and the island are in a condition of swimming toward one another" was the nearest possible approximation.

The Dwellers lived in darkness, and, like Earth's cetaceans, in a liquid medium. Perhaps they were psychologically unable to separate themselves from their environment, from their fluid surroundings. Never approaching the surface—it was presumed they could not survive in a non-pressurized environment—they had no idea of the upper limit of their world. They were surrounded by a liquid three-dimensional wholeness, not an air-earth-sky environment from which they could consider themselves separate.

A high-pitched whooping came over the speakers, and Anthony smiled as he listened. The singer was one of the humpbacks that he had imported to this planet, a male called The One with Two Notches on His Starboard Fluke.

Two Notches was one of the brighter whales, and also the most playful. Anthony ordered his computer to translate the humpback speech.

Anthony, I and a place of bad smells have found one another, but this has not deterred our hunger.

The computer played back the message as it displayed the translation, and Anthony could understand more context from the sound of the original speech: that Two Notches was floating in a cold layer beneath the bad smell, and that the bad smell was methane or something like it—humans couldn't smell methane, but whales could. The over-literal translation was an aid only, to remind Anthony of idioms he might have forgotten.

Anthony's name in humpback was actually He Who Has Brought Us to the Sea of Rich Strangeness, but the computer translated it simply. Anthony tapped his reply.

What is it that stinks, Two Notches?

Some kind of horrid jellyfish. Were they and I feeding, they and I would spit one another out. I/they will give them/me a name. I/they will give them a name: they/me are the jellyfish that smell like indigestion.

That is a good name, Two Notches.

I and a small boat discovered each other earlier today. We itched, so we scratched our back on the boat. The humans and I were startled. We had a good laugh together in spite of our hunger.

Meaning that Two Notches had risen under the boat, scratched his back on it, and terrified the passengers witless. Anthony remembered the first time this had happened to him back on Earth, a vast female humpback rising up without warning, one long scalloped fin breaking the water to port, the rest of the whale to starboard, thrashing in cetacean delight as it rubbed itself against a boat half its length. Anthony had clung to the gunwale, horrified by what the whale could do to his boat, but still exhilarated, delighted at the sight of the creature and its glorious joy.

Still, Two Notches ought not to play too many pranks on the tourists.

We should he careful, Two Notches. Not all humans possess our sense of humor, especially if they are hungry.

We were bored, Anthony. Mating is over, feeding has not begun. Also, it was Nick's boat that got scratched. In our opinion Nick and I enjoyed ourselves, even though we were hungry.

Hunger and food seemed to be the humpback subtheme of the day. Humpback songs, like the human, were made up of verse and chorus, the chorus repeating itself, with variations, through the message.

I and Nick will ask each other and find out, as we feed.

Anthony tried to participate in the chorus/response about food, but he found himself continually frustrated at his clumsy phrasing. Fortunately the whales were tolerant of his efforts.

Have we learned anything about the ones that swim deep and do not breathe and feed on obscure things?

Not yet, Two Notches. Something has interrupted us in our hungry quest.

A condition of misfortune exists like unto hunger. We must learn to be quicker

We will try, Two Notches. After we eat.

We would like to speak to the Deep Dwellers now, and feed with them, but we must breathe.

We will speak to ourselves another time, after feeding.

We are in a condition of hunger, Anthony. We must eat soon.

We will remember our hunger and make plans.

The mating and calving season for the humpbacks was over. Most of the whales were already heading north to their summer feeding grounds, where they would do little for six months but eat. Two Notches and one of the other males had remained in the vicinity of Las Madres as a favor to Anthony, who used them to assist in locating the Deep Dwellers, but soon—in a matter of days—the pair would have to head north. They hadn't eaten anything for nearly half a year; Anthony didn't want to starve them.

But when the whales left, Anthony would be alone—again—with the Deep Dwellers. He didn't want to think about that.

The system's second sun winked across the waves, rising now. It was a white dwarf and emitted dangerous amounts of X-rays. The boat's falkner generator, triggered by the computer, snapped on a field that surrounded the boat and guarded it from energetic radiation. Anthony felt the warmth on his shoulders decrease. He turned his attention back to the Deep Dwellers.

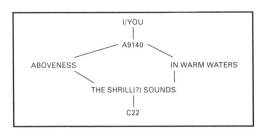

A blaze of delight rose in Anthony. The Dwellers, he realized, had overheard his conversation with Two Notches, and were commenting on it. Furthermore, he knew, A9140 probably was a verb form having to do with hearing—the Dwellers had a lot of them. "I/You hear the shrill sounds from above" might do as a working translation, and although he had no idea how to translate C22, he suspected it was a comment on the sounds. In a fever, Anthony began to work. As he bent over his keys he heard, through water and bone, the sound of Two Notches singing.

The Milky Way was a dim watercolor wash overhead. An odd twilight hung over Las Madres, a near-darkness that marked the hours when only the dwarf star was in the sky, providing little visible light but still pouring out X-rays. Cabo Santa Pola lay in a bright glowing crescent across the boat's path. Music drifted from a waterfront tavern, providing a counterpoint to the Deep Dweller speech that still rang in Anthony's head. A familiar figure waited on the dock, standing beneath the yellow lamp that marked Anthony's slip. Anthony waved and throttled the boat back.

A good day. Even after the yellow sun had set, Anthony still felt in a sunny mood. A9140 had been codified as "listen(H)," meaning listen solely in the sense of listening to a sound that originated from far outside the Dwellers' normal sphere—from outside their entire universe, in fact, which spoke volumes for the way the Dwellers saw themselves in relation to their world. They knew something else was up there, and their speech could make careful distinction between the world they knew and could perceive directly and the one they didn't. C22 was a descriptive term involving patterning: the Dwellers realized that the cetacean speech they'd been hearing wasn't simply random. Which spoke rather well for their cognition.

Anthony turned the boat and backed into the slip. Nick Kanellopoulos, whom the humpbacks called The One Who Chases Bad-Tasting Fish, took the stern line that Anthony threw him and tied it expertly to a cleat. Anthony shut off the engines, took a bowline, and hopped to the dock. He bent over the cleat and made his knot.

"You've gotta stop beating up my customers, Anthony," Nick said.

Anthony said nothing.

"You even send your damn whales to harass me."

Anthony jumped back into the boat and stepped into the cabin for a small canvas bag that held his gear and the data cubes containing the Dweller's conversation. When he stepped back out of the cabin, he saw Nick standing on one foot, the other poised to step into the boat. Anthony gave Nick a look and Nick pulled his foot back. Anthony smiled. He didn't like people on his boat.

"Dinner?" he asked.

Nick gazed at him. A muscle moved in the man's cheek. He was dapper, olive-skinned, about a century old, the second-youngest human on the planet. He looked in his late teens. He wore a personal falkner generator on his belt that protected him from the dwarf's X-rays.

"Dinner. Fine." His brown eyes were concerned. "You look like hell, Anthony."

Anthony rubbed the stubble on his cheeks. "I feel on top of the world," he said.

"Half the time you don't even talk to me. I don't know why I'm eating supper with you."

"Let me clean up. Then we can go to the Mary Villa."

Nick shook his head. "Okay," he said. "But you're buying. You cost me a customer last night."

Anthony slapped him on the shoulder. "Least I can do, I guess."

A good day.

Near midnight. Winds beat at the island's old volcanic cone, pushed down the crowns of trees. A shuttle, black against the darkness of the sky, rose in absolute silence from the port on the other side of the island, heading toward the bright fixed star that was Overlook Station. The alien, Telamon, was aboard, or so the newscasts reported.

Deep Dwellers still sang in Anthony's head. Mail in hand, he let himself in through the marina gate and walked toward his slip. The smell of the sea rose around him. He stretched, yawned. Belched up a bit of the tequila he'd been drinking with Nick. He intended to get an early start and head back to sea before dawn.

Anthony paused beneath a light and opened the large envelope, pulled out actual page proofs that had been mailed, at a high cost, from the offices of the *Xenobiology Review* on Kemps. Discontent scratched at his nerves. He frowned as he glanced through the pages. He'd written the article over a year before, at the end of the first spring he'd spent here, and just glancing through it he now found the article overtentative, overformal, and, worse, almost pleading in its attempt to justify his decision to move himself and the whales here. The palpable defensiveness made him want to squirm.

Disgust filled him. His fingers clutched at the pages, then tore the proofs across. His body spun full circle as he scaled the proofs out to the sea. The wind scattered thick chunks of paper across the dark waters of the marina.

He stalked toward his boat. Bile rose in his throat. He wished he had a bottle of tequila with him. He almost went back for one before he realized the liquor stores were closed.

"Anthony Maldalena?"

She was a little gawky, and her skin was pale. Dark hair in a single long braid, deep eyes, a bit of an overbite. She was waiting for him at the end of his slip, under the light. She had a bag over one shoulder.

Anthony stopped. Dull anger flickered in his belly. He didn't want anyone taking notice of the bruises and cuts on his face. He turned his head away as he stepped into his boat, dropped his bag on a seat.

"Mr. Maldalena. My name is Philana Telander. I came here to see you."

"How'd you get in?"

She gestured to the boat two slips down, a tall FPS-powered yacht shaped like a flat oval with a tall flybridge jutting from its center so that the pilot could see over wavetops. It would fly from place to place, but she could put it down in the water if she wanted. No doubt she'd bought a temporary membership at the yacht club.

"Nice boat," said Anthony. It would have cost her a fair bit to have it gated here. He opened the hatch to his forward cabin, tossed his bag onto the long couch inside.

"I meant," she said, "I came to this planet to see you."

Anthony didn't say anything, just straightened from his stoop by the hatch and looked at her. She shifted from one foot to another. Her skin was yellow in the light of the lamp. She reached into her bag and fumbled with something.

Anthony waited.

The clicks and sobs of whales sounded from the recorder in her hand.

◉

"I wanted to show you what I've been able to do with your work. I have some articles coming up in *Cetology Journal* but they won't be out for a while."

"You've done very well," said Anthony. Tequila swirled in his head. He was having a hard time concentrating on a subject as difficult as whale speech.

Philana had specialized in communication with female humpbacks. It was harder to talk with the females: although they were curious and playful, they weren't vocal like the bulls; their language was deeper, briefer, more personal. They made no songs. It was almost as if, solely in the realm of speech, the cows were autistic. Their psychology was different and complicated, and Anthony had little success in establishing any lasting communication. The cows, he had realized, were speaking a different language: the humpbacks were essentially bilingual, and Anthony had learned only that of the males.

Philana had succeeded where Anthony had found only frustration. She had built from his work, established a structure and basis for communication. She still wasn't as easy in her speech with the cows as Anthony was with a bull like Two Notches, but she was far closer than Anthony had ever been.

She and Anthony sat on the cushioned benches in the stern of Anthony's boat. Steam rose from the coffee cup in Philana's hand. Tequila still buzzed in Anthony's head. Conflicting urges warred in him. He didn't want anyone else here, on his boat, this close to his work; but Philana's discoveries were too interesting to shut her out entirely. He swallowed more coffee.

"Listen to this," Philana said. "It's fascinating. A cow teaching her calf about life." She touched the recorder, and muttering filled the air. Anthony had difficulty understanding: the cow's idiom was complex, and bore none of the poetic repetition that made the males' language easier to follow. Finally he shook his head.

"Go ahead and turn it off," he said. "I'm picking up only one phrase in five. I can't follow it."

Philana seemed startled. "Oh. I'm sorry. I thought—"

Anthony twisted uncomfortably in his seat. "I don't know every goddamn thing about whales," he said.

The recorder fell silent. Wind rattled the canvas awning over the flybridge. Savage discontent settled into Anthony's mind. Suddenly he needed to get rid of this woman, get her off his boat and head to sea right now, away from all the things on land that could trip him up.

He thought of his father upside-down in the smokehouse. Not moving, arms dangling.

He should apologize, he realized. We are, he thought, in a condition of permanent apology.

"I'm sorry," he said. "I'm just...not used to dealing with people."

"Sometimes I wonder," she said. "I'm only twenty-one, and..."

"Yes?" Blurted suddenly, the tequila talking. Anthony felt disgust at his own awkwardness.

Philana looked at the planks. "Yes. Truly. I'm twenty-one, and sometimes people get impatient with me for reasons I don't understand."

Anthony's voice was quiet. "I'm twenty-six."

Philana was surprised. "But. I thought." She thought for a long moment. "It seems I've been reading your papers for..."

"I was first published at twenty," he said. "The finback article."

Philana shook her head. "I'd never have guessed. Particularly after what I saw in your new XR paper."

Anthony's reaction was instant. "You saw that?" Another spasm of disgust touched him. Tequila burned in his veins. His stomach turned over. For some reason his arms were trembling.

"A friend on Kemps sent me an advance copy, I thought it was brilliant. The way you were able to codify your conceptions about a race of which you could really know nothing, and have it all pan out when you began to understand them. That's an incredible achievement."

"It's a piece of crap." Anthony wanted more tequila badly. His body was shaking. He tossed the remains of his coffee over his shoulder into the sea. "I've learned so much since. I've given up even trying to publish it. The delays are too long. Even if I put it on the nets, I'd still have to take the time to write it, and I'd rather spend my time working."

"I'd like to see it."

He turned away from her. "I don't show my work till it's finished."

"I...didn't mean to intrude."

Apology. He could feel a knife twisting in his belly. He spoke quickly. "I'm sorry, Miss Telander. It's late, and I'm not used to company. I'm not entirely well." He stood, took her arm. Ignoring her surprise, he almost pulled her to her feet. "Maybe tomorrow. We'll talk again."

She blinked up at him. "Yes. I'd like that."

"Good night." He rushed her off the boat and stepped below to the head. He didn't want her to hear what was going to happen next. Acid rose in his throat. He clutched his middle and bent over the small toilet and let the spasms take him. The convulsions wracked him long after he was dry. After it was over he stood shakily, staggered to the sink, washed his face. His sinus burned and brought tears to his eyes. He threw himself on the couch.

In the morning, before dawn, he cast off and motored out into the quiet sea.

The other male, The One Who Sings of Others, found a pair of Dwellers engaged in a long conversation and hovered above them. His transponder led Anthony to the place, fifty miles south into the bottomless tropical ocean. The Dwellers' conversation was dense. Anthony understood perhaps one word-phrase in ten. Sings of Others interrupted from time to time to tell Anthony how hungry he was.

The recordings would require days of work before Anthony could even begin to make sense of them. He wanted to stay on the site, but the Dwellers fell silent, neither Anthony nor Sings of Others could find another conversation, and Anthony was nearly out of supplies. He'd been working so intently he'd never got around to buying food.

The white dwarf had set by the time Anthony motored into harbor. Dweller mutterings did a chaotic dance in his mind. He felt a twist of annoyance at the sight of Philana Telander jumping from her big air yacht to the pier. She had obviously been waiting for him.

He threw her the bowline and she made fast. As he stepped onto the dock and fastened the sternline, he noticed sunburn reddening her cheeks. She'd spent the day on the ocean.

"Sorry I left so early," he said. "One of the humpbacks found some Dwellers, and their conversation sounded interesting."

She looked from Anthony to his boat and back. "That's all right," she said. "I shouldn't have talked to you last night. Not when you were ill."

Anger flickered in his mind. She'd heard him being sick, then.

"Too much to drink," he said. He jumped back into the boat and got his gear.

"Have you eaten?" she asked. "Somebody told me about a place called the Villa Mary."

He threw his bag over one shoulder. Dinner would be his penance. "I'll show you," he said.

✳

"Mary was a woman who died," Anthony said. "One of the original Knight's Move people. She chose to die, refused the treatments. She didn't believe in living forever." He looked up at the arched ceiling, the moldings on walls and ceiling, the initials ML worked into the decoration. "Brian McGivern built this place in her memory," Anthony said. "He's built a lot of places like this, on different worlds."

Philana was looking at her plate. She nudged an ichthyoid exomembrane with her fork. "I know," she said. "I've been in a few of them."

Anthony reached for his glass, took a drink, then stopped himself from taking a second swallow. He realized that he'd drunk most of a bottle of wine. He didn't want a repetition of last night.

With an effort he put the glass down.

"She's someone I think about, sometimes," Philana said. "About the choice she made."

"Yes?" Anthony shook his head. "Not me. I don't want to spend a hundred years dying. If I ever decide to die, I'll do it quick."

"That's what people say. But they never do it. They just get older and older. Stranger and stranger." She raised her hands, made a gesture that took in the room, the decorations, the entire white building on its cliff overlooking the sea. "Get old enough, you start doing things like building Villa Marys all over the galaxy. McGivern's an oldest-generation immortal, you know. Maybe the wealthiest human anywhere, and he spends his time immortalizing someone who didn't want immortality of any kind."

Anthony laughed. "Sounds like you're thinking of becoming a Diehard."

She looked at him steadily. "Yes."

Anthony's laughter froze abruptly. A cool shock passed through him. He had never spoken to a Diehard before: the only ones he'd met were people who mumbled at him on streetcorners and passed out incoherent religious tracts.

Philana looked at her plate. "I'm sorry," she said.

"Why sorry?"

"I shouldn't have brought it up."

Anthony reached for his wine glass, stopped himself, put his hand down. "I'm curious."

She gave a little, apologetic laugh. "I may not go through with it."

"Why even think about it?"

Philana thought a long time before answering. "I've seen how the whales accept death. So graceful about it, so matter-of-fact—and they don't even have the myth of an afterlife to comfort them. If they get sick, they just beach themselves; and their friends try to keep them company. And when I try to give myself a reason for living beyond my natural span, I can't think of any. All I can think of is the whales."

Anthony saw the smokehouse in his mind, his father with his arms hanging, the fingers touching the dusty floor. "Death isn't nice."

Philana gave him a skeletal grin and took a quick drink of wine. "With any luck," she said, "death isn't anything at all."

Wind chilled the night, pouring upon the town through a slot in the island's volcanic cone. Anthony watched a streamlined head as it moved in the dark windwashed water of the marina. The head belonged to a coldblooded amphibian that lived in the warm surf of Las Madres; the creature was known misleadingly as a Las Madres seal. They had little fear of humanity and were curious about the new arrivals. Anthony stamped a foot on the slip. Planks boomed. The seal's head disappeared with a soft splash. Ripples spread in starlight, and Anthony smiled.

Philana had stepped into her yacht for a sweater. She returned, cast a glance at the water, saw nothing.

"Can I listen to the Dwellers?" she asked. "I'd like to hear them."

Despite his resentment at her imposition, Anthony appreciated her being careful with the term: she hadn't called them Leviathans once. He thought about her request, could think of no reason to refuse save his own stubborn reluctance. The Dweller sounds were just background noise, meaningless to her. He stepped onto his boat, took a cube from his pocket, put it in the trapdoor, pressed the PLAY button. Dweller murmurings filled the cockpit. Philana stepped from the dock to the boat. She shivered in the wind. Her eyes were pools of dark wonder.

"So different."

"Are you surprised?"

"I suppose not."

"This isn't really what they sound like. What you're hearing is a computer-generated metaphor for the real thing. Much of their communication is subsonic, and the computer raises the sound to levels we can hear, and also speeds it up. Sometimes the Dwellers take three or four minutes to speak what seems to be a simple sentence."

"We would never have noticed them except for an accident," Philana said. "That's how alien they are."

"Yes."

Humanity wouldn't know of the Dwellers' existence at all if it weren't for the subsonics confusing some automated sonar buoys, followed by an idiot computer assuming the sounds were deliberate interference and initiating an ET scan. Any human would have looked at the data, concluded it was some kind of seismic interference, and programmed the buoys to ignore it.

"They've noticed us," Anthony said. "The other day I heard them discussing a conversation I had with one of the humpbacks."

Philana straightened. Excitement was plain in her voice. "They can conceptualize something alien to them."

"Yes."

Her response was instant, stepping on the last sibilant of his answer. "And theorize about our existence."

Anthony smiled at her eagerness. "I...don't think they've got around to that yet."

"But they are intelligent."

"Yes."

"Maybe more intelligent than the whales. From what you say, they seem quicker to conceptualize."

"Intelligent in certain ways, perhaps. There's still very little I understand about them."

"Can you teach me to talk to them?"

The wind blew chill between them. "I don't," he said, "talk to them."

She seemed not to notice his change of mood, stepped closer. "You haven't tried that yet? That would seem to be reasonable, considering they've already noticed us."

He could feel his hackles rising, mental defenses sliding into place. "I'm not proficient enough," he said.

"If you could attract their attention, they could teach you." Reasonably.

"No. Not yet." Rage exploded in Anthony's mind. He wanted her off his boat, away from his work, his existence. He wanted to be alone again with his creatures, solitary witness to the lonely and wonderful interplay of alien minds.

"I never told you," Philana said, "why I'm here."

"No. You didn't."

"I want to do some work with the humpback cows."

"Why?"

Her eyes widened slightly. She had detected the hostility in his tone. "I want to chart any linguistic changes that may occur as a result of their move to another environment." .

Through clouds of blinding resentment Anthony considered her plan. He couldn't stop her, he knew: anyone could talk to the whales if they knew how to do it. It might keep her away from the Dwellers.

"Fine," he said. "Do it."

Her look was challenging. "I don't need your permission."

"I know that."

"You don't own them."

"I know that, too."

There was a splash far out in the marina. The Las Madres seal chasing a fish. Philana was still staring at him. He looked back.

"Why are you afraid of my getting close to the Dwellers?" she asked.

"You've been here two days. You don't know them. You're making all manner of assumptions about what they're like, and all you've read is one obsolete article."

"You're the expert. But if my assumptions are wrong, you're free to tell me."

"Humans interacted with whales for centuries before they learned to speak with them, and even now the speech is limited and often confused. I've only been here two and a half years."

"Perhaps," she said, "you could use some help. Write those papers of yours. Publish the data."

He turned away. "I'm doing fine," he said.

"Glad to hear it." She took a long breath. "What did I *do,* Anthony? Tell me."

"Nothing," he said. Anthony watched the marina waters, saw the amphibian surface, its head pulled back to help slide a fish down its gullet. Philana was just standing there. We, thought Anthony, are in a condition of non-resolution.

"I work alone," he said. "I immerse myself in their speech, in their environment, for months at a time. Talking to a human breaks my concentration. I don't know *how* to talk to a person right now. After the Dwellers, you seem perfectly..."

"Alien?" she said. Anthony didn't answer. The amphibian slid through the water, its head leaving a short, silver wake.

The boat rocked as Philana stepped from it to the dock: "Maybe we can talk later," she said. "Exchange data or something."

"Yes," Anthony said. "We'll do that." His eyes were still on the seal. Later, before he went to bed, he told the computer to play Dweller speech all night long.

Lying in his bunk the next morning, Anthony heard Philana cast off her yacht. He felt a compulsion to talk to her, apologize again, but in the end he stayed in his rack, tried to concentrate on Dweller sounds.

I/We remain in a condition of solitude, he thought, the Dweller phrases coming easily to his mind. There was a brief shadow cast on the port beside him as the big flying boat rose into the sky, then nothing but sunlight and the slap of water on the pier supports. Anthony climbed out of his sleeping bag and went into town, provisioned the boat for a week. He had been too close to land for too long: a trip into the sea, surrounded by nothing but whales and Dweller speech, should cure him of his unease.

Two Notches had switched on his transponder: Anthony followed the beacon north, the boat rising easily over deep blue rollers. Desiring sun, Anthony climbed to the flybridge and lowered the canvas cover. Fifty miles north of Cabo Santa Pola there was a clear dividing line in the water, a line as clear as a meridian on a chart, beyond which the sea was a deeper, purer blue. The line marked the boundary of the cold Kirst current that had journeyed, wreathed in mist from contact with the warmer air, a full three thousand nautical miles from the region of the South Pole. Anthony crossed the line and rolled down his sleeves as the temperature of the air fell.

He heard the first whale speech through his microphones as he entered the cold current: the sound hadn't carried across the turbulent frontier of warm water and cold. The whales were unclear, distant and mixed with the sound of the screws, but he could tell from the rhythm that he was overhearing a dialogue. Apparently Sings of Others had joined Two Notches north of Las Madres. It was a long journey to make overnight, but not impossible.

The cooler air was invigorating. The boat plowed a straight, efficient wake through the deep blue sea. Anthony's spirits rose. This was where he belonged, away from the clutter and complication of humanity. Doing what he did best.

He heard something odd in the rhythm of the whalespeech; he frowned and listened more closely. One of the whales was Two Notches: Anthony recognized his speech patterns easily after all this time; but the other wasn't Sings of Others. There was a clumsiness in its pattern of chorus and response.

The other was a human. Annoyance hummed in Anthony's nerves. Back on Earth, tourists or eager amateur explorers sometimes bought cheap translation programs and tried to talk to the whales, but this was no tourist program: it was too eloquent, too knowing. Philana, of course. She'd followed the transponder signal and was busy gathering data about the humpback females. Anthony cut his engines and let the boat drift slowly to put its bow into the wind; he deployed the microphones from their wells in the hull and listened. The song was bouncing off a colder layer below, and it echoed confusingly.

Deep Swimmer and her calf, called the One that Nudges, are possessed of one another. I and that one am the father. We hunger for one another's presence.

Apparently hunger was once again the subtheme of the day. The context told Anthony that Two Notches was swimming in cool water beneath a boat. Anthony turned the volume up:

We hunger to hear of Deep Swimmer and our calf.

That was the human response: limited in its phrasing and context, direct and to the point.

I and Deep Swimmer are shy. We will not play with humans. Instead we will pretend we are hungry and vanish into deep waters.

The boat lurched as a swell caught it at an awkward angle. Water splashed over the bow. Anthony deployed the drogue and dropped from the flybridge to the cockpit. He tapped a message into the computer and relayed it.

I and Two Notches are pleased to greet ourselves. I and Two Notches hope we are not too hungry.

The whale's reply was shaded with delight. **Hungrily I and Anthony greet ourselves. We and Anthony's friend, Air Human, have been in a condition of conversation.**

Air Human, from the flying yacht. Two Notches went on.

We had found ourselves some Deep Dwellers, but some moments ago we and they moved beneath a cold layer and our conversation is lost. I starve for its return.

The words echoed off the cold layer that stood like a wall between Anthony and the Dwellers. The humpback inflections were steeped in annoyance.

Our hunger is unabated, Anthony typed. *But we will wait for the non-breathers' return.*

We cannot wait long. Tonight we and the north must begin the journey to our feeding time.

The voice of Air Human rumbled through the water. It sounded like a distant, throbbing engine. **Our finest greetings, Anthony. I and Two Notches will travel north together. Then we and the others will feed.**

Annoyance slammed into Anthony. Philana had abducted his whale. Clenching his teeth, he typed a civil reply:

Please give our kindest greetings to our hungry brothers and sisters in the north.

By the time he transmitted his anger had faded. Two Notches' departure was inevitable in the next few days, and he'd known that. Still, a residue of jealousy burned in him. Philana would have the whale's company on its journey north: he would be stuck here by Las Madres without the keen whale ears that helped him find the Dwellers.

Two Notches' reply came simultaneously with a programmed reply from Philana. Lyrics about greetings, hunger, feeding, calves, and joy whined through the water, bounced from the cold layer. Anthony looked at the hash his computer made of the translation and laughed. He decided he might as well enjoy Two Notches' company while it lasted.

That was a strange message to hear from our friend, Two Mouths, he typed. "Notch" and "mouth" were almost the same phrase: Anthony had just made a pun.

Whale amusement bubbled through the water. **Two Mouths and I belong to the most unusual family between the surface and cold water. We-all and air breathe each other, but some of us have the bad fortune to live in it.**

The sun warmed Anthony's shoulders in spite of the cool air. He decided to leave off the pursuit of the Dwellers and spend the day with his humpback.

He kicked off his shoes, then stepped down to his cooler and made himself a sandwich.

❋

The Dwellers never came out from beneath the cold layer. Anthony spent the afternoon listening to Two Notches tell stories about his family. Now that the issue of hunger was resolved by the whale's decision to migrate, the cold layer beneath them became the new topic of conversation, and Two Notches amused himself by harmonizing with his own echo. Sings of Others arrived in late afternoon and announced he had already begun his journey: he and Two Notches decided to travel in company.

Northward homing! Cold watering! Reunion joyous! The phrases dopplered closer to Anthony's boat, and then Two Notches broke the water thirty feet off the port beam, salt water pouring like Niagara from his black jaw, his scalloped fins spread like wings eager to take the air…

Anthony's breath went out of him in surprise. He turned in his chair and leaned away from the sight, half in fear and half in awe… Even though he was used to the whales, the sight never failed to stun him, thrill him, freeze him in his tracks.

Two Notches toppled over backwards, One clear brown eye fixed on Anthony. Anthony raised an arm and waved, and he thought he saw amusement in Two Notches' glance, perhaps the beginning of an answering wave in the gesture of a fin. A living creature the size of a bus, the whale struck the water not with a smack, but with a roar, a sustained outpour of thunder. Anthony braced himself for what was coming. Salt water flung itself over the gunwale, struck him like a blow. The cold was shocking: his heart lurched. The boat was flung high on the wave, dropped down its face with a jarring thud. Two Notches' flukes tossed high and Anthony could see the mottled pattern, grey and white, on the underside, distinctive as a fingerprint…and then the flukes were gone, leaving behind a rolling boat and a boiling sea.

Anthony wiped the ocean from his face, then from his computer. The boat's auto-baling mechanism began to throb. Two Notches surfaced a hundred yards off, spouted a round cloud of steam, submerged again. The whale's amusement stung the water. Anthony's surprise turned to joy, and he echoed the sound of laughter.

I'm going to run my boat up your backside, Anthony promised; he splashed to the controls in his bare feet, withdrew the drogue and threw his engines into gear. Props thrashed the sea into foam. Anthony drew the microphones up into their wells, heard them thud along the hull as the boat gained way. Humpbacks usually took breath in a series of three: Anthony aimed ahead for Two Notches' second rising. Two Notches rose just ahead, spouted, and dove before Anthony could catch him. A cold wind cut through Anthony's wet shirt, raised bumps on his flesh. The boat increased speed, tossing its head on the face of a wave, and Anthony raced ahead, aiming for where Two Notches would rise for the third time.

The whale knew where the boat was and was able to avoid him easily; there was no danger in the game. Anthony won the race: Two Notches surfaced just aft of the boat, and Anthony grinned as he gunned his propellers and wrenched the rudder from side to side while the boat spewed foam into the whale's face. Two Notches gave a grunt of disappointment and sounded, tossing his flukes high. Unless he chose to rise early, Two Notches would be down for five minutes or more. Anthony raced the boat in circles, waiting. Two Notches' taunts rose in the cool water. The wind was cutting Anthony to the quick. He reached into the cabin for a sweater, pulled it on, ran up to the flybridge just in time to see Two Notches leap again half a mile away, the vast dark body silhouetted for a moment against the setting sun before it fell again into the welcoming sea.

Goodbye, goodbye. I and Anthony send fragrant farewells to one another.

White foam surrounded the slick, still place where Two Notches had fallen into the water. Suddenly the flybridge was very cold. Anthony's heart sank. He cut speed and put the wheel amidships. The boat slowed reluctantly, as if it, too, had been enjoying the game. Anthony dropped down the ladder to his computer.

Through the spattered windscreen, Anthony could see Two Notches leaping again, his long wings beating air, his silhouette refracted through seawater and rainbows. Anthony tried to share the whale's exuberance, his joy, but the thought of another long summer alone on his boat, beating his head against the enigma of the Dwellers, turned his mind to ice.

He ordered an infinite repeat of Two Notches' last phrase and stepped below to change into dry clothes. The cold layer echoed his farewells. He bent almost double and began pulling the sweater over his head.

Suddenly he straightened. An idea was chattering at him. He yanked the sweater back down over his trunk, rushed to his computer, tapped another message.

Our farewells need not be said just yet. You and I can follow one another for a few days before I must return. Perhaps you and the non-breathers can find one another for conversation.

Anthony is in a condition of migration. Welcome, welcome! Two Notches' reply was jubilant.

For a few days, Anthony qualified. Before too long he would have to return to port for supplies. Annoyed at himself, he realized he could as easily have victualed for weeks.

A human voice called through the water, sounded faintly through the speakers. *Air Human and Anthony are in a state of tastiest welcome.*

In the middle of Anthony's reply, his fingers paused at the keys. Surprise rose quietly to the surface of his mind.

After the long day of talking in humpback speech, he had forgotten that Air Human was not a humpback. That she was, in fact, another human being sitting on a boat just over the horizon.

Anthony continued his message. His fingers were clumsy now, and he had to go back twice to correct mistakes. He wondered why it was harder to talk to Philana, now that he remembered she wasn't an alien.

❖

He asked Two Notches to turn on his transponder, and, all through the deep shadow twilight when the white dwarf was in the sky, the boat followed the whale at a half-mile's distance. The current was cooperative, but in a few days a new set of northwest trade winds would push the current off on a curve toward the equator and the whales would lose its assistance.

Anthony didn't see Philana's boat that first day: just before dawn, Sings of Others heard a distant Dweller conversation to starboard. Anthony told his boat to strike off in that direction and spent most of the day listening. When the Dwellers fell silent, he headed for the whales' transponders again. There was a lively conversation in progress between Air Human and the whales, but Anthony's mind was still on Dwellers. He put on headphones and worked far into the night.

The next morning was filled with chill mist. Anthony awoke to the whooping cries of the humpbacks. He looked at his computer to see if it had recorded any announcement of Dwellers, and there was none. The whales' interrogation by Air Human continued. Anthony's toes curled on the cold, damp planks as he stepped on deck and saw Philana's yacht two hundred yards to port, floating three feet over the tallest swells. Cables trailed from the stern, pulling hydrophones and speakers on a subaquatic sled. Anthony grinned at the sight of the elaborate store-bought rig. He suspected that he got better acoustics with his homebuilt equipment, the translation softwear he'd programmed himself, and his hopelessly old-fashioned boat that couldn't even rise out of the water, but that he'd equipped with the latest-generation silent propellers.

He turned on his speakers. Sure enough, he got more audio interference from Philana's sled than he received from his entire boat.

While making coffee and an omelette of mossmoon eggs Anthony listened to the whales gurgle about their grandparents. He put on a down jacket and stepped onto the boat's stern and ate breakfast, watching the humpbacks as they occasionally broke surface, puffed out clouds of spray, sounded again with a careless, vast toss of their flukes. Their bodies were smooth and black: the barnacles that pebbled their skin on Earth had been removed before they gated to their new home.

Their song could be heard clearly even without the amplifiers. That was one change the contact with humans had brought: the males were a lot more vocal than once they had been, as if they were responding to human encouragement to talk—or perhaps they now had more worth talking about. Their speech was also more terse than before, less overtly poetic; the humans' directness and compactness of speech, caused mainly by their lack of fluency, had influenced the whales to a degree.

The whales were adapting to communication with humans more easily than the humans were adapting to them. It was important to chart that change, be able to say how the whales had evolved, accommodated. They were on an entire new planet now, explorers, and change was going to come fast. The whales were good at remembering, but artificial intelligences were better. Anthony was suddenly glad that Philana was here, doing her work.

As if on cue she appeared on deck, one hand pressed to her head, holding an earphone: she was listening intently to whalesong. She was bundled up against the chill, and gave a brief wave as she noticed him. Anthony waved back. She paused, beating time with one hand to the rhythm of whalespeech, then waved again and stepped back to her work.

Anthony finished breakfast and cleaned the dishes. He decided to say good morning to the whales, then work on some of the Dweller speech he'd recorded the day before. He turned on his computer, sat down at the console, typed his greetings. He waited for a pause in the conversation, then transmitted. The answer came back sounding like a distant buzzsaw.

We and Anthony wish one another a passage filled with splendid odors. We and Air Human have been scenting one another's families this morning.

We wish each other the joy of converse, Anthony typed.

We have been wondering, Two Notches said, **if we can scent whether we and Anthony and Air Human are in a condition of rut.**

Anthony gave a laugh. Humpbacks enjoyed trying to figure out human relationships: they were promiscuous themselves, and intrigued by ways different from their own.

Anthony wondered, sitting in his cockpit, if Philana was looking at him.

Air Human and I smell of aloneness, unpairness, he typed, and he transmitted the message at the same time that Philana entered the even more direct, **We are not.**

The state is not rut, apartness is the smell. Two Notches agreed readily—it was all one to him—and the lyrics echoed each other for a long moment, *aloneness, not, unpairness, not. Not.* Anthony felt a chill.

I and the Dwellers' speech are going to try to scent one another's natures, he typed hastily, and turned off the speakers. He opened his case and took out one of the cubes he'd recorded the day before.

Work went slowly.

By noon the mist had burned off the water. His head buzzing with Dweller sounds, Anthony stepped below for a sandwich. The message light was blinking on his telephone. He turned to it, pressed the play button.

"May I speak with you briefly?" Philana's voice. "I'd like to get some data, at your convenience." Her tone shifted to one of amusement. "The condition," she added, "is not that of rut."

Anthony grinned. Philana had been considerate enough not to interrupt him, just to leave the message for whenever he wanted it. He picked up the telephone, connected to directory assistance in Cabo Santa Pola, and asked it to route a call to the phone on Philana's yacht. She answered.

"Message received," he said. "Would you join me for lunch?"

"In an hour or so," she said. Her voice was abstracted. "I'm in the middle of something."

"When you're ready. Bye." He rang off, decided to make a fish chowder instead of sandwiches, and drank a beer while preparing it. He began to feel buoyant, cheerful. Siren wailing sounded through the water.

Philana's yacht maneuvered over to his boat just as Anthony finished his second beer. Philana stood on the gunwale, wearing a pale sweater with brown zigzags on it. Her braid was undone, and her brown hair fell around her shoulders. She jumped easily from her gunwale to the flybridge, then came down the ladder. The yacht moved away as soon as it felt her weight leave. She smiled uncertainly as she stepped to the deck.

"I'm sorry to have to bother you," she said.

He offered a grin. "That's okay. I'm between projects right now."

She looked toward the cabin. "Lunch smells good." Perhaps, he thought, food equaled apology.

"Fish chowder. Would you like a beer? Coffee?"

"Beer. Thanks."

They stepped below and Anthony served lunch on the small foldout table. He opened another beer and put it by her place.

"Delicious. I never really learned to cook."

"Cooking was something I learned young."

Her eyes were curious. "Where was that?"

"Lees." Shortly. He put a spoonful of chowder in his mouth so that his terseness would be more understandable.

"I never heard the name."

"It's a planet." Mumbling through chowder. "Pretty obscure." He didn't want to talk about it.

"I'm from Earth."

He looked at her. "Really? Originally? Not just a habitat in the Sol system?"

"Yes. Truly. One of the few. The one and only Earth."

"Is that what got you interested in whales?"

Her spoon stirred idly in her chowder. "I've always been interested in whales. As far back as I can remember. Long before I ever saw one."

"It was the same with me. I grew up near an ocean, built a boat when I was a boy and went exploring. I've never felt more at home than when I'm on the ocean."

"Some people live on the sea all the time."

"In floating habitats. That's just moving a city out onto the ocean. The worst of both worlds, if you ask me."

He realized the beer was making him expansive, that he was declaiming and waving his free hand. He pulled his hand in.

"I'm sorry," he said, "about the last time we talked."

She looked away. "My fault," she said. "I shouldn't have—"

"You didn't do anything wrong." He realized he had almost shouted that, and could feel himself flushing. He lowered his voice. "Once I got out here I realized..." This was really hopeless. He plunged on. "I'm not used to dealing with people. There were just a few people on Lees and they were all...eccentric. And everyone I've met since I left seems at least five hundred years old. Their attitudes are so..." He shrugged.

"Alien." She was grinning.

"Yes."

"I feel the same way. Everyone's so much older, so much more... sophisticated, I suppose." She thought about it for a moment. "I guess it's sophistication."

"They like to think so."

"I can feel their pity sometimes." She toyed with her spoon, looked down at her bowl.

"And condescension." Bitterness striped Anthony's tongue. "The attitude of, 'Oh, we went through that once, poor darling, but now we know better.'"

"Yes." Tiredly. "I know what you mean. Like we're not really people yet."

"At least my father wasn't like that. He was crazy, but he let me be a person. He—"

His tongue stumbled. He was not drunk enough to tell this story, and he didn't think he wanted to anyway.

"Go ahead," said Philana. She was collecting data, Anthony remembered, on families.

He pushed back from the table, went to the fridge for another beer. "Maybe later," he said. "It's a long story."

Philana's look was steady. "You're not the only one who knows about crazy fathers."

Then you tell me about yours, he wanted to say. Anthony opened the beer, took a deep swallow. The liquid rose again, acid in his throat, and he forced it down. Memories rose with the fire in Anthony's throat, burning him. His father's fine madness whirled in his mind like leaves in a hurricane. We are, he thought, in a condition of mutual trust and permanent antagonism. Something therefore must be done.

"All right." He put the beer on the top of the fridge and returned to his seat. He spoke rapidly, just letting the story come. His throat burned. "My father started life with money. He became a psychologist and then a fundamentalist Catholic lay preacher, kind of an unlicensed messiah. He ended up a psychotic. Dad concluded that civilization was too stupid and corrupt to survive, and he decided to start over. He initiated an unauthorized planetary scan through a transporter gate, found a world that he liked, and moved his family there. There were just four of us at the time, Dad and my mother, my little brother, and me. My mother was—is—she's not really her own person. There's a vacancy there. If you're around psychotics a lot, and you don't have a strong sense of self, you can get submerged in their delusions. My mother didn't have a chance of standing up to a full-blooded lunatic like my dad, and I doubt she tried. She just let him run things.

"I was six when we moved to Lees, and my brother was two. We were—" Anthony waved an arm in the general direction of the invisible Milky Way overhead. "—we were half the galaxy away. Clean on the other side of the hub. We didn't take a gate with us, or even instructions and equipment for building one. My father cut us off entirely from everything he hated."

Anthony looked at Philana's shocked face and laughed. "It wasn't so bad. We had everything but a way off the planet. Cube readers, building supplies, preserved food, tools, medical gear, wind and solar generators—Dad thought falkner generators were the cause of the rot, so he didn't bring any with him.

"My mother pretty much stayed pregnant for the next decade, but luckily the planet was benign. We settled down in a protected bay where there was a lot of food, both on land and in the water. We had a smokehouse to preserve the meat. My father and mother educated me pretty well. I grew up an aquatic animal. Built a sailboat, learned how to navigate. By the time I was fifteen I had charted two thousand miles of coast. I spent more than half my time at sea, the last few years. Trying to get away from my dad, mostly. He kept getting stranger. He promised me in marriage to my oldest sister after my eighteenth birthday." Memory swelled in Anthony like a tide, calm green water rising over the flat, soon to whiten and boil.

"There were some whale-sized fish on Lees, but they weren't intelligent. I'd seen recordings of whales, heard the sounds they made. On my long trips I'd imagine I was seeing whales, imagine myself talking to them."

"How did you get away?"

Anthony barked a laugh. "My dad wasn't the only one who could initiate a planetary scan. Seven or eight years after we landed some resort developers found our planet and put up a hotel about two hundred miles to the south of our settlement." Anthony shook his head. "Hell of a coincidence. The odds against it must have been incredible. My father frothed at the mouth when we started seeing their flyers and boats. My father decided our little settlement was too exposed and we moved farther inland to a place where we could hide better. Everything was camouflaged. He'd hold drills in which we were all supposed to grab necessary supplies and run off into the forest."

"They never found you?"

"If they saw us, they thought we were people on holiday."

"Did you approach them?"

Anthony shook his head. "No. I don't really know why."

"Well." Doubtfully. "Your father."

"I didn't care much about his opinions by that point. It was so *obvious* he was cracked. I think, by then, I had all I wanted just living on my boat. I didn't see any reason to change it." He thought for a moment. "If he actually tried to marry me off to my sister, maybe I would have run for it."

"But they found you anyway."

"No. Something else happened. The water supply for the new settlement was unreliable, so we decided to build a viaduct from a spring nearby. We had to get our hollow-log pipe over a little chasm, and my father got careless and had an accident. The viaduct fell on him. Really smashed him up, caused all sorts of internal injuries. It was very obvious that if he didn't get help, he'd die. My mother and I took my boat and sailed for the resort to bring help."

The words dried up. This was where things got ugly. Anthony decided he really couldn't trust Philana with it, and that he wanted his beer after all. He got up and took the bottle and drank.

"Did your father live?"

"No." He'd keep this as brief as he could. "When my mother and I got back, we found that he'd died two days before. My brothers and sisters gutted him and hung him upside-down in the smokehouse." He stared dully into Philana's horrified face. "It's what they did to any large animal. My mother and I were the only ones who remembered what to do with a dead person, and we weren't there."

"My God. Anthony." Her hands clasped below her face.

"And then—" He waved his hands, taking in everything, the boat's comforts, Overlook, life over the horizon. "Civilization. I was the only one of the children who could remember anything but Lees. I got off the planet and got into marine biology. That's been my life ever since. I was amazed to discover that I and the family were rich—my dad didn't tell me he'd left tons of investments behind. The rest of the family's still on Lees, still living in the old settlement. It's all they know." He shrugged. "They're rich, too, of course, which helps. So they're all right."

He leaned back on the fridge and took another long drink. The ocean swell tilted the boat and rolled the liquid down his throat. Whale harmonics made the bottle cap dance on the smooth alloy surface of the refrigerator.

Philana stood. Her words seemed small after the long silence. "Can I have some coffee? I'll make it."

"I'll do it."

They both went for the coffee and banged heads. Reeling back, the expression on Philana's face was wide-eyed, startled, faunlike, as if he'd caught her at something she should be ashamed of. Anthony tried to laugh out an apology, but just then the white dwarf came up above the horizon and the quality of light changed as the screens went up, and with the light her look somehow changed. Anthony gazed at her for a moment and fire began to lap at his nerves. In his head the whales seemed to urge him to make his move.

He put his beer down and grabbed her with an intensity that was made ferocious largely by Anthony's fear that this was entirely the wrong thing, that he was committing an outrage that would compel her shortly to clout him over the head with the coffee pot and drop him in his tracks. Whalesong rang frantic chimes in his head. She gave a strangled cry as he tried to kiss her and thereby confirmed his own worst suspicions about this behavior.

Philana tried to push him away. He let go of her and stepped back, standing stupidly with his hands at his sides. A raging pain in his chest prevented him from saying a word. Philana surprised him by stepping forward and putting her hands on his shoulders.

"Easy," she said. "It's all right, just take it easy."

Anthony kissed her once more, and was somehow able to restrain himself from grabbing her again out of sheer panic and desperation.

By and by, as the kiss continued, his anxiety level decreased. I/You, he thought, are rising in warmness, in happy tendrils.

He and Philana began to take their clothes off. He realized this was the first time he had made love to anyone under two hundred years of age.

Dweller sounds murmured in Anthony's mind. He descended into Philana as if she were a midnight ocean, something that on first contact with his flesh shocked him into wakefulness, then relaxed around him, became a taste of brine, a sting in the eyes, a fluid vagueness. Her hair brushed against his skin like seagrass. She surrounded him, buoyed him up. Her cries came up to him as over a great distance, like the faraway moans of a lonely whale in love. He wanted to call out in answer. Eventually he did.

Grace(1), he thought hopefully. Grace(1).

Anthony had an attack of giddiness after Philana returned to her flying yacht and her work. His mad father gibbered in his memory, mocked him and offered dire warnings. He washed the dishes and cleaned the rattling bottlecap off the fridge, then he listened to recordings of Dwellers and eventually the panic went away. He had not, it seemed, lost anything.

He went to the double bed in the forepeak, which was piled high with boxes of food, a spool of cable, a couple spare microphones, and a pair of rusting Danforth anchors. He stowed the food in the hold, put the electronics in the compartment under the mattress, jammed the Danforths farther into the peak on top of the anchor chain where they belonged. He wiped the grime and rust off the mattress and realized he had neither sheets nor a second pillow. He would need to purchase supplies on the next trip to town.

The peak didn't smell good. He opened the forehatch and tried to air the place out. Slowly he became aware that the whales were trying to talk to him. Odd scentings, they said. Things that stand in water. Anthony knew what they meant. He went up on the flybridge and scanned the horizon. He saw nothing.

The taste is distant, he wrote. *But we must be careful in our movement.* After that he scanned the horizon every half hour.

He cooked supper during the white dwarf's odd half-twilight and resisted the urge to drink both the bottles of bourbon that were waiting in their rack. Philana dropped onto the flybridge with a small rucksack. She kissed him hastily, as if to get it over with.

"I'm scared," she said.

"So am I."

"I don't know why."

He kissed her again. "I do," he said. She laid her cheek against his woolen shoulder. Blind with terror, Anthony held onto her, unable to see the future.

After midnight Anthony stood unclothed on the flybridge as he scanned the horizon one more time. Seeing nothing, he nevertheless reduced speed to three knots and rejoined Philana in the forepeak. She was already asleep with his open sleeping bag thrown over her like a blanket. He raised a corner of the sleeping bag and slipped beneath it. Philana turned away from him and pillowed her cheek on her fist. Whale music echoed from a cold layer beneath. He slept.

Movement elsewhere in the boat woke him. Anthony found himself alone in the peak, frigid air drifting over him from the forward hatch. He stepped into the cabin and saw Philana's bare legs ascending the companion to the flybridge. He followed. He shivered in the cold wind.

Philana stood before the controls, looking at them with a peculiar intensity, as though she were trying to figure out which switch to throw. Her hands flexed as if to take the wheel. There was gooseflesh on her shoulders and the wind tore her hair around her face like a fluttering curtain. She looked at him. Her eyes were hard, her voice disdainful.

"Are we lovers?" she asked. "Is that what's going on here?" His skin prickled at her tone.

Her stiff-spined stance challenged him. He was afraid to touch her.

"The condition is that of rut," he said, and tried to laugh.

Her posture, one leg cocked out front, reminded him of a haughty water bird. She looked at the controls again, then looked aft, lifting up on her toes to gaze at the horizon. Her nostrils flared, tasted the wind. Clouds scudded across the sky. She looked at him again. The white dwarf gleamed off her pebble eyes.

"Very well," she said, as if this was news. "Acceptable." She took his hand and led him below. Anthony's hackles rose. On her way to the forepeak Philana saw one of the bottles of bourbon in its rack and reached for it. She raised the bottle to her lips and drank from the neck. Whiskey coursed down her chin, her throat. She lowered the bottle and wiped her mouth with the back of her hand. She looked at him as if he were something worthy of dissection.

"Let's make love," she said.

Anthony was afraid not to. He went with her to the forepeak. Her skin was cold. Lying next to him on the mattress she touched his chest as if she were unused to the feel of male bodies. "What's your name?" she asked. He told her. "Acceptable," she said again, and with a sudden taut grin raked his chest with her nails. He knocked her hands away. She laughed and came after him with the bottle. He parried the blow in time and they wrestled for possession, bourbon splashing everywhere. Anthony was surprised at her strength. She fastened teeth in his arm. He hit her in the face with a closed fist. She gave the bottle up and laughed in a cold metallic way and put her arms around him. Anthony threw the bottle through the door into the cabin. It thudded somewhere but didn't break. Philana drew him on top of her, her laugh brittle, her legs opening around him.

Her dead eyes were like stones.

In the morning Anthony found the bottle lying in the main cabin. Red clawmarks covered his body, and the reek of liquor caught at the back of his throat. The scend of the ocean had distributed the bourbon puddle evenly over the teak deck. There was still about a third of the whiskey left in the bottle. Anthony rescued it and swabbed the deck. His mind was full of cotton wool, cushioning any bruises. He was working hard at not feeling anything at all.

He put on clothes and began to work. After a while Philana unsteadily groped her way from the forepeak, the sleeping bag draped around her shoulders. There was a stunned look on her face and a livid bruise on one cheek. Anthony could feel his body tautening, ready to repel assault.

"Was I odd last night?" she asked.

He looked at her. Her face crumbled. "Oh no." She passed a hand over her eyes and turned away, leaning on the side of the hatchway. "You shouldn't let me drink," she said.

"You hadn't made that fact clear."

"I don't remember any of it," she said. "I'm sick." She pressed her stomach with her hands and bent over. Anthony narrowly watched her pale buttocks as she groped her way to the head. The door shut behind her.

Anthony decided to make coffee. As the scent of the coffee began to fill the boat, he heard the sounds of her weeping. The long keening sounds, desperate throat-tearing noises, sounded like a pinioned whale writhing helplessly on the gaff.

A vast flock of birds wheeled on the cold horizon, marking a colony of drift creatures. Anthony informed the whales of the creatures' presence, but the humpbacks already knew and were staying well clear. The drift colony was what they had been smelling for hours.

While Anthony talked with the whales, Philana left the head and drew on her clothes. Her movements were tentative. She approached him with a cup of coffee in her hand. Her eyes and nostrils were rimmed with red.

"I'm sorry," she said. "Sometimes that happens."

He looked at his computer console. "Jesus, Philana."

"It's something wrong with me. I can't control it." She raised a hand to her bruised cheek. The hand came away wet.

"There's medication for that sort of thing," Anthony said. He remembered she had a mad father, or thought she did.

"Not for this. It's something different."

"I don't know what to do."

"I need your help."

Anthony recalled his father's body twisting on the end of its rope, fingertips trailing in the dust. Words came reluctantly to his throat.

"I'll give what help I can." The words were hollow: any real resolution had long since gone. He had no clear notion to whom he was giving this message, the Philana of the previous night or this Philana or his father or himself.

Philana hugged him, kissed his cheek. She was excited.

"Shall we go see the drifters?" she asked. "We can take my boat."

Anthony envisioned himself and Philana tumbling through space. He had jumped off a precipice, just now. The two children of mad fathers were spinning in the updraft, waiting for the impact.

He said yes. He ordered his boat to circle while she summoned her yacht. She held his hand while they waited for the flying yacht to drift toward them. Philana kept laughing, touching him, stropping her cheek on his shoulder like a cat. They jumped from the flybridge to her yacht and rose smoothly into the sky. Bright sun warmed Anthony's shoulders. He took off his sweater and felt warning pain from the marks of her nails.

The drifters were colony creatures that looked like miniature mountains twenty feet or so high, complete with a white snow-cap of guano. They were highly organized but unintelligent, their underwater parts sifting the ocean for nutrients or reaching out to capture prey—the longest of their gossamer stinging tentacles was up to two miles in length, and though they couldn't kill or capture a humpback, they were hard for the whale to detect and could cause a lot of stinging wounds before the whale noticed them and made its escape. Perhaps they were unintelligent, distant relatives of the Deep Dwellers, whose tenuous character they resembled. Many different species of seabirds lived in permanent colonies atop the floating islands, thousands of them, and the drifters processed their guano and other waste. Above the water, the drifters' bodies were shaped like a convex lens set on edge, an aerodynamic shape, and they could clumsily tack into the wind if they needed to. For the most part, however, they drifted on the currents, a giant circular circumnavigation of the ocean that could take centuries.

Screaming seabirds rose in clouds as Philana's yacht moved silently toward their homes. Philana cocked her head back, laughed into the open sky, and flew closer. Birds hurtled around them in an overwhelming roar of wings. Whistlelike cries issued from peg-toothed beaks. Anthony watched in awe at the profusion of colors, the chromatic brilliance of the evolved featherlike scales.

The flying boat passed slowly through the drifter colony. Birds roared and whistled, some of them landing on the boat in apparent hopes of taking up lodging. Feathers drifted down; birdshit spattered the windscreen. Philana ran below for a camera. A trickle of optimism began to ease into Anthony at the sight of Philana in the bright morning sun, a broad smile gracing her face as she worked the camera and took picture after picture. He put an arm around Philana's waist and kissed her ear. She smiled and took his hand in her own. In the bright daylight the personality she'd acquired the previous night seemed to gather unto itself the tenebrous, unreal quality of a nightmare. The current Philana seemed far more tangible.

Philana returned to the controls; the yacht banked and increased speed. Birds issued startled cries as they got out of the way. Wind tugged at Philana's hair. Anthony decided not to let Philana near his liquor again.

After breakfast, Anthony found both whales had set their transponders. He had to detour around the drifters—their insubstantial, featherlike tentacles could foul his state-of-the-art silent props—but when he neared the whales and slowed, he could hear the deep murmurings of Dwellers rising from beneath the cold current. There were half a dozen of them engaged in conversation, and Anthony worked through the day and far into the night, transcribing, making hesitant attempts at translation. The Dweller speech was more opaque than usual, depending on a context that was unstated and elusive. Comprehension eluded Anthony; but he had the feeling that the key was within his reach.

Philana waited for the Dwellers to end their speech before she brought her yacht near him. She had heated some prepared dinners and carried them to the flybridge in an insulated pouch. Her grin was broad. She put her pouch down and embraced him. Abstracted Dweller subsonics rolled away from Anthony's mind. He was surprised at how glad he was to see her.

With dinner they drank coffee. Philana chattered bravely throughout the meal. While Anthony cleaned the dishes, she embraced him from behind. A memory of the other Philana flickered in his mind, disdainful, contemptuous, cold. Her father was crazy, he remembered again.

He buried the memory deliberately and turned to her. He kissed her and thought, I/We deny the Other. The Other, he decided, would cease to exist by a common act of will.

It seemed to work. At night his dreams filled with Dwellers crying in joy, his father warning darkly, the touch of Philana's flesh, breath, hands. He awoke hungry to get to work.

The next two days a furious blaze of concentration burned in Anthony's mind. Things fell into place. He found a word that, in its context, could mean nothing but light, as opposed to fluorescence—he was excited to find out the Dwellers knew about the sun. He also found new words for darkness, for emotions that seemed to have no human equivalents, but which he seemed nevertheless to comprehend. One afternoon a squall dumped a gallon of cold water down his collar and he looked up in surprise: he hadn't been aware of its slow approach. He moved his computer deck to the cabin and kept working. When not at the controls he moved dazedly over the boat, drinking coffee, eating what was at hand without tasting it. Philana was amused and tolerant; she buried herself in her own work.

On preparing breakfast the morning of the third day, Anthony realized he was running out of food. He was farther from the archipelago than he'd planned on going, and he had about two days' supply left; he'd have to return at flank speed, buy provisions, and then run out again. A sudden hot fury gripped him. He clenched his fists. He could have provisioned for two or three months—why hadn't he done it when he had the chance?

Philana tolerantly sipped her coffee. "Tonight I'll fly you into Cabo Santa Pola. We can buy a ton of provisions, have dinner at Villa Mary, and be back by midnight."

Anthony's anger floundered uselessly, looking for a target, then gave up. "Fine," he said.

She looked at him. "Are you ever going to talk to them? You must have built your speakers to handle it."

Now the anger had finally found a home. "Not yet," he said.

In late afternoon, Anthony set out his drogue and a homing transponder, then boarded Philana's yacht. He watched while she hauled up her aquasled and programmed the navigation computer. The world dimmed as the falkner field increased in strength. The transition to full speed was almost instantaneous. Waves blurred silently past, providing the only sensation of motion—the field cut out both wind and inertia. The green-walled volcanic islands of the Las Madres archipelago rolled over the horizon in minutes. Traffic over Cabo Santa Pola complicated the approach somewhat; it was all of six minutes before Philana could set the machine down in her slip.

A bright, hot sun brightened the white-and-turquoise waterfront. From a cold Kirst current to the tropics in less than half an hour.

Anthony felt vaguely resentful at this blinding efficiency. He could have easily equipped his own boat with flight capability, but he hadn't cared about speed when he'd set out, only the opportunity to be alone on the ocean with his whales and the Dwellers. Now the very tempo of his existence had changed. He was moving at unaccustomed velocity, and the destination was still unclear.

After giving him her spare key, Philana went to do laundry—when one lived on small boats, laundry was done whenever the opportunity arose. Anthony bought supplies. He filled the yacht's forecabin with crates of food, then changed clothes and walked to the Villa Mary.

Anthony got a table for two and ordered a drink. The first drink went quickly and he ordered a second. Philana didn't appear. Anthony didn't like the way the waiter was looking at him. He heard his father's mocking laugh as he munched the last bread stick. He waited for three hours before he paid and left.

There was no sign of Philana at the laundry or on the yacht. He left a note on the computer expressing what he considered a contained disappointment, then headed into town. A brilliant sign that featured aquatic motifs called him to a cool, dark bar filled with bright green aquaria. Native fish gaped at him blindly while he drank something tall and cool. He decided he didn't like the way the fish looked at him and left.

He found Philana in his third bar of the evening. She was with two men, one of whom Anthony knew slightly as a charter boat skipper whom he didn't much like. He had his hand on her knee; the other man's arm was around her. Empty drinks and forsaken hors d'oeuvres lay on a table in front of them. Anthony realized, as he approached, that his own arrival could only make things worse. Her eyes turned to him as he approached; her neck arched in a peculiar, balletic way that he had seen only once before. He recognized the quick, carnivorous smile, and a wash of fear turned his skin cold. The stranger whispered into her ear.

"What's your name again?" she asked.

Anthony wondered what to do with his hands. "We were supposed to meet."

Her eyes glittered as her head cocked, considering him. Perhaps what frightened him most of all was the fact there was no hostility in her look, nothing but calculation. There was a cigarette in her hand; he hadn't seen her smoke before.

"Do we have business?"

Anthony thought about this. He had jumped into space with this woman, and now he suspected he'd just hit the ground. "I guess not," he said, and turned.

"*Qué pasa*, hombre?"

"*Nada.*"

Pablo, the Leviathan's regular bartender, was one of the planet's original South American inhabitants, a group rapidly being submerged by newcomers. Pablo took Anthony's order for a double bourbon and also brought him his mail, which consisted of an inquiry from Xenobiology Review wondering what had become of their page proofs. Anthony crumpled the note and left it in an ashtray.

A party of drunken fishermen staggered in, still in their flashing harnesses. Triumphant whoops assaulted Anthony's ears. His fingers tightened on his glass.

"Careful, Anthony," said Pablo. He poured another double bourbon. "On the house," he said.

One of the fishermen stepped to the bar, put a heavy hand on Anthony's shoulder. "Drinks on me," he said. "Caught a twelve-meter flasher today." Anthony threw the bourbon in his face.

He got in a few good licks, but in the end the pack of fishermen beat him stupid and threw him through the front window. Lying breathless on broken glass, Anthony brooded on the injustice of his position and decided to rectify matters. He lurched back into the bar and knocked down the first person he saw.

Small consolation. This time they went after him with the flashing poles that were hanging on the walls, beating him senseless and once more heaving him out the window. When Anthony recovered consciousness he staggered to his feet, intending to have another go, but the pole butts had hit him in the face too many times and his eyes were swollen shut. He staggered down the street, ran face-first into a building, and sat down.

"You finished there, cowboy?" It was Nick's voice.

Anthony spat blood. "Hi, Nick," he said. "Bring them here one at a time, will you? I can't lose one-on-one."

"Jesus, Anthony. You're such an asshole."

Anthony found himself in an inexplicably cheerful mood. "You're lucky you're a sailor. Only a sailor can call me an asshole."

"Can you stand? Let's get to the marina before the cops show up."

"My boat's hundreds of miles away. I'll have to swim."

"I'll take you to my place, then."

With Nick's assistance Anthony managed to stand. He was still too drunk to feel pain, and ambled through the streets in a contented mood. "How did you happen to be at the Leviathan, Nick?"

There was weariness in Nick's voice. "They always call me, Anthony, when you fuck up."

Drunken melancholy poured into Anthony like a sudden cold squall of rain. "I'm sorry," he said.

Nick's answer was almost cheerful. "You'll be sorrier in the morning."

Anthony reflected that this was very likely true.

Nick gave him some pills that, by morning, reduced the swelling. When Anthony awoke he was able to see. Agony flared in his body as he staggered out of bed. It was still twilight. Anthony pulled on his bloody clothes and wrote an incoherent note of thanks on Nick's computer.

Fishing boats were floating out of harbor into the bright dawn. Probably Nick's was among them. The volcano above the town was a contrast in black stone and green vegetation. Pain beat at Anthony's bones like a rain of fists.

Philana's boat was still in its slip. Apprehension tautened Anthony's nerves as he put a tentative foot on the gunwale. The hatch to the cabin was still locked. Philana wasn't aboard. Anthony opened the hatch and went into the cabin just to be sure. It was empty.

He programmed the computer to pursue the transponder signal on Anthony's boat, then as the yacht rose into the sky and arrowed over the ocean, Anthony went into Philana's cabin and fell asleep on a pillow that smelled of her hair.

He awoke around noon to find the yacht patiently circling his boat. He dropped the yacht into the water, tied the two craft together, and spent half the afternoon transferring his supplies to his own boat. He programmed the yacht to return to Las Madres and orbit the volcanic spire until it was summoned by its owner or the police.

I and the sea greet one another, he tapped into his console, and as the call wailed out from his boat he hauled in the drogue and set off after the humpbacks. Apartness is the smell, he thought, aloneness is the condition. Spray shot aboard and spattered Anthony, and salt pain flickered from the cuts on his face. He climbed to the flybridge and hoped for healing from the sun and the glittering sea.

The whales left the cold current and suddenly the world was filled with tropic sunshine and bright water. Anthony made light conversation with the humpbacks and spent the rest of his time working on Dweller speech. Despite hours of concentrated endeavor he made little progress. The sensation was akin to that of smashing his head against a stone wall over and over, an act that was, on consideration, not unlike the rest of his life.

After his third day at sea his boat's computer began signaling him that he was receiving messages. He ignored this and concentrated on work.

Two days later he was cruising north with a whale on either beam when a shadow moved across his boat. Anthony looked up from his console and saw without surprise that Philana's yacht was eclipsing the sun. Philana, dark glasses over her deep eyes and a floppy hat over her hair, was peering down from the starboard bow.

"We have to talk," she said.

Joyously we greet Air Human, whooped Sings of Others.

I and Air Human are pleased to detect one another's presence, called Two Notches.

Anthony went to the controls and throttled up. Microphones slammed at the bottom of his boat. Two Notches poked one large brown eye above the waves to see what was happening, then cheerfully set off in pursuit.

Anthony and Air Human are in a state of excitement, he chattered. **I/we are pleased to join our race.**

The flying yacht hung off Anthony's stern. Philana shouted through cupped hands. "Talk to me, Anthony!"

Anthony remained silent and twisted the wheel into a fast left turn. His wake foamed over Two Notches' face and the humpback burbled a protest. The air yacht seemed to have little trouble following the turn.

Anthony was beginning to have the sense of that stone wall coming up again, but he tried a few more maneuvers just in case one of them worked. Nothing succeeded. Finally he cut the throttle and let the boat slow on the long blue swells.

The trade winds had taken Philana's hat and carried it away. She ignored it and looked down at him. Her face was pale and beneath the dark glasses she looked drawn and ill.

"I'm not human, Anthony," she said. "I'm a Kyklops. That's what's really wrong with me."

Anthony looked at her. Anger danced in his veins. "You really are full of surprises."

"I'm Telamon's other body," she said. "Sometimes he inhabits me."

Whalesong rolled up from the sea. **We and Air Human send one another cheerful salutations and expressions of good will.**

"Talk to the whales first," said Anthony.

"Telamon's a scientist," Philana said. "He's impatient, that's his problem."

The boat heaved on an ocean swell. The trade wind moaned through the flybridge. "He's got a few more problems than that," Anthony said.

"He wanted me for a purpose but sometimes he forgets." A tremor of pain crossed Philana's face. She was deeply hung over. Her voice was ragged: Telamon had been smoking like a chimney and Philana wasn't used to it.

"He wanted to do an experiment on human psychology. He wanted to arrange a method of recording a person's memories, then transferring them to his own...sphere. He got my parents to agree to having the appropriate devices implanted, but the only apparatus that existed for the connection of human and Kyklops was the one the Kyklopes use to manipulate the human bodies that they wear when they want to enjoy the pleasures of the flesh. And Telamon is..." She waved a dismissive arm. "He's a decadent, the way a lot of the Kyklopes turn once they discover how much fun it is to be a human and that their real self doesn't get hurt no matter what they do to their clone bodies. Telamon likes his pleasures, and he likes to interfere. Sometimes, when he dumped my memory into the nth dimension and had a look at it, he couldn't resist the temptation to take over my body and rectify what he considered my errors. And occasionally, when he's in the middle of one of his binges, and his other body gives out on him, he takes me over and starts a party wherever I am."

"Some scientist," Anthony said.

"The Kyklopes are used to experimenting on pieces of themselves," Philana said. "Their own beings are tenuous and rather…detachable. Their ethics aren't against it. And he doesn't do it very often. He must be bored wherever he is—he's taken me over twice in a week." She raised her fist to her face and began to cough, a real smoker's hack. Anthony fidgeted and wondered whether to offer her a glass of water. Philana bent double and the coughs turned to cries of pain. A tear pattered on the teak.

A knot twisted in Anthony's throat. He left his chair and held Philana in his arms. "I've never told anyone," she said.

Anthony realized to his transient alarm that once again he'd jumped off a cliff without looking. He had no more idea of where he would land than last time.

Philana, Anthony was given to understand, was Greek for "lover of humanity." The Kyklopes, after being saddled with a mythological name by the first humans who had contacted them, had gone in for classical allusion in a big way. Telamon, Anthony learned, meant (among other things) "the supporter." After learning this, Anthony referred to the alien as Jockstrap.

"We should do something about him," Anthony said. It was late—the white dwarf had just set—but neither of them had any desire to sleep. He and Philana were standing on the flybridge. The falkner shield was off and above their heads the uninhibited stars seemed almost within reach of their questing fingertips. Overlook Station, fixed almost overhead, was bright as a burning brand.

Philana shook her head. "He's got access to my memory. Any plans we make, he can know in an instant." She thought for a moment. "If he bothers to look. He doesn't always."

"I'll make the plans without telling you what they are."

"It will take forever. I've thought about it. You're talking court case. He can sue me for breach of contract."

"It's your parents who signed the contract, not you. You're an adult now."

She turned away. Anthony looked at her for a long moment, a cold foreboding hand around his throat. "I hope," he said, "you're going to tell me that you signed that contract while Jockstrap was riding you."

Philana shook her head silently. Anthony looked up into the Milky Way and imagined the stone wall falling from the void, aimed right between his eyes, spinning slightly as it grew ever larger in his vision. Smashing him again.

"All we have to do is get the thing out of your head," Anthony said. "After that, let him sue you. You'll be free, whatever happens." His tone reflected a resolve that was absent entirely from his heart.

"He'll sue you, too, if you have any part of this." She turned to face him again. Her face pale and taut in the starlight. "All my money comes from him—how else do you think I could afford the yacht? I owe everything to him."

Bitterness sped through Anthony's veins. He could feel his voice turning harsh. "Do you want to get rid of him or not? Yes or no."

"He's not entirely evil."

"Yes or no, Philana."

"It'll take years before he's done with you. And he could kill you. Just transport you to deep space somewhere and let you drift. Or he could simply teleport me away from you."

The bright stars poured down rage. Anthony knew himself seconds away from violence. There were two people on this boat and one of them was about to get hurt. "Yes or no!" he shouted.

Philana's face contorted. She put her hands over her ears. Hair fell across her face. "Don't shout," she said.

Anthony turned and smashed his forehead against the control panel of the flybridge. Philana gave a cry of surprise and fear.

Anthony drove himself against the panel again. Philana's fingers clutched at his shoulders. Anthony could feel blood pouring hot from his scalp. The pain drained his anger, brought a cold, brilliant clarity to his mind. He smashed himself a third time. Philana cried out. He turned to her. He felt a savage, exemplary satisfaction. If one were going to drive oneself against stone walls, one should at least take a choice of the walls available.

"Ask me," Anthony panted, "if I care what happens to me."

Philana's face was a mask of terror. She said his name.

"I need to know where you stand," said Anthony. Blood drooled from his scalp, and he suppressed the unwelcome thought that he had just made himself look ridiculous.

Her look of fear broadened.

"Am I going to jump off this cliff by myself, or what?" Anthony demanded.

"I want to get rid of him," she said.

Anthony wished her voice had contained more determination, even if it were patently false. He spat salt and went in search of his first aid kit. We are in a condition of slow movement through deep currents, he thought.

In the morning he got the keys to Philana's yacht and changed the passwords on the falkner controls and navigation comp. He threw all his liquor overboard. He figured that if Jockstrap appeared and discovered that he couldn't leave the middle of the ocean, and he couldn't have a party where he was, he'd get bored and wouldn't hang around for long.

From Philana's cabin he called an attorney who informed him that the case was complex but not impossible, and furthermore that it would take a small fortune to resolve. Anthony told him to get to work on it. In the meantime he told the lawyer to start calling neurosurgeons. Unfortunately there were few neurosurgeons capable of implanting, let alone removing, the rider device. The operation wasn't performed that often.

Days passed. A discouraging list of neurosurgeons either turned him down flat or wanted the legal situation clarified first. Anthony told the lawyer to start calling rich neurosurgeons who might be able to ride out a lawsuit.

Philana transferred most of her data to Anthony's computer and worked with the whales from the smaller boat. Anthony used her yacht and aquasled and cursed the bad sound quality. At least the yacht's flight capability allowed him to find the Dwellers faster.

As far as the Dwellers went, he had run all at once into a dozen blind alleys. Progress seemed measured in microns.

"What's B1971?" Philana asked once, looking over his shoulder as he typed in data.

"A taste. Perhaps a taste associated with a particular temperature striation. Perhaps an emotion." He shrugged. "Maybe just a metaphor."

"You could ask them."

His soul hardened. "Not yet." Which ended the conversation.

Anthony wasn't sure whether or not he wanted to touch her. He and Jockstrap were at war and Philana seemed not to have entirely made up her mind which side she was on. Anthony slept with Philana on the double mattress in the peak, but they avoided sex. He didn't know whether he was helping her out of love or something else, and while he figured things out, desire was on hold, waiting.

Anthony's time with Philana was occupied mainly by his attempt to teach her to cook. Anything else waited for the situation to grow less opaque. Anthony figured Jockstrap would clarify matters fairly soon.

Anthony's heart lurched as looked up from lunch to see the taut, challenging grin on Philana's face. Anthony realized he'd been foolish to expect Telamon to show up only at night, as he always had before.

Anthony drew his lips into an answering grin. He was ready, no matter what the hour.

"Do I know you?" Anthony mocked. "Do we have business?"

Philana's appraisal was cold. "I've been called Jockstrap before," Telamon said.

"With good reason, I'm sure."

Telamon lurched to his feet and walked aft. He seemed not to have his sea legs yet. Anthony followed, his nerves dancing. Telamon looked out at the sea and curled Philana's lip as if to say that the water held nothing of interest.

"I want to talk about Philana," Telamon said. "You're keeping her prisoner here."

"She can leave me anytime she wants. Which is more than she can say about you."

"I want the codes to the yacht."

Anthony stepped up to Telamon, held Philana's cold gaze. "You're hurting her," he said.

Telamon stared at him with eyes like obsidian chips. He pushed Philana's long hair out of his face with an unaccustomed gesture. "I'm not the only one, Maldalena. I've got access to her mind, remember."

"Then look in her mind and see what she thinks of you."

A contemptuous smile played about Philana's lips. "I know very well what she thinks of me, and it's probably not what she's told you. Philana is a very sad and complex person, and she is not always truthful."

"She's what you made her."

"Precisely my next point." He waved his arm stiffly, unnaturally. The gesture brought him off-balance, and Philana's body swayed for a moment as Telamon adjusted to the tossing of the boat. "I gave her money, education, knowledge of the world. I have corrected her errors, taught her much. She is, in many ways, my creation. Her feelings toward me are ambiguous, as any child's feelings would be toward her father."

"Daddy Jockstrap." Anthony laughed. "Do we have business, Daddy? Or are you going to take your daughter's body to a party first?"

Anthony jumped backwards, arms flailing, as Philana disappeared, her place taken by a young man with curly dark hair and bright blue eyes. The stranger was dressed in a white cotton shirt unbuttoned to the navel and a pair of navy blue swimming trunks. He had seen the man before on vid, showing off his chest hairs. The grin stayed the same from one body to the next.

"She's gone, Maldalena. I teleported her to someplace safe." He laughed. "I'll buy her a new boat. Do what you like with the old one."

Anthony's heart hammered. He had forgotten the Kyklopes could do that, just teleport without the apparatus required by humans. And teleport other things as well.

He wondered how many centuries old the Kyklops' body was. He knew the mind's age was measured in eons.

"This doesn't end it," Anthony said.

Telamon's tone was mild. "Perhaps I'll find a nice planet for you somewhere, Maldalena. Let you play Robinson Crusoe, just as you did when you were young."

"That will only get you in trouble. Too many people know about this situation by now. And it won't be much fun holding Philana wherever you've got her."

Telamon stepped toward the stern, sat on the taffrail. His movements were fluid, far more confident than they had been when he was wearing the other, unaccustomed body. For a moment Anthony considered kicking Telamon into the drink, then decided against it. The possible repercussions had a cosmic dimension that Anthony preferred not to contemplate.

"I don't dislike you, Maldalena," the alien said. "I truly don't. You're an alcoholic, violent lout, but at least you have proven intelligence, perhaps a kind of genius."

"Call the kettle black again. I liked that part."

Two Notches' smooth body rose a cable's length to starboard. He exhaled with an audible hiss, mist drifting over his back. Telamon gave the whale a disinterested look, then turned back to Anthony.

"Being the nearest thing to a parent on the planet," he said. "I must say that I disapprove of you as a partner for Philana. However—" He gave a shrug. "Parents must know when to compromise in these matters." He looked up at Anthony with his blue eyes. "I propose we share her, Anthony. Formalize the arrangement we already seem to possess. I'll only occupy a little of her time, and for all the rest, the two of you can live out your lives with whatever sad, tormented domestic bliss you can summon. Till she gets tired of you, anyway."

Two Notches rolled under the waves. A cetacean murmur echoed off the boat's bottom. Anthony's mind flailed for an answer. He felt sweat prickling his scalp. He shook his head in feigned disbelief.

"Listen to yourself, Telamon. Is this supposed to be a scientist talking? A researcher?"

"You don't want to share?" The young man's face curled in disdain. "You want everything for yourself—the whole planet, I suppose, like your father."

"Don't be ridiculous."

"I know what Philana knows about you, and I've done some checking on my own. You brought the humpbacks here because you needed them. Away from *their* home, *their* kind. You *asked* them, I'm sure; but there's no way they could make an informed decision about this planet, about what they were doing. You needed them for your Dweller study, so you took them."

As if on cue, Two Notches rose from the water to take a breath. Telamon favored the whale with his taut smile. Anthony floundered for an answer while the alien spoke on.

"You've got data galore on the Dwellers, but do you publish? Do you share it with anybody, even with Philana? You hoard it all for yourself, all your specialized knowledge. You don't even talk to the Dwellers!" Telamon gave a scornful laugh. "You don't even want the *Dwellers* to know what Anthony knows!"

Anger poured through Anthony's veins like a scalding fire. He clenched his fists, considered launching himself at Telamon. Something held him back.

The alien stood, walked to Anthony, looked him up and down. "We're not so different," he said. "We both want what's ours. But *I'm* willing to share. Philana can be our common pool of data, if you like. Think about it."

Anthony swung, and in that instant Philana was back, horror in her eyes. Anthony's fist, aimed for the taller Telamon's chin, clipped Philana's temple and she fell back, flailing. Anthony caught her.

"It just happened, didn't it?" Her voice was woeful.

"You don't remember?"

Philana's face crumpled. She swayed and touched her temple. "I never do. The times when he's running me are just blank spots."

Anthony seated her on the port bench. He was feeling queasy at having hit her. She put her face in her hands. "I hate when that happens in front of people I know," she said.

"He's using you to hide behind. He was here in person, the son of a bitch." He took her hands in his own and kissed her. Purest desire flamed through him. He wanted to commit an act of defiance, make a statement of the nature of things. He put his arms around her and kissed her nape. She smelled faintly of pine, and there were needles in her hair. Telamon had put her on Earth, then, in a forest somewhere.

She strained against his tight embrace. "I don't know if this is a good idea," she said.

"I want to send a message to Telamon," Anthony said.

They made love under the sun, lying on the deck in Anthony's cockpit. Clear as a bell, Anthony heard Dweller sounds rumbling up the boat. Somewhere in the boat a metal mounting bracket rang to the subsonics. Philana clutched at him. There was desperation in her look, a search for affirmation, despair at finding none. The teak punished Anthony's palms. He wondered if Telamon had ever possessed her thus, took over her mind so that he could fuck her in his own body, commit incest with himself. He found the idea exciting.

His orgasm poured out, stunning him with its intensity. He kissed the moist juncture of Philana's neck and shoulder, and rose on his hands to stare down into Telamon's brittle grin and cold, knowing eyes.

"Message received, Anthony." Philana's throat convulsed in laughter. "You're taking possession. Showing everyone who's boss."

Horror galvanized Anthony. He jumped to his feet and backed away, heart pounding. He took a deep breath and mastered himself, strove for words of denial and could not find them. "You're sad, Telamon," he said.

Telamon threw Philana's arms over her head, parted her legs. "Let's do it again, Anthony." Taunting. "You're so masterful."

Anthony turned away. "Piss off, Telamon, you sick fuck." Bile rose in his throat.

"What happened?" Anthony knew Philana was back. He turned and saw her face crumple. "We were making love!" she wailed.

"A cheap trick. He's getting desperate." He squatted by her and tried to take her in his arms. She turned away from him.

"Let me alone for a while," she said. Bright tears filled her eyes.

Misplaced adrenaline ran charges through Anthony's body—no one to fight, no place to run. He picked up his clothes and went below to the main cabin. He drew on his clothing and sat on one of the berths, hands helpless on the seat beside him. He wanted to get blind drunk.

Half an hour later Philana entered the cabin. She'd braided her hair, drawn it back so tight from her temples it must have been painful. Her movements were slow, as if suddenly she'd lost her sea legs. She sat down at the little kitchen table, pushed away her half-eaten lunch.

"We can't win," she said.

"There's got to be some way," Anthony said tonelessly. He was clean out of ideas.

Philana looked at Anthony from reddened eyes. "We can give him what he wants," she said.

"No."

Her voice turned to a shout. "It's not you he does this to! It's not you who winks out of existence in the middle of doing laundry or making love, and wakes up somewhere else." Her knuckles were white as they gripped the table edge. "I don't know how long I can take this."

"All your life," said Anthony, "if you give him what he wants."

"At least then he wouldn't use it as a weapon!" Her voice was a shout. She turned away.

Anthony looked at her, wondered if he should go to her. He decided not to. He was out of comfort for the present.

"You see," Philana said, her head still turned away, "why I don't want to live forever."

"Don't let him beat you."

"It's not that. I'm afraid…" Her voice trembled. "I'm afraid that if I got old I'd become him. The Kyklopes are the oldest living things ever discovered. And a lot of the oldest immortals are a lot like them. Getting crazier, getting…" She shook her head. "Getting less human all the time."

Anthony saw a body swaying in the smokehouse. Philana's body, her fingernails trailing in the dust.

Pain throbbed in his chest. He stood up, swayed as he was caught by a slow wave of vertigo. Somewhere his father was laughing, telling him he should have stayed on Lees for a life of pastoral incest.

"I want to think," he said. He stepped past her on the way to his computer. He didn't reach out to touch her as he passed. She didn't reach for him, either.

He put on the headphones and listened to the Dwellers. Their speech rolled up from the deep. Anthony sat unable to comprehend, his mind frozen. He was helpless as Philana. Whose was the next move? he wondered. His? Philana's?

Whoever made the next move, Anthony knew, the game was Telamon's.

At dinnertime Philana made a pair of sandwiches for Anthony, then returned to the cabin and ate nothing herself. Anthony ate one sandwich without tasting it, gave the second to the fish. The Dweller speech had faded out. He left his computer and stepped into the cabin. Philana was stretched out on one of the side berths, her eyes closed. One arm was thrown over her forehead.

Her body, Anthony decided, was too tense for this to be sleep. He sat on the berth opposite.

"He said you haven't told the truth," Anthony said.

Anthony could see Philana's eyes moving under translucent lids as she evaluated this statement, scanning for meaning. "About what?" she said.

"About your relationship to him."

Her lips drew back, revealing teeth. Perhaps it was a smile.

"I've known him all my life. I gave you the condensed version."

"Is there more I should know?"

There was another pause. "He saved my life."

"Good for him."

"I got involved with this man. Three or four hundred years old, one of my professors in school. He was going through a crisis—he was a mess, really. I thought I could do him some good. Telamon disagreed, said the relationship was sick." Philana licked her lips. "He was right," she said.

Anthony didn't know if he really wanted to hear about this.

"The guy started making demands. Wanted to get married, leave Earth, start over again."

"What did you want?"

Philana shrugged. "I don't know. I hadn't made up my mind. But Telamon went into my head and confronted the guy and told him to get lost. Then he just took me out of there. My body was half the galaxy away, all alone on an undeveloped world. There were supplies, but no gates out."

Anthony gnawed his lip. This was how Telamon operated.

"Telamon kept me there for a couple weeks till I calmed down. He took me back to Earth. The professor had taken up with someone else, another one of his students. He married her, and six weeks later she walked out on him. He killed her, then killed himself."

Philana sighed, drew her hand over her forehead. She opened her eyes and sat up, swinging her legs off the berth. "So," she said. "That's one Telamon story. I've got more."

"When did this happen?"

"I'd just turned eighteen." She shook her head. "That's when I signed the contract that keeps him in my head. I decided that I couldn't trust my judgment about people. And Telamon's judgment of people is, well, quite good."

Resentment flamed in Anthony at this notion. Telamon had made his judgment of Anthony clear, and Anthony didn't want it to become a subject for debate. "You're older now," he said. "He can't have a veto on your life forever."

Philana drew up her legs and circled her knees with her arms. "You're violent, Anthony."

Anthony looked at her for a long moment of cold anger. "I hit you by accident. I was aiming at him, damn it."

Philana's jaw worked as she returned his stare. "How long before you aim at me?"

"I wouldn't."

"That's what my old professor said."

Anthony turned away, fury running through him like chill fire. Philana looked at him levelly for a moment, then dropped her forehead to her knees. She sighed. "I don't know, Anthony. I don't know anymore. If I ever did."

Anthony stared fixedly at the distant white dwarf, just arrived above the horizon and visible through the hatch. We are, he thought, in a condition of permanent bafflement. "What do you want, Philana?" he asked.

Her head came up, looked at him. "I want not to be a tennis ball in your game with Telamon, Anthony. I want to know I'm not just the prize given the winner."

"I wanted you before I ever met Telamon, Philana."

"Telamon changed a few things." Her voice was cold. "Before you met him, you didn't use my body to send messages to people."

Anthony's fists clenched. He forced them to relax.

Philana's voice was bitter. "Seems to me, Anthony, that's one of Telamon's habits you're all too eager to adopt."

Anthony's chest ached. He didn't seem able to breathe in enough air. He took a long breath and hoped his tension would ease. It didn't. "I'm sorry," he said. "It's not…a normal situation."

"For you, maybe."

Silence hung in the room, broken only by the whale clicks and mutters rising through the boat. Anthony shook his head. "What do we do, then?" he asked. "Surrender?"

"If we have to." She looked at him. "I'm willing to fight Telamon, but not to the point where one of us is destroyed." She leaned toward him, her expression intent. "And if Telamon wins, could you live with it?" she asked. "With surrender? If we had to give him what he wanted?"

"I don't know."

"I have to live with it. You don't. That's the difference."

"That's one difference." He took a breath, then rose from his place. "I have to think," he said.

He climbed into the cockpit. Red sunset was splattered like blood across the windscreen. He tried to breathe the sea air, clear the heaviness he felt in his chest, but it didn't work. Anthony went up onto the flybridge and stared forward. His eyes burned as the sun went down in flames. The white dwarf was high overhead when Anthony came down. Philana was lying in the forepeak, covered with a sheet, her eyes staring sightlessly out the open hatch. Anthony took his clothes off and crawled in beside her.

"I'll surrender," he said. "If I have to, I'll surrender." She turned to him and put her arms around him. Hopeless desire burned in his belly.

He made love to Philana, his nerves numb to the possibility that Telamon might reappear. Her hungry mouth drank in his pain. He didn't know whether this was affirmation or not, whether this meant anything other than the fact there was nothing left to do at this point than stagger blindly into one another's embrace...

A Dweller soloed from below, the clearest Anthony had ever heard one. We call to ourselves, the Dweller said. We speak of things as they are. Anthony rose from bed and set his computer to record. Sings of Others, rising alongside to breathe, called a hello. Anthony tapped his keys, hit TRANSMIT.

Air Human and I are in a condition of rut, he said.

We congratulate Anthony and Air Human on our condition of rut, Sings of Others responded. The whooping whale cries layered atop the thundering Dweller noises. **We wish ourselves many happy copulations.**

Happy copulations, happy copulations, echoed Two Notches.

A pointless optimism began to resonate in Anthony's mind. He sat before the computer and listened to the sounds of the Deep Dwellers as they rumbled up his spine.

Philana appeared at the hatch. She was buttoning her shirt. "You told the whales about us?" she said.

"Why not?"

She grinned faintly. "I guess there's no reason not to."

Two Notches wailed a question. **Are Anthony and Air Human copulating now?**

Not at present, Anthony replied.

We hope you will copulate often.

Philana, translating the speech on her own, laughed. "Tell them we hope so, too," she said.

And then she stiffened. Anthony's nerves poured fire. Philana turned to him and regarded him with Telamon's eyes.

"I thought you'd see reason," Telamon said. *"I'll surrender.* I like that."

Anthony looked at the possessed woman and groped for a vehicle for his message. Words seemed inadequate, he decided, but would have to do. "You haven't won yet," he said.

Philana's head cocked to one side as Telamon viewed him. "Has it occurred to you," Telamon said, "that if she's free of me, she won't need you at all?"

"You forget something. I'll be rid of *you* as well."

"You can be rid of me any time."

Anthony stared at Telamon for a moment, then suddenly he laughed. He had just realized how to send his message. Telamon looked at him curiously. Anthony turned to his computer deck and flipped to the Dweller translation file.

I/we, he typed, *live in the warm brightness above. I am new to this world, and send good wishes to the Dwellers below.*

Anthony pressed TRANSMIT. Rolling thunder boomed from the boat's speakers. The grammar was probably awful, Anthony knew, but he was fairly certain of the words, and he thought the meaning would be clear.

Telamon frowned, stepped to gaze over Anthony's shoulder.

Calls came from below. A translation tree appeared on the screen.

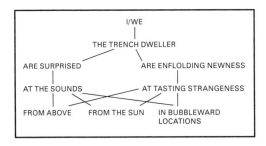

"Trench Dweller" was probably one of the Dwellers' names. "Bubbleward" was a phrase for "up," since bubbles rose to the surface. Anthony tapped the keys.

We are from far away, recently arrived. We are small and foreign to the world. We wish to brush the Dwellers with our thoughts. We regret our lack of clarity in diction.

"I wonder if you've thought this through," Telamon said.

Anthony hit TRANSMIT. Speakers boomed. The subsonics were like a punch in the gut.

"Go jump off a cliff," Anthony said.

"You're making a mistake," said Telamon.

The Dweller's answer was surprisingly direct.

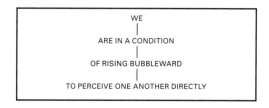

```
                      WE
                       |
              ARE IN A CONDITION
                       |
            OF RISING BUBBLEWARD
                       |
       TO PERCEIVE ONE ANOTHER DIRECTLY
```

Anthony's heart crashed in astonishment. Could the Dwellers stand the lack of pressure on the surface? *I/We,* he typed, *Trench Dweller, proceed with consideration for safety. I/We recollect that we are small and weak.* He pressed TRANSMIT and flipped to the whalespeech file.

Deep Dweller rising to surface, he typed. *Run fast northward.*

The whales answered with cries of alarm. Flukes pounded the water. Anthony ran to the cabin and cranked the wheel hard to starboard. He increased speed to separate himself from the humpbacks. Behind him, Telamon stumbled in his unfamiliar body as the boat took the waves at a different angle.

Anthony returned to his computer console. *I/We are in a state of motion,* he reported. *Is living in the home of the light occasion for a condition of damage to us/Trench Dweller?*

"You're mad," said Telamon, and then Philana staggered. "He's done it again," she said in a stunned voice. She stepped to the starboard bench and sat down. "What's happening?" she asked.

"I'm talking to the Dwellers. One of them is rising to say hello."

"*Now?*"

He gave her a skeletal grin. "It's what you wanted, yes?" She stared at him.

I'm going over cliffs, he thought. One after another.

That, Anthony concluded, is the condition of existence.

Subsonics rattled crockery in the kitchen.

```
┌─────────────────────────────────────────────────┐
│   BUBBLEWARD PLATEAU IS CONDITION FOR DAMAGE      │
│                        │                          │
│            DAMAGE IS ACCEPTABLE                   │
└─────────────────────────────────────────────────┘
```

Anthony typed, *I/We happily await greeting ourselves* and pressed TRANSMIT, then REPEAT. He would give the Dweller a sound to home in on.

"I don't understand," Philana said. He moved to join her on the bench, put his arm around her. She shrugged him off. "Tell me," she said. He took her hand.

"We're going to win."

"How?"

"I don't know yet."

She was too shaken to argue. "It's going to be a long fight," she said.

"I don't care."

Philana took a breath. "I'm scared."

"So am I," said Anthony.

The boat beat itself against the waves. The flying yacht followed, a silent shadow.

Anthony and Philana waited in silence until the Dweller rose, a green-grey mass that looked as if a grassy reef had just calved. Foam roared from its back as it broke water, half an ocean running down its sides. Anthony's boat danced in the sudden white tide, and then the ocean stilled. Bits of the Dweller were all around, spread over the water for leagues—tentacles, filters, membranes. The Dweller's very mass had calmed the sea. The Dweller was so big, Anthony saw, it constituted an entire ecosystem. Sea creatures lived among its folds and tendrils: some had died as they rose, their swim bladders exploding in the release of pressure; others leaped and spun and shrank from the brightness above.

Sunlight shone from the Dweller's form, and the creature pulsed with life.

Terrified, elated, Philana and Anthony rose to say hello.

VIDEO STAR

1

Ric could feel the others closing in. They were circling outside the Falcon Quarter as if on midsummer thermals, watching the Cadillacs with glittering raptor eyes, occasionally swooping in to take a little nibble at Cadillac business, Cadillac turf, Cadillac sources. Testing their own strength as well as the Cadillac nerves, applying pressure just to see what would happen, find out if the Cadillacs still had it in them to respond...

Ric knew the game well: he and the other Cadillacs had played it five years before, up and down the streets and datanets of the Albaicin, half-grown kids testing their strength against the gangs entrenched in power, the Cruceros, the Jerusalem Rangers, the Piedras Blancas. The older gangs seemed slow, tentative, uncertain, and when the war came the Cadillacs won in a matter of days: the others were too entrenched, too visible, caught in a network of old connections, old associations, old manners... The young Cadillacs, coming up out of nowhere, found their own sources, their own products and connections, and in the end they and their allies gutted the old boys' organization, absorbing what was still useful and letting the rest die along with the remnants of the Cruceros, Rangers, and Blancas, the bewildered survivors who were still looking for a remaining piece of turf on which to make their last stand.

At the time Ric had given the Cadillacs three years before the same thing started happening to them, before their profile grew too high and the next generation of snipers rose in confidence and ability. The Cadillacs had in the end lasted five years, and that wasn't bad. But, Ric thought, it was over.

The other Cadillacs weren't ready to surrender. The heat was mounting, but they thought they could survive this challenge, hold out another year or two. They were dreaming, Ric thought.

During the hot dog days of summer, people began to die. Gunfire echoed from the pink walls of the Alhambra. Networks disintegrated. Allies disappeared. Ric made a proposition to the Cadillacs for a bank to be shared with their allies, a fund to keep the war going. The Cadillacs in their desperation agreed.

Ric knew then it was time to end it, that the Cadillacs had lost whatever they once had. If they agreed to a proposition like this, their nerve and their smarts were gone.

So there was a last meeting, Ric of the Cadillacs, Mares of the Squires, Jacob of the Last Men. Ric walked into the meeting with a radar-aimed dart gun built into the bottom of his briefcase, each dart filled with a toxin that would stop the heart in a matter of seconds. When he walked out it was with a money spike in his pocket, a stainless steel needle tipped with liquid crystal. In the heart of the crystal was data representing over eighty thousand Seven Moons dollars, ready for deposit into any electric account into which he could plug the needle.

West, Ric thought. He'd buy into an American condecology somewhere in California and enjoy retirement. He was twenty-two years old.

He began to feel sick in the Tangier-to-Houston suborbital shuttle, a crawling across his nerves, pinpricks in the flesh. By the time he crossed the Houston port to take his domestic flight to L.A. there were stabbing pains in his joints and behind his eyes.

He asked a flight attendant for aspirin and chased the pills with American whiskey.

As the plane jetted west across Texas, Ric dropped his whiskey glass and screamed in sudden pain. The attendants gave him a morphine analogue but the agony only increased, an acid boiling under his skin, a flame that gutted his body. His vision had gone and so had the rest of his senses except for the burning knowledge of his own pain. Ric tried to tear his arms open with his fingernails, pull the tortured nerves clean out of his body, and the attendants piled on him, holding him down, pinning him to the floor of the plane like a butterfly to a bed of cork.

As they strapped him into a stretcher at the unscheduled stop in Flagstaff, Ric was still screaming, unable to stop himself. Jacob had poisoned him, using a neurotoxin that stripped away the myelin sheathing on his nerves, leaving them raw cords of agonized fiber. Ric had been in a hurry to finish his business and had only taken a single sip of his wine: that was the only thing that had saved him.

2

He was months in the hospital in Flagstaff, staring out of a glass wall at a maze of other glass walls—office buildings and condecologies stacked halfway to Phoenix, flanking the silver alloy ribbon of an expressway. The snows fell heavily that winter, then in the spring melted away except for patches of white in the shadows. For the first three months he was completely immobile, his brain chemically isolated from his body to keep the pain away while he took an endless series of nerve grafts, drugs to encourage nerve replication and healing. Finally there was physical therapy that had him screaming in agony at the searing pain in his reawakened limbs.

At the end there was a new treatment, a new drug. It dripped into his arm slowly via an IV and he could feel a lightness in his nerves, a humming in his mind. Even the air seemed to taste better.

The pain was no worse than usual and he felt better than he had since walking out of the meeting back in Granada with the money spike in his pocket.

"What's in the IV?" he asked, next time he saw the nurse.

The nurse smiled. "Everyone asks that," he said. "Genesios Three. We're one of the few hospitals that has the security to distribute the stuff."

"You don't say."

He'd heard of the drug while watching the news. Genesios Three was a new neurohormone, developed by the orbital Pink Blossom policorp, that could repair almost any amount of nerve damage. As a side effect it built additional neural connections in the brain, raised the IQ, and made people high. The hormone was rare because it was very complex and expensive to synthesize, though the gangs were trying. On the west coast lots of people had died in a war for control of the new black labs. On the street it was called Black Thunder.

"Not bad," said Ric.

The treatment and the humming in Ric's brain went on for a week. When it was over he missed it. He was also more or less healed.

3

The week of Genesios therapy took fifteen thousand dollars out of Ric's spike. The previous months of treatment had accounted for another sixty-two thousand. What Ric didn't know was that Genesios therapy could have been started at once and saved him most of his funds, but that the artificial intelligences working for the hospital had tagged him as a suspect character, an alien of no particular standing, with no work history, no policorporate citizenship, and a large amount of cash in his breast pocket. The AIs concluded that Ric was in no position to complain, and they were right.

Computers can't be sued for malpractice. The doctors and administrators followed their advice.

All that remained of Ric's money was three thousand SM dollars. Ric could live off of that for a few years, but it wasn't much of a retirement.

The hospital was nice enough to schedule an appointment for him with a career counselor, a woman who would find him a job. She worked in the basement of the vast glass hospital building, and her name was Marlene.

4

Marlene worked behind a desk littered with the artifacts of other people's lives. There were no windows in the office, two ashtrays, both full, and on the walls there were travel posters that showed long stretches of emptiness, white beaches, blue ocean, faraway clouds. Nothing alive.

Her green eyes had an opaque quality, as if she was watching a private video screen somewhere in her mind. She wore a lot of silver jewelry on her fingers and forearms and a grey rollneck sweater with cigarette burn marks. Her eyes bore elaborate makeup that looked like the wings of a Red Admiral. Her hair was almost blond. The only job she could find him was for a legal firm, something called assistant data evaluator.

Before Ric left Marlene's office he asked her to dinner. She turned him down without even changing expression. Ric had the feeling he wasn't quite real to her.

The job of assistant data evaluator consisted of spending the day walking up and down a four-story spiral staircase in the law firm, moving files from one office to another. The files were supposedly sensitive and not committed to the firm's computer lest someone steal them. The salary was insulting. Ric told the law firm that the job was just what he was looking for. They told him to start in two days.

Ric stopped into Marlene's office to tell her he got the job and to ask her to dinner again. She laughed, for what reason he couldn't tell, and said yes.

A slow spring snowfall dropped onto the streets while they ate dinner. With her food Marlene took two red capsules and a yellow pill, grew lively, drank a lot of wine. He walked her home through the snow to her apartment on the seventh floor of an old fourth-rate condeco, a place with water stains on the ceiling and bare bulbs hanging in the halls, the only home she could afford. In the hallway Ric brushed snow from her shoulders and hair and kissed her. He took Marlene to bed and tried to prove to her that he was real.

The next day he checked out of the hospital and moved in.

5

Ric hadn't bothered to show up on his first day as an assistant data evaluator. Instead he'd spent the day in Marlene's condeco, asking her home comp to search library files and print out everything relating to what the scansheets in their willful ignorance called "Juvecrime." Before Marlene came home Ric called the most expensive restaurant he could find and told them to deliver a five-course meal to the apartment.

The remains of the meal were stacked in the kitchen. Ric paced back and forth across the small space, his mind humming with the information he'd absorbed. Marlene sat on an adobe-colored couch and watched, a wine glass in one hand and a cigarette in the other, silhouetted by the glass self-polarizing wall that showed the bright aluminum-alloy expressway cutting south across melting piles of snow. Plans were vibrating in Ric's mind, nothing firm yet, just neurons stirring on the edge of his awareness, forming fast-mutating combinations. He could feel the tingle, the high, the half-formed ideas as they flickered across neural circuits.

Marlene reached into a dispenser and took out a red pill and a green capsule with orange stripes. Ric looked at her. "How much of that stuff do you take, anyway? Is it medication, or what?"

"I've got anxieties." She put the pills into her mouth, and with a shake of her head dry-swallowed them.

"How big a dose?"

"It's not the dose that matters. It's the proper combination of doses. Get it right and the world feels like a lovely warm swimming pool. It's like floating underwater and still being able to breathe. It's wonderful."

"If you say so." He resumed his pacing. Fabric scratched his bare feet. His mind hummed, a blur of ideas that hadn't yet taken shape, flickering, assembling, dissolving without his conscious thought.

"You didn't show up for work," Marlene said. "They gave me a call about that."

"Sorry."

"How are you gonna afford this taste you have for expensive food?" Marlene asked. "Without working, I mean."

"Do something illegal," Ric said. "Most likely."

"That's what I thought." She looked up at him, sideways. "You gonna let me play?"

"If you want."

Marlene swallowed half her wine, looked at the littered apartment, shrugged.

"Only if you really want," Ric said. "It has to be a thing you decide."

"What else is there for me to do?" she said.

"I'm going to have to do some research, first," he said. "Spend a few days accessing the library."

Marlene was looking at him again. "Boredom," she said. "In your experience, is that why most people turn to crime?"

"In my experience," he said, "most people turn to crime because of stupidity."

She grinned. "That's cool," she said. "That's sort of what I figured." She lit another cigarette. "You have a plan?"

"Something I can only do once. Then every freak in Western America is going to be looking for me with a machine gun."

Marlene grinned. "Sounds exciting."

He looked at her. "Remember what I said about stupidity."

She laughed. "I've been smart all my life. What's it ever got me?"

Ric, looking down at her, felt a warning resonate through him, like an unmistakable taste drawn across his tongue. "You've got a lot to lose, Marlene," he said. "A lot more than I do."

"Shit. Motherfucker." The cigarette had burned her fingers. She squashed it in the ashtray, too fast, spilling ashes on the couch. Ric watched her for a moment, then went back to his thinking.

People were dying all over California in a war over the neurohormone Genesios Three. There had to be a way to take advantage of it.

6

"You a cop, buck?" The style was different from the people Ric knew in Iberia. In Granada, Ric had worn a gaucho mode straight from Argentina, tight pants with silver dollars sewn down the seams, sashes wound around nipped-in waists, embroidered vests.

He didn't know what was worn by the people who had broken up the Cadillacs. He'd never seen any of them.

Here the new style was something called Urban Surgery. The girl bore the first example Ric had ever seen close up. The henna-red hair was in cornrows, braided with transparent plastic beads holding fast-mutating phosphorescent bacteria that constantly re-formed themselves in glowing patterns. The nose had been broadened and flattened to cover most of the cheeks, turning the nostrils into a pair of lateral slits, the base of the nose wider than the mouth. The teeth had been replaced by alloy transplants sharp as razors that clacked together in a precise, unpleasant way when she closed her mouth. The eyebrows were gone altogether and beneath them were dark plastic implants that covered the eye sockets. Ric couldn't tell, and probably wasn't supposed to know, whether there were eyes in there anymore, or sophisticated scanners tagged to the optic nerve.

The effect was to flatten the face, turn it into a canvas for the tattoo artist who had covered every inch of exposed flesh. Complex mathematical statements ran over the forehead. Below the black plastic eye implants were urban skyscapes, silhouettes of buildings providing a false horizon across the flattened nose. The chin appeared to be a circuit diagram.

Ric looked into the dark eye sockets and tried not to flinch. "No," he said. "I'm just passing through."

One of her hands was on the table in front of him. It was tattooed as completely as the face, and the fingernails had been replaced by alloy razors, covered with transparent plastic safety caps.

"I saw you in here yesterday," she said. "And again today. I was wondering if you want something."

He shrugged. It occurred to him that, repellent as Urban Surgery was, it was fine camouflage. Who was going to be able to tell one of these people from another?

"You're a little old for this place, buck," the girl said. He figured her age as about fourteen. She was small-waisted and had narrow hips and large breasts. Ric did not find her attractive.

This was his second trip to Phoenix. The bar didn't have a name, unless it was simply BAR, that being all that was said on the sign outside. It was below street level, in the storage cellar of an old building. Concrete walls were painted black. Dark plastic tables and chairs had been added, and bare fluorescent tubes decorated the walls. Speaker amps flanked the bar, playing cold electronic music devoid of noticeable rhythm or melody.

He looked at the girl and leaned closer to her. "I need your permission to drink here, or what?" he said.

"No," she said. "Just to deal here."

"I'm not dealing," he said. "I'm just observing the passing urban scene, okay?" He was wearing a lightweight summer jacket of a cream color over a black T-shirt with Cyrillic lettering, black jeans, white sneakers. Nondescript street apparel.

"You got credit?" the girl asked.

"Enough."

"Buy me a drink then?"

He grinned. "I need your permission to deal, and you don't have any credit? What kind of outlaw are you?"

"A thirsty outlaw."

Ric signaled the bartender. Whatever it was that he brought her looked as if it was made principally out of cherry soda.

"Seriously," she said. "I can pay you back later. Someone I know is supposed to meet me here. He owes me money."

"My name's Marat," said Ric. "With a silent t."

"I'm Super Virgin. You from Canada or something? You talk a little funny."

"I'm from Switzerland."

Super Virgin nodded and sipped her drink. Ric glanced around the bar. Most of the patrons wore Urban Surgery or at least made an effort in the direction of its style. Super Virgin frowned at him.

"You're supposed to ask if I'm really cherry," she said. "If you're wondering, the drink should give you a clue."

"I don't care," Ric said.

She grinned at him with her metal teeth. "You don't wanna ball me?"

Ric watched his dual reflection, in her black eye sockets, slowly shake its head. She laughed. "I like a guy who knows what he likes," she said. "That's the kind we have in Cartoon Messiah. Can I have another drink?"

There was an ecology in kid gangs, Ric knew. They had different reasons for existing and filled different functions. Some wanted turf, some trade, some the chance to prove their ideology. Some moved information, and Ric's research indicated that this last seemed to be Cartoon Messiah's function.

But even if Cartoon Messiah were smart, they hadn't been around very long. A perpetual problem with groups of young kids involving themselves in gang activities was that they had very short institutional memories. There were a few things they wouldn't recognize or know to prepare for, not unless they'd been through them at least once. They made up for it by being faster than the opposition, by being more invisible.

Ric was hoping Cartoon Messiah was full of young, fresh minds.

He signaled the bartender again. Super Virgin grinned at him.

"You sure you don't wanna ball me?"

"Positive."

"I'm gonna be cherry till I die. I'm just not interested. None of the guys seem like anybody I'd want to fuck." Ric didn't say anything. She sipped the last of her drink. "You think I'm repulsive-looking, right?"

"That seems to be your intention."

She laughed. "You're okay, Marat. What's it like in Switzerland?"

"Hot."

"So hot you had to leave, maybe?"

"Maybe."

"You looking for work?"

"Not yet. Just looking around."

She leaned closer to him. "You find out anything interesting while you're looking, I'll pay you for it. Just leave a message here, at the Bar."

"You deal in information?"

She licked her lips. "That and other things. This Bar, see, it's in a kind of interface. North of here is Lounge Lizard turf, south and east are the Cold Wires, west is the Silicon Romantics. The Romantics are on their way out." She gave a little sneer. "They're brocade commandos, right?—their turf's being cut up. But here, it's no-gang's-land. Where things get moved from one buyer to another."

"Cartoon Messiah—they got turf?"

She shook her head. "Just places where we can be found. Territory is not what we're after. Two-Fisted Jesus—he's our sort-of chairman—he says only stupid people like brocade boys want turf, when the real money's in data."

Ric smiled. "That's smart. Property values are down, anyway."

He could see his reflection in her metal teeth, a pale smear. "You got anything you wanna deal in, I can set it up," she said. "Software? Biologicals? Pharmaceuticals? Wetware?"

"I have nothing. Right now."

She turned to look at a group of people coming in the door. "Cold Wires," she said. "These are the people I'm supposed to meet." She tipped her head back and swallowed the rest of her drink. "They're so goddam bourgeois," she said. "Look—their surgery's fake, it's just good makeup. And the tattoos—they spray 'em on through a stencil. I hate people who don't have the courage of their convictions, don't you?"

"They can be useful, though." Smiling, thin-lipped.

She grinned at him. "Yeah. They can. Stop by tomorrow and I'll pay you back, okay? See ya." She pushed her chair back, scraping alloy on the concrete floor, a small metal scream.

Ric sipped his drink, watching the room. Letting its rhythm seep through his skin. Things were firming in his mind.

7

"Hi."

The security guard looked up at him from under the plastic brim of his baseball cap. He frowned. "Hi. You need something? I seen you around before."

"I'm Warren Whitmore," Ric said. "I'm recovering from an accident, going to finish the course of treatment soon. Go out into the real world." Whitmore was one of Ric's former neighbors, a man who'd had his head split in half by a falling beam. He hadn't left any instructions about radical life-preservation measures and the artificial intelligences who ran the hospital were going to keep him alive till they burned up the insurance and then the family's money.

"Yeah?" the guard said. "Congratulations." There was a plastic tape sewed on over the guard's breast pocket that said LYSAGHT.

"The thing is, I don't have a job waiting. Cigar?"

Ric had seen Lysaght smoking big stogies outside the hospital doors. They wouldn't let him light up inside. Ric had bought him the most expensive Havanas available at the hospital gift shop.

Lysaght took the cigar, rolled it between his fingers while he looked left and right down the corridor, trying to decide whether to light it or not. Ric reached for his lighter.

"I had some military training in my former life," Ric said. "I thought I might look into the idea of getting into the security business, once I get into the world. Could I buy you a drink, maybe, after you get off shift? Talk about what you do."

Lysaght drew on the cigar, still looking left and right, seeing only patients. He was a big fleshy man, about forty, dressed in a black uniform with body armor sewn into pockets on his chest and back. His long dark hair was slicked back behind his ears, falling over his shoulders in greased ringlets. His sideburns came to points. A brushed-alloy gun with a hardwood custom grip and a laser sight hung conspicuously on one hip, next to the gas grenades, next to the plastic handwrap restraints, next to the combat staff, next to the portable gas mask.

"Sure," Lysaght said. "Why not?" He blew smoke in the general direction of an elderly female patient walking purposefully down the corridor in flowery pajamas. The patient blinked but kept walking.

"Hey, Mrs. Calderón, how you doin'?" Lysaght said. Mrs. Calderón ignored him. "Fuckin' head case," said Lysaght.

"I want to work for a sharp outfit though," Ric said. He looked at Lysaght's belt. "With good equipment and stuff, you know?"

"That's Folger Security," Lysaght said. "If we weren't good, we wouldn't be working for a hospital this size."

During his time in the Cadillacs and elsewhere, Ric had been continually surprised by how little it actually took to bribe someone. A few drinks, a few cigars, and Lysaght was working for him. And Lysaght didn't even know it yet. Or, with luck, ever.

"Listen," Lysaght was saying. "I gotta go smoke this in the toilet. But I'll see you at the guard station around five, okay?"

"Sounds good."

8

That night, his temples throbbing with pain, Ric entered Marlene's condeco and walked straight to the kitchen for something to ease the long raw ache that coated the insides of his throat. He could hear the sounds of Alien Inquisitor on the vid. He was carrying a two-liter plastic bottle of industrial-strength soap he'd just stolen from the custodian's storeroom here in Marlene's condeco. He put down the bottle of soap, rubbed his sore shoulder muscle, took some whiskey from the shelf, and poured it into a tall glass. He took a slow, deliberate drink and winced as he felt the fire in his throat. He added water to the glass. Alien Inquisitor diminished in volume, then he heard the sound of Marlene's flipflops slapping against her heels.

Her eyes bore the heavy eye makeup she wore to work. "Jesus," Marlene said. She screwed up her face. "You smell like someone's been putting out cigarettes in your pockets. Where the hell have you been?"

"Smoking cigars with a rentacop. He wears so much equipment and armor he has to wear a truss, you know that? He got drunk and told me."

"Which rentacop?"

"One who works for the hospital."

"The hospital? We're going to take off the hospital?" Marlene shook her head. "That's pretty serious, Ric."

Ric was wondering if she'd heard take off used that way on the vid. "Yes." He eased the whiskey down his throat again. Better.

"Isn't that dangerous? Taking off the same hospital where you were a patient?"

"We're not going to be doing it in person. We're going to have someone else do the work."

"Who?"

"Cartoon Messiah, I think. They're young and promising."

"What's the stuff in the plastic bottle for?"

He looked at her, swirling the whiskey absently in the glass. "This cleaner's mostly potassium hydroxide," he said. "That's wood lye. You can use it to make plastic explosive."

Marlene shrugged, then reached in her pocket for a cigarette. Ric frowned. "You seem not to be reacting to that, Marlene," he said. "Robbing a hospital is serious, plastic explosive isn't?"

She blew smoke at him. "Let me show you something." She went back into the living room and then returned with her pouch belt. She fished in it for a second, then threw him a small aerosol bottle.

Ric caught it and looked at the label. "Holy fuck," he said. He blinked and looked at the bottle again. "Jesus Christ."

"Ten-ounce aerosol bottle of mustard gas," Marlene said. "Sixteen dollars in Starbright scrip at your local boutique. For personal protection, you know? The platinum designer bottle costs more."

Ric was blinking furiously. "Holy fuck," he said again.

"Some sixteen-year-old asshole tried to rape me once," Marlene said. "I hit him with the gas and now he's reading braille. You know?"

Ric took another sip of the whiskey and then wordlessly placed the mustard gas in Marlene's waiting palm.

"You're in America now, Ric," Marlene said. "You keep forgetting that, singing your old Spanish marching songs."

He rubbed his chin. "Right," he said. "I've got to make adjustments."

"Better do it soon," Marlene said, "if you're going to start busting into hospitals."

9

The next day Ric went to the drugstore, where he purchased a large amount of petroleum jelly, some nasal mist that came in squeeze bottles, liquid bleach, a bottle of toilet cleaner, a small amount of alcohol-based lamp fuel, and a bottle of glycerin. Then he drove to a chemical supply store, where he brought some distilling equipment and some litmus paper.

On his way back he stopped by an expensive liquor store and bought some champagne. He didn't want the plastic bottles the domestic stuff came in; instead he bought the champagne imported from France, in glass bottles with the little hollow cone in the bottom. It was the biggest expense of the day.

Back in Marlene's apartment he opened the tops of the nasal inhalers and drained the contents into the sink. He cleaned each and set them out to dry. He set up his distilling equipment, mixing the toilet-bowl cleaner with the liquid bleach, then bubbled the resulting chlorine gas through the wood lye until the litmus paper showed it had been neutralized. He emptied the stuff into a pan and brought it to a simmer on the stove. When crystals began forming he took it off the burner and let the pan cool. He repeated the process two more times and, in the end, he had almost pure potassium chlorate. Ric then mixed the potassium chlorate with petroleum jelly to make plastic explosive. He put it in an old coffee can in the refrigerator.

Feeling pleased with his handiwork, he opened a bottle of champagne to celebrate. He drank a glass and then set up his distilling equipment again.

He put glycerine and some of the toilet bowl cleaner in a flask, mixed it, then put it over a flame. He distilled out a couple ounces of acrolein and then put the chemical in the empty nasal spray containers. He capped them. He drank another glass of champagne, put away all his materials, and turned on the vid. Something called Video Vixens was just starting.

Ric settled into his chair. He hadn't seen that one.

10

"I made plastic explosive today," Ric said. "It's in the icebox."

"Great." Marlene had just come home from work and was tired. She was drinking champagne and waiting for the night's pills to kick in.

"I'll show you a trick," Ric said. He got some twine from the cupboard, cut it into strips, and soaked it in the lamp fuel. While it was soaking he got a large mixing bowl and filled it with water and ice. Then he tied the string around the empty champagne bottles, about three inches above the topmost point of the little hollow cone on the bottom. He got his lighter and set fire to the thread. It burned slowly, with a cool blue flame, for a couple minutes. Then he took the bottle and plunged it into the ice water. It split neatly in half with a crystalline snapping sound.

Ric took some of the plastic explosive and packed it into the bottom of the champagne bottle. He pushed a pencil into the middle of it, making a narrow hole for the detonator.

"There," he said. "That's a shaped charge. I'll make the detonators tomorrow, out of peroxide, acetone, and sulphuric acid. It's easy."

"What's a shaped charge, Ricardo?"

"It's used for blowing a hole through armor. Steel doors, cars. Tanks. Things like that."

Marlene looked at him appraisingly. "You're adjusting yourself to America, all right," she said.

11

Ric took a bus to Phoenix and rented a motel room with a kitchenette, paying five days in advance and using a false name. In the motel he changed clothes and took a cab to the Bar. Super Virgin waved as he came in. She was with her friend, Captain Islam. He was a long, gawky boy, about sixteen, with his head shaved and covered with the tattoos of Urban Surgery. He hadn't had any alterations yet, or the eye implants this group favored—instead he wore complicated mirrorshades with twin minicameras mounted above the bridge of the nose. They registered radiation in UV and infrared as well as the normal spectrum and featured liquid-crystal video displays on the backs of the eyepieces that received input from the minicameras or from any vid program he felt like seeing. Ric wondered if things weren't real to him, not unless he saw them on the vid. Captain Islam didn't talk much, just sat quietly behind his drink and his shades and watched whatever it was that he watched. The effect was unsettling and was probably meant to be. Ric could be talking to him and would never know whether the man was looking at him or at Video Vixens. Ric had first pegged him for a user, but Super Virgin said not.

Ric got a whiskey at the bar and joined the two at their table. "Slow night?" he asked.

"We're waiting for the jai alai to come on," Super Virgin said. "Live from Bilbao. We've got some money down."

"Sounds slow to me."

She gave a brittle laugh. "Guess so, Marat. You got any ideas for accelerating our motion?"

Ric frowned. "I have something to sell. Some information. But I don't know if it's something you'd really want to deal with."

"Too hot?" The words were Captain Islam's. Ric looked at his own distorted face in the Captain's spectacles.

"Depends on your concept of hot. The adjective I had in mind was big."

"Big." The word came with a pause before and after, as if Captain Islam had never heard the word before and was wondering what it meant.

Ric took a bottle of nasal mist out of his pocket and squeezed it once up each nostril.

"Got a virus?" Virgin asked.

"I'm allergic to Arizona."

Captain Islam was frowning. "So what's this action of yours, buck?" he asked.

"Several kilos of Thunder."

Captain Islam continued to stare into the interior of his mirrors. Super Virgin burst into laughter.

"I knew you weren't a fucking tourist, Marat!" she cackled. "'Several kilos'! One kilo is weight! What the hell is 'several'?"

"I don't know if you people can move that much," Ric said. "Also, I'd like an agreement. I want twenty percent of the take, and I want you to move my twenty percent for me, free of charge. If you think you can move that kind of weight at all, that is." He sipped his whiskey. "Maybe I should talk to some people in California."

"You talk to them, you end up dead," Virgin said. "They're not friendly to anyone these days, not when Thunder's involved."

Ric smiled. "Maybe you're right."

"Where is it? Who do we have to steal it from?"

"Another thing," Ric said. "I want certain agreements. I don't want any excessive force used, here. Nobody shot."

"Sometimes things happen," Captain Islam said. Ric had the feeling that the Captain was definitely looking at him this time. "Sometimes things can't be avoided."

"This stuff is guarded by an organization who won't forget it if any of their people get hurt," Ric explained. "If you try to move this kind of weight, word's going to get out that it's you that has the Thunder, and that means these characters are going to find out sooner or later. You might be tempted to give me to them as a way of getting the heat off you. Which would be a mistake, because I intend on establishing an alibi. That would mean that they're going to be extremely upset with you misleading them." Ric sipped his whiskey and smiled. "I'm just looking out for all our interests."

"A hospital," Captain Islam said. He shook his head. "You want us to take off a hospital. The one up in Flag, right? You stupid shit."

"I have a plan," Ric said. "I know their defenses, to a certain point. I know how they're organized. I know how they think."

"That's Folger Security, for chrissake," Captain Islam said. "They're tough. They don't forget when someone makes idiots out of them."

"That's why it's got to be my rules," Ric said. "But I should probably mention something, here." He grinned, seeing the smile reflected in the Captain's quicksilver eyes. "It's an inside job," Ric said. "I'm friends with someone on their force."

Virgin whooped and banged him on the shoulder with her left hand, the one with the sheathed claws. "Why didn't you say so?" she said.

"You people," Ric said. "You've got to learn to be patient."

12

Treble whimpered against a throbbing bass line. Shafts of red sunset sliced into the violet depths of the Grand Canyon. Marlene backed, spun, turned back to Ric, touched palms. She was wearing Indian war paint. Colors zigzagged across her face. Her eyes and smile were bright.

The band was dressed like hussars, lights glittering off brocade, the lead singer sweating under her dolman, threatening to split her tight breeches with each of her leaps. Her eye makeup dazzled like butterfly wings. Her lyrics were all heroism, thunder, revolution. The romantic wave against which Cartoon Messiah and Urban Surgery were a cool reaction.

Marlene stepped forward, pressing herself against him. He circled her with his arms, felt her sacral dimples as they leaned back and spun against each other. At the end of the five-bar chorus she gave a grind of her hips against him, then winked.

He laughed. While he was establishing his alibi, Cartoon Messiah were working for him back in Flagstaff. And they didn't even know it.

13

Readiness crackled from Ric's nerves as he approached the hotel door. They could try to kill him, he knew. Now would be the best time. Black Thunder tended to generate that kind of behavior. He'd been telling them he had ideas for other jobs, that he'd be valuable to them alive, but he couldn't be sure if they believed him.

The door opened and Super Virgin grinned at him with her metal teeth. "Piece of cake, Marat," she said. "Your cut's on the table."

The hotel room was dark, the walls draped in blueblack plastic. More plastic sheets covered the floors, the ceiling, some of the furniture. Coldness touched Ric's spine. There could be a lot of blood spilled in here, and the plastic would keep it from getting on anything. Computer consoles and vid sets gave off quiet hums. Cables snaked over the floor, held down with duct tape. On a table was a half-kilo white paper packet. Captain Islam and Two-Fisted Jesus sat beside it, tapping into a console. Jesus looked up.

"Just in time," he said, "for the movies."

He was a skinny boy, about eighteen, his identity obscured by the obsessive mutilations of Urban Surgery. He wore a T-shirt featuring a picture of a muscular, bearded man in tights, with cape and halo. Here in this place, the hotel room he had hung with plastic and filled with electronics, he moved and spoke with an assurance the others hadn't absorbed, the kind of malevolent grace displayed by those who gave law and style to others, unfettered by conscience.

Ric could appreciate Jesus' moves. He'd had them once himself.

Ric walked to the paper packet and hefted it. He tore open a corner, saw a row of little white envelopes, each labeled Genesios Three with the pharmaceutical company sigil in the corner. He didn't know a test for B-44 so he just stuffed the envelope in his pocket.

"This is gonna be great," Super Virgin said. She came up behind him and handed him a highball glass half-filled with whiskey. "You got time to watch the flick? We went in packing cameras. We're gonna cut a documentary of the whole thing and sell it to a station in Nogales. They'll write some scenes around it and use it on an episode of VidWar." She giggled. "The Mexicans don't care how many gringo hospitals get taken off. They'll put some kind of plot around it. A dumb love story or something. But it's the highest-rated program, 'cause people know it's real. Except for Australian Rules Firefight Football, and that's real, too."

Ric looked around and found a chair. It seemed as if these people planned to let him live. He reached into his pocket and fired a round of nasal mist up each nostril. "Sure. I'll watch," he sniffed. "I got time."

"This is a rough cut only, okay?" Captain Islam's voice. "So bear with us."

There was a giant-sized liquid-crystal vid display set up on the black plastic on the wall. A picture sizzled into existence. The hospital, a vast concrete fortress set in an aureole of halogen light. Ric felt his tongue go dry. He swallowed with difficulty.

The image moved, jolting. Whoever was carrying the camera was walking, fast, across the parking lot. Two-Fisted Jesus tapped the keys of his computer. The image grew smooth.

"We're using a lot of computer enhancement on the vid, see?" Super Virgin said. "We can smooth out the jitters from the moving camera. Except for select bits to enhance the ver—the versi—"

"Verisimilitude," said Captain Islam.

"Right. Just to let everyone know this is the real thing. And we're gonna change everyone's appearance electronically, so no one can recognize us."

Cut to someone moving into the hospital's front door, moving right past the metal detectors. Ric saw a tall girl, blond, dressed in pink shorts and a tube top. White sandal straps coiled about her ankles.

"A mercenary," Virgin said. "We hired her for this. The slut."

Captain Islam laughed. "She's an actress," he explained. "Trying for a career south of the border. Wants the publicity."

The girl stepped up to a guard. Ric recognized Lysaght. She was asking directions, pointing. Lysaght was gazing at her breasts as he replied. She smiled and nodded and walked past. He looked after her, chewed his cigar, hiked up his gunbelt. Ric grinned. As long as guards like Lysaght were around, nothing was safe.

The point of view changed abruptly, a subjective shot, someone moving down a hospital corridor. Patients in ordinary clothes moving past, smiling.

"We had a camera in this necklace she was wearing. A gold owl, about an inch long, with 3D vidcams behind the eyes. Antenna in the chain, receiver in her bag. We pasted it to her chest so it would always be looking straight forward and wouldn't get turned around or anything. Easy stuff."

"We gotta do some pickups, here," Jesus said. "Get a picture of the girl moving down a corridor. Then we tell the computer to put all the stripes on the walls. It'll be worth more when we sell it."

Subjective shot of someone moving into a woman's toilet, stepping into a stall, reaching into a handbag for a pair of coveralls.

"Another pickup shot," Jesus muttered. "Gotta get her putting on her coveralls." He made a note on a pad.

The point of view lurched upward, around, out of the stall. Centered on a small ventilator intake high on a wall. Hands came into the picture, holding a screwdriver.

"Methanethiol," Super Virgin said. "That stuff's gonna be real useful from now on. How'd you know how to make it?"

"Elementary chemistry," Ric said. He'd used it to clear out political meetings of which the Cadillacs didn't approve.

The screen was off the ventilator. Hands were reaching into the bag, taking out a small glass bottle. Carefully loosening the screw top. The hands placed the bottle upright in the ventilator. Then the point of view dipped, a hand reached down to pick up the ventilator screen. Then the ventilator screen was shoved violently into the hole, knocking the bottle over.

Airborne methanethiol gave off a horrible, nauseating smell at one-fiftieth of a part per billion. The psychology wing of the hospital was going to get a dose considerably in excess of that.

The subjective camera was moving with great rapidity down hospital corridors. To a stairwell, then down.

Cut to Super Virgin in a phone booth. She had a small voice recorder in her hand, and was punching buttons.

"Freeze that," said Two-Fisted Jesus. Virgin's image turned to ice. Jesus began tapping keys.

The tattooing shifted, dissolved to a different pattern. Super Virgin laughed. Her hair shortened, turned darker. The black insets over her eyes vanished. Brown eyes appeared, then they turned a startling pale blue.

"Leave the teeth," she said.

"Nah. I have an idea." Two-Fisted Jesus sat tapping keys for about thirty seconds. He pressed the Enter button and the metal teeth disappeared completely. He moved the picture forward a second, then back. Virgin's tongue moved readily behind her tattooed lips. The interior of the mouth was pink, a lot of gum, no teeth at all. She clapped her hands.

"That's strange, man," she said. "I like that."

"The Mexicans will probably replace her image with some vidstar, anyway," Captain Islam said. "Urban Surgery is too much for them, right now."

"Okay. I want to see this in three dimensions," Jesus said. Super Virgin's image detached itself from the background and began rotating. He stopped it every so often and made small adjustments.

"Make me taller," Super Virgin said. "And skinnier. And give me smaller tits. I hate my tits."

"We do that every time," Jesus said. "People are gonna start to twig."

"Chrome tits. Leather tits. Anything."

Captain Islam laughed. Two-Fisted Jesus made minor adjustments and ignored Super Virgin's complaints.

"Here we go. Say your line."

The image began moving. Virgin's new green eyes sparkled as she held the recorder up to the mouthpiece of the telephone.

"This is Royal Flag." It was the name of one of Arizona's more ideological kid gangs. The voice had been electronically altered and sounded flat. "We've just planted a poison gas bomb in your psychology wing. All the head cases are gonna see Jesus. The world's gene pool will be much healthier from now on. Have yourself a pleasant day."

Super Virgin was laughing. "Wait'll you see the crowd scenes. Stellar stuff, believe me."

"I believe," said Ric.

14

The video was full of drifting smoke. Vague figures moved through it. Jesus froze the picture and tried to enhance the images, without any success. "Shit," he said. "More pickups."

Ric had watched the action as members of Cartoon Messiah in Folger Security uniforms had hammered their way into a hospital back door. They had moved faultlessly through the corridors to the vault and blasted their way in with champagne-bottle-shaped charges. The blasts had set off tremblor alarms in the vault and the Folger people realized they were being hit. Now the raiders were in the corridor before the vault, retracing their steps at a run.

"Okay," Super Virgin said. "The moment of truth, coming up."

The corridor was full of billowing tear gas. Crouched figures moved through it. Commands were yammering down the monitored Folger channels. Then, coming through the smoke, another figure. A tall woman in a helmet, her hand pressed to her ear, trying to hear the radio. There was a gun in her hand. She raised the gun.

Thuds on the sound track. Tear-gas canisters, fired at short range. One of them struck the woman in her armored chest and bounced off. It hadn't flown far enough to arm itself and it just rolled down the corridor. The woman fell flat.

"Just knocked the wind out of her." Captain Islam was grinning. "How about that for keeping our deal, huh?" Somebody ran forward and kicked the gun out of her hand. The camera caught a glimpse of her lying on the floor, her mouth open, trying to breathe. There were dots of sweat on her nose. Her eye makeup looked like butterfly wings.

"Now that's what I call poignant," Jesus said. "Human interest stuff. You know?"

The kids ran away across the parking lot, onto their fuelcell tricycles, and away, bouncing across the parking lot and the railroad tracks beyond.

"We're gonna spice this up a bit," Jesus said. "Cut in some shots of guards shooting at us, that kind of thing. Steal some suspenseful music. Make the whole thing more exciting. What do you think?"

"I like it," said Ric. He put down his untasted whiskey. Jacob and his neurotoxin had made him cautious. "Do I get any royalties? Being scriptwriter and all?"

"The next deal you set up for us. Maybe."

Ric shrugged. "How are you gonna move the Thunder?"

"Small pieces, probably."

"Let me give you some advice," Ric said. "The longer you hang on to it, the bigger the chance Folger will find out you have it and start cramping your action. I have an idea. Can you handle a large increase of capital?"

15

"Is this the stuff? Great." Marlene swept in the motel room door, grinning, with her overnight bag. She gave Ric a brief hug, then went to the table of the kitchenette. She picked up the white packet, hefted it in her hand. "Light," she said. "Yeah. I can't believe people kill each other over this."

"They could kill us," Ric said. "Don't forget that." Marlene licked her lips and peeled the packet. She took one of the small white envelopes and tore it open, spilling dark powder into her cupped palm. She cocked her head. "Doesn't look like much. How do you take it?" Ric remembered the flood of well-being in his body, the way the world had suddenly tasted better.

No, he thought. He wasn't going to get hung up on Thunder. "Intravenous, mostly," he said. "Or they could put it in capsules."

Marlene sniffed at it. "Doesn't smell like anything. What's the dose?"

"I don't know. I wasn't planning on taking any." She began licking in her palm. Ric watched her little pink tongue lapping at the powder. He turned his eyes away. "Take it easy," he said.

"Tastes funny. Kind of like green pepper sauce, with a touch of kerosene."

"A touch of stupidity," he said. "A touch of…" He moved around the room, hands in his pockets. "A touch of craziness. People who are around Black Thunder get crazy."

Marlene finished licking her palm and kicked off her shoes. "Craziness sounds good," she said. She stepped up behind him and put her arms around him. "How crazy do you think we can get tonight?"

"I don't know." He thought for a minute. "Maybe I could show you our movie."

16

Ric faced the window in the motel room, watching, his mind humming. The window had been dialed to polarize completely and he could see himself, Marlene behind him on the untidy bed, the plundered packet of Thunder on the table. It had been eight days since the hospital had been robbed. Marlene had taken the bus to Phoenix every evening.

"You should try some of our product," Marlene said. "The stuff's just…when I use it, I can feel my mind just start to click. Move faster, smoother. Thoughts come out of nowhere."

"Right," Ric said. "Nowhere."

Ric saw Marlene's reflection look up at his own dark plateglass ghost. "Do I detect sarcasm, here?"

"No. Preoccupation, that's all."

"Half the stuff's mine, right? I can eat it, burn it, drop it out the window. Drop it on your head, if I want to. Right?"

"That is correct," said Ric.

"Things are getting dull," Marlene said. "You're spending your evenings off drinking with Captain Islam and Super Virgin and Krishna Commando... I get to stay here and watch the vid."

"Those people I'm drinking with," Ric said. "There's a good chance they could die because of what we're going to do. They're our victims. Would you like to have a few drinks with them? A few smokes?" He turned from the window and looked at her. "Knowing they may die because of you?"

Marlene frowned up at him. "Are you scared of them?" she asked. "Is that why you're talking like this?"

Ric gave a short laugh. Marlene ran her fingers through her almost-blond hair. Ric watched her in the mirror.

"You don't have to involve yourself in this part, Marlene," Ric said. "I can do it by myself, I think."

She was looking at the darkened vid screen. Her eyes were bright. A smile tugged at her lips.

"I'm ready," she said. "Let's do it."

"I've got to get some things ready first."

"Hurry up. I don't want to waste this feeling I've got."

Ric closed his eyes. He didn't want to see his reflection anymore. "What feeling is that?" he asked.

"The feeling that my time is coming. To try something new."

"Yeah," Ric said. His eyes were still closed. "That's what I thought."

17

Ric, wearing leather gardener's gloves, smoothed the earth over the plastic-wrapped explosive device he had just buried under a pyracantha bush. He was crouched in the shadow of a vacation cabin. Drizzle rattled off his collar. His knees were growing wet. He took the aerial for the radio detonator and pulled it carefully along one of the stems of the bush. Marlene stood next to him in red plastic boots. She was standing guard, snuffling in the cold. Ric could hear the sound of her lips as she chewed gum.

White shafts of light tracked over their heads, filtered by juniper scrub that stood between the cabins and the expressway heading north out of Flagstaff. Ric froze. His form, caught among pyracantha barbs, cast a stark moving shadow on the peeling white wall.

"Flashlight," he said, when the car had passed. Moving between the light and any onlookers, Marlene flicked it on. Ric carefully smoothed the soil, spread old leaves. He thought the thorns on the pyracantha would keep most people away, but he didn't want disturbed soil attracting anyone.

Rain danced down in the yellow light. "Thanks," he said. Marlene popped a bubble. Ric stood up, brushing muck from his knees. There were more bundles to bury, and it was going to be a long, wet night.

18

"They're going to take you off if they can," Ric said. "They're from California and they know this is a one-shot deal, so they don't care if they offend you or leave you dead. But they think it's going to happen in Phoenix, see." Ric, Super Virgin, and Two-Fisted Jesus stood in front of the juniper by the alloy road, looking down at the cluster of cabins. "They may hire people from the Cold Wires or whoever, so that they can have people who know the terrain. So the idea is, we move the meet at the last minute. Up here, north of Flag."

"We don't know the terrain, either," Jesus said. He looked uncomfortable here, his face a monochrome blotch in the unaccustomed sun.

Ric took a squeeze bottle of nasal mist from his pocket and squeezed it once up each nostril. He sniffed. "You can learn it between now and then. Rent all the cabins, put soldiers in the nearest ones. Lay in your commo gear." Ric pointed up at the ridge above where they stood. "Put some people with long guns up there, some IR goggles and scopes. Anyone comes in, you'll know about it."

"I don't know, Marat. I like Phoenix. I know the way that city thinks." Jesus shook his head in disbelief. "Fucking tourist cabins."

"They're better than hotel rooms. Tourist cabins have back doors."

"Hey." Super Virgin was grinning, metal teeth winking in the sun as she tugged on Jesus' sleeve. "Expand your horizons. This is the great outdoors."

Jesus shook his head. "I'll think about it."

19

Marlene was wearing war paint and dancing in the middle of her condeco living room. The furniture was pushed back to the walls, the music was loud enough to rattle the crystal on the kitchen shelves.

"You've got to decide, Marlene," Ric said. He was sitting behind the pushed-back table, and the paper packets of Thunder were laid out in front of him. "How much of this do you want to sell?"

"I'll decide later."

"Now. Now, Marlene."

"Maybe I'll keep it all."

Ric looked at her. She shook sweat out of her eyes and laughed.

"Just a joke, Ric."

He said nothing.

"It's just happiness," she said, dancing. "Happiness in paper envelopes. Better than money. You ought to use some. It'll make you less tense." Sweat was streaking her war paint. "What'll you use the money for, anyway? Move to Zanzibar and buy yourself a safe condeco and a bunch of safe investments? Sounds boring to me, Ric. Why'n't you use it to create some excitement?"

He could not, Ric thought, afford much in the way of regret. But still a sadness came over him, drifting through his body on slow opiate time. Another few days, he thought, and he wouldn't have to use people anymore. Which was good, because he was losing his taste for it.

20

A kid from California was told to be by a certain public phone at a certain time, with his bank and without his friends. The phone call told him to go to another phone and be there within a certain allotted time. He complained, but the phone hung up in mid-syllable.

At the second phone he was told to take the keys taped to the bottom of the shelf in the phone booth, go to such-and-such a car in the parking lot, and drive to Flagstaff to another public phone. His complaints were cut short by a slamming receiver. Once in Flagstaff, he was given another set of directions.

By now he had learned not to complain.

If there were still people with him they were very good, because they hadn't been seen at any of the turns of his course.

He was working for Ric, even though he didn't know it.

21

Marlene was practicing readiness. New patterns were constantly flickering through her mind and she loved watching her head doing its tricks.

She was wearing her war paint as she sat up on a tall ridge behind the cabins, her form encased in a plastic envelope that dispersed her body heat in patterns unrecognizable to infrared scanners. She had a radio and a powerful antenna, and she was humming "Greensleeves" to herself as she looked down at the cabins through long binoculars wrapped in a scansheet paper tube to keep the sun from winking from the lenses. Marlene also had headphones and a parabolic mike pointed down at the cabins, so that she could hear anything going on. Right now all she could hear was the wind.

She could see the cabins perfectly, as well as the two riflemen on the ridge across the road. She was far away from anything likely to happen, but if things went well she wouldn't be needed for anything but pushing buttons on cue anyway.

"Greensleeves" hummed on and on. Marlene was having a good time. Working for Ric.

22

Two-Fisted Jesus had turned the cabin into another plastic-hung cavern, lit by pale holograms and cool video monitors, filled with the hum of machinery and the brightness of liquid crystal. Right in the middle, a round coffee table full of crisp paper envelopes.

Ric had been allowed entry because he was one of the principals in the transaction. He'd undergone scanning as he entered, both for weapons and for electronics. Nothing had been found. His Thunder, and about half of Marlene's, was sitting on the table.

Only two people were in the room besides Ric. Super Virgin had the safety caps off her claws and was carrying an automatic with laser sights in a belt holster. Ric considered the sights a pure affectation in a room this small. Jesus had a sawed-off twin-barrel shotgun sitting in his lap. The pistol grip might break his wrist but the spread would cover most of the room, and Ric wondered if Jesus had considered how much electronics he'd lose if he ever used it.

23

Where three lightposts had been marked with fluorescent tape, the kid from California pulled off on the verge of the alloy road that wound ahead to leap over the Grand Canyon into Utah. Captain Islam pulled up behind him with two soldiers, and they scanned the kid right there, stripped him of a pistol and a homing sensor, and put him in the back of their own car.

"You're beginning to piss me off," the kid said.

"Just do what we tell you," Captain Islam said, pulling away, "and you'll be king of Los fucking Angeles."

24

Ric's hands were trembling so hard he had to press them against the arms of his chair in order to keep it from showing. He could feel sweat oozing from his armpits. He really wasn't good at this kind of thing.

The kid from California was pushed in the door by Captain Islam, who stepped out and closed the door behind him. The kid was black and had clear plastic eye implants, with the electronics gleaming inside the transparent eyeball. He had patterned scarring instead of the tattoos, and was about sixteen. He wore a silver jacket, carried a duffel to put the Thunder in, and seemed annoyed.

"Once you step inside," Jesus said, "you have five minutes to complete our transaction. Go ahead and test any of the packets at random."

"Yeah," the kid said. "I'll do that." He crouched by the table, pulled vials from his pockets, and made a series of tests while Jesus counted off at fifteen-second intervals. He managed to do four tests in three minutes, then stood up. Ric could see he was salivating for the stuff.

"It's good," he said.

"Let's see your key." The kid took a credit spike from his pocket and handed it to Jesus, who put it in the computer in front of him. Jesus transferred two hundred fifteen thousand in Starbright policorporate scrip from the spike to his own spike that was jacked into slot two.

"Take your stuff," Jesus said, settling back in his seat. "Captain Islam will take you back to your car. Nice doing business."

The kid gave a sniff, took his spike back, and began to stuff white packets into his duffel. He left the cabin without saying a word. Adrenaline was wailing along Ric's nerves. He stood and took his own spike from his left-hand jacket pocket. His other hand went to the squeeze bottle of nasal mist in his right. Stray novae were exploding at the peripherals of his vision.

"Look at this, Virgin," Ric said. "Look at all the money sitting in this machine." He laughed. Laughter wasn't hard, but stopping the laughter was.

"Twenty percent is yours, Marat," Jesus said. "Give me your spike."

As Super Virgin stepped up to look at the monitor, Ric brought the squeeze bottle out of his pocket and fired acrolein into her face. His spin toward Jesus was so fast that Virgin's scream had barely begun before he fired another burst of the chemical at Jesus, slamming one hand down on the shotgun to keep him from bringing it up. He'd planned on just holding it there till the boy's grip loosened, but nerves took over and he wrenched it effortlessly from Jesus' hands and barely stopped himself from smashing Jesus in the head with it.

Virgin was on her hands and knees, mucus hanging from her nose and lips. She was trying to draw the pistol. Ric kicked it away. It fell on muffled plastic.

Ric turned and pulled the spikes from the machine. Jesus had fallen out of his chair, was clawing at his face. "Dead man," Jesus said, gasping the words.

"Don't threaten me, asshole," Ric said. "It could have been mustard gas."

And then Marlene, on the ridge far above, watched the sweep hand touch five minutes, thirty seconds, and she pressed her radio button. All the buried charges went off, blasting bits of the other cabins into the sky and doubtless convincing the soldiers in the other buildings that they were under fire by rocket or mortar, that the kid from California had brought an army with him. Simultaneous with the explosive, other buried packages began to gush concealing white smoke into the air. The wind was strong but there was a lot of smoke.

Ric opened the back door and took off, the shotgun hanging in his hand. Random fire burst out but none of it came near. The smoke provided cover from both optical scanners and infrared, and it concealed him all the way across the yard behind the cabin and down into the arroyo behind it. Sixty yards down the arroyo was a culvert that ran under the expressway. Ric dashed through it, wetting himself to the knees in cold spring snowmelt.

He was now on the other side of the expressway. He didn't think anyone would be looking for him here. He threw the shotgun away and kept running. There was a cross-country motorbike waiting a little farther up the stream.

25

"There," Ric said, pressing the Return button. "Half of it's yours."

Marlene was still wearing her war paint. She sipped cognac from a crystal glass and took her spike out of the computer. She laughed. "A hundred K of Starbright," she said, "and paper packets of happiness. What else do I need?"

"A fast armored car, maybe," Ric said. He pocketed his spike. "I'm taking off," he said. He turned to her. "There's room on the bike for two."

"To where?" She was looking at him sidelong.

"To Mexico, for starters," he said. A lie. Ric planned on heading northeast and losing himself for a while in Navajoland.

"To some safe little country. A safe little apartment."

"That's the idea."

Marlene took a hefty swig of cognac. "Not me," she said. "I'm planning on staying in this life."

Ric felt a coldness brush his spine. He reached out to take her hand. "Marlene," he said carefully. "You've got to leave this town. Now."

She pulled her hand away. "Not a chance, Ricardo. I plan on telling my boss just what I think of him. Tomorrow morning. I can't wait."

There was a pain in Ric's throat. "Okay," he said. He stood up. "See you in Mexico, maybe." He began to move for the door. Marlene put her arms around him from behind. Her chin dug into his collarbone.

"Stick around," she said. "For the party."

He shook his head, uncoiled her arms, slid out of them.

"You treat me like I don't know what I'm doing," Marlene said.

He turned and looked at her. Bright eyes looked at him from a mask of bright paint. "You don't," he said.

"I've got lots of ideas. You showed me how to put things together."

"Now I'm showing you how to run and save your life."

"Hah. I'm not going to run. I'm going to stroll out with a briefcase full of happiness and a hundred K in my pocket."

He looked at her and felt a pressure hard in his chest. He knew that none of this was real to her, that he'd never been able to penetrate that strange screen in her mind that stood between Marlene and the rest of the world. Ric had never pierced it, but soon the world would. He felt a coldness filling him, a coldness that had nothing to do with sorrow.

It was hard not to run when he turned and left the apartment.

His breathing came more freely with each step he took.

26

When Ric came off the Navajo Reservation he saw scan-sheet headlines about how the California gang wars had spilled over into Phoenix, how there were dead people turning up in alleys, others were missing, a club had been bombed. All those people working for him, covering his retreat.

In New Zealand he bought into a condecology in Christchurch, a big place with armored shutters and armored guards, a first-rate new artificial intelligence to handle investments, and a mostly for-eign clientele who profited by the fact that a list of the condeco's inhabitants was never made public… This was before he found out that he could buy private property here, a big house on the South Island with a view of his own personal glacier, without a chance of anybody's war accidentally rolling over him.

It was an interesting feeling, sitting alone in his own house, knowing there wasn't anyone within five thousand miles who wanted to kill him.

Ric made friends. He played the market and the horses. And he learned to ski.

At a ski party in late September, held in the house of one of his friends, he drifted from room to room amid a murmur of conversation punctuated with brittle laughter. He had his arm around someone named Reiko, the sheltered daughter of a policorporate bigwig. The girl, nineteen and a student, had long black hair that fell like a tsunami down her shoulders, and she was fascinated with his talk of life in the real world. He walked into a back room that was bright with the white glare of video, wondering if the jai alai scores had been posted yet, and he stared into his own face as screams rose around him and his nerves turned to hot magnesium flares.

"Ugh. Mexican scum show," said Reiko, and then she saw the actor's face and her eyes widened.

Ric felt his knees trembling and he sank into an armchair in the back of the room. Ice tittering in his drink. The man on the vid was flaying alive a woman who hung by her wrists from a beam. Blood ran down his forearms. The camera cut quickly to his tiger's eyes, his thin smile. Ric's eyes. Ric's smile.

"My god," said Reiko. "It's really you, isn't it?"

"No," Ric said. Shaking his head.

"I can't believe they let this stuff even on pirate stations," someone said from the hallway. Screams rose from the vid. Ric's mind was flailing in the dark.

"I can't watch this," Reiko said, and rushed away. Ric didn't see her go. Burning sweat was running down the back of his neck.

The victim's screams rose. Blood traced artful patterns down her body. The camera cut to her face.

Marlene's face.

Nausea swept Ric and he doubled in his chair. He remembered Two-Fisted Jesus and his talent for creating video images, altering faces, voices, action. They'd found Marlene, as Ric had thought they would, and her voice and body were memorized by Jesus' computers. Maybe the torture was even real.

"It's got to be him," someone in the room said. "It's even his voice. His accent."

"He never did say," said another voice, "what he used to do for a living."

Frozen in his chair, Ric watched the show to the end. There was more torture, more bodies. The video-Ric enjoyed it all. At the end he went down before the blazing guns of the Federal Security Directorate. The credits rolled over the video-Ric's dead face. The director was listed as Jesus Carranza. The film was produced by VideoTek S.A. in collaboration with Messiah Media.

The star's name was given as Jean-Paul Marat.

"A new underground superstar," said a high voice. The voice of someone who thought of himself as an underground connoisseur. "He's been in a lot of pirate video lately. He's the center of a big controversy about how far scum shows can go."

And then the lights came on and Ric saw eyes turning to him in surprise. "It's not me," he said.

"Of course not." The voice belonged to his host. "Incredible resemblance, though. Even your mannerisms. Your accent."

"Not me."

"Hey." A quick, small man, with metal-rimmed glasses that gazed at Ric like barrels of a shotgun. "It really is you!" The high-pitched voice of the connoisseur grated on Ric's nerves like the sound of a bonesaw.

"No." A fast, sweat-soaked denial.

"Look. I've taped all your vids I could find."

"Not me."

"I'm having a party next week. With entertainment, if you know what I mean. I wonder—"

"I'm not interested," Ric said, standing carefully, "in any of your parties."

He walked out into the night, to his new car, and headed north, to his private fortress above the glacier. He took the pistol out of the glove compartment and put it on the seat next to him. It didn't make him feel any safer.

Get a new face, Ric thought. Get to Uzbekistan and check into a hospital. Let them try to follow me there.

He got home at four in the morning and checked his situation with the artificial intelligence that managed his accounts. All his funds were in long-term investments and he'd take a whopping loss if he pulled out now.

He looked at the figures and couldn't understand them.

There seemed to be a long, constant scream in Ric's mind and nerves, a scream that echoed Marlene's, the sound of someone who has just discovered what is real. His body was shaking and he couldn't stop it.

Ric switched off his monitor and staggered to bed. Blood filled his dreams.

When he rose it was noon. There were people outside his gates, paparazzi with cameras. The phone had recorded a series of requests for an interview with the new, controversial vid star. Someone at the party had talked. Ric stumbled to his office and told the AI to sell.

The money in his pocket and a gun in his lap, he raced his car past the paparazzi, making them jump aside as he tried his best to run them down. He had to make the next suborbital shuttle out of Christchurch to Mysore, then head northwest to a hospital and to a new life. And somehow he'd have to try to cover his tracks. Possibly he'd buy some hair bleach, a false mustache. Pay only cash.

Getting away from Cartoon Messiah wouldn't be hard. Shaking the paparazzi would take a lot of fast thinking.

Sweat made his grip on the wheel slippery.

As he approached Christchurch he saw a streak across the bright northeast sky, a shuttle burning its way across the Pacific from California.

He wondered if there were people on it that he knew.

In his mind, the screams went on.

THE MILLENNIUM PARTY

Darien was making another annotation to his lengthy commentary on the *Tenjou Cycle* when his Marshal reminded him that his wedding anniversary would soon be upon him. This was the thousandth anniversary—a full millennium with Clarisse!—and he knew the celebration would have to be a special one.

He finished his annotation and then de-slotted the savant brain containing the cross-referenced database that allowed him to manage his work. In its place he slotted the brain labeled *Clarisse/Passion,* the brain that contained memories of his time with his wife. Not all memories, however: the contents had been carefully purged of any of the last thousand years' disagreements, arguments, disappointments, infidelities, and misconnections… The memories were only those of love, ardor, obsession, passion, and release, all the most intense and glorious moments of their thousand years together, all the times when Darien was drunk on Clarisse, intoxicated with her scent, her brilliance, her wit.

The other moments, the less-than-perfect ones, he had stored elsewhere, in one brain or another, but he rarely reviewed them. Darien saw no reason why his mind should contain anything less than perfection.

Flushed with the sensations that now poured through his mind, overwhelmed by the delirium of love, Darien began to work on his present for his wife.

When the day came, Darien and Clarisse met in an environment that she had designed. This was an arrangement that had existed for centuries, ever since they both realized that Clarisse's sense of spacial relationships was better than his. The environment was a masterpiece, an apartment built on several levels, like little terraces, that broke the space up into smaller areas that created intimacy without sacrificing the sense of spaciousness. None of the furniture was designed for more than two people. Darien recognized on the walls a picture he'd given Clarisse on her four-hundredth birthday, an elaborate, antique dial telephone from their honeymoon apartment in Paris, and a Japanese paper doll of a woman in an antique kimono, a present he had given her early in their acquaintance, when they'd haunted antique stores together.

It was Darien's task to complete the arrangement. He added an abstract bronze sculpture of a horse and jockey that Clarisse had given him for his birthday, a puzzle made of wire and butter-smooth old wood, and a view from the terrace, a view of Rio de Janeiro at night. Because his sense of taste and smell were more subtle than Clarisse's, he by standing arrangement populated the apartment with scents, lilac for the parlor, sweet magnolia and bracing cypress on the terrace, a combination of sandalwood and spice for the bedroom, and a mixture of vanilla and cardamom for the dining room, a scent subtle enough that it wouldn't interfere with the meal.

When Clarisse entered he was dressed in a tailcoat, white tie, waistcoat, and diamond studs. She had matched his period élan with a Worth gown of shining blue satin, tiny boots that buttoned up the ankles, and a dashing fall of silk about her throat. Her tawny hair was pinned up, inviting him to kiss the nape of her neck, an indulgence which he permitted himself almost immediately.

Darien seated Clarisse on the cushions and mixed cocktails. He asked her about her work: a duplicate of one of her brains was on the mission to 55 Cancri, sharing piloting missions with other duplicates; if a habitable planet was discovered, then a new Clarisse would be built on-site to pioneer the new world.

Darien had created the meal in consultation with Clarisse's Marshal. They began with mussels steamed open in white wine and herbs, then went on to a salad of fennel, orange, and red cranberry. Next came roasted green beans served alongside a chicken cooked simply in the oven, flamed in cognac, then served in a creamy port wine reduction sauce. At the end was a raspberry Bavarian cream. Each dish was one that Darien had experienced at another time in his long life, considered perfect, stored in one brain or another, and now recreated down to the last scent and sensation.

After coffee and conversation on the terrace, Clarisse led Darien to the bedroom. He enjoyed kneeling at her feet and unlacing every single button of those damned Victorian boots. His heart brimmed with passion and lust, and he rose from his knees to embrace her. Wrapped in the sandalwood-scented silence of their suite, they feasted till dawn on one another's flesh.

Their life together, Darien reflected, was perfection itself: one enchanted jewel after another, hanging side-by-side on a thousand-year string.

After juice and shirred eggs in the morning, Darien kissed the inside of Clarisse's wrist, and saw her to the door. His brain had recorded every single rapturous instant of their time together.

And then, returning to his work, Darien de-slotted *Clarisse/Passion,* and put it on the shelf for another year.

THE BAD TWIN

There it was in my sights, for just a fraction of a second, the most infamous profile in all time. And then, before I could squeeze the trigger, Scorsese stepped into his time box and was gone.

I looked at any wrist chronometer.

15:22:16.

Scorsese had timeshifted at 15:22:14 at the latest. I decided to perform a little discreet editing.

There was a bounty on Scorsese. He was one of history's greatest time thieves, and he had never been caught. No one even knew his real name: Scorsese was an alias he'd used when he appeared at Verrocchio's studio in 1471, when Leonardo da Vinci was still apprenticed there, an appearance that resulted in the disappearance of the entire body of Leonardo's work prior to that date. We had tried to intercept him there—we'd been after lost Leonardos, too—but somehow Scorsese had maneuvered his pursuers into creating an unholy paradox so godawful that those who'd survived had been glad to get out with their lives. We had declared the whole period off limits for our own people, lest their continued tampering lose not only da Vinci's early works, but his life and the rest of his accomplishments, too.

We did know what Scorsese looked like. He'd had Leonardo paint his portrait, and some of the cartoons had survived in the pocket of one of our dead agents. His profile was unmistakable, with a Wellington beak of a nose and a high, balding forehead.

I had just seen that profile below me among the grape vines, in the split-second just before he and his time box had vanished from my present. If I could edit Scorsese and confiscate his time box laden with a genuine Bronze Age fresco, I would be entitled to the reward—plus a promotion, a medal, and if I was lucky a stay at the Time Resort in the Paleozoic.

Scorsese hadn't seen me, which meant that I wouldn't have to be looking over my shoulder while I edited him, a significant problem with combat among time travelers. Imagine a war in which the survivors of an ambush can return in time and edit out the ambushers, in turn leaving a few survivors who can hop back and edit out the editors. Thinking about it can give you a headache.

But such problems also led to a very simple rule: No Survivors Means No Headaches. If you're going to ambush someone, do it right, and do it permanently.

I was going to bag Scorsese, and I was going to do a good job of it.

Pieces of pumice crunched beneath my boots as I crossed the ridge and descended into the grape arbor adjacent to the isolated villa. When the inhabitants had fled the island after the villa's partial collapse in the last earthquake, they had abandoned some of the finest wine grapes in history to grow wild in the rich volcanic soil. Lt. Talley and I had liberated some wine jugs from the villa's cellars a few months ago, finding the contents exquisite.

Pity the whole place would be blown to hell and gone in another six months.

From the top of the small ridge I could look to the south, seeing the land fall away in the jagged terraces created by the viticulture of the inhabitants. To the northeast loomed the bulk of the volcano, rising three thousand feet above the sea. The island's inhabitants had wanted to put to use every available inch of space, and so the volcano was terraced up much of its height. The unusable parts had a mad, jagged beauty, striped in red, white, and black to mark the histories of different eruptions.

The island had many names. Before they fled, its inhabitants called it Kalliste, meaning The Fairest. Kykladic navigators sensibly called it Strongyli, Round Island. Many years later a Spartan general would conquer the place, and it would be named Thera after him. Years afterward it would take its name from its patron saint, Irene, and would be called Santorini.

At the moment it was 15:22:44, June 16, 1481 B.C.E. On December 22 the volcano would celebrate the Solstice by blowing itself to smithereens, critically wounding Minoan and Kykladic civilization in the process. The eruption was the culmination of a long series of events, begun eighteen months before when an earthquake flattened half the buildings on the island and a lava flow had obliterated a village and completely blocked one of the small harbors, while a new vent on the north side of the volcano dumped several inches of pumice blocks on the whole island and several of the nearby Kyklades. The inhabitants had fled then, all seventy thousand, in an orderly evacuation that testified to their culture's high level of organization and technology. Every so often a ship returned to see whether the current cycle of eruptions was over, and on those occasions I fired off a lot of smoke bombs and other pyrotechnics to convince them it wasn't. Thus far it had worked.

I was camped out on a nice flat piece of ground half a click from here, where a rock wouldn't be likely to fall on me. With my weapons, my armor, and my smoke bombs, I was a caretaker assigned to preserve the treasures of Thera and keep them safe from time thieves. I was a good choice for the job, insofar as I was also a U.S. Navy SEAL trained in irregular combat and survival, currently on assignment to the Time Corps of the International Time Authority at The Hague. Until six weeks ago I'd had Lt. Talley of the Royal Marine Commando to keep me company, until he developed acute appendicitis and jumped upStream to the pickup date. Since then, guardianship of the entire island of Thera had been up to me.

It was a large island for a single person, but manpower had never been the Time Corps' strong point. The Corps was kept deliberately small in order not to become a threat to the governments that sponsored it. Because it was small, the Corps had to be efficient: morale and esprit were high, and so was the level of training and commitment. We were few in number, but all history was our backyard, and we were allowed to play for keeps.

Preserving all human history, it was felt, demanded a certain degree of ruthlessness.

The governments that acted to limit the powers of the Corps had also given it a rather large task: to Preserve the Common Heritage of Humankind. The civilization of Thera represented a unique and priceless inheritance. For the better part of a century, tourists in the National Museum in Athens had been lining up to see a few frescos dug from beneath a hundred feet of ash at Akrotiri, a part of the island that had not been destroyed by the eruption.

The artwork on the rest of the island, the parts the volcano destroyed, were just as valuable, and much more numerous.

On the first of November, when the Time Stream factors were most favorable for moving a large amount of men and equipment, a collection of specialists under the guidance of Time Corps personnel would appear on Thera and salvage every pot, every fresco, every item of bronze work—every graffito, if there was time.

But, as with any major archaeological project, the pothunters had to be kept away. The island was wide open to any scrounge artist with a time box sufficiently powerful to reach to the Fifteenth Century B.C.E., and I was supposed to keep them away.

The villa itself had two storeys above ground, built of charcoal-colored stone layered with streaks of reddish-brown and creamy white, all the colors of the island blended here just as they were on the volcano that towered above us. Part of the place had collapsed in the first quake. On the far side of the villa, a tortuous zigzag path dropped with breathtaking rapidity to one of Thera's smaller ports, the one we called Agia Therasia because it lay a hundred meters or so to seaward of what would, in my century, become that splinter-island. In my own century the town had been broken, buried under a hundred feet of ash, and then submerged under the Aegean; but now, framed by dark cypress and lighter, stunted olive trees all shining with their peculiar silver-green, Aga Therasia stood in native loveliness, a crescent of black, brown, red, and white buildings, all of native stone, clinging to its fringe of dark volcanic beach. The deep turquoise Aegean, wrinkled like a baby's skin, stretched from the beach to the white horizon. The scene didn't have the wild, craggy magnificence of my century's Santorini. Here in the fifteenth century B.C.E. the island had a quieter beauty, a beauty altered and enhanced by the efforts of a now-vanished population.

Many of the buildings had crumbled, though one three-storeyed eminence, crowned with the Minoan horns of consecration, still stood above the town. The most dominant building in the town, I'd explored it and found it disappointing: it turned out to be the headquarters of a trading company from Knossos, and presumably had doubled as an embassy, architecturally dominating the Thera town as the Minoan dominated the Kykladic civilization.

It did, however, have indoor toilets even on the upper storeys, flushed by a large cistern on the roof. I thought that was an interesting detail.

In another few months it would all lie under the caldera, edited, along with the two civilizations that had built it, by a lunatic nature. I would miss it.

I walked through the deserted villa to see what Scorsese had plundered and saw how simple the snatch had been. After bracing the ceiling with some automatic jacks, Scorsese had cut away at the wall surrounding an interior fresco, covered the fresco with an aerosol preservative—he'd failed to police one of the empty cans—then attached some anti-g lifters to the fresco and pushed the whole thing into his box. I noticed that the jacks that supported the ceiling had timers on them set to drop the roof on this particular room in another hour. It would look as if earthquake damage were responsible. A clever idea, well executed.

A pity he hadn't considered my capacity for wine. I'd run out of the stuff that Talley and I had liberated from the villa, and decided to hike up the ridge and get some more. Lie under the shade of the olives, drink from an exquisite vintage, and read a copy of Sophocles' Theban trilogy I'd brought with me from my own century.

If you're ever stuck on a deserted island, by the way, I recommend reading the classics—they stay with you longer.

Now, instead of passing a balmy afternoon, I was about to kill one of the most dangerous men in history. It's a situation that Sophocles would have appreciated.

Time thieves in general are well organized and well financed. They have to be to reach as far back as they do—time travel is very expensive, and those with the private resources to build their own illegal time machine are few: some governments can't even afford it. The robberies can't be done on a very large scale, since the opportunities to move large amounts of matter through the Stream are very few, so most of their raids are in the nature of smash-and-grab—one or two men jump downStream, seize a pot, statue, or gold ornament, and then Jump upStream and away. The Time Corps edits the thieves when we find them, but unless there are records of the theft that somehow survive and get into the Corps archives, most of the stuff is simply lost, gone into private collections established hundreds, sometimes thousands of years after the theft.

Thera was an obvious target, since archaeologists had long ago established that the island had been abandoned about two years before it finally blew. The Corps sent two guards to keep the plunderers away. Usually the announcement of a Corps guard was enough to keep a place safe—there were plenty of other places to raid, after all. Scorsese had been unusually brave to raid the villa: but presumably he'd been scouting the place for some time and had been keeping tabs on my movement. He'd seen that the villa wasn't in my normal pattern; he couldn't have known that I would run out of wine and decide to hike two miles uphill, partly concealed by the series of terraces and vines, for a raid on the villa's cellar.

I took a position behind one of the olive trees to the side of the villa. I was out of sight from my earlier position behind the ridge, which would tend to reduce the possibility of a paradox. Just to make sure I glanced at my chronometer, took out the notebook that all time agents carry with them for purposes like this, and wrote a note to myself: 15:35:01 to 15:22:05. I stuck the note onto a branch of the olive tree.

Then I gave the same coordinates to my chronometer, seeing the shining numbers reflected in my specs, and waited.

I planned to head downStream to nine seconds before Scorsese's disappearance and my own appearance above the ridge. I would kill Scorsese and then Jump upStream a few hours or so in order to give my past self a chance to figure out what had happened.

For killing Scorsese would, of course, change my own past—when I heard the shots I'd pop up above the ridge line a little early, and of course see Scorsese dead below me. I assumed that I would then circle around to see if I could pick up the trail of whoever had been doing the shooting, whereupon I would find the note I'd written to myself and realize that it had been my own future self who'd been responsible.

My past self, who I'll call I-Alpha, would then take position behind the olive tree and set his own chronometer for 15:22:05. He would then jump downStream and become me, in accordance with the laws of temporal conservation, and kill Scorsese all over again.

It was complicated, but I had temporal conservation on my side. In training they'd told us that it helps to think of the universe as a lazy editor, revising a manuscript but trying to do as little work as possible. Although it is possible for a time traveler to change the past, it is harder than at first glance. To save itself the trouble of having to alter all upStream timelines, the universe tended to act to prevent paradox, attempting to solve them along the lines of least resistance. Rather than accept both I-Alpha and I-Beta materializing in the same place at the same instant, Alpha and Beta would merge.

It was 15:34:45. I braced my rifle against my shoulder and made myself ready for the edit.

At 15:35:01 I made the transit, and suddenly, in less than an eyeblink, Scorsese's time box was there in front of me, and Scorsese, with an armful of gear, was walking from the villa to its hatch.

The air cracked to the sound of shots, none of them mine.

I threw myself backward and rolled as bullets began tearing up the olive tree above my head.

Scorsese had clearly brought a friend, someone hunkered down with a rifle off to my right.

I dived behind the villa on the opposite side from Scorsese and began to work my way around to the left, behind the ridge. Bullets began thwacking into the heavy stonework of the building.

And, as I accelerated in the safe defilade of the ridge, I ran smack into myself.

Into I-Alpha, who likewise covered by the defilade was working his way toward the firing.

We both sat down and goggled at one another, ignoring the sound of the bullets spitting overhead. I had just created a paradox of duplication, and we were both in deep trouble.

"You stupid bastard," Alpha said.

"Look," I said. "You've got twelve minutes to get to an olive tree on the other side of the villa, so that you can drop back to a few seconds ago and end the duplication."

"I'm supposed to put myself in the line of fire for *you?*" Alpha asked. "You're the one who fucked up."

"We can edit out the marksman later," I said.

"Fuck that. He can edit us just as easily. Let's find out where the bastard is, first."

I doubted that the sniper would, actually, edit us. The Time Corps wasn't going to waste a lot of energy on a missing fresco, but when one of their own was killed they would spare no effort to edit the culprit, preferably before he actually committed his crime, so that his victim would remain alive.

"Circle left," I said. "There's not enough cover to our right."

We began moving to the left but the marksman managed to anticipate us. Bullets began ripping through the grape vines over our heads. It took us twenty minutes to work our way into position to hit back at him, and by that time he'd gone into the Stream and got clean away.

But more seriously, Alpha hadn't been able to get to the olive tree in time for the 14:45:01 jump downStream to become me. The odds were increasing that if he made the Jump now, he'd become not me, Beta, but a third individual, Gamma, and then there would be three of us.

We were permanently duplicated, and this was very much against the rules. Time Corps personnel were forbidden to duplicate themselves, because with an infinite number of duplications we could become an army capable of threatening the governments that employed us. Penalty for duplication was severe.

The forms would still be followed, though. A jury of our Time Corps peers would convene here on Thera, and Alpha and I would have a chance to speak in our own defense before our judges reluctantly shot one or both of us.

"Look," I said. "How about this? One of us jumps downStream for a few hours to leave a note to ourself warning him not to make this mistake."

Alpha looked at me coldly through his self-polarizing specs. His front had been smeared with black volcanic ash as he'd crawled through the grape vines, and he looked both dirty and resentful. "You're getting desperate, guy," he said. "Your thinking isn't very clear. If you succeed in changing the past, we edit *ourselves*. He lives and we don't exist any more. I don't know about you, but I have every intention of continuing to exist."

He pointed a finger at me. "And that's only if we're *lucky*. The worst is what happens if you don't succeed in editing the past. Then there'd be three of us, wouldn't there? You, me, and him. We'd be triplets."

"Oh," I said. He looked at me savagely. I hadn't realized I was capable of such anger.

"Look, sport," he said. "I was walking up to the villa for a jug of wine and suddenly I was getting shot at. It was you who fucked up. Suppose you tell me how."

"Scorsese," I said, and Alpha's surprised reaction softened the menace on his face. "He's done it again," I said. "He's protected himself by getting us involved in a paradox. We don't dare edit him for fear of making our own situation worse."

"Let's pull back and give this a think," Alpha said.

Alpha and I fell back fifty yards to a defensible outcrop of lava rock and considered the problem. We could, of course, drop back downStream to zap the sniper and Scorsese; but it would be foolish in the extreme to assume that Scorsese didn't have further backup—hell, since he didn't have to abide by any regulations about duplicating himself he could be his own backup, simply by dropping back to the same place to act as his own sniper—and if there were more Scorseses hanging about to edit our editing job then there might suddenly be four Time Corpsmen staring at one another.

We remembered how Scorsese had got six of the best of our agents involved in a paradox loop in Florence that had only been solved when they'd started killing each other. It was too easy for something like that to get started here. Every time we tried to resolve the duplication problem we risked the problem of quadrupling ourselves, or worse. If we got into a time loop as well, with all manner of catastrophe-producing ripples running upStream *and* down, the universe, ever the lazy editor, might decide that the easiest way to fix things would be to blow Thera six months early, eliminating numerous duplicate Time Corps agents and incidentally Aegean civilization. Scorsese might get blown up with the rest of us, but it would be shallow comfort.

Alpha and I worked it through over and over again, and it was all very discouraging. Alpha scratched under his boonie hat and then locked up, over my shoulder, in surprise. "Shit," he said, grabbing for his rifle, "it's *him!*"

I turned, ready for High Noon with Scorsese, but I should have realized what Alpha was really up to. By the time I started to turn back while beginning a duck and roll, all I could see was a gun butt foreshortening with remarkable speed in the instant before it crunched down between my eyes.

I landed on the ground in a puff of volcanic ash. My specs were hanging by one ear. Alpha reversed the rifle and had it pointed at me before I could go for the pistol I carried in my shoulder holster. I froze.

Alpha reached forward with a foot and kicked my shooter back behind him. "Take the pistol out with two fingers and throw it behind you," he said. "Then the belt knife, then the knife in your boot, then the little pistol in the small of your back."

Well. You can't keep these kind of secrets from yourself, now can you?

"We've got a problem here, sport," Alpha said after he'd collected all my weaponry. "There's one too many of us, and *you're* the one that fucked up. I'm clean, and I'm not responsible for the duplication. Now what does that suggest to you?"

I didn't say anything. I was too busy trying to read the expression behind the dark specs. If Alpha had wanted to kill me he would have done it by now. What else did he have in mind?

"Nothing to say, huh?" Alpha asked. He moved back a pace, well out of my range. He relaxed a trifle, though not nearly enough to make a jump worth my while.

"Well, Fubar, I can see a couple-three solutions," Alpha said. "One, I can kill you. Two, I can let you head down to Agia Therasia and let you fix up one of those old boats they've got drawn up on the beach there. If it doesn't leak too badly, you might just make it to Crete in time to warn everyone that their world is going to blow itself to hell in about six months. Maybe, if you learn Minoan quick enough, you can have a career as a prophet."

"Those boats are all junk," I said. "They were left behind for a reason. They're rotten or holed or have suffered earthquake damage."

Alpha smiled thinly. "That brings us to plan three, I believe. Here's how it goes: you and I make a jump downStream to last night, shortly after nightfall. Then I remove your wrist chronometer and let you hide yourself in the villa. I'll give you your knife so that when Scorsese shows up, you can kill him. You take his time box—I'll give it to you free and clear—and then you can run upStream for a life of crime. I keep Scorsese's body and the reward. I'll just tell our bosses that Scorsese had a partner in the box who got away before I could stop him."

"You're expecting me to edit Scorsese with a *knife?*" I asked. "Chances are he'll kill me."

Alpha's grin grew broader. "Well now, Fubar," he said. "That solves our problem, too, doesn't it?"

I looked up at the eyes masked by the dark shades, the thin, cruel grin, and I warily touched the lump hardening on my forehead.

How the hell was *I* supposed to know that I was such a bastard?

"So which'll it be, sport?" Alpha asked. "Plan one, plan two, or plan three? You decide."

"I'll go for Scorsese," I said. Alpha laughed, an unpleasant sound.

He drew a pistol and slung his awkward rifle. I was ready to make a move when he got close, but he never gave me the chance. "One word from you, Fubar," he said, "and I put two shots in your spleen."

I could feel him adjusting my chronometer—numbers flashed gold in my specs—and then he stepped back three paces and adjusted his own chronometer. Then there was a grey nothingness followed by a night wind blowing through the darkened cypresses. Brilliant stars wheeled overhead.

The Alpha approached and took the chronometer from my wrist. I was stranded in the present. Then he backed off again, and I heard two thuds by me.

"Okay," he said. "There's your survival knife, and a flashlight. The knife is awkward to throw and I know you'd miss if you tried to toss it at me."

"I would like," I said, "an entrenching tool. I want to be able to hide under the floor in there until Scorsese shows."

He paused a moment. I held my breath. I could feel how hard he was thinking, feel his mind probing at the idea, trying to work out whether the presence of an entrenching tool would alter his plans, if there was something hidden in my request.

"Okay," he said, "that's fair. When I go upStream to move our camps I'll pick up an entrenching tool, then leave it in the villa for you."

"In the wine cellar," I said. "Northwest corner. Behind one of the big pithoi, so Scorsese won't spot it if he comes here to scout."

"Northwest corner. I'll remember. Now pick up the knife and get down to the villa...and remember, I'll be watching you very carefully."

I picked up the knife and flash, and then began my walk.

The next fifteen hours were going to be a bitch.

I walked down among the grape vines where in another few hours Scorsese's time box would rest, and then, counting my steps, I paced my way to the villa. I went through the low door, turned on the flash, and carefully examined the room. There was no place to hide: the room was bare, the furniture apparently having gone abroad with its owner. The walls were bare plaster, though the fresco Scorsese was scheduled to steal was on the back of one of them.

I moved into the next room, catching a glimpse of the blue and brown of the fresco, and was luckier. The earthquake had hit harder here, and one corner of the room had come crashing down, bringing with it much of the second storey. Here I could hide myself under the rubble.

The villa had been built on the site of an older, smaller building: apparently the family was upwardly-mobile. The narrow terrace on which the villa stood had been built up and leveled by gangs of workers carrying baskets of topsoil to the terrace and dumping them here, raising the level of the ground above what it had been before. The new villa was at a higher level than the older building, with the result that the old house was used as a storage cellar.

From the kitchen in the back I went down a winding stair into the cellar. Ducking beneath the beams—the place was only about five feet tall, just a few inches taller than the big pithoi in which wine, grain and oil were stored. I breathed a sigh of relief as I found the entrenching tool that Alpha had promised me he'd hide here.

Good. I planned to use Alpha's one good deed against him. He would regret leaving me the little shovel.

It was a folding tool with a little T at the end of the handle, which made it more useful when swung as a weapon. I adjusted the blade at 90 degrees from the handle, then used the tool as a pick to chop my way through the mortared stone of the wine cellar wall. Then, reforming the tool as a shovel, I burrowed my way between the hard bedrock of the island and the looser soil of the built-up terrace, creating a one-man narrow tunnel through the soft soil of the grape arbor. When I calculated I was under the place where Scorsese's time box would appear I headed for the surface, carefully clearing away the vines' complicated root system. Eventually I pushed the blade of the E-tool up into the air, confirming the few inches between myself and the surface. I wasn't planning on breaking through just yet, so I crawled back down the tunnel to the wine cellar.

Even though my chronometer was gone, I still had a good time sense. I calculated I had a few hours before dawn, so I crawled back into the villa and found some old blankets in what I guessed were the servants' quarters. The beds were too short, so I went to sleep on the floor.

I did not sleep well.

When dawn began to creep into the room, I got up and moved to the ruined room with the fresco. I rearranged the rubble a bit, giving myself space to lie down under a beam, and then I tented a blanket over it and lay rubble and pumice over the blanket.

Making myself look like a rock. I'd seen the Apaches do it in the movies.

By the time I'd finished the sun was shining full into the room through the ruined roof, and now I could see the fresco covering the wall. Two brown children, a girl in a pleated skirt and a naked boy, were standing hand-in-hand on the seashore. Their hair was curled into long lovelocks, and their eyes were long and Egyptian. The boy was circumcised; the girl appeared to have rouged her nipples. Behind them blue-and-gold dolphins rollicked in the waves, and the dark sand beneath their feet was sprinkled with shells and starfish. It was a joyous, exuberant painting, executed in strong, bright Mediterranean colors, a paean to the childhood of mankind. To the Kykladic peoples, the Aegean was a peaceful, private lake, and the island people, protected by the naval might of Crete, were living in a golden age. Their trade in wine and purple murex dye had made them rich, and they had avoided some of the excesses, such as human sacrifice, of their Minoan cousins. No one on the planet was as civilized, or as peaceful: even in China, the Shang were sacrificing people by the thousands.

Soon the volcano would bring an end to the stability of the age, breaking the Minoan peace and bringing in the continuous violence, rapine, and pillage that made up the so-called Age of Heroes.

Well. Violence was my trade, and Alpha's. The Age of Heroes was more our style.

But still the fresco drew me—the long dark eyes of the children, the grinning dolphins torpedoing up from the wave-crests, the carefully-delineated whorls of the seashells. A painting made solely to delight, to give and express joy. I wondered if this had been the children's room, and whether the boy and girl were portraits of a boy and girl who had lived here. If so, I hoped they'd survived the quake that had brought the ceiling down.

There was little else to do, so I watched the fresco for some hours. There were other frescos in other rooms, pictures of vines and flowers, but there were a lot of blank walls and nothing as good as this carefree picture of the children. The villa had a half-finished quality: perhaps the owner had yet to commission the decorations for the rest of it. Scorsese had chosen the best.

I wanted the fresco to survive. If the Kykladic culture that had made it was doomed, I wanted at least this piece of it to come into my time, its joy and innocence intact.

When the sun was high I wriggled into my hiding place. I spent some hours there, waiting for Scorsese, moving my limbs every so often in hopes of keeping my body as alert as possible. I didn't want to lunge out at the time criminal and put my weight on a leg that had fallen asleep.

And then, some time after noon, I heard the time box drop into the grape arbor, and then a man's footsteps. I froze and tried not to breathe. I thought, very hard, about how I was only a piece of rubble.

Scorsese came into the building and moved slowly through the rooms that still stood, and then he returned to his box for his equipment. There was something about his movement that was still alert, and I decided to wait.

In the next few minutes he brought his equipment in, bolted the a-grav units to the wall, propped up the roof with his jacks, and then covered the wall front and back with an aerosol preservative. I heard the hum of the beam cutter that cut the wall free, and then the blows of a sledge that knocked the fresco clear. Then I heard the hiss of aerosols as he used his preservative on the edges of the wall, and careful steps as he floated the fresco out into the back of his time box .

Outside, Alpha and I, still one, were walking through the terraced rows of grape vines, fancying a bit of wine.

As quietly as I could, I rolled out of my hiding place and took station by the inner door. I swung the E-tool a few times for practice. It made a wicked hissing sound as it cut through the air.

Alpha, outside, was mounting the ridge line from the other side. My earlier self, Beta, would be appearing behind the olive tree in a few seconds. The sniper, who I suppose was another incarnation of Alpha—call him Alpha Prime—was probably already in position off to the northwest.

Scorsese's footsteps came closer, grew louder on the flagging of the front room. He was returning to pick up his equipment. I cocked back my arm, holding the E-tool by its T-shaped handle.

He stepped into the room, and I swung the entrenching tool.

It damn near took his head off.

I dragged the body farther into the room. Scorsese wore a kind of dark bush jacket, tan shorts similar to mine, soft boots, dark glasses, and an olive drab boonie hat—Standard Smugglers' Issue, for all I knew. He also had a government-issue wrist chronometer. I wondered if he'd got it from one of the Time Corps people during the fiasco in Florence.

Well. Four Time Corps agents were avenged. Not that I cared about that. I was in too much of a hurry to strap the chronometer to my wrist.

And once I had done that, I felt myself breathe easier. I had a way out of here.

I took his pistol, hat, specs, and jacket. The shorts and boots were similar enough to mine—I didn't feel like spending any of the next few seconds hopping from one foot to another drawing on a pair of short pants.

The chronometer showed it was 15:22:04. A second later, right on time, shots began ripping up the peace of the world, as Alpha Prime in his sniper incarnation began blasting at Beta, which is to say me.

I scuttled down into the wine cellar, entrenching tool in hand. Then I used the chronometer to jump downStream to 15:22:01 in order to give myself a few spare seconds, and then as rock 'n' roll commenced overhead again I wormed my way into the tunnel, broke through the thin layer of soil I'd left overhead, and looked through a tangle of vines at Scorsese's bright shiny time box, big and slab-sided as a delivery van.

I did not expect Alpha would let me live through this. He'd certainly never let me get away with Scorsese's time box, which would give me the ability to head downStream and edit him somehow. In his position as sniper, he was perfectly set to shoot anyone coming out of the villa. But although he covered the villa's exits, the time box stood between him and my tunnel, unless he had duplicated himself more than once—and that was dangerous, hence unlikely. He might assume that the time box jumped automatically into the Stream and got away.

And on the other hand Scorsese might be somewhere within sight, backing up himself. He, I presume, would be relieved to see someone in Scorsese's hat and jacket rise magically from the ground, throw himself into the time box, and make a clever escape. In his relief he might not notice that his famous profile was a little altered.

I could feel the imprint of a huge target symbol on my back as I scrambled from the narrow tunnel, kicking at the loose soil. I threw myself through the vines, jumped through the time box's open door, and slammed it shut behind me.

Scorsese had allowed for the possibility that he might have to make a hasty exit. The controls were already programmed for his destination, so all I had to do was press the go-button.

The windows turned black. The box had entered the Stream.

The little official-use-only wrist chronometers we Time Corps people wore were only good for traveling a few decades, perhaps a couple centuries if the Stream currents were with you. To travel longer distances more energy was needed, plus a self-contained environment with oxygen and, if the journey was long, food. The short jumps I'd made earlier in the day had seemed no longer than eyeblinks, but jumping up- or downStream for any longer distances subjectively took more time.

I looked at the gauges and saw that this journey would be up-Stream and for only four hundred years or so. It would take about half an hour, subjectively. I readjusted my jacket and hat, brushed volcanic soil from my shorts, and looked out into the darkness as the years sped by.

The island had blown in the interim. It had rained a lot of ash on Anatolia, Rhodes, and the eastern part of Crete, causing discomfort and a food shortage, but what had really smashed Minoan civilization were several major earthquakes, over the period of a year or so, caused by the collapse of Thera's caldera. The quakes had shattered the physical remnants of Cretan and Kykladic civilization, brought all the buildings down, and also caused tidal waves that had destroyed coastal towns and wiped out the Cretan and Kykladic navies, galleys drawn up on the beach.

The earthquakes spared most of mainland Greece. And without the navies of Crete to keep them down, the first of the Greek heroes began to carve their bloody paths into legend.

In the half hour it took me to jump upStream the Trojan War was fought and lost; the Dorians had swarmed into Greece and, with their systematic but orderly butchery, put an end to the chaos of the Age of Heroes; and the refugees from these new series of wars, the Pelasgians/Philistines/Peoples of the Sea, had swept south and east to be flattened by the Egyptians and in turn to flatten the Israelites.

Thera, its remaining treasures buried under tons of ash, remained uninhabited. It would keep a bad reputation, and there would still be eruptions and quakes. Eventually Plato would hear of it and write of the Round Isle of Atlantis—a curious rendering of Strongyli, one of the island's names—but he'd lose a decimal point somewhere and speak of Atlantis having existed nine thousand years before, instead of nine hundred.

Not hard to do, if you're calculating in pre-Arabic numerals.

I looked involuntarily into the back of the time box, seeing the fresco waiting for the light, as fresh as it had been when the Kykladic culture that produced it had been alive… The time of innocence and joy symbolized by those happy children was over. By now their descendents were a barbarized, conquered people, their artifacts buried, their light extinguished. The fresco of those two happy children playing on the beach was all that remained of what they once had been, until in three thousand years archaeologists began to recover some long-dead artifacts.

Suddenly I could see stars through the windows. I had completed my jump upStream.

Winds began buffeting the box and I reached for the controls to stabilize it. Below was a jagged claw of an island, all that remained of Thera now that the caldera had collapsed. Supported by the a-grav units, I was floating above dark, low, lazy rollers highlighted by a pale sheen of moonlight.

Down on the water, a half mile distant, I saw a beacon flash. A gust of wind caught the box and spun it, but I kept the beacon in sight as I corrected, and began to head for it.

I hovered above a small motor yacht, sixty feet long. Aft of the pilot house, the deck had been modified to take a helicopter, a-grav unit, or—not surprisingly—a home-made time box such as mine. I turned on my landing spots and brought the box down. I waited. I kept the landing lights on so that anyone inside would do so with dazzled eyes.

A figure came strolling aft from the pilot house. I caught moonlight glinting on blonde hair. As I opened the door of the box, she said, "Did you get it?"

I wondered who she was. Scorsese's patron? Navigator? Lover? I'd never know.

I shot her with Scorsese's pistol and then moved out of the time box and into the empty pilot house. I searched the rest of the yacht and found no one else. Nor, unfortunately, did I find a stack of lost Leonardos. I discovered that Scorsese slept with a gun under his pillow, and that his companion—who had separate quarters—favored satin sheets and Chanel.

There was also an enormously powerful time-travel rig, powered by the same heavy-duty fusion unit that provided more power than a sailing yacht would need by more than a factor of a thousand, capable of moving the entire boat back and forth thousands of years. It was a setup any major university would envy, and not a few governments.

Stashed in convenient places I found a lot of nice weaponry. All the serial numbers were burned off with acid, which was useless now because we had techniques that could read the numbers-that-were; but I appreciated Scorsese's classical approach to these things. It showed he cared.

I searched Scorsese's companion for I.D. and found none, then fingerprinted her on the off chance she was a Famous Time Criminal for whom someone might be looking. She was around thirty, dressed with elegance in casual dark clothes. She looked as if she might have been fun to be around.

She also looked somewhat familiar. I looked down at her for a moment, wondering where I'd seen her before, and then decided that she might resemble someone I'd seen in 1453 C.E. or 312 B.C.E. or on the hilltop overlooking Tyre when I'd watched Alexander lead the Silver Shields across the mole. It didn't matter. Faces repeated themselves through history. Traveling through the past, I'd always been seeing people I thought I'd recognized. It was pointless trying to keep track of them all.

I didn't want to share the yacht with a dead body, so I weighted her down and threw her overboard.

Dawn had appeared above Thera's craggy face while I had been searching. The view was somewhat disorienting: it was certainly no longer the Round Isle that I had been guarding, but it wasn't quite the modern island of Santorini, either. What would become the island of Therasia had not yet split off from the main island of Thera, and the Burnt Islands of Palea Kameni and Nea Kameni—in reality new volcanic cones growing up from the bottom of the submerged caldera—had not yet risen to the surface.

The yacht sat in the only part of the bay shallow enough for anchoring, in the inner bend of Therasia, very close to shore. I was virtually surrounded by the encircling cliffs that rose in startling majesty from the deep bay. They were striped in red, black, and pale white, and where the rising sun touched the cliffs of Therasia just to the west of me the dawn brightened and stained them so that the cliffs looked as if they were slashed and bleeding. Matching the stain on my hands, which I washed in the yacht's galley, and matching as well the color of my thoughts, which I let stand.

I jumped the yacht upStream forty hours, two nights hence, then locked everything down, put the keys in my pocket, and slept in a stateroom till dawn, a small arsenal sharing the neighboring bunk. I had a lot to think about, and I wanted to be rested when I did the thinking.

I slept very well indeed.

In the morning I took the first shower I'd had in over six months, then made myself coffee and breakfast and thought for a long moment about my good friend Alpha.

In the months since I'd been living on Thera I'd done a lot of reading in Greek mythology, and I'd noticed the prevalence of twins. There were a lot of them: Proetus and Acrisius, Castor and Polydeukes, Helen and Clytemaestra, Herakles and Iphikles, Eteokles and Polyneikes, Bellerophon and Bellerus, to name just a few. In many cases one of the twins was immortal and the other fully human, and quite often the mortal twin had to die before the godhood of his brother was proclaimed. Castor and Polydeukes had arranged to share immortality on alternate days, but the other settlements had not seemed so equitable. Often the divine twin had a hand in the death of his brother. It was clear that battle had to be done with the mortal half of one's own self, before the freedom that was godhood could be released.

I began to think about my twin. He had not been nice to me, had acted in fact like so many of those bad twins of mythology. It seemed to me that he shouldn't be allowed to get away with it. I had as great a claim to godhood as he did.

My first idea, that of becoming a time criminal, was easily dismissed. Alpha himself had suggested it, but there were problems. I didn't have enough contacts in the criminal world, and furthermore I didn't relish having to go up against my own team. I knew how ruthless the Time Corps was. From a simple survival standpoint it wasn't a good idea.

Second thought. I could head back four hundred years minus a month or two, kill Alpha, and take his place, thus solving all my problems and satisfying the demands of mythology at the same time. I found the idea unsatisfactory.

There existed, for one thing, the slight but definitely non-zero possibility that Alpha might kill me.

For another, simply *killing* Alpha wasn't good enough.

I wanted to make him suffer first.

Third idea: I could float through history for a while, perform some minor time thefts, and then arrange that the Time Corps discover evidence connecting Alpha with the crimes. This idea had its appeal, but had the misfortune of incriminating myself as well as Alpha.

Fourth idea: I could return to Alpha's time, capture him, and strand him somewhere in the past, the Age of Heroes, say. Let him become a minor character in Homer.

That struck me as the best idea yet. I pictured him wandering about the Peloponnese, struggling to learn archaic Greek and jumping into ditches to avoid the chariots of the heroes who were racing hither and yon on errands of murder and savagery.

It seemed an appropriate punishment for being a bad twin to strand him in a place where the other bad twins could take care of him. Alpha might end up responsible for a whole new myth cycle: the wandering SEAL.

And then, as I drank my third cup of coffee and wandered mentally through fantasies of revenge, one of those stray memories, unconnected to anything in my conscious thoughts, suddenly broke surface in my mind, and I remembered where I'd seen Scorsese's lady friend before.

I went to the pilot house, spent some time working out the controls, then weighed anchor and piloted the yacht out of the bay, through the deep channel—narrower than in my own time— between Therasia and Apronisi. Once away from the island, I set the autopilot to take us on a fast sweep in the general direction of Cyrenaica and spent the rest of the day methodically searching every piece of paper on the yacht, finding very little.

I did, however, find a twenty-first century map of western Greece, with a course worked on it that led into the northern entrance to the Bay of Navarino, and with some temporal coordinates marked onto it: 23:01:01, November 11, 1699 C.E.

Eleventh hour, eleventh day, eleventh month. Thieves with a sense of history. Hoodlums in general seemed to be improving.

I spent the next three days cruising in autopilot circles halfway between Kithera and Malta, well out of sight of land where no contemporary navigator would dare venture, while I went through every file I could dig out of the yacht's computer. It was all coded, of course, but the Time Corps had taught me a number of classified and for the most part highly illegal skills, and by the end of that time I'd cracked the file open.

I found that the yacht was called *Simon's Folly* and belonged to a Honduran holding company controlled principally by an interlocking directorate chartered in TanUganda, the seats of the directorate held both by private individuals and representatives of financial institutions scattered hopelessly throughout the world. The current owners were also the sixth group in four years. The papers on the boat were almost impossible to trace. No help there.

I didn't find out who Simon was, either

I did, on the other hand, recover the codes for a dozen numbered bank accounts in places like Tobago, Singapore, and the Republic of Thule. It appeared that Scorsese had a bad memory for numbers, and had to keep them in his computer files, the ones he thought were secure.

Better and better.

I moved the fresco to more spacious quarters in the yacht's cargo bay, and then jumped upStream. It took eight subjective days to reach my own present, battling the Stream currents all the way. Moving an individual costs much less energy and effort that moving a whole yacht, which is why the Theran salvage team was going the easy way, letting the Stream currents assist the move—but I had no choice. I lived, bored out of my skull in the self-contained environment of Scorsese's time box, the yacht itself not being airtight. I'd seen prison cells that were bigger. I ate canned food and kept myself amused with isometric exercises and thoughts of revenge.

I tried reading Sophocles' Theban trilogy, two plays rescued from oblivion by the Time Authority's scholars and the *Seven Against*

Thebes that had survived on its own, but the plays were about a family that went to hell, and brothers who killed each other, and I didn't want to think about that subject at all.

There was nothing else to read. All Scorsese had were magazines written in Italian, which I don't read, and adding to the frustration was the fact that most of the magazines were filled with crossword puzzles. The near-naked women illustrating the puzzle books, however. provided some consolation.

Once happily in the twenty-first century, I spent some time on the radiotelephone and made several calls to Tobago, Singapore, et cetera. I presented the codes and quietly transferred all funds to new accounts, then wiped all record of the transactions from the computer.

However this came out, I was going to be rich.

Then I routed a telephone call through several satellites and through Gibraltar, Tientsin, Aden, Nairobi, and Salt Lake City, which I hoped would confuse anyone trying to trace it. "Extension two one nine," I said, and hoped the right man would pick up.

"Macintyre," a voice said.

"Mac," I said. "Do you recognize the sound of my voice?"

The answer came after a long pause: the signal was being routed through so many satellites and exchanges it was taking nearly three seconds for my words to get to New York.

"Yes," Macintyre said. I pictured him in his wheelchair at the Time Corps regional office in New York, his beefy face lit by humming data banks.

"I need to vet some prints," I said, "but the query can't go into the record."

"Can't do it," Macintyre said, again after a long delay. His voice was Scots, modified by years of living in America. "You know I have to log every inquiry," he said. "Records go to about a dozen different departments."

"I also know," I said, "that you were one of the best time agents in the Corps, and that you know ways to make log entries disappear." I tried to put all the urgency in the world into my voice. "This is very important, Mac. It's Scorsese. "

There next silence was longer than it had to be. "Do you have the bastard?" he asked.

"Yes," I said. "Just about."

"Call back in thirty minutes. My supervisor will be out to lunch by then."

I routed the next call through Berlin, Hong Kong, Beirut, Baku, Darwin, and Bogota. There must have been B's in my mind for some reason.

"Macintyre," said the voice.

"This is Valli," I said. "Do you have my information?"

"No need for phony names," he said. "Just send me the prints, okay?" He sounded edgy.

I passed the scanner over the prints I'd taken, then waited for Macintyre's confirmation that he'd received them.

"Running," he said, and then, "I have positive I.D."

I tapped the yacht's computer. "Ready for download," I said.

I watched the file load into memory, and then I thanked Macintyre.

"Just nail Scorsese for me," he said, and hung up.

Again I pictured him in the little blank-walled duty room, a red-faced, thick-necked man in a wheelchair, putting on weight now that he wasn't as active as once he'd been.

Once he'd been an athlete, a star rugby player.

For the last twelve years he'd been pissing into a plastic bag because of the bullet Scorsese had put into his spine in Florence.

I called up the dossier and paged through it. The woman's name was Kaetie Verberne, and she was an investment counselor in Amsterdam.

I had seen her once before, on the arm of Gautier de La Tour, the comptroller-general of the International Time Authority at The Hague.

Time theft gets a lot of attention from the press, but the most sophisticated form of time crime is not theft, but investment. Once a time criminal can acquire some of the local currency—by unloading an art treasure stolen a few centuries earlier, say—he can put the money into places where he knows it will increase. Then he can take the money, buy another art treasure with it, and repeat the whole procedure until he's got enough money to live happily ever after.

In general, this brand of criminal only gets caught if he gets too greedy and calls attention to himself. The Corps doesn't have the personnel to police every investment market throughout history.

Gautier de La Tour appeared often in the tabloids, because he was a photogenic man with striking blue eyes and a halo of white hair, because he was a prominent bachelor and a very wealthy man I began to wonder if he'd inherited his money from himself.

The office of comptroller-general of the Time Authority handles disbursement of all the Corps' funds, for all periods, in all currencies. The comptroller-general doesn't have access to the operational side, but he provides funds for operations and thus was in a good position to guess where the operations would be, the better to avoid them.

If de La Tour was a time criminal, he might also have partners high in the Time Corps. I couldn't trust anyone even in my own outfit.

Except maybe one person.

I took the Folly into Malta and bought some supplies and a lot of reading material in languages I understood. All light reading, nothing about family tragedies or twins or brothers who kill each other. Then I took the Folly one week downStream and entered Palermo, where I checked into a hotel with an attached gym and spent a week getting myself into good physical condition. I rented a welding rig and spent some time making modifications to the back of the time box.

I also sent out six letters to some people I thought I could trust, with other letters enclosed and a note to mail them to the addressees enclosed if I hadn't contacted them in the next month. De La Tour might have a hard time stopping six letters from reaching six different people, or so I hoped.

Then I headed back to Thera and the thirteenth century B.C.E.

There, two hundred years following the island's destruction, I anchored for another week and got myself into shape again. I ran daily, worked out, did a lot of target practice. I was ready.

I took the time box back to 1461, at the end of July. I landed at night, high on the volcano at four in the morning, when Alpha would most likely be sound asleep—we had been taught that people sleep most soundly just before dawn. I told the time box to meet me in a few days, then watched as it winked out of sight. I found a good observation post and settled in.

I covered one area of the island thoroughly, then dropped back in time to cover another. I played it cautiously, not wanting to go into buildings on the chance he might be there, and after six days of subjective searching I found him.

He was leaving Agia Therasia on his patrol, still doing his job, keeping the principal sites under guard. Perhaps he was scared not to.

I followed him for three days. He did not seem a happy man. He looked as if he had lost weight, and he had developed a new nervous twitch, always looking over his shoulder. He was staying in shape and doing a lot of target practice and martial arts, but his exercises seemed to lack conviction.

Twice I trailed him to the villa. He worked a lot with his notebook and a pocket computer, obviously trying to find a way to go downStream and edit me without losing Scorsese in the process. He seemed very uncertain.

Once I left him there and went through Agia Therasia to find where he was living. He'd rigged some booby traps, but I knew myself well enough to look for them and had no trouble. He was living in the three-storey Minoan complex, where he had a good view of the town. He had found a bed that fit him—evidently there was a Minoan giant in residence—but his belongings were disorganized, scattered around in a random way, as if his morale was suffering.

At least he had indoor toilets.

I had worked out a number of ways to get to him, but in the end I went into the Minoan building when he was away and drugged his water supply. After he was out I disarmed him, cuffed his hands, took his chronometer, cuffed his feet to his bed, and made some coffee for when he woke up. His eyelids began to twitch, and then they cracked open. When they focused on me I gave him a nod.

"You'll notice," I said, "that I don't call you Fubar."

"Piss off," he said, without conviction, and shut his eyes again.

"I'd drink this coffee if I were you," I said. "We've got a lot to talk about." He shook his head to clear it, then opened his eyes again, staring at me uncertainly from beneath his eyebrows, and reached his cuffed hands toward me. I handed him the coffee mug. He sipped it noisily.

I waited patiently for caffeine and adrenaline to burn the drug away. Alpha looked at me levelly over the rim of the mug, saying nothing. Even considering the drug, he was more relaxed than seemed reasonable. He was slumped back against the wall behind his bed, perfectly at ease, showing no apprehension or curiosity. I began to wonder whether he had some trap set for me, but then I realized that what he was feeling was relief.

The worst had happened. He didn't have to worry any more.

"You'll be pleased to know," I said, "that I've been following your advice. I've become a time criminal—a fairly modest one, but successful. I've stolen a number of pieces, and I've stowed them in places where they're sure to turn up sooner or later. They're hidden in places traceable to me, with my—our—fingerprints on them.

"Only *I* know where they're hidden. Therefore, only *I* am able to remove the evidence and prevent myself from being arrested, sooner or later, in our own time."

I paused and made sure that I had his attention. It seemed to me that I did.

"Get it straight," I said, "you're not ever going back to our own time. If you did, you'd be arrested and tried by our friends, and the only way to explain how the evidence got there is to explain our duplication, and then they'd nail you for *that.*"

I gave him a thin smile. "*You* know what they're like," I said.

"You have plans for me, I assume," Alpha said. "Otherwise you wouldn't be here."

So I told him. He listened carefully, scratching the bristles on his chin, and when I was done, he nodded. "I agree," he said.

I thought he might.

"It may occur to you," I said, "that the time thieves may make you a better offer than I have. I don't think they'll take a shine to you. Even if they help you get rid of me your status will make them nervous, and it won't be long before they edit you."

"I guess," he said.

"Think about it," I said. "You'll see I'm right."

He said nothing, but I think he agreed with me.

I cuffed his hands behind his back and then freed his feet. We left the town and moved up the slope of the volcano to where the time box would be waiting for us, then I strapped his chronometer to his shackled wrist, set coordinates, pressed his go-button, then jumped upStream myself.

I cuffed him to the back of the time box, to staples I'd welded there. I had a cot, food, and a portable toilet for him, and for the long ride to the nineteenth century C.E. he was only slightly less comfortable than I was.

I assumed that de La Tour had backup. Now, so did I.

I steamed the *Folly* around the Peloponnese and set the autopilot to make circles beyond the horizon, off the Bay of Navarino, where fifty years downStream Greek independence had been won by the last wooden fleet to fight under sail. Then I waited for night and flew the time box to land.

On Sphacteria, the island that filled the central mouth of the bay, the Athenian fleet and army had once trapped a Spartan army, forcing it to surrender and ending their claims to invincibility. A few miles farther inland the wise king Nestor had once built his palace and lived for five generations, until the Dorians burned the palace and drove him to exile in Athens. On the southern end of the bay, the Turks had watched from their giant Byzantine-built castle as their fleet was destroyed, and their rule in Greece ended.

Alpha and I intended to make a little history ourselves.

We looked like pinups for a mercenary journal, wearing brown-and-green camouflage body armor and tight-fitting caps pulled down over our hair. Our faces and hands were smeared with camouflage paint and our boots had camouflage spats. Our packs contained a three-day supply of water and concentrated rations for two weeks. On our belts were small personal communicators with an antenna that ran around our bodies, and connections for throat mics and for the mastoid receivers in our specs. I had a silenced pistol in my armpit and another in the small of my back, specs adjustable to day or night conditions, my rifle with its sniper attachments and self-powered night scope. I had knives on my belt, boot, and my left sleeve, and strangling wires threaded through my belt, collar, and bootlaces.

I was so deadly it was ridiculous.

Alpha was similarly equipped, minus the guns. And of course the fact his hands were cuffed behind his back tended to constrain his image.

We landed the time box on the night of November 4, 1899, in a grove of tall pine. There was a gusty wind blustering in from the west, bringing the scent of the sea to mingle with the brisk pine odor. I took a pistol and shoulder holster from the storage compartment, picked up Alpha's pack, and walked across the bed of pine needles to place them under a tree. Then I returned to the time box, drew one of my pistols, and pointed it at Alpha while I released his leg irons. Then I stepped backward, gestured him to the door, and with the pistol on him released his handcuffs.

He rubbed his wrists and locked at me resentfully over his shoulder.

"Was that absolutely necessary?" he asked.

"You'd know better than I would," I said. "There's your pistol and your pack over there. You have three days to get in shape and get used to the weapon. I'll be back at sunset, November 7, and I'll expect you to have a thorough knowledge of the terrain and conditions of the island. When I get back, I'll expect to see you reclining under that tree, with your pistol placed in plain sight at least ten feet away. Got that?"

He nodded. "You're not cutting me any slack, are you?" he asked. There was a forlorn sound to his voice.

I slammed the door and jumped four days into the past.

There I did much the same thing I had told Alpha to do. I sent the time box on ahead, then scouted Sphacteria thoroughly, took bearings on local landmarks and found the best places for observing the *Folly* on the night of November 11. The island was heavily timbered with pine and wild olive and the number of good observation points were few. I made a map of everything.

Then, using my chronometer, I jumped upStream to the night before I had planned to pick up Alpha. I slept, woke before dawn, and climbed a pine tree for the day.

I saw Alpha every now and again, moving among the other pines. He came into the clearing every so often, looking very much as I had seen him when he was back on Thera, when he was staring at the villa and trying to calculate all the options. In the end he walked into the clearing, dropped his pistol on the ground, and moved off by the tree where I told him I'd meet him. There I watched while he ate some dinner and then freshened his camouflage paint.

"Hello," I said.

He looked at me without expression. I dropped from the tree, repossessed his pistol, and spread out my map. "I've worked it all out," I said.

"Glad to hear it, sport," he said. I looked at him sharply. He was flashing a superior grin. He seemed to have his confidence back, which indicated to me that he'd made up his mind.

I wondered which way.

I cuffed him again, explained the plan, and jumped us both upStream to 2100 on the night of the 11th. I pocketed his chronometer and took off his handcuffs. "Your pistol will be behind that tree," I said, jumped downStream twenty hours, put the gun behind the tree, moved about a quarter mile to the east, and then jumped to nine o'clock on the night of the 11th again.

If Alpha had made up his mind to join the opposition, there was no point in making it easy for him.

The land breeze had come up, hissing seaward through the wild olives and tall evergreen. It would make this easier.

The theory and practice of obtaining backup through time travel, as practiced by the better class of crooks, is simple: one's earlier self, one's Alpha, heads upStream to a spot overlooking the site of the planned meeting, ambush, or suspected setup, and observes whatever it is that happens to one's later self, one's Beta. If it's bad, Alpha always has a chance to assist, and if it's very bad, he can always head downStream again, become Beta, and simply not show up, creating a paradox loop that might prove dangerous for other reasons but in any case escaping the trap.

It was, therefore, imperative for me and my own Alpha to eliminate any backup de La Tour had arranged, before the backup had a chance to tell de La Tour his meeting was going to end in disaster.

My chief worry at this point was whether Scorsese and de La Tour had arranged for a private signal to be exchanged between them prior to the meet. If so, de La Tour simply wouldn't show up, and this whole exercise would be for nothing.

Moving on beds of pine needles, I moved north, walking only when the sound of wind would cover my noises. My chronometer was set to move me instantly forty-four hours and twenty-three minutes into the past, in case I was spotted—I used an oddball number, hoping that a hypothetical enemy wouldn't guess it. When I wasn't looking through my specs I was peering into my night scope.

At first sight of the figure I thought he was Alpha. He was way out of position and that meant he had joined the enemy, and at the thought he was working for the bad guys, I felt anxiety begin to gnaw at my vitals.

And then my second look showed that the still figure in my specs didn't have the right silhouette to be Alpha, but was someone shorter and a little softer-looking, dressed in commando rig with a definite Time Corps flair.

Corps surplus, maybe, and maybe the backup was Corps surplus, too. I'd have to be careful.

I scanned the trees around the sentry and saw no one.

He was lying in a fine vantage point, sweeping the island and the sea below him with night binoculars. Once he turned and swept behind him, and I dodged behind a tree and hoped he hadn't caught the movement.

Just then I heard a voice from the mastoid receiver built into my specs.

"Beta." Alpha's voice, a little hushed. "Bandit at Station Seven. He got up to take a leak, and he stepped right into me. I had to kill him. Sorry."

"Check," I whispered. I didn't want to say anything more for fear my own bandit would hear.

Alpha and I had been taught sentry removal of course: moving slowly, synchronizing movement with the sentry's breathing, moving when the wind provided cover, trying to remember not to foul one's underwear while stalking an armed and dangerous enemy.

Lucky I didn't have to do any of that.

I simply jumped downStream three days, walked out to where the sentry stood, and jumped upStream to his own time. I put my foot on his wrist chronometer to keep him in the present and dropped my rifle butt, hard, on the back of his head.

He was a little shorter than I, with a thick neck and long arms. He looked like an athlete, a wrestler maybe, who had gone a little soft around the middle. I collected a radio on his belt, then I searched him, stripped him of weapons, cuffed his hands and feet, and put my hand to my throat mic to tell Alpha.

It suddenly occurred to me that if Alpha's sentry had been equipped similarly to this man, Alpha was now armed as well as I was, and had time travel capability to boot. I could be edited at any second. I spun around and went for my rifle.

"Hello, Fubar," said Alpha.

I froze. He was holding a pistol pointed at the center of my chest. He had a belt radio like the one on the guard I'd just hammered. There was a rifle strapped over his shoulder and a Corps-issue chronometer on his wrist. No need to guess how he got here.

Alpha's eyes looked at me soberly. "I wonder," he said, "how truthful you were when you told me about all those stolen objects you'd planted on me."

"I wouldn't lie about a thing like that," I said.

Alpha gave a little frown and rubbed his chin. "Maybe," he said. "But I'd like to think about it for a while. Keep your hands where I can see them while I meditate."

He squatted down on his heels near me. He cocked his head to one side, his eyes looking at me with wary consideration. "I could," he said, "get the truth out of you one way or another. "

"You wouldn't know if it's the truth," I said. "You could take me apart, and even then you wouldn't know for certain."

Alpha gave a thin smile and rubbed his chin with his left hand again. The pistol was very steady in his right. "Maybe," he said.

I looked down through the trees and saw the lights of the *Folly* out to sea, moving in to the rendezvous point. I wondered which of us was in the pilot house, Alpha or me.

The sentry I'd knocked out began to cough, then he started rolling from side to side. With my right hand, I reached into my breast pocket and pulled out a handkerchief. I reached for our prisoner. "I'd better gag him," I said "He might call his friends."

And then, while Alpha was still making up his mind about that one, his eyes on the white handkerchief in my right hand, I slapped the prisoner on the head with my left wrist, hitting the preset go-button with the prisoner's skull.

In the space of a breath I was forty-four hours and twenty-three minutes downStream.

My chronometer showed the exact second of departure. I moved about two paces to the southeast, drew the pistol from my armpit, set the chronometer for departure in two seconds, then readied the pistol.

I saw Alpha crouched in front of me, left hand still raised to scratch his chin

"Hello yourself," I said. "Please drop the pistol and raise your left hand high."

His shoulders sagged as the breath went out of him, and he did as he was told. I handcuffed his wrists to his ankles. Searched him carefully and disarmed him.

He looked over his shoulder at me. "I wouldn't have hurt you." he said. "The worst I would have done was strand you someplace while I found out whether you were telling the truth or not."

"Maybe," I said. Once I was certain he couldn't adjust his own chronometer, I set it for him, then I set the chronometer of the guy I'd knocked out, and then my own. "Hold your breath," I told Alpha, and then, after a long moment of transit, dawn exploded over the island. I blinked in the sudden light. It was August 28th, and the crystal ocean surged below us as the western rollers came in.

I took the chronometers from Alpha's wrist and from the wrist of the sentry. He looked up at me dully, then with increasing interest. Blood was smearing tine camouflage paint on his temple.

I addressed him in English. He looked at me blankly. I tried Dutch, German, demotic Greek, classical Greek, and classical Greek with the accent of the Kyklades, all without response.

"The hell with it," I said. "I think you speak English." I shot him in the foot.

"Jesus Christ!" he said. I glanced up and happened to meet Alpha's gaze. He grinned at me.

"Your friends aren't going to save you," I told our prisoner. "They've been taken care of. You're the sole survivor. What I want to know is the time and space coordinates for meeting de La Tour."

"Jesus Christ," the man said again. Sweat patterns were appearing in his paint.

"If I don't get the information very soon," I said, "I'm going to shoot you in the knee." I dropped the pistol on his knee, hard, and watched him jump. "And then," I went on, "if you still don't tell me what I want to know, I'll find someplace else to shoot you." I pointed the pistol at his crotch.

"Just in case what you tell me is a fib," I said, "I'll gag you, tie you up, and drag you off under a tree somewhere. I bet with a foot wound like that, and the summer heat here in August, dehydration will get you inside of twenty-four hours. Your friends won't know where to look for you, even if they feel inclined to come to help you."

My prisoner made a bubbling sound and looked frantically over his shoulder at Alpha.

"What the hell's going on?" he demanded. "He's not gonna actually do it, is he?" He looked up at me again, his eyes white as he strained his neck in my direction. "You wouldn't, would you?" he asked. "Not to a fellow Corpsman?"

Alpha gave a dry chuckle. I looked at him in surprise.

"I'd tell him if I were you," he said to our prisoner. "I'm his twin brother, and look what he's done to me."

The geek looked at me again, his eyes wider than ever, and I smiled at him. It was an effective smile, I knew.

Alpha had used it on *me*.

He looked at my smile and spilled everything he knew. His name was Hogan, and he was one of only two guards. De La Tour was floating overhead at 0300 on November 19, waiting for the code that would summon him down to pick up his men. He would have to get the code on two different frequencies before he'd come down, and he'd insist on seeing two bodyguards below him.

In the absence of an anti-aircraft missile, there seemed only one way of getting to him. I scratched my chin and looked up at Alpha.

"Up to you, sport," he shrugged.

I looked down at the sea. The Folly was getting closer, and I could see the faint outline of its cabin roof illuminated faintly by its running lights. Who was behind the wheel? I wondered. De La Tour or me? I decided what I was going to do.

"Back in a second," I said. I collected most of the weaponry—there was getting to be a lot of it—jumped upStream to the point where my own time box would meet me, and stored the excess in the box. Then I took the rifle and pistol Alpha had taken from the guard he'd killed and emptied them of ammunition. I jumped back to Alpha's time and undid his handcuffs.

"Here's your guns," I said. "They won't shoot, so don't try. Pick up Hogan here, and let's move inland."

Alpha got Hogan in a fireman carry and we moved up the spine of the island. We left Hogan bound and gagged under a tree, assured him the medics were on their way, and then Alpha preceded me to the high clearing above which, in another three weeks or so, de La Tour would hover, waiting for the signal to bring him down.

Still in the cover of the pines, I handcuffed Alpha again, then put his chronometer on and set it for the time when de La Tour would expect his call. I waited for Alpha to make his jump, then jumped directly behind Alpha a few seconds before he appeared, my pistol in one hand and the keys to the handcuffs in the other. I took Alpha's chronometer and unlocked his cuffs. He straightened. "How long did you give us?" he asked.

"About two minutes. Stay at least ten meters away from me, right?"

Ten meters is enough distance to be sure of bringing down a charging man with a pistol shot. Any closer, and there's a chance he'll hit you before you can squeeze the trigger.

The Alpha nodded and pulled his cap down lower over his forehead. "Let's go."

He unslung his empty rifle and walked with me into the clearing in the pines. De La Tour would only appear overhead for a few seconds, and he had to be given the codes then, otherwise he'd vanish. Never to return, possibly, or, as was more likely, to return with a dozen heavies who would edit all our work, and us with it.

I looked up. It was a clear night, only a high, light scud of cloud between me and the Milky Way. The vast spread of stars had altered since my last night on Thera—some of the old Greek constellations were a little less obvious—and though they shone several degrees brighter than in my own time, they were clearly less brilliant than they had been on old Thera. Atmospheric pollution had already had its effect in 1899, even here in rural, windswept Greece.

And suddenly there was a shadow thrown against the Milky Way, a time box hovering after its leap through the Stream, spinning in the warm land breeze. I raised the belt radio and pressed the send button.

"Seventeen Eighty-Nine," I mumbled.

Alpha raised his own radio. "Eighteen-Fifteen," he said.

It was a simple code, if a little Francocentric. No message at all meant run and don't stop. 1812 meant the jig is up, come get us, then run. 1940 meant run without picking us up. I wonder if de La Tour honestly expected anyone to send that last message.

The time box swept lower, and then its lights stabbed on. I blinked, my glasses polarizing themselves against the glare as I threw up an arm. De La Tour apparently had no qualms about creating a UFO above Navarino in 1899.

He was expecting to see two armed men in camouflage gear, and that was what he saw. His perspective was awkward, hovering a couple hundred yards above us, and he was also busy with controlling the time box in the high breeze. Probably after his initial glance at us, he was paying attention only to his landing.

He came down clumsily, fighting the breeze, then nearly going into the trees before he relocated himself over the clearing. He stabilized and then dropped the box toward the ground. Alpha and I, still holding our hands up to shield our eyes against the lights, began walking toward him.

The box hit the ground and the lights went off. I kept on walking. I heard the sound of a door opening, and then de La Tour stepped out.

I raised my pistol and pointed it directly between his startled, much-photographed blue eyes.

"Hi there, Fubar," I said, and from the corner of my eye I saw Alpha smile.

❂

The end, I thought, was quite cinematic. On the first of November, 1481 B.C.E., a couple dozen Time Corps transports appeared above the black sand beach near Agia Therasia. They lowered themselves to the ground, and their occupants piled out. The collection of Corpsmen, archaeologists, anthropologists, art experts, classicists, and historians had scant time to adjust to the staggering beauty of the place before they saw *Simon's Folly* tearing toward them at thirty knots.

I ended with an escort of hovercraft, and from the flybridge I waved to them as I executed a smart ninety-degree turn, then threw the engines in neutral and pushed the button that kicked the anchor overboard. I lowered myself down the companion and waited on the aft landing deck for my compatriots to arrive.

The first hovercraft touched lightly, and a man jumped out. He was a man I knew slightly, a Belgian paratrooper named Rabaut.

"I think," I told him, "that I'd like some Theran wine. It's been a while."

I had left Hogan and de La Tour bound and gagged upStream in 1899, and would give the Corps their coordinates so that they could be picked up. I hadn't wanted to be burdened with them during the long journey into the past, and besides I knew there was an active Time Corps court-martial board sitting regularly around 1860 or so, and that they would be happy to deal with Scorsese's friends.

I had also wanted to deal with Alpha quietly, without any witnesses. Hogan had seen him of course, but I would simply claim I'd duplicated myself temporarily in order to handle the situation on the island.

The Corps wouldn't inquire too closely. The military rarely investigates successful operations as carefully as they do the failures.

I tied Alpha up again as soon as we'd finished with de La Tour, and then jumped downStream to where I had Scorsese's time box waiting. I shackled Alpha where he belonged, then hopped to where the *Folly* was orbiting offshore, and on the night of the eleventh I took the yacht in for the meeting that never happened.

After waiting for an hour next to my rifle just in case something had gone horribly wrong, I took the *Folly* out to sea again, made myself a very good meal, drank a bottle of wine, and then locked myself in Scorsese's time box again for a ride of almost thirty centuries.

It was night again when the *Folly* splashed out of Stream 0200:01:01, June 1, 1255 B.C.E. I brought the boat in close to the sandbar north of the island, where the Athenian forces under Demosthenes would one day beat off Spartans under Brasidas, and then I let the anchor go. The splash and roar of the chain must have awakened every shepherd for miles: they'd never heard Poseidon so angry. It might cause some questions at the court of Nestor tomorrow morning, but I'd decided I'd rather disturb the shepherds' sleep than risk having the Folly drift aground in the Bronze Age.

I drew my pistol, readied it, and walked into the time box where Alpha was waiting. He looked up.

"Doesn't the condemned get a last meal?" he asked.

"No time," I said, and unshackled him from the wall, backed out of the time box, then gestured for him to come to the rail.

I had some equipment waiting for him: concentrated rations, a couple knives, a first aid kit, water purification tablets, and a pair of flashlights. "The Trojan War will heat up in another year or two," I said. "Pylos is just over those hills, and King Nestor will be needing soldiers. Remember all those presents everyone is always giving in the *Iliad*—you can gain status out there by the quality of your gifts. Those flashlights should get you far. So should the steel knives, if you want to part with them."

He opened the pack and looked at the knives. "Too bad we don't carry swords," he said.

"Your body armor should help, if you decide to get into the local military. And I expect you can make your living as a surgeon."

He didn't look enthusiastic. I didn't blame him.

Originally I'd planned to leave him in 1899; but then I realized what chaos could result when he started coming up with nonstick fry pans, sound cinema cameras, and television, not to mention what could happen if he started putting his mind to helping one side or other in the Great War. The Bronze Age was safer by far.

Alpha raised his head, looking toward the shore. "It's good to smell the land," he said, and meant goodbye.

He hit the water cleanly, shooting through the water like the dolphins in the fresco still battened in the *Folly's* hold, and then began a steady breast stroke, a slight phosphorescence trailing out behind him in the water. I watched his bobbing head until I lost it among the dark waves, and then moved to the bridge and hauled up the anchor readying myself for Thera and my moment of fame.

I wondered what sort of legend he'd leave behind him in his wanderings through that savage era. The legends are murky enough, and clarification by time travelers is necessarily circumspect. He might well have managed to carve his way to power, if that was the path he'd chosen, and become a figure of legend.

Only I could have stopped him, and I failed to work myself up to it: I knew all along I couldn't kill him. The conflict between us was always in terms of which of us would be destined to live in the past.

In which case it was I, not Alpha, who was the Bad Twin.

I had denied my brother Olympus, and condemned him to the life of a mortal.

THE GREEN LEOPARD PLAGUE

Kicking her legs out over the ocean, the lonely mermaid gazed out at the horizon from her perch in the overhanging banyan tree.

The air was absolutely still and filled with the scent of night flowers. Large fruit bats flew purposefully over the sea, heading for their daytime rest. Somewhere a white cockatoo gave a penetrating squawk. A starling made a brief flutter out to sea, then came back again. The rising sun threw up red-gold sparkles from the wavetops and brought a brilliance to the tropical growth that crowned the many islands spread out on the horizon.

The mermaid decided it was time for breakfast. She slipped from her hanging canvas chair and walked out along one of the banyan's great limbs. The branch swayed lightly under her weight, and her bare feet found sure traction on the rough bark. She looked down to see the deep blue of the channel, distinct from the turquoise of the shallows atop the reefs.

She raised her arms, poised briefly on the limb, the ruddy light of the sun glowing bronze on her bare skin, and then she pushed off and dove headfirst into the Philippine Sea. She landed with a cool impact and a rush of bubbles.

Her wings unfolded, and she flew away.

After her hunt, the mermaid—her name was Michelle—cached her fishing gear in a pile of dead coral above the reef, and then ghosted easily over the sea grass with the rippled sunlight casting patterns on her wings. When she could look up to see the colossal, twisted tangle that were the roots of her banyan tree, she lifted her head from the water and gulped her first breath of air.

The Rock Islands were made of soft limestone coral, and tide and chemical action had eaten away the limestone at sea level, undercutting the stone above. Some of the smaller islands looked like mushrooms, pointed green pinnacles balanced atop thin stems. Michelle's island was larger and irregularly shaped, but it still had steep limestone walls undercut six meters by the tide, with no obvious way for a person to clamber from the sea to the land. Her banyan perched on the saucer-edge of the island, itself undercut by the sea.

Michelle had arranged a rope elevator from her nest in the tree, just a loop on the end of a long nylon line. She tucked her wings away—they were harder to retract than to deploy, and the gills on the undersides were delicate—and then Michelle slipped her feet through the loop. At her verbal command, a hoist mechanism lifted her in silence from the sea and to her resting place in the bright green-dappled forest canopy.

She had been an ape once, a siamang, and she felt perfectly at home in the treetops.

During her excursion she had speared a yellowlip emperor, and this she carried with her in a mesh bag. She filleted the emperor with a blade she kept in her nest, and tossed the rest into the sea, where it became a subject of interest to a school of bait fish. She ate a slice of one fillet raw, enjoying the brilliant flavor, sea and trembling pale flesh together, then cooked the fillets on her small stove, eating one with some rice she'd cooked the previous evening and saving the other for later.

By the time Michelle finished breakfast the island was alive. Geckoes scurried over the banyan's bark, and coconut crabs sidled beneath the leaves like touts offering illicit downloads to tourists. Out in the deep water, a flock of circling, diving black noddies marked where a school of skipjack tuna was feeding on swarms of bait fish.

It was time for Michelle to begin her day as well. With sure, steady feet she moved along a rope walkway to the ironwood tree that held her satellite uplink in its crown, and then straddled a limb, took her deck from the mesh bag she'd roped to the tree, and downloaded her messages.

There were several journalists requesting interviews—the legend of the lonely mermaid was spreading. This pleased her more often than not, but she didn't answer any of the queries. There was a message from Darton, which she decided to savor for a while before opening. And then she saw a note from Dr. Davout, and opened it at once.

Davout was, roughly, twelve times her age. He'd actually been carried for nine months in his mother's womb, not created from scratch in a nanobed like almost everyone else she knew. He had a sib who was a famous astronaut, and a McEldowney Prize for his *Lavoisier and His Age,* and a red-haired wife who was nearly as well-known as he was. Michelle, a couple years ago, had attended a series of his lectures at the College of Mystery, and been interested despite her specialty being, strictly speaking, biology.

He had shaved off the little goatee he'd worn when she'd last seen him, which Michelle considered a good thing. "I have a research project for you, if you're free," the recording said. "It shouldn't take too much effort."

Michelle contacted him at once. He was a rich old bastard with a thousand years of tenure and no notion of what it was to be young in these times, and he'd pay her whatever outrageous fee she asked.

Her material needs at the moment were few, but she wouldn't stay on this island forever.

Davout answered right away. Behind him, working at her own console, Michelle could see his red-haired wife Katrin.

"Michelle!" Davout said, loudly enough for Katrin to know who called without turning around. "Good!" He hesitated, and then his fingers formed the mudra for <concern>. "I understand you've suffered a loss," he said.

"Yes," she said, her answer delayed by a second's satellite lag.

"And the young man—?"

"Doesn't remember."

Which was not exactly a lie, the point being what was remembered.

Davout's fingers were still fixed in <concern>. "Are you all right?" he asked.

Her own fingers formed an equivocal answer. "I'm getting better." Which was probably true.

"I see you're not an ape anymore."

"I decided to go the mermaid route. New perspectives, all that." And welcome isolation.

"Is there any way we can make things easier for you?"

She put on a hopeful expression. "You said something about a job?"

"Yes." He seemed relieved not to have to probe further—he'd had a realdeath in his own family, Michelle remembered, a chance-in-a-billion thing, and perhaps he didn't want to relive any part of that.

"I'm working on a biography of Terzian," Davout said.

"…And his Age?" Michelle finished.

"And his *Legacy*." Davout smiled. "There's a three-week period in his life where he—well, he drops right off the map. I'd like to find out where he went—and who he was with, if anyone."

Michelle was impressed. Even in comparatively unsophisticated times such as that inhabited by Jonathan Terzian, it was difficult for people to disappear.

"It's a critical time for him," Davout went on. "He'd lost his job at Tulane, his wife had just died—realdeath, remember—and if he decided he simply wanted to get lost, he would have all my sympathies." He raised a hand as if to tug at the chin-whiskers that were no longer there, made a vague pawing gesture, then dropped the hand. "But my problem is that when he resurfaces, everything's changed for him. In June he delivered an undistinguished paper at the Athenai conference in Paris, then vanishes. When he surfaced in Venice in mid-July, he didn't deliver the paper he was scheduled to read, instead he delivered the first version of his Cornucopia Theory."

Michelle's fingers formed the mudra <highly impressed>. "How have you tried to locate him?"

"Credit card records—they end on June 17, when he buys a lot of euros at American Express in Paris. After that he must have paid for everything with cash."

"He really *did* try to get lost, didn't he?" Michelle pulled up one bare leg and rested her chin on it. "Did you try passport records?"

<No luck> "But if he stayed in the European Community he wouldn't have had to present a passport when crossing a border."

"Cash machines?"

"Not 'til after he arrived in Venice, just a couple days prior to the conference."

The mermaid thought about it for a moment, then smiled. "I guess you need me, all right."

<I concur> Davout flashed solemnly. "How much would it cost me?"

Michelle pretended to consider the question for a moment, then named an outrageous sum.

Davout frowned. "Sounds all right," he said.

Inwardly Michelle rejoiced. Outwardly, she leaned toward the camera lens and looked businesslike. "I'll get busy, then."

Davout looked grateful. "You'll be able to get on it right away?"

"Certainly. What I need you to do is send me pictures of Terzian, from as many different angles as possible, especially from around that period of time."

"I have them ready."

"Send away."

An eyeblink later, the pictures were in Michelle's deck. <Thanks> she flashed. "I'll let you know as soon as I find anything."

At university Michelle had discovered that she was very good at research, and it had become a profitable sideline for her. People— usually people connected with academe in one way or another— hired her to do the duller bits of their own jobs, finding documents or references, or, in this case, three missing weeks out of a person's life. It was almost always work they could do themselves, but

Michelle was simply better at research than most people, and she was considered worth the extra expense. Michelle herself usually enjoyed the work—it provided interesting sidelights on fields about which she knew little, and provided a welcome break from routine.

Plus, this particular job required not so much a researcher as an artist, and Michelle was very good at this particular art.

Michelle looked through the pictures, most scanned from old photographs. Davout had selected well: Terzian's face or profile was clear in every picture. Most of the pictures showed him young, in his twenties, and the ones that showed him older were of high quality, or showed parts of the body that would be crucial to the biometric scan, like his hands or his ears.

The mermaid paused for a moment to look at one of the old photos: Terzian smiling with his arm around a tall, long-legged woman with a wide mouth and dark, bobbed hair, presumably the wife who had died. Behind them was a Louis Quinze table with a blaze of gladioli in a cloisonné vase, and above the table a large portrait of a stately looking horse in a heavy gilded frame. Beneath the table were stowed—temporarily, Michelle assumed—a dozen or so trophies, which to judge from the little golden figures balanced atop them were awarded either for gymnastics or martial arts. The opulent setting seemed a little at odds with the young, informally dressed couple: she wore a flowery tropical shirt tucked into khakis, and Terzian dressed in a tank top and shorts. There was a sense that the photographer had caught them almost in motion, as if they'd paused for the picture en route from one place to another.

Nice shoulders, Michelle thought. Big hands, well-shaped muscular legs. She hadn't ever thought of Terzian as young, or large, or strong, but he had a genuine, powerful physical presence that came across even in the old, casual photographs. He looked more like a football player than a famous thinker.

Michelle called up her character-recognition software and fed in all the pictures, then checked the software's work, something she was reasonably certain her employer would never have done if he'd been doing this job himself. Most people using this kind of canned software didn't realize how the program could be fooled, particularly when used with old media, scanned film prints heavy with grain and primitive digital images scanned by machines that simply weren't very bright. In the end, Michelle and software between them managed an excellent job of mapping Terzian's body and calibrating its precise ratios: the distance between the eyes, the length of nose and curve of lip, the distinct shape of the ears, the length of limb and trunk. Other men might share some of these biometric ratios, but none would share them all.

The mermaid downloaded the data into her specialized research spiders, and sent them forth into the electronic world.

A staggering amount of the trivial past existed there, and nowhere else. People had uploaded pictures, diaries, commentary, and video; they'd digitized old home movies, complete with the garish, deteriorating colors of the old film stock; they'd scanned in family trees, postcards, wedding lists, drawings, political screeds, and images of handwritten letters. Long, dull hours of security video. Whatever had meant something to someone, at some time, had been turned into electrons and made available to the universe at large.

A surprising amount of this stuff had survived the Lightspeed War—none of it had seemed worth targeting, or if trashed had been reloaded from backups.

What all this meant was that Terzian was somewhere in there. Wherever Terzian had gone in his weeks of absence—Paris, Dalmatia, or Thule—there would have been someone with a camera. In stills of children eating ice cream in front of Notre Dame, or moving through the video of buskers playing saxophone on the Pont des Artistes, there would be a figure in the background, and that figure would be Terzian. Terzian might be found lying on a beach in Corfu, reflected in a bar mirror in Gdynia, or negotiating with a prostitute in Hamburg's St. Pauli district—Michelle had found targets in exactly those places during the course of her other searches.

Michelle sent her software forth to find Terzian, then lifted her arms above her head and stretched—stretched fiercely, thrusting out her bare feet and curling the toes, the muscles trembling with tension, her mouth yawned in a silent shriek.

Then she leaned over her deck again, and called up the message from Darton, the message she'd saved 'til last.

"I don't understand," he said. "Why won't you talk to me? I love you!"

His brown eyes were a little wild.

"Don't you understand?" he cried. "I'm not dead! *I'm not really dead!*"

Michelle hovered three or four meters below the surface of Zigzag Lake, gazing upward at the inverted bowl of the heavens, the brilliant blue of the Pacific sky surrounded by the dark, shadowy towers of mangrove. Something caught her eye, something black and falling, like a bullet: and then there was a splash and a boil of bubbles, and the daggerlike bill of a collared kingfisher speared a blue-eyed apogonid that had been hovering over a bright red coral head. The kingfisher flashed its pale underside as it stroked to the surface, its wings doing efficient double duty as fins, and then there was a flurry of wings and feet and bubbles and the kingfisher was airborne again.

Michelle floated up and over the barrel-shaped coral head, then over a pair of giant clams, each over a meter long. The clams drew shut as Michelle slid over them, withdrawing the huge siphons as thick as her wrist. The fleshy lips that overhung the scalloped edges of the shells were a riot of colors, purples, blues, greens, and reds interwoven in an eye-boggling pattern.

Carefully drawing in her gills so their surfaces wouldn't be inflamed by coral stings, she kicked up her feet and dove beneath the mangrove roots into the narrow tunnel that connected Zigzag Lake with the sea.

Of the three hundred or so Rock Islands, seventy or thereabouts had marine lakes. The islands were made of coral limestone and porous to one degree or another: some lakes were connected to the ocean through tunnels and caves, and others through seepage. Many of the lakes contained forms of life unique in all the world, evolved distinctly from their remote ancestors: even now, after all this time, new species were being described.

During the months Michelle had spent in the islands she thought she'd discovered two undescribed species: a variation on the *Entacmaea medusivora* white anemone that was patterned strangely with scarlet and a cobalt-blue; and a nudibranch, deep violet with yellow polka-dots, that had undulated past her one night on the reef, flapping like a tea towel in a strong wind as a seven-knot tidal current tore it along. The nudi and samples of the anemone had been sent to the appropriate authorities, and perhaps in time Michelle would be immortalized by having a Latinate version of her name appended to the scientific description of the two marine animals.

The tunnel was about fifteen meters long, and had a few narrow twists where Michelle had to pull her wings in close to her sides and maneuver by the merest fluttering of their edges. The tunnel turned up, and brightened with the sun; the mermaid extended her wings and flew over brilliant pink soft corals toward the light.

Two hours' work, she thought, *plus a hazardous environment. Twenty-two hundred calories, easy.*

The sea was brilliantly lit, unlike the gloomy marine lake surrounded by tall cliffs, mangroves, and shadow, and for a moment Michelle's sun-dazzled eyes failed to see the boat bobbing on the tide. She stopped short, her wings cupping to brake her motion, and then she recognized the boat's distinctive paint job, a bright red meant to imitate the natural oil of the *cheritem* fruit.

Michelle prudently rose to the surface a safe distance away—Torbiong might be fishing, and sometimes he did it with a spear. The old man saw her, and stood to give a wave before Michelle could unblock her trachea and draw air into her lungs to give a hail.

"I brought you supplies," he said.

"Thanks." Michelle said as she wiped a rain of seawater from her face.

Torbiong was over two hundred years old and Paramount Chief of Koror, the capital forty minutes away by boat. He was small and wiry and black-haired, and had a broad-nosed, strong-chinned, unlined face. He had traveled over the world and off it while young, but returned to Belau as he aged. His duties as chief were mostly ceremonial, but counted for tax purposes; he had money from hotels and restaurants that his ancestors had built and that others managed for him, and he spent most of his time visiting his neighbors, gossiping, and fishing. He had befriended Darton and Michelle when they'd first come to Belau, and helped them in securing the permissions for their researches on the Rock Islands. A few months back, after Darton died, Torbiong had agreed to bring supplies to Michelle in exchange for the occasional fish.

His boat was ten meters long and featured a waterproof canopy amidships made from interwoven pandanas leaves. Over the scarlet faux-*cheritem* paint were zigzags, crosses, and stripes in the brilliant yellow of the ginger plant. The ends of the thwarts were decorated with grotesque carved faces, and dozens of white cowrie shells were glued to the gunwales. Wooden statues of the kingfisher bird sat on the prow and stern.

Thrusting above the pandanas canopy were antennae, flagpoles, deep-sea fishing rods, fish spears, radar, and a satellite uplink. Below the canopy, where Torbiong could command the boat from an elaborately carved throne of breadfruit-tree wood, were the engine and rudder controls, radio, audio, and video sets, a collection of large audio speakers, a depth finder, a satellite navigation relay, and radar. Attached to the uprights that supported the canopy were whistles tuned to make an eerie, discordant wailing noise when the boat was at speed.

Torbiong was fond of discordant wailing noises. As Michelle swam closer, she heard the driving, screeching electronic music that Torbiong loved trickling from the earpieces of his headset—he normally howled it out of speakers, but when sitting still he didn't want to scare the fish. At night she could hear Torbiong for miles, as he raced over the darkened sea blasted out of his skull on betel-nut juice with his music thundering and the whistles shrieking.

He removed the headset, releasing a brief audio onslaught before switching off his sound system.

"You're going to make yourself deaf," Michelle said.

Torbiong grinned. "Love that music. Gets that blood moving."

Michelle floated to the boat and put a hand on the gunwale between a pair of cowries.

"I saw that boy of yours on the news," Torbiong said. "He's making you famous."

"I don't want to be famous."

"He doesn't understand why you don't talk to him."

"He's dead," Michelle said.

Torbiong made a spreading gesture with his hands. "That's a matter of opinion."

"Watch your head," said Michelle.

Torbiong ducked as a gust threatened to bring him into contact with a pitcher plant that drooped over the edge of the island's overhang. Torbiong evaded the plant and then stepped to the bow to haul in his mooring line before the boat's canopy got caught beneath the overhang,

Michelle submerged and swam till she reached her banyan tree, then surfaced and called down her rope elevator. By the time Torbiong's boat hissed up to her, she'd folded away her gills and wings and was sitting in the sling, kicking her legs over the water.

Torbiong handed her a bag of supplies: some rice, tea, salt, vegetables, and fruit. For the last several weeks Michelle had experienced a craving for blueberries, which didn't grow here, and Torbiong had included a large package fresh off the shuttle, and a small bottle of cream to go with them. Michelle thanked him.

"Most tourists want corn chips or something," Torbiong said pointedly.

"I'm not a tourist." Michelle said. "I'm sorry I don't have any fish to swap—I've been hunting smaller game." She held out the specimen bag, still dripping seawater.

Torbiong gestured toward the cooler built into the back of his boat. "I got some *chai* and a *chersuuch* today," he said, using the local names for barracuda and mahi mahi.

"Good fishing."

"Trolling." With a shrug. He looked up at her, a quizzical look on his face. "I've got some calls from reporters," he said, and then his betel-stained smile broke out. "I always make sure to send them tourist literature."

"I'm sure they enjoy reading it."

Torbiong's grin widened. "You get lonely, now," he said, "you come visit the family. We'll give you a home-cooked meal."

She smiled. "Thanks."

They said their farewells and Torbiong's boat hissed away on its jets, the whistles building to an eerie, spine-shivering chord. Michelle rose into the trees and stashed her specimens and groceries. With a bowl of blueberries and cream, Michelle crossed the rope walkway to her deck, and checked the progress of her search spiders.

There were pointers to a swarm of articles about the death of Terzian's wife, and Michelle wished she'd given her spiders clearer instructions about dates.

The spiders had come up with three pictures. One was a not-very-well focused tourist video from July 10, showing a man standing in front of the Basilica di Santa Croce in Florence. A statue of Dante, also not in focus, gloomed down at him from beneath thick-bellied rain clouds. As the camera panned across him he stood with his back to the camera but turned to the right, one leg turned out as he scowled down at the ground—the profile was a little smeared, but the big, broad-shouldered body seemed right. The software reckoned there was a 78% chance the man was Terzian.

Michelle got busy refining the image, and after a few passes of the software decided the chances of the figure being Terzian were more on the order of 95%.

So maybe Terzian had gone on a Grand Tour of European cultural sites. He didn't look happy in the video, but then the day was cloudy and rainy and Terzian didn't have an umbrella.

And his wife had died, of course.

Now that Michelle had a date and a place she refined the instructions from her search spiders to seek out images from Florence a week either way from July 3, and then expand the search from there, first all Tuscany, then all Italy.

If Terzian was doing tourist sites, then she surely had him nailed.

The next two hits, from her earlier research spiders, were duds. The software gave a less than 50% chance of Terzian being in Lisbon or Cape Sounion, and refinements of the image reduced the chance to something near zero.

Then the next video popped up, with a time stamp right there in the image—Paris, June 26, 13:41:44 hours, just a day before Terzian bought a bankroll of Euros and vanished.

<Bingo!> Michelle's fingers formed.

The first thing Michelle saw was Terzian walking out of the frame—no doubt this time that it was him. He was looking over his shoulder at a small crowd of people. There was a dark-haired woman huddled on his arm, her face turned away from the camera. Michelle's heart warmed at the thought of the lonely widow Terzian having an affair in the City of Love.

Then she followed Terzian's gaze to see what had so drawn his attention. A dead man stretched out on the pavement, surrounded by hapless bystanders.

And then, as the scene slowly settled into her astonished mind, the video sang at her in the piping voice of Pan.

Terzian looked at his audience as anger raged in his backbrain. A wooden chair creaked, and the sound spurred Terzian to wonder how long the silence had gone on. Even the Slovenian woman who had been drowsing realized that something had changed, and blinked herself to alertness.

"I'm sorry," he said in French. "But my wife just died, and I don't feel like playing this game anymore."

His silent audience of seven watched as he gathered his papers, put them in his case, and left the lecture room, his feet making sharp, murderous sounds on the wooden floor.

Yet up to that point his paper had been going all right. He'd been uncertain about commenting on Baudrillard in Baudrillard's own country, and in Baudrillard's own language, a cheery compare-and-contrast exercise between Baudrillard's "the self does not exist" and Rorty's "I don't care," the stereotypical French and American answers to modern life. There had been seven in his audience, perched on creaking wooden chairs, and none of them had gone to sleep, or walked out, or condemned him for his audacity.

Yet, as he looked at his audience and read on, Terzian had felt the anger growing, spawned by the sensation of his own uselessness. Here he was, in the City of Lights, its every cobblestone a monument to European civilization, and he was in a dreary lecture hall on the Left Bank, reading to his audience of seven from a paper that was nothing more than a footnote, and a footnote to a footnote at that. To come to the land of *cogito ergo sum* and to answer, *I don't care?*

I came to Paris for this? he thought. *To read this* drivel? *I paid* for *the privilege of doing* this?

I do care, he thought as his feet turned toward the Seine. *Desiderio, ergo sum,* if he had his Latin right. I am in pain, and therefore I *do* exist.

He ended in a Norman restaurant on the Île de la Cité, with lunch as his excuse and the thought of getting hopelessly drunk not far from his thoughts. He had absolutely nothing to do until August, after which he would return to the States and collect his belongings from the servants' quarters of the house on Esplanade, and then he would go about looking for a job.

He wasn't certain whether he would be more depressed by finding a job or by not finding one.

You are alive, he told himself. *You are alive and in Paris with the whole summer ahead of you, and you're eating the cuisine of Normandy in the Place Dauphine. And if that isn't a command to be joyful, what is?*

It was then that the Peruvian band began to play. Terzian looked up from his plate in weary surprise.

When Terzian had been a child his parents—both university professors—had first taken him to Europe, and he'd seen then that every European city had its own Peruvian or Bolivian street band, Indians in black bowler hats and colorful blankets crouched in some public place, gazing with impassive brown eyes from above their guitars and reed flutes.

Now, a couple decades later, the musicians were still here, though they'd exchanged the blankets and bowler hats for European styles, and their presentation had grown more slick. Now they had amps, and cassettes and CDs for sale. Now they had congregated in the triangular Place Dauphine, overshadowed by the neo-classical mass of the Palais de Justice, and commenced a Latin-flavored medley of old Abba songs.

Maybe, after Terzian finished his veal in calvados sauce, he'd go up to the band and kick in their guitars.

The breeze flapped the canvas overhead. Terzian looked at his empty plate. The food had been excellent, but he could barely remember tasting it.

Anger still roiled beneath his thoughts. And—for God's *sake*—was that band now playing *Oasis*? Those chords were beginning to sound suspiciously like "Wonderwall." "Wonderwall" on Spanish guitars, reed flutes, and a mandolin.

Terzian had nearly decided to call for a bottle of cognac and stay here all afternoon, but not with that noise in the park. He put some euros on the table, anchoring the bills with a saucer against the fresh spring breeze that rattled the green canvas canopy over his head. He was stepping through the restaurant's little wrought-iron gate to the sidewalk when the scuffle caught his attention.

The man falling into the street, his face pinched with pain. The hands of the three men on either side who were, seemingly, unable to keep their friend erect.

Idiots, Terzian thought, fury blazing in him.

There was a sudden shrill of tires, of an auto horn.

Papers streamed in the wind as they spilled from a briefcase.

And over it all came the amped sound of pan pipes from the Peruvian band. *Wonderwall.*

Terzian watched in exasperated surprise as the three men sprang after the papers. He took a step toward the fallen man—*someone* had to take charge here. The fallen man's hair had spilled in a shock over his forehead and he'd curled on his side, his face still screwed up in pain.

The pan pipes played on, one distinct hollow shriek after another.

Terzian stopped with one foot still on the sidewalk and looked around at faces that all registered the same sense of shock. Was there a doctor here? he wondered. A *French* doctor? All his French seemed to have just drained from his head. Even such simple questions as *Are you all right?* and *How are you feeling?* seemed beyond him now. The first aid course he'd taken in his Kenpo school was *ages* ago.

Unnaturally pale, the fallen man's face relaxed. The wind floated his shock of thinning dark hair over his face. In the park, Terzian saw a man in a baseball cap panning a video camera, and his anger suddenly blazed up again at the fatuous uselessness of the tourist, the uselessness that mirrored his own.

Suddenly there was a crowd around the casualty, people coming out of stopped cars, off the sidewalk. Down the street, Terzian saw the distinctive flat-topped kepis of a pair of policemen bobbing toward them from the direction of the Palais de Justice, and felt a surge of relief. Someone more capable than this lot would deal with this now.

He began, hesitantly, to step away. And then his arm was seized by a pair of hands and he looked in surprise at the woman who had just huddled her face into his shoulder, cinnamon-dark skin and eyes invisible behind wraparound shades.

"Please," she said in English a bit too musical to be American. "Take me out of here."

The sound of the reed pipes followed them as they made their escape.

He walked her past the statue of the Vert Galant himself, good old lecherous Henri IV, and onto the Pont Neuf. To the left, across the Seine, the Louvre glowed in mellow colors beyond a screen of plane trees.

Traffic roared by, a stampede of steel unleashed by a green light. Unfocused anger blazed in his mind. He didn't want this woman attached to him, and he suspected she was running some kind of scam. The gym bag she wore on a strap over one shoulder kept banging him on the ass. Surreptitiously he slid his hand into his right front trouser pocket to make sure his money was still there.

Wonderwall, he thought. Christ.

He supposed he should offer some kind of civilized comment, just in case the woman was genuinely distressed.

"I suppose he'll be all right," he said, half-barking the words in his annoyance and anger.

The woman's face was still half-buried in his shoulder. "He's dead," she murmured into his jacket. "Couldn't you tell?"

For Terzian death had never occurred under the sky, but shut away, in hospice rooms with crisp sheets and warm colors and the scent of disinfectant. In an explosion of tumors and wasting limbs and endless pain masked only in part by morphia.

He thought of the man's pale face, the sudden relaxation.

Yes, he thought, *death came with a sigh.*

Reflex kept him talking. "The police were coming," he said. "They'll—they'll call an ambulance or something."

"I only hope they catch the bastards who did it," she said.

Terzian's heart gave a jolt as he recalled the three men who let the man fall, and then dashed through the square for his papers. For some reason all he could remember about them were their black laced boots, with thick soles.

"Who were they?" he asked blankly.

The woman's shades slid down her nose, and Terzian saw startling green eyes narrowed to murderous slits. "I suppose they think of themselves as cops," she said.

Terzian parked his companion in a café near Les Halles, within sight of the dome of the Bourse. She insisted on sitting indoors, not on the sidewalk, and on facing the front door so that she could scan whoever came in. She put her gym bag, with its white Nike swoosh, on the floor between the table legs and the wall, but Terzian noticed she kept its shoulder strap in her lap, as if she might have to bolt at any moment.

Terzian kept his wedding ring within her sight. He wanted her to see it; it might make things simpler.

Her hands were trembling. Terzian ordered coffee for them both. "No," she said suddenly. "I want ice cream."

Terzian studied her as she turned to the waiter and ordered in French. She was around his own age, twenty-nine. There was no question that she was a mixture of races, but *which* races? The flat nose could be African or Asian or Polynesian, and Polynesia was again suggested by the black, thick brows. Her smooth brown complexion could be from anywhere but Europe, but her pale green eyes were nothing but European. Her broad, sensitive mouth suggested Nubia. The black ringlets yanked into a knot behind her head could be African or East Indian or, for that matter, French. The result was too striking to be beautiful—and also too striking, Terzian thought, to be a successful criminal. Those looks could be too easily identified.

The waiter left. She turned her wide eyes toward Terzian, and seemed faintly surprised that he was still there.

"My name's Jonathan," he said.

"I'm," hesitating, "Stephanie."

"Really?" Terzian let his skepticism show.

"Yes." She nodded, reaching in a pocket for cigarettes. "Why would I lie? It doesn't matter if you know my real name or not."

"Then you'd better give me the whole thing."

She held her cigarette upward, at an angle, and enunciated clearly. "Stephanie América Pais e Silva."

"America?"

Striking a match. "It's a perfectly ordinary Portuguese name."

He looked at her. "But you're not Portuguese."

"I carry a Portuguese passport."

Terzian bit back the comment, *I'm sure you do.*

Instead he said, "Did you know the man who was killed?"

Stephanie nodded. The drags she took off her cigarette did not ease the tremor in her hands.

"Did you know him well?"

"Not very." She dragged in smoke again, then let the smoke out as she spoke.

"He was a colleague. A biochemist."

Surprise silenced Terzian. Stephanie tipped ash into the Cinzano ashtray, but her nervousness made her miss, and the little tube of ash fell on the tablecloth.

"Shit," she said, and swept the ash to the floor with a nervous movement of her fingers.

"Are you a biochemist, too?" Terzian asked.

"I'm a nurse." She looked at him with her pale eyes. "I work for Santa Croce—it's a—"

"A relief agency." A Catholic one, he remembered. The name meant *Holy Cross.*

She nodded.

"Shouldn't you go to the police?" he asked. And then his skepticism returned. "Oh, that's right—it was the police who did the killing."

"Not the *French* police." She leaned across the table toward him. "This was a different sort of police, the kind who think that killing someone and making an arrest are the same thing. You look at the television news tonight. They'll report the death, but there won't be any arrests. Or any suspects." Her face darkened, and she leaned back in her chair to consider a new thought. "Unless they somehow manage to blame it on me."

Terzian remembered papers flying in the spring wind, men in heavy boots sprinting after. The pinched, pale face of the victim.

"Who, then?"

She gave him a bleak look through a curl of cigarette smoke. "Have you ever heard of Transnistria?"

Terzian hesitated, then decided "No" was the most sensible answer.

"The murderers are Transnistrian." A ragged smile drew itself across Stephanie's face. "They're intellectual property police. They killed Adrian over a copyright."

At that point the waiter brought Terzian's coffee along with Stephanie's order. Hers was colossal, a huge glass goblet filled with pastel-colored ice creams and fruit syrups in bright primary colors, topped by a mountain of cream and a toy pinwheel on a candy-striped stick. Stephanie looked at the creation in shock, her eyes wide.

"I love ice cream," she choked, and then her eyes brimmed with tears and she began to cry.

Stephanie wept for a while, across the table, and between sobs choked down heaping spoonfuls of ice cream, eating in great gulps, and swiping at her lips and tear-stained cheeks with a paper napkin.

The waiter stood quietly in the corner, but from his glare and the set of his jaw it was clear that he blamed Terzian for making the lovely woman cry.

Terzian felt his body surge with the impulse to aid her, but he didn't know what to do. Move around the table and put an arm around her? Take her hand? Call someone to take her off his hands?

The latter, for preference.

He settled for handing her a clean napkin when her own grew sodden.

His skepticism had not survived the mention of the Transnistrian copyright police. This was far too bizarre to be a con—a scam was based on basic human desire, greed or lust, not something as abstract as intellectual property. Unless there was a gang who made a point of targeting academics from the States, luring them with a tantalizing hook about a copyright worth murdering for...

Eventually the storm subsided. Stephanie pushed the half-consumed ice cream away, and reached for another cigarette.

He tapped his wedding ring on the table top, something he did when thinking. "Shouldn't you contact the local police?" he asked. "You know something about this...death." For some reason he was reluctant to use the word *murder*. It was as if using the word would make something true, not the killing itself but his relationship to the killing... To call it murder would grant it some kind of power over him.

She shook her head. "I've got to get out of France before those guys find me. Out of Europe, if I can, but that would be hard. My passport's in my hotel room, and they're probably watching it."

"Because of this copyright."

Her mouth twitched in a half-smile. "That's right."

"It's not a literary copyright, I take it."

She shook her head, the half-smile still on her face.

"Your friend was a biologist." He felt a hum in his nerves, a certainty that he already knew the answer to the next question.

"Is it a weapon?" he asked.

She wasn't surprised by the question. "No," she said. "No, just the opposite." She took a drag on her cigarette and sighed the smoke out. "It's an antidote. An antidote to human folly."

"Listen," Stephanie said. "Just because the Soviet Union fell doesn't mean that *Sovietism* fell with it. Sovietism is still there—the only difference is that its moral justification is gone, and what's left is violence and extortion disguised as law enforcement and taxation. The old empire breaks up, and in the West you think it's great, but more countries just meant more palms to be greased—all throughout the former Soviet empire you've got more 'inspectors' and 'tax collectors,' more 'customs agents' and 'security directorates' than there ever were under the Russians. All these people do is prey on their own populations, because no one else will do business with them unless they've got oil or some other resource that people want."

"Trashcanistans," Terzian said. It was a word he'd heard used of his own ancestral homeland, the former Soviet Republic of Armenia, whose looted economy and paranoid, murderous, despotic Russian puppet regime was supported only by millions of dollars sent to the country by Americans of Armenian descent, who thought that propping up the gang of thugs in power somehow translated into freedom for the fatherland.

Stephanie nodded. "And the worst Trashcanistan of all is Transnistria."

She and Terzian had left the café and taken a taxi back to the Left Bank and Terzian's hotel. He had tuned the television to a local station, but muted the sound until the news came on. Until then the station showed a rerun of an American cop show, stolid, businesslike detectives underplaying their latest sordid confrontation with tragedy.

The hotel room hadn't been built for the queen-sized bed it now held, and there was an eighteen-inch clearance around the bed and no room for chairs. Terzian, not wanting Stephanie to think he wanted to get her in the sack, perched uncertainly on a corner of the bed, while Stephanie disposed herself more comfortably, sitting cross-legged in its center.

"Moldova was a Soviet republic put together by Stalin," she said. "It was made up of Bessarabia, which was a part of Romania that Stalin chewed off at the beginning of the Second World War, plus a strip of industrial land on the far side of the Dniester. When the Soviet Union went down, Moldova became 'independent.'" Terzian could hear the quotes in her voice. "But independence had nothing to do with the Moldovan *people,* it was just Romanian-speaking Soviet elites going off on their own account once their own superiors were no longer there to retrain them. And Moldova soon split—first the Turkish Christians…"

"Wait a second," Terzian said. "There are *Christian Turks?*"

The idea of Christian Turks was not a part of his Armenian-American worldview.

Stephanie nodded. "Orthodox Christian Turks, yes. They're called Gagauz, and they now have their own autonomous republic of Gagauzia within Moldova."

Stephanie reached into her pocket for a cigarette and her lighter.

"Uh," Terzian said. "Would you mind smoking in the window?"

Stephanie made a face. "Americans," she said, but she moved to the window and opened it, letting in a blast of cool spring air. She perched on the windowsill, sheltered her cigarette from the wind, and lit up.

"Where was I?" she asked.

"Turkish Christians."

"Right." Blowing smoke into the teeth of the gale. "Gagauzia was only the start—after that a Russian general allied with a bunch of crooks and KGB types created a rebellion in the bit of Moldova that was on the far side of the Dniester—another collection of Soviet elites, representing no one but themselves. Once the Russian-speaking rebels rose against their Romanian-speaking oppressors, the Soviet Fourteenth Army stepped in as 'peacekeepers,' complete with blue helmets, and created a twenty-mile-wide state recognized by no other government. And that meant more military, more border guards, more administrators, more taxes to charge, and customs duties, and uniformed ex-Soviets whose palms needed greasing. And over a hundred thousand refugees who could be put in camps while the administration stole their supplies and rations…

"But—" She jabbed the cigarette like a pointer. "Transnistria had a problem. No other nation recognized their existence, and they were tiny and had no natural resources, barring the underage girls they enslaved by the thousands to export for prostitution. The rest of the population was leaving as fast as they could, restrained only slightly by the fact that they carried passports no other state recognized, and that meant there were fewer people whose productivity the elite could steal to support their predatory post-Soviet lifestyles. All they had was a lot of obsolete Soviet heavy industry geared to produce stuff no one wanted.

"But they still had the *infrastructure*. They had power plants—running off Russian oil they couldn't afford to buy—and they had a transportation system. So the outlaw regime set up to attract other outlaws who needed industrial capacity—the idea was that they'd attract entrepreneurs who were excused from paying most of the local 'taxes' in exchange for making one big payoff to the higher echelon."

"Weapons?" Terzian asked.

"Weapons, sure," Stephanie nodded. "Mostly they're producing cheap knockoffs of other people's guns, but the guns are up to the size of howitzers. They tried banking and data havens, but the authorities couldn't restrain themselves from ripping those off—banks and data run on trust and control of information, and when the regulators are greedy, short-sighted crooks you don't get either one. So what they settled on was, well, *biotech*. They've got companies creating cheap generic pharmaceuticals that evade Western patents..." Her look darkened. "Not that I've got a problem with *that,* not when I've seen thousands dying of diseases they couldn't afford to cure. And they've also got other companies who are ripping off Western genetic research to develop their own products. And as long as they make their payoffs to the elite, these companies remain *completely unregulated.* Nobody, not even the government, knows what they're doing in those factories, and the government gives them security free of charge."

Terzian imagined gene-splicing going on in a rusting Soviet factory, rows and rows of mutant plants with untested, unregulated genetics, all set to be released on an unsuspecting world. Transgenic elements drifting down the Dniester to the Black Sea, growing quietly in its saline environment...

"The news," Stephanie reminded, and pointed at the television.

Terzian reached for the control and hit the mute button, just as the throbbing, anxious music that announced the news began to fade.

The murder on the Île de la Cité was the second item on the broadcast. The victim was described as a "foreign national" who had been fatally stabbed, and no arrests had been made. The motive for the killing was unknown.

Terzian changed the channel in time to catch the same item on another channel. The story was unchanged.

"I told you," Stephanie said. "No suspects. No motive."

"You could tell them."

She made a negative motion with her cigarette. "I couldn't tell them who did it, or how to find them. All I could do is put myself under suspicion."

Terzian turned off the TV. "So what happened exactly? Your friend stole from these people?"

Stephanie swiped her forehead with the back of her wrist. "He stole something that was of no value to them. It's only valuable to poor people, who can't afford to pay. And—" She turned to the window and spun her cigarette into the street below. "I'll take it out of here as soon as I can," she said. "I've got to try to contact some friends." She closed the window, shutting out the spring breeze. "I wish I had my passport. That would change everything."

I saw a murder this afternoon, Terzian thought. He closed his eyes and saw the man falling, the white face so completely absorbed in the reality of its own agony.

He was so fucking sick of death.

He opened his eyes. "I can get your passport back," he said.

Anger kept him moving until he saw the killers, across the street from Stephanie's hotel, sitting at an outdoor table in a café-bar. Terzian recognized them immediately—he didn't need to look at the heavy shoes, or the broad faces with their disciplined military mustaches—one glance at the crowd at the café showed the only two in the place who weren't French. That was probably how Stephanie knew to speak to him in English, he just didn't dress or carry himself like a Frenchman, for all that he'd worn an anonymous coat and tie. He tore his gaze away before they saw him gaping at them.

Anger turned very suddenly to fear, and as he continued his stride toward the hotel he told himself that they wouldn't recognize him from the Norman restaurant, that he'd changed into blue jeans and sneaks and a windbreaker, and carried a soft-sided suitcase. Still he felt a gunsight on the back of his neck, and he was so nervous that he nearly ran head-first into the glass lobby door.

Terzian paid for a room with his credit card, took the key from the Vietnamese clerk, and walked up the narrow stair to what the French called the second floor, but what he would have called the third. No one lurked in the stairwell, and he wondered where the third assassin had gone. Looking for Stephanie somewhere else, probably, an airport or train station.

In his room Terzian put his suitcase on the bed—it held only a few token items, plus his shaving kit—and then he took Stephanie's key from his pocket and held it in his hand. The key was simple, attached to a weighted doorknob-shaped ceramic plug.

The jolt of fear and surprise that had so staggered him on first sighting the two men began to shift again into rage.

They were drinking *beer,* there had been half-empty mugs on the table in front of them, and a pair of empties as well.

Drinking on duty. Doing surveillance while drunk.

Bastards. Trashcanians. They could kill someone simply through drunkenness.

Perhaps they already had.

He was angry when he left his room and took the stairs to the floor below. No foes kept watch in the hall. He opened Stephanie's room and then closed the door behind him.

He didn't turn on the light. The sun was surprisingly high in the sky for the hour: he had noticed that the sun seemed to set later here than it did at home. Maybe France was very far to the west for its time zone.

Stephanie didn't own a suitcase, just a kind of nylon duffel, a larger version of the athletic bag she already carried. He took it from the little closet, and enough of Terzian's suspicion remained so that he checked the luggage tag to make certain the name was *Steph. Pais,* and not another.

He opened the duffel, then got her passport and travel documents from the bedside table and tossed them in. He added a jacket and a sweater from the closet, then packed her toothbrush and shaver into her plastic travel bag and put it in the duffel.

The plan was for him to return to his room on the upper floor and stay the night and avoid raising suspicion by leaving a hotel he'd just checked into. In the morning, carrying two bags, he'd check out and rejoin Stephanie in his own hotel, where she had spent the night in his room, and where the air would by now reek with her cigarette smoke.

Terzian opened a dresser drawer and scooped out a double handful of Stephanie's t-shirts, underwear, and stockings, and then he remembered that the last time he'd done this was when he cleaned Claire's belongings out of the Esplanade house.

Shit. Fuck. He gazed down at the clothing between his hands and let the fury rage like a tempest in his skull.

And then, in the angry silence, he heard a creak in the corridor, and then a stumbling thud.

Thick rubber military soles, he thought. *With drunk baboons in them.*

Instinct shrieked at him not to be trapped in this room, this dead end where he could be trapped and killed. He dropped Stephanie's clothes back into the drawer and stepped to the bed and picked up the duffel in one hand. Another step took him to the door, which he opened with one hand while using the other to fling the duffel into the surprised face of the drunken murderer on the other side.

Terzian hadn't been at his Kenpo school in six years, not since he'd left Kansas City, but certain reflexes don't go away after they've been drilled into a person thousands of times—certainly not the front kick that hooked upward under the intruder's breastbone and drove him breathless into the corridor wall opposite.

A primitive element of his mind rejoiced in the fact that he was bigger than these guys. He could really knock them around.

The second Trashcanian tried to draw a pistol but Terzian passed outside the pistol hand and drove the point of an elbow into the man's face. Terzian then grabbed the automatic with both hands, took a further step down the corridor, and spun around, which swung the man around Terzian's hip a full two hundred and seventy degrees and drove him head-first into the corridor wall. When he'd finished falling and opened his eyes he was staring into the barrel of his own gun.

Red rage gave a fangs-bared roar of animal triumph inside Terzian's skull. Perhaps his tongue echoed it. It was all he could do to stop himself from pulling the trigger.

Get Death working for *him* for a change. Why not?

Except the first man hadn't realized that his side had just lost. He had drawn a knife—a glittering chromed single-edged thing that may have already killed once today—and now he took a dangerous step toward Terzian.

Terzian pointed the pistol straight at the knife man and pulled the trigger. Nothing happened.

The intruder stared at the gun as if he'd just realized at just this moment it wasn't his partner who held it.

Terzian pulled the trigger again, and when nothing happened his rage melted into terror and he ran. Behind him he heard the drunken knife man trip over his partner and crash to the floor.

Terzian was at the bottom of the stair before he heard the thick-soled military boots clatter on the risers above him. He dashed through the small lobby—he sensed the Vietnamese night clerk, who was facing away, begin to turn toward him just as he pushed open the glass door and ran into the street.

He kept running. At some point he discovered the gun still in his fist, and he put it in the pocket of his windbreaker.

Some moments later he realized he wasn't being pursued. And he remembered that Stephanie's passport was still in her duffel, which he'd thrown at the knife man and hadn't retrieved.

For a moment rage ran through him, and he thought about taking out the gun and fixing whatever was wrong with it and going back to Stephanie's room and getting the documents one way or another.

But then the anger faded enough for him to see what a foolish course that would be, and he returned to his own hotel.

Terzian had given Stephanie his key, so he knocked on his own door before realizing she was very unlikely to open to a random knock. "It's Jonathan," he said. "It didn't work out."

She snatched the door open from the inside. Her face was taut with anxiety. She held pages in her hand, the text of the paper he'd delivered that morning.

"Sorry," he said. "They were there, outside the hotel. I got into your room, but—"

She took his arm and almost yanked him into the room, then shut the door behind him. "Did they follow you?" she demanded.

"No. They didn't chase me. Maybe they thought I'd figure out how to work the gun." He took the pistol out of his pocket and showed it to her. "I can't believe how stupid I was—"

"*Where did you get that? Where did you get that?*" Her voice was nearly a scream, and she shrank away from him, her eyes wide. Her fist crumpled papers over her heart. To his astonishment he realized that she was afraid of him, that she thought he was *connected,* somehow, with the killers.

He threw the pistol onto the bed and raised his hands in a gesture of surrender. "No, really!" he shouted over her cries. "It's not mine! I took it from one of them!"

Stephanie took a deep gasp of air. Her eyes were still wild. "Who the hell are you, then?" she said. "James Bond?"

He gave a disgusted laugh. "James Bond would have known how to shoot."

"I was reading your—your article." She held out the pages toward him. "I was thinking, my God, I was thinking, what have I got this poor guy into. Some professor I was sending to his death." She passed a hand over her forehead. "They probably bugged my room. They would have known right away that someone was in it."

"They were drunk," Terzian said. "Maybe they've been drinking all day. Those assholes really pissed me off."

293

He sat on the bed and picked up the pistol. It was small and blue steel and surprisingly heavy. In the years since he'd last shot a gun he had forgotten that purposefulness, the way a firearm was designed for a single, clear function. He found the safety where it had been all along, near his right thumb, and flicked it off and then on again.

"There," he said. "That's what I should have done."

Waves of anger shivered through his limbs at the touch of the adrenaline still pouring into his system. A bitter impulse to laugh again rose in him, and he tried to suppress it.

"I guess I was lucky after all," he said. "It wouldn't have done you any good to have to explain a pair of corpses outside your room." He looked up at Stephanie, who was pacing back and forth in the narrow lane between the bed and the wall, and looking as if she badly needed a cigarette. "I'm sorry about your passport. Where were you going to go, anyway?"

"It doesn't so much matter if *I* go," she said. She gave Terzian a quick, nervous glance. "You can fly it out, right?"

"It?" He stared at her. "What do you mean, it?"

"The biotech." Stephanie stopped her pacing and stared at him with those startling green eyes. "Adrian gave it to me. Just before they killed him." Terzian's gaze followed hers to the black bag with the Nike swoosh, the bag that sat at the foot of Terzian's bed.

Terzian's impulse to laugh faded. Unregulated, illegal, stolen biotech, he thought. Right in his own hotel room. Along with a stolen gun and a woman who was probably out of her mind.

Fuck.

*

The dead man was identified by news files as Adrian Cristea, a citizen of Ukraine and a researcher. He had been stabbed once in the right kidney and bled to death without identifying his assailants. Witnesses reported two or maybe three men leaving the scene immediately after Cristea's death. Michelle set more search spiders to work.

For a moment she considered calling Davout and letting him know that Terzian had probably been a witness to a murder, but decided to wait until she had some more evidence one way or another.

For the next few hours she did her real work, analyzing the samples she'd taken from Zigzag Lake's sulfide-tainted deeps. It wasn't very physical, and Michelle figured it was only worth a few hundred calories.

A wind floated through the treetops, bringing the scent of night flowers and swaying Michelle's perch beneath her as she peered into her biochemical reader, and she remembered the gentle pressure of Darton against her back, rocking with her as he looked over her shoulder at her results. Suddenly she could remember, with a near perfect clarity, the taste of his skin on her tongue.

She rose from her woven seat and paced along the bough. *Damn it,* she thought, *I watched you die.*

Michelle returned to her deck and discovered that her spiders had located the police file on Cristea's death. A translation program handled the antique French without trouble, even producing modern equivalents of forensic jargon. Cristea was of Romanian descent, had been born in the old USSR, and had acquired Ukrainian citizenship on the breakup of the Soviet Union. The French files themselves had translations of Cristea's Ukrainian travel documents, which included receipts showing that he had paid personal insurance, environmental insurance, and departure taxes from Transnistria, a place of which she'd never heard, as well as similar documents from Moldova, which at least was a province, or country, that sounded familiar.

What kind of places were these, where you had to buy *insurance* at the *border?* And what was environmental insurance anyway?

There were copies of emails between French and Ukrainian authorities, in which the Ukrainians politely declined any knowledge of their citizen beyond the fact that he *was* a citizen. They had no addresses for him.

Cristea apparently lived in Transnistria, but the authorities there echoed the Ukrainians in saying they knew nothing of him.

Cristea's tickets and vouchers showed that he had apparently taken a train to Bucharest, and there he'd got on an airline that took him to Prague, and thence to Paris. He had been in the city less than a day before he was killed. Found in Cristea's hotel room was a curious document certifying that Cristea was carrying medical supplies, specifically a vaccine against hepatitis A. Michelle wondered why he would be carrying a hepatitis vaccine from Transnistria to France. France presumably had all the hepatitis vaccine it needed.

No vaccine had turned up. Apparently Cristea had got into the European Community without having his bags searched, as there was no evidence that the documents relating to the alleged vaccine had ever been examined.

The missing "vaccine"—at some point in the police file the skeptical quotation marks had appeared—had convinced the Paris police that Cristea was a murdered drug courier, and at that point they'd lost interest in the case. It was rarely possible to solve a professional killing in the drug underworld.

Michelle's brief investigation seemed to have come to a dead end. That Terzian might have witnessed a murder would rate maybe half a sentence in Professor Davout's biography.

Then she checked what her spiders had brought her in regard to Terzian, and found something that cheered her.

There he was inside the Basilica di Santa Croce, a tourist still photograph taken before the tomb of Machiavelli. He was only slightly turned away from the camera and the face was unmistakable. Though there was no date on the photograph, only the year, but he wore the same clothes he wore in the video taken outside the church, and the photo caught him in the act of speaking to a companion. She was a tall woman with deep brown skin, but she was turned away from the camera, and a wide-brimmed sun hat made her features indistinguishable.

Humming happily, Michelle deployed her software to determine whether this was the same woman who had been on Terzian's arm on the Place Dauphine. Without facial features or other critical measurements to compare, the software was uncertain, but the proportion of limb and thorax was right, and the software gave an estimate of 41%, which Michelle took to be encouraging.

Another still image of Terzian appeared in an undated photograph taken at a festival in southern France. He wore dark glasses, and he'd grown heavily tanned; he carried a glass of wine in either hand, but the person to whom he was bringing the second glass was out of the frame. Michelle set her software to locating the identity of the church seen in the background, a task the two distinctive belltowers would make easy. She was lucky and got a hit right away: the church was the Eglise St-Michel in Salon-de-Provence, which meant Terzian had attended the Fête des Aires de la Dine in June. Michelle set more search spiders to seeking out photo and video from the festivals. She had no doubt she'd find Terzian there, and perhaps again his companion.

Michelle retired happily to her hammock. The search was going well. Terzian had met a woman in Paris and traveled with her for weeks. The evidence wasn't quite there yet, but Michelle would drag it out of history somehow.

Romance. The lonely mermaid was in favor of romance, the kind where you ran away to faraway places to be more intently one with the person you adored.

It was what she herself had done, before everything had gone so wrong, and Michelle had to take steps to re-establish the moral balance of her universe.

Terzian paid for a room for Stephanie for the night, not so much because he was gallant as because he needed to be alone to think. "There's a breakfast buffet downstairs in the morning," he said.

"They have hard-boiled eggs and croissants and Nutella. It's a very un-French thing to do. I recommend it."

He wondered if he would ever see her again. She might just vanish, particularly if she read his thoughts, because another reason for wanting privacy was so that he could call the police and bring an end to this insane situation.

He never quite assembled the motivation to make the call. Perhaps Rorty's *I don't care* had rubbed off on him. And he never got a chance to taste the buffet, either. Stephanie banged on his door very early, and he dragged on his jeans and opened the door. She entered, furiously smoking from her new cigarette pack, the athletic bag over her shoulder.

"How did you pay for the room at my hotel?" she asked.

"Credit card," he said, and in the stunned, accusing silence that followed he saw his James Bond fantasies sink slowly beneath the slick, oily surface of a dismal lake.

Because credit cards leave trails. The Transnistrians would have checked the hotel registry, and the credit card impression taken by the hotel, and now they knew who *he* was. And it wouldn't be long before they'd trace him at his hotel.

"Shit, I should have warned you to pay cash." Stephanie stalked to the window and peered out cautiously. "They could be out there right now."

Terzian felt a sudden compulsion to have the gun in his hand. He took it from the bedside table and stood there, feeling stupid and cold and shirtless.

"How much money do you have?" Terzian asked.

"Couple hundred."

"I have less."

"You should max out your credit card and just carry Euros. Use your card now before they cancel it."

"Cancel it? How could they cancel it?"

She gave him a tight-lipped, impatient look. "Jonathan. They may be assholes, but they're still a *government*."

They took a cab to the American Express near the Opéra and Terzian got ten thousand Euros in cash from some people who were extremely skeptical about the validity of his documents, but who had, in the end, to admit that all was technically correct. Then Stephanie got a cell phone under the name A. Silva, with a bunch of prepaid hours on it, and within a couple hours they were on the TGV, speeding south to Nice at nearly two hundred seventy kilometers per hour, all with a strange absence of sound and vibration that made the French countryside speeding past seem like a strangely unconvincing special effect.

Terzian had put them in first class and he and Stephanie were alone in a group of four seats. Stephanie was twitchy because he hadn't bought seats in a smoking section. He sat uncertain, unhappy about all the cash he was carrying and not knowing what to do with it—he'd made two big rolls and zipped them into the pockets of his windbreaker. He carried the pistol in the front pocket of his jeans and its weight and discomfort was a perpetual reminder of this situation that he'd been dragged into, pursued by killers from Trashcanistan and escorting illegal biotechnology.

He kept mentally rehearsing drawing the pistol and shooting it. Over and over, remembering to thumb off the safety this time. Just in case Trashcanian commandos stormed the train.

"Hurled into life," he muttered. "An object lesson right out of Heidegger."

"Beg pardon?"

He looked at her. "Heidegger said we're hurled into life. Just like I've been hurled into—" He flapped his hands uselessly. "Into whatever this is. The situation exists before you even got here, but here you are anyway, and the whole business is something you inherit and have to live with." He felt his lips draw back in a snarl. "He also said that a fundamental feature of existence is anxiety in the face of death, which would also seem to apply to our situation. And his answer to all of this was to make existence, *dasein* if you want to get technical, an authentic project." He looked at her. "So what's your authentic project, then? And how authentic is it?"

Her brow furrowed. "What?"

Terzian couldn't stop, not that he wanted to. It was just Stephanie's hard luck that he couldn't shoot anybody right now, or break something up with his fists, and was compelled to lecture instead. "Or," he went on, "to put this in a more accessible context, just pretend we're in a Hitchcock film, okay? This is the scene where Grace Kelly tells Cary Grant exactly who she is and what the maguffin is."

Stephanie's face was frozen into a hostile mask. Whether she understood what he was saying or not, the hostility was clear.

"I don't get it," she said.

"What's in the fucking bag?" he demanded.

She glared at him for a long moment, then spoke, her own anger plain in her voice. "It's the answer to world hunger," she said. "Is that authentic enough for you?"

Stephanie's father was from Angola and her mother from East Timor, both former Portuguese colonies swamped in the decades since independence by war and massacre. Both parents had with great foresight and intelligence retained Portuguese passports, and had met in Rome, where they worked for UNESCO, and where Stephanie had grown up with a blend both of their genetics and their service ethic.

Stephanie herself had got a degree in administration from the University of Virginia, which accounted for the American lights in her English, then got another degree in nursing and went to work for the Catholic relief agency Santa Croce, which sent her to its every war-wrecked, locust-blighted, warlord-ridden, sandstorm-blasted camp in Africa. And a few that *weren't* in Africa.

"Trashcanistan," Terzian said.

"Moldova," Stephanie said. "For three months, on what was supposed to be my vacation." She shuddered. "I don't mind telling you that it was a frightening thing. I was used to that kind of thing in Africa, but to see it all happening in the developed world... warlords, ethnic hatreds, populations being moved at the point of a gun, whole forested districts being turned to deserts because people suddenly needed firewood..." Her emerald eyes flashed. "It's all politics, okay? Just like in Africa. Famine and camps are all politics now, and have been since before I was born. A whole population starves, and it's because someone, somewhere, sees a profit in it. It's difficult to just kill an ethnic group you don't like, war is expensive and there are questions at the UN and you may end up at The Hague being tried for war crimes. But if you just wait for a bad harvest and then arrange for the whole population to *starve,* it's different—suddenly your enemies are giving you all their money in return for food, you get aid from the UN instead of grief, and you can award yourself a piece of the relief action and collect bribes from all the relief agencies, and your enemies are rounded up into camps and you can get your armed forces into the country without resistance, make sure your enemies disappear, control everything while some deliveries disappear into government warehouses where the food can be sold to the starving or just sold abroad for a profit..." She shrugged. "That's the way of the world, okay? *But no more!*" She grabbed a fistful of the Nike bag and brandished it at him.

What her time in Moldova had done was to leave Stephanie contacts in the area, some in relief agencies, some in industry and government. So that when news of a useful project came up in Transnistria, she was among the first to know.

"So what is it?" Terzian asked. "Some kind of genetically modified food crop?"

"No." She smiled thinly. "What we have here is a genetically modified consumer."

Those Transnistrian companies had mostly been interested in duplicating pharmaceuticals and transgenetic food crops created by other companies, producing them on the cheap and underselling the patent-owners. There were bits and pieces of everything in those labs, DNA human and animal and vegetable. A lot of it had other people's trademarks and patents on it, even the human codes, which US law permitted companies to patent provided they came up with something useful to do with it. And what these semi-outlaw companies were doing was making two things they figured people couldn't do without: drugs and food.

And not just people, since animals need drugs and food, too. Starving, tubercular sheep or pigs aren't worth much at market, so there's as much money in keeping livestock alive as in doing the same for people. So at some point one of the administrators—after a few too many shots of vodka flavored with bison grass—said, "Why should we worry about feeding the animals at all? Why not have them grow their own food, like plants?"

So then began the Green Swine Project, an attempt to make pigs fat and happy by just herding them out into the sun.

"Green swine," Terzian repeated, wondering. "People are getting killed over green swine."

"Well, no." Stephanie waved the idea away with a twitchy swipe of her hand. "The idea never quite got beyond the vaporware stage, because at that point another question was asked—why swine? Adrian said, Why stop at having animals do photosynthesis—why not *people?*"

"No!" Terzian cried, appalled. "You're going to turn people green?"

Stephanie glared at him. "Something wrong with fat, happy green people?" Her hands banged out a furious rhythm on the armrests of her seat. "I'd have skin to match my eyes. Wouldn't that be attractive?"

"I'd have to see it first," Terzian said, the shock still rolling through his bones.

"Adrian was pretty smart," Stephanie said. "The Transnistrians killed themselves a real genius." She shook her head. "He had it all worked out. He wanted to limit the effect to the skin—no green muscle tissue or skeletons—so he started with a virus that has a tropism for the epidermis—papiloma, that's warts, okay?"

So now we've got green warts, Terzian thought, but he kept his mouth shut.

"So if you're Adrian, what you do is gut the virus and re-encode it to create chlorophyll. Once a person's infected, exposure to sunlight will cause the virus to replicate and chlorophyll to reproduce in the skin."

Terzian gave Stephanie a skeptical look. "That's not going to be very efficient," he said. "Plants get sugars and oxygen from chlorophyll, okay, but they don't need much food, they stand in place and don't walk around. Add chlorophyll to a person's skin, how many calories do you get each day? Tens? Dozens?"

Stephanie's lips parted in a fierce little smile. "You don't stop with just the chlorophyll. You have to get really efficient electron transport. In a plant, all that's handled in the chloroplasts, but the human body already has mitochondria to do the same job. You don't have to create these huge support mechanisms for the chlorophyll, you just make use of what's already there. So if you're Adrian, what you do is add trafficking tags to the reaction center proteins so that they'll target the mitochondria, which *already* are loaded with proteins to handle electron transport. The result is that the mitochondria handle transport from the chlorophyll, which is the sort of job they do anyway, and once the virus starts replicating you can get maybe a thousand calories or more just from standing in the sun. It won't provide full nutrition, but it can keep starvation at bay, and it's not as if starving people have much to do besides stand in the sun anyway."

"It's not going to do much good for Icelanders," Terzian said.

She turned severe. "Icelanders aren't starving. It so happens that most of the people in the world who are starving happen to be in hot places."

Terzian flapped his hands. "Fine. I must be a racist. Sue me."

Stephanie's grin broadened, and she leaned toward Terzian. "I didn't tell you about Adrian's most interesting bit of cleverness. When people start getting normal nutrition, there'll be competition within the mitochondria between normal metabolism and solar-induced electron transport. So the green virus is just a redundant backup system in case normal nutrition isn't available."

A triumphant smile crossed Stephanie's face. "Starvation will no longer be a weapon," she said. "Green skin can keep people active and on their feet long enough to get help. It will keep them healthy enough to fend off the epidemics associated with malnutrition. The point is—" She made fists and shook them at the sky. *"The bad guys don't get to use starvation as a weapon anymore! Famine ends!* One of the Four Horsemen of the Apocalypse *dies,* right here, right now, as a result of *what I've got in this bag!"* She picked up the bag and threw it into Terzian's lap, and he jerked on the seat in defensive reflex, knees rising to meet elbows. Her lips skinned back in a snarl, and her tone was mocking.

"I think even that Nazi fuck Heidegger would think my *project* is pretty damn *authentic.* Wouldn't you agree, Herr Doktor Terzian?"

Got you, Michelle thought. Here was a still photo of Terzian at the Fête des Aires de la Dine, with the dark-skinned woman. She had the same wide-brimmed straw hat she'd worn in the Florence church, and had the same black bag over her shoulder, but now Michelle had a clear view of a three-quarter profile, and one hand, with its critical alignments, was clearly visible, holding an ice cream cone.

Night insects whirled around the computer display. Michelle batted them away and got busy mapping. The photo was digital and Michelle could enlarge it.

To her surprise she discovered that the woman had green eyes. Black women with green irises—or irises of orange or chartreuse or chrome steel—were not unusual in her own time, but she knew that in Terzian's time they were rare. That would make the search much easier.

"Michelle..." The voice came just as Michelle sent her new search spiders into the ether. A shiver ran up her spine.

"*Michelle...*" The voice came again.

It was Darton.

Michelle's heart gave a sickening lurch. She closed her console and put it back in the mesh bag, then crossed the rope bridge between the ironwood tree and the banyan. Her knees were weak, and the swaying bridge seemed to take a couple unexpected pitches. She stepped out onto the banyan's sturdy overhanging limb and gazed out at the water.

"*Michelle...*" To the southwest, in the channel between the mermaid's island and another, she could see a pale light bobbing, the light of a small boat. "Michelle, where are you?"

The voice died away in the silence and surf. Michelle remembered the spike in her hand, the long, agonized trek up the slope above Jellyfish Lake. Darton pale, panting for breath, dying in her arms.

The lake was one of the wonders of the world, but the steep path over the ridge that fenced the lake from the ocean was challenging even for those who were not dying. When Michelle and Darton—at that time apes—came up from their boat that afternoon they didn't climb the steep path, but swung hand-over-hand through the trees overhead, through the hardwood and guava trees, and avoided the poison trees with their bleeding, allergenic black sap. Even though their trip was less exhausting than if they'd gone over the land route, the two were ready for the cool water by the time they arrived at the lake.

Tens of thousands of years in the past the water level was higher, and when it receded the lake was cut off from the Pacific, and with it the *Mastigias* sp. jellyfish, which soon exhausted the supply of small fish that were its food. As the human race did later, the jellies gave up hunting and gathering in exchange for agriculture, and permitted themselves to be farmed by colonies of algae that provided the sugars they needed for life. At night they'd descend to the bottom of the lake, where they fertilized their algae crops in the anoxic, sulfurous waters; at dawn the jellies rose to the surface, and over the course of the day they crossed the lake, following the course of the sun, and allowed the sun's rays to supply the energy necessary for making their daily ration of food.

When Darton and Michelle arrived, there were ten million jellyfish in the lake, from fingertip-sized to jellies the size of a dinner plate, all in one warm throbbing golden-brown mass in the center of the water. The two swam easily on the surface with their long siamang arms, laughing and calling to one another as the jellyfish in their millions caressed them with the most featherlike of touches. The lake was the temperature of their own blood, and it was like a soupy bath, the jellyfish so thick that Michelle felt she could almost walk on the surface. The warm touch wasn't erotic, exactly, but it was sensual in the way that an erotic touch was sensual, a light brush over the skin by the pad of a teasing finger.

Trapped in a lake for thousands of years without suitable prey, the jellyfish had lost most of their ability to sting. Only a small percentage of people were sensitive enough to the toxin to receive a rash or feel a modest burning.

A very few people, though, were more sensitive than that.

Darton and Michelle left at dusk, and by that time Darton was already gasping for breath. He said he'd overexerted himself, that all he needed was to get back to their base for a snack, but as he swung through the trees on the way up the ridge, he lost his hold on a Palauan apple tree and crashed through a thicket of limbs to sprawl, amid a hail of fruit, on the sharp algae-covered limestone of the ridge.

Michelle swung down from the trees, her heart pounding. Darton was nearly colorless and struggling to breathe. They had no way of calling for help unless Michelle took their boat to Koror or to their base camp on another island. She tried to help Darton walk, taking one of his long arms over her shoulder, supporting him up the steep island trail. He collapsed, finally, at the foot of a poison tree, and Michelle bent over him to shield him from the drops of venomous sap until he died.

Her back aflame with the poison sap, she'd whispered her parting words into Darton's ear. She never knew if he heard.

The coroner said it was a million-to-one chance that Darton had been so deathly allergic, and tried to comfort her with the thought that there was nothing she could have done. Torbiong, who had made the arrangements for Darton and Michelle to come in the first place, had been consoling, had offered to let Michelle stay with his family. Michelle had surprised him by asking permission to move her base camp to another island, and to continue her work alone.

She also had herself transformed into a mermaid, and subsequently a romantic local legend.

And now Darton was back, bobbing in a boat in the nearby channel and calling her name, shouting into a bullhorn.

"Michelle, I love you." The words floated clear into the night air. Michelle's mouth was dry. Her fingers formed the sign <go away>.

There was a silence, and then Michelle heard the engine start on Darton's boat. He motored past her position, within five hundred meters or so, and continued on to the northern point of the island.

<go away>...

"Michelle..." Again his voice floated out onto the breeze. It was clear he didn't know where she was. She was going to have to be careful about showing lights.

<go away>...

Michelle waited while Darton called out a half-dozen more times, and then Darton started his engine and moved on. She wondered if he would search all three hundred islands in the Rock Island group.

No, she knew he was more organized than that.

She'd have to decide what to do when he finally found her.

While a thousand questions chased each other's tails through his mind, Terzian opened the Nike bag and withdrew the small hard plastic case inside, something like a box for fishing tackle. He popped the locks on the case and opened the lid, and he saw glass vials resting in slots cut into dark grey foam. In them was a liquid with a faint golden cast.

"The papiloma," Stephanie said.

Terzian dropped the lid on the case as he cast a guilty look over his shoulder, not wanting anyone to see him with this stuff. If he were arrested under suspicion of being a drug dealer, the wads of cash and the pistol certainly wouldn't help.

"What do you do with the stuff once you get to where you're going?"

"Brush it on the skin. With exposure to solar energy it replicates as needed."

"Has it been tested?"

"On people? No. Works fine on rhesus monkeys, though."

He tapped his wedding ring on the arm of his seat. "Can it be… caught? I mean, it's a virus, can it go from one person to another?"

"Through skin-to-skin contact."

"I'd say that's a yes. Can mothers pass it on to their children?"

"Adrian didn't think it would cross the placental barrier, but he didn't get a chance to test it. If mothers want to infect their children, they'll probably have to do it deliberately." She shrugged. "Whatever the case, my guess is that mothers won't mind green babies, as long as they're green *healthy* babies." She looked down at the little vials in their secure coffins of foam. "We can infect tens of thousands of people with this amount," she said. "And we can make more very easily."

If mothers want to infect their children… Terzian closed the lid of the plastic case and snapped the locks. "You're out of your mind," he said.

Stephanie cocked her head and peered at him, looking as if she'd anticipated his objections and was humoring him. "How so?"

"Where do I start?" Terzian zipped up the bag, then tossed it in Stephanie's lap, pleased to see her defensive reflexes leap in response. "You're planning on unleashing an untested transgenetic virus on Africa—on *Africa* of all places, a continent that doesn't exactly have a happy history with pandemics. And it's a virus that's cooked up by a bunch of illegal pharmacists in a non-country with a murderous secret police, facts that don't give me much confidence that this is going to be anything but a disaster."

Stephanie tapped two fingers on her chin as if she were wishing there were a cigarette between them. "I can put your mind to rest on the last issue. The animal studies worked. Adrian had a family of bright green rhesus in his lab, till the project was canceled and the rhesus were, ah, liquidated."

"So if the project's so terrific, why'd the company pull the plug?"

"Money." Her lips twisted in anger. "Starving people can't afford to pay for the treatments, so they'd have to practically give the stuff away. Plus they'd get reams of endless bad publicity, which is exactly what outlaw biotech companies in outlaw countries don't want. There are millions of people who go ballistic at the very thought of a genetically engineered *vegetable*—you can imagine how people who can't abide the idea of a transgenetic bell pepper would freak at the thought of infecting people with an engineered virus. The company decided it wasn't worth the risk. They closed the project down."

Stephanie looked at the bag in her hands. "But Adrian had been in the camps himself, you see. A displaced person, a refugee from the civil war in Moldova. And he couldn't stand the thought that there was a way to end hunger sitting in his refrigerator in the lab, and that nothing was being done with it. And so…" Her hands outlined the case inside the Nike bag. "He called me. He took some vacation time and booked himself into the Henri IV, on the Place Dauphine. And I guess he must have been careless, because…"

Tears starred in her eyes, and she fell silent. Terzian, strong in the knowledge that he'd shared quite enough of her troubles by now, stared out the window, at the green landscape that was beginning to take on the brilliant colors of Provence. The Hautes-Alpes floated blue and white-capped in the distant east, and nearby were orchards of almonds and olives with shimmering leaves, and hillsides covered with rows of orderly vines. The Rhone ran silver under the westering sun.

"I'm not going to be your bagman," he said. "I'm not going to contaminate the world with your freaky biotech."

"Then they'll catch you and you'll die," Stephanie said. "And it will be for nothing."

"My experience of death," said Terzian, "is that it's *always* for nothing."

She snorted then, angry. "My experience of death," she mocked, "is that it's too often for *profit*. I want to make mass murder an unprofitable venture. I want to crash the market in starvation by *giving away life*." She gave another snort, amused this time. "It's the ultimate anti-capitalist gesture."

Terzian didn't rise to that. Gestures, he thought, were just that. Gestures didn't change the fundamentals. If some jefe couldn't starve his people to death, he'd just use bullets, or deadly genetic technology he bought from outlaw Transnistrian corporations.

The landscape, all blazing green, raced past at over two hundred kilometers per hour. An attendant came by and sold them each a cup of coffee and a sandwich.

"You should use my phone to call your wife," Stephanie said as she peeled the cellophane from her sandwich. "Let her know that your travel plans have changed."

Apparently she'd noticed Terzian's wedding ring.

"My wife is dead," Terzian said.

She looked at him in surprise. "I'm sorry," she said.

"Brain cancer," he said.

Though it was more complicated than that. Claire had first complained of back pain, and there had been an operation, and the tumor removed from her spine. There had been a couple weeks of mad joy and relief, and then it had been revealed that the cancer had spread to the brain and that it was inoperable. Chemotherapy had failed. She died six weeks after her first visit to the doctor.

"Do you have any other family?" Stephanie said.

"My parents are dead, too." Auto accident, aneurism. He didn't mention Claire's uncle Geoff and his partner Luis, who had died of HIV within eight months of each other and left Claire the Victorian house on Esplanade in New Orleans. The house that, a few weeks ago, he had sold for six hundred and fifty thousand dollars, and the furnishings for a further ninety-five thousand, and Uncle Geoff's collection of equestrian art for a further forty-one thousand.

He was disinclined to mention that he had quite a lot of money, enough to float around Europe for years.

Telling Stephanie that might only encourage her.

There was a long silence. Terzian broke it. "I've read spy novels," he said. "And I know that we shouldn't go to the place we've bought tickets for. We shouldn't go anywhere *near* Nice."

She considered this, then said, "We'll get off at Avignon."

They stayed in Provence for nearly two weeks, staying always in unrated hotels, those that didn't even rise to a single star from the Ministry of Tourism, or in *gîtes ruraux*, farmhouses with rooms for rent. Stephanie spent much of her energy trying to call colleagues in Africa on her cell phone and achieved only sporadic success, a frustration that left her in a near-permanent fury. It was never clear just who she was trying to call, or how she thought they were going to get the papiloma off her hands. Terzian wondered how many people were involved in this conspiracy of hers.

They attended some local fêtes, though it was always a struggle to convince Stephanie it was safe to appear in a crowd. She made a point of disguising herself in big hats and shades and ended up looking like a cartoon spy. Terzian tramped rural lanes or fields or village streets, lost some pounds despite the splendid fresh local cuisine, and gained a sun tan. He made a stab at writing several papers on his laptop, and spent time researching them in internet cafés.

He kept thinking he would have enjoyed this trip, if only Claire had been with him.

"What is it you *do*, exactly?" Stephanie asked him once, as he wrote. "I know you teach at university, but…"

"I don't teach anymore," Terzian said. "I didn't get my post-doc renewed. The department and I didn't exactly get along."

"Why not?"

Terzian turned away from the stale, stalled ideas on his display. "I'm too interdisciplinary. There's a place on the academic spectrum where history and politics and philosophy come together—it's called 'political theory' usually—but I throw in economics and a layman's understanding of science as well, and it confuses everybody but me. That's why my MA is in American Studies—nobody in my philosophy or political science department had the nerve to deal with me, and nobody knows what American Studies actually *are*, so I was able to hide out there. And my doctorate is in philosophy, but only because I found one rogue professor emeritus who was willing to chair my committee.

"The problem is that if you're hired by a philosophy department, you're supposed to teach Plato or Hume or whoever, and they don't want you confusing everybody by adding Maynard Keynes and Leo Szilard. And if you teach history, you're supposed to confine yourself to acceptable stories about the past and not toss in ideas about perceptual mechanics and Kant's ideas of the noumenon, and of course you court crucifixion from the laity if you mention Foucault or Nietzsche."

Amusement touched Stephanie's lips. "So where do you find a job?"

"France?" he ventured, and they laughed. "In France, 'thinker' is a job description. It's not necessary to have a degree, it's just something you do." He shrugged. "And if that fails, there's always Burger King."

She seemed amused. "Sounds like burgers in your future."

"Oh, it's not as bad as all that. If I can generate enough interesting, sexy, highly original papers, I might attract attention and a job, in that order."

"And have you done that?"

Terzian looked at his display and sighed. "So far, no."

Stephanie narrowed her eyes and she considered him. "You're not a conventional person. You don't think inside the box, as they say."

"As they say," Terzian repeated.

"Then you should have no objections to radical solutions to world hunger. Particularly ones that don't cost a penny to white liberals throughout the world."

"Hah," Terzian said. "Who says I'm a liberal? I'm an *economist*."

So Stephanie told him terrible things about Africa. Another famine was brewing across the southern part of the continent. Mozambique was plagued with flood *and* drought, a startling combination. The Horn of Africa was worse. According to her friends, Santa Croce had a food shipment stuck in Mogadishu and before letting it pass the local warlord wanted to renegotiate his bribe. In the meantime people were starving, dying of malnutrition, infection, and dysentery in camps in the dry highlands of Bale and Sidamo. Their own government in Addis Ababa was worse than the Somali warlord, at this stage permitting no aid at all, bribes or no bribes.

And as for the southern Sudan, it didn't bear thinking about.

"What's *your* solution to this?" she demanded of Terzian. "Or do you have one?"

"Test this stuff, this papiloma," he said, "show me that it works, and I'm with you. But there are too many plagues in Africa as it is."

"Confine the papiloma to labs while thousands die? Hand it to governments who can suppress it because of pressure from religious loons and hysterical NGOs? You call *that* an answer?" And Stephanie went back to working her phone while Terzian walked off in anger for another stalk down country lanes.

Terzian walked toward an old ruined castle that shambled down the slope of a nearby hill. And if Stephanie's plant people proved viable? he wondered. All bets were off. A world in which humans could become plants was a world in which none of the old rules applied.

Stephanie had said she wanted to crash the market in starvation. But, Terzian thought, that also meant crashing the market in *food*. If people with no money had all the food they needed, that meant *food itself had no value in the marketplace*. Food would be so cheap that there would be no profit in growing or selling it.

And this was all just *one application* of the technology. Terzian tried to keep up with science: he knew about nanoassemblers. Green people was just the first magic bullet in a long volley of scientific musketry that would change every fundamental rule by which humanity had operated since they'd first stood upright. What happened when *every* basic commodity—food, clothing, shelter, maybe even health—was so cheap that it was free? What then had value?

Even *money* wouldn't have value then. Money only had value if it could be exchanged for something of equivalent worth.

He paused in his walk and looked ahead at the ruined castle, the castle that had once provided justice and security and government for the district, and he wondered if he was looking at the future of *all* government. Providing an orderly framework in which commodities could be exchanged was the basic function of the state, that and providing a secure currency. If people didn't need government to furnish that kind of security and if the currency was worthless, the whole future of government itself was in question. Taxes weren't worth the expense of collecting if the money wasn't any good, anyway, and without taxes government couldn't be paid for.

Terzian paused at the foot of the ruined castle and wondered if he saw the future of the civilized world. Either the castle would be rebuilt by tyrants, or it would fall.

Michelle heard Darton's bullhorn again the next evening, and she wondered why he was keeping fruit-bat hours. Was it because his calls would travel farther at night?

If he were sleeping in the morning, she thought, that would make it easier. She'd finished analyzing some of her samples, but a principle of science was not to do these things alone: she'd have to travel to Koror to mail her samples to other people, and now she knew to do it in the morning, when Darton would be asleep.

The problem for Michelle was that she was a legend. When the lonely mermaid emerged from the sea and walked to the post office in the little foam booties she wore when walking on pavement, she was noticed. People pointed; children followed her on their boards, people in cars waved. She wondered if she could trust them not to contact Darton as soon as they saw her.

She hoped that Darton wasn't starting to get the islanders on his side.

Michelle and Darton had met on a field trip in Borneo, their obligatory government service after graduation. The other field workers were older, paying their taxes or working on their second or third or fourth or fifth careers, and Michelle knew on sight that Darton was no older than she, that he, too, was a child among all these elders. They were pulled to each other as if drawn by some violent natural force, cataloguing snails and terrapins by day and spending their nights wrapped in each other in their own shell, their turtleback tent. The ancients with whom they shared their days treated them with amused condescension, but then that was how they treated everything. Darton and Michelle didn't care. In their youth they stood against all creation.

When the trip came to an end they decided to continue their work together, just a hop across the equator in Belau. Paying their taxes ahead of time. They celebrated by getting new bodies, an exciting experience for Michelle, who had been built by strict parents that wouldn't allow her to have a new body until adulthood, no matter how many of her friends had been transforming from an early age into one newly fashionable shape or another.

Michelle and Darton thought that anthropoid bodies would be suitable for the work, and so they went to the clinic in Delhi and settled themselves on nanobeds and let the little machines turn their bodies, their minds, their memories, their desires and their knowledge and their souls, into long strings of numbers. All of which were fed into their new bodies when they were ready, and reserved as backups to be downloaded as necessary.

Being a siamang was a glorious discovery. They soared through the treetops of their little island, swinging overhand from limb to limb in a frenzy of glory. Michelle took a particular delight in her body hair—she didn't have as much as a real ape, but there was enough on her chest and back to be interesting. They built nests of foliage in trees and lay tangled together, analyzing data or making love or shaving their hair into interesting tribal patterns. Love was far from placid—it was a flame, a fury. An obsession that, against all odds, had been fulfilled, only to build the flame higher.

The fury still burned in Michelle. But now, after Darton's death, it had a different quality, a quality that had nothing to do with life or youth.

Michelle, spooning up blueberries and cream, riffled through the names and faces her spiders had spat out. There were, now she added them up, a preposterous number of pictures of green-eyed women with dark skin whose pictures were somewhere in the net. Nearly all of them had striking good looks. Many of them were un-identified in the old scans, or identified only by a first name. The highest probability the software offered was 43%.

That 43% belonged to a Brasilian named Laura Flor, who re-search swiftly showed was home in Aracaju during the critical per-iod, among other things having a baby. A video of the delivery was available, but Michelle didn't watch it. The way women delivered babies back then was disgusting.

The next most likely female was another Brasilian seen in some tourist photographs taken in Rio. Not even a name given. A fur-ther search based on this woman's physiognomy turned up nothing, not until Michelle broadened the search to a different gender, and discovered the Brasilian was a transvestite. That didn't seem to be Terzian's scene, so she left it alone.

The third was identified only as Stephanie, and posted on a site created by a woman who had done relief work in Africa. Stephanie was shown with a group of other relief workers, posing in front of a tin-roofed, cinderblock building identified as a hospital.

The quality of the photograph wasn't very good, but Michelle mapped the physiognomy anyway, and sent it forth along with the name "Stephanie" to see what might happen.

There was a hit right away, a credit card charge to a Stephanie América Pais e Silva. She had stayed in a hotel in Paris for the three nights before Terzian disappeared.

Michelle's blood surged as the data flashed on her screens. She sent out more spiders and the good news began rolling in.

Stephanie Pais was a dual citizen of Portugal and Angola, and had been educated partly in the States—a quick check showed that her time at university didn't overlap Terzian's. From her graduation she had worked for a relief agency called Santa Croce.

Then a news item turned up, a sensational one. Stephanie Pais had been spectacularly murdered in Venice on the night of July 19, six days before Terzian had delivered the first version of his Cornucopia Theory.

Two murders…

One in Paris, one in Venice. And one the woman who seemed to be Terzian's lover.

Michelle's body shivered to a sudden gasping spasm, and she realized that in her suspense she'd been holding her breath. Her head swam. When it cleared, she worked out what time it was in Maryland, where Dr. Davout lived, and then told her deck to page him at once.

Davout was unavailable at first, and by the time he returned her call she had more information about Stephanie Pais. She blurted the story out to him while her fingers jabbed at the keyboard of her deck, sending him copies of her corroborating data.

Davout's startled eyes leaped from the data to Michelle and back. "How much of this…" he began, then gave up. "How did she die?" he managed.

"The news article says stabbed. I'm looking for the police report."

"Is Terzian mentioned?"

<No> she signed. "The police report will have more details."

"Any idea what this is about? There's no history of Terzian *ever* being connected with violence."

"By tomorrow," Michelle said, "I should be able to tell you. But I thought I should send this to you because you might be able to tie this in with other elements of Terzian's life that I don't know anything about."

Davout's fingers formed a mudra that Michelle didn't recognize—an old one, probably. He shook his head. "I have no idea what's happening here. The only thing I have to suggest is that this is some kind of wild coincidence."

"I don't believe in that kind of coincidence," Michelle said.

Davout smiled. "A good attitude for a researcher," he said. "But experience—well," he waved a hand.

But he loved her, Michelle insisted inwardly. She knew that in her heart. Stephanie was the woman he loved after Claire died, and then she was killed and Terzian went on to create the intellectual framework on which the world was now built. He had spent his modest fortune building pilot programs in Africa that demonstrated his vision was a practical one. The whole modern world was a monument to Stephanie.

Everyone was young then, Michelle thought. Even the seventy-year-olds were young compared to the people now. The world must have been *ablaze* with love and passion. But Davout didn't understand that because he was old and had forgotten all about love.

"Michelle..." Darton's voice came wafting over the waters.

Bastard. Michelle wasn't about to let him spoil this.

Her fingers formed <gotta go>. "I'll send you everything once it comes in," she said. "I think we've got something amazing here."

She picked up her deck and swung it around so that she could be sure that the light from the display couldn't be seen from the ocean. Her bare back against the rough bark of the ironwood, she began flashing through the data as it arrived.

She couldn't find the police report. Michelle went in search of it and discovered that all police records from that period in Venetian history had been wiped out in the Lightspeed War, leaving her only with what had been reported in the media.

"Where are you? I love you!" Darton's voice came from farther away. He'd narrowed his search, that was clear, but he still wasn't sure exactly where Michelle had built her nest.

Smiling, Michelle closed her deck and slipped it into its pouch. Her spiders would work for her tirelessly till dawn while she dreamed on in her hammock and let Darton's distant calls lull her to sleep.

❉

They shifted their lodgings every few days. Terzian always arranged for separate bedrooms. Once, as they sat in the evening shade of a farm terrace and watched the setting sun shimmer on the silver leaves of the olives, Terzian found himself looking at her as she sat in an old cane chair, at the profile cutting sharp against the old limestone of the Vaucluse. The blustering wind brought gusts of lavender from the neighboring farm, a scent that made Terzian want to inhale until his lungs creaked against his ribs.

From a quirk of Stephanie's lips Terzian was suddenly aware that she knew he was looking at her. He glanced away.

"You haven't tried to sleep with me," she said.

"No," he agreed.

"But you *look*," she said. "And it's clear you're not a eunuch."

"We fight all the time," Terzian pointed out. "Sometimes we can't stand to be in the same room."

Stephanie smiled. "That wouldn't stop most of the men I've known. Or the women, either."

Terzian looked out over the olives, saw them shimmer in the breeze. "I'm still in love with my wife," he said.

There was a moment of silence. "That's well," she said.

And I'm angry at her, too, Terzian thought. Angry at Claire for deserting him. And he was furious at the universe for killing her

319

and for leaving him alive, and he was angry at God even though he didn't believe in God. The Trashcanians had been good for him, because he could let his rage and his hatred settle there, on people who deserved it.

Those poor drunken bastards, he thought. Whatever they'd expected in that hotel corridor, it hadn't been a berserk grieving American who would just as soon have ripped out their throats with his bare hands.

The question was, could he do that again? It had all occurred without his thinking about it, old reflexes taking over, but he couldn't count on that happening a second time. He'd been trying to remember the Kenpo he'd once learned, particularly all the tricks against weapons. He found himself miming combats on his long country hikes, and he wondered if he'd retained any of his ability to take a punch.

He kept the gun with him, so the Trashcanians wouldn't get it if they searched his room when he was away. When he was alone, walking through the almond orchards or on a hillside fragrant with wild thyme, he practiced drawing it, snicking off the safety, and putting pressure on the trigger... The first time the trigger pull would be hard, but the first shot would cock the pistol automatically and after that the trigger pull would be light.

He wondered if he should buy more ammunition. But he didn't know how to buy ammunition in France and didn't know if a foreigner could get into trouble that way.

"We're both angry," Stephanie said. He looked at her again, her hand raised to her head to keep the gusts from blowing her long ringlets in her face. "We're angry at death. But love must make it more complicated for you."

Her green eyes searched him. "It's not death you're in love with, is it? Because—"

Terzian blew up. She had no right to suggest that he was in a secret alliance with death just because he didn't want to turn a bunch of Africans green. It was their worst argument, and this one ended with both of them stalking away through the fields and orchards while the scent of lavender pursued them on the wind.

When Terzian returned to his room he checked his caches of money, half-hoping that Stephanie had stolen his Euros and run. She hadn't.

He thought of going into her room while she was away, stealing the papiloma and taking a train north, handing it over to the Pasteur Institute or someplace. But he didn't.

In the morning, during breakfast, Stephanie's cell phone rang, and she answered. He watched while her face turned from curiosity to apprehension to utter terror. Adrenaline sang in his blood as he watched, and he leaned forward, feeling the familiar rage rise in him, just where he wanted it. In haste she turned off the phone, then looked at him. "That was one of them. He says he knows where we are, and wants to make a deal."

"If they know where we are," Terzian found himself saying coolly, "why aren't they here?"

"We've got to *go*," she insisted.

So they went. Clean out of France and into the Tuscan hills, with Stephanie's cell phone left behind in a trash can at the train station and a new phone purchased in Siena. The Tuscan country-side was not unlike Provence, with vine-covered hillsides, orchards a-shimmer with the silver-green of olive trees, and walled medieval towns perched on crags; but the slim, tall cypress standing like sentries gave the hills a different profile and there were different types of wine grapes, and many of the vineyards rented rooms where people could stay and sample the local hospitality. Terzian didn't speak the language, and because Spanish was his first foreign language consistently pronounced words like "villa" and "panzanella" as if they were Spanish. But Stephanie had grown up in Italy and spoke the language not only like a native, but like a native Roman.

Florence was only a few hours away, and Terzian couldn't re-sist visiting one of the great living monuments to civilization. His parents, both university professors, had taken him to Europe several times as a child, but somehow never made it here.

Terzian and Stephanie spent a day wandering the center of town, on occasion taking shelter from one of the pelting rainstorms that shattered the day. At one point, with thunder booming overhead, they found themselves in the Basilica di Santa Croce.

"Holy Cross," Terzian said, translating. "That's your outfit."

"We have nothing to do with this church," Stephanie said. "We don't even have a collection box here."

"A pity," Terzian said as he looked at the soaked swarms of tourists packed in the aisles. "You'd clean up."

Thunder accompanied the camera strobes that flashed against the huge tomb of Galileo like a vast lighting storm. "Nice of them to forget about that Inquisition thing and bury him in a church," Terzian said.

"I expect they just wanted to keep an eye on him."

It was the power of capital, Terzian knew, that had built this church, that had paid for the stained glass and the Giotto frescoes and the tombs and cenotaphs to the great names of Florence: Dante, Michelangelo, Bruni, Alberti, Marconi, Fermi, Rossini, and of course Machiavelli. This structure, with its vaults and chapels and sarcophagi and chanting Franciscans, had been raised by successful bankers, people to whom money was a real, tangible thing, and who had paid for the centuries of labor to build the basilica with caskets of solid, weighty coined silver.

"So what do you think he would make of this?" Terzian asked, nodding at the resting place of Machiavelli, now buried in the city from which he'd been exiled in his lifetime.

Stephanie scowled at the unusually plain sarcophagus with its Latin inscription. "No praise can be high enough," she translated, then turned to him as tourist cameras flashed. "Sounds overrated."

"He was a republican, you know," Terzian said. "You don't get that from just *The Prince*. He wanted Florence to be a republic, defended by citizen soldiers. But when it fell into the hands of a despot, he needed work, and he wrote the manual for despotism. But he looked at despotism a little too clearly, and he didn't get the job." Terzian turned to Stephanie. "He was the founder of modern political theory, and that's what I do. And he based his ideas on the belief that all human beings, at all times, have had the same passions." He turned his eyes deliberately to Stephanie's shoulder bag. "That may be about to end, right? You're going to turn people into plants. That should change the passions if anything would."

"Not *plants*," Stephanie hissed, and glanced left and right at the crowds. "And not *here*." She began to move down the aisle, in the direction of Michelangelo's ornate tomb, with its draped figures who appeared not in mourning, but as if they were trying to puzzle out a difficult engineering problem.

"What happens in your scheme," Terzian said, following, "is that the market in food crashes. But that's not the *real* problem. The real problem is what happens to the market in *labor*."

Tourist cameras flashed. Stephanie turned her head away from the array of Kodaks. She passed out of the basilica and to the portico. The cloudburst had come to an end, but rainwater still drizzled off the structure. They stepped out of the droplets and down the stairs into the piazza.

The piazza was walled on all sides by old palaces, most of which now held restaurants or shops on the ground floor. To the left, one long palazzo was covered with canvas and scaffolding. The sound of pneumatic hammers banged out over the piazza. Terzian waved a hand in the direction of the clatter.

"Just imagine that food is nearly free," he said. "Suppose you and your children can get most of your food from standing in the sunshine. My next question is, *Why in hell would you take a filthy job like standing on a scaffolding and sandblasting some old building?*"

He stuck his hands in his pockets and began walking at Stephanie's side along the piazza. "Down at the bottom of the labor market, there are a lot of people whose labor goes almost entirely for the necessities. Millions of them cross borders illegally in order to send enough money back home to support their children."

"You think I don't know that?"

"The only reason that there's a market in illegal immigrants is that *there are jobs that well-off people won't do.* Dig ditches. Lay roads. Clean sewers. Restore old buildings. Build *new* buildings. The well-off might serve in the military or police, because there's a certain status involved and an attractive uniform, but we won't guard prisons no matter how pretty the uniform is. That's strictly a job for the laboring classes, and if the laboring classes are too well-off to labor, who guards the prisons?"

She rounded on him, her lips set in an angry line. "So I'm supposed to be afraid of people having more choice in where they work?"

"No," Terzian said, "you should be afraid of people having *no choice at all.* What happens when markets collapse is *intervention*—and that's state intervention, if the market's critical enough, and you can bet the labor market's critical. And because the state depends on ditch-diggers and prison guards and janitors and road-builders for its very being, then if these classes of people are no longer available, and the very survival of civil society depends on their existence, in the end the state will just *take* them.

"You think our friends in Transnistria will have any qualms about rounding up people at gunpoint and forcing them to do labor? The powerful are going to want their palaces kept nice and shiny. The liberal democracies will try volunteerism or lotteries or whatever, but you can bet that we're going to want our sewers to work, and somebody to carry our grandparents' bedpans, and the trucks to the supermarkets to run on time. And what *I'm* afraid of is that when things get desperate, we're not going to be any nicer about getting our way than those Sovietists of yours. We're going to make sure that the lower orders do their jobs, even if we have to kill half of them to convince the other half that we mean business. And the technical term for that is *slavery.* And if someone of

African descent isn't sensitive to *that* potential problem, then I am very surprised."

The fury in Stephanie's eyes was visible even through her shades, and he could see the pulse pounding in her throat. Then she said, "I'll save the *people,* that's what I'm good at. You save the rest of the world, *if* you can." She began to turn away, then swung back to him. "And by the way," she added, "fuck you!"—and turned, and marched away.

"Slavery or anarchy, Stephanie!" Terzian called, taking a step after. "That's the choice you're forcing on people!"

He really felt he had the rhetorical momentum now, and he wanted to enlarge the point by saying that he knew some people thought anarchy was a good thing, but no anarchist he'd ever met had ever even *seen* a real anarchy, or been in one, whereas Stephanie had—drop your anarchist out of a helicopter into the eastern Congo, say, with all his theories and with whatever he could carry on his back, and see how well he prospered…

But Terzian never got to say any of these things, because Stephanie was gone, receding into the vanishing point of a busy street, the shoulder bag swinging back and forth across her butt like a pendulum powered by the force of her convictions.

Terzian thought that perhaps he'd never see her again, that he'd finally provoked her into abandoning him and continuing on her quest alone, but when he stepped off the bus in Montespèrtoli that night, he saw her across the street, shouting into her cell phone.

The next day, as with frozen civility they drank their morning coffee, she said she was going to Rome the next day. "They might be looking for me there," she said, "because my parents live there. But I won't go near the family, I'll meet Odile at the airport and give her the papiloma."

Odile? Terzian thought. "I should go along," he said.

"What are you going to do?" she said. "Carry that gun into an *airport?*"

"I don't have to take the gun. I'll leave it in the hotel room in Rome."

She considered. "Very well."

Again, that night, Terzian found the tumbled castle in Provence haunting his thoughts, that ruined relic of a bygone order, and once more considered stealing the papiloma and running. And again, he didn't.

They didn't get any farther than Florence, because Stephanie's cell phone rang as they waited in the train station. Odile was in Venice. "*Venezia?*" Stephanie shrieked in anger. She clenched her fists. There had been a cache of weapons found at the Fiumicino airport in Rome, and all planes had been diverted, Odile's to Marco Polo outside Venice. Frenzied booking agents had somehow found rooms for her despite the height of the tourist season.

Fiumicino hadn't been reopened, and Odile didn't know how she was going to get to Rome. "Don't try!" Stephanie shouted. "I'll come to *you.*"

This meant changing their tickets to Rome for tickets to Venice. Despite Stephanie's excellent Italian the ticket seller clearly wished the crazy tourists would make up their mind which monuments of civilization they really wanted to see.

Strange—Terzian had actually *planned* to go to Venice in five days or so. He was scheduled to deliver a paper at the Conference of Classical and Modern Thought.

Maybe, if this whole thing was over by then, he'd read the paper after all. It wasn't a prospect he coveted: he would just be developing another footnote to a footnote.

The hills of Tuscany soon began to pour across the landscape like a green flood. The train slowed at one point—there was work going on on the tracks, men with bronze arms and hard hats—and Terzian wondered how, in the Plant People Future, in the land of Cockaigne, the tracks would ever get fixed, particularly in this heat. He supposed there were people who were meant by nature to fix tracks, who would repair tracks as an avocation or out of boredom regardless of whether they got paid for their time or not, but he suspected there wouldn't be many of them.

You could build machines, he supposed, robots or something. But they had their own problems, they'd cause pollution and absorb resources and on top of everything they'd break down and have to be repaired. And who would do *that*?

If you can't employ the carrot, Terzian thought, if you can't reward people for doing necessary labor, then you have to use the stick. You march people out of the cities at gunpoint, like Pol Pot, because there's work that needs to be done.

He tapped his wedding ring on the arm of his chair and wondered what jobs would still have value. Education, he supposed; he'd made a good choice there. Some sorts of administration were necessary. There were people who were natural artists or bureaucrats or salesmen and who would do that job whether they were paid or not.

A woman came by with a cart and sold Terzian some coffee and a nutty snack product that he wasn't quite able to identify. And then he thought, *labor.*

"Labor," he said. In a world in which all basic commodities were provided, the thing that had most value was actual labor. Not the stuff that labor bought, but the work itself.

"Okay," he said, "it's labor that's rare and valuable, because people don't *have* to do it anymore. The currency has to be based on some kind of labor exchange—you purchase *x* hours with *y* dollars. Labor is the thing you use to pay taxes."

Stephanie gave Terzian a suspicious look. "What's the difference between that and slavery?"

"Have you been reading Nozick?" Terzian scolded. "The difference is the same as the difference between *paying taxes* and *being a slave.* All the time you don't spend paying your taxes is your own." He barked a laugh. "I'm resurrecting Labor Value Theory!" he said. "Adam Smith and Karl Marx are dancing a jig on their tombstones! In Plant People Land the value is the *labor itself! The calories!*" He laughed again, and almost spilled coffee down his chest.

"You budget the whole thing in calories! The government promises to pay you a dollar's worth of calories in exchange for their currency! In order to keep the roads and the sewer lines going, a citizen owes the government a certain number of calories per year—he can either pay in person or hire someone else to do the job. And jobs can be budgeted in calories-per-hour, so that if you do hard physical labor, you owe fewer hours than someone with a desk job—that should keep the young, fit, impatient people doing the nasty jobs, so that they have more free time for their other pursuits." He chortled. "Oh, the intellectuals are going to just hate this! They're used to valuing their brain power over manual labor—I'm going to reverse their whole scale of values!"

Stephanie made a pffing sound. "The people I care about have no money to pay taxes at all."

"They have bodies. They can still be enslaved." Terzian got out his laptop. "Let me put my ideas together."

Terzian's frenetic two-fingered typing went on for the rest of the journey, all the way across the causeway that led into Venice. Stephanie gazed out the window at the lagoon soaring by, the soaring water birds and the dirt and stink of industry. She kept the Nike bag in her lap until the train pulled into the Stazione Ferrovie dello Stato Santa Lucia at the end of its long journey.

Odile's hotel was in Cannaregio, which according to the map purchased in the station gift shop was the district of the city nearest the station and away from most of the tourist sites. A brisk wind almost tore the map from their fingers as they left the station, and their vaporetto bucked a steep chop on the greygreen Grand Canal as it took them to the Ca' d'Oro, the fanciful white High Gothic palazzo that loomed like a frantic wedding cake above a swarm of bobbing gondolas and motorboats.

Stephanie puffed cigarettes at first with ferocity, then with satisfaction. Once they got away from the Grand Canal and into Cannaregio itself they quickly became lost. The twisted medieval streets were broken on occasion by still, silent canals, but the canals didn't seem to lead anywhere in particular. Cooking smells demonstrated that it was dinnertime, and there were few people about, and

no tourists. Terzian's stomach rumbled. Sometimes the streets de-
teriorated into mere passages. Stephanie and Terzian were in such a
passage, holding their map open against the wind and shouting directions at each other when someone slugged Terzian from behind.

He went down on one knee with his head ringing and the taste of
blood in his mouth, and then two people rather unexpectedly picked
him up again, only to slam him against the passage wall. Through
some miracle he managed not to hit his head on the brickwork and
knock himself out. He could smell garlic on the breath of one of the
attackers. Air went out of him as he felt an elbow to his ribs.

It was the scream from Stephanie that fortified his attention. There
was violent motion in front of him, and he saw the Nike swoosh and
remembered that he was dealing with killers and that he had a gun.

In an instant Terzian had his rage back. He felt his lungs fill with
the fury that spread through his body like a river of scalding blood.
He planted his feet and twisted abruptly to his left, letting the strength
come up his legs from the earth itself, and the man attached to his right
arm gave a grunt of surprise and swung counterclockwise. Terzian
twisted the other way, which budged the other man only a little, but
which freed his right arm to claw into his right pants pocket.

And from this point on it was just the movement that he
rehearsed. Draw, thumb the safety, pull the trigger hard. He shot
the man on his right and hit him in the groin. For a brief second
Terzian saw his pinched face, the face that reflected such pain that
it folded in on itself, and he remembered Adrian falling in the Place
Dauphine with just that look. Then he stuck the pistol in the ribs
of the man on his left and fired twice. The arms that grappled him
relaxed and fell away.

There were two more men grappling with Stephanie. That made
four altogether, and Terzian reasoned dully that after the first three
fucked up in Paris, the home office had sent a supervisor. One was
trying to tug the Nike bag away, and Terzian lunged toward him
and fired at a range of two meters, too close to miss, and the man
dropped to the ground with a whuff of pain.

The last man had ahold of Stephanie and swung her around, keeping her between himself and the pistol. Terzian could see the knife in his hand and recognized it as one he'd seen before. Her dark glasses were cockeyed on her face and Terzian caught a flash of her angry green eyes. He pointed the pistol at the knife man's face. He didn't dare shoot.

"*Police!*" he shrieked into the wind. "*Policia!*" He used the Spanish word. Bloody spittle spattered the cobblestones as he screamed.

In the Trashcanian's eyes he saw fear, bafflement, rage.

"*Polizia!*" He got the pronunciation right this time. He saw the rage in Stephanie's eyes, the fury that mirrored his own, and he saw her struggle against the man who held her.

"*No!*" he called. Too late. The knife man had too many decisions to make all at once, and Terzian figured he wasn't very bright to begin with. *Kill the hostages* was probably something he'd been taught on his first day at Goon School.

As Stephanie fell, Terzian fired, and kept firing as the man ran away. The killer broke out of the passageway into a little square, and then just fell down.

The slide of the automatic locked back as Terzian ran out of ammunition, and then he staggered forward to where Stephanie was bleeding to death on the cobbles.

Her throat had been cut and she couldn't speak. She gripped his arm as if she could drive her urgent message through the skin, with her nails. In her eyes he saw frustrated rage, the rage he knew well, until at length he saw there nothing at all, a nothing he knew better than any other thing in the world.

He shouldered the Nike bag and staggered out of the passageway into the tiny Venetian square with its covered well. He took a street at random, and there was Odile's hotel. Of course: the Trashcanians had been staking it out.

It wasn't much of a hotel, and the scent of spice and garlic in the lobby suggested the desk clerk was eating his dinner. Terzian went up the stair to Odile's room and knocked on the door. When she opened—she was a plump girl with big hips and a suntan—he tossed the Nike bag on the bed.

"You need to get back to Mogadishu right away," he said. "Stephanie just died for that."

Her eyes widened. Terzian stepped to the wash basin to clean the blood off as best he could. It was all he could do not to shriek with grief and anger.

"You take care of the starving," he said finally, "and I'll save the rest of the world."

❊

Michelle rose from the sea near Torbiong's boat, having done thirty-six hundred calories'-worth of research and caught a honeycomb grouper into the bargain. She traded the fish for the supplies he brought. "Any more blueberries?" she asked.

"Not this time." He peered down at her, narrowing his eyes against the bright shimmer of sun on the water. "That young man of yours is being quite a nuisance. He's keeping the turtles awake and scaring the fish."

The mermaid tucked away her wings and arranged herself in her rope sling. "Why don't you throw him off the island?"

"My authority doesn't run that far." He scratched his jaw. "He's interviewing people. Adding up all the places you've been seen. He'll find you pretty soon, I think."

"Not if I don't want to be found. He can yell all he likes, but I don't have to answer."

"Well, maybe." Torbiong shook his head. "Thanks for the fish."

Michelle did some preliminary work with her new samples and then abandoned them for anything new that her search spiders had discovered. She had a feeling she was on the verge of something colossal.

She carried her deck to her overhanging limb and let her legs dangle over the water while she looked through the new data. While paging through the new information, she ate something called a Raspberry Dynamo Bar that Torbiong had thrown in with her supplies. The old man must have included it as a joke: it was over-sweet and sticky with marshmallow and strangely flavored. She chucked it in the water and hoped it wouldn't poison any fish.

Stephanie Pais had been killed in what the news reports called a "street fight" among a group of foreign visitors. Since the authorities couldn't connect the foreigners to Pais, they had to assume she was an innocent bystander caught up in the violence. The papers didn't mention Terzian at all.

Michelle looked through pages of follow-up. The gun that had shot the four men had never been found, though nearby canals were dragged. Two of the foreigners had survived the fight, though one died eight weeks later from complications of an operation. The survivor maintained his innocence and claimed that a complete stranger had opened fire on him and his friends, but the judges hadn't believed him and sent him to prison. He lived a great many years and died in the Lightspeed War, along with most people caught in prisons during that deadly time.

One of the four men was Belarusian. Another Ukrainian. Another two Moldovan. All had served in the Soviet military in the past, in the Fourteenth Army in Transnistria. It frustrated Michelle that she couldn't shout back in time to tell the Italians to connect these four to the murder of another ex-Soviet, seven weeks earlier, in Paris.

What the hell had Pais and Terzian been up to? Why were all these people with Transnistrian connections killing each other, and Pais?

Maybe it was Pais they'd been after all along. Her records at Santa Croce were missing, which was odd because other personnel records from the time had survived. Perhaps someone was arranging that certain things not be known.

She tried a search on Santa Croce itself, and slogged through descriptions and mentions of a whole lot of Italian churches, including the famous one in Florence where Terzian and Pais had been seen at Machiavelli's tomb. She refined the search to the Santa

Croce relief organization, and found immediately the fact that let it all fall into place.

Santa Croce had maintained a refugee camp in Moldova during the civil war following the establishment of Transnistria. Michelle was willing to bet that Stephanie Pais had served in that camp. She wondered if any of the other players had been residents there.

She looked at the list of other camps that Santa Croce had maintained in that period, which seemed to have been a busy one for them. One name struck her as familiar, and she had to think for a moment before she remembered why she didn't know it. It was at a Santa Croce camp in the Sidamo province of Ethiopia where the Green Leopard Plague had first broken out, the first transgenetic epidemic.

It had been the first real attempt to modify the human body at the cellular level, to help marginal populations synthesize their own food, and it had been primitive compared to the more successful mods that came later. The ideal design for the efficient use of chlorophyll was a leaf, not Homo sapiens—the designer would have been better advised to create a plague that made its victims leafy, and later designers, aiming for the same effect, did exactly that. And Green Leopard's designer had forgotten that the epidermis already contains a solar-activated enzyme: melanin. The result on the African subjects was green skin mottled with dark splotches, like the black spots on an implausibly verdant leopard.

The Green Leopard Plague broke out in the Sidamo camp, then at other camps in the Horn of Africa. Then it leaped clean across the continent to Mozambique, where it first appeared at an Oxfam camp in the flood zone, then spread rapidly across the continent, then leaped across oceans. It had been a generation before anyone found a way to disable it, and by then other transgenetic modifiers had been released into the population, and there was no going back.

The world had entered Terzian's future, the one he had proclaimed at the Conference of Classical and Modern Thought.

What, Michelle thought excitedly, if Terzian had known about Green Leopard ahead of time? His Cornucopia Theory had seemed prescient precisely because Green Leopard appeared just a few weeks after he'd delivered his paper. But if those Eastern Bloc thugs had been involved somehow in the plague's transmission, or were attempting to prevent Pais and Terzian from sneaking the modified virus to the camps...

Yes! Michelle thought exultantly. That had to be it. No one had ever worked out where Green Leopard originated, but there had always been suspicion directed toward several semi-covert labs in the former Soviet empire. This was *it.* The only question was how Terzian, that American in Paris, had got involved...

It had to be Stephanie, she thought. Stephanie, who Terzian had loved and who had loved him, and who had involved him in the desperate attempt to aid refugee populations.

For a moment Michelle bathed in the beauty of the idea. Stephanie, dedicated and in love, had been murdered for her beliefs—real-death!—and Terzian, broken-hearted, had carried on and brought the future—Michelle's present—into being. A *wonderful* story. And no one had known it till *now,* no one had understood Stephanie's sacrifice, or Terzian's grief...not until the lonely mermaid, working in isolation on her rock, had puzzled it out.

"Hello, Michelle," Darton said.

Michelle gave a cry of frustration and glared in fury down at her lover. He was in a yellow plastic kayak—kayaking was popular here, particularly in the Rock Islands—and Darton had slipped his electric-powered boat along the margin of the island, moving in near-silence. He looked grimly up at her from below the pitcher plant that dangled below the overhang.

They had rebuilt him, of course, after his death. All the data was available in backup, in Delhi where he'd been taken apart, recorded, and rebuilt as an ape. He was back in a conventional male body, with the broad shoulders and white smile and short hairy bandy legs she remembered.

Michelle knew he hadn't made any backups during their time in Belau. He had his memories up to the point where he'd lain down on the nanobed in Delhi. That had been the moment when his love of Michelle had been burning its hottest, when he had just made the commitment to live with Michelle as an ape in the Rock Islands.

That burning love had been consuming him in the weeks since his resurrection, and Michelle was glad of it, had been rejoicing in every desperate, unanswered message that Darton sent sizzling through the ether.

"Damn it," Michelle said, "I'm working."

<Talk to me> Darton's fingers formed. Michelle's fingers made a ruder reply.

"I don't understand," Darton said. "We were in love. We were going to be together."

"I'm not talking to you," Michelle said. She tried to concentrate on her video display.

"We were still together when the accident happened," Darton said. "I don't understand why we can't be together now."

"I'm not listening, either," said Michelle.

"*I'm not leaving, Michelle!*" Darton screamed. "*I'm not leaving till you talk to me!*"

White cockatoos shrieked in answer. Michelle quietly picked up her deck, rose to her feet, and headed inland. The voice that followed her was amplified, and she realized Darton had brought his bullhorn.

"*You can't get away, Michelle! You've got to tell me what happened!*"

I'll tell you about Lisa Lee, she thought, *so you can send her desperate messages, too.*

Michelle had been deliriously happy for her first month in Belau, living in arboreal nests with Darton and spending the warm days describing their island's unique biology. It was their first vacation, in Prague, that had torn Michelle's happiness apart. It was there that they'd met Lisa Lee Baxter, the American tourist who thought apes were cute, and who wondered what these shaggy kids were doing so far from an arboreal habitat.

It wasn't long before Michelle realized that Lisa Lee was at least two hundred years old, and that behind her diamond-blue eyes was the withered, mummified soul that had drifted into Prague from some waterless desert of the spirit, a soul that required for its continued existence the blood and vitality of the young. Despite her age and presumed experience Lisa Lee's ploys seemed to Michelle to be so *obvious,* so *blatant.* Darton fell for them all.

It was only because Lisa Lee had finally tired of him that Darton returned to Belau, chastened and solemn and desperate to be in love with Michelle again. But by then it was Michelle who was tired. And who had access to Darton's medical records from the downloads in Delhi.

"You can't get away, Michelle!"

Well, maybe not. Michelle paused with one hand on the banyan's trunk. She closed her deck's display and stashed it in a mesh bag with some of her other stuff, then walked again out again on the overhanging limb.

"I'm not going to talk to you like this," she said. "And you can't get onto the island from that side, the overhang's too acute."

"Fine," Darton said. The shouting had made him hoarse. "Come down here, then."

She rocked forward and dived off the limb. The saltwater world exploded in her senses. She extended her wings and fluttered close to Darton's kayak, rose, and shook seawater from her eyes.

"There's a tunnel," she said. "It starts at about two meters and exits into the lake. You can swim it easily if you hold your breath."

"All right," he said. "Where is it?"

"Give me your anchor."

She took his anchor, floated to the bottom, and set it where it wouldn't damage the live coral.

She remembered the needle she'd taken to Jellyfish Lake, the needle she'd loaded with the mango extract to which Darton was violently allergic. Once in the midst of the jellyfish swarm, it had been easy to jab the needle into Darton's calf, then let it drop to the anoxic depths of the lake.

He probably thought she'd given him a playful pinch.

Michelle had exulted in Darton's death, the pallor, the labored breathing, the desperate pleading in the eyes.

It wasn't murder, after all, not really, just a fourth-degree felony. They'd build a new Darton in a matter of days. What was the value of a human life, when it could be infinitely duplicated, and cheaply? As far as Michelle was concerned, Darton had amusement value only.

The rebuilt Darton still loved her, and Michelle enjoyed that as well, enjoyed the fact she caused him anguish, that he would pay for ages for his betrayal of her love.

Linda Lee Baxter could take a few lessons from the mermaid, Michelle thought.

Michelle surfaced near the tunnel and raised a hand with the fingers set at <follow me>. Darton rolled off the kayak, still in his clothes, and splashed clumsily toward her.

"Are you sure about this?" he asked.

"Oh yes," Michelle replied. "You go first, I'll follow and pull you out if you get in trouble."

He loved her, of course. That was why he panted a few times for breath, filled his lungs, and dove.

Michelle had not, of course, bothered to mention the tunnel was fifteen meters long, quite far to go on a single breath. She followed him, very interested in how this would turn out, and when Darton got into trouble in one of the narrow places and tried to back out, she grabbed his shoes and held him right where he was.

He fought hard but none of his kicks struck her. She would remember the look in his wide eyes for a long time, the thunderstruck disbelief in the instant before his breath exploded from his lungs and he died.

She wished she could speak again the parting words she'd whispered into Darton's ear when he lay dying on the ridge above Jellyfish Lake. *"I've just killed you. And I'm going to do it again."*

But even if she could have spoken the words underwater, they would have been untrue. Michelle supposed this was the last time she could kill him. Twice was dangerous, but a third time would be too clear a pattern. She could end up in jail for a while, though of course you only did severe prison time for realdeath.

She supposed she would have to discover his body at some point, but if she cast the kayak adrift it wouldn't have to be for a while. And then she'd be thunderstruck and grief-stricken that he'd thrown away his life on this desperate attempt to pursue her after she'd turned her back on him and gone inland, away from the sound of his voice.

Michelle looked forward to playing that part.

She pulled up the kayak's anchor and let it coast away on the six-knot tide, then folded away her wings and returned to her nest in the banyan tree. She let the breeze dry her skin and got her deck from its bag and contemplated the data about Terzian and Stephanie Pais and the outbreak of the Green Leopard Plague.

Stephanie had died for what she believed in, murdered by the agents of an obscure, murderous regime. It had been Terzian who had shot those four men in her defense, that was clear to her now. And Terzian, who lived a long time and then died in the Lightspeed War along with a few billion other people, had loved Stephanie and kept her secret till his death, a secret shared with the others who loved Stephanie and spread the plague among the refugee populations of the world.

It was realdeath that people suffered then, the death that couldn't be corrected. Michelle knew that she understood that kind of death only as an intellectual abstract, not as something she would ever have to face or live with. To lose someone *permanently*... That was something she couldn't grasp. Even the ancients, who faced real-death every day, hadn't been able to accept it, that's why they'd invented the myth of Heaven.

Michelle thought about Stephanie's death, the death that must have broken Terzian's heart, and she contemplated the secret Terzian had kept all those years, and she decided that she was not inclined to reveal it.

Oh, she'd give Davout the facts, that was what he paid her for. She'd tell him what she could find out about Stephanie and the

Transnistrians. But she wouldn't mention the camps that Santa Croce had built across the starvation-scarred world, she wouldn't point him at Sidamo and Green Leopard. If he drew those conclusions himself, then obviously the secret was destined to be revealed. But she suspected he wouldn't—he was too old to connect those dots, not when obscure ex-Soviet entities and relief camps in the Horn of Africa were so far out of his reference.

Michelle would respect Terzian's love, and Stephanie's secret. She had some secrets of her own, after all.

The lonely mermaid finished her work for the day and sat on her overhanging limb to gaze down at the sea, and she wondered how long it would be before Darton called her again, and how she would torture him when he did.

With thanks to Dr. Stephen C. Lee.

DIAMONDS FROM TEQUILA

1.

"**N**o," says Ossley. "No. Really. You can make diamonds out of tequila."

"Sell enough tequila," says Yunakov, "and you can buy all the diamonds you want."

"That's not what I mean," says Ossley.

We're sitting in Yunakov's room at the resort, with the breeze roaring through the windows and doors and sweeping our cannabis smoke out to sea. In one corner of the room a 3D printer hums through its routine, and in another corner is a curved wet bar with two stools and about fifteen half-empty bottles of liquor. Six or eight of us are sitting around a blocky wooden coffee table on which is perched a large clear plastic bong that Ossley had printed out on the first day of principal photography.

The movie is called *Desperation Reef*. Yunakov is the prop master, and Ossley is his assistant. The others in the room are members of the crew: a couple gaffers, a wardrobe assistant, a set dresser, and somebody's cousin named Chip.

I'm the star of the picture. In fact I'm a very big star, and the producers are spending a couple hundred million dollars to make me a bigger one; but I'm not so big a star that I can't hang with the crew.

I want the crew to like me, because they can make me look good. And besides, they have the best dank on the set.

We're in Mexico, but we're not smoking Mexican bud. Buying dank in Mexico is hazardous, largely because the dealer would likely turn you in to the cops, who in turn would put you in jail, then confiscate the weed and sell it back to the dealer. Plus of course there would be the embarrassment of having a major Hollywood guy busted in Mexico, with all the outcry and bribes that would involve.

No, this is 420 grown in California, where it's pretty much legal, and smuggled to Mexico, where it isn't, in boxes of film equipment. All of which is fine with me, because California has the best of everything, including the best herb.

In fact I'm less than thrilled to be in a foreign country, where people speak a foreign language and have foreign customs and serve Mexican food that isn't as good as the Mexican food I can get in L.A. But still, I'm a big international star, so even though I'm in a foreign country everyone is treating me very well; and that's better than being treated as a washed-up has-been in California, which is also within my experience.

We watch as Chip—the person who is somebody's cousin— sparks the bong's bowl and inhales a truly heroic amount of smoke, a binger big enough to keep him cross-eyed for hours... After an appreciative pause, Ossley says, "No, really. You have to heat the tequila up to eight hundred degrees centigrade, after which nano-scale diamonds will precipitate onto trays of silicon or steel. There are, like, industrial applications."

"You're just making this shit up," says Yunakov, but by that point someone's looked up the answer on their phone and discovered that the story is true, or at least true on the Internet. Which is not always the same thing.

At which time the 3D printer, which has been humming away in its corner, makes a final mechanical whine, and then dies. Ossley half-crawls across the tile floor to the machine and removes an object that looks like a thick-walled laboratory beaker. It isn't entirely transparent: there seem to be yellowish layers made of slightly different materials.

"Okay," he says. "Here's my latest project."

Ossley is a short man, five-four or -five, and thin. His hair hangs in tight corkscrew curls over his ears. Black-rimmed eyeglasses magnify his eyes into vast staring Rorschach blotches, and five o'clock shadow darkens his jaw line. He wears tank tops and cargo shorts bulging with tools, cables, and electronics.

Since he's established his credibility by building James Bong with his machine, we pay attention to what follows. He goes behind the bar, produces an unlabeled bottle of wine, unscrews the cap, and pours out a glass. The wine is a deep blood red, so dark it's almost purple.

"Okay," he says. "Some friends of mine have a Central Coast winery, and they sent me this stuff to practice on. It's your basic cabernet. The cab is only a couple weeks old, just old enough that fermentation has stopped. It's been racked once, so I've filtered it to take out any remaining sediment, but otherwise it's pretty raw."

He passes it around and we all take a sample. When it's my turn I take a whiff, and it doesn't smell like much of anything. I sip, and as the wine flows over my tongue I can feel my taste buds try to actually crawl away from the stuff like victims crawling from the site of a toxic spill. I swallow it only because spitting on the floor would be rude. I pass it on.

"Two things would turn this into an acceptable wine," Ossley says from behind the bar. "Time, and aging in oak barrels. Oak is perfect for wine, and hardly any winemaker uses anything else. Oak allows oxygen to enter the wine, and oxygenation speeds the other processes that go on between oak and wine. Which have to do with hydro-hydrolysable tannins and phenols and terpenes and fur-furfurals." The cannabis makes him stumble on the technical terms.

He holds up the beaker. "I've designed this to do in a few minutes what aging in oak does in months. So let's see if it works."

Ossley puts the beaker down on the bar, then pours the wine into it. He glances at us over the bar. "The reaction can be a little, ah, splattery." He finds a plate and puts it over the top of his beaker.

"Now we wait twenty minutes or so."

We go back to enjoying our evening. The bong makes another round, and I chase my hit with a beer.

Normally I wouldn't get this chewed when I know I'll be working the next day, but in fact I have no dialog to learn for the next day's shoot. All my scenes will be underwater, and I won't have to talk.

Desperation Reef concerns my character's attempt to salvage a sunken submarine, an effort made problematic by the fact that the sub is one used by a Mexican drug cartel to smuggle narcotics to the States. The sub went down with two hundred million dollars' worth of cocaine on board, making it a desirable target for my character, a commercial diver with a serious coke habit. Unfortunately the cartel wants its drugs back, and of course the Coast Guard and DEA are also in the action.

My character Hank isn't a good guy, particularly. He starts as angry and addicted, but over the course of the film, he finds love and inspiration with Anna, the sister of one of the sailors who went down with the sub. In the climax, when cartel heavies come calling, he trades his coke spoon for a Heckler & Koch submachine gun and takes care of business.

What happens in the denouement is kind of up in the air. As it stands, the movie has two endings, by two different writers. In the first, the original, Hank raises and sells the cocaine, and he and Anna head off into the sunset many millions of dollars the richer.

In the second ending, Hank learns the important moral lesson that Drugs are Bad, he turns the coke over to the DEA, and he walks away with nothing.

The first ending, which everyone likes, makes a lot more sense in terms of Hank's character. The second ending, which no one at all likes, is an act of cowardice on the part of the producers, who are afraid of being accused of making a movie promoting drug use.

Last I've been told, we're going to film both endings, and the producers will decide during editing which ending will end up on the final film. Since film producers are notorious cowards, I figure I know which ending will end up on the picture.

Unless I make a stand or something. I could just refuse to film the second ending, or I could blow every take.

But then I'm a coward, too, so that probably won't happen.

"Right, then," Ossley says. He's back behind the bar, peering at his beaker with his huge magnified eyes. "I think the reaction's over." He gets a glass and jams it in the ice bucket, then pours the contents of the beaker into the glass. From the way he handles the beaker I can see it's hot.

The wine has changed color. It's a lot brighter shade of red.

Ossley puts a thermometer into the glass and waits till the wine reaches room temperature. Then he takes the glass from the ice bucket, and he walks from behind the bar and hands the glass to me.

"Here you go, Sean," he says. "Taste it and let me know what you think."

The outside of the glass is slippery with melted ice. I look at it with a degree of alarm. "Do I really want to drink your chemistry experiment?" I ask.

"It won't hurtcha." Ossley raises the glass to his nose, takes a whiff, and then a hearty swallow. "Give it a try."

I take the glass dubiously. I recall that, in the past, people have tried to kill me. People I didn't even *know*, and all for reasons I didn't have a clue about.

"You realize," I say, "that if you poison me, the whole production shuts down and you're out of a job?"

Ossley gives me a purse-lipped, superior look. "This is actually Version Six point One of the container," Ossley says. "I've drunk from all of them. There's nothing in there that will harm you. Not in these quantities, anyway."

I hold the glass beneath my nose and give a whiff. I'm surprised. Unlike the earlier sample, this sure as hell *smells* like wine. Ossley grins.

"See?" he says. "That's vanillin you're smelling. And some lactones that give it a kinda oakey scent."

Yunakov, the prop master, gives me a wink. "It's wine, dude," he says. "I've been drinking Ossley's product all week. It's fine."

I cautiously draw a small amount of the liquid across my tongue. It tastes more or less like red table wine. Not brilliant, but perfectly acceptable.

"Not bad," I say. "Much improved." I pass the glass to the set dresser to my right.

"See?" Ossley says. "It normally takes *months* to produce a wine of that quality, and my reactant did it in twenty minutes. Imagine what would happen to the wine industry if every winery could produce *grand cru* in twenty minutes?"

The set dresser sips, then smacks her lips critically. "This is hardly *grand cru*," she says.

"It's early days," Ossley says. "In another couple years, I'll be serving up something that you won't be able to tell from Haut-Brion."

She raises an eyebrow. "How do you account for *terroir?*" she asks.

Ossley laughs. "*Terroir* isn't a mystical thing. *Terroir* doesn't happen because your ancestors wore wooden shoes and prayed to St. Valery. It's just chemistry. Give me a chemical analysis, and I can probably duplicate the result."

There follows an earnest discussion on *terroir* and *debourbage* and *encépagement,* and I return to my beer. I like my plonk just fine, but I'm not fanatic enough about wine to care about the fiddly details.

The bong goes round one more time, and then I decide it's time to go to bed. Yunakov's room is on the ground floor of the resort, so I leave by hopping over the balcony rail onto the walk beyond, and then I lope over toward my cabana.

The sea glitters in starlight. Tropical flowers sway pale in the breeze. The beach is an opalescent shimmer.

If I close my eyes, I can almost imagine that I'm back in paradise, which is to say Southern California.

I turn the corner and jump as I hear a shriek. It's one of the hotel waiters carrying a room-service tray. The bottles and dishes give a leap, and I lunge to get them all settled before something crashes. Eventually the waiter and I get everything sorted out.

"I'm sorry, Mister Makin," the waiter says. "I didn't see you coming."

The resort is in Quintana Roo, so the waiter is Mayan and maybe five feet tall, with a broad face and beaky nose and an anxious smile. I look down at him.

"That's all right," I say. "Have a good evening."

I'm not entirely unused to hearing people scream when I turn up unexpectedly, which is why I'm an unlikely movie star.

I was a cute, big-headed kid actor when I was young, and when all America invited me into their living rooms as the star of the sitcom *Family Tree*. But when I grew, I grew tall, and my head kept growing after my body stopped. It's a condition called pedomorphosis—my head is freakishly large, and my features have retained the proportions of an infant, with a snub nose, a vast forehead, and unusually large eyes.

At the moment I look even more sinister than is usual for me, since for my morally ambiguous part I've shaved my balding head and have grown a goatee. I look like someone you really *don't* want to see looming around the corner on a dark night.

My appearance explains why my career collapsed after I stopped being cute, and why I struggled to find work for more than a decade until I was rescued by an unlikely savior—a game designer named Dagmar Shaw, who employed me as the star of a production called *Escape to Earth* that was broadcast over the Internet. I played Roheen, who was sort of an alien and sort of an angel. *Escape to Earth* was an enormous hit, and so was the sequel. I'm in negotiation with Dagmar now for more Roheen projects, but in the meantime I'm trying to expand my celebrity by starring in a feature.

My freakish face guarantees that I'll never be the star of a romantic comedy, and also that I can be accepted fairly readily as a villain—during the years I was scuffling for work, I played heavies more than anything else. So in *Desperation Reef,* I'm playing a villainous character who finds redemption and turns into a good guy.

Even if I nail the part, even if I'm absolutely brilliant, it's still unclear whether people will pay to see my weird head blown up to the size of a theater screen. After all, my only successes have been in smaller formats.

Thinking about these uncertainties, I walk to my cabana. It's a white-plastered building with a tall, peaked Mayan roof of palm-leaf thatch, all oozing local color. I open the door, and I see that Loni Rowe arrived before me. She's hunched in an armchair drinking some of my orange juice and thumbing text into her hand-held, but when she sees me arrive, she puts her phone away and stands.

"Hi," she says. "There was a camera drone overhead, so I thought I'd come to your cabana and give them something to write about."

She's a pale redhead who hides from the sun, and when she's onscreen she has to slather on the makeup to hide all her freckles. She has large brilliant teeth accentuated by a minor overbite, and a lush figure that has won her admirers all over the world. There's a popular poster of Loni that's sold millions, and it's hard to picture the room of any adolescent American male without a view of Loni's cleavage in it somewhere.

Loni is an ambitious young actress, and she has a part in the movie as the mistress of a drug lord. She's also my girlfriend— or actually, my Official Tabloid Girlfriend, good for headlines guaranteed to keep our names in the public eye.

Even though our affaire is mostly for publicity purposes, we have in fact had sex now and then. The teenagers who go to sleep every night staring at Loni's poster will be disappointed to learn the experience was pleasant enough, but nothing special. There is no passion in our relationship, because both of us are far more passionate about our careers. But Loni and I are friends, even given that we're using one another, and I imagine we'll remain friends even after we've both gone on to other tabloid romances.

Loni, you will remember, is the hottie who stole me from my previous tabloid girlfriend, Ella Swift. Ella is a much bigger star than Loni, and snagging me was quite a coup for Loni. It boosted her profile enormously.

Both tabloid romances were dreamed up by my agent, Bruce Kravitz of PanCosmos Talent Associates back in Beverly Hills. *Desperation Reef* is a near-complete PCTA package—Bruce represents most of the talent and the writer who drafted the first script—a script I've never seen from a writer I've never met—as well as the other writer who rewrote the script and created the first ending, and the *other* other writer who wrote the second ending, the one that everyone hates but which will probably be used anyway.

Bruce also represents Ella Swift, and he put us together as tabloid lovers to generate headlines for us during a period when neither of us had anything in the theaters to remind viewers that we existed. For reasons best known to herself, Ella wanted to conceal the fact that she is a lesbian and in the middle of a passionate relationship with her hairdresser.

I have no idea why Ella wants to stay in the closet, because to me the thought of her with other women makes her even more exotic and interesting; but I had no one else in my life right then and played along. So we were seen at premieres, parties, charity events, and the odd Lakers game, and I slept at her Malibu house two or three nights a week—in a guest bedroom, while she shared the master suite with the hairdresser.

Then Ella went off to South Africa to make *Kimberley*, about the diamond trade, and Loni, who is at the stage of her career when any publicity at all is good for her, agreed to become the other woman who broke Ella's heart.

The triangle generated a massive number of Bruce-generated headlines, in which Ella wept to her friends, or broke down on the set of *Kimberley*, or flew to the States to beg me to come back to her. Some weeks the tabloids dutifully reported that Loni and I were fighting on the set, or had broken up; some weeks we were about to announce our engagement. Sometimes she'd catch me talking on the phone to Ella and be furious, and sometimes I secretly flew off to Africa to be with Ella.

I was always happy to see myself in the headlines, even if the stories weren't even remotely true.

If you're in the news, it means people care. I *like* it when people care. Seeing my name on the front page of the tabloids warms my heart.

But there are a few disadvantages to becoming such a tabloid celebrity, including the camera-carrying drone aircraft that paparazzi send buzzing over our living and work spaces. These are illegal, at least in the States, but you can't arrest a drone; and if you can find and arrest the operator all you have is a man with a controller, and you can't prove that he's done anything with his controller against the law.

To me, the drones are cheating. As far as I'm concerned, the tabloids are supposed to report the stories our publicists give them, not start their own air force and find out stuff on their own.

Still, Loni had known what to do when the report came of a drone camera-bombing the hotel. She'd gone from her room to my cabana, as if for a rendezvous, and made certain that the *Tale,* or the *Weekly Damage,* or whoever, had their next story. *Loni's Secret Night Visits to Sean,* or something.

"Is the drone still up?" I ask.

Loni looks at her hand-held and checks the report filed by our nighttime security staff. "Apparently not," she says. "The coast is clear."

I walk up to her and help myself to a sip of her orange juice.

"You can stay if you like," I say.

She offers a little apologetic smile. "I'll go back to my room, if that's okay. I need a few more hours on social media tonight."

The aspiring star must network, or so it seems. "Have fun," I tell her, and finish her orange juice as she heads for the door.

Exit, texting. Apparently I'm sleeping alone tonight.

2.

Next morning I'm underwater, in scuba gear, doing about a zillion reaction shots. With the camera close on my face, I mime surprise, anger, determination, desperation, and duress. I swim across the frame left to right. I swim right to left. I go up and down. I crouch behind coral heads while imaginary bad guys swim overhead. I handle underwater salvage apparatus with apparent competence.

The director, an Englishman named Hadley, sits in a kind of tent on a converted barge and gives me instructions through underwater speakers. He's not even getting his feet wet, all he's doing is watching video monitors and sipping a macchiato made by his personal barista.

"Too small," he says. "Make it bigger."

"Too big," he says. "Make it smaller."

I hate the underwater stuff. We all do. I tried to convince the producers that we could do this all on green screen, but they didn't believe me.

I'm done by twelve-thirty, but the better part of four hours in the water has me exhausted, and the diver's mask has scored a red circle around my nose and eyes. I'm lucky that everything was filmed at shallow depth, where there's ample natural light, and I don't have to go through decompression.

A powerboat takes me back to the hotel, and on the way I decide to stop by Loni Rowe's room. I'd seen the call sheets that morning, and noted that the shooting schedule's changed and I've got a scene with Loni the next day. I want to talk to her about it—I'm thinking of giving her some of my lines actually, because they're too on the nose, as they say, for my character, but would be okay for her.

She's got a ground-floor suite in one wing of the hotel, with a patio looking out on the beach, and on the patio is some lawn furniture where a bathing suit and some towels are drying in the breeze. The bathing suit is big enough to cover her whole body, like a wet suit, and aids the pale redhead in hiding from the sun. There's a cardboard sign by the door with Loni's name, *L. Rowe*, so that people from the production staff won't wake someone else by accident.

I notice that the sliding glass door is cracked—a bird probably hit it, I think, a gull or something—and then I knock on the doorframe, open the door, and step into the air-conditioned interior.

Loni lies dead on the tiles. There's not a lot of doubt about her status, because her head is a bloody mess. Her pink sun dress is spattered with a deeper shade of red, deeper even than the red of her hair. A broken coffee cup lies on the floor next to her in a puddle of mocha liquid. There's a cloying scent in the air that wraps itself around my senses.

I look around wildly to see if there's anyone else in the room, particularly anyone with a weapon. There isn't.

My heart pounds in my throat, and my pulse is so loud in my ears that I can no longer hear the breeze, the ocean waves, or my own thoughts. I'm not a complete stranger to dead bodies, but if I'm going to face death, I need more preparation.

I back out of the room and try to remember if I touched anything. As I back onto the porch I get a tissue out of my pocket, and I scrub the door handle. Then I shut the sliding glass door, and suddenly all the glass in the doorframe falls out and crashes to the ground in a huge pile of glittering rainbow shards. The sound is louder than the cry of a guilty conscience.

Again I look around wildly, but no one seems to be paying attention. I scuttle to my cabana, and then I do the obvious thing for someone in my position.

I call my agent.

3.

"So Loni's been shot?" Bruce says.

"Shot? I guess." My gut clenches, and I bend over my dinette in a sudden agonizing spasm. "I don't know how she was killed," I say. "I only know she's dead."

"But you didn't kill her."

"No."

He ticks off the next question on his mental list.

"Do you have an alibi?"

I try to think. Thinking is hard, because my mind keeps whirling, and my guts are in a turmoil, and I keep seeing Loni's body crumpled on the floor in her pink sundress.

"I was on the underwater set all morning," I say.

"So you're fine," Bruce says. There's a tone of self-congratulation in his voice, in the logical way he's handling the crisis. "You're in the clear."

"Bruce," I say, "these aren't the Beverly Hills police we have down here. These aren't kid-gloves kind of police. They might just pin this on me because I'm handy."

"That's why you only talk with one of our lawyers present," Bruce says. "I'll have someone on his way to you in a few minutes, along with a Mexican colleague."

The gut spasm passes. I straighten. The panic begins to fade.

"Sean," Bruce says. "Do you think this might have been aimed at you? Because of, you know, what happened."

What happened a couple years ago, when a surprising number of people were trying to screw up my comeback by killing me.

Bruce's question sends a wave of paranoia jittering along my nerves, but then I consider the timeline of events.

"I don't see how," I say.

Because really, all those bad times are behind me, those times when I was traveling with bodyguards and hiding in hotel rooms and complete strangers were trying to stick me with kitchen knives.

I'm a big star now. People love me. Nobody wants me dead now except for maybe a few spoilsports.

"It's all good, Sean," Bruce says. "You're absolutely in the clear. And we'll make sure you don't have any problems."

"Okay. Okay." A sense of well-being descends on me. Bruce Kravitz is an absolute wizard at conjuring up that sense of well-being. It's how he gets things done, and how he makes people happy.

"Now," Bruce says, "you should tell somebody about the body."

The paranoia returns. "Not the police!" I say.

"No," Bruce says. "Absolutely not the police, you're right. Are any of the producers on the premises?"

"I don't know."

"I'll start calling and I'll find out. Just sit tight and remember that you're devastated."

"Of *course* I'm devastated!" I say.

"I mean," Bruce says firmly, "remember that you and Loni were supposed to be an item. It's your *girlfriend* that was killed, Sean, your *lover*. You'll have to be ready to play that."

"Right." In my panic and terror I'd sort of forgotten that everything the public knew about me and Loni was a complete fabrication.

"Can you do that, Sean? Can you play that part?" Bruce sounds like he wants reassurance, so I reassure him.

"Of course I can play that," I say. "I liked Loni. I found the body. It won't be hard."

"Good. Now I'm going to make some calls, and I'll call you right back."

Once again Bruce's voice conjures up that amazing sense of well-being. I thank him and hang up and sit down on a couch, and wait for what happens next.

4.

What happens next is Tom King, the line producer. On a set, the line producer is the person who keeps everything running, who controls the budget and supervises the production, a job that requires the financial acumen of JP Morgan and the relentless tenacity of a TV cop. He's experienced with big productions like this one, and the horrific, complex troubles they can cause.

He's knocking on my door just as my phone rings, Bruce telling me he's on his way. I open the door and let him in.

Tom King is a burly, balding man of fifty. He wears a white cotton shirt and Dockers, and he holds his phone in his hand. There's an odd little triangular patch of hair on his philtrum, hair his razor had missed that morning.

He has intelligent blue eyes that are looking at me warily through black-rimmed spectacles, as if I might explode if not handled carefully.

"Bruce tells me there's a problem," he says.

"The problem is that Loni is dead," I say, a little sharply. Because this isn't some little issue in catering or shooting schedules that needs to be smoothed out, there's an actual dead body lying in one of the rooms, and Tom seems to be regarding it less as a violent crime than as a tactical problem.

His blue eyes flicker. "Can you show me?" he asks.

"Why don't you go and look for yourself?" Because I have no desire to see Loni dead again.

"I only know what Bruce told me," he says. He is still regarding me warily, as if he's suspecting me of hallucinating.

Unhinged speculation whirls through my mind. Maybe he's used to actors going off the rails and hallucinating dead bodies. Maybe this happens to him all the time.

"Please," he says.

"I'm not going inside," I say.

"Okay. You don't have to go in."

We walk back to Loni's patio. Her towels are still fluttering in the breeze. Tom steps onto the patio and shades his eyes with his hand to look inside. I stand a good fifteen feet away, where I won't be in danger of seeing anyone dead.

"The door glass is shattered," Tom says.

"I did that. The glass broke when I shut the door."

He looks at the pile of glass and frowns. "I'm sure the code requires safety glass," he says. Which is a line producer sort of thing to say.

He gives me a look over his shoulder, seems about to say something, then decides against it. I know what he's thinking: *You broke the glass when you were fleeing the scene of your crime.*

Fuck him, I think.

He opens the door carefully and steps inside, and I hear a sudden intake of breath. I step onto the patio, feeling the cool breath of air conditioning escaping through the door, and as my eyes adjust to the shade I see Tom bent over Loni's body. He's touching her leg. He straightens, still looking down at the corpse.

"She's cold," he says. "She's been here a while."

Which lets me off the hook, as he well knows. He straightens and looks at me.

"Sean, I'm sorry," he says.

"What happened?" I ask. "Do you have any idea?"

Now that he's actually in the room, he doesn't want to look at the body. I don't want to look at it, either. We look at each other instead. And then I look past his shoulder, and I see the bullet hole in the wall behind him.

"Look," I say, pointing.

Tom steps to the wall and looks at the bullet hole. My mind is starting to recover from its shock, and I'm able to process a few of the facts.

"The bullet went through the glass door," I say, "and it hit Loni, and then it kept on going into the next room."

He looks at the hole, and he nods, and then at the same instant the same horrifying thought occurs to the both of us. He spins around, his blue eyes wide.

"Who's in the next room?" he asks.

We sprint clean around the building. I'm out of breath by the time I come to the room on the other side from Loni's, with its neat cardboard sign, *E. Cousteau.*

"Emeline," I pant. She's one of the set dressers, a French-Canadian from Montreal. I jump onto her patio, and the sliding glass door is open, so I just walk in.

"Emeline!" I call. No answer. There's a faint, sweet smell in the air.

At least there's no body on the floor. But I find the bullet hole easily enough, and looking from the hole to the door, it's clear that the bullet punched through the wall and flew out through the open door.

"What's back there?" I ask, waving an arm.

"Swimming pool, and tennis courts beyond," Tom says. "And if a bullet hit anyone out there, we'd know about it by now."

"Emeline!" I call again, and I check the bedroom, but she's not in. I return to find Tom standing pensively in the front room, staring down at one of Ossley's printed bongs sitting on the table, next to a bag of bud, which explains the cannabis scent in the air. Thoughtfully, Tom confiscates both.

"I don't think we want the police finding this," he says.

"Check."

He looks at me. "If you've got anything in your place, you'd better make it disappear."

"I'm clean," I say. "I never travel with anything that could get me busted."

That's what the *crew* is for, for heaven's sake.

"I'm going to have to call people," Tom says. "You should go back to your cabana. And expect the police."

"Bruce says he has a lawyer on the way."

"Police will probably get here first." He frowns at me. "Do you have any idea who'd want to kill Loni?"

"No. No one at all."

"You and she were, you know, seeing each other," he says. "She didn't mention anyone?"

By now the shock is over and I'm getting pissed off. "She did not tell me she was being stalked by a killer, no," I say. "Oddly, that did not come up."

He's a little surprised by my vehemence.

"Okay," he says. "I believe you. But maybe you should go to your room now."

Which I do. But not before a sense begins to come over me that I've been through all this before.

5.

The fact is that people around me keep getting killed. I don't have ill intentions to anyone, it just seems to work out that they die. When I look into my past, I see a lot of blood there.

I've only killed one person myself. Well, two. But nobody knows about one of them. And I had no animosity in either case.

I don't get up in the morning thinking, "Well, who will I kill today?" I don't intend harm to anybody. I never have.

I'd hoped all that was behind me. But now Loni's been murdered by an unknown party for unknown reasons, and it's all beginning to seem horribly familiar.

By the time the police interview me, late at night, reliving my old memories has me emotionally exhausted and discouraged and depressed, and I don't have to act at all in order to seem like Loni's stunned, grieving boyfriend. It's only the knowledge that if I misstep, I might be blamed for everything that keeps me from lurching in the direction of the nearest tequila bottle and drowning in it.

The police interview goes better than I expected. Turns out that the production rates the best—very quickly the local cops are supplanted by the PFM, the Policía Federal Ministerial, who are the top investigators in the country. I'm interviewed by a very polite man in a neat gray civilian suit with excellent English skills. His name is Sandovál. He offers his condolences on my loss, and records the interview on a very new recorder with a transcription function, that displays a written version of the interview on a nine-inch screen. The problem is that it keeps transcribing the English words as whatever Spanish words seem phonetically close, and the result is complete gibberish. He doesn't know how to turn on the English function, if there is one, but he assures me that the audio recording will be all right.

He sort of looks like Charlton Heston in *Touch of Evil*, and I have a moment of grim amusement as I remember Heston's character trying to get his radio bugging device working in that film.

Sandovál has two companions, an older white-haired man, well-dressed, who sits quietly and listens without speaking. He might be the senior officer, but I think he might not be talking because his English isn't very good. And there's another man, thick-necked and blonde, in hiking boots and some kind of faded blue bush-ranger jacket with lots of pockets. He looks American, but he doesn't talk either, so I can't tell.

No lawyers have shown up, but Tom King sits in the interview as moral support, and confirms my story as I tell it.

It goes well enough until I mention that after I found the body I contacted Tom. Sandovál's eyebrows go up.

"You didn't call the police?" he asks.

"I don't know *how* to call the police in Mexico," I said. "I don't have the emergency number. I thought someone else might know."

If Sandovál finds this implausible, he doesn't say so. I finish my story, and Sandovál asks a few follow-up questions, and then he offers his sympathies again and leaves.

Speaking as someone who's been interrogated by police any number of times, this interview was about as good as they get.

After, I have no trouble sleeping. In the morning, I'm awakened by the assistant director bringing me breakfast. This is not normally part of her job, but she's offering condolences and also trying to find out if I'm functional and can carry on with the production.

I assure her that I'm okay. I ask her what's going on, and she tells me the police are still around, taking measurements and interviewing everyone. The news of Loni's death leaked, of course, and half a dozen paparazzi drones are circling the hotel, while extra police have been deployed to keep intruders off the premises.

In fact, because she speaks Spanish and overheard some of the cops yelling at each other, she knows a lot about the investigation. Apparently the local police bungled everything before the PFM got here.

"They cut out pieces of the drywall where the bullet went through," she burbles. "Both in Loni's apartment and in Emeline's. They put them in evidence bags, but they forgot to label them, and now they don't know which is which. And so many cops came into Loni's apartment to have their pictures taken that all the evidence there, like the blood spatter, is useless…" Her eyes grow big as she realizes that Loni's presumed lover is perhaps not the best recipient of this news. She puts her hands over her mouth.

"Oh gosh, Sean, I'm sorry," she says. "I shouldn't have said any of that!"

"They wanted their pictures taken with a *corpse?*" I demand. I'm sickened.

I can see the whole thing. Cops in uniforms tramping around, posing with the body, the famous scandalous Hollywood star…

Though, on second thought, maybe that's how Loni would have wanted it.

The assistant director scurries away, but she isn't the last person to bring me food. Apparently it's customary to bring food to someone in mourning, even if that person doesn't need it—after all, I'm the star of the production, and normally I get three catered meals a day, plus healthy snacks—and now my refrigerator's filling up with fruit bowls, soups, boxes of chocolate, six-packs of yogurt, cakes, bags of nuts, and a gluten-free pizza.

Plus there are lots and lots of flowers, including a perfectly giant bouquet from my agent.

The only person who doesn't express condolences is Mila Cortés, the beautiful Venezuelan who plays my character's girlfriend Anna. Mila is a complete prima donna. She's too good for the resort hotel that's housing everyone else on the production, and she's staying on a yacht berthed in Playa del Carmen, north of here. I only see her when we have a scene together, and the rest of the time she ignores me.

Worse than ignores, actually. In fact she's repulsed by my appearance, and is offended to her soul that she has to share the universe with someone as strange-looking as me. I've been strange-looking for a long time now, and people with Mila's attitude stand out from the others quite easily.

Still, most everyone else cares, and despite the ridiculous superabundance of flowers and food, I'm genuinely touched by everyone's concern. They expect me to be torn with grief, and so powerful is the force of their belief that I find myself genuinely grief-stricken. Sometimes my voice chokes and dies in mid-sentence. Tears come to my eyes. I'm in awe of my ability to embody the character of a devastated lover.

When one of the sound techs, a really beautiful California blonde named Tracee, offers to help me forget Loni, I tell her I'm too broken up to respond. So we make an appointment for late that night.

The lawyers turn up around mid-morning and I have to go through the story again, which depresses me even more.

Around noon the claustrophobia gets to me, so I decide to pay a visit to the director, Hadley. I put on a pair of shades and a stolid expression and go out into the sunlight, and suddenly the air is full of whirring as camera drones zoom in for close-ups.

Being in the tabloids always makes me feel happy and wanted, so it takes some effort for me to don the required attitude of moody bereavement and shuffle along with my hands in my pockets.

I find Hadley talking to Sandovál by the pool. Another Mexican cop is talking to Chip, the man who's cousin to somebody on the set. There's a line of people to be interviewed, so obviously this will go on for a while.

People keep walking up to me to offer condolences. The advantage of being out of doors is that I can escape them. I thank them and move on, as if I had somewhere to go.

I end up on the beach, alone on the brilliant white sand staring out at the water. I figure it'll make a great picture on the cover of the *Weekly Dish*, or some other such publication.

The ocean is a perfect turquoise blue, with surf breaking over the reef a hundred yards offshore. There are police standing around on the beach, guarding the sand or something, but they're polite enough not to approach.

I breathe in the iodine scent of the sea.

"Hi," someone says. "You doin' okay?"

I turn and see that it's the blond cop who was present at my interview the night before, the man I thought might be American. He's still in his blue bush jacket, and he's wearing Ray-Bans, like Gregory Peck in that movie about some war or other. His voice is a sort of tidewater North Carolina.

"Who are you, anyway?" I ask.

He scans the sky for any drone that might be able to read his lips.

"Special Agent Sellers," he said. "DEA."

I blink in deep surprise. "You think Loni got killed in some kind of drug crime?"

"No." He shakes his head. "I'm just tagging along with the PFM. I'm here on another matter."

A cool warning throbs through my veins. If he's after drugs, there are plenty of them on the set. And I, for one, could not pass a urine test right now.

"Another matter?" I ask. "What's that?"

He takes out a hand-held and turns it on. The display is washed out in the sunlight, so he says, "Can we move to the shade?" We find some palms and stand under them, where the drones won't be able to spy on us, and he thumbs through different pictures until he finds the one he wants. He shows it to me.

"Do you know this man?"

I push my shades up onto my forehead and look at the photograph. A feeling of recognition passes through me, and I look closer.

It's Ossley, the assistant prop guy with the fondness for chemical experiments, though in the photo he's got a shaved head and a goatee. It's the blurry eyes behind the thick glasses that give him away, that and the rather superior expression.

"What's his name?" I ask.

"Oliver Ramirez," Sellers says. "Goes by Ollie."

I say nothing.

"You look like you recognized him," Sellers probes.

"He looks like a barista I know," I say. "Works in a coffee shop in Sherman Oaks." I slide my shades down to cover my eyes and look at Sellers with what I hope is an expression of innocence. "I don't know whether his name is Ollie or not."

I'm not about to finger someone who could implicate me as a drug user, especially if the drug is more or less legal where I live.

So far as I know, Ossley's chemical experiments haven't actually hurt anybody. And for obvious reasons I'm not a big fan of my country's archaic, punitive drug laws.

I decide to change the subject.

"Do you have any idea about—" I pause, as if overcome by emotion. "About what happened to Loni?"

Sellers looks out to sea. "Nobody really knows anything yet," he says. "But there's a theory the whole thing was an accident."

I don't have to counterfeit surprise. My jaw drops open of its own accord.

Sellers understands my confusion. "See, the shot came from the water," he says. He waves a hand out to sea. "The shooter must have been in a boat some distance away, on the other side of the reef, otherwise someone would have seen him. And the police are having a hard time figuring out how the killer managed an uncannily accurate rifle shot from out to sea, in a boat that was bobbing up and down, through a glass door and into a darkened room that would have been damn near impossible to see into. And because nobody can find a motive, they're thinking that maybe it was an accidental discharge…"

He falls silent when he sees my reaction.

"That's wrong," I say. "That's not what happened."

"Yes?" he says, suddenly very interested. "How do you know?"

Because what happens around me aren't accidents, I'm on the edge of saying. *What happens around me is murder.*

But I don't say that, because my phone rings right at that instant, and it's my agent, so I have to pick up.

"Thanks for the flowers," I say.

"Are things okay?" Bruce asks.

"More or less."

"The lawyers seemed to think everything was all right."

Other than Loni's still being dead, I think.

"I'm glad they think so," I say. I'm not being very candid, since there's a DEA agent listening from less than three feet away.

There's a pause, and then Bruce goes on with the next item on his checklist.

"Have you talked to Loni's parents?" he asks. "This morning they heard about Loni's death from the news. I'm sure they'd appreciate a more personal touch."

"Oh Jesus Christ!" Because normally I'd just have my assistant send a card, you know? But I'm supposed to be Loni's boyfriend, so now I'm nearly family, and I'll probably have to spend ages on the phone faking bathos to a couple of strangers.

"I don't even know their names," I say.

"Kevin's texting you all that." Kevin being Bruce's assistant. "Are you okay otherwise?"

"I'm holding up," I say.

My phone gives a chime as the text arrives.

"I'll call them right away," I say. Because that will give me an excuse to get away from Special Agent Sellers.

Which I do. I go back to my cabana and make the phone call, which is gruesome and produces anxiety and depression in equal amounts, and then I go looking for Ossley.

6.

Ossley's room isn't even in the hotel, it's on the ground floor of some annex tucked between the main hotel and the highway. In fact I think the annex may be an older, shabbier hotel that the bigger hotel acquired. When I knock, it's not Ossley who calls from inside the room, but a woman.

"This is Sean," I say. "Is Ossley in?"

The door opens and I see Emeline Cousteau, the set dresser whose suite was punctured by the bullet. She's tall and dark-haired, with an open face that reminds me of Karen Allen, except without the freckles. She's barefoot and wears a fiesta top that leaves her shoulders bare.

"Hi, Sean, come in," she says. "I'm so sorry about Loni."

"Yeah. Me too."

Ossley's place is small, an ordinary hotel room, and has two beds and a little desk. The drapes are drawn, the room is dark and stuffy, and the air smells of mildew from the shower. Ossley is sitting at the desk working on a computer and drinking from a soda can.

I sit on the bed that hasn't been used. Ossley tells me how sorry he is about Loni. His eyes are impossible to read behind the thick glasses.

"There's a DEA agent here along with the Mexican police," I say. "They're looking for a guy named Ollie Ramirez."

You can't say my dart doesn't hit home. Ossley turns spastic in about half a nanosecond—he knocks his keyboard to the floor, his soda can jumps across the desk, and his glasses sag down his nose.

"Peace, brother," I tell him. "I didn't rat you out." Though of course that was no guarantee someone else wouldn't.

Ossley picks up his keyboard, then puts his head in his hands. "What am I going to do?" he cries, to no one in particular.

Emeline walks over to him and puts her hands on his shoulders. She massages his stringy muscles and bends over him to whisper into his ear.

"Don't worry, baby. You'll be all right."

As I watch the two, comprehension strikes me like a sandbag dropped on my chest. I think my heart actually stops beating for a while. I gape for a few seconds as I try to jigsaw my thoughts together, and I raise a hand to point at Ossley.

"They were shooting at *you*," I say. "You were in Emeline's room, and the bullet missed and went through the wall and killed Loni." And then punched a hole in her door and vanished out to sea.

I remember glass on Loni's patio when I walked to her door yesterday morning. The glass had blown *outward*, which would have been a clue as to which direction the bullet was headed, except that all the glass fell out of the door right afterwards and lay in heaps everywhere, and I'd forgotten about all that till now.

Maybe if you looked closely at the bullet hole in the wall the actual trajectory might have been more clear, but all I remembered were neat little holes. No one was paying much attention to the wall, not with a body lying right there, an obvious target for a sea-borne sniper.

Ossley and Emeline stare at me as if I've just uncovered the great secret that will send their souls screaming all the way to Hell. Which I have, maybe.

"We were—y'know—together," Ossley says. "And I lowered my head to, um—and anyway, the bullet went right over my head."

"We hid for a while," says Emeline. "And then we ran away."

I look at Ossley. "What chemical experiments have you been doing," I say, "to get both the DEA and a sniper after you?"

Ossley flaps a hand at me. "Well," he said. "You know."

Somehow I keep a hold on my patience. "No," I say, "I don't."

Emeline looks up at me. "You know," she said. "Like with the wine."

I nod. "He's making a reactor vessel—"

"Reactant," Ossley corrects.

"You're going to print drugs," I tell him.

He shakes his shaggy head. "I just lay down the precursor chemicals," he says. "They're like prodrugs in nature—they'll produce drugs once they've finished reacting with the vessel."

"The vessel," I say, "which you also print."

"Yeah."

"*Which* drugs?" I ask.

He gives a hapless shrug. "The opiates are easier," he says. "I mean, they're all closely related, you just decide how many acetyl groups or whatever you want to tag onto morphine…"

"Oxy?" I ask. "Dilaudid? Heroin?"

"Diacetylmorphine hydrochloride," Ossley says. "But that's not…" He shrugs, nods, and concedes the point. "Well yeah, it *is* heroin, yeah."

"And how much of this stuff have you made?"

He seems surprised by the question. "Um," he says. "None. My gear isn't good enough. If you're aiming at producing drugs, your printer needs to be really precise, and you have to control temperature and humidity and light really well. I've never been able to afford a printer that good. And even if I get one, I'll have to run tons of experiments before I can produce anything like a pharmaceutical grade product."

"So why is the DEA…?"

"I put some stuff on the Internet."

I nod. "Of *course* you did," I snarl. "Because the conventions of social media *demand* that you announce your growing criminality on an electronic forum searchable by law enforcement. What else could you possibly do?"

He spreads his hands in a helpless gesture. "The narcs showed up. They started talking about 'criminal conspiracy to distribute narcotics.' I decided it was time to leave town, so I cashed in the Ramirez identity and created a new one."

"You had a backup identity just lying around."

"I printed it. And then I got a job here because I know some people."

At this point I am beyond surprise, so I just nod. Ossley gives a superior grin. "I named myself after the greatest drug dealer of all time."

I'm blank. "There's a famous drug dealer named Ossley?"

"Owsley. Augustus Owsley Stanley. He practically created the Psychedelic Sixties. Made millions of tabs of acid back when it was still legal."

I rub my forehead. "I really don't care what your grandparents got up to," I say. "I'm just trying to figure out what I'm going to do with you."

Ossley's alarm is clear even behind his thick glasses. He and Emeline exchange looks.

"You can't tell the cops," he says. "I mean, everything I did was just theoretical."

"Someone," I say, "is *shooting* at you. Another innocent person could get hit." I looked up at him. "Maybe you should just disappear."

Ossley and Emeline exchange looks again. "We thought about it," he says. "But shit, we're sitting right here in the middle of this huge police presence. I figure we're safer here than outside."

"Tell that to Loni," I say.

There is a long silence. "Look," he says finally. "Nobody's going to shoot with all these cops around. It's just not going to happen."

"No?" I point at the drapes drawn over his window. "Then why don't you open your drapes? Stand out on your patio and drink a beer?"

Ossley licks his lips. He looks desperate. Emeline, who is still standing behind him, gives his shoulders a little push.

"Tell him about the paradigm shift," she says.

"I—"

She pushes him again. "*Tell* him," she insists.

His eyes blink behind the thick glasses. "Well, see, it's a shift in how everything's going to be manufactured, right? Little 3D printers in kiosks and garages, making all the tools you need."

"Including drugs," I say.

"Right. Most of the stuff now that they need big factories and assembly lines to create." He licks his lips again. "But see, if you can make—or someone in your *village* can make—stuff that used to need a factory, then nobody's going to need that factory, right?"

"So," I say, "factories go out of business."

"*Drug* factories," says Ossley. "Because once the formula gets out, people can make their medication on their own. Not just the illegal stuff, but everything else—statins for cholesterol, beta-blockers for hypertension, triterpenoids for kidney disease, antibiotics for infection…"

"It's a *paradigm shift*," Emeline says. She's desperate to be understood.

"So drug companies go crash," I say. "I get it."

"Not just drug companies," Ossley says. "But the whole mechanism by which drugs are distributed, or, um, *not* distributed. Suppressed." He gives a desperate little laugh. "See, the DEA's job becomes *impossible* if *anyone* can make the drugs they want." He grins. "It's a new world. Prohibition will go away, because there will be too many ways around it."

"That's why the DEA wants to put Ossley away!" Emeline cries. "He's not breaking the law, he's threatening their *jobs*."

I try to put my mind around what Emeline is trying to tell me. "You're saying it was the DEA who tried to shoot you?" I say.

"No," Ossley says, just as Emeline shouts *"Of course!"* They glare at each other for a minute, and then Ossley turns back to me.

"See, it's not just the cops who are out of business," he says. "It's the *criminals*."

"Ah," I say. Because right now there are elaborate networks that take coca or opium poppies or whatever, and refine the raw vegetable matter down to powerful alkaloids, and smuggle that stuff across borders, and then cut it and break it into small packages and distribute it around neighborhoods…and of course there are a lot of really hard men with guns whose job it is to make sure that business is successful, and protected from competition.

Whole organizations, reaping billions of dollars in profit, for which violence is a *first* response, and every member of which will have to go back to shining shoes, planting beans, or working at the convenience store if Ossley perfects his technology.

"You'll put the cartels out of business," I say.

"Couldn't happen to a nicer bunch of people, yeah?" he says.

"And in the meantime they're trying to kill you."

"I still think it's the damn cops," Emeline says. "How would the cartels even know you're here?"

I don't have an answer for that, or for much of anything else. I stand.

"Better print a new identity and plan your escape," I say. "You can't stay here much longer."

He chews on that while I leave.

7.

I'm sitting in my cabana that afternoon when Hadley, the director, comes to see me. He doesn't bring me food.

"Jesus Christ, we're in such fucking trouble," he says.

I'm almost grateful that he's not oozing sympathy. He wanders over to one of the baskets of fruit I've been given and starts popping grapes into his mouth.

Hadley is bearded and blond and twitchy, with a full range of nervous tics probably acquired during the course of helming a series of huge, complex films, where a single mistake on his part, or on the part of practically anyone else connected with the production, could result in a couple hundred million dollars disappearing just as surely as if it had been doused with gasoline and set on fire. He's devoted to his films with a formidable single-mindedness that's just slightly inhuman.

"We've still got Loni's two big scenes," he says. "Completion bond company thinks we can just cut them and nobody will notice."

A completion bond is the film's insurance, who guarantee that in the event of some catastrophe that threatens the production, either the film will be completed or the backers will be repaid their investment. On a big production like this, specialists from the completion bond company are on the set a lot, mostly auditing the various departments. But though they'd obviously prefer that the film be made and they don't have to pay anyone back, they don't guarantee that the film will be any *good*—and they might well be within their rights to insist that the film do without an important subplot and two important scenes. All they care about is whether the movie's in the can, preferably on time and under budget.

You can imagine my delight in the prospect of my first big feature being a hacked-up, incoherent mess.

"I've got to argue them out of it," Hadley says. He's pulled a pineapple out of the fruit basket and is absently tugging on the leaves at the top. But he's too weak to actually yank any of them out, so he loses his patience and slams the pineapple back into the basket.

"Somebody made me a casserole," I said. "It's in the fridge. Why don't you beat that up instead?"

Hadley looks at me. "You've got to help, mate."

"Damn right I will." I lead with my ace. "I'll call Bruce Kravitz."

He puts a finger to his nose. "Brilliant."

Hadley isn't a Kravitz client—all PanCosmos directors capable of handling such a big, complicated production were off on other projects—so he doesn't have access to the biggest cannon in the industry. But I do.

I call Bruce right then, and he understands the equation right away: crappy film => declining careers for PanCosmos clients.

"I'll start calling around," he says.

I'm telling the good news to Hadley when Tom King, the line producer, strides in.

"Thought you'd better know," he tells Hadley. "The cops have been running background checks on everyone connected with the production, and they've come across a problem."

I feel my shoulders tense as I anticipate the news that Ossley is about to be arrested, but that isn't what Tom is telling us.

"It's the trucking company we've hired to move our gear around on location. It's a cartel front."

Hadley and I both stare.

"It really *is* the fucking narcos?" Hadley says.

"The trucking company's owned by one Antonio Germán Contreras. His brother Juan Germán Contreras is one of the leaders of the Tricolor Cartel, which controls narcotics trafficking on the Gulf Coast."

"Fuck me all standing!" Hadley says.

Tom's blue eyes are relentless. "The Tricolors are badasses," he says, "even as cartels go. They've killed thousands of people to get where they are."

Hadley clutches his head and looks at me. "What the fuck do we *do?* If we fire them, they'll kill us. If we *don't* fire them, they'll kill us anyway."

Tom turns to me. "Sean," he says, "do you have *any* idea why the cartel and Loni are connected?"

"I don't think they are," I say, truthfully enough. I give the subject some desperate consideration. "Does the cartel have rivals?" I say. "Maybe it was a warning to the Tricolors from some other cartel."

Tom sees the implications of this immediately. He turns to Hadley. "That's our excuse to fire them. We'll say that their presence is making the production more likely to be attacked."

"And then they'll *kill* us!" Hadley says. He paces around in a frantic little circle. He is literally gnashing his teeth.

Tom gives this some more thought. "Maybe we'll have to pay them anyway."

"Completion bond company isn't going to go for that!" Hadley says.

"We'll talk about it." Tom turns to me. His blue eyes grow concerned. "Sean," he says, "how are you doing?"

"Okay, I guess." An honest self-evaluation would be something like, "I'm really tired of having to pretend to be this grieving lover," but I don't think that's in the cards.

"Because we're all going to be under pressure to finish the film," Tom says. "I want you to know that you can take as long as you think necessary to return to the set. " There is a groan from Hadley at this idea. Tom's eyes flick to the director, then back to me. "But it would be a good thing to know—"

"I'm ready to work," I say.

I can sense deep relief behind the concerned blue eyes. "Are you sure? Because—"

"Yes," I say. "I really want to get out of here and get back on location. It's the best thing for me."

This makes them very happy. They leave together to put together a revised shooting schedule, leaving me alone in my cabana amid the smell of fruit baskets and flower arrangements.

Two seconds after they roll the sliding door shut, my phone rings. I look at it and see that it's Dagmar.

Oh damn. More trouble.

8.

"I'm on vacation," Dagmar says. "I'm in the Virgin Islands with my husband and my daughter. My first vacation in years that wasn't marked by riots, murder, and the collapse of society. And you couldn't stay out of trouble for two lousy weeks, could you?"

"I'm not in trouble," I point out. "I had nothing to do with this one."

"You've lied to me before," she says, "when people were trying to kill you."

Well, I admit to myself, *that's fair.*

It has to be conceded that my relationship with Dagmar Shaw is imperfect. She's the woman who rescued me from obscurity and made me a star by casting me in *Escape to Earth* and its sequel, and for that I'm grateful—but on the other hand she's controlling and devious and driven and far too smart, and she's got an agenda that's far beyond mine.

I want to be a big star and have millions of people love me. This strikes me as a modest and understandable ambition.

Dagmar, by contrast, is basically a genius supervillain who wants to take over the world.

"I'm sending you bodyguards," she tells me. "You need looking after."

I have a hard time summoning up the moral courage to resist Dagmar. The fact is that she knows a lot more about me than I'd like.

She knows where the bodies are buried—or actually *body,* singular, not that this makes it any better from my perspective.

"Yeah, okay," I say. I've lived in a circle of bodyguards before—at times it was annoying, but most of the time it was like having servants with guns. They have to do what you tell them, and there's the extra bonus in that they keep the bad people away.

"One more thing," she says. "It's your job to make sure the guards are charged to *your* production. Not to my company."

I consider this.

"I can probably manage that." Hiring bodyguards for me would probably count as due diligence, considering both the shooting and my own past.

"And by the way," she says, "I'm very sorry about Loni Rowe."

"Most people would have led with that," I point out.

"Most people," she says, "don't know she wasn't your real girlfriend."

It never occurs to me to ask Dagmar how she knows this. She has her sources, some of them uncanny.

"Keep out of trouble, now," she says. "Don't interrupt my vacation again."

"I'll do my best," I say, and she hangs up.

It's at that point that my nerves give a snarling leap as big, booming gunshots ring out over the compound. I dive behind the sofa.

Bodyguards, I think, might not be such a bad idea.

9.

It turns out to be the Mexican police who are shooting. They've warned the tabloid reporters that the airspace above the hotel is to be treated as a crime scene, and that the drones should be recalled, but the reporters as usual ignored the warnings. Except this is Quintana Roo, not Beverly Hills, and the PFM okayed the use of shotguns to knock the drones from the skies. In addition, any stranger caught with a radio controller was dragged from his vehicle, beaten silly, and tossed in jail.

I stay indoors while the skeet shooting goes on, and falling bird-shot rattles down the palm-leaf roof and rains onto the patio. In no time at all, the airspace over the hotel is free of clutter, which makes it easier for Tracee, the sound tech, to slip into my cabana after nightfall. She thinks she's comforting me after Loni's death, but in fact she's easing my anxieties about a lot of things that I couldn't explain to her if I tried.

Next day new call sheets appear, and we find out that production will resume the following day. My bodyguards, four of them, arrive in Cancun on the same flight as Mrs. Trevanian, the agent from the completion bond company. The bodyguards are the gents carrying weapons, but Trevanian is the one who can kill the movie by cutting all of Loni's scenes and turning the story into nonsense. She's a sinister figure in a navy blue suit, with a determined way of walking that sends a cold warning shuddering up my back. She looks as if she already knows what she's willing to pay for, and what she's not.

That afternoon there's a memorial for Loni. We all get together in one of the producer's cabanas and take turns talking about how wonderful she was, and all the while I know Mrs. Trevanian is deciding my future in another room. I have a hard time finding anything to say at the memorial. Other people are effusive, chattering on about their happy memories of Loni; but I'm just depressed, struck dumb with grief at the knowledge that Mrs. Trevanian is going to destroy my chances of being a movie star.

I drag myself away from the memorial as soon as I decently can, and I try to learn my next day's lines while in a frenzy of anxiety.

Tom comes to tell me after dinner that the meeting didn't go well. Mrs. Trevanian insisted that it was not necessary to replace Loni, but only to cut all her scenes. When Hadley shrieked, tore at his facial hair, and cried that without those scenes the film would be incoherent, Mrs. Trevanian said that *Desperation Reef* was an action blockbuster, and that action blockbusters didn't *have* to make sense. "Haven't you seen the *Transformers* films?" she asked.

I sink deep into my sofa and restrain a whimper of despair. My visions of superstardom are being shot down, just like the spy drones, and I know they're not coming back. This movie is going to crash, and afterwards, nobody's going to spend another couple hundred million dollars on someone as certifiably freaky-looking as I am.

My only choice will be to go on working for Dagmar until she gets tired of me, and then I'll be back on the beach, a nobody, like I was three years ago.

"This whole thing will have been for nothing," I moan. "Loni will have died for nothing."

"Yeah well," Tom says, "what can we do?"

"Raise more money?" I say.

He gives me a skeptical look. "It's a little late for that," he says.

"Seriously," I say. "How much would it cost to shoot all Loni's scenes with another actress? We don't have to hire a big star or anything—just some competent, reliable..."

Tom is trying to be kind. "Who else has Loni's sex appeal? Who else looks as good in a bikini? The character's a femme fatale."

"California is *full* of girls who look good in bikinis," I point out, truthfully enough.

Tom goes into his tablet computer and scrolls through figures. "Not counting Loni's paycheck," he says, "reshooting all Loni's scenes will cost ten million dollars."

I stare at him. Loni's only in a few scenes. "Ten million dollars for—"

"Most of it's for the cigarette boat chase," he says.

Oh Christ, I'd forgotten about the cigarette boat chase, mainly because I hadn't shot my part of it yet. Loni had already shot her half, and after I shot my bit, the two parts would be edited together, along with many, many expensive shots, already in the can, involving stunt doubles, explosions, and gunfire, to make it seem as if I had barely managed to evade murder by Loni and a group of cartel gunmen, all of whom get blown up in a flaming crash that cost a fortune in special effects.

"Look," I point out, "if we don't shoot the rest of the boat chase, we'll save millions of dollars. Just put those millions of dollars into hiring a new actress, find some cheap substitute for the boat chase, and re-shooting Loni's scenes."

Tom looks at me blankly. "I made that suggestion. Trevanian turned it down flat. It's absolutely not approved."

"But the money's *already in the budget!*"

"*Not any more, it isn't!*"

The cords on Tom's neck are standing out. There's despair in his tone. He's already been through this argument.

For a desperate moment I consider putting up the money myself. With my savings and investments, and of course the cash sitting in the Caymans, I might just pull it off.

But no, that's insane. Motion pictures are the worst investments *in the world.* Worse than investing in brand-new factories for buggy whips and antimacassars and snoods. Hollywood has a way of making people's money disappear.

And even if no one tried to steal my money outright, even if everyone on the picture did their best, all it would take was a screwup in *one* department to make the movie a flop. The studio could demand a catastrophically bad re-edit or bungle a last-second transfer into 3-D, the composer doing the score could have a tin ear, the trailers could suck, the publicity department could be at war with the producers and sabotage the promotion, and all my money would disappear.

In which case, I'd be out of work *and* broke.

I lean back in the sofa and try not to snivel. "We're fucked."

"Hadley's on the verge of shooting himself," Tom says.

"Better if he shot Mrs. Trevanian."

"Well," Tom says, "we can always hope for a last-minute backer with a big check."

I reach for my phone. "I'll call Bruce."

Bruce's phone goes straight to voice mail. It's annoying that he has other clients and a personal life, but I suppose it's only to be expected.

I put the phone away. "I'll try again later."

Tom is looking back out the door, where one of my guards is pacing around.

"Where did the guards come from?" he asks.

"You're paying for them," I tell him. "It's your due diligence. Even Mrs. Trevanian would agree."

"*Fuck!*" he yells. But that's the only objection he makes.

10.

I go over my lines one more time, and then I hear a shotgun boom out as another tabloid drone makes a run at the hotel. I give up. No one's come to console me in a long time, thank God, and so I decide it's time to stroll over to my bar and open a bottle of reposado. A couple shots down, and I realize how to raise the money to make the movie as it ought to be made.

I knock on Ossley's door and receive a muffled, paranoid query in response. I tell him it's me, and he cracks the door open to make sure I'm not lying. When he sees my two bodyguards, he assumes they're assassins and panics, but I jam my shoe into the door, lean close, and speak in a low voice.

"Look," I say, "I can get you off the hook."

He lets me into the room. My guards take up stations outside, on either side of the door. Emeline isn't there, and without her the place has a look of despair, its only light a laptop computer running its screensaver, and a forsaken room service meal on the dresser slowly turning into compost.

I take the room's single chair, leaving Ossley to sit on the bed, where I had sat that morning.

"I see that your curtains are still drawn," I say.

"Be careful walking in front of them," he says. "You might get silhouetted."

I look at the curtains with more respect. "I'll do that," I say. And then I look at him.

"Look," I say, "they found people from the Tricolor Cartel working on the production." He winces. "They're going to keep coming after you," I assure him. "So what we need to do is make you harmless."

I'm hoping for a glimmer of hope to shine in his eyes, but what I get instead is a glimmer of suspicion.

"How do you plan to pull *that* off?" he says.

"We sell your process to the cartel."

He considers this with what seems to be impatience. His lips curls. *You cretin,* is what the lip seems to say.

"I see two problems," he says. "First, what stops them from just killing me instead of giving me money?"

"You need to have insurance. You need to have the process documented, and in the hands of people you can trust to release it if anything should happen to you."

His sneer grows. "People like you?"

"No," I say. "I don't want anything to do with it. I wouldn't understand it anyway."

"You sure don't," he says. "Because you didn't even get what I told you earlier—*there is no process.* I haven't printed any drugs, all I've done is *theory.* And all my theories are available *right on the Internet,* in forums devoted to additive manufacturing. There's nothing to sell!"

I give this some consideration. "Well," I tell him, "we could *say* that you've got a complete process. And then get money for not telling anyone about it."

Ossley jumps off the bed and paces about, waving his arms. "Tell a bunch of violent criminals I have a process that doesn't exist? And expect them to pay me to suppress it?"

"Well," I say, "yeah."

"That's crazy!" he says.

I'm on the verge of agreeing with him: yeah, it's not my most brilliant idea. But then he goes on.

"You don't know me at all!" he proclaims. "If there's one thing I believe in, it's *freedom!*"

I'm not sure what any of this has to do with freedom, but then Ossley goes on to tell me.

"I'm not interested in making money from my ideas!" he says. "I'm not interested in *patents* and *copyrights* and *trademarks!*" He practically spits the words. "All that gets in the way of freedom to use the technology, and the technology's what's important! The tech's gotta be free—free to all the people who want to use it, without some asswipe standing there with his hand out collecting the toll!"

"Even if it kills you?" I ask.

A gleam of absolute certainty shimmers through Ossley's thick glasses. "If I die," he says, "the technology's going to happen anyway! *Someone* will figure out how to do it! People are going to print drugs in their homes! It's as inevitable as people connecting their computers to phone lines and creating the Internet!"

"Yeah," I say, "and whoever figures out the answer is going to get a ton of money."

He looks down at me from the absolute heights of moral superiority. "This information needs to be free," he says. "And I'm the one to free it."

It occurs to me that the last thing I need tonight is to put up with a lecture from some sneering, megalomaniac geek. I remind myself that I'm very tall and that I look like a Klingon and that I'm a murderer, and that I could just stand up right now, pick up Ossley, throw him down on the ground, and tell him that he's going to do what I tell him, or I'll kick his stupid fucking head in.

But I don't do that. I'm not really that guy.

Instead I leave, pick up my bodyguards, and return to my cabana, where I study my lines until it's time to go to bed. I get a call from Tracee, the sound tech, but I tell her that I'm too upset to see her.

Have sex with someone three times, it's dangerously near a relationship. So I decide not to see her again.

11.

"I want it bigger," Hadley tells me. "I need you to fucking *act,* here, Sean."

When Hadley is actually being a director—when he's in his little shed or tent, surrounded by video monitors, and communicating with his minions through a headset or a loudspeaker—he's not the grimacing, twitching, half-hysterical character he is the rest of the time. When he's directing, Hadley is in his element. He's authoritative, decisive, and he tells you what he wants.

Though of course he's still a prat.

Still, I could use some direction about now. I'd rather it come from a director who's actually on the set, and knows how to talk to actors, instead of some Jehovah-wannabe off in a little room by himself with his barista, a macchiato, and a Napoleon complex, but I'll take what I can get.

Fact is, I'm beyond depressed. Mrs. Trevanian has killed the movie, the movie will kill my career, and the point of finishing the film at all has begun to elude me.

I know that I should be the living embodiment of the Three Ps (Prompt, Perky, and Professional, if you want to know) and that I should give the part everything I've got because I should be happy simply to be working; but now I'm wondering what the reward for any of that will be. I've been a hard-working professional all my life—I've even *killed people*—and annoying characters like Mrs. Trevanian and anonymous Tricolor snipers still won't let my happy place alone.

Suddenly I'm wondering why I'm even bothering trying to play the lead in a feature. I've never played the hero in a movie. And working in movies and television requires different styles of acting.

TV stars are cool. Even if their characters are less than admirable, they come across as somehow sympathetic, maybe even neighborly. They are, after all, people you invite into your home every week. If you don't like them, you won't watch them.

Movie stars, by contrast, are *hot*. They have to blaze so fiercely that they fill a screen forty feet high and demand the attention of a crowded theater.

That's why very few TV stars have graduated successfully to features. It requires not only different skills but a different personality. You have to go from amiable to commanding.

Likewise, some movie stars are simply too big for television. Jack Nicholson is riveting on screen, but you wouldn't want him in your living room week after week. The television simply couldn't contain his personality.

I *think* I'm doing well in the feature. Everyone tells me I'm great—but then they would whether I was any good or not. I could sit through the dailies and find out for myself, but I've always been too insecure to watch dailies.

But now I'm having a hard time seeing the point.

I get through it somehow, and Hadley pronounces himself satisfied with whatever energy I've been able to summon. I go back to my cabana for a shower and supper, and then—thank God—my guards tell me that the propmaster Yunakov is at the door.

He's inviting me to a party in his suite by way of consoling me for my loss. I'm so eager to get out of the depressing flower-filled environment that I jump at the chance.

It's much the same as the party the other night, except that Ossley is in hiding and there's no sign of cannabis, not least because a pair of Mexican police have joined the fun. These are uniformed state police who are here to guard us and to keep order, as opposed to the plainclothes PFM who are actually investigating Loni's murder. I assume the two police are off-duty, because they're slamming down cognac as if they've never had expensive, imported Napoleon brandy before. Both of them are Mayans around five feet tall.

I look at the pistols they're carrying on their belts—and the two Heckler & Koch submachine guns they've propped in a corner, along with a shotgun for shooting at drones—and a scheme begins to drift across my brain on feather-light feet.

I decide that the cops are going to be my friends.

I top up their glasses. I talk to them both, and ask them about their lives. Hector has the better English skills, but Octavio is far more expressive, communicating through expansive gestures, tone of voice, and a natural talent for mimicry. I ask if he's ever thought of being an actor.

They're pretty flattered that a big Hollywood star is taking an interest in them. They tell big exciting police stories which, though they may be true, I suspect didn't happen to them, but to someone else.

When the party breaks up, I take Hector and Octavio for a walk, me swaying along with a couple tipsy guys shouldering automatic weapons nearly as long as they are. They let me march along with the shotgun. I take them to the little hotel annex where Ossley is holed up, and I carefully count the number of sliding glass patio doors until I come to Ossley's room.

I offer to pay them a thousand dollars apiece if they'll shoot at that door sometime tomorrow afternoon, when I'm scheduled to be on the set. I tell them I want them to aim high, so no one will be hurt.

They're sufficiently hammered that they don't see anything terribly wrong in my request, and a thousand dollars is, after all, about three times their monthly salary. Though Hector is a little puzzled. "But why?" he asks.

"Publicity," I tell them with a wink, and that seems to satisfy him.

"Okay," Hector says. "But we need another five hundred."

"What for?"

"To pay the sergeant to make the evidence disappear."

I'm hardly sober during this conversation, but next morning I remember enough of what I'd said to stock up on some cash. We are in a part of Quintana Roo filled with Americans and American dollars, and getting a few thousand from the bank is no problem. After which I head off to my makeup call.

We're shooting another underwater scene. I'm scheduled to be on the set for six hours, but there is a raft of technical problems, more than the usual amount of chaos, a distinct lack of cooperation on the part of the ocean, the sun, and the clouds, and so many retakes that I'm working for nearly twelve long hours, much of it in the ocean. It's nearly ten o'clock by the time I'm out of makeup and back at the cabana.

My guards go into my cabana ahead of me to make certain there are no assassins lurking therein, and to their surprise discover Ossley and Emeline hiding in my spare bedroom. I affect more astonishment than I actually feel, and ask Ossley what they're doing here.

"Umm," he says. "Can we talk privately?"

My guards make sure he's not carrying anything pointy, then slip out to guard the gardens.

I sit in a chair beneath a vase filled with fading mourning blossoms. "What can I do for you?" I ask.

Ossley doesn't look good. He's unshaven, he's shambling, and his hands keep roaming over his body as if to make sure it's all still there.

"They took another shot at him today!" Emeline says in complete outrage.

I look at Ossley. "I ran for it before the police got there," he says.

I conceal my inner dance of delight. "Sorry about all that," I tell him, "but you can't hide here, you know. I don't want anyone in my place who will draw fire."

Emeline looks at Ossley. "Tell him," she says. "Tell him what you're thinking."

He gives a little twitch. "I've been thinking about what we talked about the other night."

I put on my Klingon mien and look at him seriously. "Maybe you'd better remind me. Because what I most remember is you lecturing me about freedom."

It's Emeline who's responsible for his change of heart, Emeline and of course the bullets Hector fired through his patio door. When all is said and done, I've won. And I see no damn reason why I shouldn't rub his superior little nose in it.

After I finish talking to Ossley and Emeline, I decide to let him stay in the spare room overnight, then hide him somewhere else the next day. After which I take a little walk, find Hector and Octavio, and make them and their unknown sergeant as happy as I am.

12.

Hollywood stardom opens a lot of doors. Which is why it doesn't take nearly as much effort to get an interview with Juan Germán Contreras as you might think. I go through his brother, who owns the trucking company, and when I finally get the word that he'll see me, I bring presents. A very expensive bottle of small-batch bourbon, plus Ossley's 3-D printer, the beaker he'd shown me at the party, and a container of Ossley's rotgut cabernet.

The actual meeting is all very last-second. I get some GPS coordinates texted to me, and drive to the location with my bodyguards. This turns out to be a half-completed Burger King overlooking the ocean, with the waves breaking white over the reef, and waiting for me there is the brother, Antonio. We're required to put our cellphones in a plastic bag hidden on the construction site, because cops can follow our phones' GPS. We follow Germán's Chevy Tahoe off into the jungle, where we go through several gates guarded by some very large, well-armed Mexicans, and then to a modest-sized bungalow with a tile roof, a house identical to about a million homes in California.

My guards aren't happy about any of this, but I'm the boss, and they sort of have to do what I tell them. They're warned to stay in the car. Germán's guards help me carry my gear into the house, and there I meet the man of the hour.

I'm all dressed up like the Pope of Greenwich Village. Grey tropical suit, red tie, wingtips. My goatee has been trimmed, and my head re-shaved. I'm hoping I look like a Klingon mafioso.

I suppose I should ask forgiveness for pointing out again that I happen to look sinister in a very freakish way. I terrify small children. I scare room-service waiters I meet by chance, at night.

Plus during my wilderness years, when I was struggling, if I worked at all, I played a heavy. I'm very good at projecting menace when I need to.

Germán is so menacing in real life that he doesn't have to act scary. He also didn't put on a tie. He's a trim man of around forty, dressed casually in a cotton peasant shirt, drawstring pants, and sandals. I've done my research, and I know that the most wanted man in Mexico is a former high-ranking officer in the PFM who went over to the Dark Side. He maintains what can only be described as a paramilitary bearing, and he seems to bear a reserved curiosity about what brings me here.

He smiles whitely and shakes my hand. I present him with the bourbon, and he offers me a seat on a chair so grandly carved and painted with Mesoamerican designs that it should really be sitting in a museum of folk art.

He and his brother Antonio take their seats. "I understand there has been violence on your production," Germán says.

"I'm afraid so," I tell him.

"I regret to say that I can't help you," he says. "The police have surrounded your company with their own people, and they and I—" He waves a hand ambiguously. "We do not work together."

He thinks I've come to him for protection. Instead I plan to take his money—but first, I think, a little flattery.

"I'm impressed," I say. "You speak extremely good English."

He lets the compliment pass without changing expression. "I used to work with your Drug Enforcement Agency," he says. "When I was with the police."

I think about asking him if he knows Special Agent Sellers, and then decide against it.

"My children and I enjoyed *Escape to Earth*," he says. "We watched it together."

My heart warmed as I pictured this charming domestic scene, Germán and his children absorbed in the drama while the chieftain's followers went about their murderous errands, smuggling, stabbing, shooting, and cutting off heads.

"Thank you," I say. "Those projects were very special."

We chat a bit about the picture business, and the current production here in Mexico. He expresses condolences on Loni's death. He seems to know all about *Desperation Reef,* and appears moderately amused by the story line. I'm pleased that he doesn't seem to want to cut my head off.

"I wonder," I say, "if you know Ollie Ramirez."

He looks blank.

"He's a kind of inventor," I say. "He's the person that the assassins have been trying to kill."

He seems surprised. "It was not Loni Rowe?" he says.

"Loni's death was accidental," I tell him, though I'm confident he knows that already. "May I demonstrate something?"

I go through the wine demonstration, just as Ossley had performed it in Yunakov's suite. I let Germán taste the dreadful young wine, then put the cabernet in Ossley's container, let the reaction take place, chill the result to room temperature, and hand it to him. His brows rise as he tastes the result.

"This is only one of Ollie's inventions," I say. "Some of the others you can find online." I give him a look. "If you look at some of these sites, you can see that he's working on using this technology to print drugs."

A shadow passes over Germán's eyes. I try not to shiver. He's no longer the courteous host, not entirely, but the lord of a criminal empire. Very calculating, very hard. All the warmth in the room is gone.

If my career as a major Hollywood action star weren't at stake, I wouldn't want to be within a thousand miles of him.

"Your Mister Ramirez wants to sell me this technology?" he says.

"No," I say. "That would be too dangerous." He lifts his head in a kind of query, his eyes like stone. "Once this technology is known to exist," I point out, "you can't possibly control it. All people will need to fabricate drugs is a printer and some precursor chemicals and some instructions from the Internet. People in the States would make their own drugs and could sell them cheaper than you could."

Germán regards me as a young child might regard a housefly, just before he pulls off its wings.

"May I ask," he says, "where your interest lies in all this?"

I've been on my feet demonstrating the technology. I return to the folk-art armchair and sit, looking at Germán evenly, at his own level.

"I'm trying to get Ollie Ramirez out of trouble," I say. "Someone's trying to kill him, and it simply isn't necessary."

He looks at me, unblinking. Because I've done my research, I know that his organization has killed maybe twenty thousand people in just the last few years. Not just killed, but tortured, mutilated, dismembered, blown up, and burned alive.

But I've killed, too. It's not something in which I take any particular pride, but it's public knowledge, and if Germán has done his research he knows this. Maybe on that account I'm entitled to a little of his respect.

"Killing Ollie right now would be a mistake," I say. "As soon as he realized someone was after him, he made sure that other people had custody of his research. People he could trust. A lawyer in one place, a friend in another. So if anything were to happen to Ollie, the information would be made public."

Which is true enough. Though what Bruce Kravitz, in his office high in the PanCosmos Building, made of the PDF file in his Inbox could only be conjectured.

Germán's face seems carved of stone. "Do you know any of these friends of Ramirez?" he asks.

"No. I don't want to know their names, and I don't understand the technology. I'm an actor, not a scientist."

And maybe, therefore, I won't be tortured for information that I don't have.

"And what does Ramirez want?" Germán asks.

"Fair value for his discoveries." I take out a piece of paper, and put it on the table between us.

I've done some calculations based on what I've been able to find out about Germán's business. Each year, he makes a profit of around six billion dollars on an income of twenty billion. He has something like 150,000 people who work for him in one capacity or another, not counting the corrupt officials he has on his payroll.

"In order to make certain that Ollie's discoveries never see the light of day," I say, "he asks for twenty-five million dollars. Twenty-five million *each year.*"

That figure doesn't seem unreasonable. One of the difficulties of Germán's business is finding places to put all the money he makes. Sometimes it just stacks up in garages or spare rooms. When cartel honchos are arrested, sometimes they're found with a hundred million dollars or more, all in cash, just piled in some room because they can't find a place for it.

"You can make this investment or not," I say. "You know your own business best." I nod at the piece of paper. "That's an account in the Cayman Islands," I say. "If the money appears there, we'll know that you find Ollie a good investment, and he'll find some other line of research that has nothing to do with you or your business."

Germán looks at the paper but doesn't touch it. The Cayman account is mine, as it happens, an attempt at tax avoidance by yours truly. Some of the money behind *Desperation Reef* is French, and some Japanese, and at Bruce Kravitz's suggestion I stashed most of my pay in an offshore account. The money's never been in the States, and I won't have to pay taxes on it till I bring it home.

"There's only one point I should make," I add. "This technology… it's going to happen sooner or later. Someone's going to duplicate Ollie's research, and then—" I shrug. "Then you stop paying. You'll have bought some years."

Germán's look is unreadable. "If this printing technology should break free," he says, "how do I know it's not Ramirez behind it?"

I wave a hand. "You have resources," I tell him. "You'll find out. Besides, it's not like any of these people can keep a secret—my guess is that whoever does it will be bragging in every online forum he can find."

Germán looks at his brother, and his brother looks back. Then Germán turns to me.

"I don't know this Ramirez," he says. "But what you say is interesting. I understand why someone is shooting at him."

I rise from my Mesoamerican chair. "I've taken up enough of your time," I say.

And then I shake hands with the Germán brothers and leave, carrying the printer. I'd leave it as a gift, but it belongs to the property department.

I'm modestly surprised at my own survival, and so are my bodyguards. By the time I get back to the hotel, I'm convinced the whole trip was deranged, and that the Germáns were sitting back in their bungalow knocking back bourbon and laughing at their idiot visitor.

Which is why I'm surprised when, the next day, I check my bank balance and find that twenty-five million has been deposited to the Cayman account. In cash, no less, which means that Germán not only had the money sitting in the Caymans, but was able to get someone to physically carry the money from his stash to my bank.

I go to Cancun to where Ossley's hiding in a hotel under yet another alias, and I tell him the money has arrived. In another day or two, he'll fly to Cayman, where he'll open a bank account, and I can transfer his share of the money.

"If you go back into the drug business," I tell him, "I'll kill you myself."

He should devote himself to his wine project, I tell him. Stay away from anything illegal.

I leave my cabana after supper and take a stroll through the hotel grounds. I avoid the beach or ocean views, since I spend my working day on one or in the other. I'm looking in a vague way for a gathering where I can relax, but Yunakov isn't in his room, and so I wander up to the open-walled bar by the pool and order myself a Negro Modelo.

When my eyes adjust to the murk in the bar, I see Special Agent Sellers standing in a corner, trying to communicate with the green-and-red talking parrot the bar has installed on a perch. Sellers is still wearing his Jungle Jim outfit. I stroll over with my beer in hand and take a look at the parrot.

"Got him to confess yet?" I say.

Sellers glances at me, then gives a little start—yes, I am indeed a disturbing and ominous figure to find looming over one's shoulder—and then he turns to me.

"The parrot's not talking," he says. "I think he wants his lawyer."

"Motherfucker!" the parrot shrieks. His vocabulary seems to have been strongly influenced by drunken American tourists.

"Obviously a hard case," I point out. "Why don't you take a break and have a drink?"

He joins me at the bar and orders a vodka tonic.

"Did you ever find that man you were looking for?" I ask.

"He kept dodging the interview. Then someone shot into his room and he split."

"You were looking for the props guy?" I ask in feigned surprise. He nods. "Do you know who shot at him?" I ask.

"That's confidential," he says, which I figure means he has no clue.

I decide to change the subject. "Any progress on who killed Loni?" I ask.

He looks a little uncertain whether or not he should be sharing any news, but then he decides to let his vodka tonic do the talking.

"Remember when I said it might have been an accident?" he says. I nod.

"There was some problem with the evidence at first," Sellers says, "but it got straightened out, and now it looks as if the shot was fired from the land. Maybe at someone on the tennis courts, from someone hiding in the jungle across the highway. And it punched through the wall and killed Loni purely by mistake."

It isn't hard to look shocked. I'd thought I was really clever working that one out all by myself.

"I've been thinking and thinking," I say. "And I couldn't imagine why anyone would—" I succeed in summoning a tear to my eye. "And now you say it really was an accident!" I blurt.

He nods in what is probably meant to be a comforting way. "That's how the physical evidence lines up," he says. "I said before that it could be random, but you disagreed."

"I don't know what I think any more," I say. I think about putting a quaver in my voice, but decide against it. I don't want to overact when my audience is only three feet away.

I sip my sweet, dark beer. Sellers says nothing. "Motherfucker!" says the parrot.

There's a stir in the bar, and then a half-dozen film crew come into the bar. They've obviously just come in from dinner somewhere, and among them I recognize Chip, the man who is here because he's somebody's cousin. And for some reason a memory of Germán rises to my mind. *I don't know this Ramirez. But what you say is interesting. I understand why somebody's shooting at him.*

It suddenly occurs to me that maybe Germán was telling the truth.

I nod toward the group. "Do you know the tall one there?" I ask. "The blond?"

"I was there when he was interviewed," Sellers says.

"He's not part of the crew," I say.

"He's here on vacation," Sellers says. "He's related to, ah, I think it was the assistant greenskeeper."

I consider Chip from the vantage point of the bar. "Do you know what he does for a living?" I ask.

Sellers pulls out his handheld and pages through his files. Which is probably something he wouldn't do if he hadn't had more than a couple vodka-and-tonics.

"He works for Porter-Bakker Pharmaceuticals," he says. "In marketing."

It's like an explosion in my mind, only in reverse. All the smoke and flame and debris fly together, the bits assembling to form a complete whole.

"Okay," I say. "That's interesting."

13.

It turns out that Chip is a golfer, and goes out most days to one of the many courses in Cancún. I watch him when he comes back from one of his trips, his golf bag slung over his shoulder. He walks into his suite, and he immediately realizes that someone has broken into his rooms and scattered his belongings everywhere. He drops his bag and runs to the settee in his front room, and pulls out a long box from underneath. He looks relieved to discover it's still there.

"Right," I say. "Let's go."

I and my four bodyguards leave my cabana, where I'm watching Chip's antics on video, and then stroll across the compound to Chip's suite. Two guards precede me through the open door.

"Hold on there, cowboy," I say. "We've got to talk."

Chip spins around, his face alight with what I believe is called a "guilty countenance." He stares as my guards approach him.

"What do you have in the box there?" I ask, and then—because he looks as if he's going to attempt desperate resistance—I add, "No point in fighting. A video record of this is already on a server in New Zealand."

Which is true. My guards and I broke into Chip's suite earlier in the day, put video cameras everywhere, then tossed his belongings all over the room all under the assumption that he would lead us to the box hiding under the settee—which of course we had discovered in the course of our search.

My guards, I am pleased to remark, seem to be brigands only slightly disguised in tropical suits. They would probably have taken Chip to sea and drowned him if I'd asked.

One of my guards takes the box from Chip's nerveless fingers. I look at the box with all my Klingon intensity.

"What do you want?" says Chip. His face is stony.

"Let's go outside and talk." Away from any recording devices.

My guards pat Chip down for weapons, and then we all stroll to the pool, where Chip and I sit at a wrought-iron table. The sun dazzles on the water. There is the scent of chlorine. One of my guards adjusts the table's red-and-yellow umbrella to keep us in the shade, and then the guards withdraw out of earshot.

I look at Chip, still using my Klingon face. "Let's open the conversation by agreeing that you're an idiot," I begin.

"You don't know what you're talking about," he says.

"Okay," I say. "Let's make sure we're on the same page. Because from what I can see, you came here to kill Ollie Ramirez, only you missed him and killed a *movie star.* Which brings heat and publicity down on this whole production, making it difficult to complete your mission, and so you while away your time playing *golf.* And you did this in *Mexico,* where the authorities won't even *need* to open that box, and find there a rifle covered with your fingerprints, to beat a confession out of you and throw you in jail, which you will very likely not survive because it's going to be full of violent cartel killers who will torture you to death simply for the fun of hearing you scream."

There is a moment of appalled silence, and then Chip summons the fortitude to ask a question.

"Why would I kill this Ollie Ramirez?"

I sigh. "On behalf of Porter-Bakker Pharmaceuticals, who've clearly made up their minds that Ollie's discoveries are a threat to their bottom line. I looked them up—last year they made a profit of six point three billion on income of forty-nine billion. They could hardly keep *that* up if people could print their own prescriptions in their basement." I give a contemptuous laugh. "They're *also* idiots, by the way."

Chip just glares at me. I reach into my pocket and take out a piece of paper. A piece of paper very similar to that which I'd given Germán only a few days before.

"If you don't want your rifle given to the PFM, along with a suitably edited copy of the video, I want fifty million dollars sent to this account. By tomorrow. And another fifty mil. every year, on the anniversary of Loni's death, to guarantee that Ollie Ramirez won't continue his researches."

He stares. His lips move but nothing comes out. He's beyond speech.

"That may seem like a lot to you and me," I say, "but on profits of six point three billion, it's not so much. Plus of course there's the matter of evading all the investigations, bad publicity, and the collapse of your company's stock. Along with jail for everyone concerned."

I lean back in my chair and consider the possibilities. "Of course," I say, "your superiors may decide that their most sensible action now is to kill *you*. So I suggest you stay in your room, under guard, until the money is delivered." I smile. "And since I don't trust you or your company in the least, the evidence will be hidden, and released automatically if anything unfortunate should happen to me."

I stand. My bodyguards look in my direction. Chip hasn't said anything in a long time.

"Maybe now," I say, "you should go find a phone or something."

Chip goes back to his room, and one of my guards goes in with him. And as for me, I think I shall raise a magic editing wand, perform a cinematic dissolve from this scene by the pool, and go straight to the happy ending.

Porter-Bakker Pharmaceuticals paid up. Some of their lower-level executives resigned, but by that point I wasn't very interested, because I was busy rescuing my movie. I shelled out ten million in cash, received executive producer credit and a larger percentage of the gross than I'd had previously, and Bruce Kravitz provided Loni's replacement, a fine actress named Karen Wilkes. She didn't fill a bikini as well as Loni, but added a kind of crazed evil to the part of the gangster's girlfriend that made the role memorable. The wicked Mrs. Travanian was foiled, and gathered up her cloak of evil and went back to Los Angeles.

I didn't split the Porter-Bakker money with Ossley. After all, he was *already* being paid not to continue his drug research.

So everything ends really well for me. It's unfortunate that justice wasn't meted out to Loni's killer, but even if Chip went to jail, it wouldn't bring Loni back. And of course I'm sorry that Loni had to die—but if she *had* to die, at least it was in a way that got me both publicity and a fortune. And a good movie, which is nothing to sneeze at.

Plus of course, *I* didn't die. Which is always a plus.

And the best part comes later, in a meeting with Hadley and Tom King. We're in Hadley's cabana, eating seafood tacos, drinking iced caramel macchiatos made by his barista, and hashing out the shooting schedule. We're trying to work out how and where we're shooting the ending.

I finish a taco and lick my fingers.

"And by the way," I tell Tom, "I'm not going to shoot that second chickenshit ending, the one where I give the drugs to the cops instead of selling them and living happily ever after. That's just not my character. My character keeps the money."

Hadley look up at me in alarm. "Sean," he says. "The producers *want* that chickenshit ending."

"*I'm* the producer now," I tell him, and flash him my Klingon look.

He wabbles and waffles, but in the end caves in.

What choice does he have? I'm the man who saved his picture. I'm the boy who made money from tragedy, happiness from misery, diamonds from tequila.

Desperation Reef is going to be a hit. I know this because Loni's getting killed gave it the sort of publicity that the studio would have had to pay hundreds of millions of dollars for. All the people who have seen the tabloid headlines or who watch the entertainment news will want to be part of the story—part of *my* story.

They will pay money to be closer to me. And I will let them. I will accept their love, and their love will make me happy, and in return I will give them everything I have. I will give them brilliant things.

I will give them diamonds.

MARGAUX

"**H**ey Earthgirl! I got someone for you to meet!"

Stoney was excited. He was almost *always* excited. He was one of Lamey's lieutenants, a boy who hijacked cargo that came over the sea to Maranic Port and sold it through Lamey's outlets in the Fabs. Stoney wore soft felt boots and a puffy padded jacket with rows of tiny little metal chimes that rang when he moved, and a hard round plastic hat without a brim, the clothes that all Lamey's linkboys wore when they wanted to be noticed.

Gredel came into the room on Lamey's arm. He had dressed her in a gown of short-haired kantaran leather set off with collar and cuffs of white satin, big clunky white ceramic jewelry inlaid with gold, shiny little plastic boots with nubbly surfaces and tall heels. The height of fashion, at least as far as the Fabs were concerned.

Lamey liked shopping for Gredel. He took her to the stores and bought her a new outfit two or three times each week.

Lamey had earned his name because he once had a defect that made him walk with a limp. It was something he'd got fixed as soon as he had the money, and when Gredel first met him he glided along like a prince, putting each foot down with deliberate, exaggerated care, as if he were walking on rice paper and didn't want to tear it. Lamey was only twenty-five years old in Shaa measure, but already he ran a set of linkboys, and had linkages of his own that eventually ran up to some of the Peers responsible for running places like the Fabs. He had millions, all in cash stashed in various places, and three apartments, and half a dozen small stores through which he moved the material acquired by his crews.

He also had a seventeen-year-old girlfriend called Earthgirl.

Lamey had offered to set her up in an apartment, but Gredel still lived with Nelda, the woman who had mostly raised her since Gredel's mother had been sentenced to serve on the agrarian communes. Gredel wasn't sure why she stayed. Maybe it was because Gredel hoped she could protect Nelda against Antony, her husband— Gredel's earliest memories were of cowering in the dark while Antony raged outside the door, bellowing and smashing furniture. Or maybe Gredel stayed because once she moved into a place that Lamey bought her, she'd have to spend all her time there waiting for him to come see her. She wouldn't be able to leave for fear that he'd come by and find her gone and get angry; and she couldn't have her friends visit because they might be there when Lamey turned up and that would probably make him mad, too.

That was the kind of life Gredel's mother Ava had always led, waiting in some apartment somewhere for some man to turn up. That's why Ava had never been able to see her daughter when she wanted to. Gredel's father had apparently been caught at something, but it had been Ava who had paid for it, and Gredel's father who had skipped town. Gredel had seen him maybe twice since then.

Gredel wanted a different life for herself. She had no idea how to get it, but she was paying attention, and maybe some day she'd learn.

Gredel still attended school. Every afternoon, when Gredel left her school, she'd find Lamey in his car waiting for her, Lamey or one of his boys who would take Gredel to wherever Lamey was waiting.

Gredel's attending school was something Lamey found amusing. "I'm going around with a schoolgirl," he'd laugh, and sometimes he'd remind her to do her schoolwork when he had to leave with his boys on some errand or other. Not that he left her much time for schoolwork. Her grades had plunged to the point where she would probably get kicked out of school before she graduated.

Tonight, the eve of the Festival of Spring, Lamey had taken Gredel to a party at Panda's place. Panda was another of Lamey's linkboys, and he worked on the distribution end. He'd pointed Stoney and his crew at a warehouse full of wine imported from Cavado and pharmaceuticals awaiting shipment to a Fleet hospital on Spannan's ring. The imported wine was proving difficult to sell, there not being much of a market in the Fabs for something so select; but the pharmaceuticals were moving fast through Panda's outlets and everyone was in the mood to celebrate.

"Come on, Earthgirl!" Stoney urged. "You've got to meet her!"

A warning hummed through Gredel's nerves as she saw everyone at the party looking at her with eyes that glittered from more than whatever they'd been consuming earlier in the evening. There was an anticipation there in those eyes Gredel didn't like. So she dropped Lamey's arm and straightened—because she didn't want these people to see her afraid—and she walked to where Stoney waited.

"Earthgirl!" Stoney said. "This is Caro!" He was practically jumping up and down with excitement, and instead of looking where Stoney was pointing, Gredel just gave Stoney a long, cool glance, because he was just so outrageous this way.

When she turned her head, her first thought was, *She's beautiful.* And then the full impact of the other girl's face struck her.

"Ah. Hah," she said.

Caro looked at her with a ragged grin. She had long golden hair and green eyes and skin smooth as butter-cream, flawless...

"It's your twin!" Stoney almost shouted. "Your secret twin sister!"

Gredel gaped while everyone laughed, but Caro just looked at her and said, "Are you really from Earth?"

"No," Gredel said. "I'm from here."

"Help me build this pyramid."

Gredel shrugged. "Why not?" she said.

Caro wore a short dress and a battered jacket with black metal buckles and boots that came up past her knees—expensive stuff. She stood by the dining table carefully building a pyramid of crystal wine glasses. "I saw this done once," she said. "You pour the wine into the one glass on the top, and when it overflows it fills all the others. If you do it right you fill all the glasses and you don't spill a drop."

Caro spoke with a kind of drawl, like Peers or rich people did when they made speeches or announcements on video.

"We're going to make a mess," Gredel predicted.

"That's all right, too," Caro shrugged.

When the pyramid was completed Caro got Stoney to start opening bottles. It was the wine his crew had stolen from the warehouse in Maranic Port, and it was a kind of bright silver in color, and filled the glasses like liquid mercury.

Caro tried to pour carefully but, as Gredel predicted she made a terrible mess, the precious wine bubbling across the tabletop and over onto the carpet. Caro seemed to find this funny. At length all the glasses were brimming full, and she put down the bottle and called everyone over to drink. They took glasses and cheered and drank. Laughter and clinking glasses rang in the air. The glasses were so full that the carpet got another bath.

Caro took one glass for herself and pushed another into Gredel's hand, then took a second glass for herself and led Gredel to the sofa. Gredel sipped cautiously at the wine—there was something subtle and indefinable about the taste, something that made her think of the park in spring, the way the trees and flowers had a delicate freshness to them. She'd never tasted any wine like it before.

The taste was more seductive than she wanted anything with alcohol to be. She didn't take a second sip.

"So," Caro said, "are we related?"

"I don't think so," Gredel said.

Caro swallowed half the contents of a glass in one go. "Your dad was never on Zanshaa? I can almost guarantee my dad was never here."

"I get my looks from my Ma, and she's never been anywhere," Gredel said. Then, surprised, "You're from Zanshaa?"

Caro gave a little twitch of her lips, followed by a shrug. Interpreting this as a yes, Gredel asked,

"What do your parents do?"

"They got executed," Caro said.

Gredel hesitated. "I'm sorry," she said. Caro's parents were linked, obviously. No wonder she was hanging with this crowd.

"Me, too." Caro said it with a brave little laugh, but she gulped down the remains of the wine in her first glass, then took a sip from the second. She looked up at Gredel.

"You heard of them maybe? The Sula family?"

Gredel tried to think of any of the linkages with that name, but couldn't. "Sorry, no," she said.

"That's all right," Caro said. "The Sulas were big on Zanshaa, but out here in the provinces they wouldn't mean much." Her eyes narrowed. "Why do they call you Earthgirl?"

Gredel put on her Earth accent. "Because I can talk like I'm from Earth, darling. I do the voice."

Caro laughed. She finished her second glass of wine, then got two more from the pyramid and drank them, then reached for Gredel's. "You going to drink that?"

"I don't drink much."

"Why not?"

Gredel hesitated. "I don't like being drunk."

Caro shrugged. "That's fair." She drank Gredel's glass, then put it with the others on the side table. "I don't like being drunk," she said, as if she were making up her mind right then. "But I don't dislike it either. What I don't like," she said carefully, "is standing still. Not moving. Not changing. I get bored fast, and I don't like *quiet*."

"In that case you've come to the right place," Gredel said.

Her nose is more pointed, Gredel thought. And her chin is different. She doesn't look like me, not really.

I bet I'd look good in that jacket, though.

"So do you live around here someplace?" Gredel asked.

Caro shook her head. "Maranic Town."

"I wish I lived in Maranic."

Caro looked at her in surprise. "Why?"

"Because it's…not here."

"Maranic is a hole. It's not something to wish for. If you're going to wish, wish for Zanshaa. Or Sandamar. Or Esley."

"Have you been to those places?" Gredel asked. She almost hoped the answer was no, because she knew she'd never get anywhere like that, that she'd get to Maranic Town if she was lucky.

"I was there when I was little," Caro said.

"I wish I lived in Byzantium," Gredel said.

Caro gave her a look again. "Where's that?"

"Earth. Terra."

"Terra's a hole," Caro said.

"I'd still like to go there."

"It's probably better than Maranic Town," Caro decided.

Someone programed some dance music, and Lamey came to dance with Gredel. A few years ago he hadn't been able to walk right, but now he was a good dancer, and Gredel enjoyed dancing with him, responding to his changing moods in the fast dances, molding her body to his when the beat slowed down.

Caro also danced with one boy or another, but Gredel saw that she couldn't dance at all, just bounced up and down while her partner maneuvered her around.

After a while Lamey went to talk business with Ibrahim, one of his boys who thought he knew someone in Maranic who could distribute the stolen wine, and Gredel found herself on the couch with Caro again.

"Your nose is different," Caro said.

"I know."

"But you're prettier than I am."

This was the opposite of what Gredel had been thinking. People were always telling her she was beautiful, and she had to believe they saw her that way, but when she looked in the mirror she saw nothing but a vast collection of flaws.

A girl shrieked in another room, and there was a crash of glass. Suddenly Caro's mood changed completely: she glared toward the other room as if she hated everyone there.

"Time to change the music," she said. She dug in her pocket and pulled out a med injector. She looked at the display, programed a number, and put the injector to her throat, over the carotid. Little flashes of alarm pulsed through Gredel.

"What's in there?" she asked.

"What do you care?" Caro snarled. Her eyes snapped green sparks.

She pressed the trigger, and an instant later the fury faded, and a drowsy smile came to Caro's lips. "Now that's better," she said. "Panda's got the real goods, all right."

"Tell me about Zanshaa," Gredel said.

Caro lazily shook her head. "No. Nothing but bad memories there."

"Then tell me about Esley."

"Sure. What I can remember."

Caro talked about Esley's black granite peaks, with a white spindrift of snow continually blowing off them in the high perpetual wind, and the shaggy Yormak who lived there, tending their equally shaggy cattle. She described glaciers pouring in ageless slow motion down mountain valleys, high meadows covered with fragrant star flowers, chill lakes so clear that you could see all the way to the bottom.

"Of course I was only at that mountain resort for a few weeks," Caro added. "The rest of the planet might be burning desert for all I know."

Lamey came back for more dancing, and when Gredel returned to the sofa Caro was unconscious, the med injector in her hand. She seemed to be breathing all right, though, lying asleep with a smile on her face. After a while Panda came over and tried to grope her, but Gredel slapped his hands away.

"What's your problem?" he asked.

"Don't mess with my sister when she's passed out," Gredel told him. He laughed, not exactly in a nice way, but he withdrew.

Caro was still asleep when the party ended. Gredel made Lamey help her carry Caro to his car, and then got him to drive to Maranic Town to her apartment. "What if she doesn't wake up long enough to tell us where it is?" Lamey complained.

"Whatever she took will wear off sooner or later."

"What if it's next week?" But he drove off anyway, heading for Maranic, while Gredel sat with Caro in the back seat and tried to wake Caro up. Caro woke long enough to murmur the fact that she lived in the Volta Apartments. Lamey got lost on the way there, and wandered into a Torminel neighborhood. The nocturnal Torminel were in the middle of their active cycle, and Lamey got angry at the way they stared at him with their huge eyes as he wandered their streets.

Lamey was furious by the time he found the apartment building. He opened the passenger door and practically dragged Caro out of the car onto the sidewalk. Gredel scrambled out of the car and tried to get one of Caro's arms over her shoulders so she could help Caro get to her feet.

A doorman came scrambling out of the building. "Has something happened to Lady Sula?" he demanded.

Lamey looked at him in surprise. The doorman stared at Gredel, then at Caro, astonished by the resemblance. But Gredel looked at Caro.

Lady Sula? Gredel thought.

Her twin was a Peer.

Ah, she thought. *Hah.*

❋

Lady Sula?

She wasn't even Lady Caro, she was Lady *Sula.* She wasn't just any Peer, she was head of the whole Sula clan.

Lamey's fury faded away quickly—it did that, came and went with lightning speed—and he picked Caro up in his arms and carried her to the elevator while the doorman fussed around him. When they arrived on the top floor, the doorman opened Caro's apartment, and Lamey walked in as if he paid the rent himself and carried Caro to her bedroom. There he put Caro down on her bed, and had Gredel draw off the tall boots while Lamey covered her with a comforter.

Gredel had never admired Lamey so much as at that moment. He behaved with a strange delicacy, as if he were a Peer himself, some lord commander of the Fleet cleaning up after a confidential mission.

The doorman wouldn't let them stay. On the way out Gredel saw that Caro's apartment was a terrible mess, with clothes in piles and the tables covered with glasses, bottles, and dirty dishes.

"I want you to come back here tomorrow," Lamey said as he started the car. "I want you to become Caro Sula's best friend."

Gredel fully intended this, but she wondered why Lamey's thoughts echoed her own. "Why?"

"Peers are rich," Lamey said simply. "Maybe we can get some of that and maybe we can't. But even more than the money, Peers are also the keys to things, and maybe Caro can open some doors for us. Even if it's just the door to her bank account, it's worth a try."

It was very, very late, almost dawn, but Lamey wanted to take Gredel to one of his apartments. There they had a brisk five minutes' sex, hardly worth taking off her clothes as far as Gredel was concerned, and then Lamey took Gredel home.

As soon as she walked in the door she knew Antony was back— he'd been gone for four months, working in another town, and Gredel had got used to walking in the door without fear. Now the apartment smelled different, a blend of beer and tobacco and human male and fear. Gredel took off her boots at the door so she wouldn't wake him, and crept in silence to her bed. Despite the hour she lay awake for some time, thinking of keys and doors opening.

Lamey didn't know what he wanted from Caro, not quite, he was operating on an instinct that told him Caro could be useful, give him connections, links that would move him upward in the Fabs. Gredel had much the same intuition where Caro was concerned, but she wanted Caro for other things. Gredel didn't want to stay in the Fabs. Caro might show her how to do that, how to behave, perhaps, or how to dress, how to move up, and maybe not just out of the Fabs but off Spannan altogether, loft out of the ring station on a tail of fire to Esley or Zanshaa or Earth, to a glittering life that she felt hovering around her, a kind of potential waiting to be born, but that she couldn't quite imagine.

She woke just before noon and put on her robe to shower and use the toilet. The sounds of the Spring Festival zephyrball game blared from the front room, where Antony was watching the video. Gredel finished her business in the bathroom and went back into her room to dress. When she finished putting on her clothes and her makeup she brushed her hair for a long time, delaying the moment when she would leave her sanctum to face Antony, but when she realized what she was doing she got angry at herself and put the brush down, then put her money in the pocket of her jacket and walked through the door.

Antony sat on the sagging old sofa watching the game on the video wall. The remains of a sandwich sat on a plate next to him. He was a man of average height but built powerfully, with broad shoulders and a barrel chest and long arms with big hands. He looked like a slab on legs. Iron-grey hair fringed his bald head, and his eyes were tiny and set in a permanent suspicious glare.

He wasn't drinking, Gredel saw, and felt some of her tension ease.

"Hi, Antony," she said as she walked for the apartment door.

He looked at her with his glaring black eyes. "Where you going dressed like that?"

"To see a friend."

"The friend who bought you those clothes?"

"No. Someone else." She made herself stop walking and face him.

His lips twitched in a sneer. "Nelda says you're whoring now for some linkboy. Just like your mother."

Anger flamed along Gredel's veins, but she clamped it down and said, "I've never whored. Never. Not once."

"Not for money, maybe," Antony said. "But look at those clothes on you. And that jewelry." Gredel felt herself flush. Antony returned his attention to the game. "Better you sell that tail of yours for money," he muttered. "Then you could contribute to your upkeep around here."

So you could steal it, Gredel thought, but didn't say it. She headed for the door, and just before it swung shut behind her she heard Antony's parting shot. "You better not take out that implant! You get pregnant, you're out of this place! I'm not looking after another kid that isn't my own!"

Like he'd ever looked after any kid.

Gredel left the building with her fists clenched and a blaze of fury kindled in her eyes. Kids playing in the front hall took one look at her and got out of her way.

It wasn't until the train was halfway to Maranic Town that the anger finally ebbed to a normal background buzz, and Gredel began to wonder if Caro would be at home, if she would even remember meeting her the previous night.

Gredel found the Volta Apartments quickly now that she knew where it was. The doorman—it was a different doorman this time— opened the door for her and showed her right to the elevator. Clearly he thought she was Caro. "Thank you," Gredel smiled, trying to drawl out the words the way a Peer would.

She had to knock loudly, several times, before Caro came to the door. Caro was still in her short dress from the previous night, and tights, and bare feet. Her hair was disordered, and there was a smear of mascara on one cheek. Her slitted eyes opened wide as she saw Gredel at the door.

"Earthgirl," she said. "Hi."

"The doorman thought I was you. I came over to see if you were all right."

Caro opened the door and flapped her arms, as if to say, *I am as you see me.* "Come in," she said, and turned to walk toward the kitchen.

The apartment was still a mess, and the air smelled stale. Caro went to the sink in the little kitchen and poured herself a glass of water.

"My mouth tastes like cheese," she said. "The kind with the veins in it. I hate that kind of cheese."

She drank her water while Gredel walked around the apartment. She felt strangely reluctant to touch anything, as if it was a fantasy that might dissolve if she put a finger on it.

"So," she said finally. "You want to go and do something?"

Caro finished her water and put down her glass on a counter already covered with dirty glasses. "I need some coffee first," she said. "Would you mind going to the café on the corner and getting some for me while I change?"

"What about the coffee maker?" Gredel asked.

Caro blinked at the machine as if she were seeing it for the first time. "I don't know how to work it," she said.

"I'll show you."   .

"I never learned how to do kitchen stuff," Caro said, as she made way for Gredel in the kitchen. "Till I came here we always had servants. I had servants *here,* but I called the last one a cow and threw her out."

"What's a cow?" Gredel asked.

"They're ugly and fat and stupid. Like Berthe when I fired her."

Gredel found coffee in a cupboard and began preparing the coffee maker. "Do you *eat* cows, or what?" she asked.

"Yeah, they give meat. And milk, too."

"We have vashes for that. And zieges. And swine and bison, but they only give meat."

Gredel made coffee for them both. Caro took her cup into the bathroom with her, and after a while Gredel heard the shower start to run. She sipped her coffee as she wandered around the apartment—the rooms were nice, but not *that* nice, Lamey had places just as good, though not in such an exclusive building as this. There was a view of the Iola River two streets away, but it wasn't that nice a view, there were buildings in the way, and the window glass was dirty.

Then, because she couldn't stand the mess any longer, Gredel began to pick up the scattered clothes and fold them. She finished that and was putting the dirty dishes in the washer when Caro appeared, dressed casually in soft wool pantaloons, a high-necked blouse, and a little vest with gold buttons and lots of pockets slashed one on top of the other. Caro looked around in surprise.

"You cleaned up!"

"A little."

"You didn't have to do that."

"I didn't have anything else to do." Gredel came into the front room. She looked down at one of the piles of clothing, put her hand down on the soft pile of a sweater she had just folded and placed neatly on the back of a sofa. "You have some nice things," she said.

"That's from Yormak cattle. They have wonderful wool." She eyed Gredel's clothing. "What you're wearing, that's—that's all right."

"Lamey bought it for me."

Caro laughed. "Might have known a man picked that."

What's wrong with it? Gredel wanted to ask. It was what everyone was wearing, only top quality. These weren't clothes hijacked at Maranic Port, they were bought in a *store.*

Caro took Gredel's arm. "Let's get some breakfast," she said, "and then I'll take you shopping."

The doorman stared comically as Caro and Gredel stepped out of the elevator. Caro introduced Gredel as her twin sister Margaux from Earth, and Gredel greeted the doorman in her Earth accent. The doorman bowed deeply as they swept out.

An hour later in the restaurant, Gredel was surprised when Caro asked her to pay for their meal. "My allowance comes first of the month," she said. "And this month's money supply is *gone.* This café won't run a tab for me."

"Weren't we going shopping?"

Caro grinned. "Clothes I can buy on credit."

They went to one of the arcades where exclusive shops sheltered under a long series of graceful arches of polymerous resin, the arches translucent but grown in different colors, so that the vaulted ceiling of each glowed with subtle tones that merged and flowed and blended. Caro introduced Gredel as her sister, and laughed when Gredel used her Earth accent. Gredel was called Lady Margaux and surrounded by swarms of clerks and floorwalkers, and she was both surprised and flattered by the attention. This is what it was like to be a Peer.

If she'd been merely Gredel, the staff would have been there all right, but following her around to make sure she didn't steal.

The arcades didn't serve just Terrans, so there were Torminel there, and Naxids, and some pleasure-loving Cree who wandered through the shops burbling in their musical voices. It was unusual for Gredel to see so many non-humans in one place, since she rarely had any reason to leave the Terran parts of the Fabs. But the Peers, Gredel concluded, were almost a species of their own. They had more in common with each other than they had with other folk.

Caro bought an outfit for herself and two for Gredel, first a luxurious gown with a cape so long it dragged on the floor, and next a pajama-like lounging outfit. Gredel had no idea where she would ever wear such things. Caro nodded at the lounging suit. "Made of worm spit," she said.

"Sorry?" Gredel said, startled.

"Worm spit. They call it 'silk.'"

Gredel had heard of silk, and she touched the fabric with a new respect. "Do you think it came from Earth?" she asked.

"I doubt it." Dismissively. "Earth's a hole. My mother was there on government service, and she told me."

Caro bought everything on credit. Gredel noticed that she signed only *Sula*, leaving out her first name and the honorific *Lady*. She seemed to carry a tab in every store in the arcade. When Gredel thanked her for the presents, Caro said, "You can pay me back by buying dinner."

"I don't think I can afford that," Gredel said doubtfully.

Caro laughed. "Guess we better learn to eat worm spit," she said.

Gredel was intrigued by the way everyone lined up to give Caro credit. "They know I'm good for it," Caro explained. "They know I'll have the money eventually."

"When?"

"When I'm twenty-two. That's when the funds mature." She laughed again. "But those people still won't get paid. I'll be off the planet by then, in the Fleet, and they can chase me through space if they like."

Gredel was intrigued by this, too. There tended to be serious consequences in the Fabs for people who didn't pay their debts. Maybe this, too, was different for Peers.

"So this is money your parents left you?" Gredel asked.

Caro looked dubious. "I'm not sure. My parents were caught in some kind of scheme to swindle government suppliers out of a lot of money, and they lost everything—estates, money—" She tapped her neck significantly. "Everything. I got sent to live with Jacob Biswas in Blue Lakes." This was an exclusive area outside of Maranic Town. "The Biswas clan were clients of the Sulas, and Dad got Biswas the job of Assistant Port Administrator here. I'm not sure if the money is something Dad got to him, or whether it came from my dad's clients or friends, but it's in a bank on Spannan's ring, and the interest comes to me here every month."

"You don't live with Biswas anymore, though. Did he leave Spannan?"

"No, he's still here. But he got divorced and remarried, and the new wife and I didn't get along—we were fighting every day, and poor old Jacob couldn't take it any more, so he got me the place in the Volta until it was time for me to join the Fleet."

Caro went on to explain that her family was forbidden to be in the civil service for three generations, both as punishment for what her parents had done and to minimize the chance to steal. But as a Peer she had an automatic ticket to one of the Fleet academies, and so it had been planned for her to go there.

"I don't know," Caro said, shaking her head. "I can't see myself in the Fleet. Taking orders, wearing uniforms…under all that discipline. I think I'd go crazy in ten days."

The Fleet, Gredel thought. The Fleet could carry you away from Spannan, through the wormhole gates to the brilliant worlds beyond. Zanshaa, Esley, Earth… The vision was dazzling. For that she could put up with uniforms.

"I'd do it in a second," Gredel said.

Caro gave her a look. "Why?"

Gredel thought she may as well emphasize the practical advantages. "You get food and a place to sleep. Medical and dental care. And they *pay* you for it."

Caro gave a disdainful snort. *"You* do it, then."

"I would if I could."

Caro made a disgusted noise. "So why don't you? You could enlist."

"They wouldn't let me. My mother has a criminal record."

The Fleet had their pick of recruits: there were plenty of people who wanted those three free meals per day. They checked the background of everyone who applied.

Unless, Gredel thought, someone she knew could pull strings. A Peer, say.

They took a taxi back to Caro's apartment, but when the driver started to pull up to the curb, Caro ducked into the back seat, pulled a bewildered Gredel down atop her, and shouted at the driver to keep going.

"What's the matter?" Gredel asked.

"A collector. Someone come to get money from me. The doorman usually chases them off, but this one's really persistent."

Apparently living on credit wasn't as convenient as Caro let on.

The driver let them off in the alley behind the apartment building. There was a loading dock there, and Caro's codes opened the door. There were little motorized carts in the entryway, for use when people moved in furniture or other heavy belongings.

They took the freight elevator to Caro's floor and looked for something to eat. There wasn't much, just biscuits and an old piece of cheese. "Have you got food at your place?" Caro asked.

Gredel hesitated. Her reluctance was profound. "Food," she said, "but we've got Antony, too."

"And who's that?"

Gredel told her. Caro's disgusted look returned. "He comes near me," she said, "I'll kick him in the balls."

"That's wouldn't stop him for long," Gredel said, and shivered. "He'd still slap your face off."

"We'll see." Caro's lip curled again, defiant.

"I'm serious. You don't want to get Antony mad. I bet even Lamey's boys would have a hard time with him."

Caro shook her head. "This is crazy," she laughed. "You know anyone who could buy us some food?"

"Well. There's Lamey."

"He's your boyfriend, right? The tall one?"

"He carried you up here last night."

"So I *already* owe him," Caro laughed. "Will he mind if I mooch dinner off him? I'll pay him back, first of the month."

Gredel called Lamey on her phone, and he was amused by their dilemma and said he'd be there soon.

"So tell me about Lamey," Caro said while they waited.

So Gredel told Caro about Lamey's business. "He's linked, you know? He knows people, and he moves stuff around. From the Port, from other places. Makes it available to people at good prices. When people can't get loans, he loans them money."

"Aren't the clans' patrons supposed to do that?"

"Sometimes they will. But, you know, those mid-level clans, they're in a lot of businesses themselves, or their friends and allies are. So they're not going to loan money for someone to go into competition with them. And once the new businesses start, they have to be protected, you know, against the people who are already in that business, so Lamey and his people do that, too."

"It's the Peers who are supposed to protect people," Caro said.

"Caro," Gredel said, "you're the first Peer I've ever seen outside of a video. Peers don't come to places like the Fabs."

Caro gave a cynical grin. "So Lamey just does *good* things, right? He's never hurt anybody, he just helps people."

Gredel hesitated. They were entering the area of things she tried not to think about. She thought about the boy Moseley, the dreadful dull squelching thud as Lamey's boot went into him. The way her own head rang after Lamey slapped her that time.

"Sure," she said finally, "he's hurt people. People who stole from him, mostly. But he's really not bad," she added quickly, "he's not one of the violent ones, he's *smart*. He uses his intelligence."

"Uh-huh," Caro said. "So has he used his...*intelligence*...on you?"

Gredel felt herself flush. "A few times," she said quickly. "He's got a temper. But he's always sweet when he cools down, and buys me things."

"Uh-huh," Caro said.

Gredel tried not to bristle at Caro's attitude. Hitting was what boyfriends *did*, it was normal, the point was whether they felt sorry afterwards.

"Do you love him?" Caro asked.

Gredel hesitated again. "Maybe," she said.

"I hope at least he's good in bed."

Gredel shrugged. "He's all right." Sex seemed to be expected of her, because she was thought to be beautiful and because she went with older boys who had money. For all that it had never been as pleasurable as she'd been led to expect, it was nevertheless pleasurable enough so that she never really wanted to quit.

"Lamey's too young to be good in bed," Caro declared. "You need an older man to show you what sex is really about." Her eyes sparkled, and she gave a diabolical giggle. "Like my Sergei. He was really the best! He showed me *everything* about sex."

Gredel blinked. "Who was Sergei?"

"Remember I told you that Jake Biswas remarried? Well, his wife's sister was married to Sergei. He and I met at the wedding and fell for each other—we were always sneaking away to be together. That's what all the fighting in the family was about. That's why I had to move to Maranic Town."

"How much older was he?"

"In his forties somewhere."

Black, instant hatred descended on Gredel. She could have torn Sergei to ribbons with her nails, with her teeth.

"That's sick," she said. "That man is disgusting."

Caro gave a cynical laugh. "I wouldn't talk if I were you," she said. "How old is Lamey? What kind of scenes does *he* get you into?"

Gredel felt as if Caro's words had slapped her across the face. Caro gave her a smirk.

"Right," she said. "We're models of stability and mental health, we are."

Gredel decided to change the subject.

Caro's mood had sweetened by the time Lamey turned up. She thanked him for taking her home the previous night, and took them both to a restaurant so exclusive that Caro had to give a thumbprint in order to enter. There were no real dinners on the menu, just a variety of small plates that everyone at the table shared. Gredel had never heard of some of the ingredients. Some of the dishes were wonderful, some weren't. Some were simply incomprehensible.

Caro and Lamey got along well, to Gredel's relief. Caro filled the air with vivacious talk, and Lamey joked and deferred to her. Toward the end of the meal he remembered something, and reached into his pocket. Gredel's nerves tingled as she recognized a med injector.

"Panda asked me if you wanted any more of the endorphin," Lamey said.

"I don't have any money, remember?" Caro said.

Lamey gave an elaborate shrug. "I'll put it on your tab."

Don't, Gredel wanted to shout.

But Caro gave a pleased, catlike smile, and reached for the injector in Lamey's hand.

⚫

Gredel and Caro spent a lot of time together after that. Partly because Lamey wanted it, but also because Gredel found that she liked Caro, and she liked learning from her. She studied how Caro dressed, how she talked, how she moved. And Caro enjoyed dressing Gredel up like one of her dolls, and teaching her to walk and talk as if she were Lady Margaux, the sister of a Peer. Gredel worked on her accent till her speech was a letter-perfect imitation of Caro's. Caro couldn't do voices the way Gredel could, and Gredel's Earthgirl voice always made her laugh.

Gredel was learning the things that might get her out of the Fabs.

Caro enjoyed teaching her. Maybe, Gredel thought, this was because Caro really didn't have much to do. She'd left school, because she was a Peer and would get into the academy whether she had good marks or not, and she didn't seem to have any friends in Maranic Town. Sometimes friends from Blue Lakes came to visit her—usually a pack of girls all at once—but all their talk was about people and events in their school, and Gredel could tell that Caro got bored with that fast.

"I wish Sergei would call," Caro said. But Sergei never did. And Caro refused to call Sergei. "It's his move, not mine," she said, her eyes turning hard.

Caro got bored easily. And that was dangerous, because when Caro got bored she wanted to change the music. Sometimes that meant shopping or going to a club, but it could also mean drinking a couple bottles of wine or a bottle of brandy, or firing endorphin or benzedrine into her carotid from the med injector, or sometimes all of the above. It was the endorphins she liked best, though.

The drugs weren't illegal, but the supply was controlled in various ways, and they were expensive. The black market provided pharmaceuticals at more reasonable prices, and without a paper or money trail. The drugs the linkboys sold weren't just for fun, either: Nelda got Gredel black market antivirals when she was sick, and fast-healers once when she broke her leg, and saved herself the expense of supporting a doctor and a pharmacy.

When Caro changed the music she became a spiky, half-feral creature, a tangled ligature of taut-strung nerves and overpowering impulse. She would careen from one scene to the next, from party to club to bar, having a frenzied good time one minute, spitting out vicious insults at perfect strangers the next.

At the first of the month Gredel urged Caro to pay Lamey what she owed him. Caro just shrugged, but Gredel insisted. "This isn't like the debts you run up at the boutique."

Caro gave Gredel a narrow-eyed look that made her nervous, because she recognized it as the prelude to fury. "What do you mean?"

"When you don't pay Lamey, things happen."

"Like what?" Contemptuously.

"Like—" Gredel hesitated. "Like what happened to Moseley."

Her stomach turned over at the memory. "Moseley ran a couple of Lamey's stores, you know, where he sells the stuff he gets. And Lamey found out that Moseley was skimming the profits. So—" She remembered the way Lamey screamed at Moseley, the way his boys held Moseley while Lamey smashed him in the face and body. The way that Lamey kept kicking him even after Moseley fell unconscious to the floor, the thuds of the boots going home.

"So what happened to Moseley?" Caro asked.

"I think he died." Gredel spoke the words past the knot in her throat. "The boys won't talk to me about it. No one ever saw him again. Panda runs those stores now."

"And Lamey would do that to *me?*" Caro asked. It clearly took effort to wrap her mind around the idea of being vulnerable to someone like Lamey.

Gredel hesitated again. "Maybe you just shouldn't give him the chance. He's unpredictable."

"Fine," Caro said. "Give him the money then."

Caro went to her computer and gave Gredel a credit chit for the money, which Gredel then carried to Lamey. He gave the plastic tab a bemused look—he was in a cash-only business—and then asked Gredel to take it back to Caro and have it cashed. When Gredel returned to Caro's apartment the next day, Caro was hung over and didn't want to be bothered, so she gave Gredel the codes to her cash account.

It was as easy as that.

Gredel looked at the deposit made the previous day and took a breath. Eight hundred forty zeniths, enough to keep Nelda and her assortment of children for a year, with enough left over for Antony to get drunk every night. And Caro got this every *month*.

Gredel started looking after Caro's money, seeing that at least some of the creditors were appeased, that there was food in the kitchen. She cleaned the place, too, tidied the clothes Caro scattered everywhere, saw that the laundry was sent out and, when it returned, was put away. Caro was amused by it all. "When I'm in the Fleet, you can join, too," she said. "I'll make you a servant or something."

Hope burned in Gredel's heart. "I hope so," she said. "But you'll have to pull some strings to get me in—I mean, with my mother's record and everything."

"I'll get you in," Caro assured.

Lamey was disappointed when Gredel told him about Caro's finances. "Eight hundred forty," he muttered, "it's hardly worth stealing." He rolled onto his back in the bed—they were in one of his apartments—and frowned at the ceiling.

"People have been killed for a lot less than that," Gredel said. "For the price of a bottle of cheap wine."

Lamey's blue eyes gave her a sharp look. "I'm not talking about killing anybody," he said. "I'm just saying it's not worth *getting killed over*, because that's what's likely to happen if you steal from a Peer. It won't be worth trying until she's twenty-two, when she gets the whole inheritance, and by then she'll be in the Fleet." He sighed. "I wish she were in the Fleet now, assigned to the Port. We might be able to make use of her, get some Fleet supplies."

"I don't want to steal from her," Gredel said.

Lamey fingered his chin thoughtfully and went on as if he hadn't heard. "What you do, see, is get a bank account in *her* name, but with *your* thumbprint. Then you transfer Caro's money over to your account, and from there you turn it into cash and walk off into the night." He smiled. "Should be easy."

"I thought you said it wasn't worth it," Gredel said.

"Not for eight hundred it isn't," Lamey said. He gave a laugh. "I'm just trying to work out a way of getting my investment back."

Gredel was relieved that Lamey wasn't really intending to steal Caro's money. She didn't want to be a thief, and she especially didn't want to steal from a friend like Caro.

"She doesn't seem to have any useful contacts here." Lamey continued thinking aloud. "Find out about these Biswas people. They might be good for *something*."

Gredel agreed. The request seemed harmless enough.

Gredel spent most of her nights away from Nelda's now, either with Lamey or sleeping at Caro's place. That was good, because things at Nelda's were grim. Antony looked as if he was settling in for a long stay. He was sick, something about his liver, and he couldn't get work. Sometimes Nelda had fresh bruises or cuts on her face. Sometimes the other kids did. And sometimes when Gredel came home at night Antony was there, passed out on the sofa, a bottle of gin in his hand. She took off her shoes and walked past him quietly, glaring her hatred as she passed him, and she would think how easy it would be to hurt Antony then, to pick up the bottle and smash Antony in the face with it, smash him until he couldn't hurt anyone ever again.

Once Gredel came home and found Nelda in tears. Antony had slapped her around and taken the rent money, for the second time in a row. "We're going to be evicted," Nelda whispered hoarsely. "They're going to throw us all out."

"No they're not," Gredel said firmly. She went to Lamey and explained the situation and begged him for the money. "I'll never ask you for anything ever again," she promised.

Lamey listened thoughtfully, then reached into his wallet and handed her a hundred-zenith note. "This take care of it?" he asked.

Gredel reached for the note, hesitated. "More than enough," she said. "I don't want to take that much."

Lamey took her hand and put the note into it. His blue eyes looked into hers. "Take it and welcome," he said. "Buy yourself something nice with the rest."

Gratitude flooded Gredel's eyes. Tears fell down her cheeks. "Thank you," she said. "I know I don't deserve it."

"Of course you do," Lamey said. "You deserve the best, Earthgirl." He kissed her, his lips coming away salty. "Now you take this to the building agent, right? You don't give it to Nelda, because she might give it away again."

"I'll do that right away," Gredel said.

"And—" His eyes turned solemn. "Does Antony need taking care of? Or need encouragement to leave? You know what I mean."

Gredel shrank from the idea. "No," she said. "No—he won't stay long."

"You remember it's an option, right?" She made herself nod in answer.

Gredel took the money to the agent, a scowling little woman who had an office in the building and who smelled of cabbage and onions. She insisted on a receipt for the two months' rent, which the woman gave grudgingly, and as Gredel walked away she thought about Lamey and how this meant Lamey loved her.

Too bad he's going to die. The thought formed in her mind unbidden. The worst part was that she knew it was true.

People like Lamey didn't survive for long. There weren't many *old* linkboys—that's why they weren't called link*men*. Sooner or later they were caught and killed. And the people they loved—their wives, their lovers, their children—paid as well, with a term on the labor farms like Ava, or with their own execution.

The point was reinforced a few days later, when Stoney was caught hijacking a cargo of fuel cells in Maranic Port. His trial was over two weeks later, and then he was executed the next week. Because stealing private property was a crime against common law, not against the Praxis that governed the empire, he wasn't subjected to the tortures reserved for those who transgressed against the ultimate law, but simply strapped into a chair and garotted.

The execution was broadcast on the video channel reserved for punishments, and Lamey made his boys watch it. "To make them more careful," he said simply.

Gredel didn't watch. She went to Caro's instead and surprised herself by helping Caro drink a bottle of wine. Caro was delighted at this lapse on Gredel's part, and was her most charming all night, thanking Gredel effusively for everything Gredel had done for her. Gredel left with the wine singing in her veins. She had rarely felt so good.

The euphoria lasted until she entered Nelda's apartment. Antony was in full cry. A chair lay in pieces on the floor and Nelda had a cut above her eye that wept red tears across her face. Gredel froze in the door as she came in, and then tried to slip toward her room without attracting Antony's attention.

No such luck. Antony lunged toward her, grabbed her blouse by its shoulder. She felt the fabric tear. "Where's the money?" Antony shouted. "Where's the money you get by selling your tail?"

Gredel held out her pocketbook in trembling hands. "Here!" she said. "Take it!"

It was clear enough what was going on, it was Antony Scenario Number One. He needed cash for a drink, and he'd already taken everything Nelda had.

Antony grabbed the pocketbook, poured coins into his hand. Gredel could smell the juniper scent of the gin reeking off his pores. He looked at the coins dumbly, then threw the pocketbook to the floor and put the money in his pocket.

"I'm going to put you on the street myself, right now," he said, and seized her wrist in one huge hand. "I can get more money for you than this."

"No!" Gredel filled with terror, tried to pull away.

Anger blazed in Antony's eyes. He drew back his other hand.

Gredel felt the impact not on her flesh but in her bones. Her teeth snapped together and her heels went out from under her and she sat on the floor.

Then Nelda was there, screaming, her hands clutching Antony's forearm as she tried to keep him from hitting Gredel again. "Don't hit the child!" she wailed.

"Stupid bitch!" Antony growled, and turned to punch Nelda in the face. "Don't ever step between me and her again!"

Turning his back was Antony's big mistake. Anger blazed in Gredel, an all-consuming blowtorch annihilating fury that sent her lunging for the nearest weapon, a leg that had been broken off when Antony had smashed a chair in order to underscore one of his rhetorical points. Gredel kicked off her heels and rose to her feet and swung the chair leg two-handed for Antony's head.

Nelda gaped at her, her mouth an O, and wailed again. Antony took this as a warning and started to turn, but it was too late. The wooden chair leg caught him in the temple, and he fell to one knee. The chair leg, which was made of compressed dedger fiber, had broken raggedly, and the splintery end gouged his flesh.

Gredel gave a shriek powered by fifteen years of pure, suppressed hatred and swung again. There was a solid crack as the chair leg connected with Antony's bald skull, and the big man dropped to the floor like a bag of rocks. Gredel dropped her knees onto his barrel chest and swung again and again. She remembered the sound that Lamey's boots made going into Moseley and wanted badly to make those sounds come from Antony. The ragged end of the chair leg tore long ribbons out of Antony's flesh. Blood splashed the floor and walls.

She only stopped when Nelda wrapped Gredel's arms with her own and hauled her off Antony. Gredel turned to swing at Nelda, and only stopped when she saw the older woman's tears.

Antony was making a bubbling sound as he breathed. A slow river of blood poured out of his mouth onto the floor. "What do we do?" Nelda wailed as she turned little helpless circles on the floor. "What do we do?"

Gredel knew the answer to the question perfectly well. She got her phone out of her pocketbook and went to her room and called Lamey. He was there in twenty minutes with Panda and three other boys. He looked at the wrecked room, at Antony lying on the floor, at Gredel standing over the man with the bloody chair leg in her hand.

"What do you want done?" he asked Gredel. "We could put him on a train, I suppose. Or in the river."

"No!" Nelda jumped between Antony and Lamey. Tears brimmed from her eyes as she turned to Gredel. "Put him on the train. Please, honey, please."

"On the train," Gredel repeated to Lamey.

"We'll wake him up long enough to tell him not to come back," Lamey said. He and his boys picked up Antony's heavy body and dragged it toward the door.

"Where's the freight elevator?" Lamey asked.

"I'll show you." Gredel went with them to the elevator. The tenants were working people who went to bed at a reasonable hour, and the building was silent at night and the halls empty. Lamey's boys panted for breath as they hauled the heavy, inert carcass with its heavy bones and solid muscle. They reached the freight elevator doors and the boys dumped Antony on the floor while they caught their breath.

"Lamey," Gredel said.

Lamey looked at her. "Yes?"

She looked up at him, into his accepting blue eyes.

"Put him in the river," she said. "Just make sure he doesn't come up."

Lamey looked at her, a strange silent sympathy in his eyes, and he put his arm around her and kissed her cheek. "I'll make it all right for you," he said.

No you won't, she thought, *but you'll make it better.*

The next morning Nelda threw her out. She looked at Gredel from beneath the slab of grey healing plaster she'd pasted over the cut in her forehead, and she said, "I just can't have you here anymore. I just can't."

For a moment of blank terror Gredel wondered if Antony's body had come bobbing up under Old Iola Bridge, but soon Gredel realized that wasn't the problem. The previous evening had put Nelda in a position of having to decide who she loved more, Antony or Gredel. She'd picked Antony, unaware that he was no longer an option.

Gredel went to her mother's, and Ava's objections died the moment she saw the bruise on Gredel's cheek. Gredel told her the story of what had happened—not being stupid, she left out what she'd asked Lamey to do—and Ava hugged her and told her she was proud of her. She worked with cosmetics for a long time to hide the damage.

And then she took Gredel to Maranic Town, to Bonifacio's for ice cream.

※

Ava and Lamey and Panda helped carry Gredel's belongings to Ava's place, arms and boxes full of the clothing Lamey and Caro had bought her, the blouses and pants and frocks and coats and capes and hats and shoes and jewelry, all the stuff that had long ago overflowed the closets in her room at Nelda's, that was for the most part lying in neat piles on the old, worn carpet.

Panda was highly impressed by the tidiness of it. "You've got a *system* here," he said.

Ave was in a better situation than usual. Her man was married and visited only at regularly-scheduled intervals, and he didn't mind if she spent her free time with family or friends. But Ava didn't have many friends—her previous men hadn't really let her have any—and so she was delighted to spend time with her daughter.

Lamey was disappointed that Gredel didn't want to move into one of his apartments. "I need my Ma right now," Gredel told him, and that seemed to satisfy him.

I don't want to live with someone who's going to be killed soon. That was what she thought to herself. But she wondered if she was obliged to live with the boy who had killed for her.

Caro was disappointed as well. "You could have moved in with *me!*" she said.

Shimmering delight sang in Gredel's mind. "You wouldn't mind?"

"No!" Caro was enthusiastic. "We could be sisters! We could shop and go out—have fun."

For days Gredel basked in the warm attentions of Caro and her mother. She spent almost all her time with one or the other, enough so that Lamey began to get jealous, or at least to *pretend* that he was jealous—Lamey was sometimes hard to read that way. "Caro's kidnaped you," he half-joked over the phone. "I'm going to have to send the boys to fetch you back."

Gredel began to spend nights with Caro, the nights when Ava was with her man. There was a lot of room in the big bed. She found that Caro didn't so much go to sleep as put herself into a coma: she loaded endorphins into the med injector and gave herself one dose after another until unconsciousness claimed her. Gredel was horrified.

"Why do you do it?" she asked one night, as Caro reached for the injector.

Caro gave her a glare. "Because I *like* it," she snarled. "I can't sleep without it."

Gredel shrank away from Caro's look. She didn't want Caro to rip into her the way she ripped into other people.

One night Lamey took them both to a party. "I've got to take Caro out, too," he told Gredel "Otherwise I'd never see *you.*"

The reason for the party was that Lamey had put up a loan for a restaurant and club, and the people hadn't made a go of it, so he'd foreclosed and taken the place over. He'd inherited a stockroom of liquor and a walk-in refrigerator full of food, decided it may as well not go to waste, and invited nearly everyone he knew. He paid the staff for one more night and let all his guests know the food and drinks were free.

"We'll have fun tonight," he said, "and tomorrow I'll start looking for somebody to manage the place."

It was the last great party Gredel had with Lamey and his crew. The big room was filled with food and music and people having a good time. Laughter rang from the club's rusted, reinforced iron ceiling, which was not an attempt at decor but a reminder of the fact that the floor above had once been braced to support heavy machinery. Though Gredel didn't have anything to drink she still got high simply from being around so many people who were soaking up the good times along with the free liquor. Gredel's mind whirled as she danced, whirled like her body spinning along the dance floor in response to Lamey's smooth, perfect, elegant motion. He leaned close and spoke into her ear.

"Come and live with me, Earthgirl."

She shook her head, smiled. "Not yet."

"I want to marry you. Have babies with you."

A shiver of pleasure sang up Gredel's spine. She had no reply, only put her arms around Lamey's neck and rested her head on his shoulder.

Gredel didn't know quite how she deserved to be so loved. Lamey, Caro, her mother, each of them filling a dreadful hollowness inside her, a hollowness she hadn't realized was there until it was filled with warmth and tenderness.

Lamey danced with Caro as well, or rather guided her around the dance floor while she did the jumping-up-and-down thing she did instead of dancing. Caro was having a good time. She drank only a couple bottles of wine over the course of the night, which for her was modest, and the rest of the time danced with Lamey or members of his crew. As they left the club she kissed Lamey extravagantly to thank him for inviting her. Lamey put an arm around both Caro and Gredel.

"I just like to show my beautiful sisters a good time," he said.

He and Gredel took Caro to the Volta Apartments, after which they intended to drive back to the Fabs to spend the dawn in one of Lamey's apartments. But Caro lingered in the car, leaning forward out of the back seat to prop her head and shoulders between Lamey and Gredel. They all talked and laughed, and the doorman hovered in the Volta vestibule, waiting for the moment to let Lady Sula past the doors. Finally Lamey said it was time to go.

"Save yourself that drive back to the Fabs," Caro said. "You two can use my bed. I can sleep on the sofa."

Lamey gave her a look. "I hate to put a beautiful woman out of her bed."

Caro gave a sharp, sudden laugh, then turned to kiss Gredel on the cheek. "That depends on Gredel."

Ah. Hah, Gredel thought, surprised and not surprised.

Lamey, it seems, was looking for a return on his investment. Gredel thought a moment, then shrugged.

"I don't mind," she said.

So Lamey took Gredel and Caro up to the apartment and made love to them both. Gredel watched her boyfriend's pale butt jigging up and down over Caro and wondered why this scene didn't bother her.

Because I don't love him, she decided. *If I loved him, this would matter.*

And then she thought, *Maybe Caro loves him.* Maybe Caro would want to stay with Lamey in the Fabs, and Gredel could take Caro's place in the academy and go to Earth.

Maybe that would be the solution that would leave everyone happy.

Caro apologized the next day, after Lamey left. "I was awful last night," she said. "I don't know what you must think of me."

"It was all right," Gredel said. She was folding Caro's clothes and putting them away. *Cleaning up after the orgy,* she thought.

"I'm such a slut sometimes," Caro said. "You must think I'm trying to steal Lamey away from you."

"I'm not thinking that."

Caro trotted up behind Gredel and put her arms around her. She leaned her head against Gredel's shoulder, and put on the lisping voice of a penitent little girl. "Do you forgive me?"

"Yes," Gredel said. "Of course."

Suddenly Caro was all energy. She skipped around the room, bounding around Gredel as Gredel folded her clothes. "I'll make it up to you!" Caro proclaimed. "I'll take you anywhere you want today! What would you like? Shopping?"

Gredel considered the offer. It wasn't as if she needed new things—she was beginning to feel a little oppressed by all her possessions—but on the other hand she enjoyed Caro's pleasure in purchasing them. But then another idea struck her.

"Godfrey's," she said.

Caro's eyes glittered. "Oh yes."

It was a glorious day—summer was coming on, and warm breezes flowed through the louvered windows on the private rooms at Godfrey's, breezes that wafted floral perfume over Gredel's skin. She and Caro started with a steam bath, then a facial, a lotion wrap, a massage that stretched all the way from the scalp to the toes. Afterwards they lay on couches, talking and giggling, caressed by the breezes and drinking fruit juice as smiling young women gave them manicures and pedicures.

Every square inch of Gredel's skin seemed flushed with summer, with life. Back at the Volta, Caro dressed Gredel in one of her own outfits, the expensive fabrics gliding over nerve-tingling, butter-smooth flesh. When Lamey came to pick them up, Caro put Gredel's hand in Lamey's, and guided them both toward the door.

"Have a lovely night," she said.

"Aren't you coming with us?" Lamey asked.

Caro only shook her head and laughed. Her green eyes looked into Gredel's—Gredel saw amusement there, and secrets that Lamey would never share.

Caro steered them into the hall and closed the door behind them. Lamey paused a moment, looking back.

"Is Caro all right?" he asked.

"Oh yes," Gredel said. "Now let's go find a place to dance."

She felt as if she was floating, moving across the floor so lightly that she almost danced on her way to the elevator. It occurred to her that she was happy, that happiness had never been hers before but now she had it.

All it took was getting Antony out of the picture.

The first crack in Gredel's happiness occurred two afternoons later, when Gredel arrived at the Volta late due to a blockage on the train tracks from the Fabs. Gredel let herself in, and found Caro snoring on her bed. Caro was dressed to go out, but she must have got bored waiting for Gredel to turn up, because there was an empty wine bottle on the floor and the med injector near her right hand.

Gredel called Caro, then shook her. There was no response at all. Caro was pale, her flesh cool and faintly bluish.

Another long, grating snore shredded the air. Gredel felt her heart turn over at the pure insistence of the sound. She seized the med injector and checked the contents: endorphin analogue, something called Phenyldorphin-Zed.

Caro began another snore, and then the sound simply rattled to a halt. Her breathing had simply stopped. Terror roared through Gredel's veins.

She had never dealt with an overdose, but there was a certain amount of oral legend on the subject that circulated through the Fabs. One of the fixes involved filling the victim's pants with ice, she remembered. Ice on the genitals was supposed to wake you right up. Or was that just for men?

Gredel straddled Caro and slapped her hard across the face. Her own nerves leaped at the sound, but Caro gave a start, her eyelids coming partway open, and she gasped in air.

Gredel slapped her again. Caro gasped again and coughed, and her lids opened all the way. Her eyes were eerie, blank convexities of green jasper, the pupils so shrunk they could barely be seen.

"What—?" Caro said. "What are you—?"

"You've got to get up." Gredel slid off the bed and pulled Caro by the arm. "You've got to get up and walk around with me, right?"

Caro gave a lazy laugh. "What is—what—?"

"Stand up now!"

Gredel managed to haul Caro upright. Caro found her feet with difficulty, and Gredel got Caro's arm around her shoulders and began to drag Caro over the floor. Caro laughed again. "Music!" she snorted. "We need music if we're going to dance!"

This struck her as so amusing that she almost doubled over with laughter, but Gredel pulled her upright and began moving her again. She got Caro into the front room and began marching in circles around the sofa.

"You're funny, Earthgirl," Caro said. "Funny, funny." Laughter kept bubbling out of her throat. Gredel's shoulders ached with Caro's weight.

"Help me, Caro," she ordered.

"Funny funny. Funny Earthgirl."

When she couldn't hold Caro up any more, Gredel dumped her on the sofa and went to the kitchen to get the coffee maker started. Then she returned to the front room and found Caro asleep again. She slapped Caro twice, and Caro opened her eyes.

"Yes, Sergei," she said. "You do that. You do that all you want."

"You've got to get up, Caro."

"Why wouldn't you talk to me?" Caro asked. There were tears in her eyes. Gredel pulled her to her feet and began walking with her again.

"I called you," Caro said as they walked. "I couldn't stand it anymore and I called you and you wouldn't talk to me. Your secretary said you were out but I knew he was lying from the way he said it."

It was three or four hours before Gredel's fear began to ebb. Caro was able to walk on her own, and her conversation was almost normal, if a little subdued. Gredel left her sitting on the sofa with a cup of coffee and went into the bedroom. She took the med injector, and two others she found in the bedroom and another in the bathroom, plus the cartridges of Phenyldorphin-Zed and every other drug cartridge she could find, and she hid them under some towels in the bathroom so that she could carry them out later, when Caro wasn't looking. She wanted to get rid of the liquor, too, but that would be too obvious. Maybe she could pour most of it down the sink when she had the chance.

"You stopped *breathing*," Gredel told Caro later. "You've got to stop using, Caro."

Caro nodded over her cup of coffee. Her pupils had expanded a bit, and her eyes were almost normal-looking. "I've been letting it get out of hand."

"I was never so frightened in my life. You've just got to stop."

"I'll be good," Caro said.

Gredel was sleeping over three nights later, when Caro produced a med injector before bed and held it to her neck. Gredel reached out in sudden terror and yanked the injector away.

"Caro! You said you'd stop!"

Caro smiled, gave an apologetic laugh. "It's all right," she said. "I was depressed the other day, over something that happened. I let it get out of hand. But I'm not depressed any more." She tugged the injector against Gredel's fingers. "Let go," she said. "I'll be all right."

"Don't," Gredel begged.

Caro laughingly detached Gredel's fingers from the injector, then held it to her neck and pressed the trigger. She laughed while Gredel felt a fist tightening on her insides.

"See?" Caro said. "Nothing wrong here."

Gredel talked to Lamey about it the next day. "Just tell Panda to stop selling to her," she said.

"What good would that do?" Lamey said. "She had sources before she ever met any of us. And if she wanted, she could just go into a pharmacy and pay full price."

Anxiety sang along Gredel's nerves. She would just have to be very careful, and watch Caro to make sure there weren't any more accidents.

❋

Gredel's happiness ended shortly after, on the first hot afternoon of summer. Gredel and Caro returned from the arcades tired and sweating, and Caro flung her purchases down on the sofa and announced she was going to take a long, cool bath. On her way to the bathroom Caro took a bottle of chilled wine from the kitchen, opened it, offered some to Gredel, who declined, then carried the bottle and a glass into the bathroom with her.

The sound of running water came distantly to the front room. Gredel helped herself to a papaya fizz and for lack of anything else to do turned on the video wall.

There was a drama about the Fleet, except that all the actors striving to put down the mutiny were Naxids. All their acting was in the way their beaded scales shifted color, and Gredel didn't understand any of it. The Fleet setting reminded her of Caro's academy appointment, though, and Gredel shifted to the data channel and looked up the requirements for the Cheng Ho academy, which the Sulas traditionally attended.

By the time Caro came padding out in her dressing gown, Gredel was full of information. "You'd better find a tailor, Caro," she said. "Look at the uniforms you've got to get made." The video wall paged through one picture after another. "Dress, undress," Gredel itemized. "Ship coveralls, planetary fatigues, formal dinner dress, parade dress—just look at that hat! And Cheng Ho's in a temperate zone, so you've got greatcoats and jackboots for winter, plus uniforms for any sport you decide to do, and a ton of other gear. Dinner settings!—in case you give a formal dinner, your clan crest optional."

Caro blinked and looked at the screen as if she were having trouble focusing on it all. "What are you talking about?" she said.

"When you go to the Cheng Ho academy. Do you know who Cheng Ho *was*, by the way? I looked it up. He—"

"Stop babbling." Gredel looked at Caro in surprise. Caro's lips were set in a disdainful twist. "I'm not going to any stupid academy," she said. "So just forget about all that, all right?"

Gredel stared at her. "But you have to," she said. "It's your career, the only one you're allowed to have."

Caro gave a little hiss of contempt. "What do I need a career for? I'm doing fine as I am."

It was a hot day and Gredel was tired and had not had a rest or a bath or a drink, and she blundered right through the warnings signals Caro was flying, the signs that she'd not only had her bottle of wine in the bath, but taken something else as well, something that kinked and spiked her nerves and brought her temper sizzling.

"We *planned* it," Gredel insisted. "You're going into the Fleet, and I'll be your orderly. And we can both get off the planet and—"

"*I don't want to hear this useless crap!*" Caro screamed. Her shriek was so loud that it stunned Gredel into silence and set her heart beating louder than Caro's angry words. Caro advanced on Gredel, green fury flashing from her eyes. "You think I'd go into the Fleet? The Fleet, just for *you? Who do you think you are?*"

Caro stood over Gredel. Her arms windmilled as if they were throwing rocks at Gredel's face. "You drag your ass all over this apartment!" she raged. "You—you wear my clothes! You're in my bank accounts all the time—*where's my money, hey! My money!*"

"I never took your money!" Gredel gasped. "Not a cent! I never—"

"*Liar!*" Caro's hand lashed out, and the slap sounded louder than a gunshot. Gredel stared at her, too overwhelmed by surprise to raise a hand to her stinging cheek. Caro screamed on.

"I see you everywhere—everywhere in my life! You tell me what to do, how much to spend—I don't even have any friends anymore! They're all *your* friends!" She reached for the shopping bags that held their purchases and hurled them at Gredel. Gredel warded them off, but when they bounced to the floor Caro just picked them up and threw them again, so finally Gredel just snatched them out of the air and let them pile in her lap, a crumpled heap of expensive tailored fabrics and hand-worked leather.

"Take your crap and get out of here!" Caro cried. She grabbed one of Gredel's arms and hauled her off the sofa. Gredel clutched the packages to her with her other arm, but several spilled as Caro shoved her to the door. "I never want to see you again! Get out! Get out! *Get out!*"

The door slammed behind her. Gredel stood in the corridor with a package clutched to her breast as if it were a child. Inside the apartment she could hear Caro throwing things.

She didn't know what to do. Her impulse was to open the door—she knew the codes—to go into the apartment and try to calm Caro and explain herself.

I didn't take the money, she protested. *I didn't ask for anything.*

Something hit the door hard enough so that it jumped in its frame.

Not the Fleet. The thought seemed to steal the strength from her limbs. Her head spun. *I have to stay here now. On Spannan, in the Fabs. I have to...*

What about tomorrow? a part of her cringed. She and Caro had made plans to go to a new boutique in the morning. Were they going or not?

The absurdity of the question struck home and sudden rage possessed her, rage at her own imbecility. She should have known better than to press Caro on the question, not when she was in this mood.

She went to her mother's apartment and put the packages away. Ava wasn't home. Anger and despair battled in her mind. She called Lamey and let him send someone to pick her up, then let him divert her for the rest of the evening.

In the morning she went to the Volta at the time she had planned with Caro. There was a traffic jam in the lobby—a family was moving into the building, and their belongings were piled onto several motorized carts, each with the Volta's gilt blazon, that jammed the lobby waiting for elevators. Gredel greeted the doorman in her Peer voice, and he called her "Lady Sula" and put her alone into the next elevator.

She hesitated at the door to Caro's apartment. She knew she was groveling, and knew as well that she didn't deserve to grovel.

But this was her only hope. What choice did she have?

She knocked, and when there wasn't an answer she knocked again. She heard a shuffling step inside and then Caro opened the door and blinked at her groggily through disordered strands of hair. She was dressed as Gredel had last seen her, bare feet, naked under her dressing gown.

"Why didn't you just come in?" Caro said. She left the door open and withdrew into the apartment. Gredel followed, her heart pulsing sickly in her chest.

There were several bottles lying on tables, and Gredel recognized the juniper reek that oozed from Caro's pores. "I feel awful," Caro said. "I had too much last night."

Doesn't she remember? Gredel wondered. Or is she just pretending?

Caro reached for the gin bottle and the neck of the bottle clattered against a tumbler as she poured herself two fingers' worth. "Let me get myself together," Caro said, and drank.

A thought struck Gredel with the force of revelation.

She's just a drunk, she thought. *Just another damn drunk.*

Caro put the tumbler down, wiped her mouth, gave a hoarse laugh. "Now we can have some fun," she said.

"Yes," Gredel said. "Let's go."

She had begun to think it might never be fun again.

✸

Perhaps it was then that Gredel began to hate Caro, or perhaps the incident only released hatred and resentment that had lain, denied, for some time. But now Gredel could scarcely spend an hour with Caro without finding new fuel for anger. Caro's carelessness made Gredel clench her teeth, and her laughter grated on Gredel's nerves. The empty days that Caro shared with Gredel, the pointless drifting from boutique to restaurant to club, now made Gredel want to shriek. Gredel deeply resented her tidying up after Caro even as she did it. Caro's surging moods, the sudden shifts from laughter to fury to sullen withdrawal, brought Gredel's own temper near the breaking point. Even Caro's affection and her impulsive generosity began to seem trying. *Why is she making all this fuss over me?* Gredel thought. *What's she after?*

But Gredel managed to keep her thoughts to herself, and at times she caught herself enjoying Caro's company, caught herself in a moment of pure enjoyment or unfeigned laughter. And then she wondered how this could be genuine as well as the other, the delight and the hatred coexisting in her skull.

It was like her so-called beauty, she thought. Her alleged beauty was what most people reacted to; but it wasn't her *self*. She managed to have an inner existence, thoughts and hopes entirely her own, apart from the shell that was her appearance. But it was the shell that people saw, it was the shell that most people spoke to, hated, envied or desired. The Gredel that interacted with Caro was another kind of shell, a kind of machine she'd built for the purpose, built without intending to. It wasn't any less genuine for being a machine, but it wasn't her *self*.

Her *self* hated Caro. She knew that now.

If Caro detected any of Gredel's inner turmoil, she gave no sign. In any case she was rarely in a condition to be very observant. Her alcohol consumption had increased as she shifted from wine to hard liquor. When she wanted to get drunk, she wanted the drunk *instantly,* the way she wanted everything, and hard liquor got her there quicker. The ups and downs increased as well, and the spikes and valleys that were her behavior. She was banned from one of her expensive restaurants for talking loudly, and singing, and hurling a plate at the waiter who asked her to be more quiet. She was thrown out of a club for attacking a woman in the ladies' room. Gredel never found out what the fight was about, but for days afterwards Caro proudly sported the black eye she'd got from the bouncer's fist.

For the most part Gredel managed to avoid Caro's anger. She learned the warning signs, and she'd also learned how to manipulate Caro's moods. She could change Caro's music, or at least shift the focus of Caro's growing anger from herself to someone else.

Despite her feelings she was now in Caro's company more than ever. Lamey was in hiding. She had first found out about it when he sent Panda to pick her up at Caro's apartment instead of coming himself. Panda drove her to the Fabs, but not to a human neighborhood: instead he took her into a building inhabited by Lai-owns. A family of the giant flightless birds stared at her as she waited in the lobby for the elevator. There was an acrid, ammonia smell in the air.

Lamey was in a small apartment on the top floor, with a pair of his guards and a Lai-own. The avian shifted from one foot to the other as Gredel entered. Lamey seemed nervous. He didn't say anything to Gredel, just gave a quick jerk of his chin to indicate that they should go into the back room.

The room was thick with the heat of summer. The ammonia smell was very strong. Lamey steered Gredel to the bed. She sat, but Lamey was unable to be still: he paced back and forth in the narrow range permitted by the small room. His smooth, elegant walk had developed hitches and stutters, uncertainties that marred his normal grace.

"I'm sorry about this," he said. "But something's happened."

"Is the Patrol looking for you?"

"I don't know." His mouth gave a little twitch. "Bourdelle was arrested yesterday. It was the Legion of Diligence who arrested him, not the Patrol, so that means they've got him for something serious, something he could be executed for. We've got word that he's bargaining with the prefect's office." His mouth twitched again. Linkboys did not bargain with the prefect, they were expected to go to their punishment with their mouths shut.

"We don't know what he's going to offer them," Lamey went on. "But he's just a link up from me, and he could be selling me or any of the boys." He paused in his pacing, rubbed his chin. Sweat shone on his forehead. "I'm going to make sure it's not me," he said.

"I understand," Gredel said.

Lamey looked at her. His blue eyes were feverish. "From now on, you can't call me. I can't call you. We can't be seen in public together. If I want you, I'll send someone for you at Caro's."

Gredel looked up at him. "But—" she began, then, "When?"

"*When I want you,*" he said insistently. "I don't know when. You'll just have to be there when I need you."

"Yes," Gredel said. Her mind whirled. "I'll be there."

He sat next to her on the bed and took her by the shoulders. "I missed you, Earthgirl," he said. "I really need you now."

She kissed him. His skin felt feverish. She could taste the fear on him. Lamey's unsteady fingers began to fumble with the buttons of her blouse. *You're going to die soon,* she thought.

Unless of course it was Gredel who paid the penalty instead, the way Ava had paid for the sins of her man.

Gredel had to start looking out for herself, before it was too late.

When Gredel left Lamey, he gave her two hundred zeniths in cash. "I can't buy you things right now, Earthgirl," he explained. "But buy yourself something nice for me, all right?

Gredel remembered Antony's claim that she whored for money. It was no longer an accusation she could deny.

One of Lamey's boys drove Gredel from the rendezvous to her mother's building. Gredel took the stairs instead of the elevator because it gave her time to think. By the time she got to her mother's door, she had the beginnings of an idea.

But first she had to tell her mother about Lamey, and why she had to move in with Caro. "Of course, honey," Ava said. She took Gredel's hands and pressed them. "Of course you've got to go."

Loyalty to her man was what Ava knew, Gredel thought. She had been arrested and sentenced to years in the country for a man she'd hardly ever seen again. She'd spent her life sitting alone amid expensive decor, waiting for one man or another to show up. She was beautiful, but in the bright summer light Gredel could see the first cracks in her mother's façade, the faint lines at the corners of her eyes and mouth that the years would only broaden. When the beauty faded, the men would fade, too.

Ava had cast her lot with beauty and with men, neither of which would last. If Gredel remained with Lamey, or with some other linkboy, she would be following Ava's path.

The next morning Gredel took a pair of bags to Caro's place and let herself in. Caro was asleep, so far gone in torpor that she didn't wake when Gredel padded into the bedroom and took her wallet with its identification. Gredel slipped out again and went to a bank, where she opened an account in the name of Caroline, Lady Sula, and deposited three-quarters of what Lamey had given her.

When asked for a thumbprint, she gave her own.

When Gredel returned from the bank she found Caro grop-ing with a shivering hand for her first cup of coffee. After Caro took the coffee to the bathroom for the long bath that would soak away the stale alcohol from her pores, Gredel replaced Caro's wal-let, then opened the computer link and transferred some of Caro's money, ten zeniths only, to her new account just to make certain that it worked.

It worked fine.

I have just done a criminal act, she thought. *A criminal act that can be traced to me.*

Whatever she may have done before, it hadn't been this.

After Caro's bathe, she and Gredel went to a café for breakfast, and Gredel told her about Lamey being on the run and she asked if she could move in with Caro so that he would be able to send for her. Caro was thrilled. She had never heard of anything so romantic in her life.

Romantic? Gredel thought. It was sordid beyond belief.

But Caro hadn't been in the sultry little room in the Lyone quarter, the smell of ammonia in her nostrils while Lamey's sweat rained down on her. Let her keep her illusions.

"Thank you," she said. But she knew that once she was with Caro, it wouldn't be long before Caro would grow bored with her, or impatient, or angry. Whatever Gredel was going to do, it would have to be soon.

"I don't know how often Lamey's going to send for me," she said. "But I hope it's not on your birthday. I'd like you and I to celebrate that together."

The scowl on Caro's face was immediate, and predictable. "Birthday? My birthday was last winter." The scowl deepened. "That was the last time Sergei and I were together."

"Birthday?" Gredel said, in her Earth accent. "I meant *Earth*day, darling." And when Caro's scowl began to look dangerous, she added quickly, "Your birthday in Earth years. I do the math, see, it's a kind of game. And your Earthday is next week—you'll be fifteen." Gredel smiled. "The same age as me, I turned fifteen Earth years just before I met you."

It wasn't true, not exactly—Caro's Earthday was in three months— but Gredel knew that Caro would never do the math. Might not even know *how* to do it.

There was so much Caro didn't know. The knowledge brought a kind of savage pleasure to Gredel's mind. Caro didn't know *anything*, didn't even know that her best friend hated her. She didn't know that Gredel had stolen her money and her identity only an hour ago, and could do it again whenever she wanted.

The days went by and were even pleasurable in a strange, disconnected way. Gredel thought she finally understood what it was like to be Caro, to have nothing that attached her to anything, to have long hours to fill and nothing to fill them with but whatever impulse drifted into her mind. Gredel felt that way herself—mentally at least she was cutting her own ties free, all of them, floating free of everything she'd known.

To save herself trouble Gredel exerted herself to please Caro, and Caro responded. Caro's mood was sunny, and she laughed and joked and dressed Gredel like a doll, as she always had. Behind her pleasing mask Gredel despised Caro for being so easily manipulated. *You're so stupid,* she thought.

But pleasing Caro brought trouble of its own, because when Lamey's boy called for her Gredel was standing in the rain, in a Torminel neighborhood, trying to buy Caro a cartridge of endorphin analog—with Lamey's businesses in eclipse, she could no longer get the stuff from Panda.

When Gredel finally connected with her ride and got to the place where Lamey was hiding—he was back in the Terran Fabs, at least—he had been waiting for hours, and his patience was gone. He got her alone in the bedroom and slapped her around for a while, telling her it was her fault, that she had to know that she had to be where he could find her when he needed her.

Gredel lay on her back on the bed, letting him do what he wanted, and she thought, *This is going to be my whole life if I don't get out of here.* She looked at the pistol Lamey had waiting on the bedside table for whoever he thought might kick down the door, and she thought about grabbing the pistol and blowing Lamey's brains out. Or her own brains. Or just walking into the street with the pistol and blowing out brains at random.

No, she thought. *Stick to the plan.*

Lamey gave her five hundred zeniths afterwards. Maybe that was an apology.

Sitting in the car later, with her bruised cheek swelling and the money crumpled in her hand and Lamey's slime still drooling down her thigh, she thought about calling the Legion of Diligence and letting them know where Lamey was hiding. But instead she told the boy to take her to a pharmacy near Caro's place.

She walked inside and found a box of plasters that would soak up the bruises, and she took it to the drug counter in the back. The older woman behind the counter looked at her face with knowing sympathy. "Anything else, honey?"

"Yes," Gredel said. "Two vials of Phenyldorphin-Zed."

She was required to sign the Narcotics Book for the endorphin analog, and the name she scrawled was *Sula*.

Caro was outraged by Gredel's bruises. "Lamey comes round here again, I'll kick him in the balls!" she said. "I'll hit him with a chair!"

"Forget about it," Gredel said wearily. She didn't want demonstrations of loyalty from Caro right now. Her feelings were confused enough: she didn't want to start having to like Caro all over again.

Caro pulled Gredel into the bedroom and cleaned her face, and then she cut the plasters to fit Gredel's face and applied them. She did a good enough job at sopping up the bruises and swelling so that the next day, when the plasters were removed, the bruises had mostly disappeared, leaving behind some faint discoloration easily covered with cosmetic. Her whole face hurt, though, and so did her ribs and her solar plexus where Lamey had hit her.

Caro brought Gredel breakfast from the café and hovered around her until Gredel wanted to shriek.

If you want to help, she thought at Caro, *take your appointment to the academy and get us both out of here.*

But Caro didn't answer the mental command. And her solicitude faded by afternoon, when she opened the day's first bottle. It was vodka flavored with bison grass, which explained the strange fusil-oil overtones Gredel had scented on Caro's skin the last few days. By mid-afternoon Caro had consumed most of the bottle and fallen asleep on the couch.

Gredel felt a small, chill triumph at this. It was good to be reminded why she hated her friend.

Next day was Caro's phony Earthday. *Last chance,* Gredel thought at her. *Last chance to mention the academy.* But the word never passed Caro's lips.

"I want to pay you back for everything you've done," Gredel said. "Your Earthday is on me." She put her arm around Caro.

"I've got everything planned," she said.

They started at Godfrey's for the full treatment, massage, facial, hair, the lot. Then lunch at a brass-railed bistro south of the arcades, bubbling grilled cheese on rare vashe roast and crusty bread, with a salad of marinated dedger flowers. To Caro's surprise Gredel called for a bottle of wine, and poured some of it into her own glass.

"You're *drinking,*" Caro said, delighted. "What's got into you?"

"I want to toast your Earthday," Gredel said.

Being drunk might make it easier, she thought.

Gredel kept refilling Caro's glass while sipping at her own, and so the first bottle went. Gredel took Caro to the arcades then, and bought her a summer dress of silk patterned with rhompé birds and jennifer flowers, a jacket shimmering with gold and green sequins, matching Caro's hair and eyes, and two pairs of shoes. She bought outfits for herself as well.

After taking their treasures to Caro's place, where Caro had a few shots of the bison vodka, they went to dinner at one of Caro's exclusive dining clubs. Caro hadn't been thrown out of this club yet, but the maitre d' was on guard enough to sit them well away from everyone else. Caro ordered cocktails and two bottles of wine and after-dinner drinks. Gredel's head spun even after the careful sips she'd been taking; she couldn't imagine what Caro must be feeling. Caro needed a jolt of benzedrine to get to the dance club Gredel had put next on the agenda, though she had no trouble keeping her feet once she got there.

After dancing awhile Gredel said she was tired, and they brushed off the male admirers they'd collected and took a taxi home.

Gredel showered while Caro headed for the bison vodka again. The benzedrine had given her a lot of energy that she put into finishing the bottle. Gredel changed into the silk lounging suit Caro had bought her on their first day together, and she put the two vials of endorphin analog into a pocket.

Caro was on the couch where Gredel had left her. Her eyes were bright, but when she spoke to Gredel her words were slurred.

"I have one more present," Gredel said. She reached into her pocket and held out the two vials. "I think this is a kind you like. I really wasn't sure."

Caro laughed. "You take care of me all day, and now you help me to sleep!" She reached across the couch and put her arms around Gredel. "You're my best sister, Earthgirl." In Caro's embrace Gredel could smell bison grass and sweat and perfume all mingled, and she tried to keep a firm grip on her hatred even as her heart turned over in her chest.

Caro unloaded her med injector and put in one of the vials of Phenyldorphin-Zed and used it right away. Her eyelids fluttered as the endorphin flooded her brain. "Oh nice," she murmured. "Such a good sister." She gave herself another dose a few minutes later. She spoke a few soft words but her voice kept floating away. She gave herself a third dose and fell asleep, her golden hair fallen across her face as she lay on the pillow.

Gredel took the injector from Caro's limp fingers. She reached out and brushed the hair from Caro's face.

"Want some more?" she asked. "Want some more, sister Caro?"

Caro gave a little indistinct murmur. Her lips curled up in a smile. When Gredel fired another dose into her carotid the smile broadened, and she shrugged herself into the sofa pillows like a happy puppy.

Gredel turned from her and reached for Caro's portable computer console. She called up Caro's banking files, and prepared a form closing Caro's bank account and transferring its contents to the account Gredel had set up. Then she prepared another message to Caro's trust account on Spannan's ring, instructing any further payments to be sent to the new account as well.

"Caro," Gredel said. "Caro, I need your thumbprint here, all right?"

She stroked Caro awake, and managed to get her to lean over the console long enough to press her thumb, twice, to the reader. Then Gredel handed the injector to Caro and watched her give herself another dose.

Now I'm really *a criminal,* she thought. She had left a trail of data that pointed straight to herself.

But even so she could not bring herself to completely commit to this course of action. She left herself a way out. *Caro has to want it,* she thought. *I won't give her any more if she says no.*

Caro sighed, settled herself more deeply into the pillows. "Would you like some more?" Gredel asked.

"Mmm," Caro said, and smiled.

Gredel took the injector from her hand and gave her another dose.

After a while she exhausted the first vial and started on the second. Each dose she shook Caro a little and asked if she wanted more. Caro would sigh, or laugh, or murmur, but never said no. Gredel triggered dose after dose.

After the second vial was exhausted the snoring started, Caro's breath heaving itself past the palate, the lungs pumping hard, sometimes with a kind of wrench. Gredel remembered the sound from when Caro had given herself too much endorphin, and the memory caused her to leap from the sofa and walk very fast around the apartment, rubbing her arms to fight her sudden chill.

The snoring went on. Gredel very much needed something to do, so she went into the kitchen and made coffee. And then the snoring stopped.

Ice shuddered along Gredel's nerves She went to the kitchen door and stared out into the front room, at the tumbled golden hair that hung off the end of the couch. *It's over,* she thought.

And then Caro's head rolled, and Gredel's heart froze as she saw Caro's hand come up and comb the hair with her fingers. There was a gurgling snort, and the snoring resumed.

Gredel stood in the door as cold terror pulsed through her veins. But she told herself, *No, it can't be long now.*

And then suddenly she couldn't stand still any longer, and she walked swiftly over the apartment, straightening and tidying. The new clothes went into the closet, the shoes on their racks, the empty bottle in the trash. Wherever she went the snores pursued her. Sometimes they stopped for a few paralyzing seconds, but then resumed.

Abruptly Gredel couldn't bear being in the apartment, and she put on a pair of shoes and went to the freight elevator and took it to the basement, where she went in search of one of the motorized carts they used to move luggage and furniture. There were a great many objects in the basement, things that had been discarded or forgotten about, and Gredel found some strong dedger-fiber rope and an old compressor, a piece of solid bronzework heavy enough to anchor a fair-sized boat.

Gredel put these in the cart and pushed it to the elevator. As she approached Sula's doors she could hear Caro's snores through the enameled steel. Gredel's fingers trembled as she pressed codes into the lock.

Caro was still on the couch, her breath still fighting its way past her throat. Gredel cast an urgent glance at the clock. There weren't many hours of darkness left, and darkness was required for what happened next.

Gredel sat at Caro's feet and hugged a pillow to her chest and watched her breathe. Caro's skin was pale and looked clammy. "Please," Gredel begged under her breath. "Please die now. Please." But Caro wouldn't die. Her breaths grated on and on, until Gredel began to hate them with a bitter resentment. This was so *typical,* she thought. Caro couldn't even *die* without getting it all wrong.

Gredel looked at the wall clock, and it stared back at her like the barrel of a gun. Come dawn, she thought, the gun goes off. Or she could sit in the apartment all day with a corpse, and that was a thought she couldn't face.

Again Caro's breath hung suspended, and Gredel felt her own breath cease for the long moment of suspense. Then Caro dragged in another long rattling gasp, and Gredel felt her heart sink. She knew that her tools had betrayed her. She would have to finish this herself.

All anger was gone by now, all hatred, all emotion except a sick weariness, a desire to get it over. The pillow was already held to her chest, a warm comfort in the room filled only with Caro's racking, tormented snores.

She cast one last look at Caro, thought *Please die* at her one more time, but Caro didn't respond any more than she had ever responded to any of Gredel's other wishes.

Gredel suddenly lunged across the sofa, her body moving without any conscious command, the movement seeming to come from pure instinct. She pressed the pillow over Caro's face and put her weight on it.

Please die, she thought.

Caro hardly fought at all. Her body twisted on the couch, and both her hands came up, but the hands didn't fight, they just fell across Gredel's back as if in a kind of halfhearted embrace.

Gredel would have felt better if Caro had fought. It would have given her hatred something to fasten onto.

Instead she felt, though the closeness of their bodies, the urgent kick-kick-kick of Caro's diaphragm as it tried to draw in air, the kick repeated over and over again. Fast, then slow, then fast. Caro's feet shivered. Gredel could feel Caro's hands trembling as they lay on her back. Tears spilled from Gredel's eyes.

The kicking stopped. The trembling stopped.

Gredel leaned on the pillow a while longer just to make sure. The pillow was wet with tears. When she finally took the pillow away, the pale, cold thing beneath seemed to bear no resemblance to Caro at all.

Caro was weight now, not a person. That made what followed a lot easier.

Handling a limp body was much more difficult than Gredel had ever imagined. By the time she got it onto the cart she was panting for breath and her eyes stung with sweat. She covered Caro with a bed sheet, and she added some empty suitcases to the cart as well. She took the cart to the freight elevator, then left by the loading dock at the back of the building.

"I am Caroline, Lady Sula," she rehearsed her story. "I'm moving to a new place because my lover beat me." She would have the identification to prove her claim, and what remained of the bruises, and the suitcases plain to see alongside the covered objects that weren't so plain.

Gredel didn't need to use her story. The streets were deserted as she walked downslope alongside the humming cart, down to the Iola River.

The roads ran high above the river on either side, with ramps that descended to the darkened riverside quay below. Gredel rode the cart down the ramp to the river's edge. This was the good part of Maranic Town and there were no houseboats here, no beggars, no homeless, and—at this hour—no fishermen. The only encounters Gredel feared were lovers sheltering under the bridges, but by now it was so late that even the lovers had gone to bed.

It was as hard getting Caro off the cart as it had been getting her on it, but once she went into the river, tied to the compressor, the dark waters closed over her with barely a ripple. In a video drama Caro would have floated a while, poignantly, saying goodbye to the world, but there was none of that here, just the silent dark submersion and ripples that died swiftly in the current.

Caro had never been one for protracted goodbyes.

Gredel walked alongside the cart back to the Volta. A few cars slowed to look at her but moved on.

In the apartment she tried to sleep, but Caro's scent filled the bed, and sleep was impossible there. Caro had died on the sofa and Gredel didn't want to go near it. She caught a few hours' fitful rest on a chair, and then the woman called Caroline Sula rose and began her day.

The first thing she did was send in the confirmation of her appointment to the Cheng Ho Academy.

The first day she packed two suitcases and took them to Maranic Port and the ground-effect ferry that took her across the Krassow Sea to Vidalia. From there she took the express train up the Hayakh Escarpment to the Quaylah Plateau, where high altitude moderated the subtropical heat of the Equatorial Continent. The planet's antimatter ring arced almost directly overhead.

Paysec was a winter resort, and the snowfall wouldn't begin here until the monsoon shifted to the northeast, so she found good rates for a small apartment in Lus'trel, and took it for two months. She bought some clothes, not the extravagant garments she would have found in Maranic Town's arcades, but practical country clothes, and boots for walking. She found a tailor and he began to assemble the extensive wardrobe she would need for the academy.

She didn't want Lady Sula's disappearance from Maranic Town to cause any official disturbance, so she sent a message to Caro's official guardian, Jacob Biswas, telling him that she found Maranic too distracting and had come to Lus'trel in order to concentrate on academic preparation for the Academy. She told him she was giving up the Maranic apartment, and that he could collect anything she'd left there.

Because she didn't trust her impersonation of Caro with someone who knew her well, she didn't use video, she typed the message and sent it print only.

Biswas called back almost immediately, but she didn't take his call or any of the other calls that followed. She replied with print messages to the effect that she was sorry she'd been out when he called, but she was spending a lot of time in the library cramming.

That wasn't far from the truth. Requirements for the service academies were posted on the computer net, and most of the courses were available in video files, and she knew she was deeply deficient in almost every subject. She worked hard.

She only answered one call, when she happened to be home, was able to listen to the answerware, and realized the caller was Sergei. She answered and called him every filthy name she could think of, and once her initial anger was a little spent she began to choose words more carefully, flaying him alive with one choice phrase after another. By the end he was weeping, loud gulping honks that grated over the speakers.

Serve him right, she thought.

Lamey had her worried more than Sergei or Jacob Biswas. Every day she half-expected Lamey to burst down the door and demand that she produce Earthgirl. He never turned up.

On her final day on Spannan, Biswas insisted on meeting her, with other members of his family, at the elevator terminal. She cut her hair severely short, wore Cheng Ho undress uniform, and virtually plated her face with cosmetic. If she looked to Biswas like a different girl, no wonder.

He was kind and warm and asked no questions. He told her she looked very grown up, and he was proud of her. She thanked him for his kindness and for looking after her. She hugged him and the daughters he'd brought with him.

His wife, Sergei's sister, had the sense to stay away.

Later, as the elevator carried her to Spannan's ring and its steady acceleration pressed her into her seat, she realized it was Caro's Earthday, the real one.

The anniversary that Caro would never see.

PRAYERS ON THE WIND

Hard is the appearance of a Buddha.
—Dhammapada

Bold color slashed bright slices out of Vajra's violet sky. The stiff spring breeze off the Tingsum Glacier made the yellow prayer flags snap with sounds like gunshots. Sun gleamed from the baroque tracework that adorned silver antennae and receiver dishes. Atop the dark red walls of the Diamond Library Palace, saffron-robed monks stood like sentries, some of them grouped in threes around ragdongs, trumpets so huge they required two men to hold them aloft while a third blew puff-cheeked into the mouthpiece. Over the deep, grating moan of the trumpets, other monks chanted their litany.

Salutation to the Buddha.

In the language of the gods and in that of the Lus,

In the language of the demons and in that of the men,

In all the languages which exist,

I proclaim the Doctrine.

Jigme Dzasa stood at the foot of the long granite stair leading to the great library, the spectacle filling his senses, the litany dancing in his soul. He turned to his guest. "Are you ready, Ambassador?"

The face of !urq was placid. "Lus?" she asked.

"Mythical beings," said Jigme. "Serpentine divinities who live in bodies of water."

"Ah," !urq said. "I'm glad we got that cleared up." Jigme looked at the alien, decided to say nothing.

"Let us begin," said the Ambassador. Jigme hitched up his zen and began the long climb to the Palace, his bare feet slapping at the stones. A line of Gelugspa monks followed in respectful silence. Ambassador Colonel !urq climbed beside Jigme at a slow trot, her four boot heels rapping. Behind her was a line of Sangs, their centauroid bodies cased neatly in blue-and-gray uniforms, decorations flashing in the bright sun. Next to each was a feathery Masker servant carrying a ceremonial parasol.

Jigme was out of breath by the time he mounted the long stairway, and his head whirled as he entered the tsokhang, the giant assembly hall. Several thousand members of religious orders sat rigid at their stations, long lines of men and women: Dominicans and Sufis in white, Red Hats and Yellow Hats in their saffron zens, Jesuits in black, Gyudpas in complicated aprons made of carved, interwoven human bones… Each sat in the lotus posture in front of a solid gold data terminal decorated with religious symbols, some meditating, some chanting sutras, others accessing the Library.

Jigme, !urq, and their parties passed through the vast hall that hummed with the distant, echoing sutras of those trying to achieve unity with the Diamond Mountain. At the far side of the room were huge double doors of solid jade, carved with figures illustrating the life of the first twelve incarnations of the Gyalpo Rinpoche, the Treasured King. The doors opened on silent hinges at the touch of equerries' fingertips. Jigme looked at the equerries as he passed— lovely young novices, he thought, beautiful boys really. The shaven nape of that dark one showed an extraordinary curve.

Beyond was the audience chamber. The Masker servants remained outside, holding their parasols at rigid attention, while their masters trotted into the audience chamber alongside the line of monks.

Holographic murals filled the walls, illustrating the life of the Compassionate One. The ceiling was of transparent polymer, the floor of clear crystal that went down to the solid core of the planet. The crystal refracted sunlight in interesting ways, and as he walked across the room Jigme seemed to walk on rainbows.

At the far end of the room, flanked by officials, was the platform that served as a throne. Overhead stretched an arching canopy of massive gold, the words AUM MANI PADME HUM worked into the design in turquoise. The platform was covered in a large carpet decorated with figures of the lotus, the Wheel, the swastika, the two fish, the eternal knot, and other holy symbols. Upon the carpet sat the Gyalpo Rinpoche himself, a small man with a sunken chest and bony shoulders, the Forty-First Incarnation of the Bodhisattva Bob Miller, the Great Librarian, himself an emanation of Avalokitesvara.

The Incarnation was dressed simply in a yellow zen, being the only person in the holy precincts permitted to wear the color. Around his waist was a rosary composed of 108 strung bone disks cut from the forty skulls of his previous incarnations. His body was motionless but his arms rose and fell as the fingers moved in a series of symbolic hand gestures, one mudra after another, their pattern set by the flow of data through the Diamond Mountain.

Jigme approached and dropped to his knees before the platform. He pressed the palms of his hands together, brought the hands to his forehead, mouth, and heart, then touched his forehead to the floor. Behind him he heard thuds as some of his delegation slammed their heads against the crystal surface in display of piety—indeed, there were depressions in the floor worn by the countless pilgrims who had done this—but Jigme, knowing he would need his wits, only touched his forehead lightly and held the posture until he heard the Incarnation speak.

"Jigme Dzasa. I am pleased to see you again. Please get to your feet and introduce me to your friends."

The old man's voice was light and dry, full of good humor. In the seventy-third year of his incarnation, the Treasured King enjoyed good health.

Jigme straightened. Rainbows rose from the floor and danced before his eyes. He climbed slowly to his feet as his knees made popping sounds—twenty years younger than the Incarnation, he was a good deal stiffer of limb—and moved toward the platform in an attitude of reverence. He reached to the rosary at his waist and took from it a white silk scarf embroidered with a religious text. He unfolded it and, sticking out his tongue in respect, handed it to the Incarnation with a bow.

The Gyalpo Rinpoche took the khata and draped it around his own neck with a smile. He reached out a hand, and Jigme dropped his head for the blessing. He felt dry fingertips touch his shaven scalp, and then a sense of harmony seemed to hum through his being. Everything, he knew, was correct. The interview would go well.

Jigme straightened and the Incarnation handed him a khata in exchange, one with the mystic three knots tied by the Incarnation himself. Jigme bowed again, stuck out his tongue, and moved to the side of the platform with the other officials. Beside him was Dr. Kay O'Neill, the Minister of Science. Jigme could feel O'Neill's body vibrating like a taut cord, but the minister's overwrought state could not dispel Jigme's feeling of bliss.

"Omniscient," Jigme said, "I would like to present Colonel !urq, Ambassador of the Sang."

!urq was holding her upper arms in a Sang attitude of respect. Neither she nor her followers had prostrated themselves, but had stood politely by while their human escort had done so. !urq's boots rang against the floor as she trotted to the dais, her lower arms offering a khata. She had no tongue to stick out—her upper and lower palates were flexible, permitting a wide variety of sounds, but they weren't as flexible as all that. Still she thrust out her lower lip in a polite approximation.

"I am honored to be presented at last, Omniscient," !urq said. Dr. O'Neill gave a snort of anger.

The Treasured King draped a knotted khata around the Ambassador's neck. "We of the Diamond Mountain are pleased to welcome you. I hope you will find our hospitality to your liking."

The old man reached forward for the blessing. !urq's instructions did not permit her to bow her head before an alien presence, so the Incarnation simply reached forward and placed his hand over her face for a moment. They remained frozen in that attitude, and then !urq backed carefully to one side of the platform, standing near Jigme. She and Jigme then presented their respective parties to the Incarnation. By the end of the audience the head of the Gyalpo Rinpoche looked like a tiny red jewel in a flowery lotus of white silk khatas.

"I thank you all for coming all these light-years to see me," said the Incarnation, and Jigme led the visitors from the audience chamber, chanting the sutra *Aum vajra guru Padma siddhi hum,* Aura the diamond powerful guru Padma, as he walked.

!urq came to a halt as soon as her party had filed from the room. Her lower arms formed an expression of bewilderment. "Is that all?"

Jigme looked at the alien. "That is the conclusion of the audience, yes. We may tour the holy places in the Library, if you wish."

"We had no opportunity to discuss the matter of Gyangtse."

"You may apply to the Ministry for another interview."

"It took me twelve years to obtain this one." Her upper arms took a stance that Jigme recognized as martial. "The patience of my government is not unlimited," she said.

Jigme bowed. "I shall communicate this to the Ministry, Ambassador."

"Delay in the Gyangtse matter will only result in more hardship for the inhabitants when they are removed."

"It is out of my hands, Ambassador."

!urq held her stance for a long moment in order to emphasize her protest, then relaxed her arms. Her upper set of hands caressed the white silk khata. "Odd to think," she said, amused, "that I journeyed twelve years just to stick out my lip at a human and have him touch my face in return."

"Many humans would give their lives for such a blessing," said Jigme.

"Sticking out the lip is quite rude where I come from, you know."

"I believe you have told me this."

"The Omniscient's hands were very warm." !urq raised fingers to her forehead, touched the ebon flesh. "I believe I can still feel the heat on my skin."

Jigme was impressed. "The Treasured King has given you a special blessing. He can channel the energies of the Diamond Mountain through his body. That was the heat you felt."

!urq's antennae rose skeptically, but she refrained from comment. "Would you like to see the holy places?" Jigme said. "This, for instance, is a room devoted to Maitreya, the Buddha That Will Come. Before you is his statue. Data can be accessed by manipulation of the images on his headdress..." Jigme's speech was interrupted by the entrance of a Masker servant from the audience room. A white khata was draped about the avian's neck. !urq's trunk swiveled atop her centaur body; her arms assumed a commanding stance. The clicks and pops of her own language rattled from her mouth like falling stones.

"Did I send for you, creature?"

The Masker performed an obsequious gesture with its parasol. "I beg the Colonel's pardon. The old human sent for us. He is touching us and giving us scarves." The Masker fluttered helplessly. "We did not wish to offend our hosts, and there were no Sang to query for instruction."

"How odd," said !urq. "Why should the old human want to bless our slaves?" She eyed the Masker and thought for a moment. "I will not kill you today," she decided. She turned to Jigme and switched to Tibetan. "Please continue, Rinpoche."

"As you wish, Colonel." He returned to his speech. "The Library Palace is the site of no less than twenty-one tombs of various bodhisattvas, including many incarnations of the Gyalpo Rinpoche. The Palace also contains over eight thousand data terminals and sixty shrines."

As he rattled through the prepared speech, Jigme wondered about the scene he had just witnessed. He suspected that "I will not kill you today" was less alarming than it sounded, was instead an idiomatic way of saying "Go about your business."

Then again, knowing the Sang, maybe not.

The Cabinet had gathered in one of the many other reception rooms of the Library Palace. This one was small, the walls and ceiling hidden behind tapestry covered with appliqué, the room's sole ornament a black stone statue of a dancing demon that served tea on command.

The Gyalpo Rinpoche, to emphasize his once-humble origins, was seated on the floor. White stubble prickled from his scalp.

Jigme sat cross-legged on a pillow. Across from him was Dr. O'Neill. A lay official, her status was marked by the long turquoise earring that hung from her left ear to her collarbone, that and the long hair piled high on her head. The rosary she held was made of 108 antique microprocessors pierced and strung on a length of fiberoptic cable. Beside her sat the cheerful Miss Taisuke, the Minister of State. Although only fifteen years old, she was Jigme's immediate superior. Her authority derived from being the certified reincarnation of a famous hermit nun of the Yellow Hat Gelugspa order. Beside her, the Minister of Magic, a tantric sorcerer of the Gyud School named Daddy Carbajal, toyed with a trumpet made from human thighbone. Behind him in a semireclined position was the elderly, frail, toothless State Oracle—his was a high-ranking position, but it was a largely symbolic one as long as the Treasured King was in his majority. Other ministers, lay or clerical, sipped tea or gossiped as they waited for the Incarnation to begin the meeting.

The Treasured King scratched one bony shoulder, grinned, then assumed in an eyeblink a posture of deep meditation, placing hands in his lap with his skull-rosary wrapped around them. "Aum," he intoned. The others straightened and joined in the holy syllable, the Pranava, the creative sound whose vibrations built the universe. Then the Horse of the Air rose from the throat of the Gyalpo Rinpoche, the syllables *Aum mane padme hum,* and the others reached for their rosaries.

As he recited the rosary, Jigme tried to meditate on each syllable as it went by, comprehend the full meaning of each, the color, the importance, the significance. *Aum,* which was white and connected with the gods. *Ma,* which was blue and connected with the titans. *Ne,* which was yellow and connected with men. *Pad,* which was green and connected with animals. *Me,* which was red and connected with giant sand demigods. *Hum,* which was black and connected with dwellers in purgatory. Each syllable a separate realm, each belonging to a separate species, together forming the visible and invisible universe.

"Hri!" called everyone in unison, signifying the end of the 108th repetition. The Incarnation smiled and asked the black statue for some tea. The stone demon scuttled across the thick carpet and poured tea into his golden bowl. The demon looked up into the Incarnation's face. "Free me!" said the statue.

The Gyalpo Rinpoche looked at the statue. "Tell me truthfully. Have you achieved Enlightenment?"

The demon said nothing.

The Treasured King smiled again. "Then you had better give Dr. O'Neill some tea."

O'Neill accepted her tea, sipped, and dismissed the demon. It scuttled back to its pedestal.

"We should consider the matter of Ambassador !urq," said the Incarnation.

O'Neill put down her teacup. "I am opposed to her presence here. The Sang are an unenlightened and violent race. They conceive of life as a struggle against nature rather than search for Enlightenment.

They have already conquered an entire species, and would subdue us if they could."

"That is why I have consented to the building of warships," said the Incarnation.

"From their apartments in the Nyingmapa monastery, the Sang now have access to the Library," said O'Neill. "All our strategic information is present there. They will use the knowledge against us."

"Truth can do no harm," said Miss Taisuke.

"All truth is not vouchsafed to the unenlightened," said O'Neill. "To those unprepared by correct study and thought, truth can be a danger." She gestured with an arm, encompassing the world outside the Palace. "Who should know better than we, who live on Vajra? Haven't half the charlatans in all existence set up outside our walls to preach half-truth to the credulous, endangering their own Enlightenment and that of everyone who hears them?"

Jigme listened to O'Neill in silence. O'Neill and Daddy Carbajal were the leaders of the reactionary party, defenders of orthodoxy and the security of the realm. They had argued this point before.

"Knowledge will make the Sang cautious," said Jigme. "They will now know of our armament. They will now understand the scope of the human expansion, far greater than their own. We may hope this will deter them from attack."

"The Sang may be encouraged to build more weapons of their own," said Daddy Carbajal. "They are already highly militarized, as a way of keeping down their subject species. They may militarize further."

"Be assured they are doing so," said O'Neill. "Our own embassy is kept in close confinement on a small planetoid. They have no way of learning the scope of the Sang threat or sending this information to the Library. We, on the other hand, have escorted the Sang ambassador throughout human space and have shown her anything in which she expressed an interest."

"Deterrence," said Jigme. "We wished them to know how extensive our sphere is, that the conquest would be costly and call for more resources than they possess."

"We must do more than deter. The Sang threat should be eliminated, as were the threats of heterodox humanity during the Third and Fifth Incarnations."

"You speak jihad," said Miss Taisuke.

There was brief silence. No one, not even O'Neill, was comfortable with Taisuke's plainness.

"All human worlds are under the peace of the Library," said O'Neill. "This was accomplished partly by force, partly by conversion. The Sang will not convert."

The Gyalpo Rinpoche cleared his throat. The others fell silent at once. The Incarnation had been listening in silence, his face showing concentration but no emotion. He always preferred to hear the opinions of others before expressing his own. "The Third and Fifth Incarnations," he said, "did nothing to encourage the jihads proclaimed in their name. The Incarnations did not wish to accept temporal power."

"They did not speak against the holy warriors," said Daddy Carbajal.

The Incarnation's elderly face was uncommonly stern. His hands formed the teaching mudra. "Does not Shakyamuni speak in the *Anguttara Nikaya* of the three ways of keeping the body pure?" he asked. "One must not commit adultery, one must not steal, one must not kill any living creature. How could warriors kill for orthodoxy and yet remain orthodox?"

There was a long moment of uncomfortable silence. Only Daddy Carbajal, whose tantric Short Path teaching included numerous ways of dispatching his enemies, did not seem nonplussed.

"The Sang are here to study us," said the Gyalpo Rinpoche. "We also study them."

"I view their pollution as a danger." Dr. O'Neill's face was stubborn.

Miss Taisuke gave a brilliant smile. "Does not the *Mahaparinirvana-sutra* tell us that if we are forced to live in a difficult situation and among people of impure minds, if we cherish faith in Buddha we can ever lead them toward better actions?" Relief fluttered through Jigme. Taisuke's apt quote, atop the Incarnation's sternness, had routed the war party.

"The Embassy will remain," said the Treasured King. "They will be given the freedom of Vajra, saving only the Holy Precincts. We must remember the oath of the Amida Buddha: 'Though I attain Buddhahood, I shall never be complete until people everywhere, hearing my name, learn right ideas about life and death, and gain that perfect wisdom that will keep their minds pure and tranquil in the midst of the world's greed and suffering.'"

"What of Gyangtse, Rinpoche?" O'Neill's voice seemed harsh after the graceful words of Scripture.

The Gyalpo Rinpoche cocked his head and thought for a moment. Suddenly the Incarnation seemed very human and very frail, and Jigme's heart surged with love for the old man.

"We will deal with that at the Picnic Festival," said the Incarnation.

From his position by the lake, Jigme could see tents and banners dotting the lower slopes of Tingsum like bright spring flowers. The Picnic Festival lasted a week, and unlike most of the other holidays had no real religious connection. It was a week-long campout during which almost the entire population of the Diamond City and the surrounding monasteries moved into the open and spent their time making merry. Jigme could see the giant yellow hovertent of the Gyalpo Rinpoche surrounded by saffron-robed guards, the guards present not to protect the Treasured King from attackers, but rather to preserve his tranquillity against invasions by devout pilgrims in search of a blessing. The guards—monks armed with staves, their shoulders padded hugely to make them look more formidable—served the additional purpose of keeping the Sang away from the Treasured King until the conclusion of the festival, something for which Jigme was devoutly grateful. He didn't want any political confrontations disturbing the joy of the holiday. Fortunately Ambassador !urq seemed content to wait until her scheduled appearance at a party given by the Incarnation on the final afternoon.

Children splashed barefoot in the shallows of the lake, and others played chibi on the sward beside, trying to keep a shuttlecock aloft using the feet alone. Jigme found himself watching a redheaded boy on the verge of adolescence, admiring the boy's grace, the way the knobbed spine and sharp shoulders moved under his pale skin. His bony ankles hadn't missed the shuttlecock yet. Jigme was sufficiently lost in his reverie that he did not hear the sound of boots on the grass beside him. "Jigme Dzasa?"

Jigme looked up with a guilty start. !urq stood beside him, wearing hardy outdoor clothing. Her legs were wrapped up to the shoulder. Jigme stood hastily and bowed.

"Your pardon, Ambassador. I didn't hear you."

The Sang's feathery antennae waved cheerfully in the breeze. "I thought I would lead a party. Would you care to join us?"

What Jigme wanted to do was continue watching the ball game, but he assented with a smile. Climbing mountains: that was the sort of thing the Sang were always up to. They wanted to demonstrate they could conquer anything.

"Perhaps you should find a pony," !urq said. "Then you could keep up with us."

Jigme took a pony from the Library's corral and followed the waffle patterns of !urq's boots into the trees on the lower slopes. Three other Sang were along on the expedition; they clicked and gobbled to one another as they trotted cheerfully along. Behind toiled three Maskers-of-burden carrying food and climbing equipment. If the Sang noticed the incongruity demonstrated by the human's using a quadruped as a beast of burden while they, centauroids, used a bipedal race as servants, they politely refrained from mentioning it. The pony's genetically altered cloven forefeet took the mountain trail easily, nimbler than the Sang in their heavy boots. Jigme noticed that this made the Sang work harder, trying to outdo the dumb beast.

They came to a high mountain meadow and paused, looking down at the huge field of tents that ringed the smooth violet lake. In the middle of the meadow was a three-meter tower of crystal, weathered and yellow, ringed by rubble flaked off during the hard winters. One of the Sang trotted over to examine it.

"I thought the crystal was instructed to stay well below the surface," he said.

"There must have been a house here once," Jigme said. "The crystal would have been instructed to grow up through the surface to provide Library access."

!urq trotted across a stretch of grass, her head down. "Here's the beginning of the foundation," she said. She gestured with an arm. "It runs from here to over there."

The Sang cantered over the ground, frisky as children, to discover the remnants of the foundation. The Sang were always keen, Jigme found, on discovering things. They had not yet learned that there was only one thing worth discovering, and it had nothing to do with old ruins.

!urq examined the pillar of crystal, touched its crumbling surface. "And over eighty percent of the planet is composed of this?" she said.

"All except the crust," Jigme said. "The crystal was instructed to convert most of the planet's material. That is why our heavy metals have to come from mined asteroids, and why we build mostly in natural materials. This house was probably of wood and laminated cloth, and it most likely burned in an accident."

!urq picked up a bit of crystal from the ring of rubble that surrounded the pillar. "And you can store information in this."

"All the information we have," Jigme said reverently. "All the information in the universe, eventually." Involuntarily, his hands formed the teaching mudra. "The Library is a hologram of the universe. The Blessed Bodhisattva Bob Miller was a reflection of the Library, its first Incarnation. The current Incarnation is the forty-first."

!urq's antennae flickered in the wind. She tossed the piece of crystal from hand to hand. "All the information you possess," she said. "That is a powerful tool. Or weapon."

"A tool, yes. The original builders of the Library considered it only a tool. Only something to help them order things, to assist them in governing. They did not comprehend that once the Diamond Mountain contained enough information, once it gathered enough energy, it would become more than the sum of its parts. That it would become the Mind of Buddha, the universe in small, and that the Mind, out of its compassion, would seek to incarnate itself as a human."

"The Library is self-aware?" !urq asked. She seemed to find the notion startling.

Jigme could only shrug. "Is the universe self-aware?" !urq made a series of meditative clicking noises.

"Inside the Diamond Mountain," Jigme said, "there are processes going on that we cannot comprehend. The Library was designed to be nearly autonomous; it is now so large we cannot keep track of everything, because we would need a mind as large as the Library to process the information. Many of the energy and data transfers that we can track are very subtle, involving energies that are not fully understood. Yet we can track some of them. When an Incarnation dies, we can see the trace his spirit makes through the Library—like an atomic particle that comes apart in a shower of short-lived particles, we see it principally through its effects on other energies—and we can see part of those energies move from one place to another, from one body to another, becoming another Incarnation."

!urq's antennae moved skeptically. "You can document this?"

"We can produce spectra showing the tracks of energy through matter. Is that documentation?"

"I would say, with all respect, your case remains unproven."

"I do not seek to prove anything." Jigme smiled. "The Gyalpo Rinpoche is his own proof, his own truth. Buddha is truth. All else is illusion."

!urq put the piece of crystal in her pocket. "If this was our Library," she said, "we would prove things one way or another."

"You would see only your own reflection. Existence on the quantum level is largely a matter of belief. On that level, mind is as powerful as matter. We believe that the Gyalpo Rinpoche is an Incarnation of the Library; does that belief help make it so?"

"You ask me questions based on a system of belief that I do not share. How can you expect me to answer?"

"Belief is powerful. Belief can incarnate itself."

"Belief can incarnate itself as delusion."

"Delusion can incarnate itself as reality." Jigme stood in his stirrups, stretching his legs, and then settled back into his saddle. "Let me tell you a story," he said. "It's quite true. There was a man who went for a drive, over the pass yonder." He pointed across the valley at the low blue pass, the Kampa La between the mountains Tampa and Tsang. "It was a pleasant day, and he put the car's top down. A windstorm came up as he was riding near a crossroads, and his fur hat blew off his head into a thorn bush, where he couldn't reach it. He simply drove on his way.

"Other people walked past the bush, and they saw something inside. They told each other they'd seen something odd there. The hat got weathered and less easy to recognize. Soon the locals were telling travelers to beware the thing near the crossroads, and someone else suggested the thing might be a demon, and soon people were warning others about the demon in the bush."

"Delusion," said !urq.

"It *was* delusion," Jigme agreed. "But it was not delusion when the hat grew arms, legs, and teeth, and when it began chasing people up and down the Kampa La. The Ministry of Magic had to send a naljorpa to perform a rite of chöd and banish the thing."

!urq's antennae gave a meditative quiver. "People see what they want to see," she said.

"The delusion had incarnated itself. The case is classic: the Ministries of Science and Magic performed an inquiry. They could trace the patterns of energy through the crystal structure of the Library: the power of the growing belief, the reaction when the

465

belief was fulfilled, the dispersing of the energy when chöd was performed." Jigme gave a laugh. "In the end, the naljorpa brought back an old, weathered hat. Just bits of fur and leather."

"The naljorpa got a good reward, no doubt," said !urq, "for bringing back this moldy bit of fur."

"Probably. Not my department, actually."

"It seems possible, here on Vajra, to make a good living out of others' delusions. My government would not permit such things."

"What do the people lose by being credulous?" Jigme asked. "Only money, which is earthly, and that's a pitiful thing to worry about. It matters only that the act of giving is sincere."

!urq gave a toss of her head. "We should continue up the mountain, Rinpoche."

"Certainly." Jigme kicked his pony into a trot. He wondered if he had just convinced !urq that his government was corrupt in allowing fakirs to gull the population. Jigme knew there were many ways to Enlightenment and that the soul must try them all. Just because the preacher was corrupt did not mean his message was untrue. How to convince !urq of that? he wondered.

"We believe it is good to test oneself against things," !urq said. "Life is struggle, and one must remain sharp. Ready for whatever happens."

"In the *Parinibbana-sutra,* the Blessed One says that the point of his teaching is to control our own minds. Then one can be ready."

"Of course we control our minds, Rinpoche. If we could not control our minds, we would not achieve mastery. If we do not achieve mastery, then we are nothing."

"I am pleased, then," Jigme smiled, "that you and the Buddha are in agreement."

To which !urq had no reply, save only to launch herself savagely at the next climb, while Jigme followed easily on his cloven-hoofed pony.

The scent of incense and flowers filled the Gyalpo Rinpoche's giant yellow tent. The Treasured King, a silk khata around his neck, sat in the lotus posture on soft grass. The bottoms of his feet were stained green. Ambassador !urq stood ponderously before him, lower lip thrust forward, her four arms in formal stance, the Incarnation's knotted scarf draped over her shoulders.

Jigme watched as he stood next to the erect, angry figure of Dr. O'Neill. He took comfort from the ever-serene smile of Miss Taisuke, who sat on the grass across the tent.

"Ambassador Colonel, I am happy you have joined us on holiday."

"We are pleased to participate in your festivals, Omniscient," said !urq.

"The spring flowers are lovely, are they not? It's worthwhile to take a whole week to enjoy them. In so doing, we remember the words of Shakyamuni, who tells us to enjoy the blossoms of Enlightenment in their season and harvest the fruit of the right path."

"Is there a season, Omniscient, for discussing the matter of Gyangtse?"

Right to the point, Jigme thought. !urq might never learn the oblique manner of speech that predominated at the high ministerial levels.

The Incarnation was not disturbed, "Surely matters may be discussed in any season," he said.

"The planet is desirable, Omniscient. Your settlement violates our border. My government demands your immediate evacuation."

Dr. O'Neill's breath hissed out at the word "demand." Jigme could see her ears redden with fury.

"The first humans reached the planet before the border negotiations were completed," the Incarnation said equably. "They did not realize they were settling in violation of the agreement."

"That does not invalidate the agreement."

"Conceded, Ambassador. Still, would it not be unjust, after all their hard labor, to ask them to move?"

!urq's antennae bobbed politely. "Does not your Blessed One admit that life is composed of suffering? Does the Buddha not condemn the demon of worldly desires? What desire could be more worldly than a desire to possess a world?"

Jigme was impressed. Definitely, he thought, she was getting better at this sort of thing.

"In the same text," said the Incarnation, "Shakyamuni tells us to refrain from disputes, and not repel one another like water and oil, but like milk and water mingle together." He opened his hands in an offering gesture. Will your government not accept a new planet in exchange? Or better yet, will they not dispose of this border altogether, and allow a free commerce between our races?"

"What new planet?" !urq's arms formed a querying posture.

"We explore constantly in order to fulfill the mandate of the Library and provide it with more data. Our survey records are available through your Library access. Choose any planet that has not yet been inhabited by humans."

"Any planet chosen will be outside of our zone of influence, far from our own frontiers and easily cut off from our home sphere."

"Why would we cut you off, Ambassador?"

"Gyangtse is of strategic significance. It is a penetration of our border."

"Let us then dispose of the border entirely."

!urq's antennae stood erect. Her arms took a martial position. "You humans are larger, more populous. You would overwhelm us by sheer numbers. The border must remain inviolate."

"Then allow us greater commerce across the border than before. With increased knowledge, distrust will diminish."

"You would send missionaries. I know there are Jesuits and Gelugspa who have been training for years in hopes of obtaining converts or martyrdom in the Sang dominions."

"It would be a shame to disappoint them." There was a slight smile on the Incarnation's face.

!urq's arms formed an obstinate pattern. "They would stir up trouble among the Maskers. They would preach to the credulous among my own race. My government must protect its own people."

"The message of Shakyamuni is not a political message, Ambassador."

"That is a matter of interpretation, Omniscient."

"Will you transmit my offer to your government?"

!urq held her stance for a long moment. Jigme could sense Dr. O'Neill's fury in the alien's obstinacy. "I will do so, Omniscient," said the Ambassador. "Though I have no confidence that it will be accepted."

"I think the offer will be accepted," said Miss Taisuke. She sat on the grass in Jigme's tent. She was in the butterfly position, the soles of her feet pressed together and her knees on the ground. Jigme sat beside her. One of Jigme's students, a clean-limbed lad named Rabjoms, gracefully served them tea and cakes, then withdrew.

"The Sang are obdurate," said Jigme. "Why do you think there is hope?"

"Sooner or later the Sang will realize they may choose any one of hundreds of unoccupied planets. 'Twill dawn on them that they can pick one on the far side of our sphere, and their spy ships can travel the length of human occupied space on quite legitimate missions, and gather whatever information they desire."

"Ah."

"All this in exchange for one minor border penetration."

Jigme thought about this for a moment. "We've held onto Gyangtse in order to test the Sang's rationality and their willingness to fight. There has been no war in twelve years. This shows that the Sang are susceptible to reason. Where there is reason, there is capability for Enlightenment."

"Amen," said Miss Taisuke. She finished her tea and put down the glass.

"Would you like more? Shall I summon Rabjoms?"

"Thank you, no." She cast a glance back to the door of the tent. "He has lovely brown eyes, your Rabjoms."

"Yes."

Miss Taisuke looked at him. "Is he your consort?"

Jigme put down his glass. "No. I try to forsake worldly passions."

"You are of the Red Hat order. You have taken no vow of celibacy."

Agitation fluttered in Jigme's belly. "The *Mahaparinirvana-sutra* says that lust is the soil in which other passions flourish. I avoid it."

"I wondered. It has been remarked that all your pages are such pretty boys."

Jigme tried to calm himself. "I choose them for other qualities, Miss Taisuke. I assure you."

She laughed merrily. "Of course. I merely wondered." She leaned forward from out of her butterfly position, reached out, and touched his cheek. "I have a sense this may be a randy incarnation for me. You have no desire for young girls?"

Jigme did not move. "I cannot help you, Minister."

"Poor Jigme." She drew her hand back. "I will offer prayers for you."

"Prayers are always accepted, Miss Taisuke."

"But not passes. Very well." She rose to her feet, and Jigme rose with her. "I must be off to the Kagyupas' party. Will you be there?"

"I have scheduled this hour for meditation. Perhaps later."

"Later, then." She kissed his cheek and squeezed his hand, then slipped out of the tent. Jigme sat in the lotus posture and called for Rabjoms to take away the tea things. As he watched the boy's graceful movements, he gave an inward sigh. His weakness had been noticed, and, even worse, remarked on. His next student would have to be ugly. The ugliest one he could find. He sighed again.

A shriek rang out. Jigme looked up, heart hammering, and saw a demon at the back of the tent. Its flesh was bright red, and its eyes seemed to bulge out of its head. Rabjoms yelled and flung the tea service at it; a glass bounced off its head and shattered.

The demon charged forward, Rabjoms falling under its clawed feet. The overwhelming smell of decay filled the tent. The demon burst through the tent flap into the outdoors. Jigme heard more shrieks and cries of alarm from outside. The demon roared like a bull, then laughed like a madman. Jigme crawled forward to gather up Rabjoms, holding the terrified boy in his arms, chanting the Horse of the Air to calm himself until he heard the teakettle hiss of a thousand snakes followed by a rush of wind, the sign that the entity had dispersed. Jigme soothed his page and tried to think what the meaning of this sudden burst of psychic energy might be.

A few moments later, Jigme received a call on his radiophone. The Gyalpo Rinpoche, a few moments after returning to the Library Palace in his hovertent, had fallen stone dead.

"Cerebral hemorrhage," said Dr. O'Neill. The Minister of Science had performed the autopsy herself—her long hair was undone and tied behind, to fit under a surgical cap, and she still wore her scrubs. She was without the long turquoise earring that marked her rank, and she kept waving a hand near her ear, as though she somehow missed it. "The Incarnation was an old man," she said. "A slight erosion in an artery, and he was gone. It took only seconds."

The cabinet accepted the news in stunned silence. For all their lives, there had been only the one Treasured King. Now the anchor of all their lives had been removed.

"The reincarnation was remarkably swift," Dr. O'Neill said. "I was able to watch most of it on the monitors in real time—the energies remained remarkably focused, not dissipated in a shower of sparks as with most individuals. I must admit I was impressed. The demon that appeared at the Picnic Festival was only one of the many side effects caused by such a massive turbulence within the crystal architecture of the Diamond Mountain."

Miss Taisuke looked up. "Have you identified the child?"

"Of course." Dr. O'Neill allowed herself a thin-lipped smile. "A second-trimester baby, to be born to a family of tax collectors in Dulan Province, near the White Ocean. The fetus is not developed to the point where a full incarnation is possible, and the energies remain clinging to the mother until they can move to the child. She must be feeling…elevated. I would like to interview her about her sensations before she is informed that she is carrying the new Bodhisattva." Dr. O'Neill waved a hand in the vicinity of her ear again.

"We must appoint a regent," said Daddy Carbajal.

"Yes," said Dr. O'Neill. "The more so now, with the human sphere being threatened by the Unenlightened."

Jigme looked from one to the other. The shock of the Gyalpo Rinpoche's death had unnerved him to the point of forgetting political matters. Clearly this had not been the case with O'Neill and the Minister of Magic. He could not let the reactionary party dominate this meeting.

"I believe," he said, "we should appoint Miss Taisuke as Regent." His words surprised even himself.

The struggle was prolonged. Dr. O'Neill and Daddy Carbajal fought an obstinate rearguard action, but finally Miss Taisuke was confirmed. Jigme had a feeling that several of the ministers only consented to Miss Taisuke because they thought she was young enough that they might manipulate her. They did not know her well, Jigme thought, and that was fortunate.

"We must formulate a policy concerning Gyangtse and the Sang," Dr. O'Neill said. Her face assumed its usual thin-lipped stubbornness.

"The Omniscient's policy was always to delay," Miss Taisuke said. "This sad matter will furnish further excuse for postponing any final decision."

"We must put the armed forces on alert. The Sang may consider this a moment in which to strike."

The Regent nodded. "Let this be done."

"There is the matter of the new Incarnation," Dr. O'Neill said. "Should the delivery be advanced? How should the parents be informed?"

"We shall consult the State Oracle," said Miss Taisuke.

The Oracle, his toothless mouth gaping, was a picture of terror. No one had asked him anything in years.

✺

Eerie music echoed through the Oracular Hall of the Library, off the walls and ceiling covered with grotesque carvings—gods, demons, and skulls that grinned at the intent humans below. Chanting monks sat in rows, accompanied by magicians playing drums and trumpets all made from human bone. Jigme's stinging eyes watered from the gusts of strong sandalwood incense.

In the middle of it all sat the State Oracle, his wrinkled face expressionless. Before him, sitting on a platform, was Miss Taisuke, dressed in the formal clothing of the Regency.

"In old Tibetan times, the Oracle used to be consulted frequently," Jigme told Ambassador !urq. "But since the Gyalpo Rinpoche has been incarnated on Vajra, the Omniscient's close association with the universe analogue of the Library has made most divination unnecessary. The State Oracle is usually called upon only during periods between Incarnations."

"I am having trouble phrasing my reports to my superiors, Rinpoche," said !urq. "Your government is at present run by a fifteen-year-old girl with the advice of an elderly fortune-teller. I expect to have a certain amount of difficulty getting my superiors to take this seriously."

"The Oracle is a serious diviner," Jigme said. "There are a series of competitive exams to discover his degree of empathy with the Library. Our Oracle was right at the top of his class."

"My government will be relieved to know it."

The singing and chanting had been going on for hours. !urq had long been showing signs of impatience. Suddenly the Oracle gave a start. His eyes and mouth dropped open. His face had lost all character.

Then something else was there, an alien presence. The Oracle jumped up from his seated position, began to whirl wildly with his arms outstretched. Several of his assistants ran forward carrying his headdress while others seized him, holding his rigid body steady.

The headdress was enormous, all hand-wrought gold featuring skulls and gods and topped with a vast array of plumes. It weighed over ninety pounds.

"The Oracle, by use of intent meditation, has driven the spirit from his own body," Jigme reported. "He is now possessed by the Library, which assumes the form of the god Yamantaka, the Conqueror of Death."

"Interesting," !urq said noncommittally.

"An old man could not support that headdress without some form of psychic help," Jigme said. "Surely you must agree?" He was beginning to be annoyed by the Ambassador's perpetual skepticism.

The Oracle's assistants had managed to strap the headdress on the Oracle's bald head. They stepped back, and the Oracle continued his dance, the weighty headdress supported by his rigid neck. The Oracle dashed from one end of the room to the other, still whirling, sweat spraying off his brow, then ran to the feet of Miss Taisuke and fell to his knees.

When he spoke it was in a metallic, unnatural voice. "The Incarnation should be installed by New Year!" he shouted, and then toppled. When the assistant monks had unstrapped the heavy headdress and the old man rose, back in his body once more and rubbing his neck, the Oracle looked at Miss Taisuke and blinked painfully. "I resign," he said.

"Accepted," said the Regent. "With great regret."

"This is a young man's job. I could have broken my damn neck."

Ambassador !urq's antennae pricked forward. "This," she said, "is an unusually truthful oracle."

"Top of his class," said Jigme. "What did I tell you?"

* * *

The new Oracle was a young man, a strict orthodox Yellow Hat whose predictive abilities had been proved outstanding by every objective test. The calendar of festivals rolled by: the time of pilgrimage, the week of operas and plays, the kite-flying festival, the end of Ramadan, Buddha's descent from Tishita Heaven, Christmas, the celebration of Kali the Benevolent, the anniversary of the death of Tsongkhapa... The New Year was calculated to fall sixty days after Christmas, and for weeks beforehand the artisans of Vajra worked on their floats. The floats—huge sculptures of fabulous buildings, religious icons, famous scenes from the opera featuring giant animated figures, in all tens of thousands of man-hours of work—would be taken through the streets of the Diamond City during the New Year's procession, then up onto Burning Hill in plain sight of the Library Palace where the new Incarnation could view them from the balcony.

And as the sculptures grew the new Incarnation grew as well, as fast as the technology safely permitted. Carefully removed from his mother's womb by Dr. O'Neill, the Incarnation was placed in a giant autowomb and fed a diet of nutrients and hormones calculated to bring him to adulthood. Microscopic wires were reinserted carefully into his developing brain to feed the memory centers with scripture, philosophy, science, art, and the art of governing. As the new Gyalpo Rinpoche grew the body was exercised by electrode so that he would emerge with physical maturity.

The new Incarnation had early on assumed the lotus position during his rest periods, and Jigme often came to the Science Ministry to watch, through the womb's transparent cover, the eerie figure meditating in the bubbling nutrient solution. All growth of hair had been suppressed by Dr. O'Neill and the figure seemed smooth perfection. The Omniscient-to-be was leaving early adolescence behind, growing slim and cat-muscled.

The new Incarnation would need whatever strength it possessed. The political situation was worsening. The border remained unresolved—the Sang wanted not simply a new planet in exchange for Gyangtse, but also room to expand into a new militarized sphere on the other side of human space. Sang military movements, detected from the human side of the border, seemed to be rehearsals for an invasion, and were countered by increased human defense allotments. As a deterrent, the human response was made obvious to the Sang: Ambassador !urq complained continually about human aggression. Dr. O'Neill and Daddy Carbajal grew combative in Cabinet meetings, opposition to them was scattered and unfocused. If the reactionary party wanted war, the Sang were doing little but playing into their hands.

Fortunately the Incarnation would be decanted within a week, to take possession of the rambling, embittered councils and give them political direction. Jigme closed his eyes and offered a long prayer that the Incarnation might soon make his presence felt among his ministers.

He opened his eyes. The smooth, adolescent Incarnation hovered before him, suspended in golden nutrient. Fine bubbles rose in the liquid, stroking the Incarnation's skin, The figure had a fascinating, eerie beauty, and Jigme felt he could stare at it forever.

Jigme saw, to his surprise, that the floating Incarnation had an erection. And then the Incarnation opened his eyes. The eyes were green. Jigme felt coldness flood his spine—the look was knowing, a look of recognition. A slight smile curled the Incarnation's lips. Jigme stared. The smile seemed cruel.

Dry-mouthed, Jigme bent forward, slammed his forehead to the floor in obeisance. Pain crackled through his head. He stayed that way for a long time, offering prayer after frantic prayer.

When he finally rose, the Incarnation's eyes were closed, and the body sat calmly amid golden, rising bubbles.

The late Incarnation's rosary seemed warm as it lay against Jigme's neck. Perhaps it was anticipating being reunited with its former owner.

"The Incarnation is being dressed," Dr. O'Neill said. She stepped through the doors into the vast cabinet room. Two novice monks, doorkeepers, bowed as she swept past, their tongues stuck out in respect, then swung the doors shut behind her. O'Neill was garbed formally in a dress so heavy with brocade that it crackled as she moved. Yellow lamplight flickered from the braid as she moved through the darkened counsel chamber. Her piled hair was hidden under an embroidered cap; silver gleamed from the elaborate settings of her long turquoise earring. "He will meet with the Cabinet in a few moments and perform the recognition ceremony."

The Incarnation had been decanted that afternoon. He had walked as soon as he was permitted. The advanced growth techniques used by Dr. O'Neill appeared to have met with total success. Her eyes glowed with triumph; her cheeks were flushed.

She took her seat among the Cabinet, moving stiffly in the heavy brocade. The Cabinet sat surrounding a small table on which some of the late Incarnation's possessions were surrounded by a number of similar objects or imitations. His rosary was around Jigme's neck. During the recognition ceremony, the new Incarnation was supposed to single out his possessions in order to display the continuance from his former personality. The ceremony was largely a formality, a holdover from the earlier, Tibetan tradition—it was already perfectly clear, from Library data, just who the Incarnation was.

There was a shout from the corridor outside, then a loud voice raised in song. The members of the Cabinet stiffened in annoyance. Someone was creating a disturbance. The Regent beckoned to a communications device hidden in an image of Kali, intending to summon guards and have the disorderly one ejected.

The doors swung open, each held by a bowing novice with outthrust tongues. The Incarnation appeared between them. He was young, just entering late adolescence. He was dressed in the tall crested formal hat and yellow robes stiff with brocade. Green eyes gleamed in the dim light as he looked at the assembled officials.

The Cabinet moved as one, offering obeisance first with praying hands lifted to the forehead, mouth, and heart, then prostrated themselves with their heads to the ground. As he fell forward, Jigme heard a voice singing.

Let us drink and sport today,
Ours is not tomorrow.
Love with Youth flies swift away,
Age is naught but Sorrow.
Dance and sing, Time's on the wing,
Life never knows the return of Spring.

In slow astonishment, Jigme realized that it was the Incarnation who sang. Gradually Jigme rose from his bow.

Jigme saw that the Incarnation had a bottle in his hand. Was he drunk? he wondered. And where in the Library had he gotten the beer, or whatever it was? Had he materialized it?

"This way, boy," said the Incarnation. He had a hand on the shoulder of one of the doorkeepers. He drew the boy into the room, then took a long drink from his bottle. He eyed the Cabinet slowly, turning his head from one to the next.

"Omniscient—" said Miss Taisuke.

"Not yet," said the Incarnation. "I've been in a glass sphere for almost ten months. It's time I had some fun." He pushed the doorkeeper onto hands and knees, then knelt behind the boy. He pushed up the boy's zen, clutched at his buttocks. The page cast little frantic glances around the room. The new State Oracle seemed apoplectic.

"I see you've got some of my things," said the Incarnation.

Jigme felt something twitch around his neck. The former Incarnation's skull-rosary was beginning to move. Jigme's heart crashed in his chest.

The Cabinet watched in stunned silence as the Incarnation began to sodomize the doorkeeper. The boy's face showed nothing but panic and terror.

This is a lesson, Jigme thought insistently. This is a living Bodhisattva doing this, and somehow this is one of his sermons. We will learn from this.

The rosary twitched, rose slowly from around Jigme's neck, and flew through the air to drop around the Incarnation's head.

A plain ivory walking stick rose from the table and spun through the air. The Incarnation materialized a third arm to catch the cane in midair. A decorated porcelain bowl followed, a drum, and a small golden figurine of a laughing Buddha that ripped itself free from the pocket of the new State Oracle. Each was caught by a new arm. Each item had belonged to the former Incarnation; each was the correct choice.

The Incarnation howled like a beast at the moment of climax. Then he stood, adjusting his garments. He bent to pick up the ivory cane. He smashed the porcelain bowl with it, then broke the cane over the head of the Buddha. He rammed the Buddha through the drum, then threw both against the wall. All six hands rose to the rosary around his neck; he ripped at it and the cord broke, white bone disks flying through the room. His extra arms vanished.

"Short Path," he said, turned and stalked out.

Across the room, in the long silence that followed, Jigme could see Dr. O'Neill. Her pale face seemed to float in the darkness, distinct amid the confusion and madness, her expression frozen in a racking, electric moment of private agony. The minister's moment of triumph had turned to ashes.

Perhaps everything had.

Jigme rose to comfort the doorkeeper.

"There has never been an Incarnation who followed the Short Path," said Miss Taisuke.

"Daddy Carbajal should be delighted," Jigme said. "He's a doub-tob himself."

"I don't think he's happy," said the Regent. "I watched him. He is a tantric sorcerer, yes, one of the best. But the Incarnation's perform-ance frightened him."

They spoke alone in Miss Taisuke's townhouse—in the lha khang, a room devoted to religious images. Incense floated gently in the air. Outside, Jigme could hear the sounds of celebration as the word reached the population that the Incarnation was among them once again.

A statue of the Thunderbolt Sow came to life, looked at the Regent. "A message from the Library Palace, Regent," it said. "The Incarnation has spent the evening in his quarters, in the company of an apprentice monk. He has now passed out from drunkenness."

"Thank you, Rinpoche," Taisuke said. The Thunderbolt Sow froze in place. Taisuke turned back to Jigme.

"His Omniscience is possibly the most powerful doubtob in history," she said. "Dr. O'Neill showed me the spectra—the display of psychic energy, as recorded by the Library, was truly awesome. And it was perfectly controlled."

"Could something have gone wrong with the process of bringing the Incarnation to adulthood?"

"The process has been used for centuries. It has been used on Incarnations before—it was a fad for a while, and the Eighteenth through Twenty-Third were all raised that way." She frowned, leaning forward. "In any case, it's all over. The Librarian Bob Miller—and the divine Avalokitesvara, if you go for that sort of thing—has now been reincarnated as the Forty-Second Gyalpo Rinpoche. There's nothing that can be done."

"Nothing," Jigme said. The Short Path, he thought, the path to Enlightenment taken by magicians and madmen, a direct route that had no reference to morality or convention... The Short Path was dangerous, often heterodox, and colossally difficult. Most doubtobs ended up destroying themselves and everyone around them.

"We have had carnal Incarnations before," Taisuke said. "The Eighth left some wonderful love poetry behind, and quite a few have been sodomites. No harm was done."

"I will pray, Regent," said Jigme, "that no harm may be done *now*."

It seemed to him that there was a shadow on Taisuke's usual blazing smile. "That is doubtless the best solution. I will pray also."

Jigme returned to the Nyingmapa monastery, where he had an apartment near the Sang embassy. He knew he was too agitated to sit quietly and meditate, and so called for some novices to bring him a meditation box. He needed to discipline both body and mind before he could find peace.

He sat in the narrow box in a cross-legged position and drew the lid over his head. Cut off from the world, he would not allow himself to relax, to lean against the walls of the box for support. He took his rosary in his hands. "Aum vajra satira," he began, Aum the Diamond Being, one of the names of Buddha.

But the picture that floated before his mind was not that of Shakyamuni, but the naked, beautiful form of the Incarnation, staring at him from out of the autowomb with green, soul-chilling eyes.

<hr />

"We should have killed the Jesuit as well. We refrained only as a courtesy to your government, Rinpoche."

Perhaps, Jigme thought, the dead Maskers' souls were even now in the Library, whirling in the patterns of energy that would result in reincarnation, whirling like the snow that fell gently as he and !urq walked down the street.

To be reincarnated as humans, with the possibility of Enlightenment. "We will dispose of the bodies, if you prefer," Jigme said.

"They dishonored their masters," said !urq. "You may do what you like with them."

As Jigme and the Ambassador walked through the snowy streets toward the Punishment Grounds, they were met with grins and waves from the population, who were getting ready for the New Year celebration. !urq acknowledged the greetings with graceful nods of her antennae. Once the population heard what had just happened, Jigme thought, the reception might well be different.

"I will send monks to collect the bodies. We will cut them up and expose them on hillsides for the vultures. Afterward their bones will be collected and perhaps turned into useful implements."

"In my nation," !urq said, "that would be considered an insult."

"The bodies will nourish the air and the earth," said Jigme. "What finer kind of death could there be?"

"Elementary. A glorious death in service to the state."

Two Masker servants, having met several times with a Jesuit acting apparently without orders from his superiors, had announced their conversion to Buddhism. !urq had promptly denounced the two as spies and had them shot out of hand. The missionary had been ordered whipped by the superiors of his Order, and !urq wanted to be on hand for it.

Jigme could anticipate the public reaction. Shakyamuni had strictly forbidden the taking of life. The people would be enraged. It might be unwise for the Sang to be seen in public for the next few days, particularly during the New Year Festival, when a large percentage of the population would be drunk.

Jigme and the Ambassador passed by a row of criminals in the stocks. Offerings of flowers, food, and money were piled up below them, given by the compassionate population. Another criminal—murderer, probably—shackled in leg irons for life, approached with his begging bowl. Jigme gave money and passed on.

"Your notions of punishment would be considered far from enlightened in my nation," !urq said. "Flogging, branding, putting people in chains! We would consider that savage."

"We punish only the body," Jigme said. "We always allow an opportunity for the spirit to reform. Death without Enlightenment can only result in a return to endless cycles of reincarnation."

"A clean death is always preferable to bodily insult. And many of your flogging victims die afterward."

"But they do not die during the flogging."

"Yet they die in agony, because your whips tear their backs apart."

"Pain," said Jigme, "can be transcended."

"Sometimes," !urq said, antennae twitching, "you humans are terrifying. I say this in absolute and admiring sincerity."

There were an unusual number of felons today, since the authorities wanted to empty the holding cells before the New Year. The Jesuit was among them—a calm, bearded, black-skinned man stripped to the waist, waiting to be lashed to the triangle. Jigme could see that he was deep in a meditative trance. Suddenly the gray sky darkened. People looked up and pointed. Some fell down in obeisance, others bowed and thrust out their tongues.

The Incarnation was overhead, sitting on a wide hovercraft, covered with red paint and hammered gold, that held a small platform and throne. He sat in a full lotus, his elfin form dressed only in a light yellow robe. Snow melted on his shoulders and cheeks.

The proceedings halted for a moment while everyone waited for the Incarnation to say something, but at an impatient gesture from the floating throne things got under way. The floggings went efficiently, sometimes more than one going on at once. The crowd succored many of the victims with money and offers of food or medicine. There was another slight hesitation as the Jesuit was brought forward—perhaps the Incarnation would comment on, or stay, the punishment of someone who had been trying to spread his faith—but from the Incarnation came only silence. The Jesuit absorbed his twenty lashes without comment, was taken away by his cohorts. To be praised and promoted, if Jigme knew the Jesuits.

The whipping went on. Blood spattered the platform. Finally there was only one convict remaining, a young monk of perhaps seventeen in a dirty, torn zen. He was a big lad, broad-shouldered and heavily-muscled, with a malformed head and a peculiar brutal expression—at once intent and unfocused, as if he knew he hated something but couldn't be bothered to decide exactly what it was. His body was possessed by constant, uncontrollable tics and twitches. Police armed with staves surrounded him. Obviously they considered him dangerous.

An official read off the charges. Kyetsang Kunlegs had killed his guru, then set fire to the dead man's home in hopes of covering his crime. He was sentenced to six hundred lashes and to be shackled for life. Jigme suspected he would not get much aid from the crowd afterward; most of them reacted with disgust.

"Stop," said the Incarnation. Jigme gaped. The floating throne was moving forward. It halted just before Kunlegs. The murderer's guards stuck out their tongues but kept their eyes on the killer.

"Why did you kill your guru?" the Incarnation asked.

Kunlegs stared at him and twitched, displaying nothing but fierce hatred. He gave no answer.

The Incarnation laughed. "That's what I thought," he said. "Will you be my disciple if I remit your punishment?"

Kunlegs seemed to have difficulty comprehending this. His belligerent expression remained unaltered. Finally he just shrugged. A violent twitch made the movement grotesque.

The Incarnation lowered his throne. "Get on board," he said. Kunlegs stepped onto the platform. The Incarnation rose from his lotus, adjusted the man's garments, and kissed him on the lips. They sat down together.

"Short Path," said the Incarnation. The throne sped at once for the Library Palace.

Jigme turned to the Ambassador. !urq had watched without visible expression.

"Terrifying," she said. "Absolutely terrifying."

●

Jigme sat with the other Cabinet members in a crowded courtyard of the Palace. The Incarnation was about to go through the last of the rituals required before his investiture as the Gyalpo Rinpoche. Six learned elders of six different religious orders would engage the Incarnation in prolonged debate. If he did well against them, he would be formally enthroned and take the reins of government.

The Incarnation sat on a platform-throne opposite the six. Behind him, gazing steadily with his expression of misshapen, twitching brutality, was the murderer Kyetsang Kunlegs.

The first elder rose. He was a Sufi, representing a three-thousand-year-old intellectual tradition. He stuck out his tongue and took a formal stance. "What is the meaning of Dharma?" he began.

"I'll show you," said the Incarnation, although the question had obviously been rhetorical. The Incarnation opened his mouth, and a demon the size of a bull leapt out. Its flesh was pale as dough and covered with running sores. The demon seized the Sufi and flung him to the ground, then sat on his chest. The sound of breaking bones was audible.

Kyetsang Kunlegs opened his mouth and laughed, revealing huge yellow teeth.

The demon rose and advanced toward the five remaining elders, who fled in disorder.

"I win," said the Incarnation.

Kunlegs' laughter broke like obscene bubbles over the stunned audience. "Short Path," said the Incarnation.

"Such a shame," said the Ambassador. Firelight flickered off her ebon features. "How many man-years of work has gone into it all? And by morning it'll be ashes."

"Everything comes to an end," said Jigme. "If the floats are not destroyed tonight, they would be gone in a year. If not a year, ten years. If not ten years, a century. If not a century..."

"I quite take your point, Rinpoche," said !urq. "Only the Buddha is eternal."

"Indeed."

The crowd assembled on the roof of the Library Palace gasped as another of the floats on Burning Hill went up in flames. This one was made of figures from the opera, who danced and sang and did combat with one another until, burning, they came apart on the wind.

Jigme gratefully took a glass of hot tea from a servant and warmed his hands. The night was clear but bitterly cold. The floating throne moved silently overhead, and Jigme stuck out his tongue in salute. The Gyalpo Rinpoche, in accordance with the old Oracle's instructions, had assumed his title that afternoon.

"Jigme Dzasa, may I speak with you?" A soft voice at his elbow, that of the former Regent.

"Of course, Miss Taisuke. You will excuse me, Ambassador?"

Jigme and Taisuke moved apart. "The Incarnation has indicated that he wishes me to continue as head of the government," Taisuke said.

"I congratulate you, Prime Minister," said Jigme, surprised. He had assumed the Gyalpo Rinpoche would wish to run the state himself.

"I haven't accepted yet," she said. "It isn't a job I desire." She sighed. "I was hoping to have a randy incarnation, Jigme. Instead I'm being worked to death."

"You have my support, Prime Minister."

She gave a rueful smile and patted his arm. "Thank you. I fear I'll have to accept, if only to keep certain other people from positions where they might do harm." She leaned close, her whisper carrying over the sound of distant fireworks. "Dr. O'Neill approached me. She wished to know my views concerning whether we can declare the Incarnation insane and reinstitute the Regency."

Jigme gazed at Taisuke in shock. "Who supports this?"

"Not I. I made that clear enough."

"Daddy Carbajal?"

"I think he's too cautious. The new State Oracle might be in favor of the idea—he's such a strict young man, and, of course, his own status would rise if he became the Library's interpreter instead of subordinate to the Gyalpo Rinpoche. O'Neill herself made the proposal in a veiled manner—if such-and-such a thing proved true, how would I react? She never made a specific proposal."

Anger burned in Jigme's belly. "The Incarnation cannot be insane!" he said. "That would mean the Library itself is insane. That the Buddha is insane."

"People are uncomfortable with the notion of a doubtob Incarnation."

"What people? What are their names? They should be corrected!" Jigme realized that his fists were clenched, that he was trembling with anger.

"Hush. O'Neill can do nothing."

"She speaks treason! Heresy!"

"Jigme…"

"Ah. The Prime Minister." Jigme gave a start at the sound of the Incarnation's voice. The floating throne, its gold ornaments gleaming in the light of the burning floats, descended noiselessly from the bright sky. The Incarnation was covered only by a reskyang, the simple white cloth worn even in the bitterest weather by adepts of tumo, the discipline of controlling one's own internal heat.

"You will be my Prime Minister, yes?" the Incarnation said. His green eyes seemed to glow in the darkness. Kyetsang Kunlegs loomed over his shoulder like a demon shadow.

Taisuke bowed, sticking out her tongue. "Of course, Omniscient."

"When I witnessed the floggings the other day," the Incarnation said, "I was shocked by the lack of consistency. Some of the criminals seemed to have the sympathy of the officials, and the floggers did not use their full strength. Some of the floggers were larger and stronger than others. Toward the end they all got tired, and did not lay on with proper force." He frowned. "This does not seem to me to be adequate justice. I would like to propose a reform." He handed Taisuke a paper. "Here I have described a flogging machine. Each strike will be equal to the one before. And as the machine is built on a rotary principle, the machine can be inscribed with religious texts, like a prayer wheel. We can therefore grant prayers and punish the wicked simultaneously."

Taisuke seemed overcome. She looked down at the paper as if afraid to open it. "Very...elegant, Omniscient."

"I thought so. See that the machine is instituted throughout humanity, Prime Minister."

"Very well, Omniscient."

The floating throne rose into the sky to the accompaniment of the murderer Kunlegs' gross bubbling laughter. Taisuke looked at Jigme with desperation in her eyes.

"We must protect him, Jigme," she said.

"Of course."

"We must be very, very careful."

She loves him, too, he thought. A river of sorrow poured through his heart. Jigme looked up, seeing Ambassador !urq standing with her head lifted to watch the burning spectacle on the hill opposite. "Very careful indeed," he said.

The cycle of festivals continued. Buddha's birthday, the Picnic Festival, the time of pilgrimage...

In the Prime Minister's lha khang, the Thunderbolt Sow gestured toward Taisuke. "After watching the floggings," it said, "the Gyalpo Rinpoche and Kyetsang Kunlegs went to Diamond City spaceport, where they participated in a night-long orgy with ship personnel. Both have now passed out from indulgence in drink and drugs, and the party has come to an end."

The Prime Minister knit her brows as she listened to the tale.

"The stories will get offworld now," Jigme told her.

"They're already offworld."

Jigme looked at her helplessly. "How much damage is being done?"

"Flogging parties? Carousing with strangers? Careening from one monastery to another in search of pretty boys? Gracious heaven—the abbots are pimping their novices to him in hopes of receiving favor." Taisuke gave a lengthy shudder. There was growing seriousness in her eyes. "I'll let you in on a state secret. We've been reading the Sang's despatches."

"How?" Jigme asked. "They don't use our communications net, and the texts are coded."

"But they compose their messages using electric media," Taisuke said. "We can use the Library crystal as a sensing device, detect each character as it's entered into their coding machines. We can also read incoming despatches in the same fashion."

"I'm impressed, Prime Minister."

"Through this process, we were kept informed of the progress of the Sang's military buildup. We were terrified to discover that it was scheduled to reach its full offensive strength within a few years."

"Ah. That was why you consented to the increase in military allotments."

"Ambassador !urq was instructed not to resolve the Gyangtse matter, in order that it be used as a casus belli when the Sang program reached its conclusion. !urq's despatches to her superiors urged them to attack as soon as their fleet was ready. But now, with the increased military allotments and the political situation, !urq is urging delay. The current Incarnation, she suspects, may so discredit the institution of the Gyalpo Rinpoche that our society may disintegrate without the need for a Sang attack."

"Impossible!" A storm of anger filled Jigme. His hands formed the mudra of astonishment.

"I suspect you're right, Jigme." Solemnly. "They base their models of our society on the despots in their own past—they don't realize that the Treasured King is not a tyrant or an absolute ruler, but rather someone of great wisdom whom others follow through their own free will. But we should encourage !urq in this estimation, yes? Anything to give impetus to the Sang's more rational impulses."

"But it's based on a slander! And a slander concerning the Incarnation can never be countenanced!"

Taisuke raised an admonishing finger. "The Sang draw their own conclusions. And should we protest this one, we might give away our knowledge of their communications."

Anger and frustration bubbled in Jigme's mind. "What barbarians!" he said. "I have tried to show them truth, but..."

Taisuke's voice was calm. "You have shown them the path of truth. Their choosing not to follow it is their own karma."

Jigme promised himself he would do better. He would compel !urq to recognize the Incarnation's teaching mission.

Teaching, he thought. He remembered the stunned look on the doorkeeper's face that first Cabinet meeting, the Incarnation's cry at the moment of climax, his own desperate attempt to see the thing as a lesson. And then he thought about what !urq would have said, had she been there.

He went to the meditation box that night, determined to exorcize the demon that gnawed at his vitals. Lust, he recited, provides the soil in which other passions flourish. Lust is like a demon that eats up all the good deeds of the world. Lust is a viper hiding in a flower garden; it poisons those who come in search of beauty.

It was all futile. Because all he could think of was the Gyalpo Rinpoche, the lovely body moving rhythmically in the darkness of the Cabinet room.

The moan of ragdongs echoed over the gardens and was followed by drunken applause and shouts. It was the beginning of the festival of plays and operas. The Cabinet and other high officials celebrated the festival at the Jewel Pavilion, the Incarnation's summer palace, where there was an outdoor theater specially built among the sweet-smelling meditative gardens. The palace, a lacy white fantasy ornamented with statues of gods and tall masts that carried prayer flags, sat bathed in spotlights atop its hill.

In addition to the members of the court were the personal followers of the Incarnation, people he had been gathering during the seven months of his reign. Novice monks and nuns, doubtobs and naljorpas, crazed hermits, loony charlatans and mediums, runaways, workers from the spaceport…all drunk, all pledged to follow the Short Path wherever it led.

"Disgusting," said Dr. O'Neill. "Loathsome." Furiously she brushed at a spot on her brocaded robe where someone had spilled beer.

Jigme said nothing. Cymbals clashed from the stage, where the orchestra was practicing. Three novice monks went by, staggering under the weight of a flogging machine. The festival was going to begin with the punishment of a number of criminals, and any of the culprits who could walk afterward would be encouraged to join the revelers. The first opera would be sung on a stage spattered with blood.

Dr. O'Neill stepped closer to Jigme. "The Incarnation has asked me to furnish him a report on nerve induction. He wishes to devise a machine to induce pain without damage to the body."

Heavy sorrow filled Jigme at the fact he could no longer be surprised by such news. "For what purpose?" he asked.

"To punish criminals, of course. Without crippling them. Then his Omniscience will be able to order up as savage punishments as he likes without being embarrassed by hordes of cripples shuffling around the Capital."

Jigme tried to summon indignation. "You should not impart unworthy motives to the Gyalpo Rinpoche."

Dr. O'Neill only gave him a cynical look. Behind her, trampling through a hedge, came a young monk, laughing, being pursued by a pair of women with whips. O'Neill looked at them as they dashed off into the darkness. "At least it will give them less of an excuse to indulge in such behavior. It won't be as much fun to watch if there isn't any blood."

"That would be a blessing."

"The Forty-Second Incarnation is potentially the finest in history," O'Neill said. Her eyes narrowed in fury. She raised a clenched fist, the knuckles white in the darkness. "He is the most intelligent Incarnation, the most able, the finest rapport with the Library in centuries…and look at what he is doing with his gifts!"

"I thank you for the compliments, Doctor," said the Incarnation. O'Neill and Jigme jumped. The Incarnation, treading lightly on the summer grass, had walked up behind them. He was dressed only in his white reskyang and the garlands of flowers given him by his followers. Kunlegs, as always, loomed behind him, twitching furiously.

Jigme bowed profoundly, sticking out his tongue.

"The punishment machine," said the Incarnation. "Do the plans move forward?"

Dr. O'Neill's dismay was audible in her reply. "Yes, Omniscient."

"I wish the work to be completed for the New Year. I want particular care paid to the monitors that will alert the operators if the felon's life is in danger. We should not want to violate Shakyamuni's commandment against slaughter."

"The work shall be done, Omniscient."

"Thank you, Dr. O'Neill." He reached out a hand to give her a blessing, his hand tenderly touching her face. "I think of you as my mother, Dr. O'Neill. The lady who tenderly watched over me in the womb. I hope this thought pleases you."

"If it pleases your Omniscience."

"It does." The Incarnation withdrew his hand. In the darkness his smile was difficult to read. "You will be honored for your care for many generations, Doctor. I make you that promise."

"Thank you, Omniscient."

"Omniscient!" A new voice called out over the sound of revelry. The new State Oracle, dressed in the saffron zen of a simple monk, strode toward them over the grass. His thin, ascetic face was bursting with anger. "Who are these people, Omniscient?" he demanded.

"My friends, minister."

"They are destroying the gardens!"

"They are *my* gardens, minister."

"Vanity!" The Oracle waved a finger under the Incarnation's nose. Kunlegs grunted and started forward, but the Incarnation stopped him with a gesture.

"I am pleased to accept the correction of my ministers," he said.

"Vanity and indulgence!" the Oracle said. "Has the Buddha not told us to forsake worldly desires? Instead of doing as Shakyamuni instructed, you have surrounded yourself with followers who indulge their own sensual pleasures and your vanity!"

"Vanity?" The Incarnation glanced at the Jewel Pavilion. "Look at my summer palace, minister. It is a vanity, a lovely vanity. But it does no harm."

"It is nothing! All the palaces of the world are as nothing beside the word of the Buddha!"

The Incarnation's face showed supernal calm. "Should I rid myself of these vanities, minister?"

"Yes!" The State Oracle stamped a bare foot. "Let them be swept away!"

"Very well. I accept my minister's correction." He raised his voice, calling for the attention of his followers. A collection of drunken rioters gathered around him. "Let the word be spread to all here," he cried. "The Jewel Pavilion is to be destroyed by fire. The gardens shall be uprooted. All statues shall be smashed." He looked at the State Oracle and smiled his cold smile.

"I hope this shall satisfy you, minister." A horrified look was his only reply.

The Incarnation's followers laughed and sang as they destroyed the Jewel Pavilion, as they toppled statues from its roof and destroyed furniture to create bonfires in its luxurious suites. "Short Path!" they chanted. "Short Path!" In the theater the opera began, an old Tibetan epic about the death by treachery of the Sixth Earthly Gyalpo Rinpoche, known to his Mongolian enemies as the Dalai Lama. Jigme found a quiet place in the garden and sat in a full lotus, repeating sutras and trying to calm his mind. But the screams, chanting, songs, and shouts distracted him.

He looked up to see the Gyalpo Rinpoche standing upright amid the ruin of his garden, his head raised as if to sniff the wind. Kunlegs was standing close behind, caressing him. The light of the burning palace danced on his face. The Incarnation seemed transformed, a living embodiment of…of what? Madness? Exultation? Ecstasy? Jigme couldn't tell, but when he saw it he felt as if his heart would explode.

Then his blood turned cold. Behind the Incarnation, moving through the garden beneath the ritual umbrella of a Masker servant, came Ambassador !urq, her dark face watching the burning palace with something like triumph.

Jigme felt someone near him. "This cannot go on," said Dr. O'Neill's voice, and at the sound of her cool resolution terror flooded him.

"Aum vajra sattva," he chanted, saying the words over and over, repeating them till the Jewel Pavilion was ash and the garden looked as if a whirlwind had torn through it, leaving nothing but tangled ruin.

Rising from the desolation, he saw something bright dangling from the shattered proscenium of the outdoor stage.

It was the young State Oracle, hanging by the neck.

"!urq's despatches have grown triumphant. She knows that the Gyalpo Rinpoche has lost the affection of the people, and that they will soon lose their tolerance."

Miss Taisuke was decorating a Christmas tree in her lha khang. Little glowing buddhas, in their traditional red suits and white beards, hung amid the evergreen branches. Kali danced on top, holding a skull in either hand.

"What can we do?" said Jigme.

"Prevent a coup whatever the cost. If the Incarnation is deposed or declared mad, the Sang can attack under pretext of restoring the Incarnation. Our own people will be divided. We couldn't hope to win."

"Can't Dr. O'Neill see this?"

"Dr. O'Neill desires war, Jigme. She thinks we will be victorious no matter what occurs."

Jigme thought about what interstellar war would mean, the vast energies of modern weapons deployed against helpless planets. Tens of billions dead, even with a victory. "We should speak to the Gyalpo Rinpoche," he said.

"He must be made to understand."

"The State Oracle spoke to him, and what resulted?"

"You, Prime Minister—"

Taisuke looked at him. Her eyes were brimming with tears. "I have tried to speak to him. He is interested only in his parties, in his new punishment device. It's all he will talk about."

Jigme said nothing. His eyes stung with tears. Two weeping officials, he thought, alone on Christmas Eve. What more pathetic a picture was possible?

"The device grows ever more elaborate," Taisuke said. "There will be life extension and preservation gear installed. The machine can torture people for *lifetimes!*" She shook her head. Her hands trembled as they wiped her eyes. "Perhaps Dr. O'Neill is right. Perhaps the Incarnation needs to be put away."

"Never," Jigme said. "Never."

"Prime Minister." The Thunderbolt Sow shifted in her corner. "The Gyalpo Rinpoche has made an announcement to his people. 'The Short Path will end with the New Year.'"

Taisuke wiped her eyes on her brocaded sleeve. "Was that the entire message?"

"Yes, Prime Minister."

Her eyes rose to Jigme's. "What could it mean?"

"We must have hope, Prime Minister."

"Yes." Her hands clutched at his. "We must try to have hope."

495

Beneath snapping prayer flags, a quarter-size Jewel Pavilion made of flammable lattice stood on Burning Hill. The Cabinet was gathered inside it, flanking the throne of the Incarnation. The Gyalpo Rinpoche had decided to view the burning from inside one of the floats.

Kyetsang Kunlegs, grinning with his huge yellow teeth, was the only one of his followers present. The others were making merry in the city.

In front of the sham Jewel Pavilion was the new torture machine, a hollow oval, twice the height of a man, its skin the color of brushed metal. The interior was filled with mysterious apparatus.

The Cabinet said the rosary, and the Horse of the Air rose up into the night. The Incarnation, draped with khatas, raised a double drum made from the crowns of two human skulls. With a flick of his wrist, a bead on a string began to bound from one drum to the other. With his cold green eyes he watched it rattle for a long moment. "Welcome to my first anniversary," he said.

The others murmured in reply. The drum rattled on. A cold winter wind blew through the pavilion. The Incarnation looked from one Cabinet member to the other and gave his cruel, ambiguous smile.

"On the anniversary of my ascension to the throne and my adoption of the Short Path," he said, "I would like to honor the woman who made it possible." He held out his hand. "Dr. O'Neill, the Minister of Science, whom I think of as my mother. Mother, please come sit in the place of honor."

O'Neill rose stone-faced from her place and walked to the throne. She prostrated herself and stuck out her tongue. The Treasured King stepped off the platform, still rattling the drum; he took her hand, helped her rise. He sat her on the platform on his own throne.

Another set of arms materialized on his shoulders; while the first rattled the drum, the other three went through a long succession of mudras. Amazement, Jigme read, fascination, the warding of evil.

"My first memories in this incarnation," he said, "are of fire. Fire that burned inside me, that made me want to claw my way out of my glass womb and launch myself prematurely into existence. Fires that aroused lust and hatred before I knew anyone to hate or to lust for. And then, when the fires grew unendurable, I would open my eyes, and there I would see my mother, Dr. O'Neill, watching me with happiness in her face."

Another pair of arms appeared. The Incarnation looked over his shoulder at Dr. O'Neill, who was watching him with the frozen stare given a poison serpent. The Incarnation turned back to the others. The breeze fluttered the khatas around his neck.

"Why should I burn?" he said. "My memories of earlier Incarnations were incomplete, but I knew I had never known such fire before. There was something in me that was not balanced. That was made for the Short Path. Perhaps Enlightenment could be reached by leaping into the fire. In any case, I had no choice."

There was a flare of light, a roar of applause. The first of the floats outside exploded into flame. Fireworks crackled in the night. The Incarnation smiled. His drum rattled on.

"Never had I been so out of balance," he said. Another pair of arms materialized. "Never had I been so puzzled. Were my compulsions a manifestation of the Library? Was the crystal somehow out of alignment? Or was something else wrong? It was my consort Kyetsang Kunlegs who gave me the first clue." He turned to the throne and smiled at the murderer, who twitched in reply. "Kunlegs has suffered all his life from Tourette's Syndrome, an excess of dopamine in the brain. It makes him compulsive, twitchy, and—curiously—brilliant. His brain works too fast for its own good. The condition should have been diagnosed and corrected years ago, but Kunlegs' elders were neglectful."

Kunlegs opened his mouth and gave a long laugh. Dr. O'Neill, seated just before him on the platform, gave a shiver. The Incarnation beamed at Kunlegs, then turned back to his audience.

"I didn't suffer from Tourette's—I didn't have all the symptoms. But seeing poor Kunlegs made it clear where I should look for the source of my difficulty." He raised the drum, rattled it beside his head. "In my own brain," he said.

Another float burst into flame. The bright light glowed through the wickerwork walls of the pavilion, shone on the Incarnation's face. He gazed into it with his cruel half-smile, his eyes dancing in the firelight.

Dr. O'Neill spoke. Her voice was sharp. "Omniscient, may I suggest that we withdraw? This structure is built to burn, and the wind will carry sparks from the other floats toward us."

The Incarnation looked at her. "Later, honored Mother." He turned back to the Cabinet. "Not wanting to bother my dear mother with my suspicions, I visited several doctors when I was engaged in my visits to town and various monasteries. I found that not only did I have a slight excess of dopamine, but that my mind also contained too much serotonin and norepinephrine, and too little endorphin."

Another float burst into flame. Figures from the opera screamed in eerie voices. The Incarnation's smile was beatific. "Yet my honored mother, the Minister of Science, supervised my growth. How could such a thing happen?"

Jigme's attention jerked to Dr. O'Neill. Her face was drained of color. Her eyes were those of someone gazing into the Void.

"Dr. O'Neill, of course, has political opinions. She believes the Sang heretics must be vanquished. Destroyed or subdued at all costs. And to that end she wished an Incarnation who would be a perfect conquering warrior king—impatient, impulsive, brilliant, careless of life and indifferent to suffering. Someone with certain sufficiencies and deficiencies in brain chemis—"

O'Neill opened her mouth. A scream came out, a hollow sound as mindless as those given by the burning floats. The Incarnation's many hands pointed to her, all but the one rattling the drum.

Laughing, Kyetsang Kunlegs lunged forward, twisting the khata around the minister's neck. The scream came to an abrupt end. Choking, she toppled back into his huge lap.

"She is the greatest traitor of all time!" the Incarnation said. "She who poisoned my predecessor, the Forty-First Incarnation, so that she could begin her plan. She who would subvert the Library itself

to her ends. She who would poison the mind of a Bodhisattva." His voice was soft, yet exultant. It sent an eerie chill down Jigme's back.

Kunlegs rose from the platform holding Dr. O'Neill in his big hands. Her piled-up hair had come undone and trailed across the ground. Kunlegs carried her out of the building and into the punishment machine.

The Incarnation's drum stopped rattling. Jigme looked at him in stunned comprehension.

"She shall know what it is to burn," he said. "She shall know it for many lifetimes."

Sparks blew across the floor before the Incarnation's feet. There was a glow from the doorway, where some of the wickerwork had caught fire.

The machine was automatic in its function. Dr. O'Neill began to scream again, a rising series of shrieks. Her body began to rotate. The Incarnation smiled. "She shall make that music for many centuries. Perhaps one of my future incarnations shall put a stop to it."

Jigme felt burning heat on the back of his neck. O'Neill's screams ran up and down his spine. "Omniscient," he said. "The pavilion is on fire. We should leave."

"In a moment. I wish to say a few last words."

Kunlegs came loping back, grinning, and hopped onto the platform. The Incarnation joined him and kissed him tenderly. "Kunlegs and I will stay in the pavilion," he said. "We will both die tonight."

"No!" Taisuke jumped to her feet. "We will not permit it! Your condition can be corrected."

The Incarnation stared at her. "I thank you, loyal one. But my brain is poisoned, and even if the imbalance were corrected I would still be perceiving the Library through a chemical fog that would impair my ability. My next Incarnation will not have this handicap."

"Omniscient!" Tears spilled from Taisuke's eyes. "Don't leave us!"

"You will continue as head of the government. My next Incarnation will be ready by the next New Year, and then you may retire to the secular life I know you wish to pursue in this lifetime."

"No!" Taisuke ran forward, threw herself before the platform. "I beg you, Omniscient!"

Suddenly Jigme was on his feet. He lurched forward, threw himself down beside Taisuke. "Save yourself, Omniscient!" he said.

"I wish to say something concerning the Sang." The Incarnation spoke calmly, as if he hadn't heard. "There will be danger of war in the next year. You must all promise me that you won't fight."

"Omniscient." This from Daddy Carbajal. "We must be ready to defend ourselves!"

"Are we an Enlightened race, or are we not?" The Incarnation's voice was stern.

"You are Bodhisattva." Grudgingly. "All know this."

"We are Enlightened. The Buddha commands us not to take life. If these are not facts, our existence has no purpose, and our civilization is a mockery." O'Neill's screams provided eerie counterpoint to his voice. The Incarnation's many arms pointed at the members of the Cabinet. "You may arm in order to deter attack. But if the Sang begin a war, you must promise me to surrender without condition."

"Yes!" Taisuke, still face down, wailed from her obeisance. "I promise, Omniscient."

"The Diamond Mountain will be the greatest prize the Sang can hope for. And the Library is the Buddha. When the time is right, the Library will incarnate itself as a Sang, and the Sang will be sent on their path to Enlightenment."

"Save yourself, Omniscient!" Taisuke wailed. The roar of flames had drowned O'Neill's screams. Jigme felt sparks falling on his shaven head.

"Your plan, sir!" Daddy Carbajal's voice was desperate. "It might not work! The Sang may thwart the incarnation in some way!"

"Are we Enlightened?" The Incarnation's voice was mild. "Or are we not? Is the Buddha's truth eternal, or is it not? Do you not support the Doctrine?"

Daddy Carbajal threw himself down beside Jigme. "I believe, Omniscient! I will do as you ask!"

"Leave us, then. Kyetsang and I wish to be alone."

Certainty seized Jigme. He could feel tears stinging his eyes. "Let me stay, Omniscient!" he cried. "Let me die with you!"

"Carry these people away," said the Incarnation. Hands seized Jigme. He fought them off, weeping, but they were too powerful: he was carried from the burning pavilion. His last sight of the Incarnation was of the Gyalpo Rinpoche and Kunlegs embracing one another, silhouetted against flame, and then everything dissolved in fire and tears.

And in the morning nothing was left, nothing but ashes and the keening cries of the traitor O'Neill, whom the Bodhisattva in his wisdom had sent forever to Hell.

Jigme found !urq there, standing alone before O'Neill, staring at the figure caught in a webwork of life support and nerve stimulators. The sound of the traitor's endless agony continued to issue from her torn throat. "There will be no war," Jigme said.

!urq looked at him. Her stance was uncertain.

"After all this," Jigme said, "a war would be indecent. You understand?" !urq just stared.

"You must not unleash this madness in us!" Jigme cried. Tears rolled down his face. "Never, Ambassador! Never!"

!urq's antennae twitched. She looked at O'Neill again, rotating slowly in the huge wheel. "I will do what I can, Rinpoche," she said.

!urq made her lone way down Burning Hill. Jigme stared at the traitor for a long time.

Then he sat in the full lotus. Ashes drifted around him, some clinging to his zen, as he sat before the image of the tormented doctor and recited his prayers.

WALL, STONE, CRAFT

ONE

She awoke, there in the common room of the inn, from a brief dream of roses and death. Once Mary came awake she recalled there were wild roses on her mother's grave, and wondered if her mother's spirit had visited her.

On her mother's grave, Mary's lover had first proposed their elopement. It was there the two of them had first made love.

Now she believed she was pregnant. Her lover was of the opinion that she was mistaken. That was about where it stood.

Mary concluded that it was best not to think about it. And so, blinking sleep from her eyes, she sat in the common room of the inn at Le Caillou and resolved to study her Italian grammar by candlelight.

Plurals. *La nascita, le nascite. La madre, le madri. Un bambino, i bambini...*

Interruption: stampings, snortings, the rattle of harness, the barking of dogs. Four young Englishmen entered the inn, one in scarlet uniform coat, the others in fine traveling clothes. Raindrops dazzled on their shoulders. The innkeeper bustled out from the kitchen, smiled, proffered the register.

Mary, unimpressed by anything English, concentrated on the grammar.

503

"Let me sign, George," the redcoat said. "My hand needs the practice." Mary glanced up at the comment.

"I say, George, here's a fellow signed in Greek!" The Englishman peered at yellowed pages of the inn's register, trying to make out the words in the dim light of the innkeeper's lamp. Mary smiled at the English officer's efforts.

"Perseus, I believe the name is. Perseus Busseus...d'ye suppose he means Bishop?—...Kselleius. And he gives his occupation as 'te anthropou philou'—...that would make him a friendly fellow, eh?—"

The officer looked over his shoulder and grinned, then returned to the register. "'Kai atheos.'" The officer scowled, then straightened.

"Does that mean what I think it does, George?"

George—the pretty auburn-haired man in byrons—shook rain off his short cape, stepped to the register, examined the text. "Not 'friendly fellow,'" he said. "That would be 'anehr philos.' 'Anthropos' is mankind, not man." There was the faintest touch of Scotland in his speech.

"So it is," said the officer. "It comes back now."

George bent at his slim waist and looked carefully at the register.

"What the fellow says is, 'Both friend of man and—'" He frowned, then looked at his friend. "You were right about the 'atheist,' I'm afraid."

The officer was indignant. "Ain't funny, George," he said.

George gave a cynical little half-smile. His voice changed, turned comical and fussy, became that of a high-pitched English school-master. "Let us try to make out the name of this famous atheist." He bent over the register again. "Perseus—you had that right, Somerset. Busseus—how very irregular. Kselleius—Kelly? Shelley?" He smiled at his friend. His voice became very Irish.

"Kelly, I imagine. An atheistical upstart Irish schoolmaster with a little Greek. But what the Busseus might be eludes me, unless his middle name is Omnibus."

Somerset chuckled. Mary rose from her place and walked quietly toward the pair. "The gentleman's name is Bysshe, sir," she said. "Percy Bysshe Shelley."

The two men turned in surprise. The officer—Somerset—bowed as he perceived a lady. Mary saw for the first time that he had one empty sleeve pinned across his tunic, which would account for the comment about the hand. The other—George, the man in byrons—swept off his hat and gave Mary a flourishing bow, one far too theatrical to be taken seriously. When he straightened, he gave Mary a little frown.

"Bysshe Shelley?" he said. "Any relation to Sir Bysshe, the baronet?"

"His grandson."

"Sir Bysshe is a protégé of old Norfolk." This an aside to his friends. Radical Whiggery was afoot, or so the tone implied. George returned his attention to Mary as the other Englishmen gathered about her. "An interesting family, no doubt," he said, and smiled at her. Mary wanted to flinch from the compelling way he looked at her, gazed upward, intently, from beneath his brows. "And are you of his party?"

"I am."

"And you are, I take it, Mrs. Shelley?"

Mary straightened and gazed defiantly into George's eyes. "Mrs. Shelley resides in England. My name is Godwin."

George's eyes widened, flickered a little. Low English murmurs came to Mary's ears. George bowed again. "Charmed to meet you, Miss Godwin."

George pointed to each of his companions with his hat. "Lord Fitzroy Somerset." The armless man bowed again. "Captain Harry Smith. Captain Austen of the Navy. Pásmány, my fencing master."

Most of the party, Mary thought, were young, and all were handsome, George most of all. George turned to Mary again, a little smile of anticipation curling his lips. His burning look was almost insolent. "My name is Newstead."

Mortal embarrassment clutched at Mary's heart. She knew her cheeks were burning, but still she held George's eyes as she bobbed a curtsey.

George had not been Marquess Newstead for more than a few months. He had been famous for years both as an intimate of the Prince Regent and the most dashing of Wellington's cavalry officers, but it was his exploits on the field of Waterloo and his capture of Napoleon on the bridge at Genappe that had made him immortal. He was the talk of England and the Continent, though he had achieved his fame under another name.

Before the Prince Regent had given him the title of Newstead, auburn-haired, insolent-eyed George had been known as George Gordon Noël, the sixth Lord Byron.

Mary decided she was not going to be impressed by either his titles or his manner. She decided she would think of him as George.

"Pleased to meet you, my lord," Mary said. Pride steeled her as she realized her voice hadn't trembled.

She was spared further embarrassment when the door burst open and a servant entered followed by a pack of muddy dogs—whippets—who showered them all with water, then howled and bounded about George, their master. Standing tall, his strong, well-formed legs in the famous side-laced boots that he had invented to show off his calf and ankle, George laughed as the dogs jumped up on his chest and bayed for attention. His lordship barked back at them and wrestled with them for a moment—not very lordlike, Mary thought—and then he told his dogs to be still. At first they ignored him, but eventually he got them down and silenced.

He looked up at Mary. "I can discipline men, Miss Godwin," he said, "but I'm afraid I'm not very good with animals."

"That shows you have a kind heart, I'm sure," Mary said.

The others laughed a bit at this—apparently kindheartedness was not one of George's better-known qualities—but George smiled indulgently.

"Have you and your companion supped, Miss Godwin? I would welcome the company of fellow English in this tiresome land of Brabant."

Mary was unable to resist an impertinence. "Even if one of them is an atheistical upstart Irish schoolmaster?"

"Miss Godwin, I would dine with Wolfe Tone himself." Still with that intent, under-eyed look, as if he was dissecting her.

Mary was relieved to turn away from George's gaze and look toward the back of the inn, in the direction of the kitchen. "Bysshe is in the kitchen giving instructions to the cook. I believe my sister is with him."

"Are there more in your party?"

"Only the three of us. And one rather elderly carriage horse."

"Forgive us if we do not invite the horse to table."

"Your ape, George," Somerset said dolefully, "will be quite enough."

Mary would have pursued this interesting remark, but at that moment Bysshe and Claire appeared from out of the kitchen passage. Both were laughing, as if at a shared secret, and Claire's black eyes glittered. Mary repressed a spasm of annoyance.

"Mary!" Bysshe said. "The cook told us a ghost story!" He was about to go on, but paused as he saw the visitors.

"We have an invitation to dinner," Mary said. "Lord Newstead has been kind enough—"

"Newstead!" said Claire. "*The* Lord Newstead?"

George turned his searching gaze on Claire. "I'm the only Newstead I know."

Mary felt a chill of alarm, for a moment seeing Claire as George doubtless saw her: black-haired, black-eyed, fatally indiscreet, and all of sixteen.

Sometimes the year's difference in age between Mary and Claire seemed a century.

"Lord Newstead!" Claire babbled. "I recognize you now! How exciting to meet you!"

Mary resigned herself to fate. "My lord," she said, "may I present my sister, Miss Jane—Claire, rather, Claire Clairmont, and Mr. Shelley."

"Overwhelmed and charmed, Miss Clairmont. Mr. Perseus Omnibus Kselleius, tí kánete?"

Bysshe blinked for a second or two, then grinned. "Thanmásia eùxaristô," returning politeness, "kaí eseîs?"

For a moment Mary gloried in Bysshe, in his big frame in his shabby clothes, his fair, disordered hair, his freckles, his large hands—and his absolute disinclination to be impressed by one of the most famous men on Earth.

George searched his mind for a moment. "Polú kalá, eùxaristô. Thá éthela ná—" He groped for words, then gave a laugh. "Hang the Greek!" he said. "It's been far too many years since Trinity. May I present my friend Somerset?"

Somerset gave the atheist a cold Christian eye. "How d'ye do?"

George finished his introductions. There was the snapping of coach whips outside, and the sound of more stamping horses. The dogs began barking again. At least two more coaches had arrived. George led the party into the dining room. Mary found herself sitting next to George, with Claire and Bysshe across the table.

"Damme, I quite forgot to register," Somerset said, rising from his bench. "What bed will you settle for, George?"

"Nothing less than Bonaparte's."

Somerset sighed. "I thought not," he said.

"Did Bonaparte sleep here in Le Caillou?" Claire asked.

"The night before Waterloo."

"How exciting! Is Waterloo nearby?" She looked at Bysshe. "Had we known, we could have asked for his room."

"Which we then would have had to surrender to my lord Newstead," Bysshe said tolerantly. "He has greater claim, after all, than we."

George gave Mary his intent look again. His voice was pitched low.

"I would not deprive two lovely ladies of their bed for all the Bonapartes in Europe."

But rather join us in it, Mary thought. That look was clear enough.

The rest of George's party—servants, aides-de-camp, clerks, one black man in full Mameluke fig, turned-up slippers, ostrich plumes, scarlet turban and all—carried George's equipage from his carriages. In addition to an endless series of trunks and a large miscellany of weaponry there were more animals. Not only the promised ape—actually a large monkey, which seated itself on George's shoulder—but brightly-colored parrots in cages, a pair of greyhounds, some hooded hunting hawks, songbirds, two forlorn-looking kit foxes in cages, which set all the dogs howling and jumping in eagerness to get at them, and a half-grown panther in a jeweled collar, which the dogs knew better than to bark at. The innkeeper was loud in his complaint as he attempted to sort them all out and stay outside of the range of beaks, claws, and fangs.

Bysshe watched with bright eyes, enjoying the spectacle. George's friends looked as if they were weary of it.

"I hope we will sleep tonight," Mary said.

"If you sleep not," said George, playing with the monkey, "we shall contrive to keep you entertained."

How gracious to include your friends in the orgy, Mary thought. But once again kept silent.

Bysshe was still enjoying the parade of frolicking animals. He glanced at Mary. "Don't you think, Maie, this is the very image of philosophical anarchism?"

"You are welcome to it, sir," said Somerset, returning from the register. "George, your mastiff has injured the ostler's dog. He is loud in his complaint."

"I'll have Ferrante pay him off."

"See that you do. And have him pistol the brains out of that mastiff while he's at it."

"Injure poor Picton?" George was offended. "I'll have none of it."

"Poor Picton will have his fangs in the ostler next."

"He must have been teasing the poor beast."

"Picton will kill us all one day." Grudgingly.

"Forgive us, Somerset-laddie." Mary watched as George reached over to Somerset and tweaked his ear. Somerset reddened but seemed pleased.

"Mr. Shelley," said Captain Austen. "I wonder if you know what surprises the kitchen has in store for us."

Austen was a well-built man in a plain black coat, older than the others, with a lined and weathered naval face and a reserved manner unique in this company.

"Board 'em in the smoke! That's the Navy for you!" George said. "Straight to the business of eating, never mind the other nonsense."

"If you ate wormy biscuit for twenty years of war," said Harry Smith, "you'd care about the food as well."

Bysshe gave Austen a smile. "The provisions seem adequate enough for a country inn," he said. "And the rooms are clean, unlike most in this country. Claire and the Maie and I do not eat meat, so I had to tell the cook how to prepare our dinner. But if your taste runs to fowl or something in the cutlet line I daresay the cook can set you up."

"No meat!" George seemed enthralled by the concept. "Disciples of J.F. Newton, as I take it?"

"Among others," said Mary.

"But are you well? Do you not feel an enervation? Are you not feverish with lack of a proper diet?" George leaned very close and touched Mary's forehead with the back of one cool hand while he reached to find her pulse with the other. The monkey grimaced at her from his shoulder. Mary disengaged and placed her hands on the table.

"I'm quite well, I assure you," she said.

"The Maie's health is far better than when I met her," Bysshe said.

"Mine too," said Claire.

"I believe most diseases can be conquered by proper diet," said Bysshe. And then he added,

"He slays the lamb that looks him in the face,
And horribly devours his mangled flesh."

"Let's have some mangled flesh tonight, George!" said Somerset gaily.

"Do let's," added Smith.

George's hand remained on Mary's forehead. His voice was very soft. "If eating flesh offend thee," he said, "I will eat but only greens."

Mary could feel her hackles rise. "Order what you please," she said. "I don't care one way or another."

"Brava, Miss Godwin!" said Smith thankfully. "Let it be mangled flesh for us all, and to perdition with all those little Low Country cabbages!"

"I don't like them, either," said Claire.

George removed his hand from Mary's forehead and tried to signal the innkeeper, who was still struggling to corral the dogs. George failed, frowned, and lowered his hand.

"I'm cheered to know you're familiar with the works of Newton," Bysshe said.

"I wouldn't say *familiar*," said George. He was still trying to signal the innkeeper. "I haven't read his books. But I know he wants me not to eat meat, and that's all I need to know."

Bysshe folded his big hands on the table. "Oh, there's much more than that. Abstaining from meat implies an entire new moral order, in which mankind is placed on an equal level with the animals."

"George in particular should appreciate that," said Harry Smith, and made a face at the monkey.

"I think I prefer being ranked above the animals," George said. "And above most people, too." He looked up at Bysshe. "Shall we avoid talk of food before we eat? My stomach's rumbling louder than a battery of Napoleon's daughters." He looked down at the monkey and assumed a high-pitched Scots dowager's voice.

"An' sae is Jerome Bonaparte's, annit nae, Jerome?"

George finally succeeded in attracting the innkeeper's attention and the company ordered food and wine. Bread, cheese, and pickles were brought to tide them over in the meantime. Jerome Bonaparte was permitted off his master's lap to roam free along the table and eat what he wished.

George watched as Bysshe carved a piece of cheese for himself. "In addition to Newton, you would also be a follower of William Godwin?"

Bysshe gave Mary a glance, then nodded. "Ay. Godwin also."

"I thought I recognized that 'philosophical anarchism' of yours. Godwin was the rage when I was at Harrow. But not so much thought of now, eh? Excepting of course his lovely namesake."

Turning his gaze to Mary.

Mary gave him a cold look. "Truth is ever in fashion, my lord," she said.

"Did you say *ever* or *never!*" Playfully. Mary said nothing, and George gave a shrug. "Truthful Master Godwin, then. And who else?"

"Ovid," Mary said. The officers looked a little serious at this. She smiled. "Come now—he's not as scandalous as he's been made out. Merely playful."

This did not reassure her audience. Bysshe offered Mary a private smile. "We've also been reading Mary Wollstonecraft."

"Ah!" George cried. "Heaven save us from intellectual women!"

"Mary Wollstonecraft," said Somerset thoughtfully. "She was a harlot in France, was she not?"

"I prefer to think of my mother," said Mary carefully, "as a political thinker and authoress."

There was sudden silence as Somerset turned white with mortification. Then George threw back his head and laughed.

"Sunburn me!" he said. "That answers as you deserve!"

Somerset visibly made an effort to collect his wits. "I am most sorry, Miss——" he began.

George laughed again. "By heaven, we'll watch our words hereafter!"

Claire tittered. "I was in suspense, wondering if there would be a mishap. And there was, there *was!*"

George turned to Mary and managed to compose his face into an attitude of solemnity, though the amusement that danced in his eyes denied it.

"I sincerely apologize on behalf of us all, Miss Godwin. We are soldiers and are accustomed to speaking rough among ourselves, and have been abroad and are doubtless ignorant of the true worth of any individual——" He searched his mind for a moment, trying to work out a graceful way to conclude. "—outside of our own little circle," he finished.

"Well said," said Mary, "and accepted." She had chosen more interesting ground on which to make her stand.

"Oh yes!" said Claire. "Well said indeed!"

"My mother is not much understood by the public," Mary continued. "But intellectual women, it would seem, are not much understood by *you*."

George leaned away from Mary and scanned her with cold eyes.

"On the contrary," he said. "I am married to an intellectual woman."

"And she, I imagine…" Mary let the pause hang in the air for a moment, like a rapier before it strikes home. "…resides in England?"

George scowled. "She does."

"I'm sure she has her books to keep her company."

"And Francis Bacon," George said, his voice sour. "Annabella is an authority on Francis Bacon. And she is welcome to reform *him,* if she likes."

Mary smiled at him. "Who keeps *you* company, my lord?"

There was a stir among his friends. He gave her that insolent, under-eyed look again.

"I am not often lonely," he said.

"Tonight you will rest with the ghost of Napoleon," she said. "Which of you has better claim to that bed?"

George gave a cold little laugh. "I believe that was decided at Waterloo."

"The Duke's victory, or so I've heard."

George's friends were giving each other alarmed looks. Mary decided she had drawn enough Byron blood. She took a piece of cheese.

"Tell us about Waterloo!" Claire insisted. "Is it far from here?"

"The field is a mile or so north," said Somerset. He seemed relieved to turn to the subject of battles. "I had thought perhaps you were English tourists come to visit the site."

"Our arrival is coincidence," Bysshe said. He was looking at Mary narrow-eyed, as if he was trying to work something out. "I'm somewhat embarrassed for funds, and I'm in hope of finding a letter at Brussels from my—" He began to say "wife," but changed the word to "family."

"We're on our way to Vienna," Smith said.

"The long way 'round," said Somerset. "It's grown unsafe in Paris—too many old Bonapartists lurking with guns and bombs, and of course George is the laddie they hate most. So we're off to join the Duke as diplomats, but we plan to meet with his highness of Orange along the way. In Brussels, in two days' time."

"Good old Slender Billy!" said Smith. "I haven't seen him since the battle."

"The battle!" said Claire. "You said you would tell us!"

George gave her an irritated look. "Please, Miss Clairmont, I beg you. No battles before dinner." His stomach rumbled audibly.

"Bysshe," said Mary, "didn't you say the cook had told you a ghost story?"

"A good one, too," said Bysshe. "It happened in the house across the road, the one with the tile roof. A pair of old witches used to live there. Sisters." He looked up at George. "We may have ghosts before dinner, may we not?"

"For all of me, you may."

"They dealt in charms and curses and so on, and made a living supplying the, ah, the supernatural needs of the district. It so happened that two different men had fallen in love with the same girl, and each man applied to one of the weird sisters for a love charm—each to a different sister, you see. One of them used his spell first and won the heart of the maiden, and this drove the other suitor into a rage. So he went to the witch who had sold him his charm, and demanded she change the young lady's mind. When the witch insisted it was impossible, he drew his pistol and shot her dead."

"How very un-Belgian of him," drawled Smith.

Bysshe continued unperturbed. "So quick as a wink," he said, "the dead witch's sister seized a heavy kitchen cleaver and cut off the young man's head with a single stroke. The head fell to the floor and bounced out the porch steps. And ever since that night—" He leaned across the table toward Mary, his voice dropping dramatically. "— people in the house have sometimes heard a thumping noise, and seen *the suitor's head, dripping gore, bouncing down the steps.*"

Mary and Bysshe shared a delicious shiver. George gave Bysshe a thoughtful look.

"D'ye credit this sort of thing, Mr. Omnibus?"

Bysshe looked up. "Oh yes. I have a great belief in things supernatural."

George gave an insolent smile, and Mary's heart quickened as she recognized a trap.

"Then how can you be an atheist?" George asked.

Bysshe was startled. No one had ever asked him this question before. He gave a nervous laugh. "I am not so much opposed to God," he said, "as I am a worshiper of Galileo and Newton. And of course an enemy of the established Church."

"I see."

A little smile drifted across Bysshe's lips.

"Yes!" he said,

> "I have seen God's worshipers unsheathe
> The sword of his revenge, when grace descended,
> Confirming all unnatural impulses,
> To satisfy their desolating deeds;
> And frantic priests waved the ill-omened cross
> O'er the unhappy earth; then shone the sun
> On showers of gore from the upflashing steel
> Of safe assassin—"

"And *have* you seen such?" George's look was piercing.

Bysshe blinked at him. "Beg pardon?"

"I asked if you had seen showers of gore, upflashing steel, all that sort of thing."

"Ah. No." He offered George a half-apologetic smile. "I do not hold warfare consonant with my principles."

"Yes." George's stomach rumbled once more. "It's rather more in my line than yours. So I think I am probably better qualified to judge it…" His lip twisted. "…*and* your principles."

Mary felt her hackles rise. "Surely you don't dispute that warfare is a great evil," she said. "And that the church blesses war and its outcome."

"The church—" He waved a hand. "The chaplains we had with us in Spain were fine men and did good work, from what I could see. Though we had damn few of them, as for the most part they preferred to judge war from their comfortable beds at home. And as for war—ay, it's evil. Yes. Among other things."

"Among other things!" Mary was outraged. "What other things?"

George looked at each of the officers in turn, then at Mary. "War is an abomination, I think we can all agree. But it is also an occasion for all that is great in mankind. Courage, comradeship, sacrifice. Heroism and nobility beyond the scope of imagination."

"Glory," said one-armed Somerset helpfully.

"Death!" snapped Mary. "Hideous, lingering death! Disease. Mutilation!" She realized she had stepped a little far, and bobbed her head toward Somerset, silently begging his pardon for bringing up his disfigurement. "Endless suffering among the starving widows and orphans," she went on. "Early this year Bysshe and Jane and I walked across the part of France that the armies had marched over. It was a desert, my lord. Whole villages without a single soul. Women, children, and cripples in rags. Many without a roof over their head."

"Ay," said Harry Smith. "We saw it in Spain, all of us."

"Miss Godwin," said George, "those poor French people have my sympathy as well as yours. But if a nation is going to murder its rightful king, elect a tyrant, and attack every other nation in the world, then it can but expect to receive that which it giveth. I reserve far greater sympathy for the poor orphans and widows of Spain, Portugal, and the Low Countries."

"And England," said Captain Austen.

"Ay," said George, "and England."

"I did not say that England has not suffered," said Mary. "Anyone with eyes can see the victims of the war. And the victims of the Corn Bill as well."

"Enough." George threw up his hands. "I heard enough debate on the Corn Bill in the House of Lords—I beg you, not here."

"People are starving, my lord," Mary said quietly.

"But thanks to Waterloo," George said, "they at least starve in peace."

"Here's our flesh!" said a relieved Harry Smith. Napkins flourished, silverware rattled, the dinner was laid down. Bysshe took a bite of his cheese pie, then sampled one of the little Brabant cabbages and gave a freckled smile—he had not, as had Mary, grown tired of them. Smith, Somerset, and George chatted about various Army acquaintances, and the others ate in silence. Somerset, Mary noticed, had come equipped with a combination knife-and-fork and managed his cutlet efficiently.

George, she noted, ate only a little, despite the grumblings of his stomach.

"Is it not to your taste, my lord?" she asked.

"My appetite is off." Shortly.

"That light cavalry figure don't come without sacrifice," said Smith. "I'm an infantryman, though," brandishing knife and fork, "and can tuck in to my vittles."

George gave him an irritated glance and sipped at his hock.

"Cavalry, infantry, Senior Service, staff," he said, pointing at himself, Smith, Austen, and Somerset with his fork. The fork swung to Bysshe. "Do you, sir, have an occupation? Besides being atheistical, I mean."

Bysshe put down his knife and fork and answered deliberately. "I have been a scientist, and a reformer, and a sort of an engineer. I have now taken up poetry."

"I didn't know it was something to be taken up," said George.

"Captain Austen's sister does something in the literary line, I believe," Harry Smith said.

Austen gave a little shake of his head. "Please, Harry. Not here."

"I know she publishes anonymously, but—"

"She doesn't want it known," firmly, "and I prefer her wishes be respected."

Smith gave Austen an apologetic look. "Sorry, Frank."

Mary watched Austen's distress with amusement. Austen had a spinster sister, she supposed—she could just imagine the type—who probably wrote ripe horrid Gothic novels, all terror and dark battlements and cloaked sensuality, all to the constant mortification of the family.

Well, Mary thought. She should be charitable. Perhaps they were good.

She and Bysshe liked a good gothic, when they were in the mood. Bysshe had even written a couple, when he was fifteen or so.

George turned to Bysshe. "That was your own verse you quoted?"

"Yes."

"I thought perhaps it was, as I hadn't recognized it."

"*Queen Mab*," said Claire. "It's *very* good." She gave Bysshe a look of adoration that sent a weary despairing cry through Mary's nerves. "It's got all Bysshe's ideas in it," she said.

"And the publisher?"

"I published it myself," Bysshe said, "in an edition of seventy copies."

George raised an eyebrow. "A self-published phenomenon, forsooth. But why so few?"

"The poem is a political statement in accordance with Mr. Godwin's *Political Justice*. Were it widely circulated, the government might act to suppress it, and to prosecute the publisher." He gave a shudder. "With people like Lord Ellenborough in office, I think it best to take no chances."

"Lord Ellenborough is a great man," said Captain Austen firmly.

Mary was surprised at his emphatic tone.

"He led for Mr. Warren Hastings, do you know, during his trial," Austen continued, "and that trial lasted seven years or more and ended in acquittal. Governor Hastings did me many a good turn in India—he was the making of me. I'm sure I owe Lord Ellenborough my purest gratitude."

Bysshe gave Austen a serious look. "Lord Ellenborough sent Daniel Eaton to prison for publishing Thomas Paine," he said. "And he sent Leigh Hunt to prison for publishing the truth about the Prince Regent."

"One an atheist," Austen scowled, "the other a pamphleteer."

"Why, so am I both," said Bysshe sweetly, and, smiling, sipped his spring water. Mary wanted to clap aloud.

"It is the duty of the Lord Chief Justice to guard the realm from subversion," said Somerset. "We were at war, you know."

"We are no longer at war," said Bysshe, "and Lord Ellenborough still sends good folk to prison."

"At least," said Mary, "he can no longer accuse reformers of being Jacobins. Not with France under the Bourbons again."

"Of course he can," Bysshe said. "Reform is an idea, and Jacobinism is an idea, and Ellenborough conceives them the same."

"But are they not?" George said.

Mary's temper flared. "Are you serious? Comparing those who seek to correct injustice with those who—"

"Who cut the heads off everyone with whom they disagreed?" George interrupted. "I'm perfectly serious. Robespierre was the very type of reformer—virtuous, sober, sedate, educated, a spotless private life. And how many thousands did he murder?" He jabbed his fork at Bysshe again, and Mary restrained the impulse to slap it out of his hand. "You may not like Ellenborough's sentencing, but a few hours in the pillory or a few months in prison ain't the same as beheading. And that's what reform in England would come to in the end—mobs and demagogues heaping up death, and then a dictator like Cromwell, or worse luck Bonaparte, to end liberty for a whole generation."

"I do not look to the French for a model," said Bysshe, "but rather to America."

"So did the French," said George, "and look what they got."

"If France had not desperately needed reform," Bysshe said, "there would have been nothing so violent as their revolution. If England reforms itself, there need be no violence."

"Ah. So if the government simply resigns, and frame-breakers and agitators and democratic philosophers and wandering poets take their place, then things shall be well in England."

"Things will be better in any case," Bysshe said quietly, "than they are now."

"Exactly!" Claire said.

George gave his companions a knowing look. *See how I humor this vagabond?* Mary read. Loathing stirred her heart.

Bysshe could read a look as well as Mary. His face darkened.

"Please understand me," he said. "I do not look for immediate change, nor do I preach violent revolution. Mr. Godwin has corrected that error in my thought. There will be little amendment for years to come. But Ellenborough is old, and the King is old and mad, and the Regent and his loathsome brothers are not young..."

He smiled. "I will outlive them, will I not?"

George looked at him. "Will you outlive me, sir? I am not yet thirty."

"I am three-and-twenty." Mildly. "I believe the odds favor me."

Bysshe and the others laughed, while George looked cynical and dyspeptic. *Used to being the young cavalier,* Mary thought. *He's not so young any longer—how much longer will that pretty face last?*

"And of course advance of science may turn this debate irrelevant," Bysshe went on. "Mr. Godwin calculates that with the use of mechanical aids, people may reduce their daily labor to an hour or two, to the general benefit of all."

"But you oppose such machines, don't ye?" George said. "You support the Luddites, I assume?"

"Ay, but—"

"And the frame-breakers are destroying the machines that have taken their livelihood, aren't they? So where is your general benefit, then?"

Mary couldn't hold it in any longer. She slapped her hand down on the table, and George and Bysshe started. "The riots occur because the profits of the looms were not used to benefit the weavers, but to enrich the mill owners! Were the owners to share their profits with the weavers, there would have been no disorder."

George gave her a civil bow. "Your view of human nature is generous," he said, "if you expect a mill owner to support the families of those who are not even his employees."

"It would be for the good of all, wouldn't it?" Bysshe said. "If he does not want his mills threatened and frames broken."

"It sounds like extortion wrapped in pretty philosophy."

"The mill owners will pay one way or another," Mary pointed out. "They can pay taxes to the government to suppress the Luddites with militia and dragoons, or they can have the goodwill of the people, and let the swords and muskets rust."

"They will buy the swords every time," George said. "They are useful in ways other than suppressing disorder, such as securing trade routes and the safety of the nation." He put on a benevolent face. "You must forgive me, but your view of humanity is too benign. You do not account for the violence and passion that are in the very heart of man, and which institutions such as law and religion are intended to help control. And when science serves the passions, only tragedy can result—when I think of science, I think of the science of Dr. Guillotin."

"We are fallen," said Captain Austen. "Eden will never be within our grasp."

"The passions are a problem, but I think they can be turned to good," said Bysshe. "That is—" He gave an apologetic smile. "That is the aim of my current work. To use the means of poetry to channel the passions to a humane and beneficent aim."

"I offer you my very best wishes," condescendingly, "but I fear mankind will disappoint you. Passions are—" George gave Mary an insolent, knowing smile. "—are the downfall of many a fine young virtue."

Mary considered hitting him in the face. Bysshe seemed not to have noticed George's look, nor Mary's reaction. "Mr. Godwin ventured the thought that dreams are the source of many irrational passions," he mused. "He believes that should we ever find a way of doing without sleep, the passions would fall away."

"Ay!" barked George. "Through enervation, if nothing else."

The others laughed. Mary decided she had had enough, and rose.

"I shall withdraw," she said. "The journey has been fatiguing."

The gentlemen, Bysshe excepted, rose to their feet. "Good night, Maie," he said. "I will stay for a while, I think."

"As you like, Bysshe." Mary looked at her sister. "Jane? I mean Claire? Will you come with me?"

"Oh, no." Quickly. "I'm not at all tired."

Annoyance stiffened Mary's spine. "As you like," she said.

George bowed toward her, picked a candle off the table, and offered her an arm. "May I light you up the stair? I should like to apologize for my temerity in contradicting such a charming lady." He offered his brightest smile. "I think my poor virtue will extend that far, yes?"

She looked at him coldly—she couldn't think it customary, even in George's circles, to escort a woman to her bedroom.

Damn it anyway. "My lord," she said, and put her arm through his.

Jerome Bonaparte made a flying leap from the table and landed on George's shoulder. It clung to his long auburn hair, screamed, and made a face, and the others laughed. Mary considered the thought of being escorted up to bed by a lord and a monkey, and it improved her humor.

"Goodnight, gentlemen," Mary said. "Claire."

The gentlemen reseated themselves and George took Mary up the stairs. They were so narrow and steep that they couldn't go up abreast; George, with the candle, went first, and Mary, holding his hand, came up behind. Her door was the first up the stairs; she put her hand on the wooden door handle and turned to face her escort. The monkey leered at her from his shoulder.

"I thank you for your company, my lord," she said. "I fear your journey was a little short."

"I wished a word with you," softly, "a little apart from the others."

Mary stiffened. To her annoyance her heart gave a lurch. "What word is that?" she asked.

His expression was all affability. "I am sensible to the difficulties that you and your sister must be having. Without money in a foreign country, and with your only protector a man—" He hesitated. Jerome Bonaparte, jealous for his attention, tugged at his hair. "A charming man of noble ideals, surely, but without money."

"I thank you for your concern, but it is misplaced," Mary said. "Claire and I are perfectly well."

"Your health ain't my worry," he said. Was he deliberately misunderstanding? Mary wondered in fury. "I worry for your future— you are on an adventure with a man who cannot support you, cannot see you safe home, cannot marry you."

"Bysshe and I do not wish to marry." The words caught at her heart. "We are free."

"And the damage to your reputation in society—" he began, and came up short when she burst into laughter. He looked severe, while the monkey mocked him from his shoulder. "You may laugh now, Miss Godwin, but there are those who will use this adventure against you. Political enemies of your father at the very least."

"That isn't why I was laughing. I am the daughter of William Godwin and Mary Wollstonecraft—I *have* no reputation! It's like being the natural daughter of Lucifer and the Scarlet Woman of Babylon. Nothing is expected of us, nothing at all. Society has given us license to do as we please. We were dead to them from birth."

He gave her a narrow look. "But you have at least a little concern for the proprieties—why else travel pseudonymously?"

Mary looked at him in surprise. "What d'you mean?"

He smiled. "Give me a little credit, Miss Godwin. When you call your sister *Jane* half the time, and your protector calls you *May*..."

Mary laughed again. "*The* Maie—Maie for short—is one of Bysshe's pet names for me. The other is Pecksie."

"Oh."

"And Jane is my sister's given name, which she has always hated. Last year she decided to call herself Clara or Claire—this week it is Claire."

Jerome Bonaparte began to yank at George's ear, and George made a face, pulled the monkey from his shoulder, and shook it with mock ferocity. Again he spoke in the cracked Scots dowager's voice. "Are ye sae donsie wicked, creeture? Tae Elba w'ye!"

Mary burst into laughter again. George gave her a careless grin, then returned the monkey to his shoulder. It sat and regarded Mary with bright, wise eyes.

"Miss Godwin, I am truly concerned for you, believe else of me what you will."

Mary's laughter died away. She took the candle from his hand.

"Please, my lord. My sister and I are perfectly safe in Mr. Shelley's company."

"You will not accept my protection? I will freely give it."

"We do not need it. I thank you."

"Will you not take a loan, then? To see you safe across the Channel? Mr. Shelley may pay me back if he is ever in funds."

Mary shook her head.

A little of the old insolence returned to George's expression. "Well. I have done what I could."

"Good night, Lord Newstead."

"Good night."

Mary readied herself for bed and climbed atop the soft mattress. She tried to read her Italian grammar, but the sounds coming up the stairway were a distraction. There was loud conversation, and singing, and then Claire's fine voice, unaccompanied, rising clear and sweet up the narrow stair.

Torcere, Mary thought, looking fiercely at her book, *attorcere, rattorcere, scontorcere, torcere.*

Twist. Twist, twist, twist, twist.

Claire finished, and there was loud applause. Bysshe came in shortly afterwards. His eyes sparkled and his color was high. "We were singing," he said.

"I heard."

"I hope we didn't disturb you." He began to undress.

Mary frowned at her book. "You did."

"And I argued some more with Byron." He looked at her and smiled. "Imagine it—if we could convert Byron! Bring one of the most famous men in the world to our views."

She gave him a look. "I can think of nothing more disastrous to our cause than to have him lead it."

"Byron's famous. And he's a splendid man." He looked at her with a self-conscious grin. "I have a pair of byrons, you know, back home. I think I have a good turn of ankle, but the things are the very devil to lace. You really need servants for it."

"He's Newstead now. Not Byron. I wonder if they'll have to change the name of the boot?"

"Why would he change his name, d'you suppose? After he'd become famous with it."

"Wellington became famous as Wellesley."

"Wellington *had* to change his name. His brother was *already* Lord Wellesley." He approached the bed and smiled down at her. "He likes you."

"He likes any woman who crosses his path. Or so I understand."

Bysshe crawled into the bed and put his arm around her, the hand resting warmly on her belly. He smelled of the tobacco he'd been smoking with George. She put her hand atop his, feeling on the third finger the gold wedding ring he still wore. Dissatisfaction crackled through her. "You are free, you know." He spoke softly into her ear. "You can be with Byron if you wish."

Mary gave him an irritated look. "I don't *wish* to be with Byron. I want to be with you."

"But you *may*," whispering, the hand stroking her belly, "be with Byron if you want."

Temper flared through Mary. "I don't *want* Byron!" she said. "And I don't want Mr. Thomas Jefferson Hogg, or any of your other friends!"

He seemed a little hurt. "Hogg's a splendid fellow."

"Hogg tried to seduce your wife, and he's tried to seduce me. And I don't understand how he remains your best friend."

"Because we agree on everything, and I hold him no malice where his intent was not malicious." Bysshe gave her a searching look. "I only want you to be free. If we're not free, our love is chained, chained absolutely, and all ruined. I can't live that way—I found that out with Harriet."

She sighed, put her arm around him, drew her fingers through his tangled hair. He rested his head on her shoulder and looked up into her eyes. "I want to be *free* to be with you," Mary told him. "Why will that not suit?"

"It suits." He kissed her cheek. "It suits very well." He looked up at her happily. "And if Harriet joins us in Brussels, with a little money, then all shall be perfect."

Mary gazed at him, utterly unable to understand how he could think his wife would join them, or why, for that matter, he thought it a good idea. *He misses his little boy,* she thought. *He wants to be with him.*

The thought rang hollow in her mind.

He kissed her again, his hand moving along her belly, touching her lightly. "My golden-haired Maie." The hand cupped her breast. Her breath hissed inward.

"Careful," she said. "I'm very tender there."

"I will be nothing but tenderness." The kisses reached her lips. "I desire nothing but tenderness for you."

She turned to him, let his lips brush against hers, then press more firmly. Sensation, a little painful, flushed her breast. His tongue touched hers. Desire rose and she put her arms around him.

The door opened and Claire came in, chattering of George while she undressed. Mood broken, tenderness broken, there was nothing to do but sleep.

❄

"Come and look," Mary said, "here's a cat eating roses; she'll turn into a woman, when beasts eat these roses they turn into men and women." But there was no one in the cottage, only the sound of the wind.

Fear touched her, cold on the back of her neck.

She stepped into the cottage, and suddenly there was something blocking the sun that came through the windows, an enormous figure, monstrous and black and hungry...

Nausea and the sounds of swordplay woke her. A dog was barking maniacally. Mary rose from the bed swiftly and wrapped her shawl around herself. The room was hot and stuffy, and her gorge rose.

She stepped to the window, trying not to vomit, and opened the pane to bring in fresh air.

Coolness touched her cheeks. Below in the courtyard of the inn was Pásmány, the fencing teacher, slashing madly at his pupil, Byron.

Newstead. *George*, she reminded herself, she would remember he was *George*. And serve him right.

She dragged welcome morning air into her lungs as the two battled below her. George was in his shirt, planted firmly on his strong, muscular legs, his pretty face set in an expression of intent calculation. Pásmány flung himself at the man, darting in and out, his sword almost fluid in its movement. They were using straight heavy sabers, dangerous even if unsharpened, and no protective equipment at all. A huge black dog, tied to the vermilion wheel of a big dark-blue barouche, barked at the both of them without cease.

Nausea swam over Mary; she closed her eyes and clutched the windowsill. The ringing of the swords suddenly seemed very far away.

"Are they fighting?" Claire's fingers clutched her shoulder. "Is it a duel? Oh, it's *Byron!*"

Mary abandoned the window and groped her way to the bed. Sweat beaded on her forehead. Bysshe blinked muzzily at her from his pillow.

"I must go down and watch," said Claire. She reached for her clothing and, hopping, managed to dress without missing a second of the action outside. She grabbed a hairbrush on her way out the door and was arranging her hair on the run even before the door slammed behind her.

"Whatever is happening?" Bysshe murmured. She reached blindly for his hand and clutched it.

"Bysshe," she gasped. "I am with child. I must be."

"I shouldn't think so." Calmly. "We've been using every precaution." He touched her cheek. His hand was cool. "It's the travel and excitement. Perhaps a bad egg."

Nausea blackened her vision and bent her double. Sweat fell in stately rhythm from her forehead to the floor. "This can't be a bad egg," she said. "Not day after day."

"Poor Maie." He nestled behind her, stroked her back and shoulders. "Perhaps there is a flaw in the theory," he said. "Time will tell."

No turning back, Mary thought. She had *wanted* there to be no turning back, to burn every bridge behind her, commit herself totally, as her mother had, to her beliefs. And now she'd succeeded—she and Bysshe were linked forever, linked by the child in her womb. Even if they parted, if—free, as they both wished to be—he abandoned this union, there would still be that link, those bridges burnt, her mother's defiant inheritance fulfilled…

Perhaps there is a flaw in the theory. She wanted to laugh and cry at once.

Bysshe stroked her, his thoughts his own, and outside the martial clangor went on and on.

It was some time before she could dress and go down to the common rooms. The sabre practice had ended, and Bysshe and Claire were already breaking their fast with Somerset, Smith, and Captain Austen. The thought of breakfast made Mary ill, so she wandered outside into the courtyard, where the two breathless swordsmen, towels draped around their necks, were sitting on a bench drinking water, with a tin dipper, from an old wooden bucket. The huge black dog barked, foaming, as she stepped out of the inn, and the two men, seeing her, rose.

"Please sit, gentlemen," she said, waving them back to their bench; she walked across the courtyard to the big open gate and stepped outside. She leaned against the whitewashed stone wall and took deep breaths of the country air. Sweet-smelling wildflowers grew in the verges of the highway. Prosperous-looking villagers nodded pleasantly as they passed about their errands.

"Looking for your haunted house, Miss Godwin?"

George's inevitable voice grated on her ears. She looked at him over her shoulder. "My intention was simply to enjoy the morning."

"I hope I'm not spoiling it."

Reluctant courtesy rescued him from her own riposting tongue.

"How was the Emperor's bed?" she said finally.

He stepped out into the road. "I believe I slept better than he did, and longer." He smiled at her. "No ghosts walked."

"But you still fought a battle after your sleep."

"A far, far better one. Waterloo was not something I would care to experience more than once."

"I shouldn't care to experience it even the first time."

"Well. You're female, of course." All offhand, unaware of her rising hackles. He looked up and down the highway.

"D'ye know, this is the first time I've seen this road in peace. I first rode it north during the retreat from Quatre Bras, a miserable rainy night, and then there was the chase south after Boney the night of Waterloo, then later the advance with the army to Paris..." He shook his head. "It's a pleasant road, ain't it? Much better without the armies."

"Yes."

"We went along there." His hand sketched a line across the opposite horizon. "This road was choked with retreating French, so we went around them. With two squadrons of Vandeleur's lads, the 12th, the Prince of Wales's Own, all I could find once the French

529

gave way. I knew Boney would be running, and I knew it had to be along this road. I had to find him, make certain he would never trouble our peace. Find him for England." He dropped right fist into left palm.

"Boney'd left two battalions of the Guard to hold us, but I went around them. I knew the Prussians would be after him, too, and their mounts were fresher. So we drove on through the night, jumping fences, breaking down hedges, galloping like madmen, and then we found him at Genappe. The bridge was so crammed with refugees that he couldn't get his barouche across."

Mary watched carefully as George, uninvited, told the story that he must, by now, have told a hundred times, and wondered why he was telling it now to someone with such a clear distaste for things military. His color was high, and he was still breathing hard from his exercise; sweat gleamed on his immaculate forehead and matted his shirt; she could see the pulse throbbing in his throat. Perhaps the swordplay and sight of the road had brought the memory back; perhaps he was merely, after all, trying to impress her.

A female, of course. Damn the man.

"They'd brought a white Arab up for him to ride away," George went on. "His Chasseurs of the Guard were close around. I told each trooper to mark his enemy as we rode up—we came up at a slow trot, in silence, our weapons sheathed. In the dark the enemy took us for French—our uniforms were similar enough. I gave the signal—we drew pistols and carbines—half the French saddles were emptied in an instant. Some poor lad of a cornet tried to get in my way, and I cut him up through the teeth. Then there he was—the Emperor. With one foot in the stirrup, and Roustam the Mameluke ready to boost him into the saddle."

A tigerish, triumphant smile spread across George's face. His eyes were focused down the road, not seeing her at all. "I put my dripping point in his face, and for the life of me I couldn't think of any French to say except to tell him to sit down. *'Asseyez-vous!'* I ordered, and he gave me a sullen look and sat down, right down in the muddy roadway, with the carbines still cracking around us and bullets flying through the air. And I thought, He's finished. He's done. There's nothing left of him now. We finished off his bodyguard—they hadn't a chance after our first volley. The French soldiers around us thought we were the Prussian advance guard, and they were running as fast as their legs could carry them. Either they didn't know we had their Emperor or they didn't care. So we dragged Boney's barouche off the road, and dragged Boney with it, and ten minutes later the Prussians galloped up—the Death's Head Hussars under Gneisenau, all in black and silver, riding like devils. But the devils had lost the prize."

Looking at the wild glow in George's eyes Mary realized that she'd been wrong—the story was not for her at all, but for *him*. For George. He needed it somehow, this affirmation of himself, the enunciated remembrance of his moment of triumph.

But why? Why did he need it?

She realized his eyes were on her. "Would you like to see the coach, Miss Godwin?" he asked. The question surprised her.

"It's here?"

"I kept it." He laughed. "Why not? It was mine. What Captain Austen would call a fair prize of war." He offered her his arm. She took it, curious about what else she might discover.

The black mastiff began slavering at her the second she set foot inside the courtyard. Its howls filled the air. "Hush, Picton," George said, and walked straight to the big gold-trimmed blue coach with vermilion wheels. The door had the Byron arms and the Latin motto CREDE BYRON.

Should she believe him? Mary wondered. And if so, how much?

"This is Bonaparte's?" she said.

"Was, Miss Godwin. Till June 16th last. *Down*, Picton!" The dog lunged at him, and he wrestled with it, laughing, until it calmed down and began to fawn on him.

George stepped to the door and opened it. "The Imperial symbols are still on the lining, as you see." The door and couch were lined with rich purple, with golden bees and the letter N worked in heavy gold embroidery. "Fine Italian leatherwork," he said. "Drop-down secretaires so that the great man could write or dictate on the march. Holsters for pistols." He knocked on the coach's polished side. "Bulletproof. There are steel panels built in, just in case any of the Great Man's subjects decided to imitate Marcus Brutus." He smiled. "I was glad for that steel in Paris, I assure you, with Bonapartist assassins lurking under every tree." A mischievous gleam entered his eye. "And last, the best thing of all." He opened a compartment under one of the seats and withdrew a solid silver chamber pot. "You'll notice it still bears the imperial N."

"Vanity in silver."

"Possibly. Or perhaps he was afraid one of his soldiers would steal it if he didn't mark it for his own."

Mary looked at the preposterous object and found herself laughing.

George looked pleased and stowed the chamber pot in its little cabinet. He looked at her with his head cocked to one side. "You will not reconsider my offer?"

"No." Mary stiffened. "Please don't mention it again."

The mastiff Picton began to howl again, and George seized its collar and told it to behave itself. Mary turned to see Claire walking toward them.

"Won't you be joining us for breakfast, my lord?"

George straightened. "Perhaps a crust or two. I'm not much for breakfast."

Still fasting, Mary thought. "It would make such sense for you to give up meat, you know," she said. "Since you deprive yourself of food anyway."

"I prefer not to deny myself pleasure, even if the quantities are necessarily restricted."

"Your swordplay was magnificent."

"Thank you. Cavalry style, you know—all slash and dash. But I *am* good, for a' that."

"I know you're busy, but—" Claire bit her lip. "Will you take us to Waterloo?"

"Claire!" cried Mary.

Claire gave a nervous laugh. "Truly," she said. "I'm absolutely with child to see Waterloo."

George looked at her, his eyes intent. "Very well," he said. "We'll be driving through it in any case. And Captain Austen has expressed an interest."

Fury rose in Mary's heart. "Claire, how dare you impose—"

"Ha' ye nae pity for the puir lassie?" The Scots voice was mock-severe. "Ye shallnae keep her fra' her Waterloo."

Claire's Waterloo, Mary thought, was exactly what she wanted to keep her from.

George offered them his exaggerated, flourishing bow. "If you'll excuse me, ladies, I must give the necessary orders."

He strode through the door. Pásmány followed, the swords tucked under his arm. Claire gave a little joyous jump, her shoes scraping on cobbles. "I can hardly believe it," she said. "Byron showing us Waterloo!"

"I can't believe it either," Mary said. She sighed wearily and headed for the dining room.

Perhaps she would dare to sip a little milk.

They rode out in Napoleon's six-horse barouche, Claire, Mary, and Bysshe inside with George, and Smith, Somerset, and Captain Austen sharing the outside rear seat. The leather top with its bulletproof steel inserts had been folded away and the inside passengers could all enjoy the open air. The barouche wasn't driven by a coachman up top, but by three postboys who rode the right-hand horses, so there was nothing in front to interrupt the view. Bysshe's mule and little carriage, filled with bags and books, ate dust behind along with the officers' baggage coaches, all driven by George's servants.

The men talked of war and Claire listened to them with shining eyes. Mary concentrated on enjoying the shape of the low hills with their whitewashed farmhouses and red tile roofs, the cut fields of golden rye stubble, the smell of wildflowers and the sound of birdsong. It was only when the carriage passed a walled farm, its whitewash marred by bullets and cannon shot, that her reverie was marred by the thought of what had happened here.

"La Haye Sainte," George remarked. "The King's German Legion held it throughout the battle, even after they'd run out of ammunition. I sent Mercer's horse guns to keep the French from the walls, else Lord knows what would have happened." He stood in the carriage, looked left and right, frowned. "These roads we're about to pass were sunken—an obstacle to both sides, but mainly to the French. They're filled in now. Mass graves."

"The French were cut down in heaps during their cavalry attack," Somerset added. "The piles were eight feet tall, men and horses."

"How gruesome!" laughed Claire.

"Turn right, Swinson," said George.

Homemade souvenir stands had been set up at the crossroads. Prosperous-looking rustics hawked torn uniforms, breastplates, swords, muskets, bayonets. Somerset scowled at them. "They must have made a fortune looting the dead."

"And the living," said Smith. "Some of our poor wounded weren't brought in till two days after the battle. Many had been stripped naked by the peasants."

A young man ran up alongside the coach, shouting in French. He explained he had been in the battle, a guide to the great Englishman Lord Byron, and would guide them over the field for a few guilders.

"Never heard of you," drawled George, and dismissed him. "Hey! Swinson! Pull up here."

The postboys pulled up their teams. George opened the door of the coach and strolled to one of the souvenir stands. When he returned it was with a French breastplate and helmet. Streaks of rust dribbled down the breastplate, and the helmet's horsehair plume smelled of mildew.

"I thought we could take a few shots at it," George said. "I'd like to see whether armor provides any protection at all against bullets—I'll wager not. There's a movement afoot at Whitehall to give breastplates to the Household Brigade, and I suspect they ain't worth the weight. If I can shoot a few holes in this with my Mantons, I may be able to prove my point."

They drove down a rutted road of soft earth. It was lined with thorn hedges, but most of them had been broken down during the battle and there were long vistas of rye stubble, the gentle sloping ground, the pattern of plow and harvest. Occasionally the coach wheels grated on something, and Mary remembered they were moving along a mass grave, over the decaying flesh and whitening bones of hundreds of horses and men. A cloud passed across the sun, and she shivered.

"Can ye pull through the hedge, Swinson?" George asked. "I think the ground is firm enough to support us—no rain for a few days at least." The lead postboy studied the hedge with a practiced eye, then guided the lead team through a gap in it.

The barouche rocked over exposed roots and broken limbs, then ground onto a rutted sward of green grass, knee-high, that led gently down into the valley they'd just crossed. George stood again, his eyes scanning the ground. "Pull up over there," he said, pointing, and the coachman complied.

"Here you can see where the battle was won," George said. He tossed his clanging armor out onto the grass, opened the coach door and stepped out himself. The others followed, Mary reluctantly. George pointed with one elegant hand at the ridge running along the opposite end of the valley from their own, a half-mile opposite.

"Napoleon's grand battery," he said. "Eighty guns, many of them twelve-pounders—Boney called them his daughters. He was an artillerist, you know, and he always prepared his attacks with a massed bombardment. The guns fired for an hour and put our poor fellows through hell. Bylandt's Dutchmen were standing in the open, right where we are now, and the guns broke 'em entirely.

"Then the main attack came, about two o'clock. Count d'Erlon's corps, 16,000 strong, arrayed 25 men deep with heavy cavalry on the wings. They captured La Haye and Papelotte, those farms over there on the left, and rolled up this ridge with drums beating the *pas de charge...*"

George turned. There was a smile on his face. Mary watched him closely—the pulse was beating like d'Erlon's drums in his throat, and his color was high. He was loving every second of this.

He went on, describing the action, and against her will Mary found herself seeing it, Picton's division lying in wait, prone on the reverse slope, George bringing the heavy cavalry up, the cannons banging away. Picton's men rising, firing their volleys, following with the bayonet. The Highlanders screaming in Gaelic, their plumes nodding as they drew their long broadswords and plunged into the fight, the pipers playing "Johnnie Cope" amid all the screams and clatter. George leading the Household and Union Brigades against the enemy cavalry, the huge grain-fed English hunters driving back the chargers from Normandy. And then George falling on d'Erlon's flanks, driving the French in a frightened mob all the way back across the valley while the British horsemen slashed at their backs. The French gunners of the grand battery unable to fire for fear of hitting their own men, and then dying themselves under the British sabres.

Mary could sense as well the things George left out. The sound of steel grating on bone. Wails and moans of the wounded, the horrid challenging roars of the horses. And in the end, a valley filled with stillness, a carpet of bodies and pierced flesh...

George gave a long sigh. "Our cavalry are brave, you know, far too brave for their own good. And the officers get their early training in steeplechases and the hunt, and their instinct is to ride straight at the objective at full gallop, which is absolutely the worst thing cavalry can ever do. After Slade led his command to disaster back in the Year Twelve, the Duke realized he could only commit cavalry at his peril. In Spain we finally trained the horse to maneuver and to make careful charges, but the Union and Household troops hadn't been in the Peninsula, and didn't know the drill... I drove myself mad in the weeks before the battle, trying to beat the recall orders into them." He laughed self-consciously. "My heart was in my mouth during the whole charge, I confess, less with fear of the enemy than with terror my own men would run mad. But they answered the trumpets, all but the Inniskillings, who wouldnae listen—the Irish blood was up—and while they ran off into the valley, the rest of us stayed in the grand battery. Sabred the gunners, drove off the limbers with the ready ammunition—and where we could we took the wheels off the guns, and rolled 'em back to our lines like boys with hoops. And the Inniskillings—" He shook his head. "They ran wild into the enemy lines, and Boney loosed his lancers at 'em, and they died almost to a man. I had to watch from the middle of the battery, with my officers begging to be let slip again and rescue their comrades, and I had to forbid it."

There were absolute tears in George's eyes. Mary watched in fascination and wondered if this was a part of the performance, or whether he was genuinely affected—but then she saw that Bysshe's eyes had misted over and Somerset was wiping his eyes with his one good sleeve. So, she thought, she could believe Byron, at least a little.

"Well." George cleared his throat, trying to control himself. "Well. We came back across the valley herding thousands of prisoners—and that charge proved the winning stroke. Boney attacked later, of course—all his heavy cavalry came knee-to-knee up the middle, between La Haye Sainte and Hougoumont," gesturing to the left with one arm, "we had great guns and squares of infantry to hold them, and my heavies to counterattack. The Prussians were pressing the French at Plancenoit and Papelotte. Boney's last throw of the dice sent the Old Guard across the valley after sunset, but our Guards under Maitland held them, and Colborne's 52nd and the Belgian Chasseurs got round their flanks, and after they broke I let the Household and Union troopers have their head—we swept 'em away. Sabred and trampled Boney's finest troops right in front of his eyes, all in revenge for the brave, mad Inniskillings—the only time his Guard ever failed in attack, and it marked the end of his reign. We were blown by the end of it, but Boney had nothing left to counterattack with. I knew he would flee. So I had a fresh horse brought up and went after him."

"So *you* won the battle of Waterloo!" said Claire.

George gave her a modest look that, to Mary, seemed false as the very devil. "I was privileged to have a decisive part. But 'twas the Duke that won the battle. We all fought at his direction."

"But you captured Napoleon and ended the Empire!"

He smiled. "That I did do, lassie, ay."

"Bravo!" Claire clapped her hands.

Harry Smith glanced up with bright eyes. "D'ye know, George," he said, "pleased as I am to hear this modest recitation of your accomplishments, I find precious little mention in your discourse of the *infantry*. I seem to remember fighting a few Frenchies myself, down Hougoumont way, with Reille's whole corps marching down on us, and I believe I can recollect in my dim footsoldier's mind that I stood all day under cannon shot and bursting mortar bombs, and that Kellerman's heavy cavalry came wave after wave all afternoon, with the Old Guard afterward as a lagniappe..."

"I am pleased that you had some little part," George said, and bowed from his slim cavalry waist.

"Your lordship's condescension does you more credit than I can possibly express." Returning the bow.

George reached out and gave Smith's ear an affectionate tweak.

"May I continue my tale? And then we may travel to Captain Harry's part of the battlefield, and he will remind us of whatever small role it was the footsoldiers played."

George went through the story of Napoleon's capture again. It was the same, sentiment for sentiment, almost word for word. Mary wandered away, the fat moist grass turning the hem of her skirt green. Skylarks danced through the air, trilling as they went. She wandered by the old broken thorn hedge and saw wild roses blossoming in it, and she remembered the wild roses planted on her mother's grave.

She thought of George Gordon Noël with tears in his eyes, and the way the others had wanted to weep—even Bysshe, who hadn't been there—and all for the loss of some Irishmen who, had they been crippled or out of uniform or begging for food or employment, these fine English officers would probably have turned into the street to starve…

She looked up at the sound of footsteps. Harry Smith walked up and nodded pleasantly. "I believe I have heard George give this speech," he said.

"So have I. Does he give it often?"

"Oh yes." His voice dropped, imitated George's limpid dramatics. *"He's finished. He's done. There's nothing left of him now."* Mary covered amusement with her hand. "Though the tale has improved somewhat since the first time," Smith added. "In this poor infantryman's opinion."

Mary gave him a careful look. "Is he all he seems to think he is?"

Smith gave a thin smile. "Oh, ay. The greatest cavalryman of our time, to be sure. Without doubt a genius. *Chevalier sans peur et—* well, I won't say *sans reproche*. Not quite." His brow contracted as he gave careful thought to his next words. "He purchased his way up to colonel—that would be with Lady Newstead's money—but since then he's earned his spurs."

"He truly is talented, then."

"Truly. But of course he's lucky, too. If Le Marchant hadn't died at Salamanca, George wouldn't have been able to get his heavy brigade, and if poor General Cotton hadn't been shot by our own sentry George wouldn't have got all the cavalry in time for Vitoria, and of course if Uxbridge hadn't run off with Wellington's sister-in-law then George might not have got command at Waterloo… Young and without political influence as he is, he wouldn't have *kept* all those commands for long if he hadn't spent his every leave getting soused with that unspeakable hound, the Prince of Wales. Ay, there's been luck involved. But who won't wish for luck in his life, eh?"

"What if his runs out?"

Smith gave this notion the same careful consideration. "I don't know," he said finally. "He's fortune's laddie, but that don't mean he's without character."

"You surprise me, speaking of him so frankly."

"We've been friends since Spain. And nothing I say will matter in any case." He smiled. "Besides, hardly anyone ever asks for *my* opinion."

The sound of Claire's laughter and applause carried across the sward. Smith cocked an eye at the other party. "Boney's at sword's point, if I'm not mistaken."

"Your turn for glory."

"Ay. If anyone will listen after George's already won the battle." He held out his arm and Mary took it. "You should meet my wife. Juanita—I met her in Spain at the storming of Badajoz. The troops were carrying away the loot, but I carried her away instead." He looked at her thoughtfully. "You have a certain spirit in common."

Mary felt flattered. "Thank you, Captain Smith. I'm honored by the comparison."

They moved to another part of the battlefield. There was a picnic overlooking the château of Hougoumont that lay red-roofed in its valley next to a well-tended orchard. Part of the château had been destroyed in the battle, Smith reported, but it had been rebuilt since. Rebuilt, Mary thought, by owners enriched by battlefield loot.

George called for his pistols and moved the cuirass a distance away, propping it up on a small slope with the helmet sitting on top. A servant brought the Mantons and loaded them, and while the others stood and watched, George aimed and fired. Claire clapped her hands and laughed, though there was no discernible effect. White gunsmoke drifted on the morning breeze. George presented his second pistol, paused to aim, fired again. There was a whining sound and a scar appeared on the shoulder of the cuirass. The other men laughed.

"That cuirassier's got you for sure!" Harry Smith said.

"May I venture a shot?" Bysshe asked. George assented.

One of George's servants reloaded the pistols while George gave Bysshe instruction in shooting. "Hold the arm out straight and use the bead to aim."

"I like keeping the elbow bent a little," Bysshe said. "Not tucked in like a duelist, but not locked, either."

Bysshe took effortless aim—Mary's heart leaped at the grace of his movement—then Bysshe paused an instant and fired. There was a thunking sound and a hole appeared in the French breastplate, directly over the heart.

"Luck!" George said.

"Yes!" Claire said. "Purest luck!"

"Not so," Bysshe said easily. "Observe the plume holder." He presented the other pistol, took briefest aim, fired. With a little whine the helmet's metal plume holder took flight and whipped spinning through the air. Claire applauded and gave a cheer.

Mary smelled powder on the gentle morning wind.

Bysshe returned the pistols to George. "Fine weapons," he said, "though I prefer an octagonal barrel, as you can sight along the top."

George smiled thinly and said nothing.

"Mr. Shelley," said Somerset, "you have the makings of a soldier."

"I've always enjoyed a good shoot," Bysshe said, "though of course I won't fire at an animal. And as for soldiering, who knows what I might have been were I not exposed to Mr. Godwin's political thought?"

There was silence at this. Bysshe smiled at George. "You shouldn't lock the elbow out," he said. "That fashion, every little motion of the body transmits itself to the weapon. If you keep the elbow bent a bit, it forms a sort of a spring to absorb involuntary muscle tremors and you'll have better control." He looked at the others gaily. "It's not for nothing I was an engineer!"

George handed the pistols to his servant for loading. "We'll fire another volley," he said. His voice was curt.

Mary watched George as the Mantons were loaded, as he presented each pistol—straight-armed—and fired again. One knocked the helmet off its perch, the other struck the breastplate at an angle and bounced off. The others laughed, and Mary could see a little muscle twitching in George's cheek.

"My turn, George," said Harry Smith, and the pistols were recharged. His first shot threw up turf, but the second punched a hole in the cuirass. "There," Smith said, "that should satisfy the Horse Guards that armor ain't worth the weight."

Somerset took his turn, firing awkwardly with his one hand, and missed both shots.

"Another volley," George said.

There was something unpleasant in his tone, and the others took hushed notice. The pistols were reloaded. George presented the first pistol at the target, and Mary could see how he was vibrating with passion, so taut his knuckles were white on the pistol-grip. His shots missed clean.

"Bad luck, George," Somerset said. His voice was calming.

"Probably the bullets were deformed and didn't fly right."

"Another volley," said George.

"We have an appointment in Brussels, George."

"It can wait."

The others drew aside and clustered together while George insisted on firing several more times. "What a troublesome fellow he is," Smith muttered. Eventually George put some holes in the cuirass, collected it, and stalked to the coach, where he had the servants strap it to the rear so that he could have it sent to the Prince of Wales.

Mary sat as far away from George as possible. George's air of defiant petulance hung over the company as they started north on the Brussels road. But then Bysshe asked Claire to sing, and Claire's high, sweet voice rose above the green countryside of Brabant, and by the end of the song everyone was smiling. Mary flashed Bysshe a look of gratitude.

The talk turned to war again, battles and sieges and the dead, a long line of uniformed shadows, young, brave men who fell to the French, to accident, to camp fever. Mary had little to say on the subject that she hadn't already offered, but she listened carefully, felt the soldiers' sadness at the death of comrades, the rejoicing at victory, the satisfaction of a deadly, intricate job done well. The feelings expressed seemed fine, passionate, even a little exalted.

Bysshe listened and spoke little, but gradually Mary began to feel that he was somehow included in this circle of men and that she was not—perhaps his expert pistol shooting had made him a part of this company.

A female, of course. War was a fraternity only, though the suffering it caused made no distinction as to sex.

"May I offer an observation?" Mary said.

"Of course," said Captain Austen.

"I am struck by the passion you show when speaking of your comrades and your—shall I call it your *craft?*"

"Please, Miss Godwin," George said. "The enlisted men may have a *craft,* if you like. We are gentlemen, and have a *profession.*"

"I intended no offense. But still—I couldn't help but observe the fine feelings you show towards your comrades, and the attention you give to the details of your…profession."

George seemed pleased. "Ay. Didn't I speak last night of war being full of its own kind of greatness?"

"Greatness perhaps the greater," Bysshe said, "by existing in contrast to war's wretchedness."

"Precisely," said George.

"Ay," Mary said, "but what struck me most was that you gentlemen showed such elevated passion when discussing war, such sensibility, high feeling, and utter conviction—more than I am accustomed to seeing from any…respectable males." Harry Smith gave an uncomfortable laugh at this characterization.

"Perhaps you gentlemen practice war," Mary went on, "because it allows free play to your passions. You are free to feel, to exist at the highest pitch of emotion. Society does not normally permit this to its members—perhaps it must in order to make war attractive."

Bysshe listened to her in admiration. "Brava!" he cried. "War as the sole refuge of the passions—I think you have struck the thing exactly."

Smith and Somerset frowned, working through the notion. It was impossible to read Austen's weathered countenance. But George shook his head wearily.

"Mere stuff, I'm afraid," he said. "Your analysis shows an admirable ingenuity, Miss Godwin, but I'm afraid there's no more place for passion on the battlefield than anywhere else. The poor Inniskillings had passion, but look what became of *them*." He paused, shook his head again. "No, it's drill and cold logic and a good eye for ground that wins the battles. In my line it's not only my own sensibility that must be mastered, but those of hundreds of men and horses."

"Drill is meant to master the passions," said Captain Austen. "For in a battle, the impulse, the overwhelming passion, is to run away. This impulse must be subdued."

Mary was incredulous. "You claim not to experience these elevated passions which you display so plainly?"

George gave her the insolent, under-eyed look again. "All passions have their place, Miss Godwin. I reserve mine for the appropriate time."

Resentment snarled up Mary's spine. "Weren't those tears I saw standing in your eyes when you described the death of the Inniskillings? Do you claim that's part of your drill?"

George's color brightened. "I didn't shed those tears during the battle. At the time I was too busy damning those cursed Irishmen for the wild fools they were, and wishing I'd flogged more of them when I'd the chance."

"But wasn't Bonaparte's great success on account of his ability to inspire his soldiers and his nation?" Bysshe asked. "To raise their passions to a great pitch and conquer the world?"

"And it was the uninspired, roguey English with their drill and discipline who put him back in his place," George said. "Bonaparte should have saved the speeches and put his faith in the drill-square."

Somerset gave an amused laugh. "This conversation begins to sound like one of Mrs. West's novels of Sense and Sensibility that were so popular in the Nineties," he said. "I suppose you're too young to recall them. *A Gossip's Story,* and *The Advantages of Education.* My governess made me read them both."

Harry Smith looked at Captain Austen with glittering eyes. "In fact—" he began.

Captain Austen interrupted. "One is not blind to the world of feeling," he said, "but surely Reason must rule the passions, else even a good heart can be led astray."

"I can't agree," Bysshe said. "Surely it is Reason that has led us to the world of law, and property, and equity, and kingship—and all the hypocrisy that comes with upholding these artificial formations, and denying our true nature, all that deprives us of life, of true and natural goodness."

"Absolutely!" said Claire.

"It is Reason," Mary said, "which makes you deny the evidence of my senses. I *saw* your emotion, gentlemen, when you discussed your dead comrades. And I applaud it."

"It does you credit," Bysshe added.

"Do you claim not to feel anything in battle?" Mary demanded. "Nothing at all?"

George paused a moment, then answered seriously. "My concentration is very great. It is an elevated sort of apprehension, very intent. I must be aware of so much, you see—I can't afford to miss a thing. My analytical faculty is always in play."

"And that's all?" cried Mary.

That condescending half-smile returned. "There isnae time for else, lass."

"At the height of a charge? In the midst of an engagement?"

"Then especially. An instant's break in my concentration and all could be lost."

"Lord Newstead," Mary said, "I cannot credit this."

George only maintained his slight smile, knowing and superior.

Mary wanted to wipe it from his face, and considered reminding him of his fractious conduct over the pistols. *How's that for control and discipline,* she thought.

But no, she decided, it would be a long, unpleasant ride to Brussels if she upset George again.

Against her inclinations, she concluded to be English, and hypocritical, and say nothing.

Bysshe found neither wife nor money in Brussels, and George arranged lodgings for them that they couldn't afford. The only option Mary could think of was to make their way to a channel port, then somehow try to talk their way to England with promise of payment once Bysshe had access to funds in London.

It was something for which she held little hope.

They couldn't afford any local diversions, and so spent their days in a graveyard, companionably reading.

And then, one morning two days after their arrival in Brussels, as Mary lay ill in their bed, Bysshe returned from an errand with money, coins clanking in a bag. "We're saved!" he said, and emptied the bag into her lap.

Mary looked at the silver lying on the comforter and felt her anxiety ease. They were old Spanish coins with the head of George III stamped over their original design, but they were real for all that.

"A draft from Har…from your wife?" she said.

"No." Bysshe sat on the bed, frowned. "It's a loan from Byron—Lord Newstead, I mean."

"Bysshe!" Mary sat up and set bedclothes and silver flying. "You took money from that man? Why?"

He put a paternal hand on hers. "Lord Newstead convinced me it would be in your interest, and Claire's. To see you safely to England."

"We'll do well enough without his money! It's not even his to give away, it's his wife's."

Bysshe seemed hurt. "It's a loan," he said. "I'll pay it back once I'm in London." He gave a little laugh. "I'm certain he doesn't expect repayment. He thinks we're vagabonds."

"He thinks worse of us than that." A wave of nausea took her and she doubled up with a little cry. She rolled away from him. Coins rang on the floor. Bysshe put a hand on her shoulder, stroked her back.

"Poor Pecksie," he said. "Some English cooking will do you good."

"Why don't you believe me?" Tears welled in her eyes. "I'm with child, Bysshe!"

He stroked her. "Perhaps. In a week or two we'll know for certain." His tone lightened. "He invited us to a ball tonight."

"Who?"

"Newstead. The ball's in his honor, he can invite whomever he pleases. The Prince of Orange will be there, and the English ambassador."

Mary had no inclination to be the subject of one of George's freaks.

"We have no clothes fit for a ball," she said, "and I don't wish to go in any case."

"We have money now. We can buy clothes." He smiled. "And Lord Newstead said he would loan you and Claire some jewels."

"Lady Newstead's jewels," Mary reminded.

"All those powerful people! Imagine it! Perhaps we can effect a conversion."

Mary glared at him over her shoulder. "That money is for our passage to England. George wants only to display us, his tame Radicals, like his tame monkey or his tame panther. We're just a caprice of his—he doesn't take either us or our arguments seriously."

"That doesn't invalidate our arguments. We can still make them." Cheerfully. "Claire and I will go, then. She's quite set on it, and I hate to disappoint her."

"I think it will do us no good to be in his company for an instant longer. I think he is..." She reached behind her back, took his hand, touched it. "Perhaps he is a little mad," she said.

"Byron? Really? He's *wrong,* of course, but..."

Nausea twisted her insides. Mary spoke rapidly, desperate to convince Bysshe of her opinions. "He so craves glory and fame, Bysshe. The war gave expression to his passions, gave him the achievement he desired—but now the war's over and he can't have the worship he needs. That's why he's taken up with us—he wants even *our* admiration. There's no future for him now—he could follow Wellington into politics but he'd be in Wellington's shadow forever that way. He's got nowhere to go."

There was a moment's silence. "I see you've been giving him much thought," Bysshe said finally.

"His marriage is a failure—he can't go back to England. His relations with women will be irregular, and—"

"*Our* relations are irregular, Maie. And all the better for it."

"I didn't mean that. I meant he cannot love. It's worship he wants, not love. And those pretty young men he travels with—there's something peculiar in that. Something unhealthy."

"Captain Austen is neither pretty nor young."

"He's along only by accident. Another of George's freaks."

"And if you think he's a paederast, well—we should be tolerant. Plato believed it a virtue. And George always asks after you."

"I do not wish to be in his thoughts."

"He is in yours." His voice was gentle. "And that is all right. You are free."

Mary's heart sank. "It is *your* child I have, Bysshe," she said.

Bysshe didn't answer. *Torcere,* she thought. *Attorcere, rattorcere.*

Claire's face glowed as she modeled her new ball gown, circling on the parlor carpet of the lodgings George had acquired for

Bysshe's party. Lady Newstead's jewels glittered from Claire's fingers and throat. Bysshe, in a new coat, boots, and pantaloons, smiled approvingly from the corner.

"Very lovely, Miss Clairmont," George approved.

George was in full uniform, scarlet coat, blue facings, gold braid, and byrons laced tight. His cocked hat was laid carelessly on the mantel. George's eyes turned to Mary.

"I'm sorry you are ill, Miss Godwin," he said. "I wish you were able to accompany us."

Bysshe, Mary presumed, had told him this. Mary found no reason why she should support the lie.

"I'm not ill," she said mildly. "I simply do not wish to go—I have some pages I wish to finish. A story called *Hate*."

George and Bysshe flushed alike. Mary, smiling, approached Claire, took her hand, admired gown and gems. She was surprised by the effect: the jewels, designed for an older woman, gave Claire a surprisingly mature look, older and far more experienced than her sixteen years. Mary found herself growing uneasy.

"The seamstress was shocked when she was told I needed it tonight," Claire said. "She had to call in extra help to finish in time." She laughed. "But money mended everything!"

"For which we may thank Lord Newstead," Mary said, "and Lady Newstead to thank for the jewels." She looked up at George, who was still smoldering from her earlier shot. "I'm surprised, my lord, that she allows them to travel without her."

"Annabella has her own jewels," George said. "These are mine. I travel often without her, and as I move in the highest circles, I want to make certain that any lady who finds herself in my company can glitter with the best of them."

"How chivalrous." George cocked his head, trying to decide whether or not this was irony. Mary decided to let him wonder. She folded her hands and smiled sweetly.

"I believe it's time to leave," she said. "You don't want to keep his highness of Orange waiting."

Cloaks and hats were snatched; goodbyes were said. Mary managed to whisper to Claire as she helped with her cloak.

"Be careful, Jane," she said.

Resentment glittered in Claire's black eyes. "You have a man," she said.

Mary looked at her. "So does Lady Newstead."

Claire glared hatred and swept out, fastening bonnet-strings. Bysshe kissed Mary's lips, George her hand. Mary prepared to settle by the fire with pen and manuscript, but before she could sit, there was a knock on the door and George rushed in.

"Forgot me hat," he said. But instead of taking it from the mantel, he walked to where Mary stood by her chair and simply looked at her. Mary's heart lurched at the intensity of his gaze.

"Your hat awaits you, my lord," she said.

"I hope you will reconsider," said George.

Mary merely looked at him, forced him to state his business. He took her hand in both of his, and she clenched her fist as his fingers touched hers.

"I ask you, Miss Godwin, to reconsider my offer to take you under my protection," George said.

Mary clenched her teeth. Her heart hammered. "I am perfectly safe with Mr. Shelley," she said.

"Perhaps not as safe as you think." She glared at him. George's eyes bored into hers. "I gave him money," he said, "and he told me you were free. Is that the act of a protector?"

Rage flamed through Mary. She snatched her hand back and came within an inch of slapping George's face.

"Do you think he's sold me to you?" she cried.

"I can conceive no other explanation," George said.

"You are mistaken and a fool." She turned away, trembling in anger, and leaned against the wall.

"I understand this may be a shock. To have trusted such a man, and then discovered—"

The wallpaper had little bees on it, Napoleon's emblem. "Can't you understand that Bysshe was perfectly literal!" she shouted. "I am free, he is free, Claire is free—free to go, or free to stay." She straightened her back, clenched her fists. "I will stay. Goodbye, Lord Newstead."

"I fear for you."

"Go away," she said, speaking to the wallpaper; and after a moment's silence she heard George turn, and take his hat from the mantel, and leave the building.

Mary collapsed into her chair. The only thing she could think was, *Poor Claire.*

TWO

Mary was pregnant again. She folded her hands over her belly, stood on the end of the dock, and gazed up at the Alps.

Clouds sat low on the mountains, growling. The passes were closed with avalanche and unseasonal snow, the *vaudaire* storm wind tore white from the steep waves of the gray lake, and *Ariel* pitched madly at its buoy by the waterfront, its mast-tip tracing wild figures against the sky.

The *vaudaire* had caused a "seiche"—the whole mass of the lake had shifted toward Montreux, and water levels had gone up six feet.

The strange freshwater tide had cast up a line of dead fish and dead birds along the stony waterfront, all staring at Mary with brittle glass eyes.

"It doesn't look as if we'll be leaving tomorrow," Bysshe said. He and Mary stood by the waterfront, cloaked and sheltered by an umbrella. Water broke on the shore, leaped through the air, reaching for her, for Bysshe… It spattered at her feet.

She thought of Harriet, Bysshe's wife, hair drifting, clothes floating like seaweed. Staring eyes like dark glass. Her hands reaching for her husband from the water.

She had been missing for weeks before her drowned body was finally found.

The *vaudaire* was supposed to be a warm wind from Italy, but its warmth was lost on Mary. It felt like the burning touch of a glacier.

"Let's go back to the hotel," Mary said. "I'm feeling a little weak."

She would deliver around the New Year unless the baby was again premature.

A distant boom reached her, was echoed, again and again, by mountains. Another avalanche. She hoped it hadn't fallen on any of the brave Swiss who were trying to clear the roads.

She and Bysshe returned to the hotel through darkening streets. It was a fine place, rather expensive, though they could afford it now.

Their circumstances had improved in the last year, though at cost.

Old Sir Bysshe had died, and left Bysshe a thousand pounds per year. Harriet Shelley had drowned, bricks in her pockets. Mary had given birth to a premature daughter who had lived only two weeks. She wondered about the child she carried—she had an intuition all was not well. Death, perhaps, was stalking her baby, was stalking them all.

In payment for what, Mary wondered.? What sin had they committed?

She walked through Montreux's wet streets and thought of dead glass eyes, and grasping hands, and hair streaming like seaweed.

Her daughter dying alone in her cradle at night, convulsing, twitching, eyes open and her tiny red face torn with mortal terror.

When Mary had come to the cradle later to nurse the baby, she had thought it in an unusually deep sleep. She hadn't realized that death had come until after dawn, when the little corpse turned cold.

Death. She and Bysshe had kissed and coupled on her mother's grave, had shivered together at the gothic delights of *Vathek,* had whispered ghost stories to one another in the dead of night till Claire screamed with hysteria. Somehow death had not really touched her before. She and Bysshe had crossed war-scarred France two years ago, sleeping in homes abandoned for fear of Cossacks, and somehow death had not intruded into their lives.

"Winter is coming," Bysshe said. "Do we wish to spend it in Geneva? I'd rather push on to Italy and be a happy salamander in the sun."

"I've had another letter from Mrs. Godwin."

Bysshe sighed. "England, then."

She sought his hand and squeezed it. Bysshe wanted the sun of Italy, but Bysshe was her sun, the blaze that kept her warm, kept her from despair. Death had not touched *him*. He flamed with life, with joy, with optimism.

She tried to stay in his radiance. Where his light banished the creeping shadows that followed her.

As they entered their hotel room they heard the wailing of an infant and found Claire trying to comfort her daughter Alba. "Where have you been?" Claire demanded. There were tears on her cheeks. "I fell asleep and dreamed you'd abandoned me! And then I cried out and woke the baby."

Bysshe moved to comfort her. Mary settled herself heavily onto a sofa.

In the small room in Montreux, with dark shadows creeping in the corners and the *vaudaire* driving against the shutters, Mary put her arms around her unborn child and willed the shade of death to keep away.

Bysshe stopped short in the midst of his afternoon promenade.

"Great heavens," he said. His tone implied only mild surprise— he was so filled with life and certitude that he took most of life's shocks purely in stride.

When Mary looked up, she gasped and her heart gave a crash.

It was a barouche—*the* barouche. Vermilion wheels, liveried postboys wearing muddy slickers, armorial bearings on the door, the bulletproof top raised to keep out the storm. Baggage piled on platforms fore and aft.

Rolling past as Mary and Bysshe stood on the tidy Swiss sidewalk and stared.

CREDE BYRON, Mary thought viciously. As soon credit Lucifer.

The gray sky lowered as they watched the barouche grind past, steel-rimmed wheels thundering on the cobbles. And then a window dropped on its leather strap, and someone shouted something to the postboys. The words were lost in the *vaudaire*, but the postboys pulled the horses to a stop. The door opened and George appeared, jamming a round hat down over his auburn hair. His jacket was a little tight, and he appeared to have gained a stone or more since Mary had last seen him. He walked toward Bysshe and Mary, and Mary tried not to stiffen with fury at the sight of him.

"Mr. Omnibus! Tí kánete?"

"Very well, thank you."

"Miss Godwin." George bowed, clasped Mary's hand. She closed her fist, reminded herself that she hated him.

"I'm Mrs. Shelley now."

"My felicitations," George said.

George turned to Bysshe. "Are the roads clear to the west?" he asked. "I and my companion must push on to Geneva on a matter of urgency."

"The roads have been closed for three days," Bysshe said. "There have been both rockslides and avalanches near Chexbres."

"That's what they told me in Vevey. There was no lodging there, so I came here, even though it's out of our way." George pressed his lips together, a pale line. He looked over his shoulder at the coach, at the mountainside, at the dangerous weather. "We'll have to try to force our way through tomorrow," he said. "Though it will be damned hard."

"It shouldn't," Bysshe said. "Not in a heavy coach like that."

George looked grim. "It was unaccountably dangerous just getting here," he said.

"Stay till the weather is better," Bysshe said, smiling. "You can't be blamed if the weather holds you up."

Mary hated Bysshe for that smile, even though she knew he had reasons to be obliging.

Just as she had reasons for hating.

"Nay." George shook his head, and a little Scots fell out. "I cannae bide."

"You might make it on a mule."

"I have a lady with me." Shortly. "Mules are out of the question."

"A boat...?"

"Perhaps if the lady is superfluous," Mary interrupted, "you could leave her behind, and carry out your errand on a mule, alone."

The picture was certainly an enjoyable one.

George looked at her, visibly mastered his unspoken reply, then shook his head.

"She must come."

"Lord Newstead," Mary went on, "would you like to see your daughter? She is not superfluous either, and she is here."

George glanced nervously at the coach, then back. "Is Claire here as well?"

"Yes."

George looked grim. "This is not...a good time."

Bysshe summoned an unaccustomed gravity. "I think, my lord," Bysshe said, "there may never be a better time. You have not been within five hundred miles of your daughter since her birth. You are on an urgent errand and may not tarry—very well. But you must spend a night here, and can't press on till morning. There will never be a better moment."

George looked at him stony-eyed, then nodded. "What hotel?"

"La Royale."

He smiled. "Royal, eh? A pretty sentiment for the Genevan Republic."

"We're in Vaud, not Geneva."

"Still not over the border?" George gave another nervous glance over his shoulder. "I need to set a faster pace."

His long hair streamed in the wind as he stalked back to the coach.

Mary could barely see a blonde head gazing cautiously from the window. She half-expected that the coach would drive on and she would never see George again, but instead the postboys turned the horses from the waterfront road into the town, toward the hotel.

Bysshe smiled purposefully and began to stride to the hotel. Mary followed, walking fast across the wet cobbles to keep up with him.

"I can't but think that good will come of this," he said.

"I pray you're right."

Much pain, Mary thought, however it turned out.

George's new female was tall and blonde and pink-faced, though she walked hunched over as if embarrassed by her height, and took small, shy steps. She was perhaps in her middle twenties.

They met, annoyingly, on the hotel's wide stair, Mary with Claire, Alba in Claire's arms. The tall blonde, lower lip outthrust haughtily, walked past them on the way to her room, her gaze passing blankly over them. Perhaps she hadn't been told who Alba's father was.

She had a maid with her and a pair of George's men, both of whom had pistols stuffed in their belts. For a wild moment Mary wondered if George had abducted her.

No, she decided, this was only George's theatricality. He didn't have his menagerie with him this time, no leopards or monkeys, so he dressed his postboys as bandits.

The woman passed. Mary felt Claire stiffen. "She looks like you," Claire hissed.

Mary looked at the woman in astonishment. "She doesn't. Not at all."

"She does! Tall, blonde, fair eyes..." Claire's own eyes filled with tears. "Why can't she be dark, like me?"

"Don't be absurd!" Mary seized her sister's hand, pulled her down the stairs. "Save the tears for later. They may be needed."

In the lobby Mary saw more of George's men carrying in luggage. Pásmány, the fencing master, had slung a carbine over one shoulder. Mary's mind whirled—perhaps this was an abduction after all.

Or perhaps the blonde's family—or husband—was in pursuit.

"This way." Bysshe's voice. He led them into one of the hotel's candlelit drawing rooms, closed the crystal-knobbed door behind them. A huge porcelain stove loomed over them.

George stood uncertain in the candlelight, elegant clothing over muddy boots. He looked at Claire and Alba stonily, then advanced, peered at the tiny form that Claire offered him.

"Your daughter Alba," Bysshe said, hovering at his shoulder.

George watched the child for a long, doubtful moment, his auburn hair hanging down his forehead. Then he straightened. "My offer rests, Miss Clairmont, on its previous terms."

Claire drew back, rested Alba on her shoulder. "Never," she said. She licked her lips. "It is too monstrous."

"Come, my lord," Bysshe said. He ventured to put a hand on George's shoulder. "Surely your demands are unreasonable."

"I offered to provide the child with means," George said, "to see that she is raised in a fine home, free from want, and among good people—friends of mine, who will offer her every advantage. I would take her myself but," hesitating, "my domestic conditions would not permit it."

Mary's heart flamed. "But at the cost of forbidding her the sight of her mother!" she said. "That is too cruel."

"The child's future will already be impaired by her irregular connections," George said. "Prolonging those connections could only do her further harm." His eyes flicked up to Claire. "Her mother can only lower her station, not raise it. She is best off with a proper family who can raise her with their own."

Claire's eyes flooded with tears. She turned away, clutching Alba to her. "I won't give her up!" she said. The child began to cry.

George folded his arms. "That settles matters. If you won't accept my offer, then there's an end." The baby's wails filled the air.

"Alba cries for her father," Bysshe said. "Can you not let her into your heart?"

A half-smile twitched across George's lips. "I have no absolute certainty that I *am* this child's father."

A keening sound came from Claire. For a wild, raging moment Mary looked for a weapon to plunge into George's breast.

"Unnatural man!" she cried. "Can't you acknowledge the consequences of your own behavior?"

"On the contrary, I am willing to ignore the questionable situation in which I found Miss Clairmont and to care for the child completely. But only on my terms."

"I don't trust his promises!" Claire said. "He abandoned me in Munich without a penny!"

"We agreed to part," George said.

"If it hadn't been for Captain Austen's kindness, I would have starved." She leaned on the door jamb for support, and Mary joined her and buoyed her with an arm around her waist.

"You ran out into the night," George said. "You wouldn't take money."

"I'll tell her!" Claire drew away from Mary, dragged at the door, hauled it open. "I'll tell your new woman!"

Fear leaped into George's eyes. "Claire!" He rushed to the door, seized her arm as she tried to pass; Claire wrenched herself free and staggered into the hotel lobby. Alba wailed in her arms. George's servants were long gone, but hotel guests stared as if in tableaux, hats and walking sticks half-raised. Fully aware of the spectacle they were making, Mary, clumsy in pregnancy, inserted herself between George and Claire. Claire broke for the stair, while George danced around Mary like an awkward footballer. Mary rejoiced in the fact that her pregnancy seemed only to make her more difficult to get around.

Bysshe put an end to it. He seized George's wrist in a firm grip. "You can't stop us all, my lord," he said.

George glared at him, his look all fury and ice. "What d'ye want, then?"

Claire, panting and flushed, paused halfway up the stair. Alba's alarmed shrieks echoed up the grand staircase.

Bysshe's answer was quick. "A competence for your daughter. Nothing more."

"A thousand a year," George said flatly. "No more than that."

Mary's heart leaped at the figure that doubled the family's income. Bysshe nodded. "That will do, my lord."

"I want nothing more to do with the girl than that. Nothing whatever."

"Call for pen and paper. And we can bring this to an end."

Two copies were made, and George signed and sealed them with his signet before bidding them all a frigid good-night. The first payment was made that night, one of George's men coming to the door carrying a valise that clanked with gold. Mary gazed at it in amazement—why was George carrying so much?

"Have we done the right thing?" Bysshe wondered, looking at the valise as Claire stuffed it under her bed. "This violence, this extortion?"

"We offered love," Mary said, "and he returned only finance. How else could we deal with him?" She sighed. "And Alba will thank us."

Claire straightened and looked down at the bed. "I only wanted him to pay," said Claire. "Any other considerations can go to the devil."

The *vaudaire* blew on, scarcely fainter than before. The water level was still high. Dead fish still floated in the freshwater tide. "I would venture it," Bysshe said, frowning as he watched the dancing *Ariel*, "but not with the children."

Children. Mary's smile was inward as she realized how real her new baby was to Bysshe. "We can afford to stay at the hotel a little longer," she said.

"Still—a reef in the mains'l would make it safe enough."

Mary paused a moment, perhaps to hear the cold summons of Harriet Shelley from beneath the water. There was no sound, but she shivered anyway. "No harm to wait another day."

Bysshe smiled at her hopefully. "Very well. Perhaps we'll have a chance to speak to George again."

"Bysshe, sometimes your optimism is…" She shook her head. "Let us finish our walk."

They walked on through windswept morning streets. The bright sun glared off the white snow and deadly black ice that covered the surrounding high peaks. Soon the snow and ice would melt and threaten avalanche once more. "I am growing weary with this town," Bysshe said.

"Let's go back to our room and read *Chamouni,*" Mary suggested.

Mr. Coleridge had been a guest of her father's, and his poem about the Alps a favorite of theirs now they were lodged in Switzerland.

Bysshe was working on writing another descriptive poem on the Vale of Chamouni—unlike Coleridge, he and Mary had actually seen the place—and as an *homage* to Coleridge, Bysshe was including some reworked lines from *Kubla Khan.*

The everlasting universe of things, she recited to herself, *flows through the mind.*

Lovely stuff. Bysshe's best by far.

On their return to the hotel they found one of George's servants waiting for them. "Lord Newstead would like to see you."

Ah, Mary thought. *He wants his gold back.*

Let him try to take it.

George waited in the same drawing room in which he'd made his previous night's concession. Despite the bright daylight the room was still lit by lamps—the heavy dark curtains were drawn against the *vaudaire.* George was standing straight as a whip in the center of the room, a dangerous light in his eyes. Mary wondered if this was how he looked in battle.

"Mr. Shelley," George said, and bowed, "I would like to hire your boat to take my party to Geneva."

Bysshe blinked. "I—" he began, then, "*Ariel* is small, only twenty-five feet. Your party is very large and—"

"The local commissaire visited me this morning," George interrupted. "He has forbidden me to depart Montreux. As it is vital for me to leave at once, I must find other means. And I am prepared to pay well for them."

Bysshe looked at Mary, then at George. Hesitated again. "I suppose it would be possible…"

"Why is it," Mary demanded, "that you are forbidden to leave?"

George folded his arms, looked down at her. "I have broken no law. It is a ridiculous political matter."

Bysshe offered a smile. "If that's all, then…"

Mary interrupted. "If Mr. Shelley and I end up in jail as a result of this, I wonder how ridiculous it will seem."

Bysshe looked at her, shocked. "Mary!"

Mary kept her eyes on George. "Why should we help you?"

"Because…" He paused, ran a nervous hand through his hair. Not used, Mary thought, to justifying himself.

"Because," he said finally, "I am assisting someone who is fleeing oppression."

"Fleeing a husband?"

"Husband?" George was startled. "No—her husband is abroad and cannot protect her." He stepped forward, his color high, his nostrils flared like those of a warhorse. "She is fleeing the attentions of a seducer—a powerful man who has callously used her to gain wealth and influence. I intend to aid her in escaping his power."

Bysshe's eyes blazed. "Of course I will aid you!"

Mary watched this display of chivalry with a sinking heart. The masculine confraternity had excluded her, had lost her within its own rituals and condescension.

"I will pay you a further hundred—" George began.

"Please, my lord. I and my little boat are entirely at your service in this noble cause."

George stepped forward, clasped his hand. "Mr. Omnibus, I am in your debt."

The *vaudaire* wailed at the window. Mary wondered if it was Harriet's call, and her hands clenched into fists. She would resist the cry if she could.

Bysshe turned to Mary. "We must prepare." Heavy in her pregnancy, she followed him from the drawing room, up the stair, toward their own rooms. "I will deliver Lord Newstead and his lady to Geneva, and you and Claire can join me there when the roads are cleared. Or if weather is suitable I will return for you."

"I will go with you," Mary said. "Of course."

Bysshe seemed surprised that she would accompany him on this piece of masculine knight-errantry. "It may not be entirely safe on the lake," he said.

"I'll make it safer—you'll take fewer chances with me aboard. And if I'm with you, George is less likely to inspire you to run off to South America on some noble mission or other."

"I wouldn't do that." Mildly. "And I think you are being a little severe."

"What has George done for us that we should risk anything for him?"

"I do not serve him, but his lady."

"Of whom he has told you nothing. You don't even know her name. And in any case, you seem perfectly willing to risk *her* life on this venture."

Alba's cries sounded through the door of their room. Bysshe paused a moment, resignation plain in his eyes, then opened the door. "It's for Alba, really," he said. "The more contact between George and our little family, the better it may be for her. The better chance we will have to melt his heart."

He opened the door. Claire was holding her colicky child. Tears filled her black eyes. "Where have you been for so long? I was afraid you were gone forever!"

"You know better than that." Mary took the baby from her, the gesture so natural that sadness took a moment to come—the memory that she had held her own lost child this way, held it to her breast and felt the touch of its cold lips.

"And what is this about George?" Claire demanded.

"He wants me to take him down the lake," Bysshe said. "And Mary wishes to join us. You and Alba can remain here until the roads are clear."

Claire's voice rose to a shriek. *"No! Never!"* She lunged for Alba and snatched the girl from Mary's astonished arms. "You're going to abandon me—just like George! You're all going to Geneva to laugh at me!"

"Of course not," Bysshe said reasonably.

Mary stared at her sister, tried to speak, but Claire's cries trampled over her intentions.

"You're abandoning me! I'm useless to you—worthless! You'll soon have your own baby!"

Mary tried to comfort Claire, but it was hopeless. Claire screamed and shuddered and wept, convinced that she would be left forever in Montreux. In the end there was no choice but to take her along. Mary received mean satisfaction in watching Bysshe as he absorbed this reality, as his chivalrous, noble-minded expedition alongside the hero of Waterloo turned into a low family comedy, George and his old lover, his new lover, and his wailing bastard.

And ghosts. Harriet, lurking under the water. And their dead baby calling.

Ariel bucked like a horse on the white-topped waves as the *vaudaire* keened in the rigging. Frigid spray flew in Mary's face and her feet slid on slippery planking. Her heart thrashed into her throat. The boat seemed half-full of water. She gave a despairing look over her shoulder at the retreating rowboat they'd hired to bring them from the jetty to their craft.

"Bysshe!" she said. "This is hopeless."

"Better once we're under way. See that the cuddy will be comfortable for Claire and Alba."

"This is madness."

Bysshe licked joyfully at the freshwater spray that ran down his lips. "We'll be fine, I'm sure."

He was a much better sailor than she: she had to trust him. She opened the sliding hatch to the cuddy, the little cabin forward, and saw several inches of water sloshing in the bottom. The cushions on the little seats were soaked. Wearily, she looked up at Bysshe.

"We'll have to bail."

"Very well."

It took a quarter hour to bail out the boat, during which time Claire paced back and forth on the little jetty, Alba in her arms. She looked like a specter with her pale face peering out from her dark shawl.

Bysshe cast off the gaskets that reefed the mainsail to the boom, then jumped forward to the halyards and raised the sail on its gaff. The wind tore at the canvas with a sound like a cannonade, open-hand slaps against Mary's ears. The shrouds were taut as bowstrings. Bysshe reefed the sail down, hauled the halyards and topping lift again till the canvas was taut, lowered the leeboards, then asked Mary to take the tiller while he cast *Ariel* off from its buoy.

Bysshe braced himself against the gunwale as he hauled on the mooring line, drawing *Ariel* up against the wind. When Bysshe cast off from the buoy the boat paid instantly off the wind and the sail filled with a rolling boom. Water surged under the boat's counter and suddenly, before Mary knew it, *Ariel* was flying fast. Fear closed a fist around her windpipe as the little boat heeled and the tiller almost yanked her arms from their sockets. She could hear Harriet's wails in the windsong. Mary dug her heels into the planks and hauled the tiller up to her chest, keeping *Ariel* up into the wind.

Frigid water boiled up over the lee counter, pouring into the boat like a waterfall.

Bysshe leapt gracefully aft and released the mainsheet. The sail boomed out with a crash that rattled Mary's bones and the boat righted itself. Bysshe took the tiller from Mary, sheeted in, leaned out into the wind as the boat picked up speed. There was a grin on his face.

"Sorry!" he said. "I should have let the sheet go before we set out."

Bysshe tacked and brought *Ariel* into the wind near the jetty. The sail boomed like thunder as it spilled wind. Waves slammed the boat into the jetty. The mast swayed wildly. The stone jetty was at least four feet taller than the boat's deck. Mary helped Claire with the luggage—gold clanked heavily in one bag—then took Alba while Bysshe assisted Claire into the boat.

"It's *wet*," Claire said when she saw the cuddy.

"Take your heavy cloak out of your bags and sit on it," Mary said.

"This is *terrible*," Claire said, and lowered herself carefully into the cuddy.

"Go forrard," Bysshe said to Mary, "and push off from the jetty as hard as you can."

Forrard. Bysshe so enjoyed being nautical. Clumsy in skirts and pregnancy, Mary climbed atop the cuddy and did as she was asked.

The booming sail filled, Mary snatched at the shrouds for balance, and *Ariel* leaped from the jetty like a stone from a child's catapult.

Mary made her way across the tilting deck to the cockpit. Bysshe was leaning out to weather, his big hands controlling the tiller easily, his long fair hair streaming in the wind.

"I won't ask you to do that again," he said. "George should help from this point."

George and his lady would join the boat at another jetty—there was less chance that the authorities would intervene if they weren't seen where another Englishman was readying his boat.

Ariel raced across the waterfront, foam boiling under its counter.

The second jetty—a wooden one—approached swiftly, with cloaked figures upon it. Bysshe rounded into the wind, canvas thundering, and brought Ariel neatly to the dock. George's men seized shrouds and a mooring line and held the boat in its place.

George's round hat was jammed down over his brows and the collar of his cloak was turned up, but any attempt at anonymity was wrecked by his famous laced boots. He seized a shroud and leaped easily into the boat, then turned to help his lady.

She had stepped back, frightened by the gunshot cracks of the luffing sail, the wild swings of the boom. Dressed in a blue silk dress, broad-brimmed bonnet, and heavy cloak, she frowned with her haughty lower lip, looking disdainfully at the little boat and its odd collection of passengers.

George reassured his companion. He and one of his men, the swordmaster Pásmány, helped her into the boat, held her arm as she ducked under the boom.

George grabbed the brim of his hat to keep the wind from carrying it away and performed hasty introductions. "Mr. and Mrs. Shelley. The Comtesse Laufenburg."

Mary strained her memory, trying to remember if she'd ever heard the name before. The comtesse smiled a superior smile and tried to be pleasant. "Enchanted to make cognizance of you," she said in French.

A baby wailed over the sound of flogging canvas. George straightened, his eyes a little wild.

"Claire is here?" he asked.

"She did not desire to be *abandoned* in Montreux," Mary said, trying to stress the word "abandoned."

"My God!" George said. "I wish you had greater consideration of the...realities."

"Claire is free and may do as she wishes," Mary said.

George clenched his teeth. He took the comtesse by her arm and drew her toward the cuddy.

"The boat will be better balanced," Bysshe called after, "if the comtesse will sit on the weather side." *And perhaps,* Mary thought, *we won't capsize.*

George gave Bysshe a blank look. "The larboard side," Bysshe said helpfully. Another blank look.

"Hang it! The left."

"Very well."

George and the comtesse ducked down the hatchway. Mary would have liked to have eavesdropped on the comtesse's introduction to Claire, but the furious rattling sail obscured the phrases, if any.

George came up, looking grim, and Pásmány began tossing luggage toward him. Other than a pair of valises, most of it was military: a familiar-looking pistol case, a pair of sabers, a brace of carbines.

George stowed it all in the cuddy. Then Pásmány himself leaped into the boat, and George signaled all was ready. Bysshe placed George by the weather rail, and Pásmány squatted on the weather foredeck.

"If you gentlemen would push us off?" Bysshe said.

The sail filled and *Ariel* began to move fast, rising at each wave and thudding into the troughs. Spray rose at each impact. Bysshe trimmed the sail, the luff trembling just a little, the rest full and taut, then cleated the mainsheet down.

"A long reach down the length of the lake," Bysshe said with a smile. "Easy enough sailing, if a little hard on the ladies."

George peered out over the cuddy, his eyes searching the bank. The old castle of Chillon bulked ominously on the shore, just south of Montreux.

"When do we cross the border into Geneva?" George asked.

"Why does it matter?" Bysshe said. "Geneva joined the Swiss Confederation last year."

"But the administrations are not yet united. And the more jurisdictions that lie between the comtesse and her pursuers, the happier I will be."

George cast an uncomfortable look astern. With spray dotting his cloak, his hat clamped down on his head, his body disposed awkwardly on the weather side of the boat, George seemed thoroughly miserable—and in an overwhelming flood of sudden understanding, Mary suddenly knew why. It was over for him. His noble birth, his fame, his entire life to this point—all was as naught. Passion had claimed him for its own. His career had ended: there was no place for him in the army, in diplomatic circles, even in polite society. He'd thrown it all away in this mad impulse.

He was an exile now, and the only people whom he could expect to associate with him were other exiles.

Like the exiles aboard *Ariel*.

Perhaps, Mary thought, he was only now realizing it. Poor George. She actually felt sorry for him.

The castle of Chillon fell astern, like a grand symbol of George's hopes, a world of possibility not realized.

"Beg pardon, my lord," she said, "but where do you intend to go?"

George frowned. "France, perhaps," he said. "The comtesse has…some friends…in France. England, if France won't suit, but we won't be able to stay there long. America, if necessary."

"Can the Prince Regent intervene on your behalf?"

George's smile was grim. "If he wishes. But he's subject to strange fits of morality, particularly if the sins in question remind him of his own. Prinny will *not* wish to be reminded of Mrs. Fitzherbert and Lady Hertford. He *does* wish to look upright in the eyes of the nation. And he has no loyalty to his friends, none at all." He gave a poised, slow-motion shrug. "Perhaps he will help, if the fit is on him. But I think not." He reached inside his greatcoat, patted an inside pocket. "Do you think I can light a cigar in this wind? If so, I hope it will not discomfort you, Mrs. Shelley."

He managed a spark in his strike-a-light, puffed madly till the tinder caught, then ignited his cigar and turned to Bysshe. "I found your poems, Mr. Omnibus. Your *Queen Mab* and *Alastor*. The latter of which I liked better, though I liked both well enough."

Bysshe looked at him in surprise. Wind whistled through the shrouds. "How did you find *Mab*? There were only seventy copies, and I'm certain I can account for each one."

George seemed pleased with himself. "There are few doors closed to me." Darkness clouded his face. "Or rather, *were*." With a sigh.

He wiped spray from his ear with the back of his hand.

"I'm surprised that you liked *Mab* at all," Bysshe said quickly, "as its ideas are so contrary to your own."

"You expressed them well enough. As a verse treatise of Mr. Godwin's political thought, I thought it done as soundly as such a thing can be done. And I think you can have it published properly now—it's hardly a threat to public order, Godwin's thought being so out of fashion even among radicals."

He drew deliberately on his cigar, then waved it. The wind tore the cigar smoke from his mouth in little wisps. "*Alastor,* though better poetry, seemed in contrast to have little thought behind it. I never understood what that fellow was doing on the boat—was it a metaphor for life? I kept waiting for something to *happen.*"

Mary bristled at George's condescension. What are *you* doing on this little boat? she wanted to ask.

Bysshe, however, looked apologetic. "I'm writing better things now."

"He's writing *wonderful* things now," Mary said. "An ode to Mont Blanc. An essay on Christianity. A hymn to intellectual beauty."

George gave her an amused look. "Mrs. Shelley's tone implies that, to me, intellectual beauty is entirely a stranger, but she misunderstands my point. I found it remarkable that the same pen could produce both *Queen Mab* and *Alastor,* and have no doubt that so various a talent will produce very good work in the poetry line—provided," nodding to Bysshe, "that Mr. Shelley continues in it, and doesn't take up engineering again, or chemistry." He grinned. "Or become a sea captain."

"He is and remains a poet," Mary said firmly. She used a corner of her shawl to wipe spray from her cheek.

"Who else do you like, my lord?" Bysshe asked.

"Poets, you mean? Scott, above all. Shakespeare, who is sound on political matters as well as having a magnificent...shall I call it a *stride?* Burns, the great poet of my country. And our Laureate."

"Mr. Southey was kind to me when we met," Bysshe said. "And Mrs. Southey made wonderful tea cakes. But I wish I admired his work more." He looked up. "What do you think of Milton? The Maie and I read him constantly."

George shrugged. "Dour Puritan fellow. I'm surprised you can stand him at all."

"His verse is glorious. And he wasn't a Puritan, but an Independent, like Cromwell—his philosophy was quite unorthodox. He believed, for example, in plural marriage."

George's eyes glittered. "Did he now?"

"Ay. And his Satan is a magnificent creation, far more interesting than any of his angels or his simpering pedantic Christ. That long, raging fall from grace, into darkness visible."

George's brows knit. Perhaps he was contemplating his own long fall from the Heaven of polite society. His eyes turned to Mary.

"And how is the originator of Mr. Shelley's political thought? How does your father, Mrs. Shelley?"

"He is working on a novel. An important work."

"I am pleased to hear it. Does he progress?"

Mary was going to answer simply "Very well," but Bysshe's answer came first. "Plagued by lack of money," he said. "We will be going to England to succor him after this, ah, errand is completed."

"Your generosity does you credit," George said, and then resentment entered his eyes and his lip curled. "Of course, you will be able to better afford it, now."

Bysshe's answer was mild. "Mr. Godwin lives partly with our support, but he will not speak to us since I eloped with his daughter. You will not acknowledge Alba, but at least you've been... persuaded...to do well by her."

George preferred not to rise to this, settled instead for clarification.

"You support a man who won't acknowledge you?"

"It is not my father-in-law I support, but rather the author of *Political Justice*."

"A nice discernment," George observed. "Perhaps over-nice."

"One does what goodness one can. And one hopes people will respond." Looking at George, who smiled cynically around his cigar.

"Your charity speaks well for you. But perhaps Mr. Godwin would have greater cause to finish his book if poverty were not being made so convenient for him."

Mary felt herself flushing red. But Bysshe's reply again was mild.

"It isn't that simple. Mr. Godwin has dependents, and the public that once celebrated his thought has, alas, forgotten him. His novel may retrieve matters. But a fine thing such as this work cannot be rushed—not if it is to have the impact it deserves."

"I will bow to your expertise in matters of literary production. But still...to support someone who will not even speak to you— that is charity indeed. And it does not speak well for Mr. Godwin's gratitude."

"My father is a great man!" Mary knew she was speaking hotly, and she bit back on her anger. "But he judges by a...a very high standard of morality. He will accept support from a sincere admirer, but he has not yet understood the depth of sentiment between Bysshe and myself, and believes that Bysshe has done my reputation harm—not," flaring again, "that I would care if he had."

Ariel thudded into a wave trough, and George winced at the impact.

He adjusted his seat on the rail and nodded. "Mr. Godwin will accept money from an admirer, but not letters from an in-law. And Mr. Shelley will support the author of *Political Justice,* but not his in-laws."

"And *you*," Mary said, "will support a blackmailer, but not a daughter."

George's eyes turned to stone. Mary realized she had gone too far for this small boat and close company.

"Gentlemen, it's cold," she announced. "I will withdraw."

She made her way carefully into the cuddy. The tall comtesse was disposed uncomfortably, on wet cushions, by the hatch, the overhead planking brushing the top of her bonnet. Her gaze was mild, but her lip was haughty. There was a careful three inches between her and Claire, who was nursing Alba and, clearly enough, a grudge.

Mary walked past them to the peak, sat carefully on a wet cushion near Claire. Their knees collided every time *Ariel* fell down a wave.

The cuddy smelled of wet stuffing and stale water. There was still water sluicing about on the bottom.

Mary looked at Claire's baby and felt sadness like an ache in her breast.

Claire regarded her resentfully. "The French bitch hates us," she whispered urgently. "Look at her expression."

Mary wished Claire had kept her voice down. Mary leaned out to look at the comtesse, managed a smile. *"Vous parlez anglais?"* she asked.

"Non. Je regrette. Parles-tu français?" The comtesse had a peculiar accent. As, with a name like Laufenburg, one might expect.

Pleasant of her, though, to use the intimate *tu*. *"Je comprends un peu."* Claire's French was much better than Mary's, but Claire clearly had no interest in conversation.

The comtesse looked at the nursing baby. A shadow flitted across her face. "My own child," in French, "I was forced to leave behind."

"I'm sorry." For a moment Mary hated the comtesse for having a child to leave, that and for the abandonment itself.

No. Bysshe, she remembered, had left his own children. It did not make one unnatural. Sometimes there were circumstances.

Speech languished after this unpromising beginning. Mary leaned her head against the planking and tried to sleep, sadly aware of the cold seep of water up her skirts. The boat's movement was too violent to be restful, but she composed herself deliberately for sleep. Images floated through her mind: the great crumbling keep of Chillon, standing above the surging gray water like the setting of one of "Monk" Lewis's novels; a gray cat eating a blushing rose; a figure, massive and threatening, somehow both George and her father Godwin, flinging back the bed-curtains to reveal, in the bright light of morning, the comtesse Laufenburg's placid blonde face with its outthrust, Habsburg lip.

Habsburg. Mary sat up with a cry and banged her skull on the deckhead.

She cast a wild look at Claire and the comtesse, saw them both drowsing, Alba asleep in Claire's lap. The boat was rolling madly in a freshening breeze: there were ominous, threatening little shrieks of wind in the rigging. The cuddy stank badly.

Mary made her way out of the cuddy, clinging to the sides of the hatch as the boat sought to pitch her out. Bysshe was holding grimly to the tiller with one big hand, controlling the sheet with the other while spray soaked his coat; George and Pásmány were hanging on to the shrouds to keep from sliding down the tilted deck.

Astern was Lausanne, north of the lake, and the Cornettes to the south; and Mont Billiat, looming over the valley of the Dranse to the south, was right abeam: they were smack in the middle of the lake, with the *vaudaire* wind funneling down the valley, stronger than ever with the mountain boundary out of the way.

Mary seized the rail, hauled herself up the tilting deck toward George. "I know your secret," she said. "I know who your woman is."

George's face ran with spray; his auburn hair was plastered to the back of his neck. He fixed her with eyes colder than the glaciers of Mont Blanc. "Indeed," he said.

"Marie-Louise of the house of Habsburg." Hot anger pulsed through her, burned against the cold spindrift on her face. "Former Empress of the French!"

Restlessly, George turned his eyes away. "Indeed," he said again.

Mary seized a shroud and dragged herself to the rail next to him.

Bysshe watched in shock as Mary shouted into the wind. "Her husband abroad! Abroad, forsooth—all the way to St. Helena! Forced to leave her child behind, because her father would never let Napoleon's son out of his control for an instant. Even a Habsburg lip—my God!"

"Very clever, Miss Godwin. But I believe you have divined my sentiments on the subject of clever women." George gazed ahead, toward Geneva. "Now you see why I wish to be away."

"I see only vanity!" Mary raged. "Colossal vanity! You can't stop fighting Napoleon even now! Even when the battlefield is only a bed!"

George glared at her. "Is it my damned fault that Napoleon could never keep his women?"

"It's your damned fault that *you* keep her!"

George opened his mouth to spit out a reply and then the *vaudaire*, like a giant hand, took *Ariel's* mast in its grasp and slammed the frail boat over. Bysshe cried out and hauled the tiller to his chest and let the mainsheet go, all far too late. The deck pitched out from under Mary's heels and she clung to the shrouds for dear life.

Pásmány shouted in Hungarian. There was a roar as the sail hit the water. The lake foamed over the lee rail and the wind tore Mary's breath away. There were screams from the cuddy as water poured into the little cabin.

"Halyards and topping lift!" Bysshe gasped. He was clinging to the weather rail: a breaker exploded in his face and he gasped for air.

"Let 'em go!"

If the sail filled with water all was lost. Mary let go of the shroud and palmed her way across the vertical deck. Freezing lakewater clutched at her ankles. Harriet Shelley shrieked her triumph in Mary's ears like the wind. Mary lurched forward to the mast, flung the halyard and topping lift off their cleats. The sail sagged free, empty of everything but the water that poured onto its canvas surface, turning it into a giant weight that would drag the boat over.

Too late.

"Save the ladies, George!" Bysshe called. His face was dead-white but his voice was calm. "I can't swim!"

Water boiled up Mary's skirts. She could feel the dead weight dragging her down as she clutched at George's leg and hauled herself up the deck. She screamed as her unborn child protested, a gouging pain deep in her belly.

George raged wildly. "Damn it, Shelley, what can I *do*?" He had a leg over one of the shrouds; the other was Mary's support. The wind had taken his hat and his cloak rattled around him like wind-filled canvas.

"Cut the mast free!"

George turned to Mary. "My sword! Get it from the cabin!"

Mary looked down and into the terrified black eyes of Claire, half-out of the cuddy. She held a wailing Alba in her arms. "Take the baby!" she shrieked.

"Give me a sword!" Mary said. A wave broke over the boat, soaking them all in icy rain. Mary thought of Harriet smiling, her hair trailing like seaweed.

"Save my baby!"

"*The sword! Byron's sword! Give it!*" Mary clung to George's leg with one hand and thrust the crying babe away with the other.

"*I hate you!*" Claire shrieked, but she turned and fumbled for George's sword. She held it up out of the hatch, and Mary took the cut steel hilt in her hand and drew it rasping from the scabbard. She held it blindly above her head and felt George's firm hand close over hers and take the sabre away. The pain in her belly was like a knife. Through the boat and her spine she felt the thudding blows as George hacked at the shrouds, and then there was a rending as the mast splintered and *Ariel,* relieved of its top-hamper, swung suddenly upright.

Half the lake seemed to splash into the boat as it came off its beam-ends. George pitched over backwards as *Ariel* righted itself, but Mary clung to his leg and kept him from going into the lake while he dragged himself to safety over the rail.

Another wave crashed over them. Mary clutched at her belly and moaned. The pain was ebbing. The boat pirouetted on the lake as the wind took it, and then *Ariel* jerked to a halt. The wreckage of the mast was acting as a sea-anchor, moderating the wave action, keeping the boat stable. Alba's screams floated high above *Ariel's* remains.

Wood floats, Mary remembered dully. And *Ariel* was wood, no matter how much water slopped about in her bottom.

Shelley staggered to his feet, shin-deep in lake water. "By God, George," he gasped. "You've saved us."

"By God," George answered, "so I have." Mary looked up from the deck to see George with the devil's light in his eyes, his color high and his sabre in his hand. So, she reckoned, he must have seemed to Napoleon at Genappe. George bent and peered into the cuddy.

"Are the ladies all right?"

"*Je suis bien, merci.*" From the Austrian princess.

"Damn you to hell, George!" Claire cried. George only grinned.

"I see we are well," he said.

And then Mary felt the warm blood running down the insides of her legs, and knew that George was wrong.

Mary lay on a bed in the farmhouse sipping warm brandy.

Reddening cloths were packed between her legs. The hemorrhage had not stopped, though at least there was no pain. Mary could feel the child moving within her, as if struggling in its terror. Over the click of knitting needles, she could hear the voices of the men in the kitchen, and smell George's cigar.

The large farm, sitting below its pastures that stretched up the Noirmont, was owned by a white-mustached old man named Fleury, a man who seemed incapable of surprise or confusion even when armed men arrived at his doorstep, carrying between them a bleeding woman and a sack filled with gold. He turned Mary over to his wife, hitched up his trousers, put his hat on, and went to St. Prex to find a doctor.

Madame Fleury, a large woman unflappable as her husband, tended Mary and made her drink a brandy toddy while she sat by Mary and did her knitting.

When Fleury returned, his news wasn't good. The local surgeon had gone up the road to set the bones of some workmen caught in an avalanche—perhaps there would be amputations—but he would return as soon as he could. The road west to Geneva was still blocked by the slide; the road east to Lausanne had been cleared. George seemed thoughtful at the news. His voice echoed in from the kitchen. "Perhaps the chase will simply go past," he said in English.

"What sort of pursuit do you anticipate?" Bysshe asked. "Surely you don't expect the Austrian Emperor to send his troops into Switzerland."

"Stranger things have happened," George said. "And it may not be the Emperor's own people after us—it might be Neipperg, acting on his own."

Mary knew she'd heard the name before, and tried to recall it. But Bysshe said, "The general? Why would he be concerned?"

There was cynical amusement in George's voice. "Because he's her highness's former lover! I don't imagine he'd like to see his fortune run away."

"Do you credit him with so base a motive?"

George laughed. "In order to prevent Marie-Louise from joining Bonaparte, Prince Metternich *ordered* von Neipperg to leave his wife and to seduce her highness—and that one-eyed scoundrel was only too happy to comply. His reward was to be the co-rulership of Parma, of which her highness was to be Duchess."

"Are you certain of this?"

"Metternich told me at his dinner table over a pipe of tobacco. And Neipperg *boasted* to me, sir!" A sigh, almost a snarl, came from George. "My heart wrung at his words, Mr. Shelley. For I had already met her highness and—" Words failed him for a moment. "I determined to rescue her from Neipperg's clutches, though all the Hungarian Grenadiers of the Empire stood in the way!"

"That was most admirable, my lord," Bysshe said quietly.

Claire's voice piped up. "Who is this Neipperg?"

"Adam von Neipperg is a cavalry officer who defeated Murat," Bysshe said. "That's all I know of him."

George's voice was thoughtful. "He's the best the Austrians have. Quite the *beau sabreur,* and a diplomat as well. He persuaded Crown Prince Bernadotte to switch sides before the battle of Leipzig. And yes, he defeated Murat on the field of Tolentino, a few weeks before

Waterloo. Command of the Austrian army was another of Prince Metternich's rewards for his…services."

Murat, Mary knew, was Napoleon's great cavalry general. Neipperg, the best Austrian cavalryman, had defeated Murat, and now Britain's greatest horseman had defeated Napoleon *and* Neipperg, one on the battlefield and both in bed.

Such a competitive little company of cavaliers, she thought. Madame Fleury's knitting needles clacked out a complicated pattern.

"You think he's going to come after you?" Bysshe asked.

"*I* would," simply. "And neither he nor I would care what the Swiss think about it. And he'll find enough officers who will want to fight for the, ah, *honor* of their royal family. And he certainly has scouts or agents among the Swiss looking for me—surely one of them visited the commissaire of Montreux."

"I see." Mary heard the sound of Bysshe rising from his seat. "I must see to Mary."

He stepped into the bedroom, sat on the edge of the bed, took her hand. Madame Fleury barely looked up from her knitting.

"Are you better, Pecksie?"

"Nothing has changed." *I'm still dying,* she thought.

Bysshe sighed. "I'm sorry," he said, "to have exposed you to such danger. And now I don't know what to do."

"And all for so little."

Bysshe was thoughtful. "Do you think liberty is so little? And Byron—the voice of monarchy and reaction—fighting for freedom! Think of it!"

My life is bleeding away, Mary thought incredulously, *and his child with it.* There was poison in her voice when she answered.

"This isn't about the freedom of a woman, it's about the freedom of one man to do what he wants."

Bysshe frowned at her.

"He can't love," Mary insisted. "He felt no love for his wife, or for Claire." Bysshe tried to hush her—her voice was probably perfectly audible in the kitchen. But it was pleasing for her not to give a damn.

"It's not love he feels for that poor woman in the cellar," she said. "His passions are entirely concerned with himself—and now that he can't exorcise them on the battlefield, he's got to find other means."

"Are you certain?"

"He's a half-crazed whirlwind of destruction! Look what he did to Claire. And now he's wrecked *Ariel,* and he may yet involve us all in a battle—with Austrian cavalry, forsooth! He'll destroy us all if we let him."

"Perhaps it will not come to that."

George appeared in the door. He was wrapped in a blanket and carried a carbine, and if he was embarrassed by what he'd heard, he failed to display it. "With your permission, Mr. Shelley, I'm going to try to sink your boat. It sits on a rock just below our location, a pistol pointed at our head."

Bysshe looked at Mary. "Do as you wish."

"I'll give you privacy, then." And pointedly closed the door.

Mary heard his bootsteps march out, the outside door open and close. She put her hand on Bysshe's arm. *I am bleeding to death,* she thought. "Promise me you will take no part in anything," she said. "George will try to talk you into defending the princess—he knows you're a good shot."

"But what of Marie-Louise? To be dragged back to Austria by force of arms—what a prospect! An outrage, inhuman and degrading."

I am bleeding to death, Mary thought. But she composed a civil reply. "Her condition saddens me. But she was born a pawn and has lived a pawn her entire life. However this turns out, she will be a pawn either of George or of Metternich, and we cannot change that. It is the evil of monarchy and tyranny that has made her so. We may be thankful we were not born among her class."

There were tears in Bysshe's eyes. "Very well. If you think it best, I will not lift a hand in this."

Mary put her arms around him, held herself close to his warmth. She clenched trembling hands behind his back. *Soon,* she thought, *I will lack the strength to do even this. And then I will die.*

There was a warm and spreading lake between her legs. She felt very drowsy as she held Bysshe, the effects of the brandy, and she closed her eyes and tried to rest. Bysshe stroked her cheek and hair.

Mary, for a moment, dreamed.

She dreamed of pursuit, a towering, shrouded figure stalking her over the lake—but the lake was frozen, and as Mary fled across the ice she found other people standing there, people to whom she ran for help only to discover them all dead, frozen in their places and covered with frost. Terrified, she ran among them, seeing to her further horror that she knew them all: her mother and namesake; and Mr. Godwin; and George, looking at her insolently with eyes of black ice; and lastly the figure of Harriet Shelley, a woman she had never met in life but who Mary knew at once. Harriet stood rooted to a patch of ice and held in her arms the frost-swathed figure of a child. And despite the rime that covered the tiny face, Mary knew at once, and with agonized despair, just whose child Harriet carried so triumphantly in her arms.

She woke, terror pounding in her heart. There was a gunshot from outside. She felt Bysshe stiffen. Another shot. And then the sound of pounding feet.

"They're here, damn it!" George called. "And my shot missed!"

Gunfire and the sound of hammering swirled through Mary's perceptions. Furniture was shifted, doors barricaded, weapons laid ready. The shutters had already been closed against the *vaudaire,* so no one had to risk himself securing the windows. Claire and Alba came into Mary's room, the both of them screaming; and Mary, not giving a damn any longer, sent them both out. George put them in the cellar with the Austrian princess—Mary was amused that they seemed doomed to share quarters together. Bysshe, throughout, only sat on the bed and held Mary in his arms. He seemed calm, but his heart pounded against her ear.

M. Fleury appeared, loading an old Charleville musket as he off-handedly explained that he had served in one of Louis XVI's mercenary Swiss regiments. His wife put down her knitting needles, poured buckshot into the pockets of her apron, and went off with him to serve as his loader. Afterwards Mary wondered if that particular episode, that vision of the old man with his gun and powder horn, had been a dream—but no, Madame Fleury was gone, her pockets filled with lead.

Eventually the noise died away. George came in with his Mantons stuffed in his belt, looking pleased with himself. "I think we stand well," he said. "This place is fine as a fort. At Waterloo we held Hougoumont and La Haye Sainte against worse—and Neipperg will have no artillery. The odds aren't bad—I counted only eight of them." He looked at Bysshe. "Unless you are willing to join us, Mr. Shelley, in defense of her highness's liberty."

Bysshe sat up. "I wish no man's blood on my hands." Mary rejoiced at the firmness in his voice.

"I will not argue against your conscience, but if you won't fight, then perhaps you can load for me?"

"What of Mary?" Bysshe asked.

Indeed, Mary thought. *What of me?*

"Can we arrange for her, and for Claire and Alba, to leave this house?"

George shook his head. "They don't dare risk letting you go—you'd just inform the Swiss authorities. I could negotiate a cease-fire to allow you to become their prisoners, but then you'd be living in the barn or the outdoors instead of more comfortably in here." He looked down at Mary. "I do not think we should move your lady in any case. Here in the house it is safe enough."

"But what if there's a battle? My God—there's already been shooting!"

"No one was hurt, you'll note—though if I'd had a Baker or a jager rifle instead of my puisny little carbine, I daresay I'd have dropped one of them. No—what will happen now is that they'll either try an assault, which will take a while to organize, because they're all scattered out watching the house, and which will cost them dearly in the end…or they'll wait. They don't know how many people we have in here, and they'll be cautious on that account. We're inside, with plenty of food and fuel and ammunition, and they're in the outdoors facing unseasonably cold weather. And the longer they wait, the more likely it will be that our local Swiss yeomen will discover them, and then…" He gave a low laugh. "Austrian soldiers have never fared well in Switzerland, not since the days of William Tell. Our Austrian friends will be arrested and imprisoned."

"But the surgeon? Will they not let the surgeon pass?"

"I can't say."

Bysshe stared. "My God! Can't you speak to them?"

"I will ask if you like. But I don't know what a surgeon can do that we cannot."

Bysshe looked desperate. "There must be something that will stop the bleeding!"

Yes, Mary thought. *Death. Harriet has won.*

George gazed down at Mary with thoughtful eyes. "A Scotch midwife would sit her in a tub of icewater."

Bysshe stiffened like a dog on point. "Is there ice? Is there an ice cellar?" He rushed out of the room. Mary could hear him stammering out frantic questions in French, then Fleury's offhand reply. When Bysshe came back he looked stricken. "There is an icehouse, but it's out behind the barn."

"And in enemy hands." George sighed. "Well, I will ask if they will permit Madame Fleury to bring ice into the house, and pass the surgeon through when he comes."

George left the room and commenced a shouted conversation in French with someone outside. Mary winced at the volume of George's voice. The voice outside spoke French with a harsh accent.

No, she understood. They would not permit ice or a surgeon to enter the house.

"They suspect a plot, I suppose," George reported. He stood wearily in the doorway. "Or they think one of my men is wounded."

"They want to make you watch someone die," Mary said. "And hope it will make you surrender."

George looked at her. "Yes, you comprehend their intent," he said. "That is precisely what they want."

Bysshe looked horrified.

George's look turned intent. "And what does Mistress Mary want?"

Mary closed her eyes. "Mistress Mary wants to live, and to hell with you all."

George laughed, a low and misanthropic chuckle. "Very well. Live you shall—and I believe I know the way."

He returned to the other room, and Mary heard his raised voice again. He was asking, in French, what the intruders wanted, and in passing comparing their actions to Napoleon's abduction of the Duc d'Enghien, justly abhorred by all nations.

"A telling hit," Mary said. "Good old George." She wrapped her two small pale hands around one of Bysshe's big ones.

The same voice answered, demanding that her highness the Duchess of Parma be surrendered. George returned that her highness was here of her own free will, and that she commanded that they withdraw to their own borders and trouble her no more.

The emissary said his party was acting for the honor of Austria and the House of Habsburg. George announced that he felt free to doubt that their shameful actions were in any way honorable, and he was prepared to prove it, *corps-à-corps*, if *Feldmarschall-leutnant* von Neipperg was willing to oblige him.

"My God!" Bysshe said. "He's calling the blackguard out!"

Mary could only laugh. A duel, fought for an Austrian princess and Mary's bleeding womb.

The other asked for time to consider. George gave it.

"This neatly solves our dilemma, don't it?" he said after he returned. "If I beat Neipperg, the rest of those German puppies won't have direction—they'd be on the road back to Austria. Her royal highness and I will be able to make our way to a friendly country. No magistrates, no awkward questions, and a long head start." He smiled. "And all the ice in the world for Mistress Mary."

"And if you lose?" Bysshe asked.

"It ain't to be thought of. I'm a master of the sabre, I practice with Pásmány almost daily, and whatever Neipperg's other virtues I doubt he can compare with me in the art of the sword. The only question," he turned thoughtful, "is whether we can trust his offer. If there's treachery—"

"Or if he insists on pistols!" Mary found she couldn't resist pointing this out. "You didn't precisely cover yourself with glory the last time I saw you shoot."

George only seemed amused. "Neipperg only has one eye— I doubt he's much of a shot, either. My second would have to insist on a sabre fight," and here he smiled, *"pour l'honneur de la cavalerie."*

Somehow Mary found this satisfying. "Go fight, George. I know you love your legend more than you ever loved that Austrian girl— and this will make a nice end to it."

George only chuckled again, while Bysshe looked shocked.

"Truthful Mistress Mary," George said. "Never without your sting."

"I see no point in politeness from this position."

"You would have made a good soldier, Mrs. Shelley."

Longing fell upon Mary. "I would have made a better mother," she said, and felt tears sting her eyes.

"God, Maie!" Bysshe cried. "What I would not give!" He bent over her and began to weep.

It was, Mary considered, about time, and then reflected that death had made her satirical.

George watched for a long moment, then withdrew. Mary could hear his boots pacing back and forth in the kitchen, and then a different, younger voice called from outside.

The *Feldmarschall-leutnant* had agreed to the encounter. He, the new voice, was prepared to present himself as von Neipperg's second.

"A soldier all right," George commented. "Civilian clothes, but he's got that sprig of greenery that Austrian troops wear in their hats."

His voice lifted. "That's far enough, laddie!" He switched to French and said that his second would be out shortly. Then his bootsteps returned to Mary's rooms and put a hand on Bysshe's shoulder.

"Mr. Shelley," he said, "I regret this intrusion, but I must ask—will you do me the honor of standing my second in this affaire?"

"Bysshe!" Mary cried. "Of course not!"

Bysshe blinked tear-dazzled eyes but managed to speak clearly enough. "I'm totally opposed to the practice. It's vicious and wasteful and utterly without moral foundation. It reeks of death and the dark ages and ruling-class affectation."

George's voice was gentle. "There are no other gentlemen here," he said. "Pásmány is a servant, and I can't see sending our worthy M. Fleury out to negotiate with those little noblemen. And—" He looked at Mary. "Your lady must have her ice and her surgeon."

Bysshe looked stricken. "I know nothing of how to manage these encounters," he said. "I would not do well by you. If you were to fall as a result of my bungling, I should never forgive myself."

"I will tell you what to say, and if he doesn't agree, then bring negotiations to a close."

"Bysshe," Mary reminded, "you said you would have nothing to do with this."

Bysshe wiped tears from his eyes and looked thoughtful.

"Don't you see this is theater?" Mary demanded. "George is adding this scene to his legend—he doesn't give a damn for anyone here!"

George only seemed amused. "You are far from death, madam, I think, to show such spirit," he said. "Come, Mr. Shelley! Despite what Mary thinks, a fight with Neipperg is the only way we can escape without risking the ladies."

"No," Mary said.

Bysshe looked thoroughly unhappy. "Very well," he said. "For Mary's sake, I'll do as you ask, provided I do no violence myself.

But I should say that I resent being placed in this…*extraordinary* position in the first place."

Mary settled for glaring at Bysshe.

More negotiations were conducted through the window, and then Bysshe, after receiving a thorough briefing, straightened and brushed his jacket, brushed his knees, put on his hat, and said goodbye to Mary. He was very pale under his freckles.

"Don't forget to point out," George said, "that if von Neipperg attempts treachery, he will be instantly shot dead by my men firing from this house."

"Quite."

He left Mary in her bed. George went with him, to pull away the furniture barricade at the front door.

Mary realized she wasn't about to lie in bed while Bysshe was outside risking his neck. She threw off the covers and went to the window. Unbarred the shutter, pushed it open slightly.

Wet coursed down her legs.

Bysshe was holding a conversation with a stiff young man in an overcoat. After a few moments, Bysshe returned and reported to George. Mary, feeling like a guilty child, returned to her bed.

"Baron von Strickow—that's Neipperg's second—was taken with your notion of the swordfight *pour la cavalerie,* but insists the fight should be on horseback." He frowned. "They know, of course, that you haven't a horse with you."

"No doubt they'd offer me some nag or other." George thought for a moment. "Very well. I find the notion of a fight on horseback too piquant quite to ignore—tell them that if they insist on such a fight, they must bring forward six saddled horses, and that I will pick mine first, and Neipperg second."

"Very well."

Bysshe returned to the negotiations, and reported back that all had been settled. "With ill grace, as regards your last condition. But he conceded it was fair." Bysshe returned to Mary's room, speaking to George over his shoulder. "Just as well you're doing this on horseback. The yard is wet and slippery—poor footing for sword work."

"I'll try not to do any quick turns on horseback, either." George stepped into the room, gave Mary a glance, then looked at Bysshe.

"Your appreciation of our opponents?"

"The Baron was tired and mud-covered. He's been riding hard. I don't imagine the rest of them are any fresher." Bysshe sat by Mary and took her hand. "He wouldn't shake my hand until he found out my father was a baronet. And then I wouldn't shake his."

"Good fellow!"

Bysshe gave a self-congratulatory look. "I believe it put him out of countenance."

George was amused. "These kraut-eaters make me look positively democratic." He left to give Pásmány his carbine and pistols—"the better to keep Neipperg honest."

"What of the princess?" Mary wondered. "Do you suppose he will bother to tell her of these efforts on her behalf?"

Shortly thereafter came the sound of the kitchen trap being thrown open, and George's bootheels descending to the cellar. Distant French tones, the sound of female protest, George's calm insistence, Claire's furious shrieks. George's abrupt reply, and then his return to the kitchen.

George appeared in the door, clanking in spurs and with a sword in his hand. Marie-Louise, looking pale, hovered behind him.

Mary looked up at Bysshe. "You won't have to participate in this any longer, will you?"

George answered for him. "I'd be obliged if Mr. Shelley would help me select my horse. Then you can withdraw to the porch—but if there's treachery, be prepared to barricade the door again."

Bysshe nodded. "Very well." He rose and looked out the window. "The horses are coming, along with the Baron and a one-eyed man."

George gave a cursory look out the window. "That's the fellow. He lost the eye at Neerwinden—French sabre cut." His voice turned inward. "I'll try to attack from his blind side—perhaps he'll be weaker there."

Bysshe was more interested in the animals. "There are three white horses. What are they?"

"Lipizzaners of the royal stud," George said. "The Roman Caesars rode 'em, or so the Austrians claim. Small horses by the standard of our English hunters, but strong and very sturdy. Bred and trained for war." He flashed a smile. "They'll do for me, I think."

He stripped off his coat and began to walk toward the door, but recollected, at the last second, the cause of the fight and returned to Marie-Louise. He put his arms around her, murmured something, and kissed her cheek. Then, with a smile, he walked into the other room. Bysshe, deeply unhappy, followed. And then Mary, ignoring the questioning eyes of the Austrian princess, worked her way out of bed and went to the window.

From the window Mary watched as George took his time with the horses, examining each minutely, discoursing on their virtues with Bysshe, checking their shoes and eyes as if he were buying them.

The Austrians looked stiff and disapproving. Neipperg was a tall, bull-chested man, handsome despite the eyepatch, with a well-tended halo of hair.

Perhaps George dragged the business out in order to nettle his opponent.

George mounted one of the white horses and trotted it round the yard for a brief while, then repeated the experiment with a second Lipizzaner. Then he went back to the first and declared himself satisfied.

Neipperg, seeming even more rigid than before, took the second horse, the one George had rejected. Perhaps it was his own, Mary thought.

Bysshe retreated to the front porch of the farmhouse, Strickow to the barn, and the two horsemen to opposite ends of the yard. Both handled their horses expertly. Bysshe asked each if he were ready, and received a curt nod.

Mary's legs trembled. She hoped she wouldn't fall. She had to see it. *"Un,"* Strickow called out in a loud voice. *"Deux. Trois!"* Mary had expected the combatants to dash at each other, but they were too cautious, too professional—instead each goaded his beast into a slow trot and held his sabre with the hilt high, the blade dropping across the body, carefully on guard. Mary noticed that George was approaching on his opponent's blind right side. As they came together there were sudden flashes of silver, too fast for the eye to follow, and the sound of ringing steel.

Then they were past. But Neipperg, as he spurred on, delivered a vicious blind swipe at George's back. Mary cried out, but there was another clang—George had dropped his point behind his back to guard against just that attack.

"Foul blow!" Bysshe cried, from the porch, then clapped his hands. "Good work, George!"

George turned with an intent smile on his face, as if he had the measure of his opponent. There was a cry from elsewhere in the farmhouse, and Claire came running, terror in her eyes. "Are they fighting?" she wailed, and pushed past Mary to get to the window.

Mary tried to pull her back and failed. Her head swam. "You don't want to watch this," she said.

Alba began to cry from the cellar. Claire pushed the shutters wide and thrust her head out.

"Kill him, George!" she shouted. "Kill him!"

George gave no sign of having heard—he and Neipperg were trotting at each other again, and George was bent down over his horse's neck, his attention wholly on his opponent.

Mary watched over Claire's shoulder as the two approached, as blades flashed and clanged—once, twice—and then George thrust to Neipperg's throat and Mary gasped, not just at the pitilessness of it, but at its strange physical consummation, at the way horse and rider and arm and sword, the dart of the blade and momentum of the horse and rider, merged for an instant in an awesome moment of perfection…

Neipperg rode on for a few seconds while blood poured like a tide down his white shirtfront, and then he slumped and fell off his animal like a sack. Mary shivered, knowing she'd just seen a man killed, killed with absolute forethought and deliberation. And George, that intent look still on his face as he watched Neipperg over his shoulder, lowered his scarlet-tipped sword and gave a careless tug of the reins to turn his horse around…

Too careless. The horse balked, then turned too suddenly. Its hind legs slid out from under it on the slick grass, George's arms windmilled as he tried to regain his balance, and the horse, with an almost-human cry, fell heavily on George's right leg.

Claire and Mary cried out. The Lipizzaner's legs flailed in the air as he rolled over on George. Bysshe launched himself off the porch in a run. George began to scream, a sound that raised the hair on Mary's neck.

And, while Adam von Neipperg twitched away his life on the grass, Marie-Louise of Austria, France, and Parma, hearing George's cries of agony, bolted hysterically for the door and ran out into the yard and into the arms of her countrymen.

"No!" George insisted. "No surgeons!"

Not a word, Mary noted, for the lost Marie-Louise. She watched from the doorway as his friends carried him in and laid him on the kitchen table. The impassive M. Fleury cut the boot away with a pair of shears and tore the leather away with a suddenness that made George gasp. Bysshe peeled away the bloody stocking, and bit his lip at the sight of protruding bone.

"We *must* show this to the surgeon, George," Bysshe said. "The foot and ankle are shattered."

"No!" Sweat beaded on George's forehead. "I've seen surgeons at their work. My God—" There was horror in his eyes. "I'll be a *cripple!*"

M. Fleury said nothing, only looked down at the shattered ankle with his knowing veteran's eyes. He hitched up his trousers, took a bucket from under the cutting board, and left to get ice for Mary.

The Austrians were long gone, ridden off with their blonde trophy. Their fallen paladin was still in the yard—he'd only slow down their escape.

George was pale and his skin was clammy. Claire choked back tears as she looked down at him. "Does it hurt very much?"

"Yes," George confessed, "it does. Perhaps Madame Fleury would oblige me with a glass of brandy."

Madame Fleury fetched the jug and some glasses. Pásmány stood in the corner exuding dark Hungarian gloom. George looked up at Mary, seemed surprised to find her out of bed.

"I seem to be unlucky for your little family," he said. "I hope you will forgive me."

"If I can," said Mary.

George smiled. "Truthful Miss Mary. How fine you are." A spasm of pain took him and he gasped. Madame Fleury put some brandy in his hand and he gulped it.

"Mary!" Bysshe rushed to her. "You should not be seeing this. Go back to your bed."

"What difference does it make?" Mary said, feeling the blood streaking her legs; but she allowed herself to be put to bed.

Soon the tub of ice water was ready. It was too big to get through the door into Mary's room, so she had to join George in the kitchen after all. She sat in the cold wet, and Bysshe propped her back with pillows, and they both watched as the water turned red.

George was pale, gulping brandy from the bottle. He looked at Bysshe.

"Perhaps you could take our mind off things," he said. "Perhaps you could tell me one of your ghost stories."

Bysshe could not speak. Tears were running down his face. So to calm him, and to occupy her time while dying, Mary began to tell a story. It was about an empty man, a Swiss baron who was a genius but who lacked any quality of soul. His name, in English, meant the Franked Stone—the stone whose noble birth had paid its way, but which was still a stone, and being a stone unable to know love.

And the baron had a wasting disease, one that caused his limbs to wither and die. And he knew he would soon be a cripple.

Being a genius the baron thought he knew the answer. Out of protoplasm and electricity and parts stolen from the graveyard he built another man. He called this man a monster, and held him prisoner. And every time one of the baron's limbs began to wither, he'd arrange for his assistants to cut off one of the monster's limbs, and use it to replace the baron's withered part. The monster's own limb was replaced by one from the graveyard. And the monster went through enormous pain, one hideous surgical procedure after another, but the baron didn't care, because he was whole again and the monster was only a monster, a thing he had created.

But then the monster escaped. He educated himself and grew in understanding and apprehension and he spied on the baron and his family. In revenge the monster killed everyone the baron knew, and the baron was angered not because he loved his family but because the killings were an offense to his pride. So the baron swore revenge on the monster and began to pursue him.

The pursuit took the baron all over the world, but it never ended. At the end the baron pursued the monster to the Arctic, and disappeared forever into the ice and mist, into the heart of the white desert of the Pole.

Mary meant the monster to be Soul, of course, and the baron Reason. Because unless the two could unite in sympathy, all was lost in ice and desolation.

It took Mary a long time to tell her story, and she couldn't tell whether George understood her meaning or not. By the time she finished the day was almost over, and her own bleeding had stopped. George had drunk himself nearly insensible, and a diffident notary had arrived from St. Prex to take everyone's testimony.

Mary went back to bed, clean sheets and warmth and the arms of her lover. She and her child would live.

The surgeon came with them, took one look at George's foot, and announced it had to come off.

The surgery was performed on the kitchen table, and George's screams rang for a long time in Mary's dreams.

In a few days Mary had largely recovered. She and Bysshe thanked the Fleurys and sailed to Geneva on a beautiful autumn day in their hired boat. George and Claire—for Claire was George's again—remained behind to sort out George's legal problems. Mary didn't think the renewed friendship would last beyond George's recovery, and she hoped that Claire would not return to England heavy with another child.

After another week of recuperation in Geneva, Bysshe and Mary headed for England and the financial rescue of Mr. Godwin. Mary had bought a pocketbook and was already filling its pages with her story of the Franked Stone. Bysshe knew any number of publishers, and assured her it would find a home with one of them.

Frankenstein was an immediate success. At one point there were over twenty stage productions going on at once. Though she received no money from the stage adaptations, the book proved a very good seller, and was never out of print. The royalties proved useful in supporting Bysshe and Mary and Claire—once she returned to them, once more with child—during years of wandering, chiefly in Switzerland and Italy.

George's promised thousand pounds a year never materialized.

And the monster, the poor abused charnel creature that was Mary's settlement with death, now stalked through the hearts of all the world.

George went to South America to sell his sword to the revolutionary cause. Mary and Bysshe, reading of his exploits in tattered newspapers sent from England, found it somehow satisfying that he was, at last and however reluctantly, fighting for liberty.

They never saw him again, but Mary thought of him often—the great, famed figure, limping painfully through battle after battle, crippled, ever-restless, and in his breast the arctic waste of the soul, the franked and steely creator with his heart of stone.

STORY NOTES

"Daddy's World"

My best stories don't originate as just a single idea. Instead they feature two or more ideas that come into collision, which provides conflict and complexity, or more than one idea which reinforce each other in some unexpected way.

"Daddy's World" was written at the invitation of the writer and editor Constance Ash, one of my oldest friends (we went to college together). She was putting together an anthology title *Not of Woman Born*, about the future of human reproduction.

At that time there was a good deal of enthusiasm for "uploading," which is to say digitizing human consciousness and shifting it into computer-generated virtual environments, where reality is perhaps more flexible than in our own world. Some people are extremely enthusiastic for the idea, and it's developed a cultlike following; but while I enjoy living in the virtual environments of video games, video games come to an end, and I can return to the real world. Physical reality is the thing that keeps us from becoming megalomaniacs—consider a virtual world filled only with creatures from the Id, each accustomed to mold the environment to flatter itself into grander and grander schemes. How would you escape them?

For me, living full-time in a computer-generated reality seems to combine the worst elements of a bad vacation with an indefinite jail sentence. Living in virtual would be something akin to hell.

So my two colliding ideas involved uploading along with the future of human reproduction, and the horrors of being a child raised in an artificial environment controlled entirely by adults. (This was a theme I returned to later, in the story "Incarnation Day.") The child would have no means of escape from whatever system of rewards and punishments was designed by the adults, and would be living a grownup's fantasy of childhood, not his own.

I originally wanted to call the story "The World and the Tree," but the publisher thought the title insufficiently direct.

The Science Fiction and Fantasy Writers of America were generous enough to vote this story a Nebula Award.

"The Golden Age"

"The Golden Age" was written for the anthology *Dead Man's Hand*, edited by John Joseph Adams. John wanted stories set in the Weird West subgenre, this being defined as a story that mixes stories set in the Old West with horror, science fiction, or occult fantasy.

Despite having lived in the West for most of my life, I'd never written a Weird West story before, and viewed it as an interesting challenge. (The only other Western I'd written was "The Last Ride of German Freddie," which I define not as Weird, but as Alternative History.)

I noticed that by definition the Weird Western genre mashes the Western story with another genre, but no one (so far as I know) had ever before mashed the Western with the superhero genre, and so the Commodore's eternal battle with the Condor was brought to life.

The Commodore and his cohorts were created for this story and were never reused, and though occasionally I consider writing them into a graphic novel, other projects always seem to intervene.

"Dinosaurs"

I remember very little about the origins of this story, except that it shares a fear of senility that is visible in a lot of the stories from this period. Zimmerman in *Knight Moves*, both Roon and Reno in *Hardwired*, and Telamon in "Surfacing" all suffer from a kind of senescence involving a retreat into a pampered mental infancy in which every desire is fulfilled and every problem is taken care of, often by a surrogate parent. (In "Dinosaurs," the surrogate is even named Surrogate.)

This reported theme may be autobiographical, albeit at some remove. At one point in my life I watched an aneurism turn my father from a vital, active man into a semi-invalid with no particular purpose in life, whose needs were taken care of by his devoted spouse. He was far from senile, but he *was* wandering through existence without quite knowing who he was anymore, and I found the situation terrifying.

I was not afraid of mere senility, but of senile *systems*—governmental or societal systems that had lost their reason for being, but which still wielded power without quite remembering what it was for. In "Dinosaurs," the human race has grown so vast and over-specialized that any actual reason for its existence has been lost.

The story sold to L. Ron Hubbard, of all people. He had just announced a science fiction magazine, and was paying top rates. I figured if such venerable figures as Jack Williamson, Fred Pohl, and Roger Zelazny could be a part of Elron's various publishing enterprises, then so could I.

I have to say that I wished I'd sold it to *Robert A. Heinlein's Science Fiction Magazine*, but that enterprise would seem to live only in a better universe than this one.

The check arrived on the very day the world heard that Hubbard had died. "Better cash the check *quick*," I told myself, and did. I was a little surprised the check cleared.

The magazine was canceled, but Hubbard's publishing company still had the rights to the story, so it was some years before "Dinosaurs" appeared in *Asimov's,* was nominated for a Hugo, and lost to Ursula K. LeGuin. (A word to the wise: never get nominated against Ursula, Connie Willis, or Neil Gaiman, because your defeat will be *vast.*)

"Dinosaurs" has been one of my most reprinted stories, and is probably my most popular story in Eastern Europe. After all, if they don't know what it is to be conquered by a vast, powerful, alien, and senile political system, who does?

"Surfacing"

"Surfacing" is set in the same future as my novel *Knight Moves,* though you don't need to have read the novel in order to enjoy the story.

Somehow I thought I'd failed with the novel. I was experiencing a lot of grief at the time of writing, and the grief leaked into my own attitude toward my work. I only realized that *Knight Moves* was a fine book when I reread it twenty-eight years later.

Since I thought I'd failed with the novel, I decided on a do-over, though at a more compact length. I set the story in the *Knight Moves* future some hundreds of years later, and wrote a story that shared the major concerns of the novel: love, communication, obsession, death, life, immortality, and a nigh-hopeless quest to unravel one of nature's more imponderable mysteries.

I wrote the story in a furious white-hot blaze, then stalled on the ending. I remember workshopping the incomplete story with Terry Boren and Laura Mixon, and they couldn't figure out an ending, either.

So I set the story aside for six months or so, and then went back to it. And when I read it, I discovered that I'd already written the ending I needed, but hadn't realized it.

Some people find the ending incomplete. I get that. I faced a choice where the finale was concerned. One possible ending would be "Anthony and Philana resolve to solve their problems together, and after years of therapy and one fuck of a long lawsuit against Telamon, finally achieve something like happiness." Which would have turned my novella into something the size of *Anna Karenina*, and it would have been dull, besides.

What I decided to write instead of the long, dull ending was a triumphant scene filled with ringing trumpets and hope, that would somehow imply that Anthony and Philana were on the right track, and would solve their problems in time.

A couple things "informed," as we say, the narrative. The first was a long essay I wrote a good ten years earlier, when I was living in Boston. I knew nobody there, and had no job and no money, and so I ended up spending a lot of time in a coffee shop writing long, desperate letters to everyone I knew. And one day I—having run out of friends to pity me—found myself writing a long essay on whale speech, which of course I knew nothing about. I hypothesized, however, that the black watery realm would tend to break down the barriers between the self and the environment, and result in a grammar in which object and subject were one.

I'm told this already exists in the grammar of the Navajos. "I'm going to the store," can't be said in Navajo, you have to say "The store and I are in a condition of moving toward one another." Because you and the store inhabit the same universe, and it's all part of the same circle, and everything's connected.

All of which was said in much greater detail in my essay.

Another element of the story is that Philana's condition is a metaphor for mental illness. I'd been around some people who, even if they might not fit the diagnostic description of multiple personality disorder, nevertheless seemed to have more than one person clumping around in their heads. In one case, I went to bed with a very nice, loving lady, and next day woke up with a complete stranger. (And no, it wasn't that she just needed her morning coffee.)

This and other experienced had me thinking about MPD, and that led later to my novel *Aristoi*.

So anyway: "Surfacing." Whale speech, aliens, desperate love, Hugo and Nebula nominations, and the sense that I was on the right track.

"Video Star"

Writing a novel is like pruning a tree: you want to keep the branches nearly aligned and pointing all in the same direction, and when a branch threatens to put the story on a wrong course, or grows so big that it threatens to overwhelm the plot, you lop it off.

But sometimes the bits that you prune off can make little trees of their own. "Video Star" was once a subplot in my novel *Voice of the Whirlwind,* but it grew too big, and I cut it and replaced it with another sub-story. But as I am a thrifty writer who doesn't like his own words to go to waste, I turned the reject into a story of its own. I changed the names and wrote a new ending, and sold the story to Gardner Dozois at *Asimov's.* "Video Star" retains the Arizona setting of the original chapter, and Ric wakes up in the same hospital as Steward, and gets involved with a somewhat less stable version of Steward's girlfriend.

I'm glad "Video Star" became a story of its own, because it would have made *Voice of the Whirlwind* a lot darker, and made Steward a less sympathetic protagonist.

The story also managed to predict the Grand Canyon Skywalk, though so far the Skywalk doesn't contain a nightclub.

"Millennium Party"

One year at the Rio Hondo workshop, we all got a call from the fine writer Eileen Gunn, who was then editing the online magazine *Infinite Matrix.* She challenged us each to write a short-short (defined as a story under 1000 words) either on the subject of marriage in the future, or of artificial intelligence. I wrote on both, and also included some of the food we were cooking for each other.

This is my only short-short, and I will now bring the afterword to an end before it exceeds the length of the subject.

"The Bad Twin"

Sometimes my enjoyment of complexity gets the better of me. And so here you have a story with twin protagonists who suffer from every time-travel paradox I could imagine. I stuck them on Santorini because I'd recently seen the Santorini exhibit at the National Archaeological Museum in Athens, and the artworks' joyful beauty stayed with me. Also, for dramatic reasons, my protagonist had to be isolated in a remote place.

I've also read far too much Greek mythology in my life, and some of it is here on display.

"The Green Leopard Plague"

This story was the subject of one of the most memorable critiques of my life. I submitted an early version of this story at Rio Hondo, a professional workshop I've been running in northern New Mexico for the last twenty-odd years, and Ted Chiang, deploying "back-of-the-envelope calculations," completely demolished the story's scientific premise. I was too impressed by Ted's feat to be downcast at the destruction of my story.

Fortunately I was able to call on Dr. Stephen C. Lee, a specialist in nanotechnology, to provide a far more plausible explanation.

"The Green Leopard Plague" is another of my stories in which several ideas come crashing together. I had become interested in the economics of societies based on abundance rather than scarcity. In a society in which death is impossible, death becomes the most rare thing of all. But what else is rare, and how is it valued?

Labor would seem to be an obvious answer.

Terzian's idea that a collapse in the markets for food and labor might result in state intervention amounting to slavery was an insight that I was very proud of. It wasn't until long after the story was in print that I discovered that I had been anticipated by Frederik Pohl in "The Anything Box" (1963).

Another idea, the rise of the Trashcanistans, was borrowed from an article by Stephen Kokin in a 2002 issue of *The New Republic*.

The setting for Michelle's part of the story was inspired by a scuba-diving trip to Palau. The Rock Islands, Jellyfish Lake, and the other marine lakes are real locations. Unfortunately, when I returned to Palau in 2017, I discovered that Jellyfish Lake no longer has jellyfish in it. Climate change has wiped them out, all ten million of them.

More millions, I'm certain, will follow.

"The Green Leopard Plague" began a series, though it wasn't the first story in the series. The first published story was "Lethe," but I realized that the setting of that story was too rich to be confined to a single work, so I set the future part of "The Green Leopard Plague" there. When I wrote it "Lethe" was just a story, but a second story made it a *series*. Other stories in what I've called the College of Mystery Sequence include "Pinocchio" and "Incarnation Day."

I wanted to call the story "The Pitcher Plant," but editor Gardner Dozois wanted something more science fiction-y. I considered calling it "Sex Kings of Mars," then decided on the present title.

You will notice, by the way, that the name "Gardner Dozois" keeps reappearing in these notes. His years at *Asimov's* were groundbreaking, and he published one breakout story after another from the best writers of the day. He won fourteen Hugo awards for editing, more than anyone else in the history of the award. And he also published many of the best stories by a largely unknown writer named Walter Jon Williams.

That I became a working published novelist was thanks to a great many people, but insofar as I ever became a star, that was down to Gardner. He will be truly missed.

"Diamonds from Tequila"

Some days you win, some days you lose. Some days you take home an award, some days you get banned from your own career for five long years.

"Diamonds from Tequila" is a short novella sequel to the worst-selling books of my career.

Some years ago I helped write *Last Call Poker,* an online game. It wasn't a standard online game, like a MMORPG, it was what came to be called an Alternate Reality Game, or ARG. ARGs were new, they were cool, and I desperately wanted to take this great innovation in multimedia entertainment and turn it into words printed on dead trees.

It took a few years before I could find an editor who understood entertainment that wasn't presented between cardboard covers, but eventually I sold *This Is Not a Game,* and after I delivered the first novel I was asked to write two sequels, *Deep State* and *The Fourth Wall.* They were contemporary, they were hip, they were bleeding-edge. They were, I thought, exactly what the market needed right then.

Unfortunately *This Is Not a Game* appeared in hardback in the worst moment of the 2008 recession, and it flopped. As a result, the paperback got no support, and neither did either of the sequels. Most of my readers never saw them. You'd think that *Deep State*'s predicting the Arab Spring might have given it some traction, but somehow it didn't.

Those books sold in the *hundreds*. In fact the series sold so badly that I wasn't able to sell another novel for five years. That's five years in which I could have written a novel a year, for me to profit by and you to enjoy, but all those works will now remain in some virtual world to which neither of us has access. I'm working on other stuff now.

At some point in those wilderness years Gardner Dozois asked me to write a story for the *Rogues* anthology he was editing along with George R.R. Martin. I had just the rogue in mind.

The first two novels of the *Not a Game* series were written from the point of view of game designer Dagmar Shaw as she explored a dangerous world in which the virtual realm was becoming indistinguishable from our own. By the third book I felt I'd pretty well told Dagmar's story, and also that the "Dagmar gets into serious jeopardy in the penultimate chapter" storyline might be getting a little stale. So I wrote the third novel from the point of view of former child star Sean Makin, while Dagmar, though present, was elevated to a kind of godlike eminence, a puppetmaster operating behind the scenes from the 21st century equivalent of a volcano lair.

The character of Sean was inspired by a documentary that featured former child stars, in which mature adults were shown to be hopelessly yearning for a return to their glory days, when they were, say, eleven years old. So I developed Sean, a desperately needy Frankenstein monster trapped in a Hollywoodland he never created, and haunted by the success of his younger self.

I also got to deploy many of the stories I'd heard from Hollywood writers. The writers in question have had ample time to tell these stories in print, but they won't, because they're afraid that they might offend someone and never work again. Whereas I've *already* been through my period of no work, and can write whatever the hell I like.

In *The Fourth Wall* Sean goes to work for Dagmar Shaw, finds himself the target of killers, and gets his mojo back. By the end of the book, he's got his career again.

In "Diamonds From Tequila," Sean still has his career, but now he has a chance to leap to mega-stardom—and because of his overwhelming need for the love of every single person on earth, finds himself dealing once again with killers, hackers, drug cartels, and far too many people with guns.

I've toyed with the idea of writing another story about Sean, in which his career completes its arc by going into the crapper again, and his ever-desperate attempts to hang onto stardom cause ever more death, chaos, and heartbreak.

I think that might be fun.

"Margaux"

If I had a chance to own all the cars I wanted, among the many great machines filling my garage I'd have both a Bugatti Veyron, for those days when I needed to comfortably cross the country at something close to the speed of sound, and a Volvo station wagon for making daily trips to the store. In writing, I am attracted to both the epic as well as the more modestly-sized and practical, and in "Margaux" we have both.

Twenty years ago I began an epic far-future series with *The Praxis,* a series that has yet to conclude. It's got space travel, aliens, deadly perils, and adventure—all the stuff traditionally found in far-future epics, though I like to think I handle the material differently than most. But a vast landscape is made up of the particular, and in the Praxis stories one of the particulars is "Margaux."

"Margaux" is the origin story of one of the major characters in *The Praxis.* It was written as a short story, published in *Asimov's,* then broken into bits and scattered through the novel. Though it made sense to do that in the longer work, it diluted the dramatic punch of the story, and I'm glad to see the "Margaux" here in its original form.

"Prayers on the Wind"

At some point in the Eighties military SF became a well-defined subgenre and became popular, and we were assured that whatever happened in our future, there would be war. The writer Lewis Shiner thought that an alternate point of view was called for, and asked for writers to contribute to an anthology devoted to non-violent means of conflict resolution.

I'd just read *Magic and Mystery in Tibet* by Alexandra David-Neel, a French anarchist, feminist, and convert to Buddhism who traveled through Tibet in the guise of a lady lama. Her picture of Tibetan Buddhism strongly influenced my story. Another influence may be inferred by the name !urq, pronounced something like "Kirk," and to whom I gave all of James T. Kirk's arguments for boldly going into the universe, having adventures, and conquering stuff generally.

Lew likes to give his projects titles taken from rock songs, and the anthology was called *When the Music's Over,* which I think confused people and led to its becoming more obscure than it deserved. *Give Peace a Chance* might have been too obvious a title, I have thought, but at least it would have got the point across.

"Prayers on the Wind" was nominated for a Nebula Award by the Science Fiction Writers of America.

"Wall, Stone, Craft"

Some stories I write just for me, and among these are a series of SF stories about writers. I've written about Poe ("No Spot of Ground"), Nietzsche ("The Last Ride of German Freddie"), Mark Twain ("The Boolean Gate"), and Mary Shelley in "Wall, Stone, Craft."

I've titled the series "Dead Romantics," which is possibly the most uncommercial title ever. But then the series is written for me, not for money or applause, though to my surprise the stories have received their share of both.

My idea for the story originally had no Mary Shelley at all, and was an off-the-wall idea about the middle-aged and straitlaced spinster Jane Austen conceiving a mad passion for Lord Byron, and scandalizing the world by running off with him. A brief glance at the history shows that this was impossible, as about the time Byron was awaking in London to find himself famous, Jane Austen was dying of Addison's Disease in Winchester.

Then it occurred to me that as Mary Shelley has been credited with writing the first science fiction novel in *Frankenstein,* with its keynote paradigm of technology gone wrong, an alternative Mary Shelley might be responsible for an alternative science fiction paradigm, perhaps equally as powerful. And so I set to work.

As with most of my stories with a historical setting, everyone in the narrative was a real, historical person, with the exception of the stolid Swiss farmer Fleury, and Byron's fencing master Pásmány. The Count von Neipperg really did receive instructions from Metternich to seduce the "Countess Laufenberg," and the capsizing of Shelley's boat on Lake Geneva actually happened more or less as described. (This *Ariel* should not be confused with a later *Ariel,* which also capsized and killed Shelley and his passengers.)

I am subject to impulses both wayward and perverse, and one of these impulses is responsible for my being the only author to write about the Shelley-Byron set and not arrange to get Byron and Mary in bed together. In my defense the idea was cliché, I would also like to point out that Mary didn't like Byron that much, and with good reason—his treatment of Mary's sister was appalling.

My wife Kathy Hedges is responsible for the title, which has to do with the craft of writing, Byron's stony heart, and the psychological walls between the characters.

The story was nominated for a Nebula, a Hugo, and the World Fantasy Award, which perhaps indicates confusion on the part of readers as to how exactly to categorize it.

If I'd just got Mary and Byron into bed, I might have carried home a trophy.

COPYRIGHT INFORMATION